NORTH
OF PORTSMOUTH

David Megenhardt

red giant books

Copyright © 2017 David Megenhardt

North of Portsmouth

Red Giant Books
ISBN: 978-0-9968717-3-0

All rights reserved. No part of this book may be reproduced or transmitted in any form or by any means, electronic or mechanical, including photocopying, recording or by information and retrieval systems, without the written permission of the author, except when permitted by law.

10 9 8 7 6 5 4 3 2 1

This is a work of fiction: a product of the author's imagination. All resemblance to persons living or dead is purely coincidental.

Printed in the United States of America.

www.redgiantbooks.com

Cover Photograph and Design by
Tim Lachina

Other Works by David Megenhardt

Dogs in the Cathedral

JWB

*To Claudia and Vivian
for their love and wit*

1

Unlucky

Had Paul Newcombe stayed asleep for another minute or two his life would have most likely followed a more predictable path, leading to decades of government service, retirement, and a quiet death in an anonymous one bedroom apartment perched near a dirty shoreline. As it happened, though, he experienced one of those unhappy coincidences that he would have said plagued his life, which set him off on a previously unimagined course.

He awoke with a start to the black roiling smoke of a house fire, a roaring tar paper and wood blaze, and the screaming accompaniment of the former occupants, now dispossessed and hysterical.

...a neighbor who witnessed the blaze told us... (The screen flashed from a raven-haired beauty wearing a sleeveless silk blouse, a diaphanous wonder of teasing concealment, to a sweating and distraught face of a man with patches of whiskers and boils along the jawline as he wiped his brow. His eyes held remnants of shock and fear. "We seen the smoke coming from the porch, then nothing but fire and screaming everywhere. They is fine people. This makes no sense. They don't deserve this, no way." The camera panned across a group of people standing in the street, some nervously laughing from the excitement of the fire, others covering their mouths with their hands in shock, but the majority stood mute and respectful as if members of an ad hoc street congregation made humble at the works of an unkind and arbitrary god.

Paul had become fully conscious and analyzed the screen to see if he could recognize the street where the fire had erupted. So many streets in the city looked the same and he couldn't pinpoint the location. His job as housing inspector had probably taken him to that street before, possibly to that very house, but they all ran together in his memory. He could guess the cause of the blaze: sixteen static and hand-held appliances plugged into the one working socket in the house and the constant surge of red hot electricity poured through the ancient fuse box until the whole system burned. The old, dry houses immolated quickly once flame touched the wood.

He took a drink of lukewarm water from a glass he had left on the coffee table and imagined the fire creeping up the walls and racing along the floorboards, consuming the house in a glutinous fury, conjuring beams and columns of ash where wood once stood. Deep in his gut he feared that he had inspected the house and missed an obvious violation. He would check his files first thing in the morning and prepare a defense, if necessary. He hadn't heard if anyone had died. The inquiries normally became urgent and emotional if someone had been killed. Neighbors and council worked themselves into a fury, demanding answers from the understaffed department, who kept the housing stock from burning or rotting to the ground, because no one other than government cared for the misery of the unlucky and unfortunate.

"...*as a workman excavated a gravel pit the skull rolled down the hill. The frightened workman jumped out of his backhoe and ran to find the foreman. Deputy Greg Auro was first on the scene,*" said the newscaster *whose eyes smoldered with the coals of the house fire but had miraculously transformed to a hint of hilarity, at the expense of the frightened workman, and grave concern, because after all, the workman did dig up human remains. The screen flashed to the deputy.* "*The backhoe operator saw something white rolling down the hill and when he climbed down he saw that it was a skull. He said it terrified him.*" *Suddenly, he raised the skull into the frame of the screen from below and stared into the vacant eyes. He held the position for a second then said,* "*Now we just have to find the owner of it.*" *He ended the interview with a sneering, mocking laugh.*

The sneering laugh and cockeyed expression, a face aslant, beleaguered with skepticism and cynicism. The downy brown moustache and the crooked teeth. Narrow shoulders with strange, thick Popeye arms perfect for expansive tattoos. Greg Auro. Paul lurched up and leaned toward the television, but the image vanished as quickly as it had come. *The newscaster now beamed mock concern and allowed the corner of her mouth to bend in a wry smile, a nod to the deputy's bad joke or the absurdity of the violated grave and the humiliation of the dead.* Maybe she didn't know what to make of Greg Auro and her smile was her attempt to suppress the desire to slap that laugh off his face.

Greg Auro. Paul remembered footsteps crunching across frozen ground with their feet shod in floppy rubber boots with the buckles frozen in place like ancient locks. Their breath hovered white above their heads as they trudged through a thick, bare woods to a cave. Greg ducked under a low shelf of rock and lay flat, propelling himself with his heels and hands. The opening barely allowed his thin body to pass. Paul followed and unsheathed a flashlight from his hip and pointed it toward the ground between them so Greg could piece together an oil lantern they had disassembled and stolen piece by piece from a Kmart.

Greg raised the wick and set the tip aglow. The lantern cast a circle of light that filled the center of the room and the ragged, rock ceiling. Without a sign or prompt, the boys stepped into the shadows outside the ring of light and peeled off their wet clothes, breaking off the ice from the buckles with their fists and fumbling open the buttons and zippers with raw, red hands. As practiced through repetition, the boys sprang into the crepuscular light, naked and crouched for attack. The heat in the cave had risen a few degrees from their body temperature and the flame of the lantern, but they could see their breath and feel the cold intensely on the parts of their bodies they had just exposed.

They flung karate chops and kicked at each other's red skin. They attempted judo throws and basic wrestling takedowns with little effect. They both knew each other's strategies, techniques and weaknesses so well that each match threatened to end in a stalemate. They screamed incomprehensible curses and invectives, epithets born from virgin hatred. Chins greased with spittle, the two would eventually lock arms and tear at each other's shoulders as the aroused dust choked the air. In his memory Paul watches himself grind Greg's face against the cave floor until it was black with mud, a mixture of slobber, dirt, and blood as he straddles his back, considering whether to crush the fragile vertebrae of his neck with his hands. The true accounting of these matches skewed heavily in favor of Greg because of his superior strength. Paul remembered the one in ten matches he won because of a fluke takedown or when Greg felt on the cusp of a weeklong flu or hadn't had enough sleep the night before because his dad kept him up praying because the end of days had come.

They remained friends and fought in the cave until the ceiling could barely contain their height and the square footage could not provide the space for a full-scale brawl. They had grown about a foot and a half each and they could barely slide through the opening, but they would have continued had they not made the mistake of bringing two girls one night. They had planned to get drunk and fuck them, but either Paul or Greg started talking about the wrestling matches and the girls started egging them on to see a demonstration. Each thought their boy could take the other and they began a mock argument as to their relative strength, speed and meanness. Greg and Paul protested for a while, having other plans in mind, but the girls persisted and each thought that showing they could grind the other's face in the dirt would be an effective aphrodisiac. For the loser, well, he would have to figure out how to talk his date's pants off or turn consolation into desire. They stripped naked and began close hand-to-hand combat, because the presence of the girls, a twelve pack of beer, and the already tight space made extravagant movement impossible. They fought for a long time. Neither wanted to be embarrassed and let a chance at pussy slip through their fingers. Finally, they fell to the ground and Greg's superior strength won the match. Paul ended up on his stomach and Greg straddled him as he crushed his face against the dirt. Greg sported a full erection, which sent the girls into paroxysms of laughter. He quickly dismounted Paul and when Paul turned over they saw that he had become equally aroused, which stoked the hilarity further until both girls choked and begged for the moment to end. One of them managed to say they had no idea how gay it would be. Both Paul and Greg shouted her down to no effect. Fortunately, the presence of two erections, which refused to relent because of the girls' close scrutiny, in such a close space guaranteed success of their first purpose. So they fucked them side by side with the girls laughing throughout, but their black mood refused to lift even after they finished.

Greg was a year ahead of Paul in school even though their birthdays were just three months apart. When Greg graduated and moved from the neighborhood they lost touch. Apart from two encounters, seeing each other at a checkout line at the neighborhood grocery store that smelled of salami and freshly spilled blood and at Paul's father's funeral, when, as Paul bore the casket with his brothers and cousins down the long aisle of the church to the awaiting hearse, he spotted Greg sitting alone in the last pew. The chitchat in the grocery line didn't make it past their amazement of the passing of time and their need to get together and have a beer. Greg had grown thicker through the chest and his eyes had sunk into his skull, so that he resembled his father more than he ever had as a child. They never had the beer. They didn't speak at the funeral at all, as Greg had come late, did not follow the procession to the graveyard, and left without explanation. He hadn't come to the wake either, those miserable hours when Paul and his family sat in the funeral parlor with the wax dummy that had once been his animate father. Paul felt rage when he looked at his father's dead face and saw the makeup slathered on as if applied with a putty knife. Sometime during those endless hours he buttonholed the funeral director and accused him of wanting to make his father look like a transvestite and broke a potted plant on the floor, which wasn't easy given the thickness of the pile carpet. The funeral director's face narrowed as he looked at the dirt on the otherwise immaculate carpet and told him he wouldn't charge the family for the cleaning if Paul promised never to speak to him again.

Paul wondered if his grief had invited a visage of Greg to sit in the pew and give him comfort or if he had come to mock Paul, to enjoy the sight of his weakness, and to remind him that he would always be triumphant, crushing his face in dirt of the cave floor.

Paul blinked at the screen. Greg fucking Auro. He walked over to his computer, an ancient desktop that groaned when the hard drive engaged like a car with a bad transmission, and logged onto the internet site of the station that ran the story, to see if a link had been posted. Nothing from the 11 o'clock news had been posted yet, but Paul did read old stories about three other house fires, an unexplained shooting at a Laundromat, a break-in at a lumberyard and the subsequent disappearance of the yard's security guard. He momentarily forgot about Deputy Greg Auro and first followed one link, then another, and ended in a blind alley of pop-up ads, celebrity gossip and voyeuristic photos of a minor television actress on a beach, topless and wearing a thong. He considered the poses, the crispness of the images and the endless volume of shots and realized he had become ensnared in a planned publicity stunt made to look like a creepy voyeur with a perfect camera had stumbled upon the starlet quarry. Paul rubbed his eyes for a few moments and then stared blankly at the wall, hung between thoughts and unable to go forward or backward.

His face broke into a grim smile and he felt a form of panic brewing in his gut, not unlike the feeling he had when Greg had beaten him and pushed his face in the dirt. Helpless, captured, continuing to fight but impotent to change the outcome. He paced around his apartment, holding his face as his breathing became shallow and fast. He hadn't thought of Greg in years. His father had died ten years ago and their meeting in the grocery store had occurred five years before the funeral. He walked past his bathroom door and threw a wild punch at it, then another. He pounded the door like he punched a heavy bag. Left, right, left right, left right. Greg-or-y fuck-ing Au-ro. He stopped when he smashed a hole through the one side of the hollow-core door, his knuckles bloody on both hands.

He found an old phone book jammed in a kitchen cabinet and retrieved the number to the television station. He called the general number and descended into the station's byzantine phone system that gave very specific directions on what number to press to reach different departments, but he figured out quickly that if he pushed random numbers without following the directions he would probably end in the same place, that the elaborate phone web had been spun to create the illusion of power and really just masked a contingent of sleepy interns, one who now answered Paul's call. Paul asked him in what town the story of the rolling skull had taken place.

"That's a popular story. I've already had ten calls about it."

"Really?" Paul said as he focused on remaining patient.

"One caller said that he was a phrenologist. He said that if he was just in the vicinity of a skull he could identify the person and their occupation and possibly the residual thoughts embedded in the bone. He said driving past a cemetery for him is like hearing a riot in progress. I asked him what I thought were logical questions. Why does the skull have to be of a dead person? Wouldn't this same phenomenon happen even amongst the living? Was there something in our flesh that interfered with the transmission of these facts? He became very agitated and called me an assassin. So, the question I have for you, and I never thought I would be asking this, is whether or not you practice the art of phrenology?"

"No, I do no such thing."

"That's too bad, because I want to know why I offended him."

"I know the deputy in the story. I want to know where the story took place. I want to know where Greg Auro works."

"We have a website."

"Yes, and if a site could contain more useless information I have yet to find it."

"I find it intuitive and easy to navigate."

"That's great, but there's nothing about the story on the site."

"I've pulled it up as we've been talking. Portsmouth. They found the skull outside of Portsmouth. Sometimes the sites get blamed but really it's the lack of navigation skills of the user."

"Where is Portsmouth exactly?"

"I'm thinking it's by water. There are maps one can use to find such information."

"Are you taking comedy lessons from Greg Auro?"

"Who's Greg Auto?"

"Auro."

"Is he the skull?"

"Newsroom?? Newsroom??" Paul said as he nearly frothed with contempt and he wanted to slam the phone down but he called on a wireless so he satisfied himself with throwing the receiver against the cushions of the couch. He snatched it back up and immediately dialed information. Deputy Auro's home number turned out to be unlisted, no doubt to keep the citizens of Portsmouth at bay during his off-duty hours. He would call the sheriff's department in the morning.

He tore apart heaps of paper piled on a cheap pine bookcase, looking for a map he had bought years before. He could have easily looked up the information on the internet, of course, but his last foray with the clutching desperation of the actress with the shapely ass gave him pause. Given the time of day and the fever he felt coming he could have easily spent the next two hours hopscotching across the web with no aim or purpose. Of course he wanted to search Greg Auro's name to find other quotes attributed him, maybe even a picture, but inexorably such a search, especially an image search, would lead to secondary and tertiary of searches of women, first dressed, then sporting bikinis, then undressed, then performing traditional sexual acts shot with respect and an eye for composition, color and shadow, and then on to a bedrock of perversion and the obvious and desperate needs of the thousands of women to satisfy boyfriends, husbands and pimps who themselves were burdened by a multiplicity of perversions.

The map had been tucked under a stack of old utility bills, behind an abandoned collection of shot glasses from tourist traps, within a knot of unread manuals for the TV, DVD player, clock radio, cordless phone, microwave, window fan, vacuum cleaner and aquarium pump, on a shelf jammed with other detritus that some random current washed onto the pine nook where it would lay stagnant and forgotten until an event like Greg Auro popping up on his TV screen occurred.

Pushing aside yesterday's mail he spread the map on the dining room table like a sacred parchment, careful not to tear the weakened folds of the paper. His finger slid across the tangle of cities, rivers, lakes and roads to the nipple of the state, the southernmost intrusion into Kentucky. Beside the green splotch known as Wayne National Forest sat the black dot of Portsmouth, some 250 miles from where Paul sat in Cleveland. Of all the beatings, murders, rapes and traffic fatalities that occurred in the territory between the two cities on any given day, a story about a skull being found in a gravel pit, a skull, by the way, that provided no ancestral link in the human diaspora or had not been linked, as of yet, to a famous murder or disappearance or really was not interesting in any way, seemed like an odd pick to fill the few minutes of news beamed across the region.

Paul dug the phone out of the couch and hit the redial button. After another three minute gauntlet of contradictory directions the same intern answered the phone. Paul wanted to know why the station would run a story about a skull from a small town 250 miles away when just Cleveland itself had enough buried corpses to keep the station in stories for the rest of existence and they certainly did not need to import them from Portsmouth.

"Are you going to yell at me again?"

"No," Paul barked without the slightest indication of apology.

"Well, in the *newsroom* we can uplink to satellites from other network affiliates and we must have picked this particular story from the Columbus feed. That's how things work here in the *newsroom*."

"I understand the technology. You've missed the point. What is the purpose? Why would you pick up the story? What made it interesting to you?" Paul could not have explained why he followed this line of questioning or what he hoped the intern to say, but he could not let it drop. "A skull falls out of a quarry two hundred and fifty miles away. This is news? This is worth a goddamn satellite orbiting the earth? You find Greg Auro in some rotting little river town and you send him to me to disrupt my sleep. You pull him out of a rabbit hole and beam that goddamn downy moustache across the globe, for what?"

"Sir, are you seriously meditating on the American obsession with the grotesque and trivial?"

"I wouldn't have used the word 'meditating,' but it's not inaccurate."

"Can't you see all the elements are there? There's a skull, so death plays a central role. There's a surprise, and everybody likes to put themselves in the situation so everybody watching is asking, 'What was that like? What would I have done?' There's the oddity of the rolling skull. I don't know how to explain that other than to say the rolling motion is uncommon and, shall we say, interesting. Anyway, thus begins the mystery. Viewers are vexed and they want a solution. Maybe they even cast the deputy as the small town sleuth, who, as he puts it, finds the owner of the skull. From the simplest stories can come reams of imagination."

"Believe me, you wouldn't give Deputy Auro that much credit if you knew him."

"That's the point. We don't know him and we don't have to know him. In the *newsroom* we use our instincts and we're pretty good at knowing what stories people want to see."

"Instincts! Instincts!" Paul forgot his promise not to hang up the phone and hung up. Adrenaline rippled to the tips of his fingers and toes. He chortled for an imaginary and circumspect audience. But his anger suddenly embarrassed him, even though the outburst had been private, except for the ear of the intern who probably just placed him into the crank file, next to the phrenologist and the drunk who called every night to ask for the cell phone number of the anchorwoman. How could he stand out amongst such competition? Amongst the lunatics who believed the reporters and anchors spoke directly to them or thought a vast project of government or corporate mind control had been implemented through the television? Was it possible that the sight of Greg Auro had sent him into this rage? Had the downy moustache served as his madeleine and tapped the hate in his memories? A more likely explanation would be lateness of the hour and exhaustion, not just the simple exhaustion of a single day's activities but the amassing of grinding stress, of a contagion of humiliations, unpaid bills and the ever present reminder of time passing toward a vague terminus, but he couldn't be certain.

After carefully folding the map along the greasy creases and returning it to the top of the pile on the bookcase, Paul resolutely concluded that he would never see Greg again so all the detective work was pointless. Twenty years had passed. Even though the experiences of his childhood remained intense and sensual, because he could now view the wrestling from an adult perspective with a linear history of sexual activity and compare and place it in the context of experimentation, exploration, whatever masculine term he could conjure up to gloss over getting an erection while rubbing against male flesh, what significance could it now have in his everyday life? Given the parade of devils in the guise of his girlfriends, bosses, arresting officers, bartenders, slumlords and homeowners to whom he issued citations, Paul placed Greg in a minor role, playing one of the trumpets in an out-of-tune marching band near the middle of the parade, a teaser, a foreshadow of the horribleness to come. It was a shock seeing Greg's face on television after twenty years, especially through a haze of sleep, and in the morning he would file the experience away as a strange coincidence that momentarily illuminated a part of his memory that had grown dim.

He undressed and lay in bed, fitfully turning, kicking off the sheets, then putting them back on, smashing the pillow into a number of forms with little effect. Comfort remained elusive. He would called the sheriff's office in the morning and have a conversation with the deputy. He was sure Greg could cover the past twenty years in a few sentences and then he would be free to slink back into the shadows. Maybe, if Paul remembered, he would thank him for coming to his father's funeral all those years ago, since he never had a chance to speak with him. His decision calmed him enough to where sleep became possible, but he couldn't help thinking about what he wanted to say, how he himself would sum up the past twenty years, how they would compare, who could lay claim to living life more successfully, and who ultimately had their face crushed in the dirt.

2

Enter Ghost

After a shower and a cup of coffee Paul found himself sitting at his dining room table with his phone cradled between his shoulder and ear. The Scioto County Sheriff's Department receptionist had placed him on hold while she tracked the whereabouts of Deputy Greg Auro. Paul had rehearsed a dozen greetings that he hoped would disarm the deputy and give him an edge from the start of the conversation, making him feel less than a fool for bothering the deputy after so many years. A haze of dust drifted through a shaft of sunlight that poured through the kitchen window. He couldn't remember the last time he had opened one of the windows and the thought the breathing in the dust made his nose itch and gave him a tickle in the throat. He worried his voice would crack during the opening salvo, defusing any wit he may have managed to conjure.

The wait became interminable. Leaning back and shutting his eyes, he suppressed a desire to whip the phone across the room and run down the street. He could sit at work and write a report for five hours straight without giving his body much consideration, but waiting for this ghost to walk on stage made him bristle with nervous energy.

"Ya," the deputy grunted on the other end of the line.

Paul's eyes snapped open and he lurched forward. He nearly dropped the phone.

"Now we have to find the owner of the skull? You always went for the cheap laugh." The opening was less than what he hoped.

"Who is this?"

"The owner of the skull. I would like to place a claim for its return."

"Don't waste my time, sir. I'll ask you one more time who this is?"

"Paul Newcombe."

"Goddamn TV," the deputy muttered and the conversation dropped into silence. Paul waited for him to say something else but was forced after several seconds to ask if the deputy had remained on the line.

"Ya, I'm still here. What's been going on?" the deputy said with no energy or inflection.

Paul applied the question to the last twenty years of his life and searched for a dominant image or theme that would best represent all that had happened. He became lost in a muddle of conflicting impressions.

"Nothing much. How about you?"

"Well, you know, I've been finding skulls and tracking teenage boys so they don't impregnate our girls on the side of country roads and in the cornfields. We have some pretty tough laws against public fornication."

"Sounds like important work."

"Paul, somebody has to be the guardian of the almost virgins. It's something of a calling, more than just work. The hours are long and the challenges are endless. Get the image of a swarm of bees with hard-ons into your head and you'll get the idea of my task."

"Have you found many skulls during your time?"

"Don't be stupid. Of course I haven't found many skulls. This would be my first."

"How would I know?" Paul said, stinging from the rebuke.

"You wouldn't. I suppose that's why you called. Just another curiosity seeker, right Paul? And believe it or not you're not the first. The story aired last night and I've already gotten calls and messages from a woman in Florida who thinks the skull could belong to her long lost but not forgotten husband, from a man in California who sobbed into my ear, telling me the story of his lost daughter, from a dozen crank calls from Hamlet asking for poor Yorick, from the Cleveland Museum of Natural History who wants to examine the skull and site to make sure the backhoe didn't disrupt a Hopewell burial mound, an email from Leipzig, Germany begging us to make a plaster cast of it for inclusion in a private collection that is organized around the theme of loss and abandonment . Of course, he is willing to pay for the casting costs and delivery if they are reasonable. And I was just on the phone with an NBC producer when you called. They are thinking about creating a segment on the discovery. They have two possible ideas. One to come to town and follow me about as I try to track down the clues. I told them the sheriff would take a dim view of something like that. He might consider it if they made him the detective, but otherwise that's dead in the water. The other idea is basically the same thing but they would wait until, as she said, 'The mystery is unveiled,' and then come to town and recreate the steps I took. Of course, that all depends if the truth is interesting and how quickly it all gets resolved. If it takes six months they won't be interested, I'm sure. A Hopewell burial mound is not going to make prime time. You see, Paul, you're in good company and you shouldn't be embarrassed about calling me to find out what it's all about. "

"I don't remember saying I was embarrassed."

"Something in your voice."

The deputy became quiet as if distracted by something. The line stayed silent for several seconds, even longer than the first gap, but Paul was determined to not break and ask again if the deputy has stayed on the line. In the end, he couldn't last very long and the silence drove him to ask a question.

"Was the jaw attached?"

"To the skull?"

"Of course to the skull."

"The years have not made you any brighter, have they? Jawbones don't stay attached to the skull. Sinew and muscle keep it in place and once that rots away you have two distinct pieces. Are you imagining the skull chattering as it rolled down the hill?"

"No, I can't say I imagined that."

"Then why would you ask such a question?"

"Curiosity."

"My experience tells me that curiosity usually produces more interesting questions than that."

"The thing is, the reason why I called, is that I'm going to be down your way in a couple of weeks. I thought maybe I would do some fishing and while I'm down there I'd look you up." Paul hadn't planned any of this and wondered what he would say next, as if a third person had just made up an imaginary trip with the intent of connecting with an old friend. He didn't own a fishing pole, of course, and wouldn't know what tackle to bring without a couple of hours of research. "We could knock back a few beers and talk."

"I don't fish, Paul, but I do drink like a fish. You're welcome to come, of course. My office is in the courthouse. I'll be there. I'm always there. You can buy as long as your cash lasts, which probably won't get me half drunk, but you can try."

"You use to fish all the time. Remember those trips with your dad?"

"Here we go…work beckons, Paul. We'll reminisce all the good times if you make your way down here."

The line went unmistakably dead as the deputy had hung up.

The two of them probably would not have known each other had not their backyards shared a common border. The close orbit of children that contained a few acres of grass, an overgrown woods, the miraculous cave hidden on the far end of the woods, the back lot of a dairy store, and each other, kept them close friends until Greg learned to drive. Even then, with the frequency of their meetings reduced because of the encroaching world and its multitudes of distractions, they could never break communication entirely. They were the only children of roughly the same age in the neighborhood, both products of late, menopausal pregnancies. Their brothers and sisters were much older and had all left their parents' houses before Greg and Paul had reached nine years of age. Circumstance had thrown them together and they had made the best of it. Their option had been to play alone or seek each other's company and they chose an imperfect friendship over loneliness, especially over the interminably long summer vacations.

The idea to drive to the other end of the state to see a man he most probably would not even like seemed to be a ludicrous idea, but he knew himself. Once an unhappy coincidence had occurred he would follow the ramifications until the very end. He would request vacation, drive down to godforsaken Portsmouth, and meet his old friend Greg Auro with no other purpose than to see what conclusion may result from him having seen Greg's face on the Eleven O'clock Eyewitness News. Why else would the backhoe operator hit the ground at just the right angle and dislodge a skull? Why else would he notice the white artifact rolling among the avalanche of unearthed debris? He could see no other choice than to follow the string and to discover where the terminus lay.

3

A Singing Sensation

Paul arrived at his desk in City Hall fifteen minutes late, but no one in the department paid attention to the comings and goings of their coworkers. Stacks of violations, terse correspondence from the new Housing Department Director concerning lunchtime rules and inspector conduct, scribbled reminders to himself on the backs of used envelopes and outdated department policy, half-finished to-do lists and random pieces of junk mail and advertising circulars covered his desk. He often thought of sweeping it all into a nearby trash can and waiting to see if the purging made any difference at all, if anyone anywhere missed one single piece of paper on his desk and if there would be the smallest consequence for the act. Not that he was blind to the global meaning of his desire as he understood that should a true crisis of paper take hold of him he would be finished as an inspector, given that paper and forms fueled his profession.

He inspected his stained coffee mug, saw that it held a residue of a month's worth of coffee, and filled it anyway. At home he had never poured coffee into a dirty cup but at work the act of washing the cup before reusing it seemed terribly burdensome and inconsequential. His flip calendar, pushed to the far corner by the reams of junk and work, hadn't been flipped in three weeks, and Paul read the same pithy aphorism, just as he had every day the previous three weeks: "No project deserves more time than our very lives." The sheer awfulness and blandness of the saying had struck him the moment he had ripped off the preceding day, so he decided not to change it until the awfulness wore away. He also had a genuine fear there might be worse sayings lurking behind this one.

At the desk nearest his own sat Tony Collongo, a boy singing sensation fifty years earlier, who had tacked up a series of publicity photos of his group, The Argyles, on the wall behind his desk. Tony sported the same pompadour as in the pictures, although his magnificent head of hair may have flattened a touch over the years due to minor hair loss. The smallness of his frame and the boyishness of his face, golden assets to a boy singer bent on wooing teen girls, turned against him as he aged so that now he looked like a child with an incurable disease who had rapidly aged before reaching full maturity.

The Argyles were on the cusp of national fame, as Tony told the story, when heartbreak and bad luck tore them apart. He and three friends from the neighborhood formed the group when they were all around fourteen years old. They practiced long and hard because it gave them a good excuse to be out of their houses and found that Tony had the best voice of the four, so they pushed him out front. They slogged through dozens of teen dances, municipal holiday events, carnivals, county fairs, and bowling league awards nights. They sang for whoever would listen. The organizers of events loved Tony. He looked wholesome and vulnerable and acted as if he needed their help. They could trust him with their daughters and their first deep stirrings of lust. He could sing about love and the broken-hearted, but given that he was more child than man, or so the parents thought, he was incapable of acting on the open invitations of his fans.

The Argyles got a break when they were chosen as an opening act for a boxing match pitting Junior "The Fist" McIntyre versus Boots Vincent. The Fist was on the rise like the Argyles and had become a solid regional draw when he fought. He had a gaudy record of 43-1-1 with the loss being a disqualification because he started an uppercut too low and nearly ripped the gonads off a Puerto Rican kid who screamed, "Mis testiculos son triturades!" until he fainted. He fought the draw against a lumbering German kid who had the advantage because The Fist fought while in the first throes of a virulent flu, throwing up between rounds and during the fight until the mat had become slick with his vomit. In a rematch a month later The Fist pummeled the German to the mat early in the second round.

The fight against Boots wasn't supposed to be much of a test as his managers had scheduled it as a warm-up to a much anticipated fight against Johnny Gunn, with the winner expected to attract enough backing to make a legitimate national title run, but The Fist's managers had missed two obvious facts about Boots – he was mean and had a sledgehammer uppercut. The roaring crowd of Fist backers riled up his meanness and allowed him to take horrible cranial punishment until both eyes had nearly swelled shut, but all he needed was one opening to unleash the uppercut and it occurred near the end of the seventh. The Fist connected with three quick jabs and when he stepped back to take a breath Boots launched the most devastating uppercut he would ever throw. All of the training, punishment, humiliation and pain flowed through his arm and exploded on the Fist's chin. Boots followed with a right cross, an overhand left and an overhand right and the Fist crumpled to the canvas so hard that those who sat ringside thought he had been killed.

As stunned silence seeped across the gymnasium the audience realized The Fist had no hope of beating the ten count, Phillip Markodian leaned over to his secretary and sometimes mistress, sometimes therapist, sometimes victim of his torrents of verbal abuse, Liz Sizemore, who had chosen a stunning blood red dress for the occasion, as if willing the boxers to open their veins for her, and said:

"Back to Palookaville for the Fist."

Markodian ran a local television station and had come to the fight with the idea of televising the Fist's next fight as a kick-off to a weekly Friday night series. Markodian had picked-up on the Fist's admirers and he dreamed of televising his rise to the championship. He thought of signing him to an exclusive contract so when the network boys came sniffing around they'd have to pay him off to get to the Fist. But his plans lay bleeding and gasping on the canvas and he would have to think of something else to fill the slot.

"What about the other guy? Can't you put him in a show?"

"Boots? That fucker looks like a molester. How stupid are you? If I start beaming perverts like that into households the government will shut me down. Maybe just keep your fucking ideas rattling around in that almost empty head of yours."

Liz narrowed her eyes and wondered if he had forgotten the night before when he crawled naked at her feet, kissing her ankles and calves and sobbing uncontrollably. The venom and bluster were like an ill wind blowing across a city dump. All she had to do was plug her nose and wait for a change in wind direction, away from that rotten spot inside him. She could have him on his knees any time she wanted.

"Not that guy. The boy singers. They were pretty good. Singing from a boxing ring is not the easiest of venues. The lead singer looked like he should have been holding a teddy bear."

"You're thinking a talent show? Local acts. Polka bands, tap dancers, trumpeters and harpists, goddamn yodelers and boy bands named after textile patterns. You're trying to prove you have just as much upstairs as you do down."

"You know, Phillip, I'd be a genius if I had as much up as down. As it is I'm a double threat and you better watch yourself. Maybe I'll own your station one day."

At the mention of her downstairs and business competition, Markodian very nearly began to vibrate as sweat seeped from his temples and neck, soaking the inside of his collar and thick hair. She placed a long, slender hand on his lap.

"Easy, baby, easy. I'll take care of you tonight, unless you prefer going home and having leftovers with the wife."

With the promise of future spoils Markodian's spirits soared to a place where every one of his ideas, no matter if half-formed or just a hasty sketch, was golden and his luck unbeatable. He searched out Tony in the dispersing crowd and asked if the Argyles had a manager. Tony, who had been hanging around the back door, waiting to hear news of the Fist, said his cousin sometimes handled the bookings. Markodian's eyes glowed red as he caught a whiff of hapless prey. Markodian told him to come to the television station the following week to sign a contract to be on a new variety show. The effect of such a request or command, Tony couldn't tell which, was akin to Markodian asking him to climb aboard a rocket ship to Saturn or whether or not he would like to take a spin around town in his Cadillac with his woman friend in the blood red dress.

Tony came to the station, which was just as exciting as the landscape of a distant planet, with the Argyles in tow. If you ever question the veracity of legends or myths, then you are not paying close attention to the stories in front of you, for in this case, poor boy singer, Tony the Argyle, surely was Faust and Markodian, smoking a cigar that smelled of sulfur and wearing a cologne called Eau du Brimstone, entered into a pact of doom. Tony signed the contract without really reading it and forced the other band members to do the same, missing details such as giving Markodian 98% of all record royalties, all appearance fees except a ten dollar per singer stipend per event, all rights to current and future songs, and making the band personally liable for all expenses Markodian incurred during the management and promotion of the group to be recouped from the 2% of recording royalties, and if said royalties could not cover said expenses then Markodian would loan them the money at a reasonable interest rate just two points above prime. The term was seven years, but it could have said a lifetime. For their part, the Argyles would sing on the variety show, would act as the house band and earn 1/32nd per hour of what any of the robust stamping and assembly plants in the neighborhood were paying.

Liz Sizemore looked like a genius for spotting the boys' appeal as their first appearance on the show generated a couple of thousand calls from breathless girls, wanting to know the names of those wonderful boy singers. It turned out that the boyishness and greasiness of their hair and faces, which Markodian associated with street thugs and the working class, was transformed by the lights and lens into an ether that addled the weak and willing. The second time they appeared the response was even greater, so they held their spot as regulars and every week they closed the show with a song. Liz picked what song they would perform from a catalog of standards and current Top 40 suitable for their range and image, which had begun to evolve. She dressed them in different matching outfits each week and the cost was added to their expense ledger, but the clothes had to remain at the studio in the costume department, so they came and went to their job in the same ratty and threadbare clothes they had before all the attention.

The show lasted over a year and turned them into a solid headliner in the footprint of the station's broadcast. A promoter could count on no less than 500 people when they performed, so Liz constantly fielded inquiries and booked them whenever she could. Markodian, at Liz's bequest, dropped a couple of well-placed calls to the producers of national shows and inked a deal with The Lux Hand Cream Variety Hour without the agreement of the boys. Markodian didn't outright sell his contract to Lux, but added another layer of expenses and middlemen with their hands in the boys' pockets. The Variety Hour was a summer replacement show on CBS with Vince Morningstar, an old radioman, whose lungs, it turned out, were laden with tumors of varying size, as the host. The producers of the show, who were in the employ of Lux in their advertising department, knew about soap but nothing of talent, creating weekly lineups of weak tap dancers, fading crooners, drunk and fat actors, and angry comedians. Morningstar coughed blood before and after the introductions and kept himself numb with a quart of vodka hidden offstage next to a carton of cigarettes.

None of this mattered to the Argyles, at least to Tony and Bobby, his closest friend in the group, who, when Liz told them she would be driving them to New York to appear on the Lux Hand Cream Variety Hour, an actual network television show, agreed that a headlining run at a club in New York or Chicago was just one small step away. The third Argyle balked and killed the dream before it could make itself manifest. Jimmy Portobello, the smartest of the four, had become increasingly angry over the contract they had signed and had been incessantly repeating the line, "All I get at the end of the week is ten bucks and a sore throat." Tony had wondered why the math never turned out in his favor but applause and the leers of pretty, young girls had a way of scrambling the equations until the next time his mother asked him why he never had any money. Jimmy took matters into his own hands and ran off and got married to a girl one week before they were scheduled to appear on the show. The girl had big breasts, jumbled teeth and access to a car that her brother had left when he enlisted in the army. He called Tony from Arkansas and told him he wouldn't be coming back. Tony begged and cried a little, but Jimmy was unmoved by the display.

"It's like chasing a girl you're not supposed to have. Even if you do bed her all that's going to happen is she's going to take all your money and you're going to have to worry about losing her every day."

"But, Jimmy, this is the Lux Hand Cream Variety Hour we're talking about here. This ain't no VFW hall."

"I'll make more money working in a factory and I have all the pussy I can handle. Sheila is something else. Singing to all those girls is nothing more than an empty promise, a goddamn tease."

"Why can't you quit after the show? Why are you doing this to me?" he begged.

By this point in the conversation Tony had let panic take hold of his voice, because he knew there was no replacing Jimmy. The chemistry and harmonies had taken a couple of years to build. Besides, Dominic, the fourth Argyle, wouldn't be able to sing without keying off Jimmy. They couldn't go to New York as a duet. Without Jimmy the idea of the Argyles ceased to exist.

"Please, Jimmy, please. You get one shot at something like this. Please don't do this. Please don't do this. Please...."

Before he could say it a third time the line went dead.

Tony waited a few days, the time it would take Jimmy to return from Arkansas in a creaky, oil-burning car, before telling Liz and Markodian of Jimmy's disappearance. Markodian remained silent for a few seconds then released an exhausted and knowing sigh from the depths of his throat.

"Back to Palookaville for the boy singers. The one lesson you learn from this kid is never underestimate the power of pussy. Call me if you scratch together another band."

Liz held a tear in her eye and stroked Tony's soft cheek. Whatever sexual attraction she had for Tony coalesced in that moment into a small throb of pitiful desire. If he asked she would have taken his member in her hand to make him feel better, Markodian be damned.

Tony lost his chance at fame but kept the pompadour. He tried other singers for the third and fourth Argyle spots but either they couldn't sing or lacked the time or discipline to practice or if they had both the talent and discipline they wanted creative control of the music which led to hard feelings and the nascent groups dissolved before fully forming. After a few years of trying he gave up. Musical tastes change quickly. Teenage girls are known for their fickleness and ruthlessness. He didn't like what he was hearing on the radio and at some point he wanted to move out of his mother's house. He cashed in his local fame for a job with the city. The head of human resources remembered him because his daughter had been a fan. Tony had always seemed the most clean-cut of the four.

Jimmy died in a car accident (in the same car that had made his flight possible!) a little more than a year after he abandoned the Argyles. His wife lived but the majority of her body never quite worked the same. Years later, even to the day Paul walked in late with his old friend Deputy Greg Auro on his mind, Tony could recall the shock of hearing the news from Dominic and for thinking for a minute or two that the bastard had gotten what deserved. He wondered if Jimmy would have made the same decision had he known that he would only have a year to enjoy his wife's body. Given a view of his tragic future would he have realized that a person should never turn his back on luck and good fortune because somewhere, somehow he would have to pay for the disrespect? It could be argued that Tony had been damaged by the accident even more than the girl with the jumbled teeth, because he could move neither forward nor backward. He could no longer argue with Jimmy about his rash decision and get him to admit he had made a mistake, even if the admission came years later after time had made them fat and a brood of kids had bankrupted them. Because Jimmy was no longer around to explain his actions, he would cast his friend back to utter, irrelevant anonymity as Tony had nothing else but to brood on the events between the time Markodian discovered them and the day of Jimmy's betrayal. He replayed entire conversations, concerts and practices with the intent of discovering when and how Jimmy became disaffected, had abandoned what he thought had been a communal dream of the four Argyles. He scrutinized his every response and could find nothing he did that drove Jimmy into the arms of the girl with jumbled teeth. He barely remembered what she looked like. She was so quiet and mousy that he never would have guessed that she was a much more ominous threat than Markodian himself.

This obsession with past events, especially past events that no one else cared about, took a toll on Tony. He rapidly lost his boyish openness, which had been based on the false notion that the world was basically good and fair and all one had to do was flash a winning smile and wear comfortable shoes to get by reasonably. The lost openness created a void, filled eventually by irritability and sarcasm, because a tragedy needs an audience to fulfill its purpose and the world had moved on, had dismissed the Lux Hand Cream Variety Hour as a botched, dare we say amateurish production, had rejected street corner do-wop for more aggressive and loud guitar-based music, and looked wearily at Tony as the last remaining player of an unfortunate circumstance, thus denying the events the significance of tragedy.

But the pompadour remained as a talisman of things past. One look in the mirror could conjure the thrill of singing into a crowd of tear-stained faces. The act of applying pomade to his hair was not unlike a priest pulling on his holy vestments, a soldier lacing up his boots, or a skier meticulously dressing to play in the bitter cold. The hair was his church, his armor and his protection against insult. It could have been defiance as well, one last vestige of the boy singer on the brink of stardom.

Back at City Hall the same boy singer sat in a cubicle in the housing department under failing fluorescent tubes. By now his irritation had bloomed into hostility and his bitterness had transformed into active paranoia. Not only was the world hostile and cruel, but the forces who ruled society had long ago thrown off its mantel of passivity and now actively sought out his destruction and humiliation. A person could expect nothing more than survival and any time past the age of sixty lay an unpredictable ground of soft earth and radically shifting plates. Growing older was nothing but slaughter.

Of course a person need not be entirely passive as he awaits his ultimate fate. There were ways to fight. He could keep every single memo, policy, reprimand, accommodation, email, phone message or note ever sent to him from his previous seventy-four bosses. He could memorize the personnel policies that governed the department and recite passages, right down to comma pauses and grammar mistakes, on command. He could, once the technology became affordable and portable, record every conversation in which he engaged, no matter personal or work-related, not fully understanding that such an activity might be an unintended consequence of his obsessive constructing and deconstructing the conversations that determined the fate of the Argyles. Many times during the course of his research he remarked that he wished he had recorded the conversations between

Jimmy and him to make the analyzing that much easier. First he bought a reel-to-reel recorder and placed it under his desk by his feet and could only capture the work conservations that occurred in a close orbit around his desk due to its lack of portability. Next came a cassette recorder the size of a loaf of bread that he hid in his desk drawer or a leather satchel he carried on his shoulder with the microphone peeking out of a gap. Thereafter the recorders became smaller each year and his latest version consisted of a wireless microphone in the shape of a pen linked to a wireless recorder the size of a credit card slipped behind his driver's license in his wallet with 32 GB of recording space. Each night he downloaded the day's content onto flash drives and labeled each recording with the day, approximate time, person or persons involved and the general content of the conversation. Everyone in the office and in his family knew about the recordings, though, so the conversations tended to be without much content and never included any gossip or opinions that could be damaging if ever replayed. New bosses often ran afoul of his system when they feigned ignorance or issued contradictory orders or outright lied about something they had previously said. Many a boss had blanched when Tony recited word for word a conversation they had hoped everyone had forgotten. By the time Tony finished his recitation all they could do was acknowledge the truthfulness of his recollection. The best of them soon learned how to speak to Tony and wheedled the other employees until they told him Tony's secret. The worst of the bosses fumed and spit and called Tony all kinds of names, including conjurer, magician and idiot savant.

Tony spoke in a loud and clear voice that respected every syllable of every word. Whenever he thought the person or persons in the conversation spoke too softly, quickly or mumbled or talked over each other then he would have them repeat their statements. Usually, he would restate the question or context of the speech in a louder, more emphatic voice, something like, "So, Tom what I heard you say is that policy number 10917-27 is no longer in effect as of July 15th. Is that correct? Did I hear you correctly?" Paul had witnessed Tony asking a new supervisor to repeat the same information at least six times until the man's face contorted in rage as he stared over the labyrinth of cubicles. Paul never saw the man return to Tony's desk again to deliver instructions or chat.

When Paul arrived late that morning he noticed Tony already transcribing notes onto a violation report. They looked directly at each other through a gap in the cubicle walls. Paul wondered how many hours of his voice Tony had recorded and stored in his vault at home. It gave him small comfort to know a record of his existence resided somewhere outside his own mind.

"Looks like you're got a hot one there, Tony," Paul said with his lips hovering above the rim of his office coffee cup.

Tony cleared his throat and hummed a few notes of an old pop tune, maybe the Penguins' "Earth Angel," he used as a time marker between recordings to make it easier to find and categorize later.

"I thought I've seen some filth in my time. These people yesterday," he paused and looked to the report on his desk as if it was a diorama that captured his experience in miniature. "I don't know if they're crackheads or what. They're shitting and pissing in a bucket smack in the middle of the kitchen floor. It's just sitting there not five feet from the refrigerator and, hell, I don't know, maybe half full and the whole kitchen smells like someone just laid one to rest in there. So, I'm almost dying and God bless if Elaine didn't make bacon and eggs for breakfast, so I'm dealing with a rising tide in my gut. So, I ask the woman about the bucket, and let me tell you she smelled about as bad as the bucket and she says the landlord told her that water rates had gone up so he turned it off. Turned off the water! Told her it was either that or he raised the rent. So, naturally I ask why it's in the kitchen and she tells me the stairs had collapsed a month before, so the family can't put the bucket in the bathroom upstairs. I'm not sure if they are crackheads or what. I suppose you might as well be if you're going to live like that. Everybody is a goddamn fucking animal. The lords of the manor keep tightening the screws." He ended with a dismissive wave of his hand that blotted out or cleansed everyone who either lived in or owned substandard housing.

"Roaches?" Paul asked. He always asked about roaches because he hated them the most of all the pests since he had had them in his hair, under his shirt, and even once nestled against the elastic of his boxer shorts during his tenure as an inspector.

"C'mon, always the same question. Roaches, rats, raccoons, lice, flies by the million, bed bugs, and probably a colony of bats on the second floor."

"Who owns it?"

"What? Is this your first fucking day? Am I breaking in a rook?"

"Blevins, Inc."

"Blevins fucking Inc."

Paul fell silent and let the information tumble through his mind. Tony waited ten seconds before picking up "Earth Angel" again to signal the recording had ended. Every inspector had run across Blevins Inc. during their inspections. The company owned hundreds of houses across the city, all rapidly deteriorating and crumbling back into the earth. They had practically bought up whole neighborhoods once the depression hit the streets with the intention of renting them out for as long as possible. They had become masters at stringing out the violation process, making minor improvements to satisfy minimal progress toward resolution of the violation list, all the while knowing they had no real intention of satisfying all the city codes. The true owners of Blevins Inc. were rumored to live in the foothills of the Ozarks but stayed well-hidden behind a host of lawyers and hastily organized holding companies, so that Blevins Inc. was an apparition, a phantom that could not be punished for its misdeeds because paper ownership changed so rapidly that no court had the resources or stamina to untangle the knot.

Defeat came in cycles and it could last one day or several in a row, and Paul came to think of it as his form of migraine headaches or epilepsy. He could identify obvious triggers, like Blevins Inc. and its apparent mission to spread blight and misery, but most often as of late it came on unpredictably. Sometimes it struck him on the way to work as he passed a familiar landmark, such as a grotesque billboard hawking booze or the lottery or a boarded-up building that had been vacant for over a decade with little prospect of ever finding a new purpose or a bank of low-hanging clouds that had blotted out the sun for the previous ten days. The sensation felt akin to nausea without the danger of vomiting. Sometimes he felt it after an especially good lunch at a Lebanese restaurant where he lunched every other day or after a productive morning or even during an especially productive week. Suddenly the prospect of working five more hours, or one more week, or one more month, or one more year, or the yawning stretch of years it would take him to stagger to retirement came swooping down from atop the vending machine or out of the coffee pot or from his plate of hummus and paralyzed him for the duration of its stay. During these low periods it was all he could do to look busy, to convince himself he had at least a small purpose, by shuffling papers, checking emails, pretending to listen to the phone with a dead line, and skirting along the edge of appropriate websites approved by the administration, and not nap under his desk or head to the nearest bar.

Although, Paul would not have admitted that he disliked his work. He had begun his job as inspector with some zeal, eager to eliminate substandard housing and to track down slumlords who treated their pets better than their tenants. But inevitably the volume of misery wore the zeal out of him and poverty and squalor no longer appalled him as he became resigned to the impossibility of their eradication.

He had watched minor maintenance problems blossom into catastrophe. A fissure in a waste pipe draining a second story bathroom willfully ignored until it became a gaping hole and the collective piss and shit of a family of six doused the floor below. Or a single broken pane of glass in a window led to a metropolis of invading pigeons and a cottage industry of city bird guano, which Paul had to skate across and all but ruin a fairly new pair of shoes to find the source of the invasion. He found the family, a mother and two teenage sons, trapped in a small bedroom. They had long ago ceded control of the house to the invading flock and now used a side window to enter and exit. These instances of depravity and misery sometimes repeated themselves and other times mutated and created new categories. On the days when Paul had been shown a new page from the citizenry's book of suffering, he would come back to the office and immediately engage Tony in conversation while his impressions were still fresh. Tony parsed his schedule to the minute so Paul always knew where he could be found and what he would be doing when found. He knew when he poured his second cup of coffee, when he took a dump in the third floor bathrooms, when he worked on paperwork, when he scheduled his inspections and when he would be available to record Paul's observations.

Paul poured out every excruciating detail in a loud and clear voice. Tony egged him on with grunts and clicks and asked clarifying questions when he thought it necessary. Paul gave posterity joyous rodent gambols, infants crawling through excrement and dirt, snapped joists, rotten floors, octogenarians frozen at the breakfast table because of a broken furnace and an inability to act, collapsed roofs, basements completely underwater, and rooms filled with every scrap of paper the inhabitants had touched in the last thirty years. Paul often imagined Tony's neat row of flash drives and tapes, holding his recorded voice. The recordings would bear witness to what he had seen and slowly reveal the changes in his voice, the movement from neophyte to veteran, catching the encroaching cynicism and weariness, the reveling in unfortunate detail, and the questioning of the depravity of man.

"Tony, do you have a vacation form?"

Tony stopped writing, held Paul with his eyes, and cleared his throat.

"Why do you want a VACATION FORM, Paul? " Tony said as he eased back in his chair and raised his arms over his head, providing an unobstructed path for his microphone.

"Because I have accrued time and I'm thinking of taking a vacation."

"Well, Paul, you haven't been reading your department directives, have you? Wait, don't answer. I know the answer before you even attempt to speak. However, had you read the latest directive dated June 15th you would have remembered that, because our new commissioner has determined the backlog of cases to be too vast and burdensome to the health and welfare of our rotten city, all vacation requests will be denied, flat-out refused, until October 1st, safely on the other side of summer. I could be mistaken, but I doubt that you'll be needing a vacation form. Our new commissioner has determined there will be no summer for us this year."

Paul had lived through this a dozen times. A new housing commissioner came on the job with guns ablaze, with a steady eye on promotion to a cabinet-level position. They fired off directives about vacation and being to work on-time, the two untouchable rights and unsolvable puzzles of the staff. They collectively believed in the right of everyone to be late, and for the early-risers to leave early. No number of timekeeping solutions (time clocks, signing-in at the commissioner's desk, computer time stamp) would make them desist as they found a solution to every trap. Secondly, vacation and sick-time was valued as much as a farmer valued rain and sun or a Bedouin valued potable water. Half the staff stayed on the job because of the time they could be away from it. Altering vacation rules was tantamount to pulling out a gun and threatening the staff with summary execution, so the act of taking away their summer had left them in a black mood.

"Just give me the vacation form. I'll take it right to his desk once I fill it out."

"We both know that won't happen."

Paul could feel his face flush. Tony enjoyed playing this predictable game. The echoes of screaming and gasping girls writhing under his velvety do-wop had forever altered his idea of masculinity and whoever had not tapped this vein of male attractiveness crawled through life as a coward and more than likely desperately repressed surging homosexual impulses. Given his perch of superiority, he baited his victims with disparaging comments about past or future cowardice because they had never commanded the violent tides of estrogen released by girls awakening from their asexuality. He usually ramped up the banter until his victim cracked and showed anger, at which time he would raise his hands, palms outward, in mock surrender and suggest the offended party be less defensive or plainly admit he carried dreams of submissiveness.

Paul would not engage in the banter and thought the fact that Tony still tried reflected poorly on him. Not that Paul wasn't a coward in his heart. Tony had that right. He had never bucked any of the parade of commissioners. He had no strategy for survival other than showing up more or less on-time and working at a reasonable pace. Still, coward or not, Paul thought it unreasonable that he had to spend a decade staring at Tony's publicity photos in all their youthful, grinning futility, to be reminded hourly of crushed dreams of a naïve boy singer, and that the photos provided a shield for Tony against any volley back. Their continuous presence indicated to Paul that Tony's hold on life was so tenuous that any wrong word lobbed in his direction could send him to an early death, where he would await Dion and the Belmonts, the Mello-Kings and Kathy Young and the Innocents so he could finally sing with the stars.

Tony, not one to be pitied or think anything about himself should be pitied, took Paul's silence as proof of his accusations, and his view of Paul had become so calcified and certain that no matter what act of valor Paul performed he would see it as an anemic attempt to mask his true self. Paul accepted these defeats with a tight-lipped grin followed by an unhappy chuckle.

"Are you going to give me the vacation form or not?"

With a dramatic collapse of his features, as if to say he had been beaten by a superior opponent or, in the language of do-wop, had reached the denouement of a tragic teen love song, Tony opened a drawer of his desk and produced a crisp yellow sheet of paper. Yellow had just recently chosen as the new color of vacation forms and Tony had stored away a rainbow of past choices in case new administrations preferred a previous color. He held the paper to his side and hung his head in mock resignation.

Paul lurched from his chair, coffee cup still in his hand, and retrieved the form.

"Showing off your bald spot, Tony?" he hissed, in spite of all his control and acceptance of the small defeats delivered by Tony.

Tony straightened up and unsuccessfully fought the urge to probe the crown of his head with an index finger. The hair was still holding; no skin yet.

"What kind of lowlife bastard are you?"

Paul walked away without turning around or responding, thrilled with his comeback, paper in hand.

4

Escape

The commissioner sat in his office, talking on the phone. Paul stood in the doorway and watched him quietly mouth the words into the receiver, a sure sign the call had nothing to do with housing or any other aspect of his job. The new commissioner, young and immensely under-qualified to lead the department, had graduated from a state university somewhere in Indiana and had bounced around low-rung jobs with several municipal and state governments before landing this assignment. Whenever anyone was hired in a leadership position speculation and rumors heated-up as to whom the person knew. The case against this commissioner included proof that his father was a close, personal friend of the mayor and had raised significant amounts of cash for his reelection campaign, not to mention his father's friendships with several west side councilmen. Of the son nothing really could be said of his past except he had been lucky to have been sired by such a father. The more salacious gossip centered on the new commissioner's department by department, room by room search and seizure of all the adorable and willing women in City Hall. His dizzying mastery of all things carnal outpaced all the wagging tongues, so at any given time he might he working on a conquest two or three women removed from the subject of the rumor. To call him indiscriminate would be charitable, but it all seemed like good sport until he turned his attentions to his own department and he bedded the receptionist and the administrative assistant in successive months, when the talk took a turn toward guessing the length of his tenure and openly wondering if he would last a full year until the mayor caught wind of his indiscretions.

The commissioner smiled vacantly and his lips curled around the mouthpiece of the receiver.

"I can't wait to see you tonight bay-bee. You are so beautiful and sweet bay-bee."

Paul smirked as the commissioner ended the dalliance with a half-formed "baby" that sounded like he burped softly and as a final goodbye he gently set the receiver down. Lost in a dazed reverie that drifted through favors won and favors to come, the commissioner either didn't notice the body blocking his doorway or refused to acknowledge it until the reverie had run its course. For Paul the wait felt like an eternity, but he wouldn't leave. He had learned during his years in the department to never wait for a scheduled appointment with a commissioner or director. They could so easily change the time or date at the last minute, blame other meetings for going over, pretend the meeting had never been scheduled, or just keep their door shut and never answer the knock. The best strategy was to stand at their door and interrupt, garnering an answer or clarification before the commissioner had time to hide behind formality.

The commissioner finally noticed Paul and did nothing to hide his annoyance at being interrupted.

"Yes?"

"Just dropping off a vacation form. I need you to approve it," Paul said as he tried to dull any edge that had sharpened while he had listened to the commissioner's pillow talk.

"You are?"

"Paul Newcombe."

"Housing Inspector?"

"Correct."

"It's a big department. I can't be expected to know everyone's name yet."

"No one's expecting you to."

"What's that mean exactly?"

"It means it's a big department with a lot of names. How could you know everyone's name?"

"I assume you know how to read, right Paul? I'm sure literacy was one of the qualifications when you hired on, right? But who knows what they did in the past, right? I imagine they checked to see if you were breathing and signed you up as inspector, very rigorous screening and assessment, right?"

"I have no idea in what direction you are taking this conversation," Paul said as his face had begun to flush. He could take the ribbing from Tony because of the ridiculousness of him thinking himself superior to anyone, but the same aggressiveness out of a young, ambitious commissioner with an over-sized libido stirred a well of hate.

"I think I made myself clear on vacations, Paul. The email went out last week. The backlog is just too big and I can't spare you, funny as that sounds. I don't know what the department was doing before I got here because we have mountains of violations to process and years' worth of inspections to do. I can't be responsible for all the shirking and malingering that went on before now, but this ship has to get pointed in the right direction. We're actually going to work now. We're going to dynamite that mountain down to nothing. I'll show the mayor how a department is supposed to run. So, I've made a decision that there are no vacations this summer. Once we get ahead of the curve you can take some time off, but for now it's nothing but work. Extraordinary times call for extraordinary measures." The commissioner ended the speech by placing the palms of his hands on the top of his desk as if he expected the desk to start shaking and rattling under the force of his pronouncement.

"I do understand the policy."

"Good, then we understand each other. See, maybe you came in here seeing what you could get away with just because I'm new. Maybe your wife is harping on you to take the kids to the beach. I can almost hear her now. I'd do the same. Kids love the beach and they can drive you crazy, so I'm told. A good family guy like you wants to provide. I understand, but now you know I'm serious as a heart attack and I can sniff out any of your plots. The work needs to get done. You understand that the work needs to get done, right Paul?"

Paul had never seen the work get done. For every case that he completed three more landed on his desk. The work would never end because rot never stopped. He had learned to accept that the work could never be completed, instead of panicking that he fell more hopelessly behind each day. Such realism allowed him to be productive, if not on some days industrious, as he was able to forget the larger context of an impossible task. Because why kill yourself trying to complete an impossible task, something akin to tying a string around the world without the string ever breaking? The best the new commissioner could hope for was to create an allusion of progress and cash it in for a promotion before the trick could be revealed.

"I understand the work. I truly understand."

"Well, good again! We seem to perfectly understand each other. We have found common ground. Now go do what you do and we will both be better off for it, right?"

"The thing is that my anniversary date comes up in about two weeks."

"Really? And how long have you been here, Paul?"

"Ten years. I'll have been here ten years."

"Ten years ago I was a junior in high school, Paul, but who can argue with having experience on the staff. I'm going to use all that experience to our collective advantage."

"I understand your ambition, Commissioner, and I have to say I'm a little surprised that you're willing to take on the mayor so soon after your appointment, but I'm a good soldier. I'll step in line and do what I've been told."

"What do you mean take on the mayor?"

"Oh, right, you're so new to the job that you weren't here for the last fiscal crisis. It was a real bloodbath. We lost a lot of positions and some good people, but when the mayor went to lay them off he found a hidden treasure trove of accrued vacation time. My fellow workers like to squirrel away their days for the lean times or when they've just completely gone insane. So the mayor had to pay out huge sums of money to the laid off workers just to pay out the vacation time. The mayor, as you know, has a tendency to lose his mind when pushed into a corner, so he eliminated the option to carryover vacation time from one fiscal year to the next. It absolutely violates our collective bargaining agreement, but in times of fiscal emergency the mayor is granted broad powers to trample on contracts, ignore collective bargaining agreements, forgive his own debts, and ignore the pleas of vendors. So, really, I have no option but to take the vacation days. You can't force me to lose them and I can't horde them. I'll have no choice but to file a grievance and your policy will be held up to the light of day. If you want to cross swords with the mayor I'm good with it, but otherwise sign this form and we will be set."

"He's crippled us. I won't have anyone here. Why would he do that?"

"Because the work never gets done!" Paul exploded and he felt as if he was rising towards the ceiling without the ability to return to the ground. "There's no end to misery and filth. The work will always be there piling up, suffocating us, following us home, calling us in the middle of the night and hanging up, leaving notes for us under the windshield wipers of our cars, sending us disgusting pictures through email, and cursing us through texts." He thought he might break apart in the air, become unglued, as his voice rose and tremors shook his hands. "And there's always some commissioner or director somewhere in the Hall who thinks the work can get done so they cancel vacations, they blot out summer from the calendars, they ignore overtime rules, and they grind us down to our bones. They think the work can be appeased. Just show the work you're serious, show dedication, faith, humor, tenacity and the work may loosen the grip it has around your neck. Then it will come to his senses, and then it will slink back into the shadows. Work can be reasonable, if you give every minute of your life to calm it. And we've shamed it back into the shadows on occasion, but it's always there, eyeing us and conjuring up ways to destroy us. So you see, Commissioner, you're not thinking about this correctly, work can never be appeased. It will be ever present and will never be conquered. If you understand that you'll understand the impossibility of the task you have charged us with. Accept it as a fact. "

"So, you're the spokesman for them back there? You're the shithouse lawyer? They elected you to come up here to push me around, to see if I mean what I say?"

"No, I'm just the jerk who didn't take all of his vacation time yet and who has to take the next two weeks off so you don't run afoul of the mayor."

"Trust me. I'm good with the mayor."

"I'm going to give this form to you and you can do what you want with it. I know I'm following policy and if you want to block me from that you'll be the one responsible."

"Now you're threatening me? We're not starting off on the right foot here, Paul. I don't like to be threatened by subordinates."

"That's something you'll have to get used to. The last commissioner had a gun pulled on him in the parking deck. The crew back there can get pretty cranky, so you have to know when to take your foot off of our throats. Besides, don't think an organizational chart implies that I'm a subordinate in any other way."

"Sure, and the guy who pulled the gun is sitting in jail, thinking that it probably wasn't such a good idea to handle his problems like that," the commissioner said as a brief glimpse of panic flitted across his face.

"Not exactly. He won the case in arbitration and still works here. The mayor pressured the commissioner not to press charges because he didn't want the electorate thinking his administration settled their differences with guns."

"You're lying to me."

"No, I am not."

"Who was it?"

"I really can't tell you. I think it would be a major ethical lapse on my part to reveal her name. I'm sure there's got to be something in her personnel file. At least a mention."

"Her?"

"Or him."

Of course the story was a lie. The previous commissioner had been a benevolent boozer who drank with his inspectors whenever he could engineer it, always buying and never releasing them from the party until they were dead drunk or the bar closed. They, in turn, had no problem labeling themselves as his subordinates as he proved he could drink every one of them under the table. If anything had been put in the personnel files of the staff during his tenure it most likely would have been a glowing report about dedication and honor written on the back of a cocktail napkin. His tenure ended with a one car crash into a telephone pole and his subsequent funeral.

"I'll have to talk to the mayor. I'll never get this city straightened out if he's going to tie and my hands and feet."

"Right, and he sticks a ball in your mouth and wraps a leash around your neck and makes you call him master."

"I don't like you."

"Well, Commissioner, any number of previous bosses have told us that you don't have to like the people you work with. You just have to get the job done, but, of course, as we know the job will never get done."

The phone rang and the commissioner let six rings sound off before picking up the receiver. He softened his voice into a purr and Paul thought he heard him say, "Where have I been? Where have YOU been?" His eyebrows arched in response to the answer he received. Paul half-expected the commissioner's tongue to wrap itself around the phone receiver, like a boa constrictor seizing its prey right before a slow and fatal squeeze. Paul would not leave.

"Just a sec, bay-bee," the commissioner said as he clicked his fingers and motioned Paul to the desk.

Paul lay the vacation form on the desk and the commissioner scratched a signature across the bottom, then dismissed him with a few flicks of his fingers. As Paul closed the door he heard the commissioner breathe a lustful, guttural laugh, but he wouldn't force himself to turn around and see what face he might be making. Nothing could overwhelm his new desire to flee.

Paul handed the completed form to the commissioner's administrative assistant. She had also worked for all sixteen commissioners who had reigned during Paul's tenure, and the experience hung heavily on her face. Outside of work people thought she was an emergency room nurse or a paralegal in a divorce attorney's office, such was the narrative her face betrayed. Paul had taken her on a couple of dates years before, but they found they could talk of nothing more than their jobs and City Hall gossip, which filled up a few hours until turning utterly toxic. She read the form and smiled, stifling a small, bitter laugh.

"I just sent out that email two days ago. Does he even remember what he had me write?" she asked with mock incredulity as if she hadn't seen every form of incompetence already.

"He remembers. He just was not informed about the carry-over policy the mayor set last year."

"The carry-over policy?"

"Yes."

"And when did the mayor write this policy and what does it say?"

"I hope he actually writes one before I get back from vacation. That would solve a small problem I may have. But I would suggest that as many people as possible take advantage of the policy while it's still in effect. Remember, you have to take all of your vacation before your anniversary date. The mayor is adamant about no carry-over vacation time. It seems a terrible waste to spend our summer in this building."

"You know that's impossible, right? Some of these people have years of vacation saved. "

"I know. This is just a small window to let some fresh air in."

"If he told them to take all their vacation and made them go out into the sunshine they would lose their minds and they'd have to turn out the lights because nobody would be left on the floor."

"Sometimes we have to act and worry about the consequences later. All I know is I have a signed vacation form and starting next Monday I'll be off for two weeks. He's the one that signed the form. He might even forget he talked to me by the end of his phone call."

"Not another one of those women?"

"Complete with baby talk and a snake tongue."

She made a deep-throated retching noise as she stuck a finger in her mouth, then she opened a desk drawer and pulled out a leave request form, a different color than the one Tony had given Paul. She sported a grin as she filled in the blank spaces.

5

A Brief History

Paul told no one that he planned to visit a dank Ohio River town and meet Deputy Greg Auro. Usually, he spent his vacations somewhere along the Atlantic coast with whatever woman he could convince to come with him. Once, with a woman named Tina Burns, he stayed at Rehoboth Beach in Delaware deep in the throes of new love and the salt water and blazing sun, along with Tina's collection of miniscule bikinis, spun him through a dizzying week of sex and drunkenness. She drifted away to someone, as she said, of an airier character, leaving him to pine for more weeks of carnality and thirst. On the other end of the scale sat a week he spent in Kitty Hawk, North Carolina with Kathleen Bertram. They had begun arguing the first hour of the car ride down and didn't stop until he dropped her off at her apartment a week later. She had realized before they left that she disliked him, but being of a frugal nature she didn't want to lose the deposit money she had thrown in for the condo. So, she went forward with the vacation and he slept on the couch and they didn't' so much as kiss during their stay, an especially cruel fate given the constant state of undress she exhibited while on the beach.

For the past three summers he had gone to Virginia Beach with his last girlfriend, Annie Stock. They had stopped talking three months before Paul saw Greg on the news when they both finally concluded they were partners in a failing enterprise. Annie was older than Paul, had an eight year old son from a previous marriage, and worked as a dispatcher for a trucking company in an old industrial park that a passerby might consider to have been abandoned. Her body showed signs of aging as she looked nothing like Tina or Kathleen in a bathing suit, but she was appreciative of getting away from the industrial park and the truckers, even though their crude comments often resonated in her thoughts. Paul never warmed-up to her son so she never brought him on their vacations. Paul guessed she was waiting for a marriage proposal and his health insurance, but he would never get around to asking her.

Their last fight began when Annie caught him staring at her naked body as she applied makeup in his bathroom. She usually enjoyed the attention, but something about his furrowed brow made her ask a fatal question.

"What are you thinking about?"

He thought for a moment and formulated, "Age and decay."

Annie slammed down her lipstick, causing the paint to shoot out across surface of the sink. She stormed past him and into the bedroom, where she had left her clothes. Paul followed without apology, but the sight of her angry, burning face and her suddenly animated flesh turned him on, so he ripped off his boxer shorts and caught her by the hips as she bent over to reach a crumpled blouse.

"Get off of me! What are you doing?"

He pushed her to the bed with enough force to bury her face in the tangled sheets. He slapped her abundant ass and fucked her until he was exhausted. Later, he would liken his actions to a sudden gun blast during an otherwise quiet and drowsy morning, shattering not only the silence but an otherwise perfectly workable relationship. Annie waited until he finished with a cry and then broke away. Paul could tell a torrent of words were building up behind the dam of her lips, but she dressed in silence, although she misaligned the buttons on her blouse and didn't bother to buckle her belt.

"Why am I constantly surprised by how much of a bastard you are?" she finally and unsatisfyingly said. "Shame on me for introducing you to my son. I'm just an idiot, again and again."

He tried to call her twice for dates, but she would never pick up the phone. He thought she may be overreacting, because he refused to place his hard truth within the context of a larger body of work that had Annie's inadequacies as its subject. He couldn't have said why he insisted on honesty with her other than to remind her what she wasn't or had never been. She had never been particularly good-looking or thin or intelligent or funny or able to craft experience into entertaining stories or very good at selecting men who would treat her well and appreciate the fact that she was mediocre in all things.

So the prospect of another beach vacation with Annie Stock appeared to be dim, but he believed if she answered her phone he could coerce her to go, since almost anything had to be better than another week at the trucking company, a place ruled by fat, foul-mouthed drivers. But that downy, brown moustache and crooked teeth kept up their haunting. The narrow shoulders and unnaturally thick Popeye forearms refused to slink back to the shadows. The buckles frozen in place like ancient locks and their breath trailing from their mouths like smoke as they walked through a sparse, leafless woods to the caves played like a current memory. The cold sting came back to his cheeks and he looked to see if his hands had curled into frozen claws. Annie Stock had no power to resist the lure of Greg Auro.

Paul's mother had sold the family house shortly after his father died, so he hadn't been back to their old neighborhood in years. The vision and voice of Greg Auro had opened the door and now, as Paul sat at his desk staring at his computer screen but not comprehending an email shimmering in front of him, the ghosts filed through the open doorway seeking remembrance. His mother was technically not a ghost at all, but an increasingly distracted and confused voice talking from the edge of a swamp in the interior of Florida, but a younger and stronger version of herself came on the arm of his dead father, who talked in an argot of fatherly advice, other-worldly pronouncements, and inane chatter. Secondary characters, barbers, teachers, gas station owners, baseball coaches, stood in a deferential circle as if awaiting the lead of the play to come out and take his bow. Even his parents smiled obsequiously and deferred to the entrance of Andrew Auro, who bolted through the doorway as if determined to take control of Paul's mind and put it into some kind of order. His head was clean-shaven. He had a bared chest that tapered trimly to his waist and looked like a cruder, tougher version of Greg. His eyes held a curiosity and intelligence lacking in Greg's that Paul knew he employed in the service of his meanness, to cut deeper and more accurately than someone less intelligent ever could.

Greg's father shaved his head every night with a straight razor in a bathroom right off of the Auro family kitchen. He would leave the door open as he sat on the toilet in just his underwear or with a loosely draped towel across his lap. His head would be slathered with foam and as the long blade cut a swath his pink dome shone through the cleanly sliced rows. When Paul was allowed in the house he would stand on the periphery of Mr. Auro's vision and watch the operation. Greg might try to pull him away or whisper into his ear that they should go into his room, but Paul would not be moved and Mr. Auro let them stay because he enjoyed the audience. He contorted his face into a deadly serious grimace as he finished each swath with a flick of the wrist. He never looked into a mirror, preferring to shave by the feel of his fingertips.

This display of grooming was not the only difference between the Auro household and his own. Mr. Auro's penchant for quoting the Bible in any given situation jolted Paul's budding agnosticism, which would in later years develop into a sensible atheism that he had picked up from his parents who had lost contact with the Lutheran church they presumably belonged to. But for Mr. Auro his conversation with God was constant, vibrant and consuming. He spent the majority of his time off from work sitting in a chair with an opened Bible on his lap, looking from a distance to be calm and meditative, until Paul came close enough to see the wild anger betrayed by his eyes, brought on by the reading. Sometimes he clutched the Bible to his chest in rapture, as if the book had become a wife or small child and he couldn't help but exhibit familial love. Paul sometimes heard Mr. Auro scream from the relative safety of Greg's room, as he compared the perfection of the words to the reality of the current world. He expressed to the house that he felt like Moses coming down from Mt. Sinai carrying the commandments written in God's own hand only to find his flock fornicating and drinking at the feet of God. Paul thought he would tear apart the house in rage, but fortunately he settled for screaming from his chair and pounding the arm rests of his chair. The more such scenes Paul experienced the more drawn he became to the Auro house.

Paul's parents said Auro interpreted the Bible to his own ends. Paul's dad in particular would get himself worked-up and proselytize in a faux preacher's voice that Hebrew law explicitly reads that the man of the house shall not cut grass, or paint his house, or trim his bushes, or take out the trash. In short, a man shall not tend to his house if he has a wife. The imitation would end with a scowl and a string of invective spoken under his breath. The result of Mr. Auro's interpretation, accurately mocked by Paul's dad, was the slow wearing away of Greg's mother, Maggie Auro, who tended to all her chores in a faded pink housecoat and sometimes even pink curlers in her hair. By the time she pushed their rusty rotary mower through their acre of crab grass the coils of her hair would be soaked in sweat and ready to be washed again. Mr. Auro did not believe in mowers with motors. Motors caused luxury and weakness and every good Christian knew that those were the fields in which sin bloomed. He also worried the thwacking of a motor would disturb his studies as even the rotary mower created enough sound to make him close the window and draw the shades as Maggie toiled in the yard.

Paul's father talked to Maggie at their shared property line when they both happened to be out pulling weeds from their gardens, mowing or gathering fallen branches after a storm. They would stand with mud on their arms or sweat dripping steadily from their faces and share news of their families. Maggie spent a good portion of her time railing against her husband and explaining how all the work was slowly killing her. She believed in God being in the house, but she never imagined the personal price she would pay for his residence. Raising children and keeping up the house was no small feat when a lunatic shared your bed. She always blushed when she inadvertently acknowledged the conjugal nature of marriage, even though sex between her and her husband had stopped with the birth of their last child, Greg, or so she inferred with cryptic musings on loneliness and desire.

Paul's father took it all in with stoic charm, calming her with his assuredness and stable mental capacity. He never took the bait she offered as he would not heap more criticism on Bible-thumping Andy Auro to her. Not that he agreed with Auro's approach to life. He hated the man. He agreed with Maggie and thought Auro to be crazed, lazy, and not much of a man at all, but he would not jump into the fray because nothing good would come of it. When he could muster the strength and his sweat would finally stop dripping, his father would flirt with her and compliment the dingy housecoat or the way her face had tanned over the summer. The compliments muddled her thoughts and caused her to blush from her neck to her forehead. With a little color on her face she projected a kind of youthful ruggedness, not exactly attractive, but a pioneering resolve willing to stare down tornadoes and shovel her way out of snow drifts taller than her, and Paul's father's smile became genuine and despite the odor and filth of their bodies they leaned closer. Paul thought the flirtation ended there, two mouths two feet away, their bodies clinging to the very edge of their property. Both his father and Mrs. Auro worked too hard, lived too practically, and the opportunities for rendezvous too brief for them to carry anything further. Paul thought of them as two pack mules brushing their cheeks together after climbing an arduous mountain trail before crashing into a well-earned sleep.

"No, she won't divorce him. A woman like that will stick it out to her last day," said his father to his mother as he inspected the contents of their refrigerator, unsatisfied at his prospects. "Auro has turned her off of God, but she thinks the marriage was sanctioned by the old man himself."

Paul knew that when he met Deputy Greg Auro he would have Greg's father as a trump card in his back pocket, and at some point he would bring him up and watch the color of his face grow ashen as he would not be completely able to hide his rage and embarrassment. Paul knew some of the newer stories from his mother, who, even though she had moved from the neighborhood years before, managed to keep up with the comings and goings of the old neighbors still hunkered down in the houses where they had raised their families. Old Andy Auro had let his hair grow long well below his shoulders and his beard to the middle of his chest. He had earned the nickname, Elijah, Prophet of 532, from the local store owners and cops, because of his habit of walking up and down Route 532 at all hours of the day or night, shouting. No one stopped long enough to really listen but most figured he spoke in garbled Bible speak that was as frightening as it was impenetrable. Paul did not know this incarnation of the man, but he could easily imagine him.

Certainly Paul could ask Greg the current state of his father, but he could easily lie or deflect the question because he would bank on Paul not being able to verify anything he said. But the true stake in the heart lay in the past. He would ask Greg if he remembered the camping trip they had taken with Mr. Auro when they were around the age of thirteen. If he said he couldn't recall any such camping trip he would be lying, and Paul would be prepared to tell the story in clear detail, as he had with friends over the intervening years. He would ask Greg if he remembered when Mr. Auro had suddenly been seized with the idea of camping in the deep woods with his youngest son because his color had gone pale and his arms weak from spending too much time in his room. He would also ask if he remembered begging Paul to come and talking up the campsite by creating a fantasy that it would be near a Christian girls' camp on a lake so that there would be plenty of opportunity to watch a horde of girls splashing in the water. (He would have to remember to also ask if his own fetish for women near water had made itself manifest even at this early age or if Greg had merely stumbled onto the argument by accident, assuming that wet girls provided more allure than dry girls.) Convinced, Paul turned to his leery father, who couldn't imagine trusting Andy Auro with his son for more than an hour, let alone a weekend, but Paul's insistence and his father's guilt for his deep dislike of the man's Christianity won the day, so the trip was set.

Mr. Auro drove them to West Virginia in an ancient green Rambler wagon that had succumbed to a terminal case of rust and that pulled hard toward the ditch as if it wanted to end its own life. Paul thought he was riding in a vehicle from another century as all the inside surfaces had been made of thick metal and the air smelled thickly of burning oil and gas. They listened to a rasp of static from an AM station to mask the creaks and groans of the compromised structure vibrating around them. Paul thought they may turn back once the muffler dropped to the pavement and the engine began to roar like a jet, but Mr. Auro fetched the part from the middle of the highway and rigged it back onto the car with duct tape and wire. He lay on the gravel berm a good hour before finding the solution and when he slid back behind the wheel his face and scalp were covered with flecks of rust and a smear of oil along his jawline. He had successfully muffled the roar but more smoke leaked into the cabin. Paul tried to escape certain asphyxiation by rolling down the window, but the crank came off in his hand. Fortunately, Greg had the same idea and knew how to keep his handle connected, saving them from certain death.

In the woods Mr. Auro burst ahead of them, pushing branches and tall weeds away from him with frantic slashes of his hand. His overloaded backpack tipped him from one leg to the other, making his gait more like a totter than a purposeful stride. Soon, he disappeared over a ridge and Greg and Paul purposely lagged behind, talking about baseball and the eerie dampness and quiet of the woods, which to their imaginations meant toothless mountain men fondling their sons, daughters, sisters, and any wayward traveler thanks to the movie *Deliverance*, which they had both recently seen. They each smoked a cigarette that Paul had stolen from one of his father's packs and each independently thought of breaking off from Mr. Auro and finding a spot of their own, but neither gave expression to their thoughts so the plan lay stillborn. Paul hoped if they walked slowly enough they would lose him, even though he carried the tent and most of the food.

They heard the moans before they saw the campsite. Greg stopped and looked behind him at the path from which they had just come, calculating the distance to the Rambler. Paul looked at his shoes and scraped a design in the carpet of pine needles that lay on the ground. Then came a hoot, a shriek, followed by a scream. Greg and Paul stared at each other, Greg's race reddening. Paul hoped the mountain men had found Mr. Auro, but Greg guessed differently, and, as it turned out, correctly.

They braced themselves and walked up a small rise and ducked under a low hanging pine branch. Before them at the bottom of the hill in a sun-dappled clearing Mr. Auro crouched on the ground in once-white underwear. The backpack and his clothes had been carelessly flung to the ground. A fine, gray ash covered his skin, recovered from a previous campfire, but the ash could not cover a web of rising welts. He threw more ash into the air and stood under the resulting shower, screaming. He picked up a charred log in either hand and pounded on his thighs and calves. He rolled in the ash pit and cried. He squeezed either side of his face as if trying to pulverize the flesh and bone and to kill the impurities running through his brain. He tried to formulate a prayer, but he could articulate nothing comprehensible.

Greg's neck had gone scarlet. His eyes had remained open against their will.

"If we go down there he's going to make us do that," Greg said without looking at Paul.

"What is he doing?"

"Do you know your way back to the car?"

"Ya."

"The doors don't lock. You should sleep there tonight. It's about an hour back."

"Are you coming?"

Greg kept his eyes on his father. Paul felt rooted to the ground. He didn't want Mr. Auro to see or hear him. He wished himself home. Greg turned his face toward him and he mustered a look of contempt.

"I should have never brought you here. Get the fuck out of here," he seethed.

Paul backed down the hill. Once on level ground he began running. Stumbling, staggering, he fell twice over exposed tree roots. For a moment he thought he lost the path. Dusk was falling. The woods had turned purple. He thought someone chased him, but when he turned around he guessed the sound of running footsteps were his own bouncing off the trees.

He slept in the Rambler. He half-expected Greg and Mr. Auro to come bursting out of the trailhead, naked and dirty, screaming prayers and cursing the nature of man, but they never came before he fell asleep.

Paul awoke to the smell of smoke and Mr. Auro whistling to the static on the radio. The car bounced and swayed over uneven pavement. Mr. Auro wore a halo of dirt on his bald head, just above the ears, a line formed by sweat washing the dust from his crown. Greg sat up front with his dad and wouldn't turn his head to look in the backseat. His hair was frosted with ash. Paul sensed a shift. He had abandoned him, chosen his father, and guarded a family secret against his mockery. Paul hoped they were going home. He had only had a candy bar for dinner and couldn't muster the courage to ask for breakfast. His parents might ask why the trip had been cut short, but they would be happy he had come home. For a moment

Paul thought he could hear Greg whistling along with his father.

Paul leaned back in his chair and smiled insanely at Tony, whose finger hovered over the start button of his recorder because Paul looked ready to say something especially worthy of documentation. Paul disappointed him and never gave voice to his thoughts. Really, he wanted to thank the ghost of Mr. Auro for being so insistent on being remembered, on bullying his parents and lovers to the sidelines, and for providing him with a bludgeon he could use when he met Greg.

6

Last Bit of Business

On his last day of work Paul had to visit a house against which a complaint had been lodged by a neighbor. Essentially, the neighbor thought a new garage built down on her street must be against code. Paul reread the word 'turret' two or three times in the description of the offense. The idea of a turret on a garage made him smile and he thought he'd like to meet the man who would attempt such an atrocity. Besides, the man might have some money if he wasted it on such an extravagance and Paul might be able to make a little extra cash if the man wanted the problem to go away quickly.

He checked the permit files and he found nothing for this address. The man had built a garage with a turret and had not taken out a permit. Unbelievable. He knew the neighborhood. The fact that anyone built anything on those streets qualified as a minor miracle. The complainant's name was Mary Kelly, who lived near the offense. Paul imagined her as an old woman, the last survivor of the neighborhood that had once been, her children, friends and neighbors either dead or having fled to grassier locales.

He checked out a city car and drove over to the house. As he moved through the neighborhood he noted a thousand violations and then stopped himself, content to consider the place a ruin of a past civilization, no longer viable but providing temporary shelter for a throng of refugees.

He parked in the driveway of the house. His pile of notes and copies of the complaint had scattered across the passenger side seat and onto the floor. He gathered them and clipped them to a clipboard. When he had himself organized, he turned off the car and peered through the windshield. A man with a massive belly and long gray hair limped out of the shadows, looking like a troglodyte protecting a fresh kill. Some of the inspectors had talked about carrying guns, because the desperate citizenry had had enough of government interventions. At that moment Paul wished he had something strapped to his hip that used large caliber bullets. He donned an officious mask that helped quell his fear and uncoiled himself out of the car. He walked toward the man but stopped a good distance away, to give himself time to react should the man turn violent.

"Are you the owner of this house?" he shouted.

The man had no intention of covering the ground between them to shake Paul's hand or get inside the radius for comfortable conversation.

"I am."

"My name in Paul Newcombe and I'm a housing inspector with the City of Cleveland. You are Jack Cactus?"

"I am."

"That's the name listed on the deed. You had to make that up at some point, right? I mean no one is born with a name like that, right? I would think that Cactus had never been used as a surname until folks like yourself started adding it on to provide a sense of mystery and wonder."

Paul felt his ire rising against impudence and wanton disregard of the rules: basic, common rules that everyone agreed provided the structure in which to live. He could tell Jack Cactus thought himself above or outside the law and it made him want to torture the man. A goddamn iconoclast.

"That's my name."

"And you became the owner just earlier this year?"

"Right."

"You are the only person this year to buy into this block. That's quite an achievement. All the rats are running away from the sinking ship and you're the one rat who ran onto it. Here comes the hero. Here comes the hero rat."

"I'm guessing you think you can come onto my property and be a dick because you have City Hall behind you. I haven't ever given a fuck about any of that. I'm not some worm that you can frighten with your boot. I could give a fuck where you're from or who you think you are," said Cactus Jack as his back straightened, losing the bent, old man hunch as two massive fists gathered themselves.

"Calm down, I'm here on a simple mission, really. I've come to see your permit for building that garage. That shouldn't be too hard for you. I know things can get misplaced during the chaos of building, but you look like an old hand at this construction game. I can tell right from the get-go if someone knows what they're doing. I just bet my co-worker before I left to come here that even though we received complaints from some neighbors about a garage with a turret at this address and even though there are no permits on file at City Hall anywhere, not even an application, I bet him that when I came I would find an old experienced guy who knew the whatnots and the wherefores. My co-worker said I was a fool and an optimist. He said he's seen a hundred cases like this and he said he's always found that it's some scofflaw, some miscreant who thought he could skirt the law, who thought he could ignore community standards and building codes and all the other rules and regulations that generations of citizens have fine-tuned and argued about for decades. He said that I was going to find that kind of guy, and frankly, I told him he was full of shit. He laughed at me and said when it came out the way I said it would come out it would be the first time he's ever witnessed such a conclusion. I have to say he said he hoped he was surprised, that mistakes can be honest, and that paperwork simply is not filed in the correct file and major problems could be fixed with simple solutions."

Paul felt himself smiling. The anger on Jack Cactus' face boiled over. They both took a step towards each other.

"I pulled this house off the scrap heap. Nazis lived here. I beat back a cancer cell with these two hands. I've done more work on this place in six months than all the owners had in fifty years."

"Of course, and I understand the commendation is working its way through the Mayor's office as we speak and we're hoping you'll agree to the parade and the media coverage, because you are one of the first to buy an old, decrepit house and make it passably livable. Besides, this whole city is a scrap heap. I wouldn't doubt Nazi cells are popping up everywhere. There's gunfire every night. There's fire and death. What are you thinking?"

"You know there's no permit for the garage."

They now stood a few feet apart, staring into the other's face.

"I didn't know that until you just told me. That's an unfortunate development. Now I have to go back to work and pay twenty bucks to the guy that called me a fool. That's not a good feeling. I feel terrible about it really. I mean I was on your damn side and I clutched an optimist's dream that something simple could be done. Now I don't know what to think. I know that nothing good can now come of this."

"What do you want from me?"

"I want you to go inside your house and come out with a copy of a permit to build a garage with a ridiculous turret, an element that is not in any way reflected in the architectural elements of the house."

"You know I can't do that."

"Why can't you do that? Why would you build a garage without asking anyone if you could? Why wouldn't you draw up plans so that someone could check to see if the structure would stand for more than a month? Why would someone just build something from their head? Have you got a permit for any of the work on your house? The electrical, the plumbing, and the boiler, no?"

"I don't see what business the government has in my business."

"Really? The government doesn't have a stake when your wiring catches fire or your gas pipes leak and the government has to send over firefighters to extinguish your ineptitude? Are we supposed to just let it burn and have it take the whole block with it? Is that your idea?"

"We? So you've taken the whole of the government on your back?"

"I'm a representative. It's a legitimate use of the plural pronoun. I'm not speaking out of turn."

"My God, where do they manufacture dickheads like you?

"Sir, abusive language leads us to a bad place. Neither the government nor I made the mistake of building a garage and putting a house through major renovations without seeking permits."

"So how do I get the permits?"

"If it were only so easy. See, had you sought the permit before you started building your plans would have been passed to the architectural review board and they would have taken one look at that turret and struck it down. It never would have gotten passed. They don't like flights of fancy or grandiose statements out of context."

"So you're telling me I'm going to have to take it down?"

"That's one solution. Submit some reasonable plans and modify the structure to fit within the norms of the community. Nobody is going to respond to your iconoclasm. It's all fine inside your head, but once you've committed to building something there are other interested parties who have to weigh in. You need to enter into a discussion with your neighbors, your representatives and the administrators of the government they have chosen to rule. I know you're thinking I'm making an argument for collectivism, but it's not as bad as all that. You can express yourself all you want as long as it's inside the agreed upon parameters."

"Alright, let's cut the bullshit. How much is this going to cost me?"

"A thousand dollars in cash for me and another five hundred for the permit desk to certify the permit."

Paul knew the going rate by heart. He had used it many times. At least this crazy fuck knew how the world worked. If you want to live outside the law you have to pay and pay.

"I don't have it."

"You'll have to get it."

"I don't have any place to get it."

Paul laughed. "An old pirate like you has a dozen sources to find that small amount of money. I'll give you a couple of weeks and if you don't come up with it I'll throw so much paper at you you'll spend the next year in court just trying to figure out what the charges are and in the end you'll have to tear that monstrosity down anyway."

"What does the cash buy me?"

"Everlasting peace and tranquility, unless you get the idea in your head to build a moat and drawbridge in your front yard. Then, I might be back. I can backdate the paperwork and the permit desk will stamp anything for a little cash."

"You're a fucking little bloodsucker."

"Sir, there's no need to complicate the transaction with emotion. I've provided you with a path out of your predicament. By the looks of you I thought you'd appreciate the unofficial solution, the straight out horse trade of cash for trouble, but if you want to go down the other road of official reports, housing court and fines then by all means we can proceed that way as well."

"Give me a couple of weeks and I'll get your cash."

"Here's my card. You can call me when you're ready. Don't send me an email or leave a voicemail other than stating your name. That's all public record and we want no tracks, agreed?"

Jack took the card and neither man offered a hand to conclude the deal, so an awkward moment of confusion and hesitation occurred before Paul turned and walked back to his car. When he reversed the car he took one last look at Jack Cactus' impotent rage burning in the driveway and had himself a laugh.

7

Third Eye

Paul sat in a restaurant booth with red vinyl benches and a Formica tabletop next a grimy and spotted picture window. His view included a gravel parking lot that washed against three sides of the building and beyond that a ribbon of cars and trucks roaring down the highway. Beyond the highway he could see a high blue sky and a smudge of a daytime moon. A map of Ohio lay on the tabletop in front of him. He had unfolded and folded the map a dozen times since he had happened to see Deputy Greg Auro on the local news, so he didn't need it for direction. He had memorized the route: I-71 South to Columbus, take 270 bypass, State Route 23 South to Portsmouth. He really wanted to find a diversion from his destination, something to distract him from the deputy, but nothing could draw him away, not even the Hopewell Culture burial mounds, which under normal circumstances would be one of his first stops. Even the act of stopping at this restaurant had been a delay tactic. The drive was a little over four hours and he didn't feel particularly hungry, but at least he paused his momentum, creating a brief opportunity for him to think of something else to do.

A waitress came toward him with a plate of food in one hand and a pot of coffee in the other. He smelled the cloying fragrance of fried diner fare with a musky base, emanating from her choice of cheap drugstore perfume she had slathered on to mask the scent of her work. He wouldn't have called her old or young. He had an appropriate, long view of her as she approached, but his eyes would not settle on any one part of her as she seemed formless. Her large breasts had been flattened into a shelf by her uniform. Her hairstyle, processed and lacquered, framed a dull, bitter face. Paul could not overlay a fantasy of a brighter future, of her working herself through college, or a past debutante fallen on hard times because of a tragic choice in men. Paul looked back to his map as a distraction to his analysis.

"You're going to have to move that," she said as the plate hovered near Paul's eye level, filling the air around him with the smell of eggs fried in canola oil.

He pushed the map onto the seat next to him without folding it. He wouldn't give up just yet. Something on the map would sooner or later jump out at him.

"I could never get those things folded either," she said as she set down the plate, followed by a splash of coffee that more or less ended up in his cup. "Did you find where you are going?"

"I know where I'm going. I'm just not sure I want to get there. Is there anything to do around here? If you had your choice what would you want to do?"

Once he had asked the questions, both of them thought he sounded as if crafting an oblique pick-up line and both paused to further inspect the other to clear up the confusion, either to move it a step closer to open flirtation or to let the unfortunate inference drop and treat the question for what it probably was, a simple inquiry from a bored tourist to a local expert. Paul jabbed at a tincture of grease puddled on the white of the egg. The waitress waited, her face cast in a stony glare as if bracing herself against another humiliation, but she broke before Paul because she had her other tables and the thousand tasks she had to perform weighing on her mind.

"I guess it depends on your interests. Doesn't every place have something for everyone? If you're willing to look."

"I have a map. I'm looking."

The waitress expected a different response, and she searched for a comeback that would further her cause a step or two and not let the ember of attraction die.

"Ya, I could never fold those things," she said and when she realized she had already covered that ground, embarrassment crept up from below her collar and reddened her neck and face.

The blush allowed Paul to realize something between them had happened and he began to consider if a diversion could come in the form of a formless waitress, but she fled in panic to the other patrons before he came to a conclusion. Just then, the door banged open, shaking the glass and sending the little bells tied to the handle into hysteria. In walked two women, both dressed in jean shorts and halter tops, masked with flowing black capes of patterned crepe. The lead had raven's hair and wore a large straw hat with a large, unblinking woman's eye cut from a glossy magazine pasted on the front. Her second had dishwater hair and donned a trucker's cap emblazoned with CAT. They didn't wait to be seated and strolled along the spine of the restaurant, commanding every eye in the place follow them. They sat in the booth next to Paul and smiled sweetly at him as they squeezed into their seats. They briefly engaged in a skirmish over the table placement as each woman used her considerable weight to gain an extra inch of space. The straw hat had better leverage and stronger arms and she won the extra inch. CAT had to be resigned with the table cutting into her flesh and her breasts resting on the tabletop like an oversized entrée. The magazine eye inspected Paul as CAT had her back to him.

Sensing that her hope of breaking the monotony of hard, miserable work and single-parent child rearing was slipping through her fingers, the waitress quick-stepped it back to Paul's table to fill his still full coffee cup. She leaned close, conspiratorially.

"We can't legally keep them out of here. The cops say it's a free country, but there's nothing free about those girls."

Paul did not break his stare with the third eye, but he acknowledged the waitress with a slight nod of the head. She desperately wanted to pour coffee to tell herself she came over to his table for some other reason than to intercept his interest in the whores, but really his coffee cup was already up to the rim and pouring coffee into his water glass would only amplify her desperation.

"The penicillin is over next to the cupcakes and energy drinks. Of course, the stuff passed around these days you ain't going to cure in two lifetimes," she said with enough venom and volume that three customers turned toward the table to ascertain why she had suddenly become so loud.

"Thank you," Paul said softly as he finally looked at her. "I don't want any more coffee."

The waitress looked at the coffee pot in her hand, began to turn crimson again, following the route of the first blush, and stomped away. Paul looked back to the third eye. A tattoo of a black and red rose crawled up her left breast above the halter line. Her lips were smeared with black lipstick and when she pursed them into a teasing kiss directed at Paul a hole consumed the lower half of her face. CAT turned around in her seat, the flesh of her upper arm drooped into Paul's booth.

"She wants to tell your fortune," she said in a small girl's voice, incongruous to the height and bulk of her body. Paul had expected a husky smoker's rasp punctuated by expectorating.

"How much would that cost?"

"I guess it would depend on how much it was worth to you."

"I can see my own future and it looks pretty dismal."

A look of annoyance crossed her face as she said, "You won't be needing us, then."

The third eye leaned across the table and they exchanged a whisper. They blew across the surface of their coffees and forgot about Paul. The third eye peered out the window at a pick-up kicking up a haze of gravel dust. She released a humid breath against the window and continued watching as the truck stopped as the cloud of dust followed and consumed it.

"Is that Denny?"

CAT turned her head and waited for the dust to clear.

"No, don't he drive a blue truck?"

"That's blue."

"No, that's more green than blue. His truck is like a robin's egg."

"I was hoping it was Denny, I guess"

"Maybe you should let me in on some of that."

"That's not likely. Denny pays the rent and gas bill. He's my annuity," Third Eye said playfully.

"I got rent too. I bet he could afford both of us and my kids."

"You could always move in with me. I don't bring business home and I like kids. I get lonely in that house."

"How many annuities does a girl need? You need to share some of the wealth. At least throw me that old man. He looks like he's ready to kick it."

"The old man? We're going to get married. He says he has a ring picked out and everything."

"Oh my God! That is goddamn hilarious!" shrieked CAT as she dissolved into a fit of laughter.

"I'm not doing this forever. I sometimes wonder why I just don't do it."

"You're not serious?"

Paul threw a ten on the table and slid out of the booth. Later, in a moment of reflection, he would blame his decision on the freedom of vacation, the absence of the grinding banality of work, the fresh rush of too many cups of trucker coffee, a virulent tendency toward self-destruction, and Deputy Greg Auro. At the time he did not know how the deputy was involved in the decision-making, but in the time between his choice of stopping at the women's table or walking past with a superior smile and his moment of reflection he came to know the full force of the deputy's influence.

He stopped at the women's table. From the view above they consisted of four massive breasts and four heavy arms. Their halter tops barely clung to their nipples and Paul saw that Third Eye's tattoo was not a rose, but the head of a growling ape.

"What do you see in my future?"

From across the restaurant the waitress paused as she served salad to another table. She searched for the gaze of the hostess and they shared a private look of condemnation, disbelief, and horror.

Third Eye lifted her chin. The eye pasted on the hat looked exactly like her two real eyes, down to the false eyelashes, green eyeliner and green eye shadow.

"It depends upon the questions you ask," she said in a voice, which unlike her second, CAT, was deep and shaped by a number of alcoholic liquids, screaming fights, heavy clouds of smoke, chemical-laced factory air, and a brief stint as the lead singer of a metal band called Strip Mine.

"There's really only one question worth asking. When am I going to die?"

"Nobody really wants to know that. Nobody ever asks that, so it makes me think you're not serious about the question. Ask God. Ask Jesus. I don't get into that."

"Maybe something not so morbid? Maybe I want to know..." but Paul could think of nothing he wanted to know about his future other than his exact date of death, so he had to come up with some angle to keep the conversation going. "Maybe I want to know something about my job." The correction depressed him immensely and he half-hoped that she would tell him he would be fired by the new commissioner, because even amidst the freedom of vacation his work manipulated every atom of his body and mind.

"I can't find answers in an atmosphere like this. There's a rented room across the highway in Motel Further that I use as my sometimes office. Look for 3F."

"Will your assistant be there?"

Third Eye gave CAT a long, loving look.

"When available she assists in all my explorations of the future. It can be a tricky business. She can bring me back if there's a threat that I'll be lost."

"How much is this going to be?"

"What is knowledge worth?" CAT snorted.

"College ended up costing me about twenty thousand in loans. I'm looking for something a little cheaper."

"We work on a donation basis. You'll pay what you think is fair. This is not an exchange of cash for services. I provide the service with the help of my assistant and you will determine if you want to pay so that we can continue to provide services to travelers like yourself."

"I'm not so worried about the money. I want to know if I'll remember the experience."

Third Eye and CAT shared a bemused and knowing smile.

"It won't be our fault if you don't," CAT said.

"You go and wait in the parking lot of the motel. We'll be along after we finish our coffee," Third Eye said. "It will give you time for your food to digest some."

Paul nodded his head in agreement as he left as he couldn't argue with her reasoning.

8

At the Motel Further

Paul drove past the motel and through a beaten commercial strip of car lots, failing fast food franchises, donut shops, muffler repair garages, a florist, and a funeral home. He inspected the state of the roofs he could see, cracks in the foundations, buckling asphalt of the parking lots, unsealed dumpsters breeding rats and vermin, and the mismatched zoning that could turn any pasture or swale into a hideous nowhere. He drove until the strip exhausted itself and gave way to a weed-filled wasteland, a half-forgotten place that held a large wooden sign, now weathered, that announced the opportunity for more commercial development. The landowners of this frontier had held out hope for years that the cancer would spread to their holdings, but the strip remained stubbornly beyond the edge of their properties.

Paul played with the radio as he returned through the tangle, past the entrance ramp to the highway. He stared at the radio dial so as not to be tempted with flight. He drove to the other end of the strip and back again. This time when he passed the motel he saw Third Eye and CAT walking across the parking lot toward the building. He pulled into a gas station and filled his tank before returning to the motel.

When Paul opened the door of 3F a light draft carrying the cloying smell of perfume greeted him, but a more persistent and acrid stench of industrial cleaner followed. The sound of running water came from behind the bathroom door. A fold-up card table leaned near the foot of the bed and two fold-up metal chairs had been carefully positioned on either side of the table. In the center of the table sat a glass ball, glinting even in the weak light and resting inside a soup bowl. Trapped forever inside the ball hung a bat with its fragile wings outstretched and its tiny feet and claws extended as if intent on drilling the jugular of the onlooker. The little mouth screamed, revealing a row of razor teeth. Paul had felt pity for bats since one flew through an open window of his apartment and bashed itself senseless against the walls and ceiling in a panic. Of course, Paul didn't help matters by snapping a towel at it as it passed and screaming, but he did feel remorse after it lay bloody on the floor and he extinguished its life with a plunger.

The bathroom door opened and out came Third Eye. She still donned the hat but the trucker-hooker ensemble had been replaced by a short crimson robe made of silk, patterned with a hundred vines of filigree that just reached the top of her thighs, which chafed as she walked to the card table. The robe provided little support to her unruly flesh as she bounced and shook across the mauve carpet. She sat heavily on the chair nearest her and she pointed to the other chair across the table. The idea of ripping off the robe and plunging his face between her breasts suddenly seized him. She narrowed her eyes and crafted a bemused smile as she watched the idea take hold.

"First, the future," she said in a deliberate, prophetic cadence.

Paul stared into the photo eye and thought it may have been crying. Crying, no doubt, for him and his collection of perversions that stood in his way of attaining stability in a relationship with a woman. Crying for all of his lost opportunities he had stowed somewhere like a gathering of broken, plastic toys. He suddenly felt like weeping himself and a part of his consciousness broke away and stood as a third person to determine what exactly was happening to him. Before he could come to any conclusion, he spied CAT through the open bathroom door as she meticulously shaved her pussy in front of the bathroom sink. Entirely naked, her body seemed to be made up of cascading flesh rushing from a spring near her neck. She had taken off the trucker cap and had combed her hair to a shine. He forgot about his weeping.

Third Eye turned the bat so that the tiny, shrieking head faced her. She raised the ball and gently kissed the glass. From Paul's point of view it looked as if she had put the entire head inside her mouth, which kick-started a bout of nausea deep in his gut. He felt weak. First, the threat of sobbing and now barely holding down his breakfast. Comically clutching his stomach, he wondered if the spurned waitress had poisoned his food. His skin felt itchy as if a thousand welts were sprouting to the surface. He tore off his clothes and stood before them with a full erection. The air on his skin, the unfolding of his body, the releasing of his penis that had become twisted and pinched under his clothes dampened the nausea, although his face dripped with sweat and he felt like he could not bring his eyes into perfect focus. The women watched him, slightly amused, but their concern that he might he having a heart attack or stroke right in the middle of their office held their amusement in check. They could run and leave him dead on the carpet but enough truckers and state troopers had visited 3F that there wasn't a cave deep or dark enough where they wouldn't be found.

"Do you need a glass of water?" CAT called from the bathroom, sporting one last swath of shaving cream rising from her vagina.

"Sure, it must be dry in this room or something."

The women allowed themselves to laugh, unable to temper their mockery even though they risked making him angry. He had somehow forgotten that he stood in front of two experts of male desire and saying anything except what was absolutely true and unfiltered was ridiculous.

"I want to fuck your tits. I want to fuck you in the ass. I want both of you to suck my dick at the same time. I want to stick my tongue in your assholes. I want you to do the same for me. I want you to sit on my face until I pass out. I want to fuck you from behind while you eat out your assistant. I want to fuck you until the sensation has been completely rubbed out of my dick. I want…" Paul sat down and the metal chair that felt ice cold next to his feverish body.

The Eye objectively assessed him. The Eye knew that deviance could not exist because in order for behavior to be deviant there would have to be indisputable proof that a norm existed in the first place. In all of its experiences the Eye had yet to witness the same two behaviors, so who could really say what behavior represented the path from which all other behaviors deviated? His testicles crept away from the cold metal, but his erection showed no signs of abating even though he had no use for it as of yet.

Third Eye's other two eyes rolled into her head, leaving a white void, and she spoke in a language of moans, grunts, clicks and glottal humming that caused two conflicting urges within him, either to chase his erection out of the room and end this sordidness alongside a desire to cover her mouth with his lips and lick the dribble from her chin that had begun forming. Paragraph after paragraph of nonsense poured from her mouth. Then, suddenly, she snapped awake and looked at him with new, clear eyes, with a hint of playful mischief that had not been present before.

"You being here speaks of a great need to know future events. I won't be able to tell you what happens as a journalist would, but I am given hints, whispers, impressions, and glimpses of the possibilities. If we think of the past as cast in stone, carved and discarded. Sometimes we pull out the best and worst of what we done and give it a once over and then throw it away again. We should think of the present as full of infinite possibilities but most of us live predictably because the grooves we have worn in time, the patterns we slavishly follow, because of the limits of our imaginations and our primal fear of being lost and alone. The present is comforting and so slippery. We so easily fall into analyzing the past or dreaming about the future. But I must tell you, the future is a swirl of dust manipulated by the wind, holding the potential of infinite forms but certainly influenced by the stone past and the patterned present. Today, I won't give you a roadmap or a sculpture or a story with a linear narrative. I'll give you a sketch written in the sand amidst a raging hurricane. The danger in knowing the unknowable is that you may be tempted to change the present based on what you see, to try to change your pattern or jump from your groove too quickly, without carefully considering all the consequences of such rash behavior. Disaster awaits those who try to cheat. Do you still have the need to know the unknowable?"

Paul nodded as his eyes drifted from Third Eye back to the bathroom where CAT soaped her breasts with a washcloth.

"You must use words."

"Yes, I want to know the future," Paul said in a coarse whisper.

"Then look into the eyes of the bat and ask a question."

"How should I address him? The holiest of holies? Sir? Father?"

"First of all it's a female bat and all you have to do is ask the question. There are no formalities and we try to keep a lid on ceremony."

"Let's start with something simple. Will I get married someday?"

CAT stopped soaping herself and looked at the bat as if expecting her to burst out in a mocking cackle.

"No," Third Eye said flatly.

"No?"

"No, that answer came through as clear as a bell."

"Seems harsh. How can the answer be no, anyway? There are so many women out there looking to get married. One of them would settle for me, I think. Seems ridiculous the answer would just be a flat out no. It didn't even seem like you consulted anything. That was no swirl of dust."

"I'm in no position to argue with what is communicated to me. The answer was clear. Do you want me to give you a pep talk or reveal your future?"

"So, does it come in words or images?"

"Images, scenes, sometimes through letters, speech or song."

"How did that answer come to you?

"In sound, like a football stadium filled with 70,000 fans chanting, 'No, no, no!' in unison. Rarely are the answers that clear and unequivocal. Maybe because you are the first man to ever ask if you will be married. Sadly, that is a central question of women as their deepest neurotic fear is a lonely and loveless future. Ask another question before the connection goes stale."

"How long will I be at my current job?"

The magazine eye remained inscrutable as horror shaped the other two.

"Oh, wow," she couldn't help herself saying.

"That bad?"

"I see a highway with no end. The scenery at the sides of the road is a blur, not because you are moving too fast, but because you lack the energy and will to turn your head and look at what you are actually passing, so you blur the edges, conjure up speed, ignore possibilities and cross streets. The asphalt lifts from the ground, slowly at first. You sail into the clouds and then the incline becomes steeper and the road breaks away from the earth's atmosphere. You follow the double yellow line past Mars and Jupiter and eventually out of the solar system. At the end of this endless highway lies your answer."

"That sounds close to forever."

"I guess it could be interpreted that way."

"Can you tell me if the car radio is playing an endless cycle of do-wop music? Are all my random thoughts recorded?"

"I don't see a car and I don't hear music. I just see the endless road. You can ask one more question."

"Near Portsmouth they found a skull. I want to know who's the owner of the skull." Paul felt the need to steer the questions away from his personal life as he knew the answers better than the bat ever could know.

"You saw that too!" CAT shouted as she walked toward him from the bathroom, still naked and completely free of pubic hair. "I would have freaked out when that skull started rolling toward me. Can you imagine? And that deputy is hilarious."

CAT stopped behind Paul and pushed herself against his back so that her breasts hung just above the crown of his head. She leaned over and began stroking his chest. The bat shuddered as a tremor passed through Third Eye's arms.

"I see a teenage girl wearing a pink jumper, shapely and very alluring. Her face is so beautiful it causes a wake of pain as she passes. She is watching Roy Rogers do lasso tricks. She loves the powder blue hue of his shirt and the way the rhinestones sparkle. He sees her watching and smiles in appreciation, but he suddenly feels self-conscious by being watched by such a beauty, so he calls her a "rotten nympho' and turns away his rouged face. Then, he mimes that an idea has occurred to him and he throws the lasso over her head and draws it tight. Her smile fades to panic then resignation. Her skin and flesh fade to bone. The skull teeters and falls from the body. Once it lands on the ground it rolls away on its own volition. "

"Was Roy Rogers by any chance whistling a do-wop song?"

"No, I don't think I would recognize what do-wop music is anyway."

"Fortune shines upon you."

"Sometimes."

"Is that all there is. I get three lousy answers to three lousy questions?"

"Sometimes it fades in and out like that."

CAT yanked on the back on his chair, separating him from the table, and pulled him to his feet. She walked to the front of him, sank to her knees, and put the knob of his penis in her mouth. Paul began his ascent to the apex of his erotic life. The room spun. Four massive breasts crushed against him. Hands and lips covered his body. Labia smashed against his nose. Heaps of flesh rose and fell. They teased his erection but knew the moment to back off and not let it get too hot or rub the sensation away.

The first session lasted over an hour. Paul finally came as he fucked CAT from behind as her ample buttocks seized him and wouldn't let go until he found release. For good measure, Third Eye kneeled behind him and worked a couple of fingers up his asshole past the second knuckle. The fell in a tangle on the bed, caught their breath, and started up again in fifteen minutes. All the sensation had been rubbed out of Paul, but he felt like Mr. Auro prostrating himself in the campfire ash. He had found his altar and he gave himself freely. He wanted to stay between the four breasts and bawl at the hardness and complexity of his rapidly crumbling world. He pulled the two women closer to him and for a moment he had no decisions to make, nothing to fight, and no demands. He felt free in his abandon between them. Had he been able to breathe properly, he would have stayed there the rest of his life.

When he stumbled out of 3F he found that night had fallen, bringing to a close his first day of vacation. He had spent half the money he had set aside for his entire two week trip on CAT and Third Eye, but the budget was miserly and unrealistic anyway. At one point as he lay between them and took inventory of his exhausted body, he calculated the expense of putting his desire into a practical plan and renting them for the duration of his time off and burrowing into the musty confines of the motel room. He figured he could have negotiated a discount rate and smothered himself in flesh. What better tonic for misery at work and gnawing loneliness?

He never brought himself to negotiate. Deputy Greg Auro awaited him and even the most advantageous cost for their services would have been exorbitant. He would never be able to afford both of them for the whole two weeks. He would not humiliate himself and ask them to donate time, even the dead of night when they slept. Besides, the magical properties of the breasts slowly faded the more he watched them. So, the moment he should have been drifting into a happy sleep amongst the stewards of his religion, he found himself behind the wheel of his car, passing low budget competitors to the Motel Further. He chose one with a sign of a winking peacock standing astride a fluffy feather bed.

Minivans, SUVs, and beat-up car models from the previous decade jammed the lot. Some pulled jet skis, others were covered in bicycles, and all had the unmistakable signs of long hours on the road. Interiors arranged in nests of pillows, blankets, books, computers, snack bags and soda bottles. Exteriors, dusty and baked, with a splatter of insect remains on the windshield, headlights, and grilles. The superheated engine blocks pulsed heat as if a line of fires died to embers on the asphalt. Paul pulled between a van that for sure carried a mother, son, son and daughter as indicated by the iconic row of stickers on the back window. A father figure had mostly disappeared, with only his legs just above his knees remaining, but it was unclear if the sticker had failed or the marriage. A monster truck that looked capable of smashing through the forest and terrorizing woodland creatures and campers alike towered above him on his other side.

He had every intention of renting a room for the night when he pulled into the lot, but exhaustion and the worry about his smashed budget got the better of him. So, instead of walking to the office and completing the transaction, he pushed his seat into full recline and almost immediately fell asleep. He dreamed of the bounty of America and how she effortlessly produced such enormous and sensual creatures as CAT and Third Eye.

9

Ra-ma-da

Paul slipped into Portsmouth around noon. The air smelled of a rainstorm and generations of flooding, a slow, inexorable rot. Low slung buildings tumbled toward the river bank, holding a flicker of their past as a bustling port city when rivers were highways. He couldn't help feeling disappointed in his destination, although he couldn't have said what he had expected. The downtown felt melancholy and abandoned and he suspected a commercial strip outside of town with cheap food, easy parking, and the hum of creation and destruction by modern commerce, to have been the town's undoing. Paul could never look at a cityscape, a street, or even a house and not want to remake it, to blot out past mistakes and reengineer false starts and obvious blunders. He would never bring himself to admit this same impulse had driven planners and developers to create commercial spaces with vast, soulless parking lots and groves of vapor lights, to sacrifice robust municipal life and gathering places in the name of efficiency and a greater spending-per-customer ratio.

He passed an old J.C. Penny and a furniture store whose customers must have been funeral homes. He stopped at a traffic light. To his left stood a cluster of buildings that looked unmistakably like a community college or a low rung state university. The architecture artfully combined the monumental aspirations of government planners, the utilitarian floor plan of a factory, the remoteness and strangeness of a prison, and the sharp-edged professionalism and landscaping of a corporate headquarters. To his right sat a police station, a dirty cream building with massive Doric columns holding up a tiny porch roof. The columns looked like a part of a much grander plan that never came to fruition because of budget cuts or a failure of imagination because the roof would have needed to be five times its size to warrant the heft and stolidity of the support. Rust leaked from window air conditioners and stained the façade all the way to the ground. A woman with two small children in tow slowly climbed concrete steps toward a door that looked as if it had been sealed and disappeared into the shadows of the columns. Across the street from the police station rose a five story hotel, created as a perfect rectangle without a single distinguishing feature. Next to the hotel sat a convenience store with a large orange sign in the window that read, "Fill up your oxygen here."

He continued going straight and found himself on a bridge over the Ohio River and soon a sign announced he had crossed into Kentucky. He stole views of the water through the passing girders of the bridge. Rivers unsettled him. All motion and turbulence, rivers destroyed, swept away, actively sought life to drown. He thought of rivers in linear terms, where he stood a mere point on a churning timeline, never being able to forget there were places upriver and downriver and the place where he stood, or right now where he drove, was transitory. The constant flow of a thousand tributaries, streams, creeks, brooks, storm drains, sewer pipes all rushing through the watershed toward oblivion.

Paul drove back to the hotel and asked for a room. The clerk, a freshly-minted high school graduate who had more pimples along his jaw than prospects, looked at him in disbelief.

"You know what weekend this is, right?"

"No, I don't know what is happening this weekend. What could it be?"

"The Roy Rogers Festival. Does that ring a bell?" the clerk said, clearly incredulous.

Paul stared at the desk clerk as his face transformed into a sarcastic sneer. Paul assumed the expression a result of the clerk finally finding someone who knew less about a subject than he himself knew, so no small amount of adrenalin pumped through his veins as a result of the victory.

"Do you have a room or not? Someone may have cancelled in the time we have been talking."

"We've been booked up for months, sir. We're jammed with cowboys."

"Are you going to look or do I have to call the manager over here?"

The clerk rolled his eyes at Paul's wishful idiocy as he typed the search on his keyboard. A guest had cancelled not fifteen minutes before, leaving open a room on the top floor overlooking the river and a floodwall. The clerk's face collapsed as he lost his advantage and he thought about not telling Paul about the room, but he worried not releasing a room could get him fired, even though Paul didn't seem connected to the festival. People booked a year in advance and some who were shutout begged for rooms to no avail. This guy saunters in and snatches the last room with the best view right under everyone's nose. The clerk felt the wrong committed against the humble pilgrims of the festival but had no power in his grasp to right it.

"You are a lucky man. You just won the lottery. We have a penthouse room."

"Seriously, are you forced to call it that? Is it carpeted in fur and have a champagne fountain?"

"It's on the top floor."

"With an expansive view of the floodplain, no doubt, and all the civilization sinking back into the mud. Sounds lovely. I'll take it for the week."

The clerk completed checking him in and tried not to raise his eyes during the entire process to communicate that he did not approve of his good fortune and really did not appreciate the sarcasm with which he met his tremendous luck. At the end of the transaction he handed Paul a brochure and agenda for the festival that spanned the next three days. For the first time Paul noticed a button pinned on the clerk's shirt that read "WWRD?" which, of course, stood for "What Would Roy Do?"

In his room Paul watched the river churn for a few minutes before drawing the curtains closed. He lay on the bed and watched television with the sound muted. He fell asleep, woke, and fell asleep again. He had muddled dreams about Third Eye and CAT, in which the narrative was shattered and the dialogue unintelligible but the overarching themes were longing and fear. When he awoke the second time he stumbled over to the windows and opened the curtains again. The muddy course of the river had fallen into shadow and lights blinked alive as dusk settled over the city. He retrieved a wad of paper from his pants pocket, a single sheet of paper he had worried into a ball, and dialed the number he had meticulously transcribed between the lines. He asked for Deputy Greg Auro when a voice answered his call.

"Auro speaking."

"Well, I made it. I said I might come down and so I did." Several seconds of silence passed and Paul wondered if the deputy had hung up the phone or was distracted by an email or internet video. "This is Paul, Paul Newcombe. I'm in Portsmouth on vacation."

"In Portsmouth? On vacation?"

"I'm at the hotel on the river. The Ramada."

"You know TV is some kind of bad magic. I conjured you. My ugly mug flies through the air, bounces off a dish circling the globe and comes back down fully charged and loaded. All hell breaks loose and out of the dust walks my old pal Pauly Newcombe, calling to me and saying he's taking his vacation in the city where I work. If you asked me a hundred times if this would have been one of the possible outcomes of a backhoe driver finding a skull in a gravel pit I would answered a hundred times without including you. I would have said that talking to you would be about the last outcome I would ever expect."

"Are you drunk, Greg?"

"I'm on duty, old friend. No alcohol allowed for a deputy on-duty. I have certain standards too live by. I have limits to my behavior. I have very distinct lines that I cannot cross. It actually makes living easy. Don't act on any natural impulse. No drinking on the job, no unreasonable violence, no chasing after high school girls, no gunplay, no extortion of money. Color inside the lines. Serve and protect. The sheriff runs a tight ship, but with rules so clear how can you not follow them?"

"I suppose it makes sense."

"You have no idea what I'm talking about. Don't be insincere."

"I am aware of the rules of behavior."

"I'll meet you at the Ra-ma-da Inn bar around ten o'clock. If you have to, get started without me. I'll listen to you as long as you are buying, because you obviously have something on your mind and when I'm off-duty my drinking habits change considerably. Get your story straight and I'll see you then."

The line went dead.

10

Meet the Deputy

Paul rode the elevator down to the bar a few minutes before ten o'clock. He worked his way through a larger than expected crowd and found a high tabletop and two bar stools, the table being just high enough to be awkward and uncomfortable but it did give him a vantage point to spot the deputy when he came in. The table sat next to a large picture window that overlooked an indoor pool, empty except for a hirsute man slicing through the water as he finished an hour's worth of laps. Seven muted televisions hung from the walls and ceiling so every angle Paul could look included dancing light, except if he watched his feet. Briefly, five of the seven screens showed the same commercial for fungal cream and he felt a grip of concentration order his thoughts, but when they resumed flashing contrasting colors and patterns the order dissolved. Over the top of low conversations, clinking glasses and forks screeching across porcelain plates, rock music with big, slow guitar and heavy, earnest vocals filled every last corner and pocket of quiet. Most often, Paul deconstructed the elements of his environment and raced headlong toward obsession and irritation with the choices made by those with the power to create it. Why bombastic rock music? Why decorate the walls with pennants, flags and signs of Ohio sports teams? Why high tables that provided no opportunity for comfort or relaxation? Did any of it make the patrons drink faster or buy another round of potato skins? He constructed a familiar and redundant wager that if he designed a bar with absolute quiet and no decoration then men would drink shots until then fell on the spot where they once stood and women would dance on the bar without their tops, such was the need to quell the raging neurosis of most anyone over drinking age.

Paul turned his head and found Deputy Auro seated across the table from him, crunching a peanut between his teeth and already motioning to the bartender to bring along two tall beers.

"That's a pretty good trick. I didn't even know you were there."

Paul stuck out his hand for a handshake and Deputy Auro grabbed it hard as he stared directly into Paul's face as if trying to uncover a lie or coax a confession.

"Paul, my God, what's happened to you? You look like hell."

Unfortunately, Paul could not say the same about the deputy. He looked trim and fit in his uniform, a dark brown ensemble with gold piping down the outside of his pant legs and sleeves. To find equilibrium, Paul tried to force the thought that Greg resembled a security guard more the a sheriff's deputy, but any chance he had of minimizing the effect of his presence was quickly dispelled when Paul caught sight of the gun strapped to his hip and the gold star pinned to his shirt. The gun had obvious killing power, but the star transformed the hokey uniform into a garment of authority and power, something to be obeyed. It occurred to Paul that the deputy might have stayed in uniform to gain an advantage, to succinctly delineate who held power and who needed to stay in line.

"Don't they have laws around here about drinking in uniform?"

"I am the law, remember?"

"Well, *deputy,* do you really think it's a good idea to bring a gun into a bar or have the citizenry see you splatter that pretty uniform with vomit and piss, since they did buy it for you."

"Look, Paul, I ran over here right after my shift ended. Nobody is going to mind if I have a few pops unless I shoot one of these cowboys in the face," he said as he pointed to a table with four cowboys in powder blue, fringed cowboy shirts, with black bolo ties and white, crisp, and hardly-worn cowboy hats. Each had their shirts buttoned to the top button and all of their clothing, including their pants, chaps and black cowboy boots looked like it just come from the dry cleaners. The only inauthentic and anachronistic item on their person was the WWRD? button each one of them wore over their hearts.

"Looks like this town can get a little wild sometimes, eh?"

"Don't be a jerk."

Each took a sip of beer and watched the chorus of televisions vomit up a model ship skipping through a foamy surf, hand cream and hemorrhoid cream commercials that became one in their consciousness, a news anchor dressed in a powder blue suit mouthing her stony love for the world, a replay of a towering homerun from that night's Brewers-Cardinals game hit by a simian first baseman who had foregone shaving and bathing and whose gritted teeth and twitchy eyes created an impression that he may be on the cusp of a PED meltdown, a movie preview that consisted of a montage of monuments to human achievement, the Parthenon, St. Peter's Basilica, Stonehenge, the Hoover Dam and a host of lithe and fresh actors with amazingly full hair and spotless skin, being blown apart, melted and vaporized by tongues of blue flame and concentrated blasts of pure energy from the fingertips of aliens who had, as prurient as it sounds, penises for heads and dark green skin, and snatches of a sitcom rerun that had been created around the talents of the star whose range apparently extended as far as dressing up in drag as an old woman with enormous tits and gesticulating wildly. First Greg, then Paul broke away from the onslaught.

"So, why are you here, Paul? What do you have to tell me in person that you couldn't have said over the phone?"

"I don't have anything specific to say. I was just down this way and I thought I'd look you up."

"Have a little reunion, catch-up, see what kind of a screw-up I turned out to be? Are you that sure of your own choices that you can come down here to play a little judge and jury pantomime out in your head?"

"Maybe, the way you were back when I knew you I would have thought you'd be in a line of work less...conservative. I have to say seeing you in the uniform is pretty unbelievable."

"Oh, so you thought because I liked to smoke weed behind my parents' garage and I never changed out of my AC/DC shirt or showered that I would end up homeless or working in a convenience store mopping floors, stealing from the register and reciting scripture."

"I was hoping."

"I bet. When I got out of the army I was kicking around and didn't know what to do. I knew a guy who worked for the sheriff and he got me in. Somehow I stuck and I've been doing it close to fifteen years."

"You were in the army?"

"Unbelievable, right?"

"Surprising."

"Since I'm such a surprise to you, tell me how I should have lived. Tell me what you've been doing all these years? I'm sure I'll feel the rot of envy once you get done ticking off your successes."

"Right now I'm working for the City of Cleveland as a Housing inspector."

"And you've been doing this for how long?"

"Too long, I guess."

"You obviously didn't come down here to rub my face in your success. Married? Hot wife with beautiful little children? Win the lottery? Fired? Suddenly unmoored from the workaday world? Cancer? Softball-sized tumor in your head and you need a summing up? A reckoning? Recently discover a new perversion and decided to do a little sleuthing into your past to find its origin?"

"I don't have a bad job."

"That's fine if you've hunkered down in a comfy little cubicle, waiting for the end. Just don't expect me to be awed by it."

"Tell me, deputy, how's your dad?"

The deputy's eyes drifted back to the televisions where six narrations were bouncing along in a syncopated beat. He drained his glass of beer and set the glass back on the table exactly in the ring of condensation it had created. He rested his index finger on the lip of the glass and tapped out the rhythm of the song "Bad Company" by Bad Company, which swelled above the conversations, careening through the air like a distressed blimp. Paul thought he had struck him deep and all of his controlled movements stifled a boiling rage that could only end with him pulling his gun on his old friend.

"That's probably the one thing I envied about you, Paul. You had a normal family without all the Bible and Jesus talk. You had an actual color television set and not an old black-and-white that made every show look like it had been filmed in a snowstorm." He drifted away momentarily but came back before the televisions seized his interest. "You know, sometimes I would try to think about what was happening in your house, eating hamburgers or pizza in front of that color television, watching all the shows and laughing together, while my old man stood in the kitchen in his underwear and shouted *Romans* at us, not letting us eat until he finished. I sometimes had to do my homework by flashlight because he would get really angry when he saw my history book because it failed to mention the country had been founded solely on Christian principles. So, when you ask how he is doing you know the answer already. He's doing what he has always done, except his voice is a little weaker and he's lost his congregation except for my mom, and she's deaf."

"They still live in the neighborhood?" Paul asked, the force of his parrying now diminished.

"They'll never leave. Where did your mom move to?"

"Florida. She moved there years ago. She has a new husband, a guy named Manny, but I haven't met him except for a few conversations over the phone."

"Have you seen what the new owners have done to your old house?"

"No, I haven't been back in a long time."

"They built a giant garage where your dad's garden used to be and it looks like they store heavy equipment in it. The house is trashed. There's junk everywhere in the yard and they cut down almost all the trees, except they left them just lying on the ground like they were going to cut them up for firewood and then got distracted. It's weird. It looks like a battle was fought on the lawn and nobody bothered to clean it up. I was up there last month and I remember thinking that if your dad saw how these people live it would send him right over the edge."

Paul hadn't expected a return volley so skillfully shot, and he couldn't help thinking that he had misplayed his trump card. Instead of feeling triumphant and superior to the deputy he had become confused, swamped with memories and outrage of a lost childhood. He recognized the cloying nostalgia for what it was and his job as inspector had disabused him of the notion that anything ever stayed the same, even patches of ground and gardens where someone had grown to maturity, but knowing this made it no easier to shake the sense of loss.

The deputy knew he had skillfully fended off any further inquiry into his dad's habits. The sheriff had taught him well how to cover weakness and he couldn't help smiling a little as he watched all the blood squeezed from Paul's heart. He ordered two more beers and let silence reign long enough for the wound to become established and have a place from which to grow. The deputy relented, a little bored.

"A giant of a man came to the jail tonight and confessed to killing the girl we found in the gravel pit. He said all the years of guilt have been eating him up, but long ago he had committed himself to confessing should the body ever be found. He described how he strangled her and what color her eyes turned as she died. Not surprisingly, the color was red. He described how his back felt after all the digging and that he threw up three times during the course of the disposal. He said she was young, an innocent, a lamb, a sacrifice to the Holy Spirit. Of course, nobody believes a word of it. The sheriff himself interviewed him and he thought he was nuts. I think he pounded down a bottle of Everclear and doesn't know a damn word he's saying. He's a frequent visitor and he's going to wake up in the morning and have no idea why he's in the can or what he said. We get this kind of thing more than you can imagine. People come in and say they killed Christ and that they should be chewed in the jaws of Lucifer for all eternity, right next to Timothy McVeigh, Osama Bin Laden, and Hitler. Their sins are many. They confess to plots to blow up the Vatican inside CBS, they see monster serpents poking their head from the waters of the river, they are witness to skies full of UFOs, they follow a black shadow who commits every crime in the county and he seems especially fond of staring through open windows and watching old ladies undress. We hear this crap all the time. Most of the time we don't write any of it down because they're just products of bad alcohol, dementia, or flat-out I've-been-watching-too-much-television-paranoia, but this is the first that I've seen someone actually confess to a murder that could have happened. Well, it's pretty loose to say it could have happened. I guess what I'm trying to say is that he's the most convincing even in the face of a mountain of contradictory facts. Either he feels giant-sized guilt about something else he's done or he's drinking something new that will drive whole populations insane."

"Or maybe the simple fact is that he killed her," a voice said, coming from behind them.

They turned and faced a man in wrinkled khaki pants and an untucked button-up shirt. His beard was graying along his jaw and under his nose. His hair had receded past the crown of his head. The deputy scowled and turned back around.

"Nice to see you again, deputy," he said as he extended his hand toward Paul.

"Randall Highland. I cover this area for WKKJ Television."

Paul did not shake Randall's hand and offered neither his name nor a brief biography, but he did manage to produce a dead smile.

"Randall made some money off the skull story, so he thinks he's a professional. He even hired on as a guide for the NBC crew when they came to town and he fetched coffee for them and shined their shoes, so now he likes to stalk me to try to find out what I know, except he doesn't know how close he is to being charged with harassment of a public official. He's shown up at my kid's little league game, stopped my wife at the grocery store, and even tried to get himself invited to a barbeque at my house. The man has neither dignity nor an off switch."

"The sheriff said it was ok for me to come to the barbeque."

"At my house?"

"Since he was going to be there I thought I should ask him."

"Randall wants to know everything."

'Correction, Deputy, I want to be the FIRST to know everything."

"Knowledge is valuable."

"Are you asking for a bribe, Deputy?"

"Are you a complete idiot, Randall? If I wanted to be bribed by someone I wouldn't ask a guy who lives out of his car and smells like boiled vomit and piss."

"Then what are you saying?"

"I'm saying you want to be first so you can sell the information to the highest bidder. You're hoping that NBC crew will come back, even though the skull has stopped rolling. You're hoping that someday you won't have to sleep in the backseat of your car."

"I could bribe you if I wanted. I have resources."

"Really, and what would you give? Those wrinkled pants? A used steno pad? Your ratty Corolla, sorry, I mean your house?"

"Who do you have in the cell, Deputy?"

"A drunk."

"A drunk who confessed to murder? That seems a little out of the ordinary."

Paul saw a devious plan hatch in the deputy's mind. Some things never changed with age, wrinkles and weight, and Greg could not change the way his face slanted to the left and his mouth formed a puppet-like, vacuous grin, when he birthed some form of evil. Paul had seen the look every time they committed a petty larceny, every time he tried to convince girls to come to the cave, as well as every time he challenged Paul to a wrestling match. Randall completely missed the clue.

"I'll tell you what, Randall. Would you like to interview him?"

"Who?"

"Our confessor. Our murder suspect."

"Really? When?"

"It would have to be now. The sheriff gets in around 4:30 AM. As you know, he permits nothing outside of orthodoxy, but I can get you access. Or you can wait until he's out, but I'm sure you want to talk to him when you have bars between you and him."

"Can I bring my camera?"

"What good is a television interview without a camera? Don't you need to sell tape to the station?"

Randall scanned the deputy's face to determine the sincerity of the offer. Other than the insane smile he looked earnest.

"I have a camera in the car. It's not tape anymore. Everything is digital, man."

"Of course you do. Where else would it be? Digital, tape, what does it matter?"

"I'm just saying that I'm ready to go whenever you are."

"Paul, do you want to see a killer of girls?"

"Why not? I've never had the pleasure."

"Ah, that's the vacation spirit. Some people go to the Caribbean or Key West so they can walk around with their junk hanging out of their pants and Paul comes to Portsmouth to see a girl killer."

"Greg, you know I came to see you."

"Which is even more bizarre. I haven't figured out your angle for being here, so until I do we might as well pass the time trying to make sense of the insane," the deputy said as he lurched off his stool, punctuating his purpose by draining the glass of beer.

"What's his name?" Randall asked before he took a step to follow the deputy's lead.

"That's a funny thing. I'm sure you know the Kinnell family."

"That redneck brood that lives on Elm?"

"The very same."

"Which one?"

"Garrison."

"I think he's the youngest."

"And the biggest."

"I don't think he's that old. How could he have committed a crime like that?"

"How do you know how old the crime is? Flesh rots off the bone in a year or so. Besides, you're forgetting they have amazing redneck powers. I've seen redneck children married and divorced before the age of ten. I've seen redneck eight year-olds declare bankruptcy and let's not even mention that rednecks have redefined the phrase 'babies having babies.' With all that junk food and hormone-laced milk they drink I think the girls start having their periods around seven years old."

"So how long has the girl been in the ground?"

"That's classified information, Randall."

"Well, it has to be more than a few years. Did Kinnell kill the girl when he was ten years old?"

"Redneck powers, Randall, redneck powers. They sometimes have the strength of three men, even as babes in their mommy's arms."

"I gotta see this."

"Yes, you do, Randall, yes, you do."

They drove to the courthouse in the deputy's car. Paul sat up front next to the shotgun and Randall sat in the back, behind the wire mesh screen. Over the radio a dispatcher crooned "That's the Night the Lights Went Out in Georgia" before Greg barked into the microphone for him to shut his mouth. A quick burst of rain had wetted the streets and all the streetlights, security lights and stoplights reflected off every surface they touched, creating a brief illusion of bustle and crowding that masked the emptiness through which they drove.

Greg pulled into the parking lot of the courthouse, a limestone square mass that towered over an auto parts store and a cluster of wooden houses that looked like they had been made of sticks. To Paul, the building looked like a neo-classical bunker with poor lighting, a governmental stand against chaos washing up against its foundation. The deputy unlocked a non-descript side door that looked so inconspicuous that no one could have guessed it was the door through which prisoners were transferred from their cells to waiting prison vehicles. They walked down a hallway that smelled of disinfectant and roach spray and came to a desk where another deputy stared at two black-and-white monitors, one that showed a video feed from the jail cells and the other the hallway they had just walked down. Directly behind the seated deputy stood the door that led to the cells.

"Didn't you just leave?" the seated deputy said without taking his eyes off the screens.

"Can't stay away. You could learn something from me."

"Mostly what not to do."

"We're going to see our killer."

With some effort, the deputy lifted his eyes and inspected Deputy Auro's guests.

"Case in point. This is highly irregular, Deputy Auro. What would the sheriff say? "

"The sheriff is a fan of mine."

"You sure about that?"

"He's coming to my barbeque. We've had to keep the guest list tight, otherwise we would have invited you and your child-bride."

"She's nineteen."

"Right, you might want to check her birth certificate and get her back in middle school. There's no substitute for a good education."

"Your barbeque sounds lame, anyway."

"You'll have to ask someone who's invited if that's the case. How's the killer, by the way?'

"Charles Manson is sleeping it off on one of our luxurious cots."

"He wouldn't want to miss visitors, would he?"

"Well, that crazy-ass girlfriend of his has already been around here twice. She was pounding on the outside door not twenty minutes ago, right through the rain. She wouldn't leave until I went out there and shooed her away. She said she wanted to be arrested so she could be with him and she finally got it that if I arrested her there would be no one on the outside to bail Kinnell out tomorrow morning. She knows the drill, fortunately."

"Has he been in jail a lot," Randall asked as he held a pen poised over a steno pad and tried to keep the strap of his video camera from slipping off his shoulder.

The second deputy guffawed. "He probably sleeps on one of these cots more than he does his own bed, if he has a bed. The prosecutor has stopped charging him, most of the time. Last time he was in here because we found him naked on the Kentucky Bridge, throwing punches at passing cars. What are you going to charge him with?"

"Public indecency, perhaps?" Randall bristled.

"Nobody seen a bigger cock than that, ever. It's so goddamn big it's like comical. I think the prosecutor thought it was funny that Kinnell kept the boredom away for a while, so didn't even charge him."

"Deputy Chip, you know that wasn't the prosecutor's decision. That was the sheriff's mercy," Deputy Auro cut in, wanting to move along the conversation. "Now time's a wasting, open up the can." He felt suddenly impatient as he remembered his wife and two children at home and that the children sometimes gave his wife a hard time if they didn't get to see him before they fell asleep.

Deputy Chip shrugged his shoulders and pushed a button hidden under his desk that popped open the door leading to the jail cells. The light quality in the hallway resembled an operating room. Three cells were lined up on either side of the hallway and Kinnell lay in the farthest cell on the right. The deputy waved to the camera and then formed a gun with his index finger and thumb. He carefully aimed and took a shot at the camera, whereupon the red light under the lens suddenly went dark. He bounded back toward the cell and Randall and Paul stumbled over each other as they tried to make a path for him.

"Hey Garrison! I brought a couple of visitors to see you! Get up! I brought a court-appointed lawyer to defend you and the prosecutor as well. I thought we might as well get this trial over tonight since you're ready to confess. I'll be the judge. The sheriff has given me special powers that don't extend beyond these walls, but they can be pretty darn convenient. Your lawyer here can make sure you confess in the proper way to stand up to appeal," he said as he appointed at Randall, making Paul the prosecutor by inference.

"I don't like it, deputy. Tell him I'm a reporter. I don't like to get information under false pretenses," Randall said in the volume of a stage whisper.

"What about the time you came to my door dressed like a pizza delivery boy? Wasn't that subterfuge? A bit of clever undercover work?"

"I was actually delivering pizzas."

"Oh, I guess the journalism business is hit or miss, eh?"

"Sometimes you can run into a dry patch."

"You'll never be unemployed for long if you keep those delivery skills sharp."

"What do you faggots want?" said a soft, immature voice from inside the cell.

The mass on the cot began to move and slowly Garrison Kinnell unfolded himself and sat up on the edge of the cot frame. Kinnell had a pumpkin-shaped head with no hair from his ears upward but a full beard started just below the ears and extended downward in a tangle, terminating six inches below the edge of his chin. His skin and clothes were soiled like a farmer or mechanic who had just left work, except for his hands, which had been recently washed and looked so pink that at first glance someone could have thought he wore gloves. He shifted his weight, all 400 pounds of it, with agility uncommon in persons of such heft. Paul sounded off an audible "Christ" before he could catch himself.

"We grow them big down here, don't we Paul?" the deputy said in obvious delight of Paul's reaction.

"Jesus Christ," Paul responded.

"How tall is he, Deputy?" Randall asked.

"Hell, I don't know. He looks to me to be about eleven or twelve feet tall without heels."

"The Portsmouth Giant Killings! A family of giants loose in southern Ohio!" Paul exploded.

"See, Randall? Paul has the right idea. He knows how to turn dreck into a story. A compelling, can't-take-your-eyes-off-of-it story!"

"What you faggots want with me? I need my sleep."

"Kinnell, what exactly constitutes a faggot in your worldview?" the deputy snapped.

After a long, thoughtful pause Kinnell said in his soft baby voice, "Anybody that ain't my family, I guess, and a couple of them I wonder if they ain't faggots too."

"Then, according to you, the world is plain full of faggots. In fact, you, Kinnell, are in the minority. You are the hetero freak. The last damn bastion of manhood we have left."

"Why are you still talking if you ain't going to tell me what you want?"

"What have you been drinking, Kinnell? It smells like a kerosene pump in here."

"Maybe I been drinking kerosene."

"Then it won't be long before you start pissing fire."

Kinnell started laughing, a high-pitched twitter that should have been coming from a pre-pubescent child instead of a bald 400 pound giant. The three observers watched him list on the bed under the influence of hilarity, waiting for the cot to collapse under the massive, roiling weight. Then, the muse faded and he started sucking torrents of air and they thought the attack might be over. But once he regained his breath a peel of laughter burst from his mouth and the cycle began all over again.

The deputy became agitated after the fourth of fifth repetition. His face blanched and his glare became fixated on the large, bald head. He told Kinnell to be quiet, and then he told him to shut his mouth. He put his hands on the bars and leaned his face close to a gap. He screamed for quiet. Kinnell was either oblivious of the commands or chose to ignore them. Whatever the reason, each command made him laugh louder and faster and blood began pooling in his cheeks and the dome of his skull. Within a minute, the entire mass of his head became a dangerous looking red and his body seemed poised on the verge of a seizure. He clutched his enormous belly as if it was about to split in two. Then, the fluidity of the laughter stuttered as it became altogether impossible for him to breathe. His hands slipped from his belly and gripped to fistfuls of worn blanket. His mouth remained open, but now no sound came out and no air went in, so he froze with a startled or paralyzed look on his face, like he could have been experiencing the first salvos of a massive stroke, aneurysm or heart attack.

The deputy moved swiftly as he retrieved a key ring from beyond the door, opened the jail cell and pounced on Kinnell with a small, black club in his hand.

The first blow struck him on the shoulder as he turned his blood-filled head just in time, but the second blow landed square on the cheek. The deputy shifted his position and landed another swat across his thighs, which broke loose the blockage in his throat. Paul thought he might suck the cell free of oxygen and fill it again with a thick kerosene fog when he exhaled. The deputy cracked him on the knee, but Kinnell had enough wherewithal to swing one of his arms in defense, connecting solidly with the deputy's chest. The deputy staggered backward toward the door and managed to stumble out of the cell before Kinnell could get up and follow the first blow with more punishment. Wheezing, the deputy locked the door and thought that he had been lucky to smash Kinnell's knee and thighs, otherwise he would have caught him and killed him with his hands.

The deputy sank to his knees and tried to regain his breath. Randall and Paul did nothing except look at each other to see if the other was going to do something to help the deputy. Kinnell gulped and swallowed air as his face turned from crimson to pink again. After a few minutes the deputy stood up, brushed the dirt from his knees, and hooked the club back on his belt. He threw a crooked smile at Randall and Paul.

"Like I said, rednecks have the strength of twenty or thirty men. Have you gentlemen seen enough for tonight?"

"I brought my camera, Deputy. I'd like to interview him if I could," Randall whined.

Paul felt exhausted. The beer had pushed him over the edge and he would have lay down in one of the cots in an empty jail cell if he hadn't feared Greg locking the door and leaving him inside for the duration of his vacation.

"Right, I forgot about your scoop. Your million dollar interview. When you get a job at the network remember to come back and do a human interest story on the simple ways of small town life in a rotting river town. I could be the star, upholding the values and ideals of a lost America. What do you think?'

"It sounds like a darn good idea, Deputy. Maybe we should do it even if this interview goes nowhere."

"I've already got a start. I mean, right now I'm hot. I'm the deputy with the skull. A goddamn small town Hamlet with the skull of Juliet, but you'll need financing, a better camera, a crew. I'm not going to waste my time with a homemade movie shot on a camera you bought at Walmart."

"I'll do what I can."

"That's the spirit, Randall. Kinnell, you ready to talk to your attorney? He's going to film you because the man has no short-term memory since the accident. His poor, beautiful wife was horribly mangled. Swimming champ, 4-H champ, homecoming queen. Tragic, tragic."

"What? You think your billy messed me up? It would take more than that to stop me," Kinnell taunted.

"I think you broke a couple of my ribs and compromised my sternum. The next time I come I'll bring a bullwhip and a torch or maybe a taser locked on the elephant setting."

"Bring whatever you think you need, faggot, and I'll be waiting here for you."

"Kerosene brings out the worst in you, Kinnell. Alright, Randall, you have ten minutes with the killer of girls. Don't back away from altar of stardom."

Randall fumbled with his camera and worked at finding the right angle and height through the bars, toying with the focus to soften the garishness of the overhead fluorescence.

"I'm a little disappointed you're not going inside," the deputy teased.

"Sound travels just fine through the bars and this camera has an excellent zoom ratio. I could focus on one of his freckles if I wanted to."

"Alright, but your first step toward the network is that of a baby's."

Randall turned on the camera and filled the frame with Kinnell's head.

"Any of you all got a drink?' Kinnell asked. "My knee is hurting like hell. I think you broke my kneecap."

Deputy Auro slid a small flask from his pants pocket and slid it across the floor to Kinnell's feet.

"You want to turn off the camera there, Randall. The last thing I need is a video of me giving booze to a prisoner. Record over whatever you just recorded."

Randall trashed the few seconds of record and checked the battery life. He had half a charge left and he had forgotten the power cord in the back seat of the car, which was still parked outside the Ramada. Kinnell picked up the flask, which looked ridiculously small in his hand, and drained the contents in two gulps. He set it back on the ground and sent it careening across the floor and it banged hard against one of the bars and spun into the hallway.

"You better not have dented my flask, you fucker."

"Maybe it's a little disturbing that you carry both a flask and a gun," Paul interjected.

"The booze is for purely medicinal purposes. I can use it to take away a toothache of sterilize a gunshot wound."

"Very ingenious."

"Kinnell, I'm going to ask you a few questions. I'm going to start with your name."

"That didn't sound like a question."

"What did he say?" Randall asked the deputy and Paul.

"Pose it in the form of a question."

"Oh, for goodness' sake. Kinnell, what is your name?"

"You know my damn name. You just said it."

"Full name…What is your full name?"

"Garrison Kinnell."

"What is your occupation?"

"What?"

"Where do you work?"

"I don't work. The doctor said I have flat feet. And I have an allergy to corn that if I eat too much, like a tub of popcorn, my tongue swells up to the point where I can barely breathe."

"And how does that stop you from working?"

"You ever try to lift something or even walk around with a swollen tongue?"

"You could avoid corn and keep your tongue from swelling."

"I could stop breathing or drinking water too, but I don't see how that would help me work."

"I can't help thinking that a physique like yours should be put to some productive use."

"You ain't good at asking questions."

"He's got a point there," the deputy leaned toward Randall's ear and whispered. "Get on with it. You don't have all night."

"So, Garrison, why are you sitting in that cell? What could you have done to deserve this?"

Kinnell's gaze traveled across the floor, up the bars, and settled on the black lens of the camera.

"I killed that girl. I killed her while she was sleeping. I done it a long time ago and now the deputy found her. She came out of the ground yelling and screaming at me. She said at first she thought I was a dream, a demon come to scare her in the night. But she woke up just in time to realize I was flesh and blood and that the air she had in her lungs was the last she was ever going to breathe. Maybe it was my hands or maybe it was someone else's. I don't know, but it was my face she seen last. She was a little bird with brown hair and crooked teeth. A white neck. My girlfriend sometimes hears what people are thinking. She's an antennae. They mostly worry about what they want to eat or who they want to fuck, but she says there are a lot of hateful thoughts out there. Rage and violence are in the air. Sometimes I wake up in the morning and expect to find everyone dead, for there to be bodies rotting in the streets and blood on the pavement. The little bird with the brown hair and the crooked teeth fell victim to a violent thought. She got snagged and choked and was left to rot in a pile of gravel. It'd be a pity I suppose if it didn't happen every goddamn day."

"I'm not following, Garrison. Did you kill her or not?" Randall asked without taking his eye out of the viewfinder.

"It could've been me. I'm fully capable of killing anything at any time. I have a strong feeling that my hands are around her neck at the very end of her life. What I can't tell if it's my thought or someone else's that came flying into my thinking. That'll be something the jury will have to sort out."

"She probably died a long time ago. You would have been a child."

"I ain't never been a child."

"I see. Who was the girl?"

"A beauty. A little bird with a fast-thumping heart. A little thing that fit into the palm of my hand. She never went by a name because everybody knew who she was because there has never been anyone else like her. When she disappeared no one knew what name to shout into the air, so they all picked their favorite names or names of dead children or names of children they wish they had. It was a riot of grief. For a short time. Then she was forgotten and thought lost forever. The holes in the hearts of those who loved her never grew back properly, but enough scar tissue covered the wounds to let them live, poorer and sadder than before. She screamed for a long time, but nobody heard her because she was under the gravel. First her voice gave out and then her will to be found. She figured that she was already a rotting corpse by then and already in the ground, so what was the point of ripping up her abused throat any further just to be dug up and reburied again. She figured all her family already knew she was dead somewhere and they didn't need to be reminded. But the deputy had to find her and unleash all her anger. She's pissed off. She'd fuck my throat with a hammer if she could become real again"

"Everybody makes that mistake. They think I found the skull. I was just the one on TV. They would have interviewed the backhoe driver but he stuttered so bad that they couldn't commit him to video," Deputy Auro whispered into Paul's ear.

"But why did she have to die? Why sacrifice such innocence? How could you harm something so small and vulnerable?" asked Randall.

"You start with a little pressure and you keep squeezing. You squeeze right past what you thought was your limit to inflict pain and you keep going. By that time you start to feel like you need to push yourself into new territories. You can feel the twitching, the clawing of her fingernails on your arms, the cracking of bone, but it's now a game and those markers of reality, sight and sound and touch, are secondary to the purpose at hand. I was just trying to answer a basic question, something like 'Can I actually crush the windpipe of this little bird?' And I answered very strongly that I could."

"Shouldn't you keep him locked up as a matter of principle?" Paul asked the deputy.

"During my first couple of months as deputy I use to fall asleep at night with thoughts of massive prison barges floating up and down the river or whole cities converted into rambling penitentiaries. Not the most original thought. I think there's a couple of dozen movies like that but I couldn't see anyway else out of the problem. Kinnell's right. There's a murderer lurking in every heart and it took me a long time to understand that and accept it and that my job isn't so much to prevent the violence but to hose down the aftermath. Like how can I tell when a churchgoing father of three finally has had enough of paying bills and scratching by and decides to beat his wife's face to a pulpy mess. I've given up trying to guess."

"You faggots going to leave me alone anytime soon? My head is roaring."

"A brief period of lucidity, followed by more faggot talk, such are the crosses we bear. Garrison, that pain you feel is your body processing that kerosene you drank. It doesn't like violation."

"You all better get me some more by the morning or I'll puke all over this cage."

"Like I said, I hose down the aftermath."

"You better have a big hose."

"I can always call the fire department. They will do a nice job."

"One more question, Kinnell," Randall interrupted, as he could see him rapidly fading. "What punishment do you think you deserve?"

Kinnell tried to focus on the lens again, but his aim was off to the left and short by five feet.

"I guess a judge will have to decide that, but I'll tell him that it shouldn't be anything short of the electric chair or hanging by the neck until I'm dead."

"Those methods have been determined barbaric. It's all by injection now," corrected the deputy.

"Do they stick you with rat poison?"

"Basically, but first they sedate you with something one or two proofs higher than homemade kerosene or Everclear, then they kill you with rat poison."

"Better for this to end sooner than later."

As punctuation Kinnell retched and sent a voluminous stream of vomit onto the floor and then another. Randall, Paul and the deputy turned away and involuntarily let out a harmonic groan of disgust.

"He wasn't lying. He gave you fair warning," said Paul.

They all walked to the exit door to the soundtrack of more vomiting and retching and sobbing between the bouts of sickness.

"Cleanup in Aisle 5," Greg smirked as he passed the deputy on-duty.

"What the fuck did he do? He didn't shit himself again, did he?" the deputy whined.

"Not yet. Sometimes God grants small favors."

Deputy Auro led them outside where he lit a cigarette and shook his flask to see if Kinnell had left a drop, which he hadn't. He looked for constellations but they had been blocked out by a bank of low-flying clouds. Paul looked at the same dark sky and thought more rain imminent as Randall inspected the camera and was happy to find the battery had held out through the entire interview.

"Can you imagine being that kid?"

"What kid? The one in the ground or the one in the cell?"

"The end for the one in the ground was no doubt awful and terrifying probably. I'm thinking of Kinnell. I've personally picked him up a dozen times, mostly disorderly conduct, public drunkenness, vandalism, unlawful display of public affection, namely having his girlfriend blow him on the hood of a car in a parking lot, but he has taken a dark turn. I should have expected it. All that shit he drinks has to have some affect, but this won't end well."

"I thought there was a murderer lurking in every heart?" Paul said in a tone laden with sarcasm.

"There is, but whatever we just saw isn't in every heart. True self-destruction is rarer than you think. Why do you think every single criminal we pick up or who is sitting in a penitentiary right now claims they're innocent or are adamant that there are extenuating circumstances? Most take no responsibility for their crimes because they're trying to save their necks. They can't help but to want to survive and if survival means lying or rationalizing then that's what they do. One in a million prefers execution over lying and none of them lie to be executed. That's why I'm saying it's rare."

"What'll you do with him?"

"He'll sober up after he purges every ounce of fluid in his body and he'll realize he's in jail and that he has confessed to a capital murder and he'll say he's sorry for the inconvenience and we'll let him go and we'll see him again when he drinks too much and gets himself in trouble. The other possibility is that he sticks to his story and the prosecutor, really the sheriff, will have to figure out what to do. They may seek an indictment just to stop others from making false confessions. It's one thing to feign guilt, but something completely different sitting in front of a prosecutor and judge trying to explain your motives. If word gets out that Kinnell has done this then we'll get a couple dozen copycats calling up confessing to every damn thing. There has to be some deterrent."

"You mean like seeing an interview with him on some local channel?" asked Paul.

The deputy looked at Randall and the camera, considered him for a moment, and decided the chances of the interview ever airing anywhere to be so infinitesimal that he needn't worry about his decision to grant him access to Kinnell.

"We'll see."

"You said it was rare for someone to confess to a crime they hadn't committed. Yet, you just said you can expect a couple of dozen calls. Which one is it, deputy?"

"I don't think you understand. The copycats who call are schizophrenics, shut-ins, manic-depressives who can be imprinted with an idea and be impelled to act because their sickness tells them to confess. Kinnell seems to be an original. The story of the skull could have imprinted him, of course, but we've had so much contact with him over the past couple of years I think it would have come out before now."

"What happens if the owner of the skull is a young girl and the timeframe matches?"

"I don't think it's likely."

"But it could happen, right?'

"Then we would have a confessed murderer to burn at the stake. Do you need a ride back to the hotel?"

"No, I'm going to walk. Hopefully I'll miss the rain."

"So, you are really staying in town?"

"God yes, I wouldn't want to miss the Roy Rogers festival. "

"You've turned out weirder than I could have ever expected."

"You have no idea, really."

"Maybe I'll have you over to the house. I'm having a barbeque this weekend."

With a salute, Paul walked into the gloom, his feet splashing as he went. He didn't know if he was walking the right way, but neither Greg nor Randall offered him directions so he continued, relying on knowledge of city plans and smell of the river to find his bearings.

David Megenhardt

11

A Wall Against the Rising Water

Paul slept until noon the next day. The maid had knocked four times during the course of the morning and each time he pressed two pillows to either side of his head and mumbled for her to go away. Luckily, he had remembered to push the deadbolt the night before, because the maid was either persistent or afraid to lose her job as she used her pass key during her last attempt, rattling the door knob and testing the strength and positioning of the deadbolt. He had slept naked and he thought of answering the door without dressing, but he had the sense the maid and her peers had suffered similar humiliations dozens, if not hundreds, of times, depending on the length of their service, so the idea died before gaining momentum. He had read somewhere or he once knew a maid who admitted that men hotel guests like to parade naked, whether just out of the shower or post-coital or fresh from erotic dreams or erect from a session of early morning pornography on the pay-per-view, whether possessing small penises or mythically large ones, in front of the nameless uniformed workers who had been sent to sponge up their fluids and scrub their indiscretions, really mercenaries sent in to bring order to the chaotic lives of the guests. These sad men never acted on their urges, never once touched her or themselves in her presence. She had come to expect such behavior from the gender with the unruly piece of meat hanging between their legs, but the women surprised her. A healthy body of anecdotal evidence revealed that a surprising percentage of women would open the door with their breasts exposed or wearing nothing at all, as if playing out a fantasy of employing a private dresser whose opinion and erotic thoughts mattered so little that they could be invited into the most intimate of settings without shame. The maid who rattled Paul's door understood the game and had taken to staring at the guests' genitals or breasts, nothing judgmental or mocking, just an honest assessment and comparison to what she had seen before. She found a straightforward appreciation earned her bigger tips.

For some reason the cowboy convention brought out this kind of behavior in the guests. This very morning she had suffered through a topless middle-aged woman with sheriff star pasties trying to lasso her from atop the bed and an even older gentleman who answered the door with nothing on but a black cowboy hat, a bolo tie and a cock ring.

The last rattle woke him up for good, so he rolled out of bed, dressed, and walked down to the hotel restaurant. He passed the maid in the hallway as she came out of another room, holding towels that looked soiled by Vaseline and spray paint. She was young, pot-bellied and teetering on the loss of all her sexuality and teeth through miserable work, bad food, and recalcitrant children. She had also learned to never smile at a guest or acknowledge them in the hallway, especially if she had seen them naked, lest they think her vagina forced the smile in order to be sated.

Paul ordered a coffee and a slice of cherry pie and ate as he scanned his map again. He had ruined vacations before because of poor planning or a poor choice of locations, but never so dramatically as this. He understood the deputy had been the draw, but other than Indian burial mounds nothing in a hundred mile circumference held any interest to him, unless he included Pittsburgh, Columbus or Charleston. Going to museums, restaurants, strip clubs, and bars in an unfamiliar city seemed worse than going home and doing the same in the city he knew. He tried to push out of his mind that he would have another year of his job before being able to leave again, because dwelling on the increasingly obvious truth that he was misspending his life could lead him to do something rash like quitting his job or putting in for a promotion so he would never have to descend into the bowels of a basement filled with rat feces, turgid water, broken toys and moldering clothes. His instability may even lead to a marriage and that could only go horribly wrong.

A flash of blue passed by his table. A teenage hostess led a man dressed in a matching powder blue pants and shirt. Over his oily hair he wore a white hat. His western-cut boots, bespangled with rhinestones and faux gems, sparkled and twinkled even in the dim restaurant light. In the sunlight, Paul thought, the boots must set his feet ablaze. When he turned, the blue cowboy presented the rest of his ensemble to the lunchtime diners, which consisted of a silver bolo tie, the clasp of which had been polished to a showy sheen, a belt buckle that looked six inches in diameter that showed an Alpine scene of dancing goats, and his western style shirt with an intricate hand-stitched floral pattern emblazoned across the chest. Above his collar he had tied a red kerchief around his neck and it bloomed over his shoulders in two wide petals. He took off his hat and revealed a head of perfectly furrowed hair that had not been dented or mussed by the heavy cowboy hat. He had high cheekbones that gave his face a feminine cast and his skin shone clear and unbroken by splotches or whiskers, except for two rosy circles that resided over the very same cheekbones. Paul, even from a considerable distance, could tell Blue Cowboy wore makeup: certainly mascara, a hint of eye shadow, and even a light coating of lipstick to make his lips look engorged with blood and to create an intoxicating contrast with his clear, pale skin. He sat and drew the chair closer to the table. He carefully unfolded his napkin and laid it on his lap with movements so controlled and precise that Paul had the urge to tip over Blue Cowboy's table or, at the very least, confuse his place setting.

Paul looked to the other patrons to guess if they shared his hallucination, but he found he had overlooked the fact that most of them wore articles of cowboy paraphernalia, a kerchief here, a bolo tie there, a flannel button-up shirt that marvelously revealed a long line of cleavage and a wave of belly fat, a chaw of tobacco in that cheek, a silver belt buckle glinting in the light over there, and a platoon of very expensive cowboy boots on all their feet. They lacked hats, except for Blue Cowboy's, which sat on a chair by itself as if he was dining with his favorite possession instead of it being in service of his costume. Paul guessed the boots were a compromise for most, given that in an age of central air-conditioning and heat, of automobiles with roofs, daily showers, easily bought shampoo, of lives lived mostly squirreled away from the sun and wind made the hat at best obsolete and at worst an impractical nuisance so that only those with the strongest combination of artifice, vanity and western devotion managed to don a hat and keep it on for more than an hour. The obvious fallback was the boot. All credentials for passion and knowledge of the west-that-never-was were poured into boot designs, which became more detailed and reflected better craftsmanship as the market developed to the point of being classified as a fetish. While the hat had serious drawbacks in modern life, the boot was practical and necessary and if you weren't willing to sink considerable cash into the purchase of art from the best leather artisans then you could not call yourself anything other than a casual fan of nostalgia.

Paul locked eyes with Blue Cowboy and the cowboy winked at him and mouthed something along the lines of, "Yo, dere pardnor" or "Take me farther" or

"Call your father." Paul quickly averted his eyes and made sure not to look back in Blue Cowboy's direction should his look be misinterpreted as returning his advance. After he finished his pie, Paul ventured another glance in the cowboy's direction. Blue Cowboy's eyes waited for him, as if they had never looked in any other direction through the preceding interval and he silently said, "Do you mind if I stare?" or "I once killed a black bear," or "I have enough to share." Paul scowled as he did not like any of the possibilities. He flagged down the waitress, asked her to compute his check in her head, and slipped her enough money to cover the food and an overly generous tip. When she responded, "Thanky, Pardnor," Paul responded with "For God's sake, has everyone turned into an asshole?" and the waitress retreated before he could calculate the percentage of his tip more in his favor.

In the lobby a large-boned matron wearing a stiff blonde wig slammed into him as he made his way out of the hotel. Her right knee and his left knee collided and Paul skidded against the wall and kept himself upright by taking ahold of a potted rubber tree plant

"Sorry, honey," she belted out in a voice several octaves lower than he expected.

The collision had not affected her so she stood with her hands on her hips and her legs spread wide apart as if she braced for a terrible wind to come roaring through the lobby. Paul sank to the floor because the pain in his kneecap would not fade and began to throb like it had been pounded with a crowbar. The woman, dressed in a star-spangled mid-calf skirt, matching vest, a white shirt covered with tiny, laughing cowboy heads, and a black kerchief tied around her neck, grew impatient as Paul did not recover quickly and she felt obliged to stand there until he could walk. She offered him a hand and pulled him up with a jerk. She straightened his shirt and placed her large hands on his shoulders as she faced him.

"You should always be mindful of where you're walking. There's no telling what trouble you will find," she said seriously as if revealing a hidden truth.

Paul wilted a little under her gaze, in the orbit of her body heat, suddenly a satellite to her force and bearing. Paul would have guessed he was under the influence of a man brimming with testosterone, except for her enormous breasts squeezed under the vest and the absence of whiskers along her jaw.

"I will be mindful."

"No you won't. You haven't in the recent past, which is why I had to scoop you off the ground, and you won't be in the future," she said before letting fly a braying laugh that filled the lobby.

"Remember, what would Roy do?"

"I'm not here for the convention."

"That would explain the lack of apparel. You here to see the flood wall? They done a beautiful likeness of Roy on it. That alone would be worth the drive."

"No."

"Indian Head Rock?"

"No, I don't even know what that is."

"What else is there?"

"I'm here on business."

"What do you sell? Embalming fluid or iron lungs? The braying laugh burst from her again. "Even a businessman can take the time to see the floodwall. You won't be sorry." She trotted off, reasonably assured she had not broken any of Paul's bones.

Paul asked the front desk clerk where the floodwall could be found and the clerk returned a blank-eyed stare before managing to respond with, "By the river," and Paul asked him what part of the river as it traveled about 1,000 miles between the confluence of the Allegheny and the Monongahela rivers and the motherfucking Mississippi. The clerk braced himself against a surging apoplexy.

"Since you're asking as you stand in Portsmouth, Ohio doesn't it stand to reason the wall will be close? And since we are practically a riverfront hotel doesn't it stand to reason that the wall is at our doorstep, for God's sake."

"We are a riverfront hotel? We? Are you part of the ownership group of this fucking dump? Are you working for your investment or are your investments working for you?"

"Sir, what are you talking about?"

"I'm just fascinated with your use of a plural pronoun when describing the hotel."

"We consider ourselves a team, sir. Just go out the front door and walk straight ahead and you'll run into the floodwall."

"Was that so goddamn hard? A simple answer to a simple question."

"I don't know what you mean, sir," the clerk said as he flashed a sarcastic smile.

"Maybe you want to go outside and let me wipe that smile off your face?"

"On duty, sir. I get off at eight if you would like to meet me. I have to warn you, though, that I'm a student of mixed martial arts and you look old, slow and bloated from too much boozing and jacking off."

"I'll see you at eight."

"I'll be waiting."

They had managed to argue without raising their voices so that anyone more than a few feet away would have thought the exchange just matter-of-fact banalities, but Paul was seething when he turned away and walked out of the hotel, finally. He couldn't help but feel defeated as he was the one who had to walk away.

Outside, Paul pounded his open palm and shouted a jumble of syllables. A man and his wife, two shrunken ancients who wore matching red kerchiefs and pink cowboy shirts, bore witness to the invective and became afraid that Paul might turn his anger on them so they bowed their heads and moved as quickly as they could to the relative safety of the hotel. Paul stormed down a short hill and stopped at the foot of the floodwall. The brief exercise, really no more than a seventy yards of walking, cleared enough of his anger to make his impulse to find a sledgehammer and blast a hole in the wall a shallow and impotent flicker.

Before him stood two hundred years of Portsmouth history painted in massive squares on the face of the wall, creating an impressively long mural. The wall had to be twenty feet high, meant to keep the surging river water from the town, and the painted section had to stretch a couple thousand feet. The panel before him depicted the present day city at twilight, a glowing, yellow oasis as seen from the dark recesses of Kentucky. A ripple of humpbacked hills rise in the background and a girder bridge spans the calm Ohio in the foreground. He drifted to the side and was swept along by the images towering above him. Three Shawnee tribesman conference while their women huddle on the ground preparing food. All around them is covered with a powder of snow. Behind them a village of wooden frame huts composed of tree bark and animal hides stretches to the river. Huts can be seen on the other bank as well, a twin city rising in the light. Maybe estranged brothers who needed the distance of the river and the challenge of its current between them.

The 1913 Portsmouth Motorcycle Club roars past him. The artist has painted a reproduction of a 1913 photograph showing twenty-five motorcycle enthusiasts astride their bikes, facing the camera in a line, in the thrall of motorized two wheels, road conditions be damned. Underneath the photograph the canvas includes two rows of motorcycles on either side that stretch back to the past, the technology growing cruder as time slips by. A gleaming Harley-Davidson hog sits in front, suggesting the love affair continues until this day although it was uncertain whether the club had a continuous existence. In the center of the composition resides a pair of aviator sunglasses atop a crumpled leather jacket thrown onto the ground, the apex of American cool. The river, the road, and a white roadside cottage are reflected in the lens of the glasses, beckoning the riders to straddle their machines and hit the open road.

The sons of Portsmouth huddle over a cannon as the ball explodes from the mouth, on its way toward the Confederate line. Smoke mars the blue sky of Gettysburg. The hillside is littered with stones that look like tombstones awaiting a date of death to be carved on their faces.

The Portsmouth Earthworks, a circular mound structure created by the Hopewells around the time of the first Roman Republic was founded, stretches out before him as maybe a Hopewell traveler may have seen it from a nearby hill or riding the back of an eagle. The land is bathed in a primordial, pristine light. Behind the picture is an architectural drawing of the earthworks and around the edges are depictions of totems and pipes the traveler may have carried on his trade route, walking through the bountiful land toward the sea.

On his way he walks past Pierre Joseph Céleron de Blainville as he meets the Shawnee and English fur traders at the confluence of the Scioto and Ohio Rivers and proudly, if not arrogantly, lays claim to the entire Ohio Valley and the tributaries to the river for France. The expedition buried lead plates along the river to prove their claim just, coming as a surprise to all who lived there. Céleron looks appropriately ridiculous in a flowing cape and tri-corner hat, pointing to the French flags, with a small contingent of armed military and men and a monk haunting the space behind him as the traders lounge about in buckskin and the Shawnee stand or sit shirtless, looking incredulous, but worrying about the coming plague.

Next came an homage to a scrum between the Green Bay Packers and the Portsmouth Spartans. The Spartan running back is breaking through the arm tackles on two defenders as the referee signals touchdown in the background. The bruisers wear leather helmets and their faces looked smashed flat. A side panel highlights the history of the Spartans: admitted to the NFL in 1930, first NFL night game between Spartans and Brooklyn Dodgers, first NFL Championship game was played in 1932 between the Chicago Bears and the Spartans, and the Spartans subsequent abandonment of Portsmouth for the booming city of Detroit to become the Lions in 1934.

Following the mud and blood, an ode to a century of shoe manufacturing rose before him. Showing the interior of a factory, an assembly line of workers stitching together shoes, making brands such as Selby's, Irving Drew, Excelsior and Williams, the mural also speaks of abandonment. The factories did not move to Detroit, the last of which closed or left in 1977, but took a southerly route in search of cheap labor and societies willing to tolerate worker oppression. Of course, when the new workers began to wise up production was shifted to the waiting hands of hungry Asians.

From this nostalgic height of American industrial might the content came crashing down to a depiction of the Portsmouth Greyhound bus station, built in the art deco style and harkening back to the time when bus travel was clean, modern, thrilling, and worthy of the investment and care of good design, instead of carting around the desperately poor, the too young, and the insane. Paul felt melancholia descend upon him. If the bus station still existed he couldn't imagine what state it could be in. In his experience the simple passing of time rotted away history, and nothing could be done to stop the decay. Looking at something in the state it had once been, with fresh paint and newly fired bricks, the hope it exudes in the staying of time, either led to the delusion that not everything ended as a ruin or gave one a sense of such hopelessness that no one would build anything every again. Even the mural of the floodwall would chip away and be forgotten, the victim of vandals and graffiti artists yet to be born. A book on the lives of the past lies unread and moldering.

His spirits buoyed some with the set jaw and smiling face of Branch Rickey, who had been born near Portsmouth. Rickey went on to be the President and part-owner of the Brooklyn Dodgers and integrated baseball with the signing of Jackie Robinson. In the mural around the smiling head of Rickey float his achievements in a dream-like cloud: owner, manager, author, coach, innovator and orator. Robinson and the Portsmouth Redbirds (because Rickey pioneered the use of the minor leagues while he was an executive with the St. Louis Cardinals) are prominently displayed to his left and right. Paul imagines Rickey's luck in escaping the shoe factories because of his love of baseball.

Or did he escape the steel mills? Perhaps his grin is an acknowledgement of not spending his life slaving over rivers of molten steel as he looks upon a triptych of another ghost industry, steelmaking. He would be long dead before the last of the mills closed in 1980, ending a century run of this area of manufacturing as well. The late 70s could not have been happy times in Portsmouth with its twin identity of shoemaking and steelmaking ending within three years of each other. The painting shows a mighty ladle pouring molten steel, so elemental and powerful that is seems impossible for a company to ever shutter a factory. Has a volcano ever been closed by something as trifling as a downturn in auto or appliance manufacturing?

    The narrative, such as it is, falls back to football in the form of Jim Thorpe, who coached and played for a semi-pro team called the Portsmouth Shoe-Steels in his last years of playing football. Paul could imagine a heavy and slow Thorpe hoofing it across the mud, taking the best shots from warehouse workers and bargemen who regale listeners in their old age of the days when they brought the great Thorpe to the ground. Leading with his nose that had been smashed flat and running on gimpy knees, Thorpe bounces through the line, legs churning, always churning, giving everything so that Shelby Shoes and the Whitaker-Gleasnor Steel Mill would continue their sponsorship, hence the awkward push and pull of the team's name. The crowds who watch him, factory workers from the shoe factories and mills, hate the inconvenient marriage forced upon them and can hardly mouth the name, so they retreat to the neutral ground of the name of the city that carries their shared destiny.

    Thorpe, wincing and out of breath, runs past Julia Marlowe, an incomparable Shakespearean actress who reached the height of her popularity in the early 1900s. She looks at him with doe-eyes and her exposed neck and low-cut tragedian's dress reveals milk-white Victorian skin. Her family lived for a time in Portsmouth between stops in Kansas and Cincinnati after emigrating from England. For twenty-five years she acted on Broadway and worked touring companies that canvassed America, bringing Lady Macbeth, Portia, Cleopatra and Beatrice to the swamps, to the cities that had suddenly befouled themselves with smoke and ash, across the endless seas and corn and wheat, to feed them the poetry of Shakespeare, which had to sound like birdsong to people tending belching fires and living in the roaring wind. Her talent and popularity amongst audiences long dead earned her a place on the floodwall.

    Paul passed depictions of a stagecoach, a street car, and a bustling street scene of the 1940s, all nostalgic glimpses of past living patterns, before the ubiquity of cars and the dominance of big box stores, strip malls and highway life. Only in famine or some other dystopian future could Paul imagine an artist rendering a golden view of Walmart or Home Depot, because no one could deny the landscape had been scarred by a sense-resistant case of smallpox for the sake of convenience and consumerism. But the body of America had endured contagions and plagues before and compared to the disease of industrialization with its symptom pollution, the consumer phenomenon looks a little like a disfiguring case of acne instead of anything life-threatening.

Paul's attention began to waver and he barely gave a look to an ode of the great depression realist painter turned surrealist Clarence Holbrook and the tip of the hat to a long-standing double century bike ride known as the Tour of the Scioto River Valley. Not even a depiction of the infamous Portsmouth Gaseous Diffusion Plant could draw his complete attention back to the floodwall. The plant had enriched weapons grade uranium for the U.S. Atomic Energy program and the U.S. nuclear weapons program from 1954 to 2001, contaminating a good portion of the 3,777 acre site and the citizens of the county lucky enough to land a good job with enriched radiation. Paul began to think of taking a break or doing something else when he saw the Blue Cowboy on the wall. Dressed in powder blue pants and shirt and a white hat, the cowboy sits astride his Palomino Trigger, as the horse rears on his hind legs, a mighty beast under the sure command of his master. Both wave to their audience, the cowboy with a reassuring hand and the horse with its two front hooves. The King of Cowboys himself, Roy Rogers, sending a greeting from a grassy plain with a soaring, Rocky Mountain range in the background. When Paul read the inscription he turned cold as he thought of the two whores in the motel room and the prophecy of Third Eye. How could she conjure the Blue Cowboy's visage from a screeching bat? He realized that this image, the cowboy on the back of a friendly horse, had been what he used as a place holder when she brought up Rogers' name during the telling of the future. He had seen it before a dozen times and forgotten it an equal number. How could the bat know about him? Or was the bat just a conduit for the spirit world, much like Third Eye herself? Could his truck stop beauty actually hold the combination to the mysteries of the universe and its link to our sub-consciousness? Who else could hold such information except low-life outcasts because no one could maintain a bourgeois life knowing the next step? Certainly, a Hollywood cowboy dressed in powder blue would have no chance of understanding the tenuous line between reality and the shadow world.

"She's a beauty, ain't she?"

The voice and the idle of a car motor sounded a few feet from Paul's back. When he turned, Paul looked into the face of the Blue Cowboy, a degraded copy of

Rogers, a cheap impersonator aping the purity of the original.

"I wouldn't know. I don't really remember what he looked like."

"You're probably a little too young. I fear the memory of him is fading. How many of us are left who saw him in movie theaters?"

"Tragedy is all around us. The world collapses and is reborn every day."

"He's dead now. Just as well, I suppose. He must be turning over in his grave to see what's happening to this country. That there," here he pointed to the mural, "are the glory days with Trigger. I think it's pretty common knowledge that he was never really the same after Trigger died. That took the joy of living away from him."

"Trigger, Jesus."

"I'm a little disappointed that he didn't put Bullitt in the picture. You remember Bullitt, the amazing wonder dog."

"No."

"A thousand times smarter than Lassie and not really as prissy. I want to get a picture with me in front of the painting. I've done it every year since the panting was done. I see the pictures as a kind of existential passing of time and proof that my love of Roy has stayed steady and true through all the vagaries of my life."

Paul agreed. Blue Cowboy pulled his car to the side of the road and bounded out, holding a small plastic camera. The wind caught his kerchief and made it dramatically ruffle, providing a last touch of over-the-top flair. Paul looked in either direction of the street and hoped no one would see him with the man. Blue Cowboy had left his car stereo on and had turned up the volume so he could hear it across the street while he posed. The lyrics clearly rang out.

> Eye! Eye! Eye!
> Way out in cold Montana long ago
> Where prairie dogs prowl and the night snarls and blows, a
> Lonely cowboy's voice rang out "Hello!" and
> Echoed though the village below
> Then came back a lass' response loud and clear
> Cowboy grinned wide and shook his spurs, said
> He, "I'll take you from your family and goats, Bil-
> Lings, they say, is far away, but there's a preacher there, then
> She just grabbed his hips, she was very strong, so

Strong, oh my, and then he made a reply, Oh! Oh! Oh!

They rode the night and two days after
Billings town was some ninety miles away, but
When at last they gamboled up the street, the
Cowboy's ache was really hard not to see
On his arm his dusty, lusty girl a carrying, but
Beneath the church's little crucifix, said
She, "The last man didn't insist on marrying,"
His face got red, then he said, "What other man is this?" If
Another has come before, you'll walk home for sure, "One
Or twelve, a herd of lone rangers," said she
Then he was heard to say, "No! No! No!"

Blue Cowboy stood in front of the Rogers mural and Paul fired off three quick shots. The third had been the best, because Paul had captured a wide grin on Blue Cowboy's face as he thought of the golden times astride Trigger. He rushed over to Paul and took the camera from his hands and held it like it was something extremely fragile like a painted egg fashioned out of spider webs and dust.

"You here for the festival?" Blue Cowboy asked.

"No, I stumbled on it purely by accident."

"Now that's a happy accident,"

"That's one way of looking at it."

"And what are the other ways of looking at it?" Blue Cowboy said as he repositioned a wad of chewing tobacco and spit a brown stream onto the pavement.

"Well, I suppose you would have to be a fan of the western to get the purpose."

"You're not a fan of America then? Not a fan of men and women who stepped into the wilderness and survived by using nothing but their hands and wits?"

Paul wished he had his own wad of chew so he could return fire. He could feel bile rising in his throat and he wondered if he started punching Blue Cowboy if he could ever stop himself.

"That's enough, Roy, stop rattling your spurs. What do I know about westerns? I haven't watched one in twenty years. You could have been the King of the Cowboys or Midnight Cowboy for all I know."

"You think I dress like this outside of the festival?"

"What do I know about all the variations of the human condition?"

"I get nothing but abuse if I wear this outfit to the mall. Folks today are depraved and perverted."

The man had obviously missed or deliberately ignored the cultural shift of acceptable men's garments and that a blooming kerchief no longer meant cattle drives, a mask for dust or, if employed for nefarious reasons, bank and train robberies, but, along with the blue suit and makeup, signified the existence of glory holes, sweaty dance clubs, and politicians hell-bent on establishing a western gay credibility.

"I can only imagine the comments. Do you get many requests for anonymous oral sex?"

"Did I miss a class somewhere? How would you know that?"

"Call it a gift if you wish, but you are the first person I've ever seen walking around like that, so you're open to categorization and there are only a few options."

"Well, Roy never had an organ in his mouth."

"It sounds much worse when you put it that way."

"It seems blasphemous to be talking about this under his painting. He must have a low opinion of me."

"Why is he on the wall?"

"He lived here as a kid. His house used to be open for tours, but the new owners are a paranoid bunch and they won't let anyone through. Ironic isn't it? The King of the Cowboys grew up on the river in the foothills of the Appalachians."

"That's not exactly ironic. That's just Hollywood tripe, no? John Wayne wasn't a real cowboy either."

"You're a slippery one. I can't tell if you are a complete bastard or a few fries short of a Happy Meal."

"Don't ever use metaphors that include marketing for fast food chains. It's a cardinal sin. It's an offense to the world's collective intelligence. For you, it would be akin to jerking off to Roy's creamy white skin and befouling this painting with the product of your lust."

"You are a sick bastard. In all my years of being a Roy Rogers fan I never once thought of doing that."

A song with a cowboy yodel and a honkey tonk guitar ended and another began with barely a pause. The distinct 78 RPM hiss and pop could be heard even over the cheap car speakers. Blue Cowboy held an index finger to his lips, shushing

Paul and his impure thoughts.

> Way out west, in a nest from the rest, dwelt the bestest little Bronco Boy.
> He could ride, he could glide o'er the prairies like an arrow.
> Every maid in the glade was afraid he would take his little heart away.
> So each little peach made a nice little speech of love to him.
>
> Pony Boy, Pony Boy, won't you be my Tony Boy.
> Don't say no, here we go, off across the plains.
> Marry me, carry me, right away with you.
> Giddy up, giddy up, giddy up, whoa!
> My Pony Boy, boy.
>
> Till one day, out that way, so they say, came to stay a fluffy, ruffle girl.
> She made eyes, she surprised, and he found his heart lassoed.
> When he thought, he was caught, how he fought, but she taught this pony boy to love.
> But he balked, when she talked of a trip to New York, so she sang to him.
>
> Pony Boy, Pony Boy, won't you be my tony Boy.
> Don't say no, here we go, off across the plains.
> Marry me, carry me, right away with you.
> Giddy up, giddy up, giddy up, whoa!
> My Pony Boy, boy.

As the song ended Blue Cowboy leaned into the car and turned off the stereo. When he straightened his back, he wiped a tear from his cheek and tried to blink away the sudden emotion.

"My grandma used to sing that to me. Every time I hear that song I think of her and Roy and Dale. She just walked into his life and lassoed his heart. He could have picked anyone as he had his choice of the litter, but there was only one Dale."

Paul viewed the conversation from the point of view of a third person standing in a semi-circle with the other two, much like the Céleron de Blainville mural as he arrogantly identifies the river valley as a possession of France. Paul would be Céleron's scribe whose job it is to record the proceedings with a jaundiced eye toward France and to make Céleron sound more poetic, courageous, and patriotic than one person could possibly be, because the man had political aspirations beyond leading expeditions into the wild. In the current instance, however, Paul's third person scribe stopped writing because the conversation had veered beyond reason. How could he make sense of this sentimentality for the detritus of American pop culture, a painted floodwall, listening to a hit song from 1909 as he talked to a weepy cowboy in a powder blue ensemble? Something like this would never make it into the official record.

"Why Roy Rogers? Of all the third-rate celebrities why would you pick him?" Paul couldn't help himself. He knew he invited an explanation he had little interest in hearing, but his third person demanded reasons for Blue Cowboy's behavior.

Blue Cowboy had been asked this question several times before and for someone who had driven across the Appalachians from Baltimore, who had taken vacation time to attend the festival, who had argued with his wife about her refusal to come, who had filled a spare bedroom and basement with Roy Rogers memorabilia and he was considered one of the top five collectors in the nation by those who know the breadth and quality of his collection, the question had the surprising power to irritate him. He rolled his chew along his tongue, gathered a reservoir of juice, and landed a shiny splotch on the asphalt.

"Well, I guess people have plum forgot about the way America used to be."

"I don't think cowboys ever wore powder blue pants."

"I'm not an idiot, sir. I'm fully aware that Roy wasn't a *real* cowboy in that he didn't make his living on a ranch. Everyone likes rubbing my face in the fact that he was a product of Hollywood, created to sell tickets to the movie house and hawk records. His real name was Leonard Slye until a bunch of sharpies came up with the Roy Rogers name and near as I can tell it's a pitch perfect American name. You start thinking that he was Will Rogers' son or nephew. And Lenny Slye is from Ohio and not Montana or Wyoming or Oklahoma and he grew up on the river and not on a sweeping plain. All that you probably know and you're ready to needle me with the facts and your erudition, but you're missing the point if you go down that road. First of all, a lot of cowboys came from the east and thought the wide open west a better place to throw down a claim than in a cramped and stifling city of the east. You have to start looking at Roy as a symbol, no less than the flag. Think of the America that would raise him up and celebrate and adulate him. Think of the values of the people who wanted a sharp-dressed cowboy with a golden singing voice to put the world right. He projected honesty and integrity and possessed the ability to look spectacular in cowboy garb. I prefer him over anything the culture has produced in the last fifty years. Think about who's his equal who's living right now. Who right now has the balls to sing cowboy songs while saving the country from terrorists, schemers, industrialists, and crooked bankers? Who right now could launch a chain of restaurants and just by the force of his name pretty much guarantee a healthy western meal served in three minutes? Kenny Rogers was the last to try and you saw where that ended up. There's almost nothing left of his footprint in the U.S. and the only place he could get traction was the Philippines, for God's sake, and that took less than twenty years to come crumbling down around his head. The question, my friend, is not 'Why Roy Rogers?' but instead 'Why not Roy Rogers?' I want an America that looks to him for comfort and not some twenty year-old skank whose only discernible talent is showing her beaver to her adoring fans. I'm from Baltimore and there have been times when I'm the only person to show up to the Baltimore chapter of the Roy Rogers Campfire Circle, that's our name for the fan club. The only person in the whole of Baltimore metro area. The only thing that tells me is that I'm not out of step with America but that America has lost her way. Even his museum is closed down now. They even tried moving it from California to Branson, but the crowds just weren't there. They've kept the archive intact and we'll always have his movies and recordings to get us through."

"Right, I remember, he stuffed Trigger and put him on display. The little dog too?"

"Everybody who knows a little something about him goes right to that fact. They like to take a noble gesture and make a mockery of it. That horse was a star. He was a superhero to millions of kids. You can't just let a magnificent beast like that just molder in the ground."

"That would be a shame."

"We've been trying to track down Trigger to bring him to the festival. The insurance and travel costs are a killer. A few folks here have been holding fish fries in order to raise money, but we haven't made much over our expenses. I've told the wife if they ever decide to sell him then I'm going all in. I'm taking a second mortgage and I'll build a wing onto the house if I have to. The Holy Grail comes up for sale only every other lifetime, you know what I mean?

"Having Trigger here would build attendance." Paul couldn't help but be swept along.

"That's just a dream I've thought too much about. Instead, this year we're putting on a play. I had to come out here early to gather the cast and rehearse. We wanted to do a stage version of *The Bells of Coronado* but damn if we could secure the rights. Well, we could have secured the rights, but the movie company wanted more money than it would have taken to get Trigger here, so one of the festival organizers wrote a play based on "Bells." Of course, just to be safe, we can't put that on our flyers because that might land us in hot water, even though this version doesn't bear much resemblance to the original. Guess who I'm playing?"

"Trigger."

"There's no Trigger. The stage isn't big enough for a full grown horse. I'm Roy, for goodness sakes."

"That is something I should have known," Paul deadpanned.

"You know how many people wanted to be Roy?" Blue Cowboy said as his anger against Paul rose, not without good cause. The Rogers part had been difficult to get and required extensive lobbying and promises of favors, even granting one of the producers permission to handle one of Blue Cowboy's replica pistols that had been made from the same mold as the Rogers' original. Even with all that work, he only secured the role after the first choice, Jim Aberdeen, who really was a dead ringer for Rogers and who was a much better singer than Blue Cowboy had been fired from his job and he couldn't afford the trip to Portsmouth.

"Everybody wants to be Roy, but almost nobody gets the chance."

Blue Cowboy tipped his hat, a habit he had acquired to emphasize an important point, and let fly another gob of spit.

"Couldn't have said it better myself," Paul responded and then in a lower voice as if just to himself, "Everybody wants to be Roy, goddamn."

Paul heard a car come to a stop behind him. Before turning around he knew who would be driving the car and wondered when the first wisecrack would fly. Blue Cowboy tipped his hat and said, "Morning, Deputy," which made Paul's face grow warm, even though it was exactly who he had expected. He turned and looked into the deputy's smiling face. The deputy had shaved and sleep had brought some color back to his cheeks. He wore a wide brim brown hat with a star on the front, mirrored sunglasses and a reasonably pressed uniform.

"I see you made a new friend, Paul. It doesn't take you long to fit in." He motioned him closer to the cruiser and then said in a voice just above a whisper, "When I was overseas I saw that Belgians went for guys in cowboy outfits. They couldn't get enough of those western men. Paul, you never struck me as…Belgian, but nothing surprises me anymore."

"Do you ever have a normal conversation?"

Deputy Auro made a show of looking over his sunglasses at the cowboy and then at Paul, back to the cowboy, and then back to Paul.

"You may want to ask *yourself* that question. Of course, if you were doing more than talking I have to warn you we still have laws against sodomy on the books and my job is to serve, protect, and enforce the will of the people."

"He's here for the festival. He's playing Roy Rogers in a play."

"That's right, Deputy, and I'd be much obliged and honored really if you and your wife would come to the opening." Blue Cowboy said as he pulled the tickets from the front of his shirt pocket, walked toward the cruiser and held them in front of the deputy.

Something sad and dark passed through the deputy's face that vanquished all the mockery and sarcasm he had been ready to unleash.

"That ought to be some spectacle," the deputy said as he took the tickets and threw them on the passenger side seat. "Anyway, the reason I used the taxpayer's dollar to track you down is that my wife would like to meet you and wants me to invite you over for a barbeque we're having on Wednesday night, if you're still going to be in town and you haven't exhausted all of our cultural offerings by then," he said as he found himself staring at Blue Cowboy.

"I'll be in town Wednesday."

"I'm sure you will. Anyway, I printed out directions to our house from the hotel. For some reason I didn't think you would have access to a computer. Come around seven."

"That will be fun. I'm looking forward to it."

"I don't know how you can say that since you've never been to one of our parties, but if you want to liven things up you can bring your friend here as long as you promise to behave. I'm an open-minded man, but I have a family to protect."

"Thanks for the invitation, Deputy, but I'll be in rehearsal all Wednesday night. We've had last minute rewrites and if I didn't show up the whole project would come crashing to the ground."

"That's a pity. My wife would have enjoyed your company."

"Maybe next year."

"Jesus, let's not get ahead of ourselves. You can't start wishing away years."

"But I'll see you on opening night on Friday, right? I could meet your wife then."

Deputy Auro spotted the tickets lying on the seat and breathed a heavy sigh.

"If we can get a babysitter, we'll see."

"And I'm sure I can get your friend here to come to," Blue Cowboy said as he obviously winked.

"I'm sure he'll be there with bells on his toes. Hell, he might even be in the play if you asked him."

Deputy Auro pulled the car away before Paul could formulate a comeback. Blue Cowboy turned toward Paul.

"I'm sorry I can't go to the party. I really do have to rehearse."

"I understand."

A moment of awkward silence and feet scraping passed before Blue Cowboy got in his car and drove away.

12

Hear the Bells of Coronado

The next morning at breakfast in the hotel restaurant as Paul attacked a plate of pancakes and bacon, Third Eye walked past his table wearing a cowgirl outfit at least three sizes too small and hanging on the arm of an old geezer who stooped as he walked and whose sad gray moustache almost covered his mouth entirely. Her thigh rubbed against his shoulder as she passed, but not a glint of recognition flickered across her face. Her breasts were so squeezed and pushed that more than half of their volume hung open to the air over the top button of her blouse. The skirt raised anticipation in the room that in the event she bent over or sat down the diners would be treated to an unobstructed view of either side of her privates. Creeping shame clawed its way out of the pit of his stomach, the motel memories in the form of a black and slimy beast newly born, creeping out of the seventh circle of regrettable acts where it had been assigned. The poor creature experienced a brief rally before Paul's glowing anger beat it back into the shadows.

She had described the King of the Cowboys in her fortune and when he saw Blue Cowboy in the restaurant and then the Rogers portrait on the floodwall his skin crawled with a small acceptance of hidden mysteries. He had accepted that Third Eye had tapped into a psychic current which flowed through the head of the bat, but the truth lay in the fact she had been on her way to the festival to work the crowd, to sell her pussy in the shadow of the altar to the King of Cowboys to men and a few women who had no hope of picking anyone up but each other, dressed as they were as old and overweight ranch hands. She threw in Roy, abused his memory really, so that the prophecy would sound authentic and metaphysical. The belief she had granted him had been snatched away by her being on the arm of the old man.

For the second time in a few days Paul walked over to a table in a restaurant and accosted the same prostitute, such were the turns and twists of his life. The old man, sunken in his crisp cowboy clothes, looked like a withered fruit nestled inside a garish husk. He eyed Paul with the meanest glare he could summon. Third Eye calmly stared at him with serene patience, unblinking and mesmerizing.

"Pretty good trick, showing me Rogers in a dream. You almost sent to tumbling over the edge. A pretty good trick, but I don't think you know what could have been the consequence. That goddamn bat could have led me right back to church." Paul sounded angry and hurt and Third Eye seemed delighted at his distress as a glint of light played across her eyes.

"Why's the man talking bats, honey?" the old geezer croaked.

"A technique learned from one of my masters. She told me to find an object that best symbolizes the future and channel my fortunes through it. What better symbolizes the future than a screeching bat, coming towards you, mouth open, teeth bared, wings spread, hell-bent on destroying you with a bite from its rabid mouth. My customers tell that screaming little head everything and through his little lips comes the news of their doom. They eat it up like cake and ice cream."

"I've always thought of the future as a warm ray of sunshine," the old man said. "It sounds corny saying it but I think if you're reaching the end, honey, and everybody reaches the end, you're allowed a little comfort, no matter how foolish or false the comfort may be."

Third Eye patted him on the knee and slid the same hand high up his inner thigh.

"There, son, you have your explanation. Sounds reasonable, don't it? Don't seem much like a trick to me. Ain't nothing wrong with you believing what a bat head told you."

"I don't like to be tricked. I must have told you I was coming to Portsmouth and you figured I would see a blue cowboy somewhere so you threw in that detail just to fuck with my head. I'm not sure what your agenda was but when I saw Blue Cowboy I almost jumped out of my skin. So maybe you could have just told me that I was going to get into a car accident or I was to meet my true love at a meat counter or I would discover an unacknowledged passion for sculpting dryer lint into animal shapes."

"Maybe you can show me that bat when we go back to the room, eh sweetie?" the old man interjected.

"Oh, honey, you don't have much future left. Why spoil it by knowing it?"

The old man nodded in agreement and shrank further into his clothing so that he looked to be in danger of disappearing behind the collar. Paul suddenly felt terribly fatigued and ridiculous. He sat down at their table and drank the old man's water. The old man tried to rally and protest this intrusion but he retreated before an offensive could gather steam.

"I see you two have some business to attend to. Farah, I'll be up in my room and I'm assuming our arrangement still stands?"

"That agreement is ironclad, sugar. I'll be up in your room no later than an hour. I wish you wouldn't go. He has no appointment with me."

"Clear the deck of him and then we'll have our fun. I don't want him haunting us again."

They watched the old man stand up and shuffle through the tables and they didn't talk until he had disappeared through the door.

"So, you're displeased with my methods? You have five minutes to tell me what you want and after that if you bother me again I'll cut you ear to ear. I'm on the clock because J.C. has me for the entire festival. His wife died a few years ago and he hates coming to the festival alone. It brings up too many memories."

"He bought you for the festival?"

"Renting me. And why not? The man needs some companionship and he has more money than the rest of the people in this restaurant combined, including you."

"That's too bad. Where's your assistant, CAT Trucker Cap?"

"If you mean my assistant Miss Melissa? She's my advance scout for the Dean Martin festival in Steubenville. There's always a line of old Italians willing to drop a load of cash for the opportunity to squeeze these." She pressed her breasts together and but for the nipple snagging on the stitching on the top of her bra cup her whole right breast would have flopped out of her shirt. "We've found success on the festival circuit. Last year we raked in so much money at the Mothman Festival over in Point Pleasant that I was able to go to Florida for a week just to relax. Of course I ended up blowing three frat guys on the beach to earn the bus money back to Ohio. We've had luck at the Pumpkin Festival up in Circleville too. My little girl came in second in the Little Miss Pumpkin Pageant, so I think her title was like First Attendant. I think I cost the poor thing the title of queen. That was in my wilder days and I showed up drinking Jack and wearing next to nothing. We've also gone all the way up to Twinsburg for the Twins Day Festival. The place is full of twins and gawkers who have a fetish for twins. I've ended up in situations I didn't think possible. The last time I was there I thought I was hallucinating and I started giving it away for free. Very bad business plan. I had to hitch a ride back home with these twins that called themselves Tweedle Dum and Tweedle Dee who didn't want much more than to rub my belly and stroke my hair, but they talked in unison and were identical right down to the freckles on their testicles."

"I need a date on Wednesday night. I have a party I have to go to."

"I'm already engaged."

"I'll pay you double."

"Plus food and free drinks?"

"Of course, they won't make you pay at a party."

"What kind of party is this?"

"Just a nice suburban barbeque with boring, nice people. "

"What would I have to do?"

"Be yourself."

"Which means?"

"If one of the husbands ask you to blow them behind the garage take them up on their offer but show a little discretion. Otherwise, come as you are."

"I don't know. What would I wear?"

"C'mon, haven't you ever been to a backyard barbeque?"

"Not really. Unless it involved twins, a hot tub and lube."

"You should dress in what makes you comfortable. What you're wearing now would be fine."

"Christ, like I'm not going to drop the cowgirl disguise the minute I leave J.C.'s room? You'll pay double for the night?"

"Yes, I said I would."

"You know that'll be like two hundred bucks? You sure you have it?"

"I'm renting the penthouse suite. I have the cash."

"I'll see what I can do to get out. The old man falls asleep about seven o'clock anyway. Sometimes he calls out his wife's name in the night and wants to climb between my boobs, but I'll figure out a way to make it up to him. He's easy to please."

"It'll only be a few hours anyway."

"If I'm going to leave him then I need a guarantee."

Paul fished in his pocket and produced a crumpled wad of cash that added up to sixty-seven dollars and he placed in on the table in front of her.

"Are you staying in the hotel?" he asked.

"I made my reservation the day after last year's festival. I knew I wouldn't have to pay for it."

"I'll meet you in the lobby at 6:30 Wednesday evening."

"I told you J.C. doesn't sleep until 7:00."

"Ok, 7:00."

"7:30."

"What is he a baby you have to put down?"

She lurched out of her chair and stood.

"You didn't even eat your breakfast."

"Oh, J.C. will order room service for me. He knows I can't stay away from him and plus, he loves food play. I love feeding him. It brings us so close together."

She walked out of the restaurant and a waitress came over to Paul and asked if he would be using both tables for his dining experience. Paul sheepishly retreated from the restaurant after extravagantly giving the waitress a twenty dollar tip for a seven dollar breakfast on a credit card, not to smooth over his holding down two tables during the breakfast rush but to remind her that she too could be bought, his lesson being lost on her as she calculated the percentage of the tip. As he left he passed Blue Cowboy, who stood in line, waiting for a table.

"Howdy, pardnor!" Blue Cowboy said as a big grin broke out across his face.

"Give it a rest, Blue Cowboy."

The smile disappeared as quickly as it appeared.

"Not everyone can be as cheerful as you," Paul continued.

"I'm excited, friend. I'm grabbing a quick breakfast and then I'm off to all day rehearsals. It's all coming together. We're putting together a real hootenanny."

Paul acquired the word hootenanny for future use on Tony back at the Housing Department. The idea of the scowl that the word would produce on Tony's face lightened Paul's attitude toward Blue Cowboy. He realized that such acquisitions were often hard to come by and his lightened mood turned toward charity even before he opened his mouth.

"Are the rehearsals open to the public? I would like to see the creative process at work."

Paul had been bored on vacation before. He had watched candles being made, candy bars being molded, taffy being pulled, classic muscle cars being waxed and tended to like a lover who is loved to the point of obsession, and reenactments of pioneer, colonial and western history that embarrassed both the audience and the poor saps who acted in the travesties, but he wouldn't know until after the rehearsal whether or not he had reached a new floor for his vacation activities.

Blue Cowboy flushed in the face and neck in response to the unexpected interest shown by Paul, but be rebounded quickly and told Paul to come to the Sixth Street Missionary Baptist Church in an hour or two, really anytime until midnight, because the cast and crew had committed to work all day. They were far from professionals, Blue Cowboy confessed, but what they lacked in technical expertise they made up with passion. Paul's mind darkened, his charity had been exhausted, and he shuffled away before he would say anything sarcastic or cutting to the beaming Blue Cowboy.

"I'll try. I'll try," Paul mumbled as he walked over to the front desk.

The same clerk with whom he had tangled stood behind the counter. Paul tried to ignore the animus that had grown between them from their previous encounters.

"Good morning, sir. And how are *we* enjoying the penthouse?" the clerk said through gritted teeth. "The room must be so comfortable that you slept right through the time of our appointment. I waited for you, but you never came."

"I expected something better than carp caviar, but other than that I have no complaints." Paul continued on with a joke he had formulated on his way to counter, completely ignoring the clerk's aggression.

"Sir?"

"Can you tell me the room number of a woman who is staying here?"

"Moved on to other things I see, but remember the invitation is open. Do you know her name?"

"She wears a cowboy hat with a magazine eye pasted on it."

"We have a hotel full of ladies wearing cowboy hats. I haven't noticed any extra eyes."

"She's the only one dressed like a hooker."

"Well, sir, you obviously weren't down at the bar last night. Let's just say the women left their modesty in their rooms. This hotel hasn't seen a party like that in a while."

"She's buxom. A highway goddess. A turnpike witch. She's in the company of an old withered fuck who looks like a sick child in his father's clothes."

"Sir, I'm not allowed to search room numbers based on a description like that."

"You know who I'm talking about." Bile caught in Paul's throat as the clerk stepped back, thinking Paul might lunge across the counter at him. "All the men have seen her and know who she is."

"I don't know who you're talking about, sir."

"She's a seer and a fraud, a castaway and a pariah, a queen on her own island of the damned."

"Sir, I'm going to bring the manager over. You're starting to freak me out."

"Don't bother. I'm leaving. I hope you understand that you are blocking me from a path of happiness. You're too goddamn young to understand, but whatever little honey with pimples on her chin that you happen to be banging is a pale reflection, a nineteenth generation clone, degraded and faltering, a wan offspring of Third Eye."

"What are you saying?"

"Don't play stupid."

Paul went back to his room. He fell on the bed and searched the pay-per-view channels for pornography or a mainstream movie rated R for heavy sexual depictions involving young and serious actresses with downy pubic hair, but the mainstream Hollywood movies were all action and violence, jet fighters and beheadings, flames, floods and eviscerations. He drifted to the porn selections and settled on a camcorder masterpiece called *Mountain Valley High School Cheerleading Butt Whores* in which 35 year old actresses, whose careers were plummeting down through the quality rungs of production houses, tried to pass themselves off as high school cheerleaders for a minute before shedding their costumes and fucking their mute teachers, gym coaches, guidance counselors, bus drivers, crossing guards, principals, assistant principals, custodians, the rest of the cheerleading squad, and a few fellow students, all men and women their age, all tan and meticulously shaved. The camerawork was impressively assertive as the videographer practically climbed up the assholes of the participants and kept focus most of the time.

Paul lay back and dozed off before he could summon the energy to jackoff. He woke to a blank screen a couple of hours later with regret that he had spent $18.95 without getting off. He considered leaving, this moment, anywhere, without packing the few items the clothing and toiletries scattered around the room, because everything he owned was cheap and replaceable, to a beach, a national monument, a national forest, a mountain, a path, a river with white water, a famous house or an ordinary house of someone famous or infamous, anywhere but in this place where his urge to muck about in the deputy's stupid life could gain momentum, to alter the course he had taken, the outcome of which seemed increasingly clear and inevitable.

He really hadn't expected an invitation to his house, but now he would have an audience of his closest friends and his wife. If Third Eye didn't cause enough of a disturbance there hanging on his arm, busting out of her clothes, with her perspective of society as nothing more than an erect dick searching for a landing spot, any landing spot, anywhere, a simple and base commercial transaction, then he could conjure up a story. He'd wait until the children were shuffled off to bed and everyone had enough beer, wine or whiskey in them to feel cordial and off-guard, maybe even feeling charitable toward Third Eye with her abused body and tunnel-like perspective, he would trot out an old story that he had used to great effect a few times before when he wanted to cast doubt on his sanity, not so much for the content but for the retelling. He was reasonably certain the incident never happened, but it had such great effect that he had not resolved never to use it again. At least the story sent people reeling, and exposed their own unruly desires.

The story begins in the cave in the woods and the two battle until they are slobbering and exhausted and then one of them, it didn't really matter who, suggests they suck each other's cock. They do, with the stipulation they bring the other all the way to climax. Thrown down as a challenge both lick and suck until they swallow hot cum. Both immediately know upon the first touch of penis to lips that they are not homosexual and neither, as far as he knows, gained further experience beyond this banal introduction. Still, the story, usually introduced as how Paul realized he had few homosexual desires, had a way of causing discomfort and not a little defensive anger, ideal for a suburban barbeque hosted by the deputy and his adoring wife. Throw in Third Eye and the partygoers might think the world had unraveled and beasts now reigned.

Why would he bring up a minor act of experimentation and embarrass himself in front of a party of strangers? What was this flagellation? He asked himself these questions, yet wouldn't admit the possibility that he had taken this vacation for the sole purpose of finding a chink in the deputy's armor and to exploit it, to be an avenging ghost with a long memory and a need to cause the deputy damage. The cocksucking story and Third Eye would weaken the Deputy. He thought of Third Eye in her sleaziest outfit she owned, which, in his imagination fueled by recent observation, would be just shy of nudity. He would figure out a way to steer the conversation to the four thousand "dates" she had had with men, their purpose, outcome, and the amount of money she had earned with her services, just to leave no doubt about who she was and the complete lack of respect Paul showed by bringing a prostitute to an old friend's house. This would not be the first time Paul acted with no other purpose than destruction.

Not wanting to waste another $18.95 on another porno and trying to get the thought of Third Eye's body from his mind, Paul walked to the Fourth Street Missionary Baptist Church to watch the play rehearsal, starring none other than Blue Cowboy. Paul walked through an open side door and inside smelled heavily of oil paint. The cast had grouped at the altar, which doubled as a stage for the run of the play. Some, like Blue Cowboy, were in full costume while others wore t-shirts and shorts. The congregation of the church had been unsuccessful in its attempt to raise money to fix the air-conditioning so the air in the morning felt tolerably stuffy and thick, but throughout the day the sun beat down on the aluminum roof until the temperature rose to numbers appropriate in a sweat lodge and any movement at all became an act of will.

Paul had walked in on an argument, a shouting match between Blue Cowboy and a man holding a paint brush dripping with gray paint. Paul sat on a folding chair near the back of the hall. Blue Cowboy's face had become red and his fists were clenched at his sides.

"Who told you to paint the goddamn backdrop during rehearsal?" Blue Cowboy screamed.

The man looked back at him with an imperturbable, slack face.

"Do you want a white background or do you want electric towers and power lines and desert scenes? I could just as well leave it white or you can have that cross up there as a background."

Everyone looked at a massive cross hanging on the wall behind them. The laminate veneer spoiled the gravitas of the symbol and made it look like two intersecting lunch counters.

"Fuck you, Sal! You know we can't have a cross as a backdrop and they aren't going to let us take it down. We need scenery. You should have done it yesterday or this morning before we got here. You're going to asphyxiate us. At least you could use latex paint and not kill us!"

"I was putting in a deck yesterday. Some of us have to work."

"Some of us keep our word."

"Stand in front of a white desert, for all I care," Sal said as he dropped the brush in the paint can and stormed off the altar and out the side door.

Blue Cowboy stared at his back and then at the spot where his back had been and could not speak for a minute of two. The rest of the cast lurked along the periphery of the altar, whispering about the unfinished set and the muddled script. In fact, most objective observers would have agreed that the script was a mess. The group had worked on it over the previous year through telephone calls, emails and faxes, but it never really took shape. The problem lay in their first decision to stage a movie western with a singing cowboy. They had begun with a straight transcription of the original movie, but the movie relied so much on action, such as horses galloping as fast as European coupes, smoking gun battles, hair-trigger tempers, flying fists and panoramic shots of the Californian desert that once the transcription was finished they found little dialogue with which to work. They needed horses, lots of horses, a uranium mine, an electrical tower, the Coronado dam, a crystal-clear reservoir, a prop plane and endless expanses of desert. They had an empty altar inside a building that had the acoustics of a tin can.

Also Blue Cowboy questioned whether the audience would remember enough of the past to follow the plot. Screenwriter Sloan Nibley dropped the King of the Cowboys smack in the middle of two 1950s obsessions in the west, uranium and electrification. The plot of the movie is that a uranium shipment is hijacked by a band of thugs. During the robbery the owner of the mine is clubbed and rolls into Coronado Lake, a reservoir created by the Coronado dam. He dies later that day in the office of Doc Harding. The insurance company that holds the policy on the shipment contacts Roy Rogers, insurance investigator extraordinaire, and asks him to go undercover in Coronado to find the thugs and the shipment. Roy's Chinese cook, Shanghai, appears long enough to say, "I car you Mr. Logers. Two men rike to see you. He say very important."

Rogers goes to Coronado and finds a job at the local power company, which is stringing electrical wire from the dam to blooming population centers. Themes emerge. Nature at work for America. America taming the power and violent impulses of the wilds in grand public works style. Bounty through hard work. Roy meets Dale Evans, who also works for the power company, and they have a misunderstanding, during which she steals Trigger, who, by the way, is more than happy to gallop away from an open-mouthed Roy. The producers billed Trigger as the smartest horse in the movies, which is obvious in this scene because of his ability to advance the plot and shine a light on Roy and Dale's budding and chaste romance. It turns out that Doc Harding is an old family friend of Roy's and the good doctor even delivered baby Roy into the world. Roy blabs to all that will listen that he is an undercover insurance investigator, yet somehow manages to run an effective investigation. Sure, he doesn't want the insurance company to have to pay out a large settlement for the lost shipment, but he also doesn't want it to be taken from the country and put into the hands of a foreign power. He sings his praises to Coronado and figures out that Doc Harding is the mastermind behind the smuggling ring. Roy's worst fears have come true; Doc and his band of thugs have given up on America and are trying to get the uranium into the hands of a possible enemy. The movie had been filmed five years after the end of World War II, so the script casts a wary eye toward the old enemy and recycles what appears to be a Nazi boogeyman, although his country of origin is never explicitly named, for an audience with fresh reasons to hate and fear him.

So, the fear of losing the atomic genie pushes the action along and smiling and singing Roy keeps the uranium in the country of its origin and suffers the betrayal of an old, trusted friend with aplomb. The final scene takes place on an electrical tower. The number one thug, Doc's right hand, seeing his fellow thugs slaughtered and captured takes off on his horse. With the whole desert in front of him he decides to climb an electrical tower to escape. Now if Roy skewed just a few sufficient degrees toward reasonableness or cautiousness he would have camped under the tower and waited for the thug to die of sunstroke or dehydration or both or even used him for target practice to work out the leftward drift of some of his shots. But Roy is a man of action so he climbs the tower after him! Hounded by this imperturbable insurance investigator, who doesn't sweat, who is able to repel sand and dirt from his skin and clothing with the power of his mind, who never acknowledges the blistering oppression of the desert sun, the thug loses his will, slips, and falls to an ignominious death on the sand.

Roy and Dale sing their praises for Coronado. Electricity is progress. The uranium is ours.

Blue Cowboy had seen the movie fifty or sixty times to learn Rogers' acting style, which ranged between an easygoing smile with a musical lilt in his voice to a blank face coupled with a rigid monotone that suggested a degree of seriousness. Sometimes his hat flew off when a punch landed on his jaw and he grimaced slightly as if the punches hurt him as much as his reciting his lines. Blue Cowboy had mastered every tick, flinch and blink of Roy's face in the movie, but unfortunately the troupe could not secure the rights from the Rogers estate to perform the movie verbatim. The letter they received back from the estate in response to their inquiry ordered them to cease and desist and threatened legal action if the play was staged. The letter further hinted that a remake was being considered by the studios with Kenny Rogers as the lead since the crop of singing cowboys from which to choose grew smaller each year. So, they used the same basic plot line of the stolen uranium, the estate couldn't have a copyright on plotlines as creaky as that, and jumbled the dialogue so that Blue Cowboy's memorization of Roy's facial expressions made even less sense now given a new context and dialogue that didn't exactly match.

Blue Cowboy barked for the troupe to pick up where they were before the paint fumes almost toppled him. A gaunt fellow who looked like a convenience store clerk recently hypnotized by the endless wobble of an illuminated slurpee cup, hobbled up to Blue Cowboy with the script in his hands. They bowed their heads slightly and then Blue Cowboy began.

BLUE COWBOY

Sparrow, I'm going to tell you something that can't be told to anyone else. I'm not some journeyman, rolling into Coronado for work. I've signed up with an insurance company and we insure uranium. I know it sounds crazy but we will insure anything that has value, except, of course, parakeets and fish because you can't expect them to last that long. Anyway, I've been sent here undercover to find the stolen uranium shipment.

SPARROW

I would have thought that would be a job for the FBI or Homeland Security. Are you sure Ray you don't work for the government?

BLUE COWBOY

You know I'm as patriotic as they come, but I would never become a blood-sucking maggot and work for the government. Bureaucracy and corruption are not my game, Sparrow. I work for the free market. Corporations keep us safe because they worry about the bottom line.

SPARROW

Ray, you better not let Mr. Bennett find out. He took over the mine after Mr. Martinez got himself killed and he'll be hopping mad if he finds out you're something more than an itinerant worker with an empty belly.

BLUE COWBOY

It's bigger than Mr. Bennett. What happens if Martinez was murdered? Maybe even Mr. Bennett is involved. I do know that an investigator like me, who balances the welfare of the nation and his corporation, has to keep an open mind and suspect everyone.

SPARROW

Now why would someone kill ol' Mr. Martinez for a wagon-load of uranium? It ain't worth all that much. More trouble than it's worth really. Eat you inside out if you're not really careful.

BLUE COWBOY

Not worth much to you or me or even our government since we have a vast uranium supply, but how much do you think it would be worth to North Korea or Iran or any other terrorist bent on the destruction of our way of life, to the enemies of life and liberty.

SPARROW

I think you've been reading too many detective stories.

BLUE COWBOY

Maybe so, Sparrow, but maybe you should pick up the paper every once in the while and then maybe you would understand a little more about what goes on outside of the skull of yours.

The scene crashed into an awkward silence as Sparrow flipped through the script to find some direction for what he should do next. Blue Cowboy put his hands on his hips and choked back rising bile in the back of his throat.

"Are you lost?" asked Blue Cowboy.

"Sort of. Don't you think that last line makes Roy sound like a grade A asshole? We know that Sparrow is as dumb as a box of rocks, but Roy wouldn't rub his face in it. He's not that mean. That's not who he is. Frankly, he sounds like a little bitch."

"Church, we've been through this a dozen times."

"And a dozen times you've been wrong. What does that prove?"

A collective groan came from the crew and the other actors as they had heard nearly the same exchange a dozen times as well. Paul stopped listening as he considered Blue Cowboy's performance. He played the part with easy nonchalance, a singsong assurance in his voice, and a slightly quizzical tilt of his head. Blue Cowboy channeled Ronald Reagan. The cowboy clothes, the shock of black hair, emboldened by the belief that a poor man can walk into the desert friendless and lost and can come out remade, rich, popular beyond his imagination, and convinced of his own righteousness. A grid of connections suddenly illuminated Paul's thoughts. He had vaguely understood the connection between Reagan and western myths as defined by Hollywood B moves, but something in Blue Cowboy's performance opened a previously closed door in Paul's understanding of the Reagan phenomenon. He imagined the millions of children soaking up the lessons of American goodness, of its rising ascendency over cultures in ashes, of the cleansing properties of the desert as it applies to both religion and capitalism, spoon-fed to them by a cowboy superhero who never really is in danger, who solves every problem with his wits, his fists, a really smart and fast horse, and a devoted woman hanging on his arm who, besides being a loyal companion, is capable of landing a bullet on any part of a thug's anatomy. All Reagan had to do was don a cowboy hat and millions of voters in their 30s and 40s gushed with nostalgia for horses that could gallop faster than trains, of singing honeyed tones that exalted the waste nothingness of scrub lands and made poetry out of the monstrous electrical towers, for men and women who could keep American invention and God-given natural resources out of the hands of unfriendly governments and a willingness to slaughter anyone who becomes an obstacle in the path of righteousness.

Sparrow had shuffled off, muttering to himself because he had lost the battle for Roy's soul. Blue Cowboy had been joined onstage by an old potbellied man who swayed side to side when he walked, his girth providing a challenge for his balance. He had memorized his lines and took very seriously the axiom that a person in the back row should hear his lines as clearly as those sitting in the front as he shouted and blanched all nuance and craft from his performance. Blue Cowboy had his back to him and fiddled with something that approximated the lock of a safe. The potbellied man played the part of Doc, the kindly old friend of Roy and mastermind of the uranium smuggling plot.

DOC

Did you misplace something, Roy?

BLUE COWBOY

I'm glad you showed up, Doc. You would save me a whole bunch of trouble if you would just open this safe. I've been trying number after number but I'm getting nowhere.

DOC

It' a combination lock, Roy. That has 64,000 possible permutations. You might be good at riding a horse and punching people in the jaw, but I've never taken you for a math whiz.

BLUE COWBOY

I've never needed any help balancing a checkbook. Open the safe, Doc.

DOC

What's inside that safe is my personal property. You have no business asking me for my property. Our constitution guarantees the right to personal property. I don't have to turn anything over to the government.

BLUE COWBOY

I don't work for the government. I work as an insurance investigator.

DOC

Why in God's name would you take that job?

BLUE COWBOY

Don't worry about my career choices. When the sheriff gets here you'll be under arrest for the murder of George Martinez.

DOC

That old man fell into the lake after he ran away from my gang. The idiot tried to run up Coronado dam and slipped and fell. That is not the legal definition of murder, Roy. At worst, I could be charged with involuntary manslaughter

BLUE COWBOY

(draws his gun) I had Martinez's body exhumed. I have the coroner's report in my hand. The coroner found that he had been poisoned and suffocated, along with the water in his lungs. He guessed a cocktail of anti-freeze and rat poison was injected into his body. George Martinez came into this office alive and you killed him, Doc.

DOC

I underestimated you, Roy. No one questioned me about the death of Martinez. It was the weakest link in the chain. I tried to kill him six different ways until I just smothered him with my hand. The man was a regular Rasputin.

BLUE COWBOY

Yes, we found bruises on his face that exactly match your fingerprints.

DOC

I should have worn gloves.

BLUE COWBOY

You should have stopped yourself from becoming a murderer and a traitor to your country.

DOC

(He opens the safe with a flick of the wrist) Here's the uranium sample you are looking for (he hands the sample to Roy). That little nugget is going to light up the whole of North Korea.

BLUE COWBOY

Or goes into the making of a bomb that could land on the town of Coronado!

DOC

I'm old, Ray, what do I care if this town is vaporized? (A man walks in behind Ray. He has been hiding behind a curtain or potted plant. He carries a gun pointed at Ray.) I would have gotten away with it too, if you hadn't brought that Geiger counter and the righteousness of the insurance company with you. Now, listen closely, if I were you I would turn around slowly. One of my men has a bead on you.

BLUE COWBOY

C'mon, Doc, you don't expect me to fall for that old trick do you? (The man puts the pistol against Ray's back.)

DOC

Because you're an old friend and I brought you screaming into the world, I'm going to make it easy on you. I'll mix you a cocktail that will put you asleep and you won't have to worry anymore about what happened to your beloved town of Coronado.

BLUE COWBOY

It's not going to be one of your rat poison and anti-freeze concoctions is it, Doc?

DOC

Yes, indeed it is.

BLUE COWBOY

You're a doctor. Can't you come up with something better than that?

DOC

I graduated from the Togolese Institute of Medical Research and Broadcasting. Chemistry was not a strong suit of the school.

BLUE COWBOY

I'd rather die fighting.

Blue Cowboy jumps on the man holding the gun and they fight across the stage. They grapple and fall to the ground. They roll back and forth grunting and shouting. Doc stares toward the audience, impassively waiting for the fight to be over. The man knocks Blue Cowboy out. He stands up and tames his unruly hair.

DOC

Nice work, Jim. Give Ray this potion. (He hands him a neon green liquid in a beaker.) We'll be long gone before he dies in his own blood and vomit.

The phone rings. It is a rotary dial desk phone that looks too heavy to pick up.

DOC

Hello, yes, he is. I see. No kidding. Yes, I know you wouldn't kid about something like that. Are you completely sure? No, I don't think you are a moron. Have I doubted you in the past? Well, yes...well, I had reason to doubt you in the past. The fact is your information is almost completely unreliable, so when you call me and say that Jim is a federal agent it gives me pause. (He looks at Jim.) Oh, wait, I have to go. Yes, yes, I'll see you at the rendezvous point. (Doc hangs up and pulls a gun on Jim.)

JIM

What's up?

DOC

Just this, my strapping and handsome young man, I just found out you're an agent of the government.

JIM

Well, jeez, Doc, you didn't think a wagon full of top grade uranium could just go missing without somebody in Washington caring, do you?

DOC

Those rocks are worth a lot of money.

JIM

And nothing but trouble in the wrong hands.

Blue Cowboy springs to life and knocks the gun from Doc's hand. After a brief struggle, Blue Cowboy pushes Doc away and picks up gun. Doc lunges at Blue Cowboy one more time and he empties his gun, shooting Doc six times in the face and chest. Doc crashes to the ground. Blue Cowboy spins the gun in his hand and then holsters it. After this flair, he shakes Jim's hand. Jim stands stunned at witnessing such swift brutality.

                             JIM

I guess it couldn't be helped.

                         BLUE COWBOY

You saw him lunge.

                             JIM

But still, a seventy year-old country doctor...he did commit treason against our country.

                         BLUE COWBOY

Good to know you, Jim.

                             JIM

I didn't have a chance to tell you that I am working for the government until we were rolling around on the ground together. I thought you might knock me out before I could tell you. Thanks for believing me and going along with the trick of pretending to knock you out. I could have just been a thug telling you a story.

                         BLUE COWBOY

You have the arms and thighs of a government man.

                             JIM

You are quite a specimen yourself, Ray.

    Jim broke character as a look of exasperation crossed his face.
    "C'mon," Jim said. "This script is starting to sound like gay porn. What in God's name are you trying to do to Roy Rogers? My minister promised to come to

the show on Saturday, so I can't be cavorting up here spitting these lines. Besides, do you really need to shoot Doc six times? Roy isn't a butcher. He only commits violence when he's pushed into it, when it is absolutely necessary, when it is either his or someone else's life. You have him just gun down an unarmed man."

"Can we just get through the rehearsal? The script can't be changed now. We all agreed to this."

"I think you threw in a bunch of stuff in here at the last minute to get your jollies. I bet you don't even like Roy for the right reasons."

"And what reasons would those be?"

"That's between you, God, and Roy."

The side door opened and in walked Third Eye. She had replaced her psychic hat with a black cowboy hat with rhinestones encrusted around the band. She wore a black bra under a see-through white shirt and a black thong under an equally revealing, sheer mid-calf skirt.

"Am I late?" she bellowed.

"About two hours south of late," Blue Cowboy responded.

"I have so many demands on my time. I can give you three hours today."

"And look at her," Jim blustered. "Dale was not a whore. Not in one single movie did she play a kitten in a cathouse. We're not respecting their legacy. If we're going down this route I don't even know why we are doing the play. Is there a point to soiling Ray and Dale?"

The side door opened again and in walked Teddy, the old man who was at the restaurant with Third Eye. Her gifts had drained him of life as he looked considerably more frail and bent than before. He bent his knees and back with considerable effort and Paul thought his jaw looked permanently clamped shut. He shuffled to the front row and fell into a chair. Third Eye blew him a kiss. For a moment Paul wished he had been the recipient of her public display of affection, but he quickly scattered the thought with a quiet, mocking laugh.

The cast perked up with the inclusion of Third Eye, precisely, as Jim pointed out, because she had cast herself as a whore and the stage suddenly took on the flavor of a bachelor party or a gangbang. She commanded the stage but the command felt tenuous as the feverish men could have lost their reason and attacked. Aware of the danger she rocketed words off the back wall of the church from her bellow-like lungs. She enveloped the cast, the onlookers, the bricks, mortar and tin roof and led them in rhythmic desire as she swayed. A song started softly and rose.

Hear the bells of Coronado
Softly ringing across the desert sand
Hear the bells of Coronado
Bring me back across the Rio Grande

Her voice was golden and clear and by the third or fourth note she could have ordered them to do anything and they would have obeyed. Had Blue Cowboy been able to figure out how to keep her onstage the entire play he would have been guaranteed a roaring success, but even after all the rewrites, when they had a chance to reimagine the narrative and build around the strength of their cast, they slavishly followed the structure of the movie, which relegated Dale to a minor role of comedic relief. Third Eye should have been given the Roy Rogers part as the gifts of Blue Cowboy shrank in the presence of a brighter star, but gender swapping was still a few years away from acceptability at the festival, so they could only hope that the amps Third Eye produced during her time onstage carried the rest of the play.

The song ended as Third Eye held the last note longer and stronger than any of the other cast members. Even though the song was supposed to be sung in a chorus most of the cast had retreated to a breathy whisper after the first bar, except for Blue Cowboy who tried to hang with her as long as he could before also fading to silence near the end. The old man clapped as hard as he could, which produced a sound resembling two skeletal hands clanking together. Third Eye bowed and Paul thought with the sudden shift in weight she would crash to the ground, but she popped back up after plunging past the 45 degree mark.

"Ok, ok, people, we need to run through this at least three more times, at least until Sparrow can recite his lines without reading the script. And let's see if Dale can act as well as she can sing," Blue Cowboy said to break Third Eye's charm and reestablish control over the group.

"This is a travesty! I don't think she should be in the play. There'll be children in the audience!" Jim yelled as he slammed his script to the floor.

The assembled men growled, kicked and spit at the idea of kicking Third Eye out of the production. Even Paul and the old man stomped their feet and whistled their disapproval.

"You're all just a bunch or perverts. You like those melons swinging in your face. What are your wives or daughters going to say when they see this play with her in it? They'll know your thoughts. They'll know the darkness of your hearts."

"This is uncalled for, Jim," Blue Cowboy muttered.

"Of course it's called for. I'm a Christian, standing inside a Christian church."

Third Eye gathered herself, drew her body to a greater height and more dominant bearing.

"Have you gotten a blowjob on an altar? Because if I blow just one more preacher on God's stage I'll have to start counting with something other than my hands. You Christian folks love spilling your seed all over holy ground."

"'That's it!" Jim screamed as he kicked his script across the floor. He stormed out of the side door. The door didn't close behind him and after a few seconds of him being gone he stuck his head back through the doorway and said, "Maybe you should change the name of the play to *The Whores of Coronado*!" His head disappeared again.

"That wasn't worth coming back for! That was weak and insipid!" Blue Cowboy shouted at the empty doorway. Then, he turned to the cast and crew. "Does anybody else want to quit? We have no scenery. We have no Jim. Sparrow is just barely hanging in there. Maybe it's time to just shut the whole thing down."

The prospect of losing the opportunity to watch Third Eye rallied the group.

"I'll be Jim," the old man said as he tried to get out of his chair, which proved harder than normal given his weakened state. He tried three times and three times he failed to gain the sufficient angle to rise to his feet and fell back again.

Third Eye walked over to him and pressed his flushed face against her breasts.

"You poor thing. I've nearly killed you."

He sobbed and stained her blouse with his tears, all the while thanking her for her existence and benevolence. Third Eye pointed toward Paul.

"What about him? He could play a fed convincingly. He looks like a narc," she said to Blue Cowboy.

"You in the back, do you want to be in a play?"

Paul squirmed in his chair as his role of mocking voyeur suddenly changed to an active participant in the carnage on the altar. He tried to ignore the invitation, but he was trapped because Blue Cowboy was both persistent and desperate. He had already tried every one of the remaining crew in speaking parts and they either suffered from stuttering (prop man), a paralyzing fear of public speaking (sound and foley guy), illiteracy (ticket taker and usher), or an unintelligible Tagalog accent (lighting), and they all already had important non-speaking roles of ranch hands, electrical workers, thugs, and foreign agents.

Paul walked toward the altar. Third Eye started laughing when he came close enough to be recognized. The old man did not share in her humor and summoned his most ferocious scowl, which was mitigated by his red and puffy eyes and tear-stained cheeks.

"Isn't THIS a surprise!" Third Eye shouted. "Boys, I couldn't have thought of a better narc in ten years of thinking than this man right here."

"First of all, I think I'm the one who's supposed to be surprised," Paul came back with some heat.

"Don't blame me for your lack of imagination. A girl can't be anything else if she has psychic powers?"

"Not exactly. And what does the narc comment mean? You're just making stuff up to hear yourself talk."

"I'm going out on a limb here and guessing that you two know each other," Blue Cowboy interjected.

"I'm ok with including you as long as I don't have to break up a fight between you and the old man."

The three looked at the old man in unison. He tried to rise for vanity's sake but his arms could not generate enough power to push himself off the chair.

"If he acts like a gentleman then we'll have no problems," the old man said between gasps of breath.

"Is that the only scene that Jim is in?" Paul asked, ignoring the mean-spirited comments he created in his mind as responses to the old man's challenge.

"You're in just about every scene, but that's the only time you speak. You're part of the chorus, too, but if you can't sing just act like you're singing."

"What the hell, I have nothing else to do. "

"Except go to a party tomorrow night," whispered Third Eye, "with me, right?"

"I wouldn't miss it, for anything else in the world."

For a moment Paul thought of a dandelion seed being swept from the ground and buffeted by the wind. The seed rose with the warm currents and slowly fell to earth in Portsmouth, Ohio. There it germinated under rainstorms and sun. The first tender root clawed the ground like a finger.

13

After the Rehearsal

Paul spent the next two and a half days in rehearsal. What Blue Cowboy lacked in talent and critical analysis he made up for with organization, focus, and an unrelenting drive to see his version of *Bells of Coronado* staged, although in moments of self-doubt he might have admitted he stood alone in this desire. Paul quickly became his favorite on the set, because he learned his lines quickly, he didn't sing loudly enough to throw the chorus out of tune, and during the fight scene he didn't use the opportunity to pass along a groin shot or an eye poke as Jim had done once the production began to slide away from his values. Paul didn't worry much about nuancing his lines and delivered them with clarity and force. He had testified dozens of times in housing court against slumlords, absentee owners, the destitute and the aged, really anyone who would not or could not maintain their homes or apartment buildings, so he had grown comfortable with speaking publicly and confronting hostility, not that he expected much hostility from the audience of the play, but he couldn't guess how conservatives might take the interpretation of the text. This would be the first occasion that he would be wearing a black and rhinestone cowboy hat, a pair of leather chaps, and a bolo tie with a silver clasp that looked like it had been cast from a mold of bull testicle, but somehow if felt no different than wearing a dress shirt and tie.

The only issue he had was keeping his eyes off of Third Eye while they were on stage together and controlling his reverie as his thoughts drifted back to the motel room, the bed, and the feeling of being enveloped in flesh and musk. Fortunately there were large gaps in the play in which his only duty was to stand on the periphery as part of a crowd of either thugs, workmen, townspeople, or miners, so he had hours to watch her. His penis rose and fell with his thoughts and he had the bad luck of being fully engorged during a run-through of the wrestling scene with Blue Cowboy, who obviously felt the hard-on being pressed against him and who felt confused as to the meaning behind it. Paul could take no more and during the next break he pulled Third Eye aside for a blowjob, a handjob, a withering assessment of his length and girth, anything to relieve some of the pressure building inside of him.

"I'm off the clock, honey. If I do you I'll have the whole cast and crew lining up behind you, begging for relief. They work better when they're horny and bothered."

"Please, I'm prepared to beg."

"No, for this small slice of my life I'm an actress and a singer. I suggest you take care of that yourself." She pointed to the bulge in my pants. "And you better get a grip on yourself before the curtain because there might be a law against sporting a boner in a church in front of wives and children." A little smile played on her lips. "But I do have to change my shirt. I'm just about soaked through."

She unbuttoned her blouse and unhooked her bra and threw the wet clothes close to her gym bag. All the men who hadn't stepped outside to smoke or drink stopped talking or moving and watched her dry off her pits, arms and breasts. The little storage rooms they could have used as dressing rooms were ten degrees hotter than the altar, so dressing and undressing always took place out in the open, but none of the men, amateurs in the theater as they were, ever tired of watching the spectacle. Her breasts were so large and perfect that thoughts of crawling between them flooded Paul's brain. His erection grew to a personal best and he staggered out of the side door before he added to his humiliation by passing out on the floor.

Outside, Paul found that night had fallen and the humidity of the day had just begun to thin. The smokers and drinkers of the cast and crew had moved away from the church building and stood by their cars in the parking lot. Paul walked to the other side of the building from where they stood, dropped his pants and underwear to his ankles, and jerked himself off. At climax he steadied himself against the church, still radiating heat from the sun, with his left hand and ejaculated on the cinder blocks. He stood outside a cone of illumination from an overhead vapor light, but he wasn't entirely invisible either as the night was clear and a large yellow moon hung in the sky.

"I could have taken care of that for you," Blue Cowboy said from nearby. "The night air must feel good on your cock. It's so goddamn hot in that church."

Paul spun in the direction from which the voice came without first pulling up his pants, so any hope for reclaiming a shred of modesty or discretion was lost.

"Were you watching me?" Paul said as he realized his pants and underwear lay bunched around his ankles and pulled them up.

"You're not very private about your business."

"That does not mean, Blue Cowboy, that you are supposed to watch."

"I shouldn't rubberneck at a traffic accident and I shouldn't watch the local news because all they report on is murder, rape, and bribes. My name is Franklin by the way."

"I'm happy to report, Blue Cowboy, that I was thinking of our very own Dale Evans and not you in those blue pants."

"I can't even count the number of times I've jerked off to a vision of Dale Evans. She's something of an obsession of mine."

"I'm talking about flesh and blood. I'm talking about Third Eye on the stage with those magnificent tits."

"She's a stand-in for Dale."

"No, she's not."

"Obsessions and fetishes can mutate and disguise themselves."

"Look, I fucked her and an associate in a motel room a couple of days ago. I wasn't thinking about Dale Evans then and I wasn't thinking about her now. I haven't seen a Roy Rogers movie in decades and I own absolutely no cowboy clothes. I didn't know that festival was going on. I came down here to see an old friend who I saw on the Cleveland news because a backhoe driver found a skull in a gravel pit."

"Yet, here you are at the festival, playing a part in *The Bells of Coronado*, wearing cowboy clothes, and jerking off on a church as you think of a prostitute dressed like Dale Evans. Obsessions take many turns, my friend."

"Don't project your insanity on me."

Blue Cowboy laughed genuinely at first and then turned it into a knee-slapping western guffaw that signaled he felt nothing but braying derision.

"I'm going to slap you," Paul muttered through clenched teeth.

"Just because I find your definition of insanity to be hilarious? I'd say you're a couple of miles further down the road toward that destination than I am."

"That's not even a good colloquialism."

"I came out here to fetch you. We're ready to start again, that is if you've finished abusing yourself."

"Maybe I should just leave. Then who would you get for Jim?"

"And leave Dale's magnificent breasts? They have a gravitational pull all their own. Besides I could have Roy and Doc talk to an empty space where Jim is supposed to stand and I could have Ray roll around on the ground fighting himself. We'll call it a hallucination caused by the uranium. And maybe that's a better motive or reason for Doc to act the way he does anyway. Maybe he has gone nuts because of contact with high grade uranium. In the movie his actions make no sense. Why would a kindly old country doctor become a traitor to his nation? What's he going to do with the money, really? He's old. He's' worn out. He has status. He's one of the respected town elders and he throws it all away for some filthy lucre. Uranium poisoning could explain it all away."

They started walking back.

"I get it. I'm dispensable."

"I wouldn't say that. I sort of can't wait to see what you'll do next."

"At least I'm entertaining."

"That's all Roy and Dale every wanted to be."

"Do all roads lead to Roy with you?"

"They used to come to the festival, you know. It was bigger then. More people remembered the movies. Sometimes the local TV station even ran them on Saturday afternoons. We would hold parades and once word got back to Roy that something was happening in his old hometown they started attending. They drove a powder blue, convertible Cadillac with a white interior and a white rag top. They always wanted to be positioned right in front of the parade, after the color guard and the fife and drum corps. Roy looked more Indian than he did on screen. His dad was a full-blooded Choctaw, so it's no wonder, but you have to think it gave him just enough exotic appeal to push him over the top and that most people didn't even figure it out so they could safely adore him without worrying about muddying their genetic lines. Anyway, a few years before Roy's death, must have been the mid-90s, was the last time they could come to the festival. They were pretty frail by then. I was taking a leading role in the festival and I was responsible for the parade. The sky was growing dark when we started and about halfway through a sudden cloudburst poured on us. They had the top down, of course, on the Cadillac and by the time I got to them they looked as though they were under gunfire. They were so old and fragile. I ran over to them with an umbrella as the driver climbed out to put up the top. They smiled at me and looked like two wrinkled, lost children. They were so happy I stopped the rain from pelting them. I had been walking alongside the Caddy the whole time to be safe. I didn't think anybody would bother them but I couldn't be sure because there are so many whackos in the world. Roy pulled Dale close and wrapped his arms around her. He instinctively wanted to protect her, even from the rain, even when he was just as scared and confused as she was. I helped the driver snap the top in place and they sped off back to the Columbus airport. The last I saw of them was those two taillights in the rain. They had kept my umbrella so I had to walk back to the hotel in the pouring rain. I didn't care about the umbrella or the rain. I felt confirmed and right. So, yes, maybe this is a long way for me to answer that all roads lead to Roy or maybe better said, all roads lead from Roy. He is a source, a spring, and not a destination."

They had reached the door. Blue Cowboy pushed it open and Paul paused at the threshold, thinking he could just as easily walk back to the hotel, lock himself in his room, and use his remaining vacation to arrest his relentless drive toward humiliation and self-debasement, but he caught sight of Third Eye stretching her arms over her head as she flirted with the crew as the old man impotently watched, and he took a long stride into the church. Blue Cowboy slammed the door behind him. He knew Paul's hesitation was nothing but an act, as impotent as the old man, as he could no more leave than Blue Cowboy himself.

They rehearsed until midnight, came back early next morning and worked until the late afternoon, when they broke for the day because Paul and Third Eye explained they had to attend a barbeque being given by Deputy Auro. Blue Cowboy expressed disappointment, but even he looked forward to a couple of shots of whiskey at the hotel bar and then hunkering down in his hotel room on the too soft bed and forgetting the play for a few hours. The rest of the cast and crew jumped in their cars and screeched out of the parking lot before Blue Cowboy could change his mind. Paul asked Third Eye if she wanted a ride back to the hotel to shower and change. The day had been especially hot and both were soaked through with sweat.

"Of course, the old man slipped away hours ago. He's such a gentleman. He spared us a scene with the transfer from him to you. If he was forty years younger I'd probably marry him."

She squeezed into the passenger side of his twelve year-old Camry. The cabin had been baked all day in the sun and the heat inside felt like a fresh assault against their exhausted and wet bodies. Paul held himself from leaning over and kissing her bare shoulder, even though he didn't have to worry about when and where to make advances, since the date was costing him at minimum 25 dollars an hour as a base with an escalator clause for any sexual congress in which they may engage. He had never been on a date before with a guaranteed conclusion, secured by his own money, so he fell into a more traditional role of the gentleman searching for clues, looking for encouragement, and ready to pounce once a door had been opened long enough to permit entry. So, with this cast of mind, as unexpected as it was, he felt thrilled to hold her hand on the way to the hotel as they chatted about their chances for success on opening night and whether or not Blue Cowboy would die of a heart attack or aneurysm during the performance or before.

They stopped at the hotel, showered and changed clothes. Third Eye had brought her gym bag full of possible outfits and she modeled one after the other for Paul. The first consisted of khaki capris and a loose-fitting sleeveless blouse that looked appropriate for a run to the supermarket or a little league game. Paul rejected it out of hand as far too conservative and bland, because he thought he wanted no question as to who she was, what she did for a living, an why he brought her to a family barbeque. Certainly, he could bring her incognito and at the end of the night, after a dozen or so drinks, have her strip off her clothes and blow a few of the husbands and make dates with the rest, but such a strategy could put his culpability in question, because he might not know that such a sweet and overweight woman had the heart of a whore. He sent her back to the bathroom by saying the capris made her ass look enormous.

The second outfit looked closer to what he wanted as she wore a mid-thigh skirt, a halter top and button-down shirt with the top four buttons opened, revealing an unobstructed view of the top half of her breasts squeezed under the halter. He sent her back with instructions not to look like a spinster. So, her third attempt produced the effect he wanted, including jean shorts cut above the depth of the pockets and the same halter without the button-down. The halter could not stay below her navel and the shorts could not stay above her ample belly. Without the button-down the halter looked downright indecent with its inability to sufficiently cover or at least mask the size and shape of her breasts.

When Paul told her she looked perfect, Third Eye inspected herself and broke into a wry smile. She had been used this way before. Twice she had been paid as an announcement of the buyer's renunciation of an old and exhausted world as they entered a period of experimentation with the wilder, seedy, and dangerous side of life. She had been used as a prop. Dressed as the biggest whore on the planet, her role was to shock family, friends and colleagues into understanding the payer had renounced decency in favor of debasement. Results varied. The first time she had been hired by a man in his 40s who had found out a couple of months before he had a fast-growing, inoperable tumor inside his brain and she was one of the manifestations of his bitterness. Together they went to a graduation party for a buck-toothed boy virgin with the vague plan of introducing carnality to the boy. Not only was she to be the man with cancer's announcement of hatred toward the raw deal he had been dealt, but she was to play the dual role as a present to the boy. Straight-out nudity would have been less offensive than the clothes she wore, so it took the family only a couple of minutes to smoke out the meaning of her presence, both roles in fact. They shielded her from the boy virgin and openly wept for the man. Two men broke out a Bible and sang psalms. They gave her a robe and held her hand. Soon the party swayed to the music of the verses. They stoked the man's diseased head and wiped away his angry tears. They invited her to church the following Sunday, but she knew better than to take them up on their offer.

The second time she had been hired by a man who was despondent about being passed over for promotion in favor of a younger, more educated and more personable rival. She thought he wanted to end his career with the company with a grand and vile gesture at the company holiday party. He had her dress in black fishnet stockings, a leather mini-skirt, a sheer black bustier, and a spiked leather collar around her neck. She guessed the man's plan somehow included a blowjob in sight of his boss and his boss' boss. It was hard to get him to articulate his ideas. He showed up at her apartment already drunk and muttering that, "They'll see what I think of their plans. They can blow me. She can blow me. She will blow me. I'll be blown and that will be what I think of Jeff." By the time they reached the party they found most everybody either drunk on vodka or high on cocaine so they were barely noticed when they entered. Before they could set their plan in motion, however, a splinter group from accounting corralled Third Eye in the copy room and took turns licking her pussy and snorting cocaine off her breasts. Fortunately, the man did find a way to be fired by vomiting on the boss' new Salvator Ferragamo Python loafers and passing out near his desk in a puddle or his own urine.

"Why do you want to bust up this party? Why don't we get a bottle and we fuck until you've had your money's worth," Third Eye said as she pinched a roll of fat hanging over the beltline of her shorts. "I can't tell if I'm gaining or losing."

"They're expecting me. It would be rude to disappoint them. The deputy's wife wants to meet me."

"Deputy? I don't need trouble, friend. Portsmouth is on my circuit. I pull down some nice fees here. If I go and start fucking with the law they're arrest me every time they see me."

"The deputy will get the joke. He won't be mad at you. He might want to beat the crap out of me, though, depending how his wife reacts."

"You're aiming pretty low. This is just a cheap trick and it doesn't seem worth the effort. I should change back into the khakis and we'll see how things develop."

"You wouldn't understand."

Of course she understood everything. Hadn't she participated in the very same joke twice already? But she felt too ambivalent and exhausted to carry the argument further, so she headed toward the door without another word.

They drove to the party in silence. She kept her hands in her lap and stared at the passing buildings as they thinned and gave way to fields of sumac and acres of damp, black forest. They drove for twenty minutes as Paul consulted his directions. Finally, Paul turned into a gravel drive and crept toward a sprawling farmhouse. Several cars were already parked out front. Children's toys lay scattered across the lawn: a bike with training wheels, two soccer balls, a plastic hut and slide, a rusty wagon with a missing handle and thus no discernible way to pull it.

Paul pulled onto the lawn like those who had come before, climbed out of the car, and conducted a closer survey of the deputy's home. He could see no other neighbor as the expansive home lay nestled between fields and trees. A new barn rose behind the house, gleaming with perfect angles and plum lines, exhibiting the hubris of new construction before gravity and weather took its toll. Two new model SUVs sat parked in front of the barn and by their positioning looked to belong to the family. The house itself really was composed of two houses, the original sensible farmhouse and an addition twice as big as the original jutting off toward the woods from the opposite side of the driveway. The addition had not kept the perfect crispness of the barn but still looked absurdly new next to the original as the front corner had settled dramatically, throwing the roof line of the porch in a downward arc. The windows had been replaced but the style conflicted with the century-old architecture. Unfortunately, new plastic shutters had been tacked on and the chimney looked ready to crumble as most of the mortar on the driveway side had fallen out. While most observers would become blinded by the overall impression of success and familial communion, Paul prided himself in spotting the frayed seam, the crack in the otherwise perfect veneer.

They heard laughing coming from behind the house, so they walked down the drive and into the party. Paul could feel a knot growing in his gut as they came into view of the hosts and their guests. No one comically produced a double-take, or gaped open their mouths, or dropped their drinks in shock, but gave a sidelong glance here and there, acknowledging that two new guests had arrived. The deputy held court over a silver grill that looked like it had been polished just for the occasion. He held a beer with one hand and a pair of barbeque tongs with the other as he eyed eight sizzling steaks on the grill. Three other men stood around him with beers in their hands. They watched the deputy's technique closely and thought they each had better barbeque skills, but they were glad not to have the responsibility and it didn't matter if he burned the meat into leather.

Paul recognized Randall Highland, the reporter who had accompanied them to the jail, but not the other two who looked like they had picked their clothes from the Suburban Man's Barbeque and Lawn Games catalog as they were dressed almost identically in khaki shorts, leather sandals, and untucked polos of soft summer hues. Another man sat in a lawn chair away from the barbeque team with a grouping of four empty beer bottles already at his feet. He pretended to listen to the conversation, but he was sitting too far away to really hear, so he occasionally nodded his head to the ebb and flow of the banter as he watched their wives chatting in a cluster on the patio near the back of the house. Third Eye broke his concentration when she passed through his line of sight. He betrayed his interest by holding the bottle's mouth close to his lips long after he had poured a mouthful and swallowed. Then he closed his eyes, rubbed his temples, and when he reopened his eyes the visage of Third Eye surprisingly remained. He pushed himself off the chair and walked directly toward them.

"So it begins. I hope you're ready for what you started," Third Eye muttered to Paul, who was scanning the lawn for a cooler of beer, which he spotted sitting at arm's length from the vacated chair.

"He looks harmless enough."

"You are a terrible judge of character."

"There must have been quite a storm in heaven to blow one of its angels to the ground," the man said a little too loudly because he had started talking before he had reached a comfortable conversational distance.

Third Eye waited for him to come the rest of the distance before she said, "Or I was kicked out for other reasons."

"I've heard tell that St. Peter doesn't permit much in the way of deviant acts in his territory."

"The fact is I got caught blowing St. Peter and they couldn't very well kick him out of heaven because of the scandal that would have caused, so the punishment came down on my head alone. One minute I'm in the clouds with the very best of humanity and the next I'm at a backyard barbeque talking to you. Frankly, some of the rules of heaven baffle me. For instance, how can a person exist for eternity without oral sex, but you know what they say, heaven is always about 500 years behind the rest of the cosmos."

The man narrowed his eyes and took a long drink from his beer.

"There's nothing wrong with spreading a little wit around you. I've always appreciated a woman with a sharp mind."

"I'm happy to be appreciated."

"I'm the sheriff. You probably didn't know that."

Third Eye did not betray shock or fear and held out her hand in a mock feminine position, fingers pointed to the ground, wrist raised but bent submissively, and allowed the sheriff to take ahold of her fingers and give them a little tug.

"I was on my way to take a piss and I thought I'd welcome you to the party."

"We appreciate you taking the detour, don't we honey?"

Paul missed the cue as his mind had wandered to thinking of retreat strategies should his joke be met with unusual hostility. For some reason he had not planned on other law enforcement personnel being at the party, but given the deputy's job what circle of friends and acquaintances did he expect him to have?

"He can be so absent-minded," Third Eye continued. "Look at him there staring off into space."

"What?" Paul asked as he came back to the conversation.

"I was saying we appreciate the sheriff coming to talk to us."

"In my line of work if you drift off like then you'll more than likely end up dead."

Third Eye reached out her hand and stroked the sheriff's bicep. His demeanor softened as he watched her nails slide down his arm. Deputy Auro spotted them talking to the sheriff and he handed the tongs over to Randall after a detailed list of instructions on how and when to flip the meat. He retrieved two beers from the cooler and brought them over to Paul and Third Eye.

"Evening, Paul, I see you brought a friend. I see the sheriff has made you at home."

"This is..." Paul paused because he came up against the fact that he did not know her name, did not want to know her name, would never commit the name to memory, and did not want to explain how she became to be known as Third Eye, "...my fortuneteller and costar of the Roy Rogers play *The Bells of Coronado*, which will be premiering on Friday I'll have you know."

"Paul, for you to be my costar you would have to play Roy." She turned and to the deputy in a stage whisper, "He actually just plays a bit part of a federal agent afflicted with spontaneous erection."

"That sounds like Paul."

"I take offense to being called a bit part."

"The role or the erection?" Third Eye retorted.

The deputy laughed. The sheriff lost interest in the banter, inspected his empty beer, and drifted back toward the cooler. The deputy watched the sheriff closely and waited for him to sit down before resuming the conversation with Paul and Third Eye.

"So, you're an actress?" the deputy asked.

"Among other occupations."

"Have any of the duties of these other occupations brought you in contact with the Portsmouth jail or the police force of this jurisdiction?"

"Are you sure prior convictions are admissible evidence?"

"When they directly relate to the crime at hand, I believe they are. If I was suggesting you are trespassing then previous convictions of trespassing would certainly be admissible."

"Are you suggesting we're trespassing, Greg?" Paul interjected. "Remember, you invited me."

"I invited you. I half-expected you to bring the cowboy in the blue pants. I was prepared for that spectacle."

"What are you saying, Deputy?" Third Eye asked softly and sweetly.

"I'm saying it's been a long time since I've seen my old friend, Paul Newcombe, but knowing what I know about him and seeing what I now see I'd guess a day doesn't go by in which he doesn't break some law or another."

"You have to admit that some laws are pretty stupid. You can't follow everything."

"I don't write law or interpret law. I enforce law. The day I start talking about which laws should be followed and which ones should be ignored is the day I quit."

"How very ethical of you. I'm very impressed."

A woman, no doubt the deputy's wife, had watched them as she chatted in a group on the patio. She excused herself and took a step or two in the direction of her husband and two new guests, but the deputy artfully raised a palm that stopped her. She pretended like she had forgotten what she wanted to do, made a show of remembering, and strode over to the cooler to check on the supply of beer.

"Where's your wife, Greg? I'd love to meet her and thank her for the invitation."

The deputy narrowed his face and excused himself and Paul from Third Eye, drawing him to an open patch of grass more or less out of earshot from the rest of the party.

"What are you doing? What is your game?"

"I don't understand what you are asking."

"I invite you to my house to meet my wife and you bring a prostitute? Did you think I wouldn't notice or did you think it would be funny to rub our faces in the slime and disease out there? I'm not the one who drove the entire length of the state just to see what you were doing. I hadn't thought of you for twenty years, but now you want to come here and try to dirty up my life, knocking us out of our equilibrium, maybe introduce a little chaos into our bubble. Is that your purpose?"

"I wish I knew what you are talking about. I met Third Eye at the play rehearsals and hit it off. I think there's a pret-ty good chance I'll be getting laid tonight if all goes well at this party."

"What's wrong with you, Paul? Are you jealous I was on TV? Do you hate cops? Are you fucking lonely and scared? Did you think you'd step into the past in the hopes of catching some sympathy for your cowardice?"

"Catching sympathy? Is that supposed to be a fishing metaphor? It's doesn't work on any level."

"Look, I want you and your prostitute to get off my property. I don't have to deal with you and I won't deal with her. I see enough of this nonsense every day, and there's no reason to expose my wife and guests to it, too. Understand? Get the fuck out."

"Too late, Deputy," Paul said as he pointed over the deputy's shoulder.

The deputy turned around and saw that his wife had snagged Third Eye and drawn her into the circle of women.

"For God's sake." The deputy turned back to Paul. "I'll remember this," he seethed and added an exclamation point by jabbing an index finger hard against Paul's chest.

"I think you're taking this the wrong way."

The deputy stalked off with the purpose of extracting Third Eye from the group of women, but they were already laughing at some story she had begun, and as he passed the grill he smelled burning meat so he chose to intervene in the most pressing matter and took the tongs out of Randall's hands. Paul drifted back closer to the center of the party and settled next to the drunken sheriff in the lawn chair. It felt the most comfortable place to land.

"That's quite a woman you got there."

He looked up at Paul from his chair, but he made no movement to stand and establish an equal conversation, choosing to let Paul lean toward him to hear. His eyes were encased in black, fleshy bags and the whites of his eyes had turned the color of grapefruit flesh.

"You like her?"

"That's how I like them, so fat they can barely keep clothes on. And she doesn't seem shy either. My wife was shy. We would come to a party like this and she wouldn't say three words all night and she would never leave my hip. Sometimes you have to talk about titties and baseball and there ain't a man alive going to do that with his mute wife standing by his side. But here I am talking her down and when she died four years ago I haven't never been the same. I like them big, fat, brassy girls that come into a room all tits and ass, but I married and loved a quiet one."

They each took a drink of beer. Paul scanned the groupings to find another conversation, but the gender split had held as the women stayed on the patio and the men now stood glumly around the grill. Greg's expression had notably changed, but Paul couldn't tell if he or the burnt meat had been the author of the change of mood.

"How do you know Greg?" Paul asked absently.

"Seeing how I'm the sheriff and he's a deputy I'm sure it doesn't tax your logic to figure out how I know him."

Paul apologized for the question and stopped watching the grill.

"I've been sheriff close to thirty years. I just keep getting elected. I think people are so used to voting for me that they'll elect me after I'm dead. That's the funny thing about politics. You have the right name and you keep your dick clean you can pretty much expect to keep a job like mine until you die."

"I work in City Hall in Cleveland. I've seen plenty of people come and go."

"Oh, hell, Cleveland. I would expect that up there. You have roving packs of dogs, whole neighborhoods sinking into the ground, a murder or two a day, rogue barges terrorizing the shores of the lake, and entire schools filled with illegitimate children."

"The problems are no worse than any other place."

"I don't have to contend with that kind of scale. We've got our poverty and pill mills and meth labs. I think the problem is that nobody wants to stay conscious for more than an hour or two a day, however long it takes to secure the substance that's going to make them unconscious. They prefer to stare at the wall and shrivel away to nothing"

Paul finally committed to the conversation by finding another lawn chair and setting it down next to the sheriff, bringing two fresh beers, although the sheriff could reach the cooler himself without leaving the chair.

"If these idiot kids would just stick to beer they would be able to squeeze out five or six decades before their bodies got old and fat and they died after an assault of hemorrhages."

"Do you think the skull belongs to a kid like that?"

"You mean that one that Tuck Handy found in the gravel pit?"

"Are there others?"

"Not like up in Cleveland. I've heard some of the buildings have skulls for foundations, that you might find one in the gutter or on the sidewalk anytime day or night."

"Really that's only in the area of town called Dachau. I mean even the Bergen-Belsen district is cleaned up now."

"There's still lots of theories. Some folks from your neck of the woods at the Natural History Museum called me, thinking Tuck dug right through an Indian burial mound. This area was thick with the mounds once and they say they're planning on coming down, but it's probably just a pile of gravel."

"It would be interesting if the skull turned out to be Indian, no?"

"You don't know the story about Indian Head Rock?"

"I can't say that I do."

"Well, I've had an eight ton sandstone boulder sitting in the police garage for the past two years and I'm about to rent me out a jackhammer and pulverize the damn thing so nobody can say no more about it. See it's this big ol' rock that use to sit in the middle of the river and people liked to swim out to it or take a little rowboat out to it and they would stand on it. Maybe if they had the time and patience they would carve their names or initials on it. Sandstone isn't that hard to carve. This was forever ago—I'm talking the 1890s. And there was always this one carving—round head, little nub ears sticking out to the sides, round eyes, round nose, and a mouth that's not quite committed to a smile. If someone told you that it was supposed to be Charlie Brown you wouldn't disbelieve them. Some people say it's a carving made by an Indian, a petroglyph and some think it was made by a bored boatman as some kind of marker. Maybe he was ambivalent about Portsmouth and didn't know whether to smile or not. Anyway, the Charlie Brown head gave the rock its unofficial name, but around 1920 they dammed a portion on the river and the rock was submerged under almost 16 feet of water. So, a couple of years ago a local historian runs across these pictures of ladies in their petticoats and big hats standing on the rock in the middle of the river. The rock becomes something of an obsession with him. He puts on scuba gear, finds the rock, and hires a dive team to pull it out of the silt. The poor man started an unholy shitstorm. You would have thought the poor sap broke off the hands of the Lincoln Memorial. The Army Corps of Engineers charged him illegal dredging, even though he took a goddamn rock OUT of the shipping channel and the great State of Kentucky screamed like someone was pulling off their fingernails with a pair of pliers. Unfortunately, that sandstone rock with the Charlie Brown head does actually belong to Kentucky since they technically own this portion of the river, but they didn't hire a dive team to bring it up to the surface or give two fucks about it until someone else did. Now, even the House of Representatives in both Kentucky and Ohio have passed competing resolutions demanding the end of the conflict in their favor. Then, the Kentucky Attorney General charged our historian with violating the Kentucky Antiquities Act and the poor man's hair started falling out by the handful. The law is clearly on the Kentucky side, but Ohio has to hold out just a little longer to make the rock even more treasured. In a couple of more months of frustration Kentucky is going to start believing we have the sword of King Arthur or the helmet of Beowulf, when all they're really going to get is a Charlie Brown head. I just hope it ends up in a Kentucky museum. Shit, I hope they build a museum just for the rock and I live to see the Kentucky masses flocking to see it. Everyone taking a pilgrimage to pray to their round-headed idiot god." He added an exclamation point to his story by draining half of his beer.

Paul used the pause to excuse himself, adding unnecessarily that he had to find the toilet. The story complete, the sheriff no longer had need for him, so he nodded, inspected his beer, found it empty, and opened another one. Paul walked toward the group of women on the patio and stepped into the conversational circle just as Third Eye was wrapping up a story about Blue Cowboy's basement shrine in his home in Baltimore. The plotline somehow revolved around plaster-of-Paris statues of Roy and Dale and a colony of mice. The women winced and groaned and Paul couldn't tell if the story had been entertaining or just disgusting. He, of course, did gather that Third Eye had visited Blue Cowboy's house in Maryland. He wondered, for the sake of his own disappointment and cynicism whether or not she applied roaming charges for out of state work or charged him a flat per diem on top of her regular fees. An extraordinarily pretty woman with gold eyes turned her face toward him.

"You must be Paul. We've been entertained by your friend's experiences and her vision of the world."

He could not tell whether she held back anger, true fascination, or horror, but something raged behind her controlled tone. Paul noticed the first hints of lines projecting from the corners of her mouth and eyes. He paused a moment over the eyes as they were vivid gold. She had auburn hair with the few flecks of color loss. Paul couldn't help himself from turning squarely to face her and leaning forward to smell the scent of her neck.

"She can do that. She's quite the raconteur," he said and winced shortly after, disgusted at his attempt to display a vocabulary that really wasn't all that deep to impress someone he had supposedly come to shock.

"I'm sure. She tells me you met at play rehearsals."

"In a manner of speaking. I have gotten to know her this past week rehearsing the play, but she probably didn't tell you that we actually first met when she told my fortune. She can be a little shy about her talents."

"That's not something I like to broadcast," Third Eye said, revived somewhat from her storytelling by taking long drinks from her beer.

Hearing about Third Eye's fortunetelling ability, the other women had perked up as well. As a group they seemed pretty and trim, not as a result of anorexia, but athletically strong and radiant. Paul felt a tremor of disgust directed at Third Eye, if not because of her fleshy, oversized body, then because of his desire to touch and possess it. The woman with the gold eyes introduced herself as Jenny, the deputy's wife, and Paul's heart sank further into outright jealousy. She introduced the other women, Julie Highland, a librarian and Randall Highland's breadwinning wife, Bev Morgan, a real estate agent, whose real estate agent husband had bowed out of the party because of a wicked hangover and his dislike of the deputy, Trish Summer, wife of attorney Bill Summer whose political ambitions began with replacing the doddering and fey county prosecutor the next or the following election cycle and who now stood near the deputy and looked comfortable, but alert to opportunities, Tammy Keys, divorced and whose emotions followed her finances plunging downward, who had just finished her third tumbler of wine and who felt both nauseous and unhinged, and Leslie Whitehurst, another divorcee that Tammy had brought along with her and who none of the other women knew. Leslie had just completed her shift at Walmart and even though she had time to go home and change she still wore her uniform of khaki pants, a blue polo, and a navy blue vest with an enormous yellow smiley face on the back. One wondered as to her economic status before the divorce, because she took pride in the shame of wearing the uniform in a social situation, like showing off a scar of a near fatal accident. Tammy and she had shared a dozen private jokes through the course of the conversation with Third Eye as over the previous few months they had formed a tragic-comedic friendship, based on the fact they felt bereft and damned and they craved company during the arc of their free fall.

Tammy, being by far the most drunk of the women at this stage of the party, asked Third Eye to tell her fortune. Third Eye, ever the entrepreneur, knew she would have to provide free services at the party, but she hoped she could turn one or two of the women into paying customers, expanding her foothold in Portsmouth. With the old man and a few regular psychic gigs she could gain a little stability and have a chance of growing her businesses bigger.

"To perform I would need a quiet space and a little privacy. Most folks don't want their fortunes in front of a crowd and it takes a lot of concentration to find the threads of the future."

"What fun is that?" Tammy blurted. "I don't give a crap who knows what's going to happen to me. I think everybody knows at this point it isn't going to be good."

"Right!" Leslie jumped in. "You're going to end up naked and raped in the gutter like me!" she continued as everyone now knew how much she had had to drink, which everyone guessed had to be more than her doomed friend, although Leslie had kept her enunciation from slipping, so it was hard to tell.

"Not necessarily," Third Eye corrected. "How you feel at this moment has almost nothing to do with the future. Maybe the immediate future, maybe how this night will end, but tonight, this moment, is only one data point on a large graph. We're so busy living day-to-day we miss the trend line. Have you ever seen a stock market trend line for like five years? Each day the line jumps up and down but the long term trend is either sloping upward or downward. In the happy talk of Wall Street everything is always improving, always progressing, but we know better than that. Either you're gaining a few points every month, after horrific swings up and down or you're losing a few points even though you could point to moments of extreme joy. Discovering the future is like trying to find the trend line with only a few data points, and you have to sort through the daily highs and lows. There are millions of influences and variables with which to contend."

"You never know when a blue cowboy walks out of the mist and into your life," said Paul and the women ignored him.

"We're among friends," Tammy asserted. "I don't mind."

"I suppose I could," Third Eye teased as she then lapsed into a long silence.

"C'mon, this whore's life is like an open book, anyway," slurred Leslie.

Jenny narrowed her eyes and decided at that moment that she had had enough of Tammy's drunk friend and determined that if these were the kind of friends Tammy now had she would drop all future invitations until she could find her equilibrium and return to her former sanity. Third Eye could sense the acrimony brewing.

"Well, if the hostess is not disagreeable I can attempt a reading or two. I don't want to step on any toes because sometimes Christian folk take offense to fortune-telling. They often mistake it for the work of the devil and I do point out to them that Jesus knew he was going to be sacrificed on the cross."

For a moment Jenny did not pick up that the question had been posed to her as hostess, but as everyone looked to her and waited for a response she shook off her interior dialogue and granted permission for the show to proceed. Actually, she felt a small thrill building, based on the possibility that the monotony of the party could actually be broken. How much longer could she take the droning on about children and incompetent husbands, the chatter about vacation spots she had no interest in visiting (namely Caribbean cruises and weeklong stays on the property of Disney World), and the retelling of old stories from their youth that had begun to creep into the territory of outright myth when they had more energy and intensity and were less ossified by jobs and children?

Third Eye pulled two chairs together, facing each other. Paul tried to help, but she waved him away and looked irritated at his interference. She offered Tammy a seat and settled into the other chair. She moved closer so that her knees touched the front of Tammy's chair between her spread legs. The size of Third Eye's thighs splayed Tammy's legs to nearly a split. Paul thought he recognized her impulse to lean forward, make herself vulnerable, to crawl close to her, to surrender and to bury her flushed face between Third Eye's breasts and sob. Third Eye held her right hand, palm upward, between her own hands. She leaned backward and rolled her eyes upward so that only the whites shone through the barely opened slits of her lids. She drew in a deep breath and swelled her breasts. Tammy gasped and pushed her knee toward Third Eye's pussy, but her thighs blocked the advance. Third Eye broke into a horrible, insane grin, flicking her tongue between her teeth before she began to speak. All the women except Leslie exchanged looks, neither approving nor disapproving, but to check in and make sure the scene was actually right in front of them on Jenny's patio. Leslie focused on Tammy's knee trapped between Third Eye's thighs and bit her lip until she tasted blood.

"You wear pain like it was jewelry," Third Eye began. "To be cast on when you want to adorn yourself with the bad breaks, your unfortunate heredity, and the betrayals of those once closest to you. Sometimes you think you'll be driven insane by the thoughts of your ex-husband sleeping with the OTHER woman. Maybe her body is in no better shape than yours. Maybe most people would say that your face is prettier than hers and holding up better and longer. Maybe she applies too much makeup and the colors she chooses mark her as a direct descendent of trailer trash. But you can't stop thinking about his penis that used to be against your belly, that you fondled and sucked and had seen in every one of its states, probably a little undersized but it fit you perfectly, and now she blows him and he mounts her from behind and not once does he think of you and what the two of you once had. Since he informed you that he was abandoning the marriage, each day gets a little harder, a little worse, and recently you've begun to think that you've fallen down a bottomless rabbit hole."

Tammy began crying, but she could not pull away from Third Eye or stop looking at her face. She muttered, "It's time. It's time," under her breath.

"And with such an obvious downward arc you would expect me to tell you of an unfortunate end to your misery and pain, a car wreck, an accidental drowning, too much booze and too many pills, but the voices aren't telling me these stories at all. You're strong and maybe you don't care as much about your ex-husband as you think. He had annoying habits. He tasted like sulfur and pumice. Violence was always a possibility, brewing, a first resort. He spoke of you in low terms. I see happy children, two or three. I feel their arms around your neck. I see you leaving a dingy and cramped apartment to a house with an attached garage and a whirlpool tub. I see a late-model car and a new cell phone. A wind that blows is dry and gritty. The temperature feels like over one hundred and your face is tight with sunburn. Through a kitchen window you see a soft face, the features are blurred by rain or mist or probably the sand carried by the wind. You don't have to see the smile or the kind eyes to know you have found your soulmate. Corny sounding, sure, but you've never felt surer of anything than this face. Sometimes you stand on a little rise littered with scrub and rock and look back east, at least you hope it's east because the sun is so high and potent you feel a little disoriented, but you look to what you think is east and you thank your philandering ex-husband for shining a light of your true path that you would have never seen except for his accidental guidance."

Tammy began to sob convulsively and several of the other women wiped tears from their eyes. Leslie came up behind her and placed a hand on her back, which broke the spell between Third Eye and Tammy. Third Eye released her hand and knee and Tammy turned in her chair to hug Leslie and sob on her shoulder.

"Anybody else want to give it a try?" Third Eye asked as her gaze settled on Deputy Auro standing on the periphery of the circle, holding a serving plate of steaks. "Do you want to know your future, Deputy?"

"Or does anybody want to hear a salacious story about the past?" interjected Paul. Since no one knew him and he had really only spoken to the sheriff he had no standing or command at the party so they ignored him again.

"I would say the immediate future better include you all eating steaks because they're done and cooling fast. Beyond that I don't want to think much about it."

The smell and sight of meat and the desire to be past an uncomfortable transition broke the group apart. Couples paired off and piled their plates with potato salad, deviled eggs, baked beans, green bean casserole and a steak selected by the deputy. They sat around two old banquet tables and ate the strangely tasteless food. The dishes were not poorly executed, seasoned inappropriately, or cooked beyond the range of acceptability, but they had eaten these combinations of flavors so many times in the past their palates went to sleep from the boredom. Paul sat next to the sheriff on his left, Leslie on his right, and Jenny across the table from him. Leslie, of course, sat next to Tammy and Third Eye sat on the other side of Tammy and Paul felt like he was losing contact with her. He turned to his left and nodded to the sheriff, who had grease dribbling down his chin and who had already nearly cleaned his plate. He didn't look so much drunk as exhausted and he obviously did not want to be bothered by chatter as he ate. Leslie all but turned her back on him as she directed all of her energy to Tammy, who stayed composed, although red-eyed and sniffling. Leslie's hand glided over her shoulders and spine and finally rested on the small of her back. That left Jenny for Paul to talk to and she listened to snatches of conversations from all the pairings at the tables. Paul stared in her direction just as her eyes drifted toward him and the awkwardness of the moment forced them to talk.

"Are you from Portsmouth originally?" he asked.

"God, no. I'm from Philadelphia."

"How did you end up here?"

"That is what you call a very long story and unfortunately not particularly interesting. Not even to me, and I lived it."

Paul felt like he may be in the least interesting conversation at the tables. Laughter and spite erupted around him and he was stuck pulling words out of her like they were impacted molars. She may have been distracted as she watched the deputy chat with Third Eye. His demeanor toward her had shifted and he smiled as he talked toward her cleavage. Either Jenny contemplated the possibility of his infidelity with a common whore or she monitored the half-full tumbler of bourbon and wondered how much he had drunk and when the stupidity would start. Neither possibility left much room for holding up her end of the conversation with Paul so he thought he would shock her into paying attention to him.

"You don't seem happy."

She turned her eyes toward him and gave him a full inspection.

"That is a ridiculous statement coming from the likes of you."

"What is that supposed to mean?"

"Anyone can see you are past the point of even faking happiness. I don't need a lecture from you on any of that."

"I wasn't aware I was lecturing."

"Train wreck," she muttered under her breath and abruptly stood up to clear her untouched plate of food.

Paul couldn't tell if she was describing him, her husband, or the general state of her own life. He did marvel at the graceful way she strode away so he hoped she hadn't meant him, even though he wouldn't argue very long or stridently should the label be given him. She fussed with a few dishes on the serving table and then disappeared into the house. He thought of following her, but he couldn't conjure up a reason strong enough to warrant the action. Should he find her in the kitchen what would he say? Would he compliment her on her sinew and athleticism? Would he kiss her on the back of the neck and ask her if she preferred train wrecks to well-oiled, perfectly functioning machines? He turned toward Leslie to see if she had finished attending to Tammy. Her patient had stopped sniffling after downing a glass of red wine, but Leslie wasn't any less attentive. Paul turned again to the sheriff who had finished his plate and had gone back to beer. He had yet to wipe the grease from his chin. He winked at Paul as he tried to get out of his chair to walk somewhere, anywhere. The sheriff stayed him by talking ahold of his arm.

"Where are you going, son?"

"I thought I might take a piss, if that's alright with the law. Do you know where the john is?"

"Where are the kids?"

"I don't know. How many are there?"

"Three."

"Maybe they wanted an adult party. Maybe they're staying with their grandparents," Paul said as he couldn't help but imagine Andy Auro rolling naked in the dirt, screaming prophecies over the heads of three tow-headed toddlers.

"Not likely. None of the grandparents live in town. Jenny is from Philadelphia and the deputy never talks about his parents."

"Then I don't know."

"You're going to say I'm bat-shit crazy, full of guano up to my eyeballs, but I believe that the skull has brought bad fortune into the life of the deputy. You're his old friend. You should talk to him and tell him to let it go, to give up the chase, because it's not going to matter who it belonged to since they're still going to be dead."

"Are you saying the skull is cursed, sheriff?

"Why wouldn't it be?"

"I don't understand."

"You don't end up in a gravel pit on your own accord. Something wicked visited her and whatever is attached to her has the deputy by the short hairs. He's really the only one who cares. I don't mean to tell you there's still no interest. I mean television has maintained a bit of interest, but he's the only one who really cares. And I question his motives. What's it to him, really? I think Jenny has had enough of it."

"I didn't take you for a nattering old gossip, sheriff. I'm thinking the skull is not at the heart of their troubles."

"Then you'll admit there are troubles."

"This is the first time I've met his wife. How would I know?"

"Who are you?"

"Does it matter?"

The sheriff looked suddenly confused as if he thought Paul to be someone else entirely or as if he had awakened from a dream and the place where he had become conscious was wildly different from where he remembered falling asleep. Paul used the moment to break free and after a few strides he realized he needed a destination, so he turned toward the serving table. As he scanned the remnants of the feast, he quickly realized the flaw in his plan, if you could call it that, because if he made another plate of food he would have to go back to the table and sit next to the sheriff since no one but Jenny had left the tables. He recalculated and walked toward the deputy who spoke to Third Eye with a bemused smile on his face, although the position of his torso showed he had not yet completely succumbed to her charms. Paul interrupted a tale of a cuckolded husband, a borrowed shotgun and a naked lover cowering behind a forsythia bush and the deputy flashed a look of annoyance as Paul asked him where he could relieve himself.

"Behind the barn or in the house," the deputy said before returning to his story.

Paul figured the deputy dusted off the story or others like it whenever he wanted to portray the job as something other than the drudgery it must be. He walked through the back door and into the kitchen, where he expected to find Jenny, preferably donning an apron with her hands in the sink and her back to the door, but the kitchen was empty. The space had been recently remodeled as the cabinets were scratch and nick free and the granite marble tops had yet to collect stains and discolorations. Nothing of the preparation for the barbeque remained. They cleaned. They believed in creating order. He wandered through and found a small bathroom down a short hallway where the walls were covered in family photos, mostly of three blonde girls in various states of play. The bathroom smelled of lavender, had been decorated in a woodland creature theme, and existed in a state of cleanliness that the bathroom in Paul's apartment had never seen. The hand towels smelled freshly laundered and perfumed with the essence of something pure and natural. He avoided looking at his face in the mirror.

When he left the bathroom he spied Jenny sitting at the dining room table on the other side of the short hallway. She stared into a glass of bourbon with ice and didn't look up when Paul walked into the room and stood across the table from her.

"Was it something I said?"

"No, I loathe parties. Actually, no, that's not true. I like the idea of parties and preparation and anticipation, but when they actually occur there's some point I have to hide and clear my mind. It happens every time."

"So, I'm bothering you. But I have to say this isn't much of a hiding place."

"Any place more remote and complicated would be downright rude. This is just a landing spot to catch my breath."

"When a hostess leaves the party what are the guests to think?"

"They don't even notice I'm gone, especially with Lisa there to entertain them."

"Who?"

"Lisa, your date? Please tell me you know her name."

"Technically, no, I've been with her for only a few hours and that's the first time I've heard what she purports to be her real name. It sort of dampens the mystery somehow."

"I don't know whether it's necessary to feel shocked or disgusted."

"It's ok to feel both. Most people react to me that way."

"Fortunately for you she doesn't seem like she's going to steal anything with the deputy and sheriff here. She actually seems like she has a sweet personality hidden beneath that costume."

"I wouldn't put money on such a supposition."

"Really, I'm not that naïve. She's added a little spice to our backyard barbeque. What's the harm?"

"I can't imagine anyplace needed spice where you are."

Jenny frowned into the bourbon as she brought it to her lips.

"You're not hitting on me, right? Because if you are hitting on me I would have to jump out of my skin and find a much better hiding place, like under the foundation of the house or at the bottom of our backyard cistern."

"Am I that disgusting?"

"Creepy is a better word. It took all my good will to forgive you for bringing a prostitute to our party. And now you want me after you've had your prostitute. I have no reserves left dealing with you trying to get some off of me."

"You said Lisa was the hit of the party."

"Right, after I decided I can be ok with it. My kids aren't home and I'm not all that sheltered. By the way I'm glad you've learned her name so quickly."

"I'm a quick study."

"I have to go back to the party. I can only hide for so long," she said as she snatched the bourbon off the table.

"Did Greg ever tell you the story of when we took turns sucking each other's cocks?"

"What did you say?"

"It was before either one of us had ever been blown and we were asking each other what it might be like. Then one of us had the bright idea of performing quid pro quo fellatio."

"He hasn't shared that particular story. Is that why you've come down here, to see if you could rekindle old feelings, maybe have another go round?"

"Actually, I think it cured me of any stray homosexual thoughts I might have had. Halfway through I knew I never would do it again. I didn't like the idea of a dick in my mouth much less the taste. He did cum though, surprisingly."

"What exactly is the purpose of telling this story?" Jenny said in a tone that betrayed a rising anger.

"I wondered if he ever told you the story."

"Why would he tell me that story? There would be no time or place when I can see him divulging that information. I mean, we all experiment. I'm not that surprised, I guess."

"What does that mean?"

"Never mind what it means. You are not somebody I would ever confide in or talk seriously about what it means to be a human being on a lonely planet."

"You keep saying some pretty awful things to me. I don't know what the deputy has told you about me, but I'm really not that much of a monster."

"He told me nothing about you, until about an hour before the party started and he told me he invited you. My own intuition tells me to be repulsed. Now if you will excuse me I prefer to be in a crowd now. I crave being in a crowd."

She followed her drink out of the dining room and back to her guests. Paul readied himself to sit down at the table to assess the damage he had done when he heard a general rise of excitement coming from the backyard as if a fresh crop of lively guests had arrived or the collectively consumed alcohol had finally surged and coaxed them out of their shells at the same moment. He half-expected to see Third Eye with her top off or giving another guest a lap dance, but when he came through the back door he saw nothing of the kind. Some of the guests stood on the patio and others still sat at the table. Deputy Auro and Randall prepared something in the middle of the yard. Paul accidently stopped next to the sheriff who had a beer in each hand, each emptied to about the halfway mark. When he noticed Paul he clicked his tongue and winked. Paul nodded his head in response, but he didn't understand what had been communicated between them, as he looked for Third Eye. He found her sitting close to Leslie and Tammy, whispering into their attentive ears.

"He found some gun powder when he was renovating the barn. Gunpowder, a gold coin, and a stack of waterlogged porno magazines, he told me. I think it's a better idea to break out the pornos depending on what they are and their vintage, because gunpowder can get awfully unstable. Damn fool wants to light it, thinks it's some kind of goddamn entertainment."

The deputy and Randall had created a small stage with a piece of scrap wood and a couple of bricks. In the center stood a cone of gunpowder with an ignition trail traveling from the edge of the cone to the edge of the wood, about a foot away. The deputy whistled shrilly and even Third Eye paused her conspiracy to look up.

"Ladies and gentlemen, I give you fire!"

The deputy lit a wooden match and bent over the gunpowder to ignite the line. When he match touched the powder an enormous ball of green and orange flame shot upwards and engulfed the deputy's head and shoulders. The light was followed by the sound of the air ripping and a surprised gasp from the deputy. The flame disappeared as quickly as it appeared, nothing more than a flash. The deputy spun a half turn away from the staging area as his hands came to his face. Sections of his hair were on fire. He fell to his knees and crushed the box of matches. Randall jumped to his side and put out the burning hair with his hands and the dregs of a club soda he had been drinking. Tammy and the sheriff were the second and third to respond as everyone else had been stunned by the ball of fire. Jenny took a sip or bourbon and sat down in a chair. The air suddenly smelled of burnt hair. Randall and the sheriff held him upright while Tammy checked his face and eyes. Before long they had him on his feet and they led him to the house. He blinked rapidly and couldn't hold a straight line while walking, leaning alternatively on the sheriff and then Randall. They disappeared into the house with Tammy close behind.

Jenny downed her glass and went to the table to fill another. One of the men who Paul had not yet been introduced to sidled up to Jenny as she stood next to the table, pondering whether or not to put ice into his glass. Paul moved a few steps towards her back to hear the conversation, but not many words passed between them. The man said something like, "It must be hard." Jenny blinked off into the distance and responded with, "I can't take much more of this shit." He placed a gentle hand on her shoulder and it became obvious that if they weren't already fucking they would be very soon.

Whether it was her outright rejection of him or her lack of reaction to her husband's head being engulfed by flame, Paul could feel a budding nugget of anger toward her gathering in the pit of his stomach. He felt the sting of unfairness on behalf of Greg; he being the father of her three children who could very well be blind and she securing future dalliances with one of the most bloated of her guests, not counting the sheriff, of course. Even to him her actions felt too dramatic and attention-seeking. Any spouse with an ounce of feeling left toward her partner would have rushed to his side as he sat stricken on the ground and followed the injured party inside to check on his condition, yet here she stood. As it was she assumed the role of aggrieved wife and she expected sympathy for being married to an idiot husband. The fat suburban man looked all too ready to exploit her grievances to his own ends, but beyond his obvious motives no one else assumed a corresponding role in her play. The unspoken consensus was that the scene bespoke deep fissures within the marriage if not an outright break and to engage the wife would show complicity in the union's dissolution. No one, yet, was sure which side to be on, except the bloated suburban man, not even Leslie who had honed her aggrieved wife and then aggrieved ex-wife role in a series of pitch-perfect performances. She had Third Eye on her mind now, and now that Tammy was busy nursing the deputy she could focus all of her energies on Third Eye's glorious body and her stories of inept and frail men.

The other man Paul had not been introduced to walked up to him, held out his hand and called himself something sounding like Blaggert Girthball. Paul gave him the once over and felt the name suited him just fine, so he did not ask him to repeat it for clarification.

"Was the deputy always like this?" Blaggert asked.

"Miserable and desperate?"

"No, was he always a pyro. Every time I come over here he's blowing something up or setting something on fire. You've known the guy forever, right?"

Paul reviewed his memories and came up with at least five examples of fire play when they were children: starting a bonfire in a dead thicket, catching a sewer ditch on fire with a gallon of gasoline, melting army men in a horrific reenactment of Hiroshima, setting their jeans on fire using butane, and destroying every hand-built plastic model, whether it be a car, truck, airplane, movie monster or the Hindenburg using gasoline, firecrackers and matches.

"Yes, I suppose it's safe to say he's probably always been like this."

Blaggert's attention had drifted away as he stopped considering Greg's pyrotechnic history the moment he asked the question.

"What's your name again?"

"I never told you."

"Ok, what's your name then?"

"Paul."

"That exchange was a lot harder that it had to be."

"Nothing in life should be easy."

"Is this a personal philosophy you've developed?"

"Well, Blaggert, you may have seen my line of inspirational and motivational chotskies, coffee mugs, posters, key chains, and vibrators emblazoned with my personal motto, "Live Life Hard." Did you pick up the double entendre with the vibrator, Mr. Girthball? As a matter of fact I have a fresh shipment of them in the trunk of my car so if you like to have your wife shimmy foreign objects up your bung hole they are just the ticket. The only flaw in the design is that they are rather short and I'm thinking you like to take it deep, so tell your wife to hang onto the end or it's going to be a long night in the ER for you with lots of explaining to do."

"Maybe, Paul, I should punch you in the face."

"Oh, Blaggert."

"Stop calling me that."

"Then I would have to return several punches to your head and you would bleed all over those JC Penny khakis and ruin your best barbeque outfit."

"You're drunk."

"Sadly, no."

"Then you're an asshole."

"But I'm not YOUR asshole, because if I were I would be inflamed and engorged from too much input and not enough output."

Blaggert Girthball walked away as he stared at Paul, hoping to produce a menacing retreat. Paul blew him a kiss, but still had a strong enough grip on his rational side to wonder about the purpose of provoking Blaggert until he felt abused enough to warrant a fistfight. He took a couple of steps towards Blaggert's new position, but his progress was impeded by the reemergence of the sheriff out of the back door. Paul watched the sheriff walk over to Jenny and inform her of the deputy's condition. She took a sip of bourbon and shook her head slowly in resignation, fury, or refusal. Her expression remained unchanged and her body sank deeper into the chair. The sheriff staggered over to the cooler and pulled out a beer for each hand and then settled back into the chair he had occupied before dinner. Tammy came out of the back door and also beat a path to Jenny. Jenny politely smiled at her and nodded her head as she listened to a rather long and detailed explanation of her husband's condition. Greg bounded out of the door, wearing a fresh shirt and having combed and slicked back his burned hair just as Leslie finished giving the diagnosis.

The deputy walked over to the cooler and reached down to open the lid. He missed twice and then fumbled for the edge before he successfully opened it up and retrieved a beer. He tried to read the label from several distances, but none of the positions produced satisfactory results. He sauntered over to the largest knot of people and tried to fit in, all the while squinting and blinking. He happened to end up standing next to Paul, who was now half-listening to a conversation between Third Eye, Leslie and the last man at the party he did not know. They were soon joined by Randall Highland. They talked about tattoos and, of course, Third Eye had the most to say about the subject as she had seen a multitude of designs and locations in her travels and had even "dated" one or two tattoo artists in the past. Paul couldn't be sure, but he thought she said her favorite of all time belonged to a man who had transformed his penis into a sea serpent, whose mouth opened to bare fangs when the member became fully engorged. The men winced at the thought of such a canvas and guessed they would never be able to pull off the audacity of such a work of art.

Paul tuned to the deputy who pretended to follow the conversation, but he really was engaged in a struggle to stay on his feet and suppress cries of pain. His neck, right ear, and the right side of his face had turned an angry red and parts had begun swelling. Topical burn cream gave his face a greasy sheen. The majority of both eyebrows had been burned off. Paul looked a little closer and thought his eyelashes were gone as well and that his forehead looked three inches higher than it had before he lit the gunpowder. Sweat and burn cream dripped from his chin.

"How you feeling there, pal?" Paul asked.

The deputy turned his head and winced through the movement.

"I'm good. I'm good. You enjoying the party?" He blinked six times without clearing whatever blocked his vision, apparently.

"That's going to sting in the morning."

Third Eye just then made a hissing noise and used her hand to mime a striking cobra, which she followed with a loud and lusty laugh. Leslie joined in and they sounded ready to do something wicked. Paul planned on being present when their desires bubbled into action. Paul again inspected Third Eye, hoping at some point to be repulsed by her body and personality, but he found that hope so distant as to be considered impossible. Why not try to land one of the trim divorcees with a straightforward advance? They seemed unhinged enough to sleep with him. Maybe they could strike-up a cross state romance. He had never dated someone who lived three and half hours away and the idea suddenly appealed to him. God, he thought, I need to do something besides chasing after a fat whore.

He turned back to the deputy in time to see him wobble, try to brace himself against an imaginary solid, and fall to one knee, while keeping his beer from spilling. Paul watched as once again Randall and Tammy sprang into action. They stood on either side of the deputy and propped him up by keeping ahold of his shoulders. Tammy relieved him of his beer and tossed it on the ground. Jenny finally stirred and came over to where the deputy stood, holding a fresh bourbon in a new and larger glass.

"He really needs to go to the emergency room and get checked out," said Randall as Jenny approached.

"I can't take him, Randall. I have a yard full of people and somebody will have to pick up the kids tonight."

"I think we'll all understand, Jennifer, if the party ends a little early, for goodness sakes."

"I'm not taking him, Randall. If you want to take him, super."

"I'm ok. I just need to lie down," the deputy said to Jenny.

She gave him a withering look and took a sip of her drink.

"Seriously, Greg, gunpowder? That was your idea of entertainment?"

"The sheriff said it was unstable."

"Think about that for a moment. The sheriff has more commonsense than you do? Is this what I have to look forward to?"

"No, no, no, no, no, no," the assurances trailed off to a whisper and then became inaudible under his breath.

"Look, I'm Leslie's ride and we might be in the ER for hours," said Tammy.

"My God, this yard is thick with compassion. He was just trying to give us a thrill," Randall sneered.

"You take him, then," Jenny countered. "Or let's call an ambulance."

"No, I'll take him. Can you make sure my wife gets home somehow? She's going to be so goddamn mad at me for stranding her here," he said as he pointed to Jenny. "You owe me big time."

"Ah, Randall, just add it to my debt. I'd advise you, though, to get your claim in before I declare bankruptcy. My debt load is so large I can barely keep up with the payments."

Randall turned on Paul with sudden fury. "Can you at least help me get him to the car?"

"I didn't know I had any responsibility here."

"Just help me get him to the car, so these ladies can get back to their party. God knows I don't want to be a wet blanket."

"You're so very thoughtful, Randall," Jenny said acidly.

"I can get up on my own. I was just a little dizzy."

The deputy lurched up and would have landed face first in the grass if not for the quick hands and strength of Tammy and Randall. After they steadied him Paul moved in to replace Tammy, hooking his arm under Greg's arm. They walked him to Randall's car, a beat-up ten year old Civic with three missing hubcaps and a constellation of small dents that pocked its skin. The deputy wheezed through his nose as the burned areas grew crimson from the additional motion. He asked his escort if they had seen what happened, if he had accidently touched the match to the large pile of gunpowder. Both shrugged and didn't give voice to their answers. He asked again and Paul reminded him that the sheriff said the gunpowder had been unstable and too old.

"The sheriff is right about almost everything. You wouldn't know by looking at him."

"Or talking to him," Randall added.

They wrangled him into the front seat of the car and Randall drove away with a scowl on his face. Paul fingered the keys in his pocket and wondered if he had done enough or if he had done anything. Had he been a mere witness to a disaster already in motion or had he been the provocateur who had added the last chemical to an unstable brew? Whatever the case he felt what he considered guilt and guessed he would share in the blame once the details were sorted and the narrative formed, even though he had nothing to do with the sequence of bad decisions that led to the gunpowder exploding in the deputy's face. How could his introduction of Third Eye not somehow be linked to the deputy's accident? Paul guessed that by tomorrow the two threads would forever be sewn together as the deputy's burned face would not make sense unless some time was spent explaining that a prostitute had come to the party and upset the balance of the barbeque and led him to perform a rash and ill-conceived trick. On the other hand if a guest wanted to tell the story of the time they went to a backyard barbeque and a fiend from Cleveland showed up with a real working whore-fortuneteller, how could they not bring it all to a rousing conclusion with the burning of the deputy? Paul accepted the inevitability that the deputy's second-degree burns would morph into complete and irrevocable blindness, scorched lungs, his scalp covered in third-degree burns, showing bone, and even death. The death card was indeed used by the sheriff at a Memorial Day picnic a few years later in a drunken response to a teenager's inquiry if any of his deputies had ever been killed on the job. The sheriff dwelled on Third Eye, described her costume, her nine inches of cleavage, and told the boy her perfume smelled like pussy, before going into the tragic end of the deputy who sucked fire into his lungs. Befuddled, the boy couldn't tell if the story would have any bearing on his decision to pursue a career in law enforcement or not.

Paul leaned against his car and did not feel compelled to go back to the party now that the deputy had been carted away, even when he thought of Leslie's intentions for Third Eye. He tried looking at the sky, growing gray and the moon, hanging heavy, but the contrast between eternal placidity and his raging and tangled thoughts highlighted his growing sickness. He closed his eyes and let his thoughts reign. He entertained an idea of falling asleep on the grass, but he knew it would be hours before sleep would come to him. Blaggert Girthball came around the corner with his wife in tow. They didn't acknowledge Paul even though they passed a few feet from him on their way to their car. Next came suburban man and his wife. He walked a few feet in front of her and she looked half-drunk and angry as she kicked up stones with every step, the purpose of which seemed to be to hit suburban man in the back of the legs.

"How is he?" suburban man asked as he passed.

Paul shrugged. "You tell me."

"How the hell would I know?"

"What do you know? What do you know?" his wife shouted. "You've got everything to say to everybody. Oh, man, trotting out stories I've never heard, laughing, telling jokes like you're practicing a stand-up routine. But just wait until you get into the car. I won't hear another word from you for the rest of the night. Get ready everybody, he's about to turn to stone. I married a goddamn statue, unless you introduce him to a whore, then he lights up."

They reached their car and suburban man slipped behind the wheel without returning fire and he stared blankly at the play of fireflies through his windshield. The wife got in and continued the badgering but fortunately the windows remained up and the diatribe was effectively silenced. Paul stood at his car until he was tired of waiting for the others as he thought the party would break completely up. As he walked back he passed the sheriff and Randall Highland's wife, who were leaving as well. The sheriff looked as straight as if he had just drunk his first morning cup of coffee, even though he had just consumed more than a case of beer. Randall's wife, mousy and slump-shouldered, followed in his wake with her eyes focused on the ground.

"There he is. I didn't think you'd leave that woman behind. Now's about the time she earns her keep. I bet she's a pistol."

Randall's wife rolled her eyes and tried to hang back in case in case more inappropriate comments followed.

"More like a thirty ought six." While Paul could barely summon the energy to finish the joke, it had a great effect on the sheriff who nearly doubled over with laughter.

Randall's wife crossed her arms and waited for the gale to blow over.

"Can we just go," she said.

The sheriff's laughter stopped short and he leered at her through a squinted eye. "Maybe you could learn a thing or two from her old girl. I guarantee it would keep Randall in the barn."

"That's not something I have to worry about."

"Sure, sure, the number one attribute of men is fidelity."

"That's enough, sheriff. I can walk home."

"Elizabeth, you know it's seven miles of lonely country road between here and your house. You and I both know you're not walking. We're going to lose all the light in about twenty minutes. Maybe just try to roll with the jokes and you'll feel fine."

The sheriff started walking to his car and she let him take five or six steps before she followed. When she passed Paul she whispered under her breath, "I don't know how he keeps getting elected. Can you imagine voting for a man like him?"

"I heard that, Elizabeth. Maybe next time you or Randall can try to take me out," the sheriff said over his shoulder, punctuated by a braying laugh.

Elizabeth's face turned crimson, but she followed him to the car.

Paul walked to the backyard, but it had been abandoned. The remnants of food and drink sat on the tables, plastic cups lay on the ground, and the chairs remained cocked at various angles from where conversations had taken place. Even the cooler from which the sheriff drank and his chair remained in place. Paul entered the house through the back door and checked the kitchen, dining room and the balance of the first floor but he could find no signs of Jenny, Third Eye and the other two. He went back outside and tried the barn doors, but they were locked. He went around to the back of the barn and saw that the yard sloped down to a thick pasture toward a creek bed. Halfway down the slope stood a line of mature trees, planted in a row decades ago. Through the trees he could see a small yellow light and movements of shadow.

He scuffled toward the movement. He thought of the deputy's father squatting in the dust, humbling himself before his savior, and he hoped the old man didn't live on the property. As he approached he heard the rumbling of a motor and once he passed the trees he could see the outline of three forms inside the hot tub. Having just held the memory of Andy Auro in the throes of religious ecstasy,

Paul may have confessed to being a little disappointed at the discovery, since he was half-expecting to discover a blood sacrifice being performed in the dark woods. He hung in the shadows for a moment and watched Tammy and then Leslie kiss Third Eye on the mouth and rub her tits. Third Eye stayed in the center, warmly accepting the return of each satellite as they alternated engaging her. Paul was not much of a voyeur, as he preferred action to watching, so he stepped out of the shadows and walked to the edge of the tub.

"I don't remember agreeing to a sublease. I've paid good money for these services and I turn my back for a half hour and catch you double, well actually, triple-dripping. You have to love your entrepreneurial spirit," Paul said as the women paused.

"Who said this isn't part of the service? What man hasn't dreamed of stumbling upon three naked wood nymphs who are as horny and drunk as they are naked," said Third Eye.

"And we can only hope the lost traveler has the cock of a horse and the stamina of a tri-athlete..." Tammy said as she started laughing, which set off Leslie in a howl, before she could get through stating her challenge and fantasy.

"Sadly, ladies, I will only disappoint if you begin with those expectations."

"Let's see what you've got!" Leslie blurted more loudly and aggressively than she intended, so it sounded more like a guttural demand than a sexy come-on.

Paul didn't know what to do and he looked to Third Eye for guidance. She gave him a kind smile and beckoned him into the water. He would have preferred the other two drown so he could nestle against her flesh unmolested, but he didn't hesitate to undress and join them. Both Tammy and Leslie gave an encouraging cheer when they caught sight of his cock that had already become half erect. Tammy reached out, grabbed the knob, and pulled him into the circle as if his penis was the handle to a pull toy. She pulled him to his knees and he suddenly became aware that he could be the blood sacrifice he had been expecting, that he had actually stumbled upon a satanic ritual and that they had been waiting for him to complete the ceremony. He leaned forward to bury his face between Third Eye's wet and shimmering breasts. As he did so a mouth kissed his right ear, another mouth kissed him on the neck, a finger went up his asshole, and a foot pressed against his cock and balls. Paul marveled at the variety of life as a week before he had never had sex with more than one woman at a time and now he perched on the edge of consummating his second such session. He couldn't yet understand if this development in his life would turn out positive or negative, but he knew he had Third Eye to thank for it all and he figured he would have to find a way to keep her in his life to see what might come next.

As for actual sex very little happened in the hot tub beyond fingering and stroking. They fumbled, groped, and kissed but everyone's genitals were encased in hot water and the women remained too practical to risk pushing communal water up their vaginas. Paul thought he saw Jenny looking stern, with arms folded and her face molded into a glare, standing on the edge of the shadows. He busied himself with the nipples of Leslie and waited for Jenny to either join them or stop the festivities with a rant about decency and etiquette, but neither happened and when Paul looked at the spot where he thought she had been she had disappeared.

After all of them had been rubbed raw, had their faces turn beet red from the steam, and had the alcohol blunted from the heat and grinding, Tammy decided she really wanted to be fucked and Third Eye granted her wish because the truth be told she found herself wanting to be back in the hotel room with the old man snoring beside her while she watched pay-per-view rather than being the fourth in this sad quartet. Leslie also backed away because Tammy's wound was fresh, the pain of her divorce more palpable, and her drive toward self-annihilation more real than her own. Leslie, in rare moments of candor, would admit that she long ago had processed and dispatched the pain of her divorce, but she held onto the unmarried life, the alcohol, the weed, the frequent and diverse population of sexual partners, and the frantic and desperate clutching onto experiences no matter how sordid or counter to the principles she claimed once to hold, because she preferred this life to the monotony of marriage. She only had to remember her drunken ex-husband snoring and farting in front of the television and she wishing by some miracle that he would die in his sleep to cure her of any impulse of running back into matrimony.

Leslie regretted her acquiescence as she watched Tammy and Paul climb out of the tub and Paul take her from behind right next to a child's plastic toy lawn mower and a sandbox. Leslie turned to Third Eye who welcomed her into her arms and cradled her against her tits, understanding the sacrifices you sometimes had to make for friends. Paul knew that had he been left on his own to pick up and fuck Tammy in the space of an evening he would have had zero chance of success. He exhibited no charm, mystery, or hint of dangerous excitement that could charm women. His success had always come with a slow erosion of a woman's defenses as he understood that given time and patience a woman would settle and succumb if nothing better came along. But he was not ungrateful for the opportunity because Tammy had a lovely shape. Her hips were full and round and her skin felt incredibly soft and was free of pimples, scars, or sun damage. He worked on her a long time as the alcohol and heat had dampened his sensation, but they managed to orgasm at roughly the same time. Their combined cry echoed through the weeds and woods and even Third Eye turned to watch the collapse of their passion.

They climbed back into the hot tub. Tammy squirreled in between Third Eye and Leslie. Paul was left by himself on the opposite side. He understood the clear message behind the positioning that the sex was meant to be practically anonymous and Tammy would have preferred either Third Eye, Leslie or both to have had a dick to accomplish the deed and that he shouldn't feel any ownership or pride due to his random genetic accomplishment.

Soon, the quartet took on a post-coital atmosphere of remorse, like when a drunken couple wakes up reasonably sober and embarrassed at their choice of partners and at the impulses that pushed them to make such a bad and desperate choice. Really, only Tammy suffered such a crisis of conscience and brought all the others down, since nothing could be satisfactory about a contrite exhibitionist. She turned toward Leslie and put a hand on her shoulder.

"Do you think I'm a freak?" she asked. "That wasn't like me."

Leslie laughed. "Oh, darling, I would have been right down there with you if he had two dicks. I'd do it now, but he's not getting it up again."

Leslie hugged her to her chest and as they began to kiss Paul looked toward Third Eye. He knew Leslie's assertion had been made to salve Tammy's worried mind. He could get erect again immediately, but he wanted to leave, so he let the challenge pass. Third Eye also wanted to go so they crawled out of the hot tub and stood naked in the grass. They hadn't brought towels, of course, so they had to slip on their clothes over their wet bodies, which was less of an issue for Third Eye since so little cloth covered her skin. They walked back in silence as the hum of the hot tub motor drifted over the lawn. They looked like dispirited fans whose team had just lost on a shot at the buzzer as they walked away from the jubilant fans of the home team. Their mood lightened once they reached the car and they could no longer hear the motor.

"Do you think we will be invited back?"

Third Eye laughed. It was an honest, full-bellied release and Paul smiled because he had elicited it from her.

"It's been my experience that once you get naked at someone's house without permission and without involving one of the hosts, you aren't asked back."

"Like a swinger's house. That would involve one or both of the hosts. They would want you to be naked and they would probably ask you back."

"Would you really want to go back to a swinger's house? Really?"

"What's your beef with swingers? Do they cut into your market share?"

"You know, the old man never brings up that I'm a whore. He pays his money and buys the illusion along with the sex. You, on the other hand, never let it go. You never stop thinking about the money. You want to flog yourself with the idea that you paid to have a friend. You're a complete asshole. Do you ever wonder why you have to pay for companionship?"

"I just wanted to know what problem you have with swingers. It doesn't seem logical to me."

"Look, at least the men that pay me think sex is worth *something*. You know, divide my fee by the number of hours a guy has to work in order to earn the money and you start to get a greater appreciation about how much it means to them. I have *value*. But a woman swinger is thinking just the opposite. Her pussy has no value. She believes in free access and her need is bottomless. I guess you could argue in the economics of that world the husband or boyfriend uses her pussy as a commodity to get new pussy, but it seems to me that it has been devalued to the point of being worthless. No one looks forward to fucking her. They expect it. She's a receptacle. That's the definition of swinging to me. It's not like I have anything against them. For me, if I'm going to fuck everyone who comes along they are going to pay for the privilege."

"I don't think that answers my question. You asked why I would want to go back to a swinger's house once I got naked with them. It seems like a pretty good deal to me."

"You mean like tonight. You were lucky tonight. Any man at that party could have banged that poor sap Tammy, even the deputy after he burned his face off. Plus you had me as a commodity. You need to bring a woman as the price of admission. You need something to barter, right? So, if you want to fuck some new and strange pussy you better bring some old and familiar pussy to gain access. I don't see you being able to do it. I think you want people to believe you're nihilistic, but I don't believe it for a second. You would have liked to go to that party with a real girlfriend and lightly flirted with the wives and talked golf or whatever with the khaki crew. You would have liked someone to ask you about your job and stay interested throughout the detailed and boring explanation. You might be bored sometimes or frustrated that you haven't gone farther, but you still believe in the system and you believe in society as a whole. You think it will all work out for you one day. You'll find the right woman. You'll find the right job. You can't walk away. You can't chuck it all or burn it all to the ground. You'll be like the old man, still looking until your last breath. So, if you think swinging and nihilism is the way to go just know it won't be like tonight. Swinging would be like everybody gets into the hot tub and you get to spank some hot little wife while right next to you a line of guys pulls a train on your girlfriend or she blows a horse cock that makes your dick look like a hanging clit. I could feel you getting jealous of those two ladies rubbing on me and I'm not even close to being your girlfriend. So, no, I don't think it would be a good deal for you. You'd be a mess watching your girlfriend blow someone else. Some men can do it and believe me when I tell you those are people you want to stay away from. Those are the true nihilists, right to their core. It's one thing to hate the government or the cops but to not feel the slightest bit possessive about your woman is one of the darkest places to live."

"It sounds like you have personal experience on this topic."

"If you think I'm going to tell you anything about my personal life you are sadly, sadly mistaken."

"Why not?"

"Because I once shared some personal stories with a client and afterwards he thought he was my boyfriend. Even he felt possession, for God's sake. It was all I could do to keep him off my back. I carried a .38 for a year after that."

"Don't worry. I'll never think of you as my girlfriend. I am free of possession. But now you're making me think that's a bad thing."

"It can spring up on you when you don't expect it. Christ, is it really that late? The old man will be wondering where I am at? He won't sleep until I get there."

"Sounds like a boyfriend."

"Shut up and drive. I'm so damn tired. All this talk has wiped me out."

They fell silent and within a couple of minutes Third Eye softly snored. Dense black forest towered above them on either side of the road. Paul rolled down the window and let humid summer air slide across his arm. He smiled at the thought of the deputy's burned face and he silently thanked Third Eye for her contribution.

14

The Bells of Coronado

Paul did not see Third Eye again until the night of the play. He chalked it up to her having to make up to the old man. The morning and afternoon after the party he stalked the restaurant and lobby, but he had no luck seeing her. By early evening he felt exhausted and jittery until the hotel staff finally drove him to his room by asking for the third or fourth time if he needed any help. He knew his behavior gave proof to Third Eye's observations of the previous night, because he was, in fact, acting like a jealous boyfriend. But he didn't care. He just needed to see her, talk to her, and maybe touch the flesh of her arm while they talked. He couldn't risk humiliating himself with a phone call. The old man would probably answer and his fever would be exposed. He decided to stay in his room until the play. He kept the curtains closed, ordered room service for all his meals, and never turned the television off.

Paul arrived at the church an hour before Blue Cowboy had asked him to come, and he found that all the other cast and crew had arrived as well, all except Third Eye. Blue Cowboy acted highly agitated as he bounded between helping to secure the scenery, to checking the sound system, to giving the script one last read through before the performance. He did it all dressed in a luxurious white robe with RR embroidered over his heart and his best pair of cowboy boots that had the complete lyrics to *Home on the Range* stitched into the leather. His forehead already glistened with a sheen of sweat as the church sweltered under an early afternoon sun and the robe was really too thick to be worn anytime other than the dead of winter.

Paul found his costume and meticulously dressed. He tried eight different positions for the kerchief tied around his neck. He finally settled on a broad triangle below his chin as if the kerchief had just been used as a mask, possibly in a bank hold-up or as protection in a dust storm. Nevertheless, the kerchief spoke to Paul of virility and action, danger and self-reliance. These motifs collapsed, however, as he assembled the rest of his outfit. The shirt was too tight and the checker pattern too broad as if purposely introducing the notion of parody and his jeans were too tight and slick so that effeminacy gathered steam as well. The cowboy boots looked elfin as they slightly curled up at the end because of disuse. His belt was too thin, so instead of looking indestructible and at home on the range it looked appropriate to hold up dress pants in a climate-controlled glass box built between a strip mall and a cow pasture. He rallied though once he donned the cowboy hat, a crisp black beauty with a vaguely Native American pattern around the band, and leather chaps, which effectively covered the pants and framed his crotch in such a way as to make it look dynamic and robust.

Third Eye and the old man arrived about an hour before the performance was to begin. Apparently, Blue Cowboy had been in phone contact with her several times so he managed to hold his panic to a tolerable level. She came dressed for the part, wearing a denim min-skirt that ended just under her buttocks, a denim vest with bare cowgirls stitched on either side of the buttons, pink cowboy boots, and a pink cowboy hat that had been flecked with glitter. Because of the heat, she decided not to wear a shirt under the vest so that her smashed and lifted breasts created a shelf and a line of cleavage perpendicular to her sternum. Paul judged the costume indecent even by her standards, but he figured no one under fifty would be in the audience, so no one could use the excuse of protecting children from the sight of a woman's body as a reason for their indignation. Paul imagined Third Eye coercing the dicks of the assembled men into a standing ovation as their wives dreamed of flaunting their bodies in front of a room full of hungry and excited strangers.

Blue Cowboy finally dressed himself. He had been right to wait, because when he was assembled he dazzled the cast and crew and some may have privately thought that Roy Rogers himself had never looked better. His pants and shirt were matching blue, of course, but the fabric caught the light in such a way as to create an aura of luminescence. His boots had been buffed until the leather had taken on the qualities of a mirror. His bolo tie had been fashioned out of a buckeye, an obvious and effective nod to Rogers' Ohio roots as well as the site of the festival, but tasteful enough not to be considered pandering. The red kerchief that he tied around his neck appeared starched and without a misplaced crease or wrinkle. His cowboy hat looked like it had been taken from a sealed room free of dust, ultraviolet light, and the greasy touch of human hands. Paul thought it looked like a crown of glory rather than a practical invention to keep heat and light away from a cowboy's head. When Blue Cowboy walked a pair of spurs jangled against the floor, leaving little nicks wherever he stepped, a desecration sure to make the Baptists hopping mad.

The audience was late arriving and a half hour before the curtain was to rise Blue Cowboy resigned himself to performing for the old man and an overweight couple who dressed in the same shades of pastels. His anxiety lessened, though, as people began to file in, griping that the church did not have a clearly marked address and the driveway had been hard to find as it was blocked from the street by a line of overgrown hedges. Soon, all the seats were taken. Opening night was a sellout and a few of the latecomers even decided to suffer the inconvenience of standing along the back wall through the performance, but most felt the heat radiating out of the door, saw the overcrowded room, and decided to find something else to do.

The cast had retreated into the office of the pastor that was located just off the altar behind a hollow wood door that felt like it weighed nothing when opened or closed. The office had been decorated sparsely with a large wood crucifix hanging on the wall above a single metal desk and a beat-up faux leather chair. The pastor's diploma from Maranatha Baptist Bible College hung on the opposite wall from the crucifix next to three photos, one of a blond woman, radiating clean living through radiant skin and polished teeth, and one each of a pair of twin daughters who looked like cloned replicas of the mother. Paul thought their happiness palpable and their philosophy for living righteous and sure.

The crew had strung a curtain from the edge of the door to the altar/stage so the characters could come and go with some cover. The buzz and heat from the audience came through to them through the curtain and each one of them, even Third Eye, took turns peeking at the full house. Besides Paul, Third Eye and Blue Cowboy, the cast consisted of five other men who played all of the parts of the chorus, gang members, foreign terrorists, and the other bit parts, as they were really just props to the resplendent display that was Blue Cowboy and Third Eye. Two of them were retired school teachers. A junior high biology teacher who had moved to within fifty miles of Roy Rogers' California ranch once he had put his time in and a social studies teacher who in his later years as an educator became bored with the European immigration into the Americas, the diaspora of the Africans, the American Revolution, the Civil War, settlement, expansion, and Manifest Destiny, really the bulk of his curriculum, although he could sometimes get excited about the Teapot Dome scandal, Chester Arthur and the building of the Erie Canal, so his lectures drifted toward pop culture and by his last two years Roy Rogers films and other westerns taught his students everything they would need to know about the American West. The third had been a railroad engineer who began his career with the Baltimore and Ohio Railroad, who regaled his audience with tales from the rails whenever a railroad or, for that matter, Monopoly, happened to be mentioned. The fourth was a working television and radio voiceover specialist whose most recognizable work had been for a wart elimination cream and a decade's long campaign for a medicated foot powder. His trained voice rose above the attempts of the rest of the cast and he had the most natural acting ability, but his morbid obesity and terror of performing in front of a live audience sabotaged his advancement towards securing leads. The fifth extra had given himself the label of unemployed for the five years he had been coming to the festival, but now it felt more like a cover story than an actual status, so the festival-goers filled in the gaps, coming up with drug dealing, stolen car selling, a hidden trust fund, and a never seen wife who worked like a dog so he could pursue his transitory dreams as possible sources of income. All six men, including Blue Cowboy, took turns eyeing Third Eye and giving Paul approving nods or winks as they imagined her flesh next to theirs, to simmer down the giddiness and panic they felt, given they were about to make complete asses of themselves in front of their families and friends.

As impressive as Third Eye's flesh was, no one could doubt that Blue Cowboy was the real star of the show and had the most to gain or lose with the performance as he strode around the office in a tight circle in the small space, his spurs clicking. They all felt small and dirty next to him. Paul inspected his own haphazard costume and accepted himself as the fool in Blue Cowboy's court. Paul experienced a random thought of unzipping Blue Cowboy's pants and sucking his cock, not for the sexual nature of the act but as an act of complete submission. In the world of Roy Rogers fandom there could only be one king and his acolytes and hangers-on should cater to his whims. Since Paul may have had a cock in his mouth only once before he had trouble using his faint memories for the basis of his humbling act, but he could think of nothing else that would make manifest the powerlessness that he felt. Finally, he broke the impulse by thinking of Tammy splayed on the grass before him and calculated if it would be economically feasible to hire Third Eye as a guide to introduce him to the world of anonymous group sex.

The lights dimmed and Blue Cowboy barked an order to get ready. Paul was about to go onstage with a full-fledged erection pressing against his weird jeans. Still, he couldn't really be sure if his excitement came from his speculative homosexuality or his reverie of the hot tub.

The cast walked onstage. Blue Cowboy and Third Eye led and the extras hung in the back. When the lights came up they sang "The Bells of Coronado" as an overture. The notes came weakly at first but by the end of the first pass through they charged the audience with confidence and volume. The extras drifted offstage and Third Eye and Blue Cowboy sang the song again as a duet. After they finished they embraced and Blue Cowboy sang the third passthrough a cappella. The audience leaned forward, riveted, as he sparkled in the light and his baritone shook the walls.

As he held the last note the lights went down. The play had begun with a triumph. Blue Cowboy stayed onstage and mimed a general ranch task, either fixing a wire on a fence or slicing the throat of a deformed calf to make a veal dinner. Two men approached him from the left, the two school teachers looking official in bowler bats and black vests.

ERNIE

Well, if it isn't old Ray Regan, himself.

BERNIE

That's certainly him, working his ranch and making the land work for him.

RAY

Hey Ernie! Hello Bernie! What brings you all the way out here? I know you didn't come out here on a cordial visit with your busy schedules.

BERNIE

Well, Ray. First of all you don't have a phone, so what choice do we have but to come out here?

ERNIE

Secondly, we have an assignment. That is if you can break away from the ranch work.

RAY

You know I'm always ready. That is if the assignment doesn't include assassination, the disabling of an economy, or fermenting general unrest in an unsuspecting populace. I'm retired from that work. That's a young man's game and I have my cows, my Chinese cook, and all the open space I'll ever need to live in freedom.

ERNIE

I thought we were never to speak of that work, Ray.

BERNIE

We're amongst friends and the culpable, Ernie

ERNIE

We still agreed to never speak of it.

RAY

My apologies. What do you boys want with me, anyway?

ERNIE

We own insurance companies now, Ray.

BERNIE

There's a fortune to be made every day. There's so much fear and anxiety. The house always wins, know what I'm saying, Ray?

RAY

Sounds like that idea you have of building a casino in the desert.

ERNIE

Just waiting on some creative financing.

BERNIE

People will be lined up, wanting to throw their life savings at us. They can't stand having the filthy lucre in their hands. They don't want to think about what it took for them to earn it, save it, resist the temptation of spending it. Oh, Ray, I'll have to hire a fleet of Brink's trucks to haul away my money.

RAY

Well, you boys always seem to know how to make money. Sometimes I think you have a printing press hidden somewhere and you just print the money you want.

ERNIE

Governments start getting ruffled when you print their money. They take too big of a cut to make it profitable.

BERNIE

You don't look like you've done so bad for yourself, Ray.

RAY

America has opened herself wide for this half-Cherokee boy.

ERNIE

See, Ray, it's like this. We've taken a gamble. A big gamble.

BERNIE

We should have known better. We should have known it was a sucker bet.

ERNIE

See, a couple of years back we started insuring mining operations. Basically, you're insuring against cave-ins and collapses, but these don't happen as often as you think and it's pretty easy to prove negligence against the company. They are always using rotten timbers to brace the walls or old dynamite and they throw out just about every safety precaution for the sake of production.

RAY

I'm not proud to say you're losing me here, Ernie.

BERNIE

What Ernie is trying to say, Ray, is that we took a flyer...

ERNIE

A bigger risk than we usually take.

BERNIE

That's right, we got into uranium.

RAY

That stuff is pretty hot from what I hear.

BERNIE

Bombs and energy. It'll power everything in the future. I'm willing to bet in twenty years your toaster will be run on nuclear energy. Maybe everyone will have a little reactor right there in the toaster itself.

ERNIE

One of the shipments is missing, Ray. Hijacked right off the trail. The mine owner is dead, so we know he wasn't trying to pull a fast one, or if he was he's the victim of a double cross.

BERNIE

If we don't find the shipment we'll be ruined. The payment is huge. Our damned underwriters forgot to include acts of theft. A rookie mistake, but, nevertheless, our dreams of desert casinos will be up in smoke.

RAY

And you want me to go to the mine and find out what happened?

ERNIE

And find the shipment. We suspect foreign nationals or terrorists. This is high grade stuff.

RAY

Where's the mine?

BERNIE

Coronado, just west of the Rata Sucia Mountains and east of the Bolas de Baja River.

RAY

I know it well. I went to the university there for a time. I often think of the lush valley and the groves of poplar and elm.

ERNIE

There's no university there, Ray.

BERNIE

You're getting your pasts mixed up again. Are you sure you're up for another job?

ERNIE

The place was built on scrub land. There's not a decent-sized tree in sight. We're talking about the desert here, friend. A wasteland.

BERNIE

We know you were one of the best, but maybe all these years out here with your Chinaman has dulled your senses.

RAY

Boys, boys, easy now. I'm just the same as I've always been. This has nothing to do with the Chinaman.

ERNIE

Good to hear, Ray.

BERNIE

So, find the shipment, Ray, and we'll pay you handsomely. You'll be able to keep the Chinaman in rice for the rest of his natural life.

ERNIE

And you'll be able to sleep at night, knowing that the uranium is out of the hands of the terrorists.

RAY

I'm a darn good insurance investigator.

BERNIE

Without insurance where would we be?

ERNIE

In caves, Ray, living in caves and afraid to do anything for the fear of being sued.

BERNIE

You don't want to see the world without insurance, Ray. A world without managed risk is....unthinkable.

ERNIE

I'll tell you what it would be like. It would be like a world without oil or electricity.

RAY

I hate to break it to you, boys, but I have neither oil nor electricity on the ranch.

BERNIE

Oh, sure, Ray, that's good enough for you because you don't mind living in the Stone Age, but electricity is coming to every godforsaken corner of the earth. And good roads! The interstate!

ERNIE

We could have called you, Ray, or driven out here, instead of riding all this way on a horse and getting saddle sore. Do you know how much commerce has happened since we've left our offices? Whole national economies have risen and fallen in the hours we've spent on those two nags.

BERNIE

Before I forget, you're going to need this. (He picked up a box from the floor and handed it to Ray.)

BERNIE

A Geiger counter. It will help you find the uranium.

(Ray picked up the wand and turned on the machine. He pointed it at Bernie and nothing happened. Then, he pointed it at Ernie and the counter started wildly clicking and emitted a Theremin sound.)

ERNIE

Don't ask.

BERNIE

I tell him he's like a ticking time bomb, but will he listen?

(Ray turned off the machine.)

RAY

Next stop Coronado!

(The lights went down.)

SCENE TWO

The radio announcer (the character Sparrow) stood on stage alone, trying to do rope tricks with very little success. He came across as a good-natured idiot. Blue Cowboy entered stage right. He broke out a wide grin at Sparrow's idiocy. He acted as if he was neither a threat intellectually nor physically, so he broke into a relaxed and easy gait.

RAY

Sparrow, old friend, are you still working on your rope tricks?

SPARROW

(does not really break his concentration) Oh hi, Ray. They won't have you on cattle drives if they know you can't use a rope.

RAY

That's the greeting I get after all these years.

SPARROW

A man's got to know his rope work, Ray.

RAY

How many cattle drives are there now, Sparrow? They ship them mostly by train now, right? You've heard of a cattle car I take it?

SPARROW

(He looked at Ray blankly) A man has to know his rope.

RAY

(He broke into another wide and superior grin, delighted by Sparrow's incompetency once again.) Let me see that rope.

Sparrow handed him the rope. Ray tested the weight, found the right hold and tightened the lasso. His face fell expressionless and he began twirling the lasso at his side. The loop became a blur as Ray spun his wrist. He let out the rope and the lasso crept forward like a predator and threatened to break loose from his control, but with a flick it retreated and became his pet once again. He spun it harder and raised it over his head. The rope took on the qualities of a tornado and Ray looked like an avenging judge stepping out of the mists of purgatory. Ray took a step or two toward the audience and they recoiled in fear and mistrust that he could keep the rope's power from harming them. He raised the rope to its apex and widened its circumference until it seemed like it could consume the whole stage. Ray whipped his arm furiously to keep it aloft and the sound of his whipping arm and the rope slicing through the air combined to create a low growl. Then, tired of the monster at the end of his arm he let the rope collapse and crash into a pile around his feet and what looked like a mistake at first turned out to be a transitional move, bridging the gap between the ferocious beast and a playful kitten gamboling at his feet in a series of tumbles, figure-eights, and waves. Sparrow stood off to the side, hands on his hips, shaking his head in disbelief.

Anamorphic shapes jumped from the rope: a snake, a bear, a horse with rider, and an eagle. The audience clapped as each one appeared and several among them thought they would have been sufficiently entertained with more rope and fewer words. Blue Cowboy's instinct had been right to insert the act early in the play as he had now generated enough good will to carry it to the end. As a finale he gave a quick recap of all of the tricks in his arsenal and then pounded the rope three times against the stage and each time it bounded high into the air. The fourth time he threatened to bang the rope, but he simply let go of it. The rope quivered, shuddered, and fell limp. The audience roared and spontaneously jumped to their feet. Blue Cowboy broke character and bowed. It was a brief moment of absolute triumph. Blue Cowboy handed the rope back to Sparrow.

RAY

Here you go, Sparrow. I hope I taught you something.

SPARROW

You make me feel small, Ray.

RAY

You're a good friend. Maybe not the best with a rope, but a good man.

SPARROW

Why'd you come back to town, Ray? I was just feeling better about myself from the last time you came to town and now you've gone and undone all that good feeling.

RAY

The story is that I'm a drifting journeyman looking for work.

SPARROW

But everybody in town already knows you. I mean, sure we've had some newcomers but even they have heard the stories about the last time you came to town. We buried a lot of folks and there was some talk about charging you in the death of the preacher.

RAY

Sparrow, I'm going to tell you something that you can't tell anyone else. I'm not a journeyman looking for work in Coronado. I've signed up with an insurance company and they have insured the mine. I know it might sound a little corny, but you can insure pert near anything except parakeets and air. Anyway, I've gone undercover to find the missing uranium shipment so the company doesn't have to pay out.

SPARROW

I would have figured that the government boys, like the FBI or CIA would have handled it. Are you sure you haven't signed up with the government, Ray?

RAY

You know I'm as patriotic as the next guy, but just take me out to pasture and put me down if I ever sign up with the government. Bureaucracy and corruption are not my game, Sparrow. I work for the free market. Corporations keep us safe because they worry about the bottom line. Corporations are the purest form of organization and efficiency. Hope for the future of the world lies within the corporation model.

SPARROW

Be careful, Ray. Don't let Mr. Bennett find out. He took over the mine after Mr. Martinez got himself killed and he'll be more than hopping mad if he finds out you are an insurance investigator.

RAY

It's bigger than Mr. Bennett. What if Martinez was murdered? Maybe Bennett is involved. He's taken over control of the mine. He certainly had a motive, no? A good investigator balances the welfare of the nation and the bottom line of the corporation. He keeps an open mind, suspects everyone, and punishes anyone who is guilty.

SPARROW

Why would someone kill old Mr. Martinez for a wagon full of rocks? They ain't worth that much anyway. More trouble than they're worth, if you ask me.

RAY

Not worth much to you or me or our government since we have a vast uranium supply, but how much do you think it's worth to North Korea or Iran or some other rogue nation that's bent on the destruction of truth, liberty and the American way?

SPARROW

Ray, I think you've been reading too many detective stories.

RAY

Maybe so, Sparrow, but maybe you should pick up a newspaper every once in a while and then maybe you'd understand a little more about what goes on outside of that thick skull of yours.

SPARROW

That may be so, but at least I don't have blood on my hands.

RAY

Ah, you'd be surprised how easy blood washes off.

SPARROW

I suppose you'd be the one to know because of what happened last time.

RAY

A man learns from his past. (He took a deep breath.) The air of Coronado smells so sweet. It feels like I've come home.

SPARROW

Oh, Christ. I better get started on digging graves.

The lights went down.

The lights came back up.
All of the extras stood in a group. The two teachers had changed hats to signal that they now inhabited new characters. Paul hung in the back. Even though he did not have a speaking part, he could feel adrenalin pumping at the end of his fingers. Blue Cowboy had directed them to act like a gang of bullies who terrorized the town. They laughed loud, obviously drunk. They slapped each other on the back and began hooting and hollering when Third Eye (Duchess) entered from the left.

GANG MEMBER #1

Hey, sweet cheeks! You want to take a ride to the top of the Rata Sucia and train this old dog some new tricks.

GANG MEMBER #2

I think you have enough for the both of us.

DUCHESS

I'd rather swallow my own tongue.

GANG MEMBER #2

Who do you think you're talking to?

DUCHESS

I don't know. A filthy weasel and his friend?

GANG MEMBER #1

If you want to stay in this town you better learn your manners.

DUCHESS

(She laughed a throaty, mocking laugh.) A weasel teaching me manners? I have a suggestion for you as well. Why don't you all form a circle and take care of each other. I mean, you all work on Circle Jerk ranch, right?

(Gang Member #1 pulled a knife and brandished it in front of Duchess' face. The rest of the gang quickly surrounded her with obvious menace.)

GANG MEMBER #1

There aren't many women out in this scrub so I'd hate to slice you up, but there's a limit to my patience, even for you.

DUCHESS

(She turned around, looking for an escape.) I see you boys are already pretty good at forming circles.

Ray entered from the right.

RAY

Hey, boys! I wonder if you all can help me?

(The gang turned and the circle loosened. Duchess stepped out from them and walked to the other side of the stage behind Ray.

GANG MEMBER #1

And who are you?

RAY

I heard they're stringing electrical wire and building towers somewhere around these parts. This is Coronado, right? I'm just a worker looking for work, hoping to make a little cash bringing the modern marvel of electricity to the desert.

GANG MEMBER #1

Those are mighty fancy pants for a working man.

RAY

I must admit I'm not used to a man commenting on my pants.

DUCHESS

These men have a peculiar standard of manners.

GANG MEMBER #2

The line is out in the Barba del Diablo valley, west of the Cantando Bebé Rocas.

RAY

Much obliged. I'll walk you out ma'am.

DUCHESS

I don't think so. I don't need no fancy pants looking after me.

Duchess stormed off, her body all jiggle and shake. Ray produced a condescending smile. Paul had calmed down by now and lost his erection, so he became aware of where he was and what he was doing. He caught sight of a bald man with a large white bandage over his ear sitting in the front row at the periphery of the stage lights. When he noticed the man a second time he recognized the uniform and, now that he had shaved his head, the striking resemblance to Andy Auro.

GANG MEMBER #1

We'll have to keep an eye on that one. There's something not right about him.

Paul launched into an improvisation that nearly brought the entire scene down, since no one onstage had enough experience or talent to diverge from the memorized script.

PAUL

He looks like he works for the government, if you ask me. Like maybe he couldn't think of what else to do and maybe an opportunity fell in his lap and he took it and now that he's forty, he's got to be around forty, right? Now that he's forty he's starting to dwell on his missteps, the passing of time, and a future of disease and loss. He's thinking about his impact on the world or his absence of impact on the world. He's a dangerous man. He's untethered and alone. He'll be unpredictable and irrational. He could take us all down. The best solution, if you ask me, is that we kill him right now. Let's follow him on his way to the electrical towers and shoot him through the heart. That will take care of him once and for all.

The other gang members stared at him, not a little angry because they were supposed to be off the stage by now. They collectively realized that one of them should respond to Paul's speech, but no one could come up with a line.

PAUL

And how about Duchess? Did you get a load of those tits?

Anger and shock rose from the audience. All of the men in the building might have been thinking the same thing, but they had not assigned Paul the right to give voice to their thoughts. The women seethed at the crudeness. The science teacher, experienced in handling hostile crowds, came to the rescue.

GANG MEMBER #3

Now, now, Bobby, we all know you're crazy and barely hanging onto reality, but if you open your mouth one more time I'm going to knock out all of your teeth and beat you so bad you'll wish you had never been born.

Now that their anger had been expressed, the audience relaxed some, leaning back in their seats and exhaling. Emboldened, the social studies teacher piped in.

GANG MEMBER #4

Right, we don't even know if he works for the government and you just want to shoot him down like a dog in the dust, and we don't talk about women like that.

PAUL

Hold on, we were about to rape her a minute ago and now we can't talk about her tits?

The audience was less shocked this time around, even with the introduction of the rape theme, but impatience grew out of their anger and some thought of standing up and walking out at that moment. But they stayed, hoping there would be more songs and rope displays and the words would end or dramatically decrease. Paul saw the deputy smiling broadly. He was not one of the people thinking of leaving.

GANG MEMBER #3

You had the wrong idea. We were just trying to scare the gal. We don't believe in rape, for goodness sakes.

PAUL

Jesus, you don't BELIEVE in rape. It's something you do because you are unhinged and violent. Anyway, at least we agree on fancy pants. He's not one of us. It's almost like I'm getting a whiff of pedophilia from him, you know what I mean?

"Shut up! Shut up!" Blue Cowboy shouted from offstage. They all looked toward the source and then back at each other. They waited for Blue Cowboy to stride onstage and take command of the scene, but it was Paul who mercifully relented and put the play back on the rails.

PAUL

Sounds like the boss is mad at me again. I suppose we should go tell him about the blue cowboy directly. He'll tell us what to do. Damn, I have a headache.

They all shuffled offstage, feeling confused and shamed, except Paul, who thought the additions had added to the play. The lights dimmed. Paul passed Blue Cowboy behind the curtain and he whispered in Paul's ear to please not fuck up the production, that everyone had really worked hard on it, that he knew he meant well but when an actor went off script bad things usually followed, and to please, please, refrain from using crude language because they were, after all, in a Baptist church and saying "tits" to an audience in a Baptist church was equivalent to flashing the Pope or pissing on the Dali Llama, and that if he couldn't handle his responsibilities then they could easily shift the cast around and he could go back to his hotel room to sleep off whatever disturbance he was now experiencing. Paul reassured him that he could stick to the script and waved him off. Subsequently, Blue Cowboy was late to his mark to begin the next scene, leaving the audience in the dark an uncomfortably long time.

The crew had moved a life-sized skeleton hanging from metal stand, a chair, and a desk onto the stage. The radio announcer stood in the center. He had thrown on a white lab coat and stethoscope around his neck. He had taken off his cowboy hat and replaced it with a head reflector, an old-timey silver disk that was used to reflect light toward the source of a patient's ailments, particularly effective projecting light inside a person's mouth. Some experienced nostalgia for the head reflector because they too had been examined by an old doctor wearing such an apparatus, although pocket flashlights had effectively killed their use decades ago. Blue Cowboy finally entered from the left just as Doc examined the hand of the skeleton.

RAY

Doc! I see you're still up to your old tricks.

DOC

(He quickly dropped the skeleton hand as if caught doing something illegal or immoral.) Well, if it isn't Ray Reagan. I thought at first my old eyes deceived me, but there you are, standing right there. What brings you back to town? (They vigorously shook hands.)

RAY

I heard there was a little trouble with a uranium shipment, so I've come to find a solution.

DOC

The last time through you were working for the railroad, no? Trying to subvert the building of a highway across the desert.

RAY

No, no, the last time I was through I was scouting locations for A-bomb testing. Remember, Coronado was in the top five, but you all lost to Nye County. The place was more godforsaken than the other finalists, plus Nevada came up with some cash that made the feds happy.

DOC

That was our darn luck. I hear Nye County is booming. (He laughed at his own joke.)

RAY

(He acted as if he didn't hear the joke or understand the pun.) It has been a boon to their economy. Restaurant business in the county has gone through the roof and the government has poured a lot of money into building the site. Those bombs are the best fireworks you could ever hope to see, times a thousand. The last time I saw one though it gave me a headache that I couldn't shake for weeks.

DOC

I imagine a man like you sees much. You are privy to the machinations of the world.

RAY

But the reason I came to see you, Doc, is that I understand you treated Mr. Martinez after the cart was hijacked.

DOC

Ah, yes, tragic indeed. He died right there on my examination table.

RAY

What was the cause?

DOC

Blunt force trauma to the head. Maybe with the handle on a gun or with an ordinary rock picked up from the side of the road. I suppose the instrument of death does not matter much.

RAY

You know better than that, Doc. One piece of information can lead to another piece and if you just keep going the case will solve itself.

DOC

Ok, Ray, then he died of foolishness. He was asking for it when he decided to move a load of high grade uranium down a mountain path in a cart without guards. Almost anyone could have taken it, even me with my rheumatism, astigmatism, and vertigo.

RAY

Well, thanks, Doc, I'll be posing as a common worker while I'm conducting my investigation. I'll trust this will remain between you and me.

DOC

You know I can keep quiet. A didn't say a word when you were a location scout for the A-bomb testing or when you were an agitator on the Apache reservation or when you were rooting out communist infiltrators from the local ranches. I'll keep quiet when you come back again with a new mission. God knows this desolate piece of wasteland gets its share of action.

RAY

You are a great friend, Doc, and an even better American.

(They shook hands and Blue Cowboy left the stage. Doc waited a beat and picked up the phone on his desk. He began speaking without the aid of dialing.

DOC

(His voice changed from a kindly old country doctor to a menace.) I know the man in the fancy pants. He's a narc. I want you to take care of him the old fashioned way. (pause) Not that old fashioned, for God sakes, do you really think we have time for a crucifixion? With a bullet, dummy. Mr. Martinez was brought to my office alive. He bumped his head, so I had to clean up your mess with a sedative and a pillow. He could have fingered each and every one of you and we all would be sitting behind bars right now. I don't want any mistakes this time. Call me when the deed is done. I want Ray Reagan dead.

The lights went dark.

The crew removed the office and left the stage empty. Third Eye walked onto stage. Her left breast looked very close to springing out of her costume into the open air. Paul had noticed but he didn't say anything to her so he would have the opportunity of watching one hundred simultaneous heart attacks sweep through the audience.

The lights came back up.

DUCHESS

(She stalked the stage in an agitated state. Her face was dirty and her hair mussed.) That darn horse of mine. Sees a little old rattlesnake and she shakes me off like a bad case of fleas. I can see the dust from her hooves as she races home. I'll have a ten mile walk in this blistering heat.

Actually, this last line carried quite a bit of force with the audience as the temperature in the church had steadily risen and now hovered somewhere in the high 90s. The air had become a hot, wet blanket closing in from all sides. Blue Cowboy walked onto stage, looking fresh and cool.

RAY

What's a pretty little lady like you doing all the way out here without a horse or water?

DUCHESS

Oh, it's you, the bedazzler, the blue barker with the gleaming teeth.

RAY

Are you in need of assistance ma'am?

DUCHESS

Can you go fetch my horse, you blue-loined wizard? Can you knock some sense into that old nag of mine so she won't buck me off every time she sees an adolescent snake? You don't see me bucking and running do you? And I've got a six foot tall blue-skinned snake standing right in my path.

RAY

Are you really calling me an adolescent snake, ma'am?

DUCHESS

If the blue skins fits, don't shed it.

RAY

(He laughed, as if fending off a child's insult, sure of both his power over her and her weakness.) Ma'am, why don't you just get on the back of my horse?

DUCHESS

(She moaned with desire.) Those blue pants sure are inviting.

They stalked each other with sudden heat and as their faces drew close they began to sing "Pony Boy," the song Paul had heard coming from Blue Cowboy's car earlier in the week. They sang the duet as if in a hallucination or delirium. Lust and desire, long, lonely desert nights, fire, sweat, and the throb of sweet connection rang from their voices. The audience grew nervous that they would consummate their lust right there on stage, but appreciated the long and slow kiss that served as an exclamation point for the song. When they broke Blue Cowboy had become visibly excited through his tight pants and Third Eye gasped for breath.

DUCHESS

You go on. I can manage by myself. If I wanted to be taken care of by a man I would have stayed in the city.

RAY

Look at me, ma'am, you've left me in a state. I if I didn't want to be taken care of I would have stayed on my horse.

Third Eye fell to her knees and drew Blue Cowboy toward her with an inviting finger. He strode toward her, legs apart, all cock and swagger. He stopped in front of her and grabbed his belt. As her face leaned toward his groin she looked up at his face.

DUCHESS

While it is impressive, I suggest you take it behind that cactus and relieve yourself of its demands.

The audience laughed and groaned. They were scandalized, titillated, and disappointed at the same time. Since Paul's outburst they were unsettled and expected further shocks, but they were not going to act appreciative of the subversion. The old man, who sat next to Deputy Auro, looked ready to faint or die. Sweat glistened off the deputy's forehead as he leaned forward and chewed his lips. He had come alone as Jenny had stayed home with the kids. Third Eye rose to her feet and mockingly laughed. Blue Cowboy tipped his hat and flashed a gleaming smile, as if to say one day soon she would not be able to resist him and that she would weep with joy once she had known the pleasure of his company. Blue Cowboy stalked offstage. Third Eye stopped laughing. She looked up at the sun and fanned herself with her hand.

DUCHESS

I didn't know the sun or a man could be so hot. But I'll be darned if I get on his horse. Once you get on a man's horse you can never really get off. I'd rather crawl on my hands and knees back to town than to start up with him. But surely tonight

I will dream of blue pants.

Third Eye walked offstage. The lights dimmed, then went black. The temperature in the church had gone over one hundred degrees with the moist exhalations of the audience pushing the humidity over 95% Sweat dripped from every head and pooled in the creases and nooks of their bodies. One comedian yelled out, "I thought the desert was supposed to have a dry heat," which caused a ripple of laughter and dozens of ensuing comments amongst friends, wives, and husbands about the heat, the need for air-conditioning, and the immediate five day forecast as seen on the local news. The din became so load and persistent that even after the lights came up, revealing a group of miners standing outside a lopsided door frame, labeled above as "Uranium Mine" and glowing Day-Glo green from inside, the audience continued talking until a wave of shushes rolled through the church. The miners also faintly glowed green from head to toe as if a fine mist had been sprayed on their clothes. Glowing bricks had been strewn on the ground and had been gathered in a small pile near where the miners stood. Paul played Miner #4 and had no lines in this scene, but he felt the same unmooring as he had before when he waked onstage. He had found a small degree of calm and equilibrium backstage during the scene between Blue Cowboy and Third Eye. Fortunately, he had been blocked from seeing Third Eye fall to her knees in front of Blue Cowboy's crotch, as witnessing that might have sent him over the edge of reason. As it was, he sat in the corner away from the other extras who crowded around the door waiting for the kiss and ensuing compromising position. Somehow they had missed that she worked as a whore and could essentially be rented by the hour. If asked she would give them access to her treasures, but for reasons of nostalgia for simpler times or notions of propriety or willful naivety, they relegated their desires for her to voyeurism and fantasy. Paul held his face in his hands and successfully rubbed some of the tension away.

Onstage, he caught sight of the deputy again, looking maniacal and unhinged himself with a wide, insane grin and now wearing a pair of aviator sunglasses. Paul felt the desire to perform for the deputy, to stand out from the other extras and reveal to him the pathos residing within. He had not understood his impulsive outburst the first time but now he did. He understood the insane, mocking smile and it was as if the intervening decades melted away and they were still capable of sharing a joke between them that no one else could possibly understand. The deputy waited for a sign that Paul understood the connection, understood the world should be greeted with a cockeyed expression of cynicism or sarcasm because the world was run by fools, women were untrue, and the prospects for a couple of working class kids like themselves had always been dim.

I have never given you the proper credit for shaping my philosophy, Paul thought. I do understand you. I should have believed years ago and then maybe my life would have taken a better path.

The play roared along as he drifted away and, fortunately, the action did not require his full attention or attuned participation to be successfully performed.

Ray walked up to the miners and touched the brim of his hat in greeting. The miners slowly straightened their backs and set down their glowing rocks to prepare for a conversation with the blue stranger, except for Paul who hung onto his rock and stared at the dark lenses of the deputy's glasses, waiting for a signal.

RAY

This must be the uranium mine.

All the miners, except Paul, looked at the sign above their heads, the glowing rocks, their glowing clothes, and at the glowing entrance into the mine. The Lead Miner stepped forward and put his hands on his hips in a challenging way.

LEAD MINER

I see you like to flaunt your deductive reasoning.

RAY

I hear you lost a shipment recently.

LEAD MINER

Yessir, more likely stolen than anything else. I don't reckon it's exactly lost. We don't know where it is, but somebody out there is sitting on a valuable pile of rocks.

RAY

Who do you think stole it, then?

LEAD MINER

I would have thought you would have used that brain of yours to figure that out. That's a bit out of my purview, that's thinking above my pay grade, but I don't reckon it's too hard to figure out.

RAY

No?

LEAD MINER

Who wants the genie but can't rub him out of the lamp themselves? You got your terrorist networks, your rogue states, and your first world competitors all looking for an upgrade. Everybody wants the best genie, I reckon, and they'll do just about anything to get their hands on it.

RAY

Did you know the man who was killed very well?

LEAD MINER

I should say so. Been in these mines twenty years with him. I've drug him out of saloons when he was dead drunk. I've let him sob on my shoulder when his wife and two children disappeared in the night with an itinerant tinker with the velvet voice and two black horses. I was even his nursemaid when he was laid up with his head injury.

RAY

Head injury?

LEAD MINER

He was part injun, anywhere's from a half to a quarter, and alcohol never did set well with him. Sometimes when he got drunk he turned mean and he wouldn't be satisfied unless he fought every man in the bar and sometimes he took on all the women too, if they were game. One night he ran into a tough hombre south of the border who wasn't as drunk as he was and ol' Martinez took such a pounding that his head cracked open like an eggshell. The sumofabitch somehow survived a wagon ride to the train station and a train ride into the city where a doctor there put three or four plates in his head to keep it all together. After that he could flick his finger against his scalp and you might start thinking he was made of steel, maybe like a robot. It gave him an unfair advantage in the fights to come. He'd use that metal head as a battering ram. There hasn't been a punch that has been thrown or a bottle made that could hurt that titanium.

RAY

Does Doc know about this?

LEAD MINER

Doc in Coronado? I don't know. He patched him up a couple of times. It might have come up in conversation but you can go to Doc if you need a simple suture or if you've got the clap, but everything else you figure he's going to get wrong.

RAY

Doc? No, he's a trusted professional. He's a pillar of the community. He wears glasses and he's old, therefore he symbolizes wisdom, stability, and 'merican endurance.

LEAD MINER

(He laughed.) Maybe ten or fifteen years ago, before he started sampling the native plants and started chasing injun tail on the reservation.

RAY

Our Doc?

LEAD MINER

He's not my doc. I personally won't even see him for the clap. That's about the last place I want him touching. I've just learned to get used to the burning.

RAY

(He produced a small vial of pills from his back pocket.) This will take care of it.

LEAD MNER

Much obliged.

RAY

I'm happy to help as long as you don't tell me you caught it from Duchess.

LEAD MINER

(He laughed again.) I'd have more chance of catching it from her horse.

RAY

Why do you say that?

LEAD MINER

Every man in town has taken a run at her and not a one has been able to get past the gate.

RAY

The gate?

LEAD MINER

You know what I'm saying.

RAY

No, I don't.

LEAD MINER

The barn door is closed.

RAY

What does that have to do with Duchess?

LEAD MINER

No entry.

RAY

What?

LEAD MINER

She has not allowed a man to stick his penis inside of her.

RAY

I should knock you down for speaking about a lady like that.

LEAD MINER

Shouldn't you be leaving? Isn't there a shipment of uranium to find?

RAY

Is she really a virgin?

LEAD MINER

As fresh as the newly fallen snow, as far as anybody can tell.

RAY

What does that mean?

LEAD MINER

It's just speculation. One would have to stick a penis inside her vagina to ascertain whether or not her hymen is intact, that's all I'm saying. Otherwise, we are just interpreting her coolness towards the male gender as her jealously guarding her hard-won virginity, keeping the barbarians at the gate.

RAY

It's a wonder you have any teeth left in your mouth with the way you speak about women. Someone someday is going to punch them free of your gums. Now, I have to go find the uranium shipment and stop it before it gets to whatever nefarious place it's going. You've been helpful, except for that part about Duchess. I'll settle up with you later on that subject.

Ray exited stage right. The miners looked at each other, then all filed into the glowing mine entrance. Paul was the last to go in and he still held his rock, but the majority of the audience missed the incongruity of a miner carrying a rock back inside the mine. The stage went black.

The extras quickly changed out of the glowing clothes and into workingman overalls. The stage crew changed the scene into an endless desert horizon with a line of electrical towers growing smaller as they grew more distant.

The extras rushed onstage. Paul still wore his glowing hat. The lights came up on a crew of electrical workers building a tower deep in the desert. Suddenly, they broke into song as Ray entered from stage right. Paul pretended to sing by opening and closing his mouth and aping the arm gestures of the rest of the crews. They sang "The Workingman's Song."

> The land's been dry for a million years
> Useless scrub, scorched and forgotten
> Cursed by God, named for the Devil's sneers
> Where death comes quickly, and often!
>
> But Franklin and Edison, Americans both
> Taught us about electricity
> A current can give us what we crave most
> Refrigeration! Light! Simplicity!
>
> Oh! Gonna string this wire o'er mountains and streams
> > Gonna string that wire for you and me
> > Gonna string that wire on towers of metal
> > Gonna string that wire from sea to shining sea!

RAY

You boys have some golden pipes!

IN UNISON

Thanks, Ray.

WORKER #1

What brings you our here, Ray? It's been a time since we've laid eyes on you.

RAY

I've joined your crew fellas, but I have some business to take care of and I'd be much obliged to you if you reported that I showed up and worked a full day.

WORKER #2

That's ghost work, Ray.

WORKER #1

That doesn't seem right or fair to the likes of us. I mean our brains are bubbling right out our skulls it's so blasted hot out here.

RAY

You boys know I believe in an honest day's work for an honest day's pay. I wouldn't ask you if it wasn't a question of national security. I'll donate my pay to the whore house...er...I mean the home where the used up whores go to retire.

WORKER #1

OK, whatever you say, Ray.

WORKER #2

I say it's a slippery slope. Next he'll come here telling us he killed a man without a trial all in the name of frontier justice. Maybe he'll turn vigilante against us over some perceived slight. We've overlooked his transgressions for far too long.

RAY

You know everybody I killed deserved it. I've only shot a few in the back when they were running away. It's not easy to run in these boots, so they would have escaped and you can't have that, right? You can't have criminals running around without fear of justice and retribution, no?

WORKER #2

Are you qualified, Ray, to make a judgment of who's a criminal and who isn't? You can make a snap judgment like that, calculate the sentence, exhaust all of his appeals, and ignore new evidence and stays of execution in the split second it takes to pull the trigger? You are a one man modern marvel.

RAY

What are you saying?

WORKING MAN #1

We've been in the sun all day, Ray.

WORKING MAN #2

Don't blame my objections on my exhaustion. I have serious reservations that have nothing to do with heat stroke.

RAY

Alright, boys, I was hoping for your help, but maybe I'll ask you how you feel in the future when North Korea has the bomb or a terrorist cell takes out a city on the eastern seaboard.

WORKINGMAN #2

Jesus, Ray, why don't you just name the city? Why the veiled reference to a city on the Atlantic?

RAY

I don't want to cause undue panic. Plus, I can't predict when or where they will strike.

WORKINGMAN #2

But you're sure it's going to be the eastern seaboard?

WORKINGMAN #1

He's talking about the bomb, alright? I think we can give him some cover while he makes us safe from annihilation, don't you think?

WORKINGMAN #2

Another day working out in this heat and I won't care if a bomb is dropped directly on my head.

They all laughed hilariously and a little desperately.

> RAY

Ok, boys, I'm off to find the uranium.

> WORKINGMAN #1

Oh, sweet Jesus, uranium is missing?

> RAY

A whole cartful of grade A stuff.

> WORKINGMAN #2

How do you suppose they'll get it out of the country?

Paul stepped forward with a lurch and looked about to speak, but he caught the eye of Blue Cowboy and the teachers, who were performing the speaking parts, and he stopped and stepped back into the shadows.

> RAY

Hey, you, step back out here.

> WORKINGMAN #3

(Paul stepped out from the line.) What can I do for you, Ray?

> RAY

That's a mighty funny hat you're wearing.

> WORKINGMAN #3

What do you mean? I've had this hat for years. I mean if you think it's funny that

I've soaked it through with my sweat a thousand times.

>   RAY

Let me see the hat.

>   WORKINGMAN #3

You don't ask for a man's hat.

>   WORKINGMAN #1

That doesn't sound right.

>   WORKINGMAN #2

I thought my eyes were playing tricks on me. That hat is certainly glowing.

>   RAY

Let me see the hat.

>   WORKINGMAN #3

A hat is a personal and rather intimate item, Ray.

Ray pulled out one of his guns and leveled it at Workingman #3's chest. Paul reluctantly handed over the hat. Ray kept the gun on him as he knelt down and turned on the previously unmentioned Geiger counter. With his free hand he waved the wand over the hat and it began excitedly chirping and clicking. Ray stood up with a frightening scowl on his face.

>   RAY

Your hat is as hot as a two dollar pistol at an all-night shoot out.

WORKINGMAN #1

I'm shocked that you have any hair left at all.

WORKINGMAN #2

I'd hate to think what's going on inside that skull of yours.

Paul had forgotten his line so he stared at them blankly for a beat before he made up his own.

WORKINGMAN #3

Don't worry what's going on inside my head. My tumors are my own.

RAY

(He forged ahead even though he sensed Paul was lost.) Who are you working for?

WORKINGMAN #3

These tumors inside my head could have had nothing to do with the radiation on the hat. I may have been born with the seeds of them, little malformed masses that grew and grew silently and stealthily as I passed the milestones of my ordinary life: the first time I wiped my ass independently, my first sip of alcohol, the first time a stuck a finger or two inside a girl. All the while the tumors gained momentum and mass, crowding and pushing against the circuitry until one day they had grown so big they had to step out from the shadows and announce their presence in a fanfare of excruciating pain and abject fear. What could I do? It's my goddamn brain. This mass, these masses that my body had created lay deep inside the folds of matter, hungry to consume all the space allocated for the brain. So I went to Doc and he shined a flashlight up my nose and held a lantern next to my ear. He told me the closest x-ray was in Albuquerque and he gave me some powder for the pain. He told me I might be bewitched or that a devil might have impregnated my brain through my ear with a demon seed. The powder only worked some if I mixed it with a quart of whiskey. In Albuquerque they showed me a picture of my brain and damned if it didn't look like an Octopus' garden. I've got at least eight tendrils wrapped this way and that. The real Doc up there told me they would basically have to take out my entire brain in order to clean out all the tumors. I told him that it wasn't likely that I would be taking that option. So, I came back here pretty darn blue. I mean I have a wife and kids to think of. What's going to happen to them?

WORKINGMAN #2

He's not married.

WORKINGMAN #1

I think he's talking about that squaw he ruts with up at the reservation and those little half-breeds they produced.

WORKINGMAN #2

Oh, that's not exactly the same thing as a wife and kids.

WORKINGMAN #3

I met with Doc in town and he told me that it was a tough break and that there's never a way to tell who's going to get the short straw. But Old Doc took care of me, told me a way I could make some extra money before the pain and dysfunction became so bad I would only be able to lie in my squaw's room and hope to die.

WORKINGMAN #2

Isn't it unseemly the way he uses the word "squaw." It sounds so demeaning coming from a white man's lips who just happens to be a lover of native tail. Although, I find myself unable to conjure much sympathy for his savage bride.

WORKINGMAN #1

I would hate to die in the dust and poverty of a reservation. I'd rather fall off one of these towers or have a scorpion crawl inside my boot.

WORKINGMAN #3

Ya, ol' Doc told me to help him with a project and I could make enough money to take care of Desert Bloom and the children for a decade or more after my death.

WORKINGMAN #2

Do you think that is her real name?

WORKINGMAN #1

No, the Indian school gave her the name of Pam Jones. She knows no other name. Desert Bloom is strictly his fantasy and creation.

WORKINGMAN #2

I hear she's quite good looking, though.

WORKINGMAN #1

I wouldn't know. I don't look at them like that.

Just then Third Eye staggered in. She was in obvious distress. Her hair was a tangle and her cheeks and forehead had been smeared with swaths of dirt. Her top had all but been pulled off of her breasts but somehow the cloth managed to shield her nipples from the audience. When he saw her, Ray rushed to her side and caught her before she fell in a heap.

RAY

What happened?

DUCHESS

I'm a fool, a fool. I should have taken that ride with you. I've been wandering in the desert for hours. I got lost, even though I know this desert like the back of my hand. I don't know what has caused this delirium, probably the heat and that fool horse of mine.

RAY

You should have climbed on my horse.

DUCHESS

You'll split me open like a coconut and leave me broken and used up.

RAY

I have a Chinese cook named Hop Wang and a thousand acre ranch. I have eighteen hundred head of cattle and a burning for you deep inside me that no water can quench.

DUCHESS

I don't even know your real name.

RAY

You can call me your pony boy.

DUCHESS

It's more than I could have ever dreamed. This must be a hallucination brought on by heat stroke.

She fainted away and her weight was too much for Ray to hold so she crumpled to the ground. Paul, still acting as Workingman #3, remembered his cue to run away. Ray, however, saw the escape attempt, drew his pistols and emptied all twelve shots into Paul's back. Paul jerked with each shot, fell to his knees with the third, fell on his face with the fifth and accepted the final seven from a prone position.

WORKINGMAN #1

Jesus, Ray, I considered him a friend.

RAY

You have a poor judge of character. He was a dirty rat who sold out his country for thirty pieces of silver.

WORKINGMAN #2

Really, he wouldn't have gotten more than twenty years in jail for that. He was no mastermind. Besides if he thought his squaw could live for ten years then the salary was considerably higher than thirty pieces of silver.

WORKINGMAN #1

The judge might even have shown some mercy given his brain was a host for a cancer octopus.

WORKINGMAN #2

Right, I guess you could say he was already on death row.

RAY

The man helped sell uranium to an enemy of the state. What more reason did I need?

WORKINGMAN #1

Oh, Ray, sometimes I think you are a simpleton.

WORKINGMAN #2

I wish I had your quality to see the whitest whites and the blackest blacks without a shade between.

WORKINGMAN #1

You believe yourself to be an agent of change, a protector of virtue, and a policeman of natural resources. I see a pawn slouching in front of me.

RAY

I control my own fate.

All the actors laughed except Third Eye and Ray. It turned out to be the best punch line of the night as the audience roared, but an objective observer couldn't have discovered whether the audience laughed because the actors laughed so heartily or whether they shared a bitter awareness of Ray's naivety.

RAY

Leave his body in the desert where the coyotes can eat it. It's what he deserves. And help me get Duchess on my horse. She needs medical attention.

WORKINGMAN #1

First of all, I'm not going to be party to abusing a corpse and remember, Doc is the only medical attention in town you're going to find. Do you actually think he has the training to save her?

RAY

Then you can dig his grave. I'll bet it will take the rest of today and part of the next to dig a hole deep enough to keep him away from the coyotes. When you try to dig it feels more like granite than dirt.

WORKINGMAN #2

We'll take care of it. We'll use dynamite if we have to, on the ground and not the body.

They all helped lift Third Eye onto Ray's shoulder. From his vantage point from the floor, Paul witnessed her top snagging a buckle or ring and being pulled down to her waist. If Paul had been fortunate enough to be lying on a knothole he would have fucked the floor immediately. As for the audience the breast baring was so obviously a mistake brought about by bad costuming and awkward stage blocking they considered them in all their glory along the lines of a broken microphone, a forgotten line or a missed cue, like all the hazards of live performance, instead of a gratuitous act of adolescent titillation. Third Eye did not break character to cover herself as she was supposed to be in a dead faint. Blue Cowboy did not know of the problem until they were offstage because he had her over his shoulder and she faced away from him, so the breasts hung behind his back. Besides, the act of carrying her was next to impossible for him and he worried about dropping her or injuring something deep within his core, so he wouldn't have been concerned with a flash of nudity anyway. The rest of the cast onstage just stared, paralyzed from acting by their own desires. Blue Cowboy turned and almost toppled over. He walked offstage with his back to the audience so that with every step first the right breast and then the left bounced against his shoulder blades. The light man waited for a few seconds after they left the stage before he turned off the lights, as if holding the image in his head to commit to long term memory.

When the lights did go out exhaustion descended on the audience and in the dark with the hot, humid air a majority closed their eyes as if willing sleep to come. A few did manage to nod off for a well-deserved, although brief, rest as sweat dripped from their noses and eyebrows. The deputy leaned forward and tried not to touch his face where it had been scorched. The worst area, along his jawline, was covered in a sopping bandage, but the rest lay open to insult although it had been once covered in salve that had been washed away by his freely sweating pores. His fingers played across his cheek and he winced. His shirt had soaked through, front and back. He looked to his left to share an observation with his wife, as the left turn had grown into something of a habit over the years of marriage, but his wife had not come tonight, so when he turned he saw again a fat women, flushed and overheated, desperately fanning herself with the play program. He hoped the next time he looked she would finally turn into his wife and he could share his opinion with her.

By now sweat ran freely down Paul's face and his color had turned ashen. His mind felt oddly disconnected from the movements of his body. He knew he would perform an act for the deputy. He couldn't formulate its parameters or purpose, but somehow he had to bring forth all those hours they had spent together in their youth, to blot out the intervening years. As the crew changed scenes Blue Cowboy stood in the office and waited. He shot Paul a glance and furrowed his eyebrows at what he saw.

"Are you up for this?" he asked.

"Absolutely. Never been more ready," Paul responded as he tried to hide his trouble with a weak smile.

"We can scratch your part. The audience probably isn't following what's happening anyway. I can just shoot old Doc in the face and be done with this."

"I don't want to let you down, Blue Cowboy."

"No more grandstanding. Your speeches are too wordy. No one understands what you are saying. It's like babbling."

"I'll stick to the script as best as I can."

Blue Cowboy shook his head at the thought and strode onstage when given his cue. They were back in the Doc's office. Blue Cowboy held the Geiger counter at his side. A gun hung from his other hand.

DOC

Hello, Ray, what can I do for you now?

RAY

You can stop being a traitor to this country and you can stop trying to destroy one of the greatest insurance companies the world has ever seen.

DOC

Ray, what are you babbling about now?

RAY

Maybe you remember the lost shipment of uranium? I think you are the mastermind behind the plot.

DOC

You're talking nonsense.

RAY

I don't think so. You told me that Mr. Martinez died of a blunt force against his skull. Well, Doc, I called in the State Coroner and had the body exhumed. Mr. Martinez had so much anti-freeze in his veins he could have cooled down a V-8 roaring across the desert. How do you explain that?

DOC

Maybe I gave him the wrong shot.

RAY

What does anti-freeze cure, Doc?

DOC

Meddling fools like you. (He clumsily searched his desk for a weapon, finally picking up a rock and feebly threw it at Ray. Ray easily dodged the projectile.)

Ray pointed his gun at Doc.

RAY

That will be enough of that, Doc. You're not going to out physical me.

DOC

You're a beast.

Ray found the rock onstage, all the while keeping his gun trained on Doc. He flicked on the Geiger counter and waved the wand over the rock. The counter started wildly chirping and buzzing. Ray walked over to Doc and waved the wand over his head, chest, back, and arms. With each pass the counter became louder and more insistent that radioactivity had been found.

RAY

I've got bad news for you, Doc. You should have been more careful when handling these rocks. I'd say in a couple of weeks you're going to be a tumor with legs.

DOC

Is that your professional opinion?

RAY

Make fun of me all you want, but you probably shouldn't have put a chunk of radioactivity on your office desk. Even a country doctor should know that.

DOC

What are you going to do about it?

RAY

You're under arrest.

DOC

Wait a minute, insurance investigators don't have those powers under the Constitution.

RAY

Not yet. So you knew all along?

DOC

Of course, that fool Sparrow told me not five minutes after you talked to him.

RAY

Why that rat!

DOC

He's not a rat, you fool. He told me because he thought I was on your side, that I'm one of the town fathers looking out for the welfare of the citizenry. Blasted idiot.

> RAY

Isn't that exactly what you are supposed to be?

Paul stepped onstage, gun drawn,

> JIM

Drop the gun, Blue Cowboy.

Ray knew Jim had the drop on him so he dropped the gun.

> DOC

I'm going to bury you so deep in the ground that they won't find you until the earth splits in two.

> RAY

What would be the point of finding me then? All life on earth would basically perish.

> DOC

Never mind the hyperbole. Jim, take that damn Geiger counter away from him too. The man is a menace with that thing.

Jim walked over toward Ray. As he reached for the Geiger counter, Ray made his move. He karate-chopped the gun from his hand, smashed the Geiger counter against Jim's arm, and grabbed him in a bear hug. The two stood face to face, awkwardly close. Paul was supposed to tussle with Blue Cowboy on the ground, pretend to kill him, and while Ray played dead get the rendezvous spot from Doc where the uranium would be handed over to terrorist or foreign hands. At that point Ray would jump up, knock out or kill Doc, and race to the rendezvous to foil the transaction. Paul broke the bear hug and pushed Blue Cowboy hard. Blue Cowboy stumbled backward, tripped over the Geiger counter, and crashed to the ground. Paul chased him and pounced on his prone body, landing with his knees on the gut of poor Blue Cowboy. He let out a cry and Paul slapped him in the face, then he brought the back of his hand across the other side.

PAUL

Are you going to put your hands on me again, motherfucker? Huh? (Paul slapped Blue Cowboy again, who by now held up two ineffective hands against the onslaught and who was trying his very best not to sob in terror.) Maybe I'll fuck you in the ass so you'll remember who I am! You come here and try to get between a man and his money! A man and his birthright! A man and the future viability of his family! I'll show you! I'll show you! Paul unbuckled Blue Cowboy's belt, forcibly turned him over on his stomach, and then ripped his pants down, exposing his ass to the audience. Ass rape is as old as the hills. But maybe you already know. (Paul ripped down his own pants and exposed his fully engorged member. Doc, the crew, Third Eye and the audience all realized around the same time that something had gone horribly wrong and the play was now spinning out of Paul's mind. Blue Cowboy was moaning and bleeding from the nose. Paul grabbed his own cock and aimed it at Blue Cowboy's ass but paused. He stood up. His pants dropped down to his ankles.) I have a better idea. Where's Duchess? I want to fuck Duchess! I want to fuck Duchess! I want to fuck Duchess! I want to fuck Duchess! (He tried to run around the stage, but his pants were still around his ankles and he couldn't kick them off over his boots, so his short, hobbled steps took some of the menace from the performance. By now the audience had started to scream, cover their eyes, pound their fists, and cry. Those who knew the deputy to be a member of the law enforcement community looked to him to do something, because everyone agreed they were witnessing several laws being broken, not the least of which was exhibiting an erection in a Baptist church, which had to rise above the threshold of a felony. Third Eye walked onstage, dressed modestly in a long, white cotton robe.

DUCHESS

Did somebody say they wanted to fuck me?

Paul turned and hobbled toward her, his dick bobbing as he went. His back was to the audience and Deputy Auro used this as an opportunity to spring from his seat and run up behind him. Third Eye saw the deputy approaching and backed away to keep Paul occupied. The deputy caught him from behind and yanked him backward by the collar. Paul had no way to keep his balance and he landed hard on his back. The deputy had him on his stomach with his arm twisted and immobile within seconds. Blue Cowboy turned over, still dazed, and exposed himself fully to the audience. Eventually, he pulled up his pants. The old man lurched out of his chair and wobbled over to where Paul lay and kicked him in the ear. The deputy screamed at everyone to stay back and he would arrest them as well. Some of the crowd, those not bent on gawking, rushed through the door to find air and a sense of equilibrium. Others stood in place and screamed for someone to pull up the criminal's pants. A few prayed for forgiveness to God because of the offense committed in HIS house for fear HE would think they had been party to the desecration because they had paid money to watch the offense. The rest took a few steps forward and looked at each other and wondered if they had the beginnings of a lynch mob. All they needed was a small amount of tinder, maybe another step or two by the most offended in the audience, and they would have dragged Paul to the nearest tree with a thick horizontal branch and hanged him. But the leader never emerged and the deputy pulled up his pants and buckled the belt. Unfortunately, he had to stuff Paul's cock back through the fly and trap it behind the zipper, but all the years of sweeping up shattered glass of bad accidents involving families and the aftermath of bad ideas and violence had prepared him for almost anything. Once the cock was covered tensions in the audience eased. One woman commented that it was the first erect penis she had seen in twenty years, which produced a smattering of guffaws from those in earshot to which her husband replied that had he been given sufficient reason to get erect he would have done so long ago. The husband's comment produced no laughter as the unspoken consensus found his retort mean-spirited since both husband and wife had become misshapen from a river of pies, wines, colas and processed foods.

The deputy cuffed Paul's hands behind his back, pulled him to his feet, and walked him out of the door. He pushed him into the back of an SUV next to a booster and baby seat.

"Stay here. If you try to run I'll shoot you in the back, just like ol' Roy Rogers," the deputy said behind a threatening finger.

He returned with both Blue Cowboy and Third Eye. Neither was handcuffed, but judging by their downcast eyes, the tilt of their head, and their apprehensive gait they also had been placed under arrest. The deputy made Blue Cowboy sit in the front seat as he unclipped a booster seat so Third Eye could squeeze into the back. A group from the audience had followed them out, but when the deputy had finished securing Third Eye he barked at the gawkers to go back inside. They stood their ground as they preferred the cooler air and watching the arrest to a church full of sweaty old people jabbering away about what they had witnessed. Blue Cowboy began to plead his case as soon as the deputy slid behind the wheel and started the engine.

"Look, I didn't know. How was I to know that the man is deranged? I had no idea that he would do something like that. How could I know? If you can tell me how I was supposed to know he would do something like that then I can accept some responsibility. I will. I really will. But I don't think any reasonable person could conclude from what I'm saying that I'm responsible. He went way off script. I would never write a scene in which a man exposes his genitalia to the audience, especially in relation with Roy Rogers, who himself stood for wholesomeness. I just wouldn't do it, and I wouldn't even have included him but at the last minute I had a cast member quit on me and was desperate for an actor. I had no way of vetting him. I couldn't have known. I think it's really unfair to arrest me when I couldn't have known."

"Are you the producer of the play?" the deputy asked, more to stop Blue Cowboy from talking than to take a first stab at his reasoning that led to the arrest.

"Yes, I guess, officially, yes, you could say I am the producer."

"The program said you are the producer, right?"

"Yes."

"I'm guessing that you wrote the program as well, right?"

"Yes."

"So, being as there is no confusion as to your title and role in producing the play, I believe you to be responsible for all the content of the production, which included Paul waving his hard cock at the audience, which happens to violate every decency law on the books."

"Officer, I *understand* that what he did was against the law. It was very lewd and unsettling, but my point is that I didn't ask him to do that. It wasn't in the script. I am not responsible."

"That would be something you can explain to the judge. I witnessed a crime being committed on your stage in your play by your actor."

Blue Cowboy opened his mouth to begin his defense all over again, but the deputy raised a warning finger.

"And if you keep talking I'll slap a pair of cuffs on you and a gag."

Blue Cowboy closed his mouth.

"I'd like to know why I've been arrested," Third Eye chirped. Her indignation, if you could call it that, felt weak and shallow as she remembered the behaviors, public acts, wild desires and appetites that led to her being arrested one hundred times.

"The official reason might be for flashing your tits in a Baptist church, but you know if you fuck in a law enforcement officers' tub without permission there will be consequences to pay. My wife got an eyeful of you and those whores."

"No one actually fucked in the tub. We were just making out. Your friend fucked on the grass."

"I had to drain the tub into my back yard and scrub it out."

"In your condition? Do you think it's smart to work with your face injured like that? You have to take care of yourself."

"You never mind about my face."

"Boys shouldn't play with matches," Third Eye giggled mockingly.

"And girls shouldn't sell their pussies for profit."

This made Third Eye laugh even harder, so the deputy retreated to the comforting fact that Third Eye would soon sit in a cage and he would be the keeper of the key.

It was a short drive from the Baptist church to the jail. The deputy ordered Blue Cowboy and Third Eye out of the car and he helped Paul get out of the back seat because he had left him cuffed. When they went inside the attending deputy broke into a wide grin when he saw the troupe appear. He was new to the job and still susceptible to the vagaries of human existence and amazed at the seemingly endless combinations of misery, woe and stupidity. The veterans on the force warned him the luster would wear off once the combinations started repeating themselves or after he had seen so many he lost his moorings in normalcy and he couldn't distinguish what was odd and what was not. But tonight two cowboys and a whore walking through the door constituted wonderment and awe and produced in him a drive to know every detail of the story that brought the three of them to the jail. Unfortunately, Deputy Auro waved him off before he began his familiar barrage of questions with a promise to tell him later if he spared him now.

"Kinnell is back again tonight," the attending deputy said as he stared at the players, searching for a visual clue of their crime.

"What? What did he do this time? Is he still talking about the killing?" Deputy Auro asked.

"He was drinking hard and ended up beating the snot out of an old man."

"Which one?"

"Chester Finney"

"Jesus, did he live through the beating? I've been expecting a strong wind to kill him one of these days."

"From what I know he's in the hospital getting checked out."

"Take this one to the woman's cell and I'll take these two to spend the night with Mr. Kinnell."

"In the same cell?" Paul asked with not a little anxiety. He hadn't planned to break his silence, but he also did not want to be killed over a dumb prank.

The deputy did not answer but escorted them down the same hallway they had walked down a few days before. The deputy shoved Paul into the cell directly across from Kinnell and Blue Cowboy next to Paul.

"Really, Greg, do you think this is necessary? Are you trying to teach me a lesson?" Paul asked in the most sincere tone he could muster.

"Well, frankly, I don't think you would be the best judge of what is necessary and what isn't. I can't have you flipping your cock on the street corner of my fair city, now can I?"

"I've never done that before."

"Except in front of one hundred and fifty witnesses, who by now are probably convinced you had sex with a goat right in front of them. So, let's not worry about what you've done before."

"It's not like any of those people are going to follow-up and see if I'm in jail or if I had to pay a fine. I mean they'll forget about it by tomorrow."

The deputy brayed with laughter. "I don't think so. For some of those people you might be the memory that comes to them along with their last breath."

The deputy locked their cell doors and started walking down the hallway, when he said, "I'll see you all Monday morning," which elicited a chorus of explanations why each one of them couldn't possibly stay in jail for that length of time because all had previous commitments.

For Blue Cowboy it was his role as one of the main organizers of the festival that would keep him busy, culminating with a gala "Dinner with the Stars" the following evening. This year they had been able to secure six actors who had played in dozens of westerns on both TV and film throughout the 50s and 60s, such as Pepe Henderson, a veteran of 89 film and television productions who was of mixed Columbian and Croatian heritage but looked close enough to a Mexican that, combined with a brilliant, sneering Mexican accent, made him a favorite among casting directors looking for banditos, town drunks, and oppressed farmers. Another of the guests was Myrna O'Shaunessy, who made her name as a scene-stealing character actor who was often cast as a grouchy town spinster, a brothel madam, or an unnamed bystander who had to deliver the best wisecrack in the entire picture. Such was her dominance in this niche' that it was rumored that screenwriters one-upped each other by embedding one-liners in the script just for her. A couple of her lines made it briefly into the lexicon of pop phrases that often were repeated to cover for the users' lack of inherent wit. None of it had anything to do with the inherent value of the words as the screenwriters were terrible poets, but everything to do with Myrna's delivery of the line, which was why a cadre of western screenwriters vied for her services. Who wouldn't want their line to be famous even if you only managed to come up with something like, "Crime makes for stretched necks," or "He's a thistle among thorns," or "That sweet, randy dandy makes me want to eat his candy." All surged into the popular consciousness for a month or two after the films were released and Myrna spent a lifetime repeating those and others to the delight of western fans.

 Myrna would no doubt be hanging on the arm of Brent Hart, an actor with leading man looks but who never made it into their ranks because of a lack of charisma, bad luck, intermittent alcoholism or a combination of all three. He played the rival with the smaller cock and slower horse, the best friend without the shooting skills or rodeo acumen of the lead, the loser in a love triangle or a villain's number one henchman. He was too good-looking to be the main villain, with his sandy hair and his combination of sharp cheekbones and a strong, manly jaw because villainy could not be that attractive and be believable. What could drive a man who looked like that into darkness? He could be under a villain's control though because such casting spoke to the vulnerability and fecklessness of beauty in the face of corruption, and, on a much deeper and subconscious level, acknowledged the possibility of homosexuality on the range of vast lonely plains, because what mastermind with a distaste for women wouldn't want to keep such a specimen as Bret Hart for himself and slowly turn him over to evil?

The fourth, Bruce Harmon, an aerospace engineer by vocation, made a few brief appearances in TV westerns in the 50s and by accident stumbled upon the nostalgia market when he tried to check into the wrong hotel and was told the place was full due to a convention of early sitcom actors, writers, directors and crew and Bruce very clearly saw the line of the paying public stretch out the door and halfway down the block. Thinking quickly, he tried to check himself in at the "stars" registration table and, of course, they didn't have him on the list, so he threw out a smile that he had learned from the leading men with whom he had worked, which could be described as a, "I know you are an incompetent moron struggling through each day, creating chaos with you inadequacies, disappointing everyone you meet in some fashion and mangling each and every direction you are given, but I, in my munificence will overlook your faults, the state of disorder you have created, and the obvious inconvenience you have placed in my path if you fix your error now, satisfy my request, and throw in the opportunity to fondle your breasts and kiss your neck as I so please." The woman at the table became so flushed in the onslaught of the smile her ears turned bright red and she couldn't understand why she prepared herself to submit to a paunchy and balding man who wore his pants too high. The spell rushed her toward acquiescence, until she asked what shows Bruce had been in. When he rattled off the eight westerns that had exploited his talents, the flush drained from her face and she parried with her own smile that could have been interpreted as, "I know you have been living off your brush with stardom a thousand years ago in shows written for children and adults with no cultural comprehension, shows in which the writers used the very obvious crutches of killing or hanging to sum up each and every episode, but I am sorry to inform you that this is a *sitcom* convention and we have no use for a ranch-hand, cowboy, or townsman decked out in chaps and spurs as we have a strict policy of keeping to the theme as we have already had to escort out a group of variety show performers who wanted to argue about our definitions." Although the smile denied him star status, she felt enough compassion to allow him to jump the line ahead of the plebeians snaking out of the door. Inside amongst the exhibits of memorabilia, the autograph tables, the aging actors who looked both familiar and strange (like seeing a fat or wizened friend at a high school reunion), the childlike adulation, the electric thrill crackling in the air, he had the thought that the same scene had to be happening for all those kids who grew up on TV westerns, who always had cap guns strapped on their hips in flimsy holsters and who wore cheap cowboy hats that dyed their hair and foreheads whatever color the hat happened to be when the gunfight, cattle round-up, or horse race caused them to sweat, who, no doubt, would take off from their jobs or plan a weekend to see the heroes of their formative years and bathe in nostalgia. The idea became firmly rooted when he struck up a conversation with Richard Von Longerson, the actor who played Mr. Peeps the butler in the ABC series *Benedict and Me* (1962-1966), while standing side-by-side at a set of urinals. Longerson, cock in hand explained the nostalgia circuit and his vision of cashing in until the last fan of *Benedict and Me* croaked, which, he had to admit, might be sooner than he wanted because of the show's meager popularity and the alarming death rate of the already small fan-base. At the time he figured he had between five and ten years left before he never heard the familiar shout on the streets, "Mr. Peeps! I am in need of your service!" from a starstruck fan. Harmon thanked Longerson for the advice and immediately left the convention to research the market for fat and bald cowboys. He knew the viewing public had turned against westerns about the time the actual scale of the native and buffalo slaughters entered the public consciousness. For how long can you take a rooting interest in an unwashed and violent brute who out of ignorance and malice wipes out entire indigenous populations and species? So, he found the western market not to be as robust as the sitcom market, but he found enough events, signings, and memorabilia shows that supplemented his social security and 401K income and paid for a trip to the Honduras coast every year, where he indulged himself in a week-long bacchanal at a two-story whorehouse holding fourteen women not a day over eighteen. Of late, Harmon had noticed the same disturbing demographic deterioration that had haunted Von Longerson. The audiences were thinning and rapidly growing older. No doubt a percentage died each year and took their cowboy memories with them. In a few years who will remember the name Roy Rogers except the patrons of the remaining restaurants of the once mighty fast food chain? Harmon had had a good run given his tenuous involvement in show business, so how could he complain? He had yet to find a convention for old-time aerospace engineers where fans stalked him for autographs and offered him the occasional blowjob, so he would roll with the cowboy circuit as long as he could.

    The fifth celebrity Blue Cowboy had booked was Emily DeSoto, a beautiful young actress in her younger days with a pin-up body and without a lick of acting ability. Casting directors tried to give her speaking parts because producers saw cash in her breasts and hips, but no director born had been able to coax anything resembling a performance out of her, so she accumulated an impressive list of screen credits playing mute whores wearing as little clothing as the censors would allow. She even shared a scene with Myrna O'Shaunessy in a flop called *She Wore a Blue Bonnet* that both women now hinted could have included an on-set romance of illicit love that simply never happened. Myrna and she never talked beyond superficial chat while on the set and neither remembered the other until they talked one day at an autograph table and realized their paths had crossed decades before, but they became quite good friends on the nostalgia circuit and if coaxed would playfully kiss each other for the camera of an aging fan who could still be hooked by his lesbian fantasies. DeSoto's breasts had taken her to Europe in the 60s where she played the loose American in a series of Italian sex romps where she revealed more of her aging body with each passing year, where her horrendous acting could be dubbed away by an Italian actress with fewer endowments but with inflection in her voice, until she accepted the role of Ishtar in a pornographic retelling of the myth Gilgamesh in *The Three Ways of Gilgamesh* (1968). For a month on the Italian Adriatic coast both Gilgamesh and Enkidu pounded away at her aging flesh and they shot enough film for three movies. At the end of the shoot she decided her acting career had come to an end and hoped the film would never find a distributor in the States, which it never did, but it became something of a cult classic in Italy for the cheesy sets, the hokey dialogue, and although not at her peak, DeSoto's alluring body. The minor fame resulted in a twelve year marriage with a sculptor living in Rome and she would have still been with him in that perfect city had she not lost him to cancer. Sometimes before sex he would project *The Three Ways of Gilgamesh* (he bought one of the 35mm copies) onto the wall and he would sing love songs to her vagina. She had been so deeply in love his vibrato could make her come.

The last celebrity scheduled for the dinner was a late addition called AKA Chief Zero, a Northern Arapaho tribesman who grew up on the Wind River Reservation. He had worked in over 70 movies in the course of his career and had been killed 53 times. He had worked under six different names and finally and officially changed his name to AKA Chief Zero a few years before to blot out his memories and to avoid being found through internet searches, although he had never achieved the status of Chief as even he had fallen victim to Hollywood bravado and puffery. He despised Roy Rogers for never fully acknowledging his Native American heritage and passing himself off as the All-American boy. He was an enigma at these conventions and festivals as he was more likely to speak about the disastrous Treaty of 1868 that left the Arapaho without a land base than any dumb movie he had been in. He would often stand at the periphery of the crowd, scowling, so the attendees didn't know whether he was performing an act, some mean Indian shtick, or if he was really very angry. The Indians who lived in their subconscious were stone-faced, inscrutable, unhinged, raving breasts, crashing wave after wave on the wagon trains or white settlements, so the slightest show of unhappiness from AKA Chief Zero sent them into something akin to panic, which, once he saw the fright in their eyes, allowed him to display his more affable side. He couldn't cause so much fear that he would never be asked back. The other actors always grumbled when they heard he had been booked at a festival where they would be appearing. They too had been mistreated, beaten, tricked, and forgotten by bosses, lovers, husbands, wives, congressmen and mayors so what made the Arapaho so special that their betrayal should be mourned 150 years later? When confronted by such insensitivity, AKA Chief Zero would shake his head slowly and wish for more misery to be visited on their heads. He had been in the audience for the staging of *Bells of Coronado* and he had been shocked like everyone else, except he hoped Paul to be a prophet, portending the doom of the white race and its idiotic amusements, because how much farther could the decadence sink below the ridiculing of an erect penis until the society breaks apart from madness.

Blue Cowboy held his head in his hands and perseverated on just how much of a disaster the dinner would be without him there to organize it. But even if the authorities allowed him to make bail in time would his fellow committee members let him into the dinner now that he had befouled himself, the festival and Roy Rogers? No salve could cure this wound. Had he been a religious man and committed a deadly sin such as he had, the church fathers would have laid out some path for redemption, no matter how arduous and humiliating. Since he had never attended a church service outside of funerals and weddings he was left bereft, alone to find his own way back without the aid of his friends or Roy. He began to sob.

Third Eye took off her clothes, which felt too restricting, and lay on the cot. She figured if the cells had closed-circuit cameras the attending deputy would get an eyeful, but what did she care about that? The deputy had not bothered to frisk them or take away any of their personal belongings, so she found her cell phone nestled in her pile of clothes and called the old man. He answered the third call with a mumble and a cough. She cooed in his ear and explained that she was lying in a jail cell, naked, alone, and thinking of him. Within a few minutes he was begging her to allow him to help her. She accepted the offer and told him that she was fingering her pussy at that very moment. She hated lying, especially to the old man, so she dutifully lay a finger on her clitoris to cover the deceit. Much to her surprise she found herself warm and ready and her fingers felt electrically charged as they explored her favorite and well-worn spot. She told him she held a vision of him in her mind as she masturbated. He tried to shake some life into his penis and with each soft moan and whisper he grew more panicked. She finished long before he did, something that always charmed her, and she coaxed him to the end, whispering a filthy string of wants. By the end he was out of breath, frantic, and wheezing that his cock was balls deep inside of her. She stayed on the line until he fell asleep and started softly snoring into the phone. If anybody could get her out of jail quickly it would be the old man. His love for her would make him a scourge.

Paul felt caught in the beginnings of a hangover, but he couldn't remember drinking a single beer or ingesting a single pharmaceutical since the deputy's party. His head roared in pain and his sight had begun to blacken around the periphery. He battled rising acid in his throat but came up with a quick plan to decide where he would vomit should he relent to the pressure within. He lay on the cot and for a while listened to Blue Cowboy's sobs before his own thoughts muffled them. He thought about work, of waking up at the same time every day, eating the same cereal, wearing a variation of the same set of ten pairs of pants, twenty shirts, and thirty neck ties, the same seven minute shower, the same commute down the same stretch of road, avoiding the same potholes, vaguely recognizing some of the same cars and sometimes luckily seeing the same beautiful women, suited and made-up, holding a remote and cold expression as if boredom and disgust were the two poles of their personalities, parking in the same space, making the same 1,000 step walk to his office, greeting or not greeting the same scowling faces, walking through and past the same bitterness, disappointment, rage, fear, anxiety, frustration and revulsion that the staff brought with them every day, to the same desk, to the same work, to the same onslaught of misery and decay, existing as the standard-bearer for a standard that cannot exist and will never be met, the same retreat home, greasy, exhausted, probably a little heavier from an unhealthy lunch and a lack of exercise, carrying the dust and detritus from the houses he had inspected that day, but hopefully not the cockroaches and mites, stripping naked in the hallway, knowing that if he had the money he would burn the pile clothes with lighter fluid where they lay, the same ungainly walk through his apartment, battling the urge to walk outside naked and lie on the sidewalk to take a nap.

And what would he come home to? Six hours of evening and 48 hours of weekend time that were shaped by the inclusion or lack of a woman that had been like sparks from a fire, jettisoned from the main flame, burning with brightness and force before extinguishing, consuming themselves in the darkness after a weird and chaotic path. His interests, which had included at one time or another tennis, golf, woodworking, computer strategy, watching baseball, *Star Trek*, Roman History, and internet porn ate away some of the time, but mostly left huge gaps he had trouble filling, leading to the same troubled sleep with increasing trips to the bathroom to urinate in the night and more dreams of murder, torture, and being held against his will in a suffocating box at the bottom of the sea or buried underground. How many days like these had he fought against until he realized that comfort and control could be found in the repetition? 1,000 or the full 5,000 days he had been employed by the City, during which he had commiserated about, sneered at, struggled against the mundane, mind-numbing, soul-killing (or so everyone assumed) machinery of it all? Maybe not until this very moment of lying on a jail cell cot, listening to a man in powder blue pants sob over the end of his influence in the Roy Rogers memorabilia circuit and smelling the flesh of Third Eye waft through the bars, did he fully understand that he could not exist outside the boundaries of structured work-time, boredom and repetition. He had created, or accepted, the exact right life, and for him to think for a minute that he could step outside of those boundaries had been foolish, if not altogether impossible. It was also impossible to think that a prosecutor or judge would believe a few minutes of jail-time could bring forth such an epiphany since the official judicial system thought in terms of months and years, in court costs, lawyer fees, and higher insurance premiums. Where in this money-grab did a simple act of contrition fit? No guilty defendant has ever been given a twenty minute sentence, although Paul would have made the argument that someone could internalize the wrongness of their deed and make the same promise to society never to repeat the offense as someone ending a thirty year prison term.

"Shut up! Stop your fucking sobbing!" Paul suddenly shouted at Blue Cowboy, exhibiting none of the contrition he felt, since he had been the one to reduce Blue Cowboy to this state.

Paul returned to the thoughts tumbling through his head and decided it was not an opportune time to return home, maybe. He had discovered a couple of major truths in his short trip, all that a person could ask from a vacation. He found and passed the limits to his actions where regret and contrition began. Certainly exposing himself to an audience of blue hairs now marked a new low in his history of bad decisions, one that he hoped would never be matched, but his quick condemnation of his actions and his heartfelt remorse proved that he had limits, however low and humiliating. He had also accomplished what he had wanted to do by spending his time off in Portsmouth. He had sought out an old friend, abused his hospitality, offended his wife, and probably offended the moral sensibility of the remaining Roy Roger fan-base, if not the entire town of Portsmouth. He could not even think how the Baptists would react once they found out what had happened on their altar. He figured his act of exhibitionism had severed his last tie to the past. He couldn't have articulated this purpose at the beginning of the trip, but it was now clear to him that this was what he had wanted to do. The false memory of the cocksucking did not embarrass or disgust him. How do you know you really aren't gay unless you try an act or two and then realize it's the last thing you ever want to do again? He guessed he still held a minority opinion on this subject so he usually kept this observation to himself.

A ghost had come to him through the TV and he hunted him down and destroyed the power he once held over him. This particular ghost would never haunt him again, so the second grand truth on his journey was that the past could always strike from anywhere, from a chance meeting at a grocery store to a story on the local news, and he would be ready to kill any notion of sentimentality or nostalgia before he could be caught in its thrall. A third truth, more personal in nature than the other two, could be gleaned from the first two, that he wanted to forget everything that had happened to him roughly from the ages 12 to freshman year in college and many of those hours had been spent with the deputy. Certainly the shame and awkwardness of adolescence had something to do with his desire to blot out the period. What person living would ever pick adolescence as their favorite period? Possibly Deputy Auro had more to do with his desire than he first suspected.

There were other periods of his life he would sooner forget, especially the time between his twenty-ninth and thirty-second birthdays when he had become entangled with an anorexic whose superpower was that she could calculate the calories, grams of saturated fat, trans fat, sodium, sugars, etc. just by holding the food in her hand to feel the weight and staring at its essence. He suspected she memorized the labeling on packaged foods, but this didn't explain her uncanny ability to break down chicken tikka masala or Chinese beef and broccoli to within a few calories. Every meal, snack, beer became a calculation and every day a sum of overindulgence and fear. If he would have been offered the opportunity to relive those years without her he would have taken the offer without hesitation. Instead of approaching and winning her, lured by the sight of her long, lean body clad in spandex bike clothes, he would have passed by, momentarily appreciating her body but recognizing the torture and pain required to retain that shape. Of course, Paul rebelled against the regimen and accumulated a bulging gut and thought he felt tits developing at a fairly rapid pace. He stopped gorging on pizzas and ice cream after she finally left and the weight fell off of him. He thought it would be fairly easy to eradicate her influence, although it took several years not to think of a banana as 105 calories, 1 mg sodium, 27 g of carbohydrates, 3 g fiber, 14 g fiber and I g protein. He glossed over his attraction to Third Eye as a still relevant and alive reaction to his time spent with the woman who could not eat.

    The deputy had been harder to blot out. He had to go to the extremes of his own behavior to accomplish the task, but it had been done. Once he left Portsmouth, he hoped he would never think of him again, except in terms of these new memories, the scorched face, the bald head, fucking a strange woman in the deputy's own backyard, none of which had the same power and reach as his adolescent memories but he could rely on their newness as a shield against the tricks of the past.

    Paul looked through the bars and saw that Kinnell had come to the door of his cell and had been staring at Paul. He became impressed with his size all over again. His massive head sat atop a body that cascaded down from his neck in a series of ledges and ripples. His hands looked big and strong enough to crush a human skull or bend the bars as if they were made of tin. Kinnell pressed his forehead against the bars. His face held a deep flush, and his nose wheezed a nearly perfect G as he breathed. Kinnell beckoned him with a finger. Paul imagined Kinnell slamming his head against the bars until he set himself free. His legs felt rubbery, indicating terror at the prospect of approaching Kinnell although two sets of bars separated them, hoping he didn't actually possess the superpowers he had granted him. He pressed his face against the bars and it helped calm his feverish brow.

    "I smell pussy," Kinnell rumbled.

    "That would be the young lady in the cell next to you who has shed her clothing."

Paul thought of Kinnell and Third Eye posing for a snapshot, each with an arm around the back of the other, presenting an abundance of flesh, sex and murder in the heartland. They would have made a good couple, matching power with power, attribute with attribute, and the child they might produce would resemble a Minotaur if male or a wildly sexual gorgon if female.

"Do you see her? Kinnell growled.

"No, she's in the shadows."

"Tell her to come to the door. You can describe her to me."

Paul did not tell him that he could have described her by simply closing his eyes and giving voice to the thousand angles of memory that raged through his thoughts.

"She's not going to listen to me. She is off the clock," Paul said instead letting Kinnell share his obsession.

"I want to know what she looks like."

Paul walked back to his cot.

"Come to the door. Come to the door. Come to the door," Kinnell singsonged, which sounded more a demand than a request.

A soft snoring came from Third Eye's cell. She had obviously become accustomed to sleeping anywhere exhaustion overtook her.

"She's asleep, Kinnell. Who knows, maybe she'll dirty-talk you when she wakes up. You can always ask."

Kinnell stopped using words, but the song continued with a hum from the back of his throat. Blue Cowboy had stopped sobbing and Paul was undecided whether he preferred Blue Cowboy's sob to Kinnell's horrible song. He lay on the cot and soon fell into a troubled sleep.

David Megenhardt

PART II

15

With the Deputy

Deputy Auro lay on the couch in his living room with an ice bag over the right side of his face. The skin on his neck and along his jaw felt like someone had taken a potato peeler to it. The ice kept the throbbing down but only exacerbated the lack of elasticity and rawness of the burned area. He had slept on the couch in his clothes because his moaning and thrashing had kept his wife awake and her deep unrelenting anger made him think his face would never heal. Outside of her influence on the couch he could think more clearly and remind himself that with time, a few weeks at most, the skin would grow completely back, however imperfectly. He understood her anger, but he did not entirely accept it. Sure, his old neighborhood friend brought a prostitute to the party and fucked one of her friends in the open air, and the sheriff drank so hard that twice he pissed on the floor instead of the toilet bowl in the downstairs bathroom, and, yes, he had very nearly blinded himself with his pyrotechnics and was lucky not to need plastic surgery to erase the mistake, but, of course, she had conveniently forgotten that the party had been her idea and when she first brought up idea he had protested that he didn't much like parties and couldn't think of who he would want to entertain at their house. She called him anti-social, a misanthrope, and everything in between, so he relented with the warning that the chances of pulling off a successful party were slim. Now, he was willing to accept the fact the party had been a success but that only seemed to make her angrier. He tried to explain it was only a matter of expectations, because when he thought of unsuccessful parties he thought of deadly boredom, of guests milling around holding crappy food, with tight smiles and tighter assholes, of droning on about insurance, weather, or the electrical grid.

But her anger rose from far deeper places than her reaction to a wild party. She had been acquiring and storing for years so a minor explosion or a revelation that he had once engaged in a homosexual act, had sucked a cock were late additions to an ungainly and growing tumor of disappointment and hate. About the cocksucking she seemed a little disgusted and bewildered. He wasn't entirely sure it ever happened. He had a recollection they were wrestling in the cave and he became erect from rubbing the underside of his dick against Paul's dick as he pinned him on the dirt floor. He was just then thinking what torture to inflict on his vanquished enemy when he felt the tightness and hardness against his belly and he relaxed his hold. Paul was about ready to take advantage of the opening when he too noticed the boner. Greg slid off of him and for a moment they both stared at it, trying to read its purpose or intent. Paul figured it out first and offered to blow Greg if he would reciprocate. His cock became impossibly hard at the suggestion and he agreed to the deed. He had never had a blowjob before so he had no idea what to expect. Paul had never given a blowjob before and could honestly say had never much thought of doing so until he saw Greg's erection, the first erection he had seen other than his own, he fumbled and made several false-starts before committing to a rhythm. Paul's lips and tongue felt electric against his cock and his body felt so completely alive he could momentarily forget the strangeness of the act. He came in long, paralyzing shudders and Paul swallowed all of it. Paul broke away, gagging a little, and when he looked at Greg as he was wiping his mouth he had the expression of a scientist whose experiment had gone terribly wrong, who had the knowledge that his concoction was about to eat the flesh from his bone. Greg had the worst of the deal. Paul's part in the experiment had been all impulse at the sight of the cock ready for sex, but Greg's part was premeditated, and by being able to watch Paul, he knew something terrible loomed before him. He thought about fighting Paul so he wouldn't have to complete the deal, but if he backed out now after Paul had made him come he would be a coward and Paul could always lord it over him that he had won the contest. He would never be able to change that even if he later submitted and blew him. Of course, if he lost the contest the consolation would have been that he didn't have to suck cock, but in that moment of challenge this nuance had been lost.

    Paul straightened out his legs and spread them. His cock just lay there flaccid. He had a bigger dick than Greg, which had always caused some jealousy, and now that he had to put it into his mouth the jealousy turned to the brink of rage. Greg hadn't seen enough dicks to know whether he was on the smallish side and Paul was on the larger side of the ledger, but when he saw it every time they wrestled he alternated between feeling weak and inadequate to wanting to fight that much harder and crush Paul in all of his abundance. He tugged and pulled on Paul's cock until it became adequately hard. He crawled on his hands and knees, lowering his head and closing his eyes just before the dick blotted out his vision. He tasted dirt, sweat, and a tangy musk. Paul flinched and moaned and Greg knew he was experiencing that same electric shock that he had. The knowledge that he was giving pleasure helped him through the ordeal. The cock felt hot and unlike anything that had ever been in his mouth. The glans was a doorknob and the shaft the handle of a broom or shovel. He grabbed the base with his right hand and buried his forefinger in the soft sponge on the scrotum. He worked his had up and down as Paul cradled his head in his hands. Greg felt the reemergence of his own erection that was so hard and stiff he felt he could have hung three winter coats from the shaft without bending it. He lost himself in a rhythm and forgot about the taste. Paul gave a warning grunt, but Greg kept his lips sealed and let the semen shoot into his mouth. He fought a furious gag reflex and kept his head down. Four or five spurts later he had taken all he could and broke away, swallowing. He forced himself to not look panicked and disgusted and he gave Paul an I-can-do-anything smile, leaving cum on his lips for a few seconds before wiping it off. Suddenly his father's church dogma rose like bile up and into his throat. He remembered tightening every muscle in his body to keep from vomiting. He half-expected the cave to explode into hellfire or worse have his father poke his head through the entrance and smell the cock on his lips.

    Paul looked to be in the same state of distress for reasons other than condemnation from the church, since Paul's family never attended. His father had told him that Paul would be his ruination and he had obviously been right, now that he had tasted cock and semen and he could expect a lifetime of increasingly bizarre sex, of leather bars and glory holes, or trysts with closeted school teachers and priests, of shame, condemnation and rejection. The immediate danger of vomiting passed as Paul said he never wanted to do something like that ever again and Greg answered by slowly shaking his head, pretending that he could not even conjure words to describe how much he never wanted to have a cock in his mouth again, although he knew he was now in danger of dropping down in front of any man who asked or who looked agreeable to the exchange. Because they felt so strange, disgusted with themselves but thrilled that something monumental and weird had just occurred, they could not separate or dress, but sat cross-legged, cocks hanging heavy and flaccid, facing each other and speaking little. For a moment they had gone past embarrassment because they shared it so completely.

Later when they hung out Greg had hoped they could repeat the exchange and he guessed that Paul hoped for the same, but neither had the nerve to ask the other lest he be considered a full-blown homosexual. The first blowjob could be blamed on the accidental boner, adolescent curiosity, and a rash decision to follow stray impulse only if it also remained the last blowjob. A second of third act could not be explained away so easily so they fought hard against any residual curiosity the first act had not satisfied.

Greg contented himself with masturbating until he rubbed his dick raw, until he found a girlfriend willing to give blowjobs and intercourse, so any lingering danger of returning to Paul was thoroughly doused. The girl, Sylvia McNamee, and he fucked like castaways at a buffet table, but they both were still in high school with no easy place to meet since both of their families lived under a shroud of Christian guilt and perfection. She tired of fucking in the cave and getting dirt in her ass and pussy and by the time that winter came along she refused to undress in the cold. They broke up as the criticisms started building in their minds as he thought her sense of humor lacking and her thighs a little chubby and she thought him weird, sometimes unable to articulate a coherent thought and other times so completely sarcastic as to drain all the joy from the world.

The ice had gone warm and as his face heated up the dull throb returned. He had barely slept and could feel the exhaustion in his chest and joints. He sat up slowly and surveyed the room, waiting to feel the depth and frequency of the throb. Toys littered the floor: a mower that chattered its teeth when pushed, a garden corral complete with flowers, a faux brick wall, a mailbox, tomatoes and a gate, a dozen horses and cows, three stuffed kittens, and a pink and blue Cinderella baby stroller with the baby hanging by her arm over the edge. Since the injury the deputy had kept the girls at bay and had only played with them perfunctorily. He had fallen asleep trying to read them a story and when they brought their dolls over for him to play a part he became confused about the names of all the characters and their relationships and whether they were queens or princesses or if they lived in a mountain or ocean kingdom. He missed them climbing on his back and believing his torso to be a ladder meant to carry them to unexpected heights. He missed wrestling with them and allowing them to power slam him as they hurtled themselves from the edge of the couch onto his ribs as he lay on the floor. Most of all he missed sleeping with them. They had both recently negotiated themselves back into his and Jenny's bed and he had become used to the tangle of bodies, the punches and kicks in the night, and the sudden screams of night terrors. Although he never slept as well with them in the bed because he could not move for fear of rolling on top of them and sex with his wife was out of the question, he never felt more purposeful than when lying down with them because he had command over the shadows of the night and he could protect them from their fears.

The girls were probably now sleeping with Jenny, a fist jammed in her stomach, another hand in her hair. She unable to turn but sleeping more soundly than she ever had. Or did she have a worried mind? Had she spent the night pulling apart the threads of their marriage, untangling the recriminations, the disappointments, all the misused and untimely words that twisted and knotted themselves up until they could no longer recognize themselves or the person they once loved. Jenny blamed him for being the more dramatic of the two, always creating catastrophes where they didn't exist, always seeing evil agendas in the simple acts of their neighbors, planning for economic collapse and cannibalism in the streets, but even she agreed, he thought, that their marriage only held together because of the glue of the children. How long could their union last without them having the ability to rage at the universe, reveal their deepest secrets, or at least have the possibility of complete forgiveness when they transgressed? He doubted the marriage would last until the children were out of the house but he could say with a degree of certainty that that one of them would file for divorce on the day after the youngest one's graduation.

Once his face throbbed in earnest, he lurched from the couch, and padded into the kitchen with the ice bag at his side, hanging like a dead sea creature. He thought of filling it back up and icing his face again, but he wouldn't have time for it to be effective since he had to get ready for work. The sheriff had told him to use sick time, but he couldn't stay at home for a couple of reasons. First, Jenny's fuming and storming about the house put his teeth on edge and he couldn't help but clench his jaw, which made the burn hurt all the more. Secondly, the story of the accident was already making the rounds of the department and the surrounding sheriff and police departments and he believed he could blunt some of the mockery if the punch-line didn't include his inability to perform his duties. His ear could have been burned down to a nub and he would have shown up to work, because he could not stand a personal problem interfering with his duty, which was a persistent source of conflict with Jenny since she couldn't understand how work could be more important than pre-school graduations, birthday parties, weddings, and ballet recitals. She had an increasingly harder time accepting the sacrifices the families of law enforcement officers had to make although she hadn't tired of the perks of never having to worry about a speed limit, stoplight, and any other traffic command as long as it didn't result in the loss of life, limb or automobile.

He spooned coffee in the coffeemaker and waited for it to brew by leaning heavily against the counter. The caffeine would make the injury throb even more, but he didn't want to add a caffeine-withdrawal headache on top of the existing pain. He only waited until two cups had brewed and he cheated the pot by draining it of its meager accomplishment into his cup. He was late, probably. The clock on the stove had broken and now blinked a wildly inaccurate time, although he still looked at it expecting accurate information even though it had been close to a year since the problem occurred. Every morning he reminded himself to call the repairman, because he had no idea how to fix it, and by the time he turned away he had forgotten all about it until the next morning. He took a sip of coffee and set the cup down on the counter to cool. Either the dogs had not heard him or they were too exhausted to stir because usually when they heard the morning's first stirrings they stretched, whined, and mouthed his hands in an attempt to direct him to the back door so they could have a quick trot around the backyard. He picked up the cup again and walked out the backdoor. With the turn of the doorknob the dogs could no longer resist and they clamored through the kitchen and bolted past the deputy without pausing for a scratch or pet.

He took a drink and the coffee had gone cold and he wondered if he had dozed in the chair or paused in the kitchen longer than he thought he had. He took longer and faster sips, but he could find no depth with the right warmth. He set the cup down on the stone patio, adding it to the collection of bottles and plastic cups lying about that were the aftermath of the party. None of the clutter had been cleaned. The serving table held pans of rotting food. The dining table and chairs were covered with dirty plates and utensils. Raccoons and skunks had feasted on the debris every night since the party so all had been knocked askew from their aggressive and insistent supping.

Jenny had refused to clean the mess, filibustering with her argument that since he had acted like an out-of-control teenager the least he could do was to clean up the mess he had created. He told her an army of coons would be at their backdoor, but she dismissed him or refused to consider real consequences. For his part he had decided he would never clean the patio because even if it had been his responsibility, and there were some serious questions about that premise, his injury had given him a pass, no matter if it had been self-inflicted, adolescent and bizarre. He created a code on the fly that stated once flesh had been burnt, bones broken, or muscles ripped all standard notions of responsibility should be nullified and the able-bodied should not question their enhanced responsibilities. His arguments enraged her even more, especially when she considered what she had witnessed in the hot tub.

He wanted her to remember the sequence of events because he wanted the images to produce in her the same level of horniness that they created in him, but Jenny could not be so easily titillated and she could not get past the fact that fucking took place on the grass where her children sometimes played, although they owned acres and acres of land where animals shit, died of disease, murdered each other and died in the jaws of the dogs, and fucked themselves, so he couldn't accept the revulsion. Sometimes she trotted out her worldliness and used it as a club to denigrate the small-minded, cloistered, and ignorant townsfolk, and other times she retreated behind indignation to clearly demonstrate a deed, impulse or use of words that lay beyond her realm of understanding.

The cocksucking was a perfect example. She had gone to a very expensive liberal arts college where she practically minored in muff-diving during her tenure. While the family never directly spoke of the subject he gathered by the mutterings, innuendos, half-told stories, and reminisces of holidays past that there had been some question, maybe even outright concern, that she would live her life as a lesbian and provide no more branches of the family tree. Even early in their marriage and as late as two years ago, a trickle of single women, sometimes with a man in tow, made the pilgrimage to their house in search of something, a rekindled spark, a revelation of past events, or an investigation of how and why someone so free and beautiful and unhinged could end up in Portsmouth married to a deputy, a man who actually wore a uniform for a living. She pretended to forget these women or slough off their visits as old friends passing through instead of pilgrims trekking to the very source of their desires. So, the deputy felt unnerved when she assumed the role of shocked, suburban mommy because anyone capable of partitioning off their minds so that past experiences did not influence present judgments could be capable of condemnation, such as the morning after the party when his face felt the worst, like he had been dragged along asphalt or, instead of the flash of the explosion, he had fallen asleep with his face in a blistering hot cast iron skillet, when his stomach had turned sour from the beer, booze, and pain medication, when he kept feeling his scalp for hair that was no longer there, she stood over him on his side of the bed wearing black panties and one of his t-shirts that had been given to him by a six-pack bowling league looking for advertising opportunities. She stood so close he could smell her pussy and he wondered if he could withstand the pain if he buried his face in the thin cotton. But as he was thinking of the best angle of approach she launched into an inquiry concerning the cocksucking incident, which took him by surprise because he didn't think at that time Paul would go that low. This argument took place before the performance of the play when the deputy, of course, understood the limitless depth of Paul's perversions.

At first he denied the act ever occurred, but she persisted with airtight logic and the fundamental belief that a person wouldn't drive the length of the state just to deliver a made-up story like that. The deputy questioned Paul's sanity, his veracity, and his motives, which had some impact but she kept coming back to the fundamentals and couldn't rest until she secured a confession. Whether it was her pussy a foot from his face or the injury or his exhaustion to blame for his confession mattered little because he finally told her what could have been the truth, although he left out some details such as the mutual swallowing as a test of manhood and the random thoughts of wanting to repeat the act. Suddenly, his worldly, sometimes lesbian wife became a hanging judge and she quickly formulated a guilty verdict, not so much for the act, because the thought of a cock in the deputy's mouth actually made her laugh, but the guilt of his non-disclosure, of withholding evidence of his humanity, of repeating the same inane stories with the same jokey punch-line conclusions, but forgetting to mention the one story that probably would have made her love him more, because he just might be more curious and daring than he would ever likely admit. Instead, she said, she had to hear it from a stranger and a psychopath in her home during a godawful barbecue and even when she directly asked him about the incident he denied it for a half-hour until she finally dragged it out of him. His lack of candor, the carefully built wall around his impulses, all except pyromania, drove her to fury. He reminded her of his face and said the wall had obviously been breached, which only managed to send her stomping away. He did not understand the conversation or the anger. When would have been a good time to bring up the cocksucking? It has been well documented through porn sites, college dares, and magazines exclusively analyzing and presenting daytime fantasies that a super-majority of men have a fascination with lesbians. The deputy, for his part, could not stop thinking about those three women sitting naked in his hot tub, kissing and fingering each other since his wife had told him the story. He had not heard of women sharing such a fascination and guessed that over ninety percent would think of breaking off the relationship if they thought their husband or boyfriend guilty of man-on-man sexual contact.

One particular incident came upon him in a rush. It happened a couple of years into their marriage. They hadn't yet moved to Portsmouth and both of them had bad jobs in Columbus. A college friend of Jenny's had come in and the two of them went drinking all night. They called him at least twice to come join them, but he felt exhausted and wanted to watch a baseball game. They rolled in after midnight stinking of booze, both wearing silk shirts half-unbuttoned. Her friend looked as good as Jenny, maybe a little taller, with auburn hair and a lithe body. Jenny wobbled up to him as he sat in front of the TV. The baseball game had ended and he hadn't fallen asleep as expected. She whispered in his ear that she planned on taking the friend into their bedroom and fuck her. She may have bitten his earlobe before staggering away to the bathroom to take a shower together. By the time the water started running he had an enormous erection and the sound coming from the TV no longer made sense. They lived in a small, cheaply built apartment so he could hear them laughing and giggling, but couldn't hear exactly what they were saying. After a while the water turned off and he imagined them toweling each other. He felt rooted to the couch. He tried to imagine himself walking down the short hallway, peeling off his clothes as he went, opening the bathroom door, and joining in on the fun, but he couldn't move. He hadn't been asked so a misplaced sense of politeness and propriety kept him from acting. He could have interpreted Jenny's actions as an invitation, the calls from the bar, coming back to the apartment where she knew he was, the explicit explanation of what would be happening in the bedroom, and the bite on the ear. Collectively, weren't all these clues just as clear as if she had asked him to fuck both of them after they showered? His hands trembled when he thought of them in bed together and when the soft moaning started he closed his eyes and wrapped a pillow around his ears.

Eventually he fell asleep and woke up sometime near morning when the friend slipped past him out the door. Jenny came out a few minutes later and fetched him. He fell back asleep holding her hand and in the morning, battling what had to be a ferocious hangover, she gave him a long and tender blowjob to reaffirm their marriage and that nothing had changed between them. But something had changed inalterably between them, most notably her insatiable desire for his body as if she wanted to make up to him again and again, as if her guilt knew no end or she wanted to keep her lesbian tendencies at bay so she fucked him every time a stray thought entered her head. What had really changed, though, was that she had opened herself to him and let him inspect her every desire, emotion and secret and his view of her progressed from an idealized and naïve image of a young and mannered impossibility to a flesh and blood animal with desires as intense as his. Innocence to experience, a glossy magazine photo airbrushed and color-balanced to a Polaroid catching her unaware, from guessing to knowing, from wanting her showered and perfumed before sex to preferring her sweaty, with a whiff of underarm odor and the folds of her pussy dank and fecund.

Not that they had sleepwalked through the first few years of marriage, but they really knew very little about each other. Greg shielded himself from her, never letting on to the full horror of living with his Bible-thumping dad, and even at that moment missing the chance to tell her about the cocksucking, as he had missed the opportunity at a threesome with two extraordinarily beautiful women. To admit he once acted on the same impulses would have been to lessen her grief and possibly turn her off from him. He couldn't bring himself to confess and admit to his past, even to his wife who lay open before him, even though the admission more than likely would have brought them closer as he would have assuaged her guilt and stopped her from flaying her own skin. How could she not be grateful for such a magnanimous act? The truth was that Jenny's lesbianism gave him an advantage in the marriage. Because she felt so guilty that she had cheated on him right in their own bed while he was in the apartment and she acquiesced or initiated sex as often as he could muster the desire for it was certainly the primary benefit of the advantage, but it could be used in larger decisions about where they lived, who were their friends, how often they visited her parents and even what they watched on TV. Jenny, sensing her disadvantage, knew that sex with her alone would not heal the wound, so she offered up her friend as a kind of consolation and to even the score. The friend came to their apartment while Jenny conveniently shopped for groceries and asked to come in even after he told her that Jenny was not home. They spent the next hour and a half engaged in an awkward conversation, avoiding the only topic they had in common, fucking Jenny. Only when she asked, "Are we going to do this or what?" did he finally realize that she had been an offering of apology. Stupidly, at that moment he believed he could gain greater advantage by turning her away, by carrying the grievance around in his back pocket instead of enjoying the friend's body, so he sent her away. She looked confused and angry, because she thought the deal had already been struck coupled with the likely fact that no one had ever refused to touch her. She left without a word and Jenny and he never spoke of the incident again. The friend must have reported back to Jenny that nothing transpired between them, but she never asked why and the incident, for him, slipped into the regret column of lost opportunities, much like the night he couldn't join them to make a threesome. For Jenny, whether or not he took the offer, her debt had been repaid so her attentions receded to a more typical schedule of sex, neither as torrid or frequent.

    He dressed with difficulty. He had to make sure not to scrape the wound with his shirt and any dramatic incline of his head set off a torrent of pain. Tying his shoes became a race against time to successfully complete the task before the throb turned into the migraine or unconsciousness. The struggle made him less worried about the completeness of his shave, the crispness of his uniform or the polish of his shoes, so in total he slid into an unkempt appearance compared to his former attention to detail. Fortunately, only the most severe critic would have noticed the change in the form of a few wrinkles or a scuff on his shoes when half of his face had been scorched, his eyebrows had been burned off, and all of his hair had been shaven off his skull.

    He climbed into his Chevy Trailblazer that he had leased six months before. He had mostly kept his wife and kids from using the truck so the seats held a minimum of cracker crumbs in the seams and random juice stains everywhere else. He suddenly remembered he hadn't kissed the girls goodbye, a habit or superstition he had fallen into because of the nature of his job. Not that he would have characterized his job as extremely dangerous. No one had been killed in the line of duty in more than two decades. Coalminers and ironworkers had it much worse, he calculated, because they could die at any moment when on the clock. He only had to grapple with someone like Kinnell once or twice a week when they were crazy from Oxycontin or Vicodin or a time-tested brain scrambler like 190-proof Everclear grain alcohol, citizens bent on killing him because he had taken the form of an avenging angel, their long dead father or the Mothman come to convince them to stop destroying themselves with prescription drugs and alcohol.

    He kissed his children because of the traffic accidents, the house fires, the explosions, the fathers falling from roofs, the elderly falling down stairs, the children downing in pools or the river, the suddenly dead, the mangled and broken who reminded the deputy every day that everyone walked on a high wire a thousand feet in the air and one slip or one wrong decision could lead directly to the end. So when he left the girls he compulsively thought it might be the last time he ever saw them. Jenny's driving was erratic and she skewed toward absent-mindedness. The stairs leading to the second floor were narrow and steep. The gas furnace looked like a bomb. When would they be old enough to lift the hot tub lid? If they fell in and managed to stand up would their mouths be above the waterline? How had he failed to teach them to swim by now? Maybe they could just walk into the woods on a winter's day and never be found again. He imagined them stumbling through the trunks of barren trees, sobbing.

He couldn't risk going back to the house. If he kissed them and they waked, they would pepper him with a half hour of questions like when would he be home, when would his face look normal and feel better, was he going to die, would his eyebrows grow back, why did he sleep on the couch now, who was in jail, when would he shoot his gun for them and could he take them swimming soon because they had more fun when he took them to the lake or the pool because he would launch them into the air and catch them and play shark and play motorboat while mom tended to stand in one place and make sure they didn't go too deep, citing the frigidity of the water as the reason for her lack of movement and games? The goodbye kiss would turn into twenty kisses and an equal number of hugs and he would be even later for his shift. They were perfect in every way and he would never be able to keep them safe.

16

Angel of the Donuts

The deputy started the truck and backed out of the drive. He drove to a Dunkin' Donuts that had been recently built alongside a Taco Bell, a BP gas station with a mini grocery store of processed treats sheathed in plastic and drinks so carbonated they could have been considered a gas, and a Chick-fil-a that had hosted nearly three thousand people who showed up for its midnight opening to get a free chicken sandwich that looked and smelled like it could have been fileted from a large, brown rat. He had to work security that night and several times he thought of pulling out his gun and shooting it into the air to scatter the crowd but by the looks of half of them they brought their own weapons and a single shot could have incited a bloody skirmish on the newly poured asphalt.

He walked inside the donut shop. The manager already had the air-conditioning blasting so his burn tingled as he broke through the curtain of chilled air. Sabina stood behind the register, cashing out a trucker buying a dozen donuts that one suspected he would eat all himself. She inspected Greg over the shoulder of the trucker and her eyebrows arched at the sight of his head. Once the trucker cleared, already reaching into the box to retrieve a donut, the deputy stepped to the edge of the counter and leaned his torso in as he steadied himself by holding onto the edge.

"Jesus, what did you do to your face?" Sabina spoke with a trace of a southern Lithuanian accent that stubbornly clung to her English.

The deputy stared at the shelves of donuts, battling the growling of his stomach as he couldn't remember the last time he ate.

"I'll ask you again, what happened to your face? You do not look as pretty as before."

"Nothing permanent."

"The sheriff says you like a little boy and play with fireworks."

The deputy figured the old slob had been eyeing her, but until that moment he didn't think the sheriff knew anything about the affair he and Sabina conducted.

"Did the sheriff say anything else?"

"He said only men with small wieners like explosions as much as you do. I had to agree, right? Men like this must be angry about something to crave destruction and mayhem, no?"

"You could have disagreed."

"Yes, well, the cream sticks are very good and the toe curlers and the bend-me-overs are new and very popular. We can barely keep them upright and on the shelves. The powdered pillows you want to put your face in them and bite the corners and basically let the goodness run down your face. Personally, I like the filled donuts because with every bite and lick you don't know what will end up in your mouth."

The deputy already had an erection burrowed against the zipper of his pants as it had escaped through the fly of his boxers. He pushed against the counter, aware as he was about being in public in his uniform and not wanting anyone to notice his arousal. Sabina sensed his discomfort.

"Too bad I need this job to pay rent because I would more than likely be on my knees in front of you right now."

"Give me a large coffee and a dozen donuts for the boys."

"Oh, I see, you came for donuts and not me. I will add the maple-glazed cinnamon roll for the fat, drunk slob. He's already been in here an hour and a half ago and eaten one but if you take him another he will be in a good mood all day. He'll think he's ascended to heaven on the wings of an angel."

"When can I see you again?"

She acted as if she really considered the question, but she also knew the pausing only deepened his interest. He was being thought of and considered. Unfortunately, she could not come up with an answer that advanced the flirtation.

"I don't often sleep with burn victims. Have you seen yourself in the mirror? You look crazed and wounded. I can't say that I'm counting down the hours until we are together again."

"What does that mean?"

"You have no hair, Deputy, and I love hair and it looks like someone has taken a potato peeler to your face. Maybe you should let your wife nurse you back to health before you think of resuming your old life. Maybe your old life was not so good and it led you to this or maybe you should think why did you blow up your face."

"It was an accident."

"You know I don't believe in accidents. There are only causes and effects."

"This has nothing to do with us."

"Cause equals you blowing up your face. Let's not even talk about why you would do such a thing because in other scenarios the explosion would be an effect, ok, but in this case it is a cause and the corresponding effect is that I have no desire to be with you so our affair is at an end."

"Why?" Greg said with more panic in his voice than he wanted to show. "Does this have something to do with the sheriff?"

"No, the old, fat drunk has nothing to do with this."

"Then why are you saying this?"

"By definition the sex must be consensual between two people said to be having an affair, yes? Without the sex there is no affair, just an ex-affair and believe me when I tell you there will be no sex until you grow back your hair and eyebrows. Then you will have to wait until I get this image of you as a cancer patient out of my head, which could take a very long time. By then you may find other donut girls with whom to pass the time. Affairs are very fragile, fleeting things. I have not married you and I do not have to wait. I have not said I will accept the worst of you, which I am looking at right now. That is your wife's cross to bear."

"I came in here to find some comfort."

"I am sorry to disappoint the poor burned man."

The sugar and grease smelled offensive to him. He felt light-headed. He would have liked to sit down and hold onto a table to find his elusive equilibrium and she would sit down across from him and stroke his hand and show concern for his pain and discomfort. Her face would have been kind and gentle and probably would have been the last image his memory would have held before he fell into unconsciousness. But sitting down could also been interpreted by her as an act of defiance or antagonism or absolutely and irrevocably pathetic. He wasn't exactly clear on why she wanted to punish him, but he could find the exact reason another day when he felt stronger. The key to their future as lovers lay in this moment, his reaction to her stopping their lovemaking. He closed his eyes to gather himself but this only made the dizziness worse. When he opened them again he was surprised to find himself still standing upright.

"I'll be back when I have made a full recovery. Then we'll see what tune you are whistling." The words came out in a half-croak and the cadence was weak, so the aura of irresistibility he wanted to portray never made it much past his lips. Sweat began to bead on his forehead and upper lip.

"I hope so, lover. I hope you will show what you got again," Sabina said with poor charity. Neither believed in the possibility right now, but she didn't want him to leave completely defeated.

He staggered from the shop, but he couldn't remember if he had said goodbye to her. What did that matter, though? He tried to look professional and in-control as he jumped into his truck, but a casual observer would have considered it a half-tumble. He knew better than to close his eyes so he stared straight ahead, which encompassed the dumpster of the Chick-fil-a and the gas station beyond. Out of his periphery walked Sabina. She held his box of donuts with an enigmatic smile smeared across her face. She rapped on the driver's side window with a knuckle and he fumbled to put the keys in the ignition so the automatic window would go down.

"You forgot your donuts. Was this some kind if trick to get me out to your car? Are you going to arrest me and take me to a hotel where you will enter me through the rear?"

"No, I get that I'm a mutant right now. I must look like such a goddamn freak."

"Poor Deputy. So easily pushed aside. Maybe this also is a symptom of having a small penis. Explosions and no tenacity?"

"You're confusing me. I'm too sick to be confused."

"Ok, ok, here are your donuts. Maybe the next time you should bring fruit to the officers. Your belly is beginning to hang over your belt. I am not in love with men with bellies."

The deputy took the box without responding, so unlike him that she grew concerned about his well-being. She blew him a kiss as he drove out of the parking lot and half-expected him to smash into a telephone pole as she watched. The affair had begun six months before as the outcome of a long-standing flirtation he had been engaged in since she had been hired to work the counter of the donut shop. He began the game when he complimented her ability to rapidly fill a box of donuts with her graceful hands and she responded that she liked the way his Glock hung from his belt, certainly a quick escalation of innuendo, but it served the purpose of hooking him in the match. On another visit he complained that she had to have her beautiful mane of hair pinned back to avoid contaminating the donuts when in fact he would consider a stray follicle or two from her head as a prize worth keeping should he find them nestled amongst his order, to which she responded that she didn't think he should be able to wear his shirt so tight because of the distraction it caused. Who couldn't help but break a few laws when they saw him in that shirt? Soon after he asked how she kept her perfect shape amidst so much sugar and fat. She answered that her desires could not be sated with flour and confectioner's sugar, so the donuts proved to be no temptation. But she found the appeal of particular customers to be her greatest test. He caught the plural noun and felt challenged by unknown rivals.

There was really no telling when the levee would break. Two days later he ventured that designer of her uniform should be given a reward as Dunkin' Donuts had created the best walking away pants in the entire fast food industry, if not the hospitality sector of the economy, to which she replied how she couldn't help noticing the outline of his cock beneath his pants. Neither could breathe. The grease and sugar smell in the shop turned into a heavy animal musk. He stayed away for two weeks. He showered his wife with affection and tried to up the frequency of their sex, but they only managed to fuck once in the intervening two weeks because Jenny had a couple of debilitating migraines, he had to work security for a couple of high school football games, and both girls had ear infections that kept them up later than usual. The one time they did have sex, which occurred exactly one week after Sabina mouthed the word cock to him not three feet from his face, they were so exhausted, so distracted, and so completely unable to muster any passion that Jenny silently wished they had waited until they both felt better and the deputy wished he had taken care of himself behind the barn with a underwear circular that had come in the mail that had a model that resembled Sabina if he squinted with the word cock ringing in his ears. The deputy knew that they should try again for the sake of the marriage, a perfect opportunity never presented itself and their latest attempt had been so lackluster that he felt like a fool attempting again, at least until their affection recalibrated or the girls' ear infections cleared.

He went back to the shop and stood at the counter a long time before she came over to wait on him. He thought she might ignore him until he left, but she finally relented and gave him an icy and critical inspection from across the counter. She said she had not been wrong about his physical attributes nor his constitution. She always knew he would be the one to turn away before they leapt off the cliff together. He reminded her that he was now standing in front of her and that he had turned away from nothing. She shrugged her shoulders and wrote down her address on the back of a blank receipt. She included the days and hours when she would most likely be home.

"I think you will not keep the appointment. You don't have the stomach for it."

He showed up during the first hour of the first day of the calendar she had provided him. She lived in a trailer set in the middle of a copse of trees, so the closest parking spot was a landing of mud and gravel two hundred feet from her front door. Off to the side a small patch of ground had been tilled and was now covered by dead tomato plants. A single, soft tomato hung from one of the vines, the mother of springtime volunteers. She met him at the door as if she had been expecting him, freshly showered, hair blown dry, a trace of lipstick highlighting her perfect lips, wearing a robe that hung only to her upper thighs, open to her navel.

They never made it past the doorway or far enough inside to be able to close the door properly even though the autumn air had turned crisp. They fucked half inside and half outside as the deputy's naked ass pumped and clenched in the air, hidden behind the stand of trees. Their kisses created voltage, enough to power the trailer for a few days off the grid. It took three months for them to get past the doorway, although a few weeks in they made the concession of closing the door against the encroaching winter air. Once they graduated to the couch or her lumpy bed their lovemaking lost some of the spontaneity but technique and calculation filled the void and the fucking was not less pleasurable.

The deputy accepted the fact that he was a liar and a cheat about the time they moved to the bedroom when, through happy circumstance, he fucked Jenny in the morning before they had a chance to brush their teeth or even hand-comb their hair and he fucked Sabina not five hours later during an extended lunch. He took a shower afterwards at Sabina's and as he soaped himself up he felt a sense of accomplishment at having bedded two beautiful women within hours of each other as if he had reached the zenith of his power and that he might be on the cusp of an era in which he dominated and had his desires fulfilled when and where he wanted. Then he remembered the smile Jenny had given him at the conclusion of their coupling and his pride soured into remorse. He would not give up Sabina just yet, but some kind of accommodation had to be made to avoid the clawing guilt, so he resolved never to sleep with both of them on the same day. While the frequency appealed to his ego his conscience simply would not let the possibility stand. His guilt momentarily assuaged, he stepped from the shower and tracked down Sabina to take her from behind. It wasn't until the second time he rinsed off and was toweling himself that all the pieces of his flexible reasoning jammed themselves together. His rutting, animal nature could not be constrained by structure and clever conventions, namely family and marriage, and the foundation on which the rest of his personality had been built consisted of nothing more than craven deceit, so he acknowledged the fact, catalogued it as a disappointing admission of his own weakness, that should the opportunity of doubling up on sex present itself on any given day he would not be able to pass it up. The infrequency of the sex with Jenny made it seem improbable that his resolution would be tested any time soon, but not two weeks later the same occurred. The only difference in this occurrence and the one previous was the time between the two sessions was considerably shorter, not more than a half-hour between the last playful lick of Jenny's labia and penetrating Sabina as she jackknifed over the back on her musty couch. Accepting one's weaknesses can be the first step toward mending your ways or it can give a person permission to plunge headlong into infamy. The deputy chose the latter course.

17

The Fat Man Weighs In

He walked into the department almost an hour late for his shift. He had been late every day that he had been scheduled since the accident. Every day he showed up surprised his colleagues and the sheriff, but there was some grumbling amongst the ranks that if he planned to work then he should be on time. Punctuality had become something of a fetish in the department because the sheriff, acting as the wellspring, parsed his time to the second as a reaction to the increasing frequency of his hangovers and the depths of his drinking bouts. His rationale rested on the belief that no one could effectively criticize his personal pursuits if they in no way affected his official time, so he tracked time with the precision of a nuclear engineer. The sheriff's belief conveniently excluded the flask of Wild Turkey in his desk drawer that had once been preserved for convictions resulting from successful investigations, a validation of the efficiency of the department, but that he now used to celebrate the successful completion of an hour at work or a particularly tiresome day.

Of course the time fetish rubbed off on his employees and a competition arose not as to who could be the earliest or who could work the most hours or who could use his or her time most effectively in keeping the streets of Portsmouth free of crime, but who could most closely work the required number of hours per week that the county demanded in order to be considered a full-time employee. Once they started to pay attention, the deputies, clerks, administrative staff and maintenance staff realized how infrequently they worked an exact 40 hour work week. The nature of their work was emergency and response and anything outside the rule of law could throw their day into chaos. The 40 hour cult grew because of its rarity and at the end of pay periods an observer could spot a staff person puzzling over their time card and wondering if they could have done anything different to have not lost more minutes of their life than was completely necessary by contract.

The deputy threw the boxes of donuts on the counter in the break room. He knew by experience that he did not have to announce their arrival because several deputies had an extraordinary ability to sense confectioner's sugar in the building and they would tip off those less fortunate by parading their napkin swaddled trophy through the offices, the first pup from a cloying litter.

The deputy sat at his desk. The fever had returned. Sweat stained his underarms and he could feel hundreds of beads covering his forehead and temples, but he couldn't wipe them away because he felt he would accidentally scrape his wounds, which would more than likely set off another round of deep nausea. No one had verbally said hello. Maybe a couple of head nods and a look of incredulity. The skinhead, psycho killer look had more impact than he had first imagined. The loss of his eyebrows cast him past style and into the realm of weirdness. With eyebrows he looked like badass military. Without eyebrows he looked like a man who tortured animals and preyed on children as they walked home from their elementary school. Thank God he didn't own a van or have a side job as a clown. He would have had to arrest himself based just on a suspicious profile.

He scanned the detritus of unfinished work on his desk. A splayed pile on the right held the entire investigation of the found skull. A series of photos of the skull showed where it finally came to a rest after the long tumble down the gravel slope. The mandible and cranium had detached but they tumbled together and ended up a few feet from each other. The forensics report from the Columbus coroner stated that she had been an adolescent female, approximately 16 years old, who had been in the ground approximately 30 years, thus placing her death around 1980. More photos of the excavation of the ground around where the skull had been released revealed no other skeletal remains other than vertebrae C1 through C4. The head had been placed in the ground with a short extension of neck. Markings on vertebrae C4 clearly show the scrapes from the tool used to sever the head from its body. He imagined the head resting on the ground as a depraved lunatic dug the receiving hole. The head being picked up and placed in the hole. The wide, surprised eyes staring at the killer before their vision was blotted out by the first shovel of dirt. The pile of papers also had newspaper clippings from the Columbus Dispatch and the Portsmouth Daily Times and dozens of printed pages from the internet where the story had run, from the website of the Dallas Morning News to an entry on deathmask.com to citations on blogs dedicated to grisly and unsolved murders. Many of the writers had misinterpreted his quote, "Now we just have to find the owner of it," as the babbling of a moronic hick and not as the joke he had meant, as if he did not have the mental capacity to understand that he held the owner in his hands. Still, the rolling of the skull down the slope of the pit and his quote made for a solid web presence.

Also jammed amongst the files, photos and clippings were a hundred phone messages meticulously transcribed by the department receptionist and assistant to the sheriff. Everyone in the department had begged the sheriff at one time or another for an automated voicemail system, but he knew the technology would cost him his assistant and he was rather fond of Clarisse, a faded beauty of German descent whose clothes were always too tight for the age and state of her body and whose hair was always two shades too red, but in a certain light of a certain part of the day, maybe the dregs of twilight or the first kiss of morning sun, her former radiance shown through and the deputies would become uncomfortable because of where their musings had taken them. The sheriff had ceased considering women, so he did not protect her for any base sexual reasons. His disinterest began with a strong dose of stress and alcohol induced impotence, his desires languished in a black and foul pit and could only be summoned to the surface with a most severe onslaught of pornography and absolute concentration. So, he kept Clarisse for her other abilities, like her uncanny ability to know and keep track of the state of his staff's personal lives, every break-up, death, marriage, and fondness for fried foods, and her clairvoyance when it came to deciphering true from false rumors, which was especially important given the sheriff's unsteady relationship with the mayor and council. Clarisse trained her ability to support her fierce loyalty for the sheriff and he knew he would keep her until he died or lost at the polls, with death being the more likely cause because his name in Scioto County could not be beaten.

The deputy knew the sheriff thought he had political ambitions of his own, because, in brief moments of lucidity, he would refer to future contests by saying something like, "It's a damn shame about your last name. It wants a consonant at the end. Nobody in this county votes for a name that leaves their lips in the position to suck cock. You could change it or find out its original form before someone hacked it in half to make it more palatable for the American tongue. I can imagine a Sheriff Aurock or Aurot, but that 'o' just hanging there might as well be a child molestation charge in your past because it will stop you dead in your tracks." But the sheriff, informed by Clarisse, had it wrong. The deputy had no political aspirations presently and could not think of a time when he ever considered it. If he wanted the job his name wouldn't stop him, of that he was sure. The sheriff had forgotten that he had once been a dynamo during his first three terms in office and their subsequent elections. He jammed his schedule with barbeques, weddings, birthdays, Little League trophy presentations, American Legion Fish Fry Fridays, bowling leagues, the county fair, graduations, and funerals. He haunted every coffee shop and restaurant in the county. He stopped people at gas stations and harangued them about his qualifications to keep them safe to pursue happiness. He talked from morning to night until his voice gave way and his arches throbbed in protest. No one had worked like him to secure votes and by the time the elections rolled around he won in massive landslides never before seen in the county. Once a mayoral candidate died in a traffic accident a week before the election and even this dead candidate received more votes than the sheriff's opponent that year. But the sheriff had forgotten his work had gotten him elected, that his drive to convince the generations of voters that he was and would always be the only viable man who could keep order had been so compelling that those voting for him actually did believe his vision as he laid it out for them. Now closing in on completing a fifth term and sure he would run for a sixth, he had convinced himself that his name had carried him, had induced a trance on the electorate whereby the slightest suggestion of his continued eminence and worthiness would allow him to carry the day. His name, Felix Brust, looked good on signs, was short and memorable, had the required German origins that made at least 20% of the voting public comfortable, and had a meaning that translated to "lucky breast." How could he ever lose?

Behind the stack of paper stood a line of photos of Jenny and the children. His wife had framed the pictures and given them to him as a birthday present, but he could never decipher the intent of such a gift in his mind. Was it a simple token of affection, a group talisman to ward off drudgery, the irritations, the moments of abject misery, a hint of the joy he felt when he first fell in love with her and when he saw the girls' squished faces for the first time or had she intended the pictures to be sentinels of control, to remind him who he had left at home and that they would be unforgiving judges should any of his transgressions see the light of day? They spied on him and thought him sad as he sat behind the desk reading paperwork.

The deputy did not know how long his phone had been ringing when he finally picked up the receiver. Clarisse breathed into his ear. He listened for three or four breaths before he spoke.

"Clarisse."

"Are you ok over there?"

"I'm fine."

"Did the fire burn the eardrums out of your head?"

"No, my ears are just fine."

"So, usually, the protocol around here is that when a phone rings we answer it. When we pick up the phone we say hello and then state our position and name. So, in your case you would say, 'Hello, Deputy Auro speaking.'"

"Is there a purpose to this call, Clarisse, or has the sheriff implemented spot training?"

"The sheriff wants to see you, pronto."

The deputy hung up the phone without saying goodbye to complete his break with office etiquette. He lurched to his feet and fought an onslaught of dizziness. He must have teetered or held his hands out to find his equilibrium, because after the sensation passed and he came to everyone still left in the office stared at him, expecting him to collapse to the floor and sat poised on their chairs to rush to help him. The deputy refused to acknowledge them and tottered through the desks to the sheriff's office. He had to pass Clarisse's desk, which all but blocked access to the sheriff's office door, facing outward toward the staff and all their interruptions and irritations. A consensus developed among those who saw the arrangement that nowhere had the physical manifestation of the title "gatekeeper" been so perfectly executed in an office environment. When someone had the luck to be granted an audience he or she had to sidle through the strategically placed filing cabinets, potted plants, banker boxes and her desk chair so an acolyte either had to sidle past, sometimes pirouetting past a strategically placed obstacle.

The sheriff sat behind the desk, hands together in front of his face posed like a church steeple. Before him crowding his desk stood a lineup of 18 and 20 inch action figures, all menacingly facing the door with weapons ready or glares drawn. Front and center a huddle of *Star Wars* figures posed. The familiar and original set that began his collection included Luke Skywalker, Darth Vader, Han Solo, Chewbacca, C3PO, R2D2, Obi Wan Kenobi, and Princess Leia. On the periphery of the core group stood Lando Calrissian, Yoda, Boba Fett, and the Emperor. To the left a group that contained Hellboy, Leatherface, Arnold Schwarzenegger and the Alien from *Predator*, the Alien from *Alien*, Freddy Krueger, Jason, a skinned Terminator, Rambo and Michael Meyers. Behind this grouping was another copse of Aragorn, Legolas, Gimli, Gandalf, Boromir, Frodo, Samwise Gamgee, Merry, and Pippin. The right side of the desk was covered by Spiderman, The Hulk, Superman, Batman, Captain America, Wonder Woman, Thor, Captain Marvel, Daredevil, Ant-Man, Human Torch, Silver Surfer, The Thing, The Tick, Robin, Catwoman, Kitty Pryde, Judge Dredd, Wolverine, The Joker, Magento, Dr. Doom, The Punisher, Swamp Thing, Electra, Emma Frost, Lex Luthor, Dr. Strange, Green Lantern, Poison Ivy, and Rasputin. The sheriff had not used the desk in at least two election cycles, although the scraps of surface that could be seen at the feet of the figures looked polished and the figures themselves were free of dust.

On the four walls shelves filled with diminutive versions of the action figures competed with photographs, certificates, and plaques that charted the popularity of the sheriff's reign, so that the tiny growling faces reflected off the glass of certificates of appreciation from the Rotary Club, Junior Achievement, the 4H club, and the Ladies Auxiliary for his earnestness, dedication to service and his ability to grant favors that skirted ethical boundaries so effectively that the association or organization gushed with appreciation, since they were practically guilt-free, once their favor had been granted. The office seemed to be half the size of its actual square footage with all the crowding of genuflecting and fantasy. The deputy could never properly breathe in the space although it was the cleanest room in the building and had shortest swing in temperature throughout the year. He sat down in a chair across the desk from the sheriff before he could be asked.

The sheriff leaned back in his chair. Morning sunlight poured in from the left and blazed on the heads of the figures before them, leaving the sheriff's face in half-shadow. The sheriff stared at the deputy a long time. After a minute, which felt like ten or fifteen minutes of uncomfortable silence, the deputy realized the sheriff expected him to speak first. Sometimes the sheriff followed a protocol that only he knew and that could be changed with every capricious thought.

"You wanted to see me, sheriff?"

"I assume you're aware that the facilities provided by the taxpayers of Scioto County, which I'll have you know are gettin' more scarce than a virgin in a college dormitory, aren't to be misused in the pursuit of a personal vendetta?"

"Sir?"

"I walk in this morning and all the little birdies were chirping in my ear about how you busted-up a theatrical performance that had the chops to make an off-Broadway run. Not only did you stomp on the magic of live theater, damn near pissed on the spell of drama and pathos those brave actors spent months chasing through countless hours of rehearsal, but I've got three of them in my jail. Poor Roy Rogers messed his pants and had been sobbing for thirty-six hours straight. That friend of yours, the deputies tell, has nearly rubbed the skin right off his cock he's been jacking-off so much. The sonofabitch is wallowing in his own jizz and I'm going to have to get that cell scoured clean once we get this all cleared up. Then, not that the other two aren't bad enough, we have Miss Goddess, refusing to put any clothes on even under the threat of sedation and beatings, both of which, she says, she charges a hefty price. I've got a whole floor of deputies walking around with boners and making copies of the surveillance tape. The word I hear is that friend of yours and Miss Goddess banged your wife in the hot tub and this was your way of exacting revenge. Now, that's a strong rumor with a ton of potential truth behind it. Remember, deputy, I was at that very same party and while I think it's unlikely that was the way things turned given the mood of Jenny most of the night, there is the problem of the hot tub. That's what you get for buying one. What else do people do but skinny-dip and have orgies with their neighbors in those goddamn things? You get a hot tub you are going to start tongues a wagging. When I was your age I bought a Camaro Z28 with a 305 cubic inch small block V-8. It was white with double red stripes down the middle. I bought that car because I was a gearhead and I loved driving it, hauling ass down the country roads, thinking I was flyin', but you can't do things for your own reasons without leaving a snail trail of gossip. The mockingbirds started making up all kinds of reasons why I would buy a hot car. I heard my marriage was failing, that I had a small cock, that I was worried about male-pattern baldness, that I was a dipshit and a hillbilly and that I liked passing by the high school to pick up girls who could still be impressed by a car. I supposedly got more blowjobs than Sir John Holmes, the king himself. So here I was, I liked the look of the car and the goddamn growl of the engine and that it could take a turn with the best of them, but that wasn't good enough. People are going to project on you what they need to see, so instead of a gearhead in love with speed I was an unhappy husband, tasteless, sexually inadequate, with a powerful fear of age and a drive toward pedophilia and a fetish for oral sex, and that was based on a factory-made American production car. So my advice to you, deputy, is either get rid of the hot tub or suffer through the rumors and innuendo."

"Something happened but it wasn't like you said. It had nothing to do with Jenny."

"But enough to do with her for her to stop talking to you?"

"That, and disinfecting the tub. I don't think she'll ever go back in, so I might be getting rid of it after all."

"Truth be told, I did get my fair share of oral sex in the Camaro. The fact didn't make all the other rumors true. My wife was the one doing the blowing. She loved that car more than I did. That engine growl got her all hot and we had a lot of fun in that goddamn car."

"Millie was a nice woman. I really don't need to know..."

"That she loved cock?"

"Sheriff, c'mon, please."

"Just because she's dead doesn't make her a saint. She knew some tricks that would make Larry Flynt blush."

"Sure."

"You don't believe me?"

"Sheriff, there are just so many combinations. I get the analogy but I don't see how she could be ahead of Larry Flynt on that curve."

"You don't look well, Auro."

"I don't feel particularly well, sir."

"For a moment you looked like a burning matchstick after that gunpowder went off. The whole goddamn yard smelled like burnt hair."

"That's what I've been told."

"Hell of a party, though."

"We certainly provided enough entertainment to keep everyone's interest."

"I've done some checking. You really should be more careful who you invite to your home." He reached for a file balanced on the edge of the desk at the feet of Emma Frost.

"I didn't invite her. My friend, Paul, brought her along."

"We know all about Paul, don't we?"

"I haven't seen him a long time. I don't know anything about him, really."

He opened the file and flapped it toward the deputy's face. "A common whore! She told us her name is Juicy Cocktail, which isn't even appropriate for a stripper name. I had a hunch and we ran her prints and we got hits all over the state. I didn't even bother with Kentucky and West Virginia but I imagine the list is just as long. Let me give you an idea of what some of her aliases have been. Let's see, here: Avalon Shores, Dixie Wonder, Eveline Tender, Ariel Lush, Pink Clover, New

Jagger, Lucy Whisper, Lucy Sigh, Lucy Scream, Savannah Cream, Hello Kitty-Star, Golden Pie, Lamb Lust, Lamb Found, Betty Hole, Whole Liberty, Chrysanthemum Supple, LaLa Push, Spanky Dallas, Sweet Jane, Velvet Throb, Virginia Head, Brandy Bendover, Crystal Glitterstockings, Dreamy Soft-Toes, Chesty McCheese, Busty Strider, Olivia Gush, Roxy Crush, Pussy Rush, Pussy Cream, Pussy Star, Pussy Found, Pussy Lost, Pussy Crown, Pussy Royale, Pussy Wilde, Pussy Near, Pussy Dear, Pussy Forth, Pussy Dazzle, Pussy Down, Pussy Up, Pussy Clear, Pussy Hand, Pussy Head, Pussy Toes, Pussy Princess, Pussy On, Pussy Dream, Pussy Babylon, Pussy Stamp, Pussy Highway, Pussy Depot, Pussy Pussy, Pussy Fall, Pussy Whisper, Pussy Clover, Pussy Comfort, Pussy Key, Pussy Field Forever, Pussy Thermal, and Pussy Saraswati."

"Where are we going with this, sir?"

"What I'm telling you is she has so many arrests up and down the I-77 corridor that we damn near got a hit from every jurisdiction from Portsmouth to Cleveland."

"I'm not surprised. I can see her for what see is."

"What did she do at the church?"

"She exposed her breasts during the play. I brought her in on indecent exposure."

"Son, that old man who she has by the short hairs called me up crying. The man must know some people too because I got calls from county commissioners, mayors and even the Deputy Chief of Staff for the Governor. My take on the whole thing is that there's nothing indecent about those titties and there isn't one member of that audience that is sorry they saw them, the truth be told. The old man insists and ol' Roy Rogers in the soggy pants concurs that nothing was intended and what you saw was the Portsmouth variation of a wardrobe malfunction."

"You don't want to go any farther with the charges?"

"The old man weeps on the phone to me. It's the saddest damn thing you'd ever want to hear. Besides, I have to get my deputies back in line. Clarisse is tired of seeing their boners. You'd think I employed a gang of satyrs."

"What about the Blue Cowboy?"

"The man messed his pants."

"You said that."

"And he sat in his own shit for over a full day."

"Whatever."

"I don't think the man had anything to do with it. He's come to this town for twenty years straight without a problem. We're practically his home away from home."

"You got more calls about him?"

"The entire Roy Rogers fan-base. Clarisse tells me she's going to quit because her ear is getting hot from all the calls. I guess he's something of a legend among the fans. The crew tells me your buddy was a late, desperate addition because other actors quit. They tell me the likelihood of, what's his real name...." he said as he fumbled through a second file that held the secret of Blue Cowboy's real name. "Victor Stanpipe, right, the likelihood of him sullying the name and reputation of Roy Rogers is absolutely nil. Of course, the fans and crew told me in no uncertain terms that poor Vic is ruined in the community. He'll be lucky to be simply shunned. If they catch him they may tie him to a tree using his own intestines. They are goddamn hopping mad at him, but they know he didn't do anything on purpose. It's just he'll never be trusted again. He's done. Anyway, I doubt he'll have much yearning to come back to Portsmouth, knowing this is the place where he publicly shit his pants."

"So, we're not pressing charges."

"No, and that leaves your friend."

"He was my neighbor twenty years ago."

"Who you invited to your house."

"Who fucked one of our guests on the lawn..."

"By the hot tub, no doubt."

"Yes, by the hot tub, and who came onto my wife and who brought a prostitute in full bloom to my home and introduced her to my wife and who finger-fucked another guest while he had his tongue down the prostitute's throat."

"Somewhere in the vicinity of the hot tub."

"In the hot tub, Sheriff, in the hot tub. So, I came to the play to have a talk with him afterwards. Maybe I wanted to find out why the hell he's such a pervert and bastard that he would disrespect me and my wife, especially after not seeing him for twenty years."

"It gets worse, Deputy. He's telling every other deputy who will listen that he used to suck your cock."

"And this lunatic pulls out his cock and starts waving it at all the blue hairs. How could I not arrest him? That wasn't a proper part of the play. Roy Rogers never played in a porno."

"Did you hear me?"

"Yes, I heard you."

"Do you have anything to say about that? I personally have never been accused of cocksucking, but I thought it would be something that you'd take some notice of."

"What am I supposed to say about that? The man is a goddamn fruit loop. He was always a little weird, but I wouldn't have thought he's gone this crazy."

"Said the bald man with no eyebrows."

"What are you saying, Sheriff?"

"I'm saying that this past week hasn't been your best."

"Agreed."

"What kind of pain medication do they have you on?"

"Just prescription-strength Tylenol. I told them I'd be working."

"Jesus Christ." The sheriff mimed the act of thinking a moment, opened the left-hand drawer of his desk, and finally produced a business card. As he watched the sheriff over the heads of the action figures, the deputy caught the glare of Hellboy and looked away toward the window. Once the sheriff was ready to hand him the card their hands met over the desk both stretching to make sure none of the figures were disturbed. The deputy took the card and analyzed it. The sheriff had signed the back.

"Go over to the Allied Health Management and Wellness Clinic over on Lawndale. They pass out Oxy like it's Halloween night."

"Who is Dr. Gideon Kneebender?"

"He takes care of me. My back and neck haven't been right since I had that car accident. Once you get past his name you'll understand what a valuable resource I've just given you. He'll take care of you. He knows that card comes from me."

"Thanks, I guess, for pushing a narcotic on me."

"My guess is that you're not strictly on Tylenol, anyway. I bet you raided the medicine cabinet for Oxy or Percodan, but you couldn't have had that many. There's no reason to feel pain, Deputy. Go get the prescription and work on getting healed."

"Thank you for real, Sheriff. It is thoughtful."

"You know Kinnell is back?"

"No, I didn't know."

"Deputy Worter picked him up on another public intoxication. He started talking again about that girl. That skull of yours. He keeps babbling that he's the killer. What do you make of all of that?"

"He would have been a child, if not an infant, at the time of her death. My educated guess is that he had nothing to do with the killing. There may be others, possibly several others that he's responsible for, but not this one. What sense does it make?"

"How old would be have been at the time of her death?" the sheriff asked.

"I don't remember exactly, but no more the three or four, probably."

"Is there an outside chance?"

"That a toddler murdered a teenager, drove her to a remote site, cut off her head and buried her head and body in two separate locations?"

"Has it happened before?"

"Not to my knowledge, Sheriff. I could check the FBI database on infant and toddler crime. We might get a hit."

"Ok, smartass, you must be feeling better."

"No, I'm not really."

"My advice to you is you break it off with that girl at Dunkin'. That's not going to end well."

"What are you talking about? I thought we were talking about the skull?"

"I can see the powdered sugar falling off of you. You practically leave a trail wherever you go. She's a nice girl and doesn't deserve to be all gummed-up with a married man."

"I can't see how any of this is any of your business, Sheriff."

"I've got to keep order and discipline in my department, don't I?"

The deputy leaned forward and crossed his arms across his chest as if readying himself to jump out of a plane or sail down a waterslide. He couldn't help but remember the nature programs his father let him watch as a child, during which they would inevitably get around to showing a wounded zebra or wildebeest get torn apart by a pride of lions or a pack of sneering hyenas. There always seemed to be a moment when the wounded animal stood bleeding and panting, his fate assured, as he stared down his killer right before the final assault. He couldn't remember, though, a time when he felt more like that bleeding zebra than this moment in the sheriff's office.

"How I choose to conduct my personal life has nothing to do with my work."

"Well, Deputy, if you want to cover the same ground we both just walked across I will too. I'm willing to accept that maybe there are some limits of my interest in how you conduct your personal business, but those limits tend to fly out the window when you show up to work without eyebrows and unfit for duty. Then, your personal life tends to be business. Remember, you do carry a gun in the name of Scioto County and the great State of Ohio."

"I'm fit and ready to go."

"Your wife must have busted all the mirrors in the house."

"Funny."

"Has Jenny ever noticed the powdered sugar in your pubes?"

The deputy listed and now felt the hot breath of the lion on his neck and heard the crack of his vertebrae before all went black. When he came back around to consciousness he found himself thinking about falling to his knees in front of the sheriff and taking his cock into his mouth. He had leaped from belligerent prey to complete submission without much transition. As the sheriff's testicles slapped his chin, in fact, he did realize that the cock tasted like a glazed Dunkin' brand donut. He laughed to brace himself against the surging feelings of revulsion and fear.

"Is that funny to you, Deputy?"

"Not particularly."

"Laughter usually indicates that you find something amusing."

"I have never had any sugar in my pubic hair."

"I'm putting you on Indian Head Rock duty."

"What?"

"Kentucky is making noise they want the damn thing back again. There's some worry they'll send SWAT over to claim it. Those crazy fucks are serious about starting a border war over the head. The mayor wants a guard. I have no budget for that, but I do have you. We'll put a folding chair in the garage and you can guard the head until you can stand up and stay up or you stop sweating like you've come down with malaria, goddamn."

"I don't want to guard the head."

"Then you'll have to stay home with your mad wife."

"Sheriff."

"And stop fucking the donut girl."

"Sheriff."

"And stop playing with matches."

"Sheriff."

"And stop sucking dick and bringing your perverted friends into town."

"Sheriff."

"And sell that goddamn hot tub!"

"Sheriff!"

"And paint on some eyebrows, for God's sake, so you don't look so demented. Your face is not good for the morale of the department."

"Sheriff!"

The deputy grabbed Darth Vader from the desk and smashed it on the corner. Vader's arms shot to the left and right his and head bounced straight into the air, rattled off the heads and arms of Swamp Thing and Electra, and fell ingloriously at the feet of the sheriff, where it stopped face down. He squeezed the headless, armless body, but the plastic would not yield, so he slammed it against the floor. The doll landed with an unsatisfying soft thud as the deep pile carpet protected it from any further damage.

"You're lucky that's not an original, but a later knock-off. I keep the originals in the basement," the sheriff said as bent down and picked up Vader's head, inspected it, and jammed it into the front pocket of his shirt. His anger was immense, but he wouldn't release it, at least not yet. "I should suspend you for blatant insubordination, but I figure protecting the head is punishment enough. If I didn't want to give a favor to the mayor and governor I don't know what I would have done with you, Auro. Smashing Vader just earned you another week of head duty, I can tell you that."

"Sheriff, I can pay for the doll or find you another one like it."

"I don't want your money or your apologies. I don't want to see your face, either. And don't think you're going to sneak away from the municipal garage, either. There's a bunch of good ol' boys over there that owe me years' worth of favors, so they'll tell me everything that goes on over there, when you piss, when you sleep, when you arrive and when you leave. Now, get out of my office before I shoot you."

The deputy stood up and gathered his balance by holding the arm of the chair under the withering gaze of the sheriff.

"I had my eye on you, Auro. I thought maybe you could be sitting at this desk someday. I saw the way you handled the media with the skull, and I thought to myself that there might be a man ready to handle the pressures of the job. I think you were damn close to getting laid by that producer of Diane Sawyer. She thought you were so funny and the way she kept touching your arm. But look what's happened to you after a little bit of notoriety. If I had your constitution, imagine what would have happened to me when I caught that family of pot growers or that high school teacher pedophile. You didn't see me taking up sucking dick and burning all the hair off my head, now did you? The electorate is a fickle beast. You can keep the fucker tamed but once you give them a reason to vote against you they'll cast a vote just to spite you."

"I never said I wanted to be sheriff."

"That's not something we have to worry about now, anyway, that's my point."

The deputy let him have the last word and left the office, shutting the door behind him. He wished be had kept the mutilated Vader body so he could show it to Clarisse or the other deputies as a token of resistance, that what they thought happened in the sheriff's office had come out quite differently than anyone expected.

"Say hello to Charlie Brown for me," said Clarisse with a sarcastic smile. Her chemically whitened teeth looked phosphorescent next to the blood red of her painted lips.

When the sheriff sent the deputy to guard the rock the controversy had been far from settled and there had been a good amount of saber-rattling on both sides of the river. One Kentucky legislator, in the grip of righteous fever, suggested to his fellow Kentuckians that they muster an armed raiding party to rescue the stolen artifact. This same legislator, a three-term representative who had previously failed as a Baptist preacher and an aluminum salesman, had also suggested forced sterilization of any woman seeking an abortion, the abolishment of all income, sales, business, and real estate taxes, and the decriminalization of polygamy, so when he advocated an armed raid most everyone ignored him, except those who still held a grudge against the Ohio River for being the border between North and South in the Civil War, between being a fugitive slave and a free man, between slaveholding and abolition. Nevertheless, the threat gave the sheriff the context for him to justify sending the deputy to guard the head. Clarisse, of course, had designed the punishment and whispered it to the sheriff behind a closed door where she spent most of her time with him. The sheriff had told her about the deputy's infidelity, the arrival of a working prostitute at his party and the strange history between the deputy and the man who exposed himself in church full of old ladies.

She would see to it the deputy was drummed out of the department, because if the sheriff was right and the deputy stood a chance of becoming sheriff one day, she didn't think she would be able to work for a pervert such as the deputy. The better plan would be to take him out now and not worry about future elections.

The deputy walked to his desk and did not acknowledge the stares and smirks from the other deputies and staff. He would give them no indication that his career had just derailed in the sheriff's office. Sabina and the sheriff were obviously fucking and they had made a pact to attack him from both sides. He had become accustomed to deferring to the sheriff, but the thought of losing a woman or even sharing a woman like Sabina with him gave the deputy thoughts of taking a sledgehammer and blowtorch to the sheriff's doll collection. She had the supplest skin he had ever felt and her scent, the musk buried in the folds and pits of her body under the flour and sugar, cast him headlong into delirium. She could not be lightly given up, especially now that he knew the sheriff had been behind the separation. He might have been able to accept a natural parting of ways from boredom or exhaustion, but he couldn't abide an outside agent being the author of the affair's premature destruction.

The deputy gathered the top half of his files related to the found skull and jammed them into a cloth bag that had been a giveaway by a Taser company he had picked up at a law enforcement convention a few years earlier. Splitting the pile was like cutting a deck of cards, the arbitrary division revealed a card that had long been buried in the other leads, statistics, photos, and phone messages from the media. On that card the deputy had written the address of a girl who had disappeared within a year or two of the time the skull had been buried. She had lived in Waverly, a town north of Portsmouth on State Route 23, thirty years ago. He had been meaning to drive there to see if a relative still lived in the house or if the neighbors remembered anything about her, but he had forgotten the lead in the tumult of media inquiries and then the accident. He shoved the card in his breast pocket, threw the cloth bag over his shoulder, packed up the remaining pile of information, and tucked it under his arm. As he walked past Deputy Morris, the deputy he liked the least of any of the deputies, he heard him say under his breath either, "Goddamn dicklicker," or "Go drink some liquor, or "That goat is a good kicker." He didn't ask for clarification or acknowledge he had heard anything but walked past the deputy's desk with his eyes focused on the exit door. When he finally made it to the threshold of the exit he breathed as he was released from the curiosity, anger, disgust and maybe a touch of sympathy embedded in the glares of his co-workers. Maybe guarding the head wouldn't be so bad after all.

He threw the files in the backseat of his SUV between the two child car seats. A sob caught in his throat and the emotion passed as quickly as it came. He knew from previous experience it could strike at any moment or be set in motion by the most mundane of objects: a set of used crayons, forgotten and too small clothes, or a sippy cup with a lost top. He would be suddenly reminded that he had children and a wife and that the family had settled him and made him as happy and content as he had ever been and after this realization would strike he would inevitably wonder how long had he gone without remembering such important and basic facts about the arc of his life.

Why did he have to be reminded? Why did guilt wash over him when he saw the small clothes or the tracks of his children's eating habits? It was not precisely a "why" question. He knew why he felt guilty, because he had gone hours at a time without thinking of his children. The question really was how did they slip so easily out of his conscious mind? He had let them down, enormously, he guessed, but after the guilt had gone stale and he promised himself to live by a pure and righteous creed, he would begin to question what he owed his children and what could really be expected of him as a father. Should he stay with Jenny for the sake of them even though her lesbian experimentation always threatened to blossom into full expression? Should he be there? Did he need to be there every day even though the girls obviously preferred their mother over him? He could keep their attention for some time when he acted a fool, but they quickly tired of him and remained suspicious of his motives. Even at that moment, after he had all but been fired from his job, after he had fallen to the lowest rung in the department, after he had been publicly humiliated and slunk out of the department in shame, he thought about his children. Why did he owe them that? It was as if he sat inside a room that had caught fire, that flames licked the ceiling and shimmied across the floorboards toward him and all he could do was stare at a picture of his lovely girls, unable to move, unwilling to act, waiting for immolation.

18

Indian Head Rock

He drove over to the municipal garage, parked, and walked through an open garage door, past two salt trucks, one having been disgorged of its engine that lay in pieces on the floor. He walked through another door and there sat the rock, diminutive in the large garage area. He approached it, sought out the Charlie Brown head, and stood close to the carving. Next to the head a more recent ancestor had chiseled "EDC 1856." The deputy moved on and examined all the inscriptions of the shoemakers and other residents of Portsmouth past. He completed his assessment in under a minute, unable to conjure a reason sufficient enough to warrant the guarding. Somebody at the garage must have given prior notice of his arrival as a lone metal folding chair stood facing the garage door at a distance of ten feet from the rock.

The chair shrieked as he sat and every movement thereafter produced a sound equivalent to a sheet of metal being torn asunder by an irresistible force. The deputy couldn't put his hands to his face to rest his head, so he dropped his chin against his chest and fell into a light sleep within a matter of minutes. Images flashed through his mind that weren't exactly the product of dreams but were more like a cleansing of synapses as they slowed. Many of them centered on Clarisse, the sheriff's assistant, holding a panoply of weapons from a machete to an Uzi to a rigid endoscope employed for sigmoidoscopies. She, being the dominant theme to the cleansing, did relent some space to Paul Newcombe's head bobbing over his penis and Paul Newcombe spraying ejaculate onto the blue hair of an assembled audience of elderly ladies.

He woke up and the manager of the garage stood over him. He may or may not have kicked the deputy's feet to wake him up.

"How does sleep fall into the duties of a guard?" asked the manager in a sneering tone as he waited for the deputy to find his bearings. "Jesus, man, you look a goddamn mess."

"Look at that. The rock is still here. I didn't sleep through a crack team of mercenaries come to fetch the treasure."

The manager looked over the deputy's shoulder at the rock and let out a mocking laugh, then suddenly he grew thoughtful and serious.

"I find the rock is a blessing. It's given the politicians something to do. As long as they are worried about this goddamn thing they can't do much damage to us. The only problem is the mayor's been here a dozen times with reporters, friends, and dignitaries. Each time his chest sticks out a little more and his tail feathers grow to a bigger display."

"Little ol' Portsmouth is just a hotbed of news," said the deputy to see if his moment of fame still had any traction.

"That's right. Of course, none of the network beauties came out to see the mayor like they did you. Did you really bang Diane Sawyer?"

The deputy considered the question and surmised he didn't have the energy for mythmaking at that moment, so he retreated back to the truth. "No, I talked with her over satellite at the TV station. Her producer said she doesn't leave the studio much. Says there's talk that she's even given up her apartment and just sleeps in her dressing room."

"That's too bad. Some rumors you hope are true. I like thinking about her having a big cock up her slit as she's reading a story about the Russian oil oligarchy or some such shit."

The deputy could think of nothing to say in response so silence hung between them until the image of the sensation following the image passed. He felt his eyelids involuntarily closing and he could do nothing to stop their descending. The manager shuffled off. He wanted to tell the deputy to go home and rest, but he was worried what the sheriff might think.

The deputy now fell fully asleep and the dream that eventually took hold felt less like a dream and more like a straight-forward retelling of a past event. When he remembered the dream he might have confessed that it had been a memory, so convincing was the detail. But it actually was a dream and it unfolded like this. His father sat at their dining room table reading the Bible, no doubt the book of Obadiah because his father reveled in the scathing language of the prophet and the atmosphere of impending doom that pervades the book. His father's head had just been freshly shaven. A small nick high on his forehead bleeds freely and a rivulet of blood descends to his eyebrow, where it pools and drips onto the pages of the book, slowly but steadily. Greg approaches from the front. The table is twice as long as he remembers it. He has the musky, salty taste of dick in his mouth. He is running his tongue across his teeth and trying to swallow away the taste. His father looks at him as he approached and recites from memory: *In the day they stoodest on the other side, in the day that he became a stranger; neither shouldest they have rejoiced over the children of Judah in the day of their destruction; neither shouldest they have spoken proudly in the day of distress. Thou shouldest not have entered into the gate of my people in the day of their calamity; yea, thou shouldest not have looked on their affliction in the day of their calamity; nor have laid hands on their substance in the day of their calamity. Though thou exalt thyself as the eagle, and though thou set thy nest among the stars, thence will I bring thee down.* Greg touches his arm and notices for the first time that his father has no shirt on and he suspects he had no pants on either but the table provides a modest screen. Greg touches his arm again, which is nothing but sinew and bone. He touches the blood, but it has dried and does not come off on his fingertips. The air is humid around his father. The moisture is rolling off him in waves. The words of condemnation have excited him. His upper lip is twitching. The muscles on his arms involuntarily flex. His mother walks into the room and sits at the opposite end of the long table. She has brought a bowl of stew along with her. She is bent and twisted from rheumatoid arthritis. She can barely lift her face high enough to clear the edge of the bowl. She raises a heaping spoonful of stew, half of which goes into her mouth as the other half falls from the spoon and back into the bowl.

With her mouth full his mother says, "Have you told the boy your news?"

The veins in his father's temples swell and the color of rushing blood breaks through the skin. "I'm leaving the postal service in order to study the Bible full-time. The temporal world is too much in my thoughts. I find no room is left for God."

Greg takes a moment to survey the scene. He notices he is wearing a uniform, but it is not his deputy's uniform. The epaulettes are made of long pieces of sparkling wire. He looks like a member of a marching band of a school whose colors are white and lime green. He thinks he might be wearing a dress uniform of an obscure or discontinued branch of the military.

"What will you and mother live on? I can't imagine you've saved that much money on a postal worker's salary."

His father's anger has been replaced by calm as a beatific smile has captured his face. "Son, God will provide. He always does. I've relied on the postal service too much in my life. Now it's time to turn my fate over to God. If I am of pure heart and mind, I can find the path that leads directly to God."

Greg felt anger stirring as he had been bludgeoned by the power and threat of The Word since he could remember. In his younger days his father had not been much of a churchgoer and had actually gone on record two or three times saying the whole structure of belief was really nothing more than repression and lies to keep the populace from tearing the oligarchy limb from limb. His mother, uncles, and aunts were tight-lipped about this era of Andy Auro's life and what little Greg could glean came through snatches of overheard conversations at family gatherings or when his mother spoke on the telephone when his father tinkered in the garage. He could never discover what brought about the change, whether it was a sudden, shocking break or a slow collapse into the dark thicket of faith.

"And one more thing, son. Stop fornicating with the girl in the donut shop. I raised you with a better set of morals than that. You've broken your vows and debased yourself for the sake of that piece of meat hanging between your legs. Each act creates another scar."

"Dad, the sheriff has stolen her away from me. I will never fuck her again."

His father's nostrils flared, creating two additional mouths in the middle of his face. "Being denied and actually repenting are not the same thing. While I am not unhappy the sheriff has taken that whore away from you, he is not your conscience nor the heart you are to give unto God."

"You're nothing to me, father. I don't have to listen to you or your nonsense. When you run out of money don't come knocking on my door, because I won't answer. I'll never answer. I'll never open the door. And I'm going to get the donut girl back and I'm going to fuck her in the ass and I'm keeping the hot tub and I may even fuck her in the ass in the hot tub while my wife and children are asleep in the house!"

The deputy jolted awake. He was on the floor on his knees, sweating heavily. The rock was gone. He wobbled to his feet and put his hand on his pistol. He turned wildly, almost losing his balance and falling back to his knees. He spotted the rock where he had last seen it. When he fell off the chair he landed at an angle, causing the momentary disorientation. Panic and rage subsided and were replaced by his full acceptance that he was, in fact, in no condition to work. He had very nearly pulled his gun on a rock, so what could follow but hallucinations and tragedy? He wiped the sweat from his eyes with his fingers, causing a fresh violation to his face. Nausea crept up to the top of his throat. He had the irrational belief that if he stood still he would vomit and if he walked he could keep the churn down and maintain some dignity. He made it to the floor drain in the middle of the bay and released into the grate. His body wanted to turn itself inside out and he dry heaved five or six times in the attempt. His face, scalp, and neck blossomed in throbbing pain. He thought he had splattered vomit on his shoes and pant legs, but he was in no condition to do anything about that right now. He left the bay in a slow and steady gait, as if he didn't want to wake a sleeping dog or an armed guard.

He found his truck and resisted the urge to crawl into the back seat and fall asleep. He knew he should seek out the garage manager and tell him he was too sick to guard, but he didn't think he could get back on his feet. He also knew that he should call the department to tell them the same, but the sheriff had put Clarisse in charge of tracking employee time-off, which meant he would have to explain his situation to her. At the moment, he thought going AWOL preferable to engaging in another unpleasant conversation with Clarisse. Lies, fake illnesses, forged doctor's notes and absenteeism in general had dramatically increased because of Clarisse's control of the process, but the sheriff would have to figure that out by himself. Since Clarisse provided him with the information and created the reports herself, the sheriff had no chance of ever understanding that his department had the highest absenteeism rate of all the departments in the state.

The deputy leaned his head back and the shift in equilibrium caused more tendrils of nausea to creep out of his stomach. He remembered the sheriff's recommendation and retrieved the business card for Dr. Gideon Kneebender of the Allied Health Pain Management and Wellness Clinic. He knew every street and building in the county so he knew exactly where the clinic was located, which made the sheriff's act of giving him the card all the more curious. He flipped the card over and the on the back the sheriff had scrawled something, but the letters were so shaky and twisted the words were indecipherable. The deputy couldn't remember if he saw the sheriff write anything on the card before he handed it to him. He flipped the card over again and dialed the number of the clinic to make an appointment. A woman answered with a pleasant, husky voice.

"I would like to set-up an appointment to see Dr. Kneebender."

"Ok, we're booked nearly through August. We're very busy this time of year.

There have been many... injuries and...suffering. Pain seems to be on the move... spreading. More people are in its grip..." Her voice trailed off and the process of scheduling ground to an uncomfortable, silent halt.

"I'll be healed by then."

"Yes, that is often the complaint, but folks will keep the appointment anyway. Dr. Kneebender's time is...precious."

"I'll make an appointment."

"I have a 7:30 a.m. available on the 28th of August."

"What day of the week is that?"

"Friday."

"Ok, put me down. My name is Greg Auro."

"Oh, *Deputy* Greg Auro?"

"Yes."

"Oh, oh, you should have said so, Deputy. Dr. Kneebender has been expecting your call."

"Why would he be expecting my call?" he asked even though he knew exactly why the clinic would be expecting his call, but he wanted her to say it, wanted her to tell him that the sheriff had called, to stoke his paranoia and confirm that the sheriff believed he could manipulate any situation to end at his preferred outcome.

"Oh, did I say...*expect*? I'm sorry. I must have misspoken. I apologize. I do. The good news is that Dr. Kneebender can see you anytime today. There's no need for an appointment. We will be...flexible."

"Then how did you know I was a deputy?"

"Oh my, I obviously have to watch my words around you men in law enforcement. Show a little drop of blood and you're on me like a pack of hyenas."

"Did you answer my question?"

"Deputy Auro. Everybody in town knows you ever since...."

"I was on the news?"

"Well, yes, that started it I suppose, but I was thinking more about Diane Sawyer. That's an awfully shiny trophy to win, Deputy. The gals in the office have been wondering about you. You must be some kind of man."

"I'm driving there now. Try not to show your disappointment."

The deputy hung up the phone and considered his irritation. A rumor that he had bagged a celebrity news anchor was not bad for his reputation, he supposed. All the ladies who heard it or passed it along again gave him a second look, considered his power, visualized him with hair and eyebrows, and wondered if he would tell them just how much soft focus and makeup was needed to maintain the illusion that Diane had retained her beauty. His irritation grew from his suspicions that Clarisse had begun the rumor either at the sheriff's bequest or as a bit of her own freelancing. Had she wanted to damage or destroy him since the sheriff anointed him the leading candidate to possibly replace him when he was damn ready to retire or had become too incapacitated to speak or eat? But how would planting a story in which his virility is celebrated serve her ends? He knew she was a master with no equal and that he had almost no hope of understanding her strategies and motives. He had, though, almost started to believe that he had had sex with Diane Sawyer and that his virility must hang from him like a perfectly ripe and irresistible fruit.

19

Pain Management

The deputy stopped in front of a cinder block and glass storefront that had housed several generations of commerce, including sewing supply, a video arcade, a head shop, sporting goods, video rental, bagels, fantasy clothes and marital aides, and now pain management, which was emblazoned across the glass in foot high red letters. All the other storefronts in the small plaza had shuttered except a hair salon at the opposite end, called appropriately enough, Hair Cutters, so the deputy could deduce the multitude of cars in the lot belonged to the staff and customers of the clinic.

The waiting area was indeed filled with patients sitting in plush chairs against the walls, standing by the front window, and leaning against any open wall space they could find. The deputy first thought of an emergency room after a catastrophe, some industrial accident or force of nature that caused no visible sign of injury but jammed the hospitals and doctor's offices with the injured, nevertheless. Without moaning or open wounds the analogy didn't stick so he next thought of a failing store giving away a cheap promotional item, a toaster that charred bread even on the lowest setting or a chance to win a gas grill or season tickets to the Single A affiliate of the Pittsburgh Pirates, because the mood of the room seemed to him extraordinarily patient but expectant, with a quiet assurance that whatever happened at the clinic would be the best development of the day and would be worth the wait. Even if they didn't win a toaster or the gas grill at least they were in the game, and a slight opportunity of winning was better than sitting on the couch at home with no chance at all.

The deputy regretted walking into the clinic wearing his uniform. Whatever mood had been present before he walked in evaporated as the patients looked up, saw the uniform, the bald head, no eyebrows, and filled in the gaps, using their own imaginations, sympathies, prejudices, and fear. The most kind in the room thought him to be a cancer patient looking for relief. A woman knitting a pink sweater projected that he may be stocking up for his inevitable end. The guilty in the room assumed the clinic was being raided and that within seconds a mob of other law enforcement would be piling through the doors, seizing computers and files, handcuffing the doctor, his nurses and patients, and tossing them into the back of the van and speeding them to jail or detox, depending on their current state of intoxication or involvement in the process. Whereas the sympathetic shot him doe eyes and tears, the guilty just looked terrified and scouted the nearest exit besides the front door, of which there were none except for the door leading to the doctor's examination room. The cynics in the group leered and snickered because they knew why they sat in the clinic lobby, so if a deputy, a henchman for the ruling class, an actual uniformed official goon of government, a man bestowed with a badge and a gun, came through the same door as they had, then they had proof of what they assumed all along, that the rot had reached all the way to the top and it could all come tumbling down today, tomorrow, or next week.

 The deputy had become practiced in ignoring the reactions to his uniform, all law enforcement officers have to, because no matter where he went for whatever reason somebody would react to the clothes and badge. Sometimes he forgot he was wearing it until somebody reacted, suddenly nervous or sneering at the memory of past speeding tickets or lock-ups. He was often surprised at the lack of deference shown him when he wore civilian clothes, when a clerk didn't reflectively flash an obsequious smile or share a private aside concerning the stupidity of the world in general and the imbecility of the other shoppers in particular, except for the clerk in the bright red smock and, of course, the deputy in his sharp uniform, sharing as they did a kinship of authority. No doubt he should not have come to the clinic in the uniform. Maybe the sheriff didn't remind him because he expected the deputy to understand by now, given the years he had accumulated in the department, when to slide in under the radar or the sheriff or maybe Clarisse had set a trap, sending him to the clinic so he could be indicted on a future date, swept away for good, the cloud of drug dependence following him.

 The sheriff would receive two calls about the deputy within the span of an hour; one for leaving his post at the Head from the maintenance garage manager because he tried to stay on the sheriff's good side due to his daughter who had been in and out of trouble since she had been fourteen with men, meth, prescriptions, theft, and public intoxication, so any official empathy he could garner might alleviate her suffering and two, from a frantic Dr. Kneebender, who wanted to know if sending uniformed goons to his clinic signaled a change in the relationship between the good doctor and the sheriff. The deputy thought about going home, but given his losing streak the last thing he wanted to do was engage his wife in conversation or be in her sight, to remind her of all that he had done. Nothing good would come of it. Nothing good could happen this day.

The deputy walked to the receptionist's counter, which was encased in shatterproof, bulletproof glass. The receptionist broke out the reassuring, obsequious smile like he had been a regular customer, that she loved the presence the uniform and the panic and agitation breaking out in the waiting room was a delightful aspect of her job.

"Good morning, Deputy. You can step through the door. I'll buzz you in. The doctor will see you."

"Really? I just got here."

"Oh, we can't keep you...waiting in the lobby...now can we? Anyone can see how...injured you are. You don't look well....deputy...if I may say. You should have come to see us sooner."

She buzzed the door open and the deputy walked through. Whereas the lobby approximated a doctor's office with the plush chairs, carpeting, and fresh paint on the walls, the interior of the office looked like an afterthought, temporary and dirty. They used the linoleum floor of the previous generations of commerce. Metal studs and drywall had been thrown up to create two large rooms with a narrow hallway in between. The drywall pieces had been taped together and the screws had been mudded over but nothing had been sanded or painted. A scale was pushed up against a wall in the hallway, but considering the angle of the beam that shot cockeyed into the air as if no amount of counterweight could balance it, no one had been weighed on it since the clinic had opened its doors. Two posters hung on the walls, one by either door leading into the two examining rooms. One showed a detailed map of the circulating system (veins in red, arteries in blue) and the other was a cut-away of a man's head, his face placidly staring to the left as a section of his skull hovered in the air above him, revealing the compact mass of his brain. Helpful arrows pointed to the exact locations of the different parts. Why did the artist leave hair on the section of skull hovering in space? Was there blood coming out of the poor man's ears?

The nurse led the deputy into the room on the right, behind the cut-away skull. The space was too large for an examination room, easily six or seven times larger than normal, and sparsely furnished with an examining table close to dead center, two metal folding chairs folded and propped against an unpainted wall, and a companion poster of the cut-away head, showing the entire brain levitating above the skull. The skull cap had been nudged out of the frame so the overall impression looked a little less disturbing, but the man held the same impassive gaze off to the left as he waited for his brain to be returned to him.

The deputy walked to the examining table and lay down. He rested his hand on his gun more out reflex and habit than worrying about a doctor or nurse taking it from him. He calculated that he would be able to hear the door open and footsteps across the linoleum floor so the benefits of closing his eyes outweighed any liability that might arise from a light doze. He fell into a hard, deep sleep immediately and awoke minutes or an hour or two later with the doctor standing over him showing a tight smile.

"When I walked in here I thought we lost you. Hazards of the job. Always thinking the worst."

"It's been a bad week."

"We can turn the bad to good, the painful to the delightful, from having no life to having a life, from misery to joy. That's it, really, we eliminate misery. And let me tell you, if I could find the fountain from which all misery springs I'd cover it up with rocks and put myself out of business because there just doesn't seem to be an end to it all. It's like this life is nothing but torture for most people. I'd put myself out of business and make myself a farmer. I'd have my hands in dirt all day, that's what I would do."

The deputy sat up. He felt like he could sleep for another ten hours.

"So," the doctor continued. "Have you been experiencing pain?"

"Yes, my neck, face, scalp, a lot of headaches."

"Of course, of course, and you've recently had an accident?"

"Some gun powder blew up in my face."

"Work related?"

"No, strictly pleasure."

The doctor arched an eyebrow and assumed he had meant to say "personal" instead of "pleasure."

"How does gunpowder blow up in your face?"

"You light it."

"Of course. And what did the hospital give you for pain relief? Baby aspirin?"

"That's about right."

"Are you having trouble sleeping, thinking, walking, eating, having sexual relations, working, or participating in any other normal activity at all?"

"All of the above."

"Of course, of course. We'll start you off with a small dose and ramp it up from there, if necessary. This is not baby aspirin," he said as he produced a pill from the pocket of his lab coat and held it before the deputy with it pinched between his thumb and forefinger.

The deputy held out his hand palm up and the doctor dropped the pill from the height of an inch or so.

"What is it?"

"Truth be told, I'm an oxy man. I could give you morphine, but I've had more luck with Oxycontin. Fewer side effects. The pill is a wonder. The little lab rats who died during its invention should be given the Medal of Honor. Do you know how many lives those little bastards saved? Take the pill. You'll get your life back, whatever is left of it."

"What does that mean?"

"You'll need water."

The doctor spun on his heel and walked to the sink against the far wall where he filled up a Dixie cup with water. He returned holding the cup in front of him as the sound of his hard soled shoes clicking on the linoleum reverberated across the bare room. The deputy swallowed the pill and water as the doctor scribbled out a prescription.

"I'd take this to the pharmacy up on Scioto Trail by the cinema. They won't give you a hassle there. Of course, wearing that uniform I'd doubt anybody would give you much of a hassle."

"Why would they give me a hassle for a prescription, Dr. Kneebender?"

"You know my actual name is Nuebensphender, but I couldn't find a receptionist who could pronoun it so I simplified it. Besides it was an accidental stroke of marketing genius. My practice quadrupled its size once I made the change. Scioto County just needed a name they could pronounce and remember for them to acknowledge the pain they lived with each and every day. The power of advertising, right? We Americans shouldn't be too awed by the ability to sell through suggestion, but when you actually experience it you feel like you've tapped into one of the essential truths of the universe."

Both men were aware that the doctor hadn't answered the question, but the deputy decided to let it drop. Maybe in the future, if he was still employed by the department, he would try to find the connection between Kneebender and the sheriff and quantify the number of prescriptions that the doctor was writing. The investigation could wait until he had healed, though, until he could think clearly again, until he could formulate a plan of how to depose the sheriff and Clarisse and plant a stake in the heart of their tyranny.

"You should call if you experience hallucinations, night sweats, extreme bouts of nausea, sudden suicidal tendencies, a sudden loss of your will to live, bleeding from your rectum or penis, loss of vision, swelling of joins, limbs, lips, and eyelids, sudden and irrevocable fainting, a drop in blood pressure, somnolence, euphoria... er...hair loss, severe testicle pain and/or severe bouts of anxiety."

"Those are possible side effects?"

"Oh, no... not really. You should just call nevertheless. And thank you for coming in, deputy and letting us coordinate your pain management needs. I'll have the nurse take you out the back door, if you don't mind? We really don't want to provoke the patrons, now do we? We lost a few of them after you arrived. I guess they couldn't process the fact that deputies can have pain too. Besides, some of the pills I have them on cause such paranoia they would have run if they spotted anyone in a uniform, and that includes priests, baseball players, or waitresses from Denny's. Now, you wait here and the nurse will be in presently. Remember to call if things don't go as expected," he said as he handed him the prescription.

The doctor didn't offer him his hand, but turned crisply and walked out of the room, creating a martial beat with his heels. The door remained shut less than ten seconds and the nurse bolted in, bearing a frozen smile. She moved across the floor with intermittent squeaks from her sneakers and led him out, turning right toward the back, instead of the way he had come. The unpainted walls ended abruptly, some ten feet from the exterior cinderblock wall. The space was used for storage and held boxes of thread and an ancient sewing machine, shelving, a broken hockey stick, an exercise bike, softball uniforms, a display cabinet with a smashed glass, dildo boxes with the contents long since pilfered and employed, straps and leather and chains, bagel boxes and totes, a deflated basketball, dress patterns, outdoor signs that read *Buttons and Thread Sewing Shoppe, Rick Army Sports Emporium, Schmagels Bagels,* and *The French Connection Phantasy Boutique,* a three-ring binder of bagel recipes, and three dress mannequins, no doubt the work of a bored nurse or Kneebender himself, costumed as a football referee, a bagel clerk, and a leather clad slave with easy access openings.

The nurse placed a hand on the deputy's back and guided him through the junk, out the back door, and into a dead back lot of split asphalt and calf-high weeds, car tires, and trees gnarled as if the ground had been poisoned and only the meanest plants could grow. The dumpster reminded him, like all dumpsters did, of the time he and Deputy Connelly pulled a dead baby from one after it had been accidently discovered by a pizza delivery boy, who had decided to use that dumpster to receive the accumulated trash (undelivered pizzas, receipts, crushed fountain drink cups and an invoice for a new front tire that had wiped out a paycheck) from his car. When the call came from the dispatcher both the deputy and Connelly responded and arrived at the dumpster in separate cars. The pizza boy acted catatonic as he sat on the front fender of his car. The deputy ran to the dumpster and peered over the edge. Amongst the cardboard boxes, trash bags, fast food bags, and a crate of rotting lettuce the little blue face looked upward toward the light. He leaned in and stretched, but the baby lay too deep. Connelly grabbed ahold of the side of the dumpster and mounted the edge with the strength and grace of a gymnast. He gently placed a foot down on a bag of trash and lowered himself down. The trash crumpled and collapsed as his weight shifted the balance, threatening to send the baby into a crevasse toward the floor of the dumpster. The deputy heard the sound of an ambulance approaching. Connelly, once he felt stable, crouched down and snatched the baby from the trash with a swift move. Suddenly, he held the baby before him, offering her to the deputy. He received the baby and cradled her in his arms to support the neck, but she was stiff, cold, and the color of a deep bruise. She had wisps of brown hair and hazel eyes. She weighed about as much as a gallon of milk and she still wore a diaper and a bodysuit with a penguin blowing a trumpet on the chest. He couldn't set her down on the asphalt or weeds, but he didn't know how much longer he could hold her. Her bare legs lay against his bare forearm and he couldn't understand how anything could be so cold. Connelly jumped out of the dumpster and now looked into the face of the infant.

"Jesus motherfucking God," Connelly said as he closed her eyes.

Connelly stumbled over to the pizza boy whose entire statement consisted of, "That just fucks me up, man. That's a…fuck…that's…you can't see that and expect to stay right in the head."

The ambulance came and the paramedics whisked her away, leaving within five minutes, without turning on the lights or siren. The three remaining men, humbled that they were chosen to rescue the baby from an ignoble burial, shared a moment of exasperation concerning the cruelty of the world and the panic and desperation of its inhabitants. They could remain in that frame of mind for only a few minutes because it felt like the first step toward utter dejection, leading to a complete loss of faith that any goodness could be maintained in the face of such fury and numbness, shellshock and paralysis.

The deputy came to realize that his job involved dumpsters or alleys and back lots with dumpsters or heaping piles of trash more than he had first understood. He tried to avoid them when he could, but the aversion was equivalent to never turning left or never going through a four-way stop. Then, the sheriff brought him into office too, striking a more conciliatory and advisory tone because it happened years before the skull had been found when the sheriff acted as a mentor, and he said:

"Auro, we all know what you and Connelly found in the dumpster. I don't worry so much about Connelly because he's not smart enough to think much about it, but I have my concerns about you. There's nothing worse than seeing new life extinguished. I've seen my share of car wrecks and every time I could feel my heart climb right up into my throat as I approached the car, hoping against hope that I wasn't going to see a goddamn car seat in the back. It's bad enough seeing the kids in their tuxes and gowns or the beauties all mangled and bloody, but the little kids I found I couldn't stop thinking about all of them. Sometimes I remember perfectly what I saw, right down to the expressions on their faces and the nature of the wounds that killed them, then other times, could be a minute later, I see the infants and toddlers walking and crawling around as perfect as the day they were born. I think those are the spirits, perfect and pure, coming to visit me and tell me they are ok, that they have climbed into the lap of God. It might sound ridiculous but that's what I believe."

The deputy nodded slightly, aware that for him the path of prayers and belief had been overgrown with weeds, ruddy vines, and virulent seedlings from the nearby trees, so that the path had all but been obliterated.

"We found the mother. She's maybe eighteen, at least that's what she's saying, but I'd guess she's significantly younger than that. She's telling us she's eighteen because she thinks adults can do what they want once they reach that age. I suspect it was her daddy that knocked her up. We can't get her to stop blubbering long enough to ask her a full run of questions. I suspect she should have just climbed into that dumpster with her little baby and they could have died together. I'd say she's broken and ruined and not it's just a matter of what drug is going to take her out and how long her constitution lasts and how much havoc she's going to cause on her way out. I've seen firsthand the resiliency of humankind, but my God, how do you move forward after you've dumped a baby in a dumpster? Goddamn American gothic, front and center."

The deputy pushed the memories down, the cold, hard skin, the terrified, stricken eyes, the tiny quarter moons of dirt underneath the fingernails, and moved on to other disasters, tragedies, and a collection of grisly scenes when adult life expired, further burying the discarded infant. He paused at the edge of a wasted field and contemplated the idea of walking through the weeds, past the copse of scrub trees, and continue walking until his legs could not take another step, then falling asleep where he fell and waking up the next morning and doing the same day after day until he walked out the gnawing disappointment and boredom inside him or he collapsed into a ditch and took his last breath with his face touching a stagnant pool of water. He rejected the idea before it could truly form because it reminded him of his father and all of his Old Testament excesses. He tried to remember if his father had gone on such a trek, whether or not he had stolen the idea from him, but his mother tried to shield the children from whatever dangerous and impulsive attempts Andy Auro made toward speaking with God that she could, so the deputy did not have access to his full catalog. She couldn't mask the fasts because his father might not come to dinner for a month straight or the sudden impulse to rip off his clothing and stand naked before the supreme being, dirty and unadorned, as he had done once on the camping trip with Paul, but she could lie to them if he went missing for a few days and returned with deep scratches all over his body, with feet so swollen he could barely walk, as the injuries were explained away as the natural consequence of helping fellow church members build a garage or lay a patio or clear off a thistle-choked field so a Little League diamond could be built. The children knew it was the work of his terrible God.

20

So Many Pills behind the Counter

The deputy drove to the pharmacy the doctor had suggested. The pill he had been given had already begun working. His face felt like something akin to rubber, but the pain had receded for the first time since the accident. He could physically feel his mood lifting. Power came back into his arms. He thought possibly he might just start laughing, mocking last week's events as a comedy of errors and thinking any damage done could be undone with a little concentrated effort. He felt buoyant, free from the anchor and lead weights that had been chained across his chest and legs.

He quick-footed it into the store. He felt like running, but he didn't want to startle the clerks. He strode over to the pharmacy drop-off counter and a woman in a lab coat looked at the deputy with an arched eyebrow as is she was delighted to see him and she couldn't wait to see what he had brought her to fill. The deputy thought her beautiful, which, by any reasonable and rational standard, was true, but before they had even exchanged a formal greeting the deputy had already begun imagining her replacing Sabina, now that the sheriff had thrown his hooks into her. The pharmacist's name was Sheila as it had been stitched over her left breast in cursive red thread on the lab coat. A person had to employ considerably more intelligence to dispense possibly lethal drugs than make and sell donuts. Sheila probably did not live in trailer where the floor in winter felt more like frozen ground than actual shelter. She wouldn't taste like confectioner's sugar and burnt oil. Maybe she would be able to converse on topics other than the collection of derelicts satelliting fried dough. Sheila asked him how she could be of help and based on the evidence of how she formed her words with her perfect lips he thought she may be an angel. Not a religious angel come to enforce The Word, but a woman of perfect form and personality who radiates nothing but beauty and goodness and who can charm the darkest of cynics.

The deputy slid the prescription across the counter and when she read what it was for and who had written it her face drained of radiance and she looked to his eyes to determine the meaning of his offering.

"You are hurt?" she said as her eyes lingered over his injuries.

"I've been burned."

"I see. That looks quite painful. Your...doctor...should have prescribed rest as well as the pills."

Her hands were on the counter as were his. He wondered when they would reach out and hold each other's hands and slowly lean forward and kiss each other. At some point his luck would have to turn and who better than an angel to be the one to alter its course.

"It will take a few minutes to fill this. I will call you when it is done. Please browse the store while you wait or you can come back in ten minutes and it should be ready."

She flitted away and the deputy barely controlled an impulse to reach out and grab her arm. He couldn't be sure if he could control his impulse should she come back in reach, so he sidled off to the belly of the store. He wandered through the candy bar, nail polish, and school supply aisles before landing at the magazine rack. A crowd of tanned and oily faces stared back at him from the shelves. They whispered their secrets, come-ons, demands to him but there was such a cacophony of voices he couldn't discern all they said. He picked up a hot rod magazine that had no faces or bodies on the cover, just fast, sleek cars with purring engines. But when he randomly splayed it open a bikini-clad model lay on the hood of a turbo-charged Bugatti Veyron, moaning and throwing out invitations with a hint of boredom in her voice, repeatedly saying, "I would very much like you to fuck me on top of this Bugatti," except she pronounced Bugatti like "Bug-a-tea," thus letting the seduction of gearheads slip right through her fingers.

The deputy jammed the magazine back on the shelf and noticed a man standing in the same aisle pretending to be reading a romance novel with a cowboy and a buxom milkmaid on the cover. The man visibly blanched when the deputy looked his way. The deputy remembered him from somewhere and when he took a few steps toward him the man looked about ready to flee. It was Roy Rogers, the producer of the play, the Blue Cowboy in the flesh, except he wore loose jeans that were pulled too high over his hips and a polo shirt. The deputy stopped his approach when he recognized him.

"I see you've been released," the deputy said with some venom.

"I'm heading back to Maryland. My ulcer has flared up and I need a prescription filled for the trip back."

"Have the charges been dropped?"

"I've been told that they have. I hope they have. Do you know something different?"

"You're lucky our good sheriff doesn't like trouble."

"I don't know what you mean."

"The Roy Rogers faction in this town didn't want your indiscretions to go public. A public trial would have made you an official part of this town's history, and who wants that, really?" The deputy was aware of his innate ability to sound rational and official, but as he spoke he became more interested in the bridge between Blue Cowboy's nostrils and the softness of his face. He looked like he never needed to shave.

"They've shamed me. They've cast me out. You'll be happy to hear I won't be coming back to Portsmouth, Ohio any time soon, if ever, unless in the dead of the night, wearing a disguise. The committee met last night and approved a lifetime ban, unanimous no less, but I don't know what they are thinking because they really have no legal authority or standing. They can't keep me out of the festival if I want to come, but why would I want to come back to a festival that is going to be so lame once I stop coordinating it. You should hear their ideas. Every year, and I mean every year for the past decade, Gus Frapp says we should host a real rodeo and I even looked into it to shut him up. The setup costs, the liability costs, just the amount of working capital you need to launch something like that, none of that stops ol' Gus Frapp from hanging his hat on the idea. Diane will keep pushing the parade even though no one comes to parades anymore. I know there are some big ones left, and sometimes you'll see some small town that'll have 5,000 people turn out for a Memorial Day parade to watch fire trucks and window installation companies pass by, but by and large, parades are dead. People have enough spectacle in their lives now. But when Roy would come, we had a draw. Since he's passed we have no finale, no trump. Our king is dead. We even had a couple of guys on the committee want to organize a cowboy-themed Texas Hold-em tournament, not to promote Roy's Christian values, but because they are gambling addicts and want to throw around any loose change they manage to accumulate."

"Do prostitutes and exhibitionists promote Roy's Christian beliefs?"

"Your friend ruined me. What is his problem?"

"He is not my friend."

"You had him in your mouth. That's a sure sign of friendship," cracked Blue Cowboy before he had time to consider his words and the reaction he may elicit from a uniformed officer of the law.

"Shut up! That never happened," the deputy said through clenched teeth.

Blue Cowboy narrowed his eyes and a look of jocularity spread across his face.

"Oh, Deputy, everyone has done things they are ashamed of or would like to do over again. How could it be otherwise? How could you ever trust someone who has lived a pure life, a perfect life?"

"That sentiment seems in direct conflict with your devotion to Roy Rogers. Isn't he Christ in a fringed shirt and cowboy hat?"

Blue Cowboy's cheeks and neck turned red and his eyes darted from side to side, looking for an escape route.

"That's an entirely different idea."

"I don't think so. Roy Rogers was a human being with human weaknesses. Do you think he did things that made him ashamed? Do you think he blew the Lone Ranger or the Gipper himself?"

"I wish you wouldn't talk like that. It makes me uncomfortable."

"Because Roy Rogers was the son of God?"

"I never said that."

The deputy thought about his father and the family quest for prophets and prophecies crafted out of the thinnest of signs and allusions. He thought of the months he had to call his own father Elijah, Isaiah, Jeremiah, Ezekiel, Daniel and Jonah. Sometimes he would be one of them solely and sometimes the family had to string together the whole canon of prophets to properly address him since they all resided within him at the same time. The deputy hadn't the energy to unspool the reasons why striving for perfection was destruction, impossible and only undertaken by a fool. He knew Blue Cowboy would be such a fool.

"You've assumed his personality. You are Blue Cowboy."

"Not anymore. I've been cast out. You see what I'm wearing."

"You're no longer in the community, but you haven't been cast out of your own head. Aren't most prophets abandoned by their church, their society, and their family? Isn't it the fate of the prophet to blaze his own path, alone?"

"My collection is known to be the deepest on the eastern seaboard."

"Of course."

"I have an entire closet just for my fringe shirts and another just for my cowboy pants and hats."

"Well, you are the Blue Cowboy."

"They released all of us, you know, even your...friend...or whatever he is. I think they dropped all the charges. There wasn't much of an explanation."

"I knew they would release you and the fat prostitute."

"I think your...friend should have been kept in jail. There's something unsettled about him. I'm not sure what he'll do next, what he's actually capable of."

"Hopefully he will go home and Portsmouth will never hear from him again, much like I hope happens with you, because I know if I ever see you again I'm going to arrest you and beat the piss out of you and then I'll throw you in a goddamn dumpster behind a doctor's office amongst the other bits of trash. Understand?"

"You can't..."

"What you said to me is enough to keep me mad for a lifetime. I swear to God I don't ever want to see you back in Portsmouth, even under the cover of darkness and even dressed like Dale Evans."

The pharmacist called both Blue Cowboy and the deputy's name over a tinny loudspeaker. The deputy wouldn't move until Blue Cowboy broke his stare and walked past. The deputy leaned his shoulder to graze Blue Cowboy as he passed and closely followed him to the counter, staring at his perfectly shaved neck and the shine of his hair. He felt the urge to perform an act of violence, to knock Blue Cowboy from his stride or beat the neck black-and-blue. The pharmacist processed Blue Cowboy first and he nearly ran out of the store with the prescription, sensing as he did the deputy's descent and understanding he would be the victim of its outcome, should he act upon the tyrannical forces that drove him.

The deputy stepped up to the counter and closely inspected the pharmacist as she rang him out. She had a few pock marks along her jawline and wrinkles had begun to spider from the outside corners of her eyes. Maybe her breasts were less than perfectly ample and some of her teeth were a jumble, but intelligence and mischief radiated from her eyes. The deputy thought her endlessly curious about the world and amused at the infinite combinations of possible interactions.

"I think we should go out some day and we could swap stories of what we've seen," said the deputy as she handed him his prescription and took his debit card in return.

"I don't think I want to know what you've seen."

"You're probably right. You have to tell the stories just right for them to be amusing."

"We could compare our wedding rings, talk about the funny things that happened at our weddings, talk about our spouses and our children. That might be fun."

"You disappoint me."

The pharmacist laughed loudly, without restraint.

"You must be disappointed a lot," she said. "There are lots of married ladies out here that aren't looking for another man. One's enough for me and I happen to love him."

"Again, a disappointment."

"I'll give you credit, though. I think you are the first man fresh from the burn ward to take a run at me. The first man to try to start up an affair who had no eyebrows. Well, that's not entirely true. I've had cancer patients take runs at me, but I just chalked that up to desperation and sadness, trying to squeeze a few minutes of flirtation and romance in before incapacitation. But you, this," she waved her hands to encompass the deputy's bald head, "is a new experience for me."

"I am in need of comfort. I need safe harbor."

"Then go home to your wife. Besides, I've never been referred to as a harbor, either. I'm not sure I like it. I imagine lots of ships and boats of all shapes and sizes coming and going and I'm just not that easy."

"That's not what I meant."

"Of course, but you're the one that lobbed the nautical metaphor at me like it was going to impress me or weaken my resolve."

"Ok, so given my condition I need a fresh virgin forest or a stone castle high upon a hill in order to find comfort."

"You're not very good at this game. I would have thought a big, strong deputy in a uniform would have more command of the situation. Isn't that what you are paid to do? Be in command? Maybe by the time you get your prescription refilled you'll feel better. You have a 30 day supply. Maybe we can try it again, unless, of course, your wife picks it up for you and then the game will be at an end."

"What's wrong with what I said?'

"Besides everything? I won't give you clues. You're going to have to work on your own game, that's all I'm saying. Come back with a better grasp of a woman's ideal image of herself, which, of course, probably does not include a poor virgin forest just waiting for a big, bad lumberjack to come harvest her or an isolated ice queen hiding behind stone walls four feet thick on top or a cold, windy hill, a woman so frigid and blue that the blood in her veins has turned to slush. Those two images are definitely not appropriate...ah, see? I've gone and given you too many clues. I need to learn to shut my mouth."

"But it's such a lovely mouth. Your lips..."

"Oh, gawd! Stop before it becomes a rout."

The phone rang and she hopped over to the receiver to answer it. She began a long conversation with a doctor's office on the advisability of mixing two particular prescriptions given the patient was taking eight others on a daily basis. She handed the deputy his card, receipt and a pen as she talked. He wrote his name and cell number on the receipt and pushed it toward her across the counter. She leaned over, giving him a long look down the front of her lab coat and blouse, and revealed the full wreckage of her teeth with a broad smile. She twirled a finger at her temple, indicating she thought him crazy. Nevertheless, she scooped up the receipt and jammed it into the front pocket of the lab coat instead of the register where it belonged, before returning her full concentration to the phone call.

The deputy turned toward the door, but his progress was soon delayed by the displays of sundry items and store specials: a pyramid of 36 ounce tomato juice cans, unsold Fourth of July decorations now 75% off the original price, flimsy lawn chairs designed to hold no one over 130 pounds, rack after rack of bagged candy, shelves of inexplicable makeup, radiating a thousand different hues that made the deputy think about the parts of a woman that were manipulated, changed, and masked and how exhausting it must be to fight one's own nature, battling an unruly beast forever. Next to the makeup sat an aisle of plastic toys made to last as long as the lawn chairs if the child could warm to the rudimentary purpose of the toy long enough to break it.

The toys sent him reeling through a thousand memories of his children, the last of which included their horrified faces when they woke up and trundled downstairs to find their daddy asleep on the couch with a freshly shaven head and a bandaged face and hands. He caught a sob in his throat when he thought about their little hands around one of the toys. He knew they bravely held back their tears when they saw him and questioned him what had happened to his face. He tried to launch a joke and he couldn't smile through the pain, so he looked like he meant to reprimand them when his words were meant to be light. He had failed them, introduced pain and insecurity into their lives over a stupid stunt. They didn't deserve to see him stricken and he thought by the expressions on their faces they bore witness to the creeping shadow of death taking residence in his body. They would have nightmares of his passing because, in their minds, he had taken a long leap towards his end.

He picked out two matching pink mirrors with reflective plastic, decorated with the head and shoulders of a raven-haired princess. They would discard them within a day, leave them in the middle of the floor to be picked up and stowed away or throw them in the high grass to be chopped apart by the mower, but he wanted them to smile when he came home and anything would do, as long as it distracted them from the foreshadowing of his death. He skipped buying something for his wife because everything in the store ran counter to her tastes and, considering the current state of their marriage, he really couldn't chance another opportunity for derision and mockery as he handed her drugstore eye shadow of the wrong color or a box or off-brand chocolates that would end up stuffed down the sink disposal or in his own stomach.

He remembered water to lubricate the pill-swallowing and managed to weave his way over to the refrigerated wall filled mostly with beer and energy drinks. He wanted to take his items back to the pharmacy counter to take another run at the pharmacist, but he figured he really needed to wait at least until his eyebrows grew in and he felt more stable, back in control of his thoughts and actions before starting up another affair. He would have to replace Sabina with someone. Now that she had gone over to the sheriff he had no use for her, could not conjure up the old lust for her, and did not think he would miss her body although she carried so many perfect curves, had such the perfect full ass, because the sheriff's touch had made her wither and waste away like she had contracted a virulent pathogen.

He finally made it to the truck after paying for the water and toys. He fished out a pill from the prescription bottle, which seemed too full. He inspected the label and next to the word quantity hung a question mark, next to refills she had typed "as many as you need," in the direction space she had written "come back when you are feeling better" and where his name should have been she had written "He-who-played-with-fire" in a tiny font.

He swallowed the pill and chased it with a swig of water. He slipped another pill out of the bottle before closing it and sliding it back in the bag. He went to put the pill in his front shirt pocket and found the index card on which he had written the lead of the missing girl in Waverly up Route 23 from Portsmouth. Keeping a pill on his person seemed unnecessary, seeing how it was unlikely too much distance would develop between the prescription bottle and him, but he figured at the first hint of the return of pain he could take it and keep the throbbing at bay.

    He considered the card. He sat a few blocks away from Route 23 and Waverly lay about 25 miles to the north. When else would he have a chance to follow the lead? The sheriff would no doubt not let him out of his sight now, if he kept him working for the department and didn't use the AWOL as a grounds to fire him. The deputy had always felt a little uneasy about the publicity he had received over the skull. By all rights the sheriff should have been and the imaginary love of Diane Sawyer, since he acted as the de facto spokesman of the department and secured all the votes that kept the department in balance. The original Columbus newsreporter had insisted on talking to the law enforcement officer who had responded to the scene because the sheriff had several minutes of screen time over the previous month due to the controversy over Indian Head Rock and the release of a study that named Scioto County as the leading consumer population of prescription drugs per capita in the entire United States. The sheriff blustered and bloviated through the interviews, spoke of vague crackdowns and acceded that the population had lived hard lives full of pain and misery, had worked too much and broken their bodies, had wrung their hearts dry to scrape and survive and was it any wonder, really, that they needed a little pill to get them through the day without screaming and cursing against their collective fate? Holders of prescriptions also voted and the sheriff knew how to count. It was one of his many gifts. Privately, he told the deputy that the FBI no doubt had read the same report and had to be planning a shitstorm for their fair, beleaguered hamlet.

    So, when the story of the skull broke the surface of the national consciousness for a few moments and the attention rained down upon the deputy, he worried that the sheriff's jealousy would find some expression in the very near future. Truthfully, he hadn't expected it this soon. The sheriff sometimes waited years to even a score. Everyone who knew him guessed he kept a running list in his head of all the transgressions that had been launched against him alongside the twisted plots he formulated in response. When the reporter performed a perfunctory interview with the sheriff without the camera running and subsequently and elaborately staged the deputy's interview in front of the gravel pit that had made the offering of the skull, he made the sheriff understand that no small town despot would make him do anything he didn't want to do. Now the check had come to the table and the deputy had to pay it.

A fresh panic flooded his thoughts. The sheriff had sent him to the clinic, had all but driven him there, and he himself said the FBI had to have an interest in the pill mills now that the study had been released. No agency likes to be embarrassed. How could they ignore it? The deputy could very well be on a surveillance tape with a line feed to both the FBI and the sheriff's office. Look how easy it had been to set him up and oh, God, would they come down on him hard. Once corruption threatens to bring down the illusion of control the law feeds upon, the response can be swift and brutal. They would make an example of him, flog him unmercifully, because, they will argue and the public will believe, he had used his office and the power bestowed on him by the people as a means for personal gain, for coercing women to submit, for having favors granted, prescriptions filled, for acting on every whim and desire without heeding basic community standards. It would come down on his head from the invisible hand of the sheriff.

At some point he started the car but remained motionless in the parking lot, staring out the windshield. A persistent air-conditioned breeze whistled through the vents, but sweat poured from his head. He took the pill from his shirt pocket swallowed it, and replaced it with another from the bottle. The front pocket had become a staging area of sorts and would remain so throughout the life of the prescription. He would go to Waverly, follow the lead, see if anyone in the neighborhood remembered the girl or the story of her disappearance or know about her reappearance or verified demise. The official records of the department from that era often lagged behind the pace of life. The missing girl could be married with children and completely unaware that she had been included in the statistics of the children who had been lost.

21

On to Waverly

He turned onto Route 23 and headed north. During the drive the sheriff's office called twice about ten minutes apart, no doubt to inquire why he had left his post guarding the Head from crazed Kentuckian anthropologists looking to take back what had been stolen from them. The deputy did not pick up either call and soon after the second call his wife texted him the message, "Where r u? S wants to kno." He turned off the phone. He would remain lost a little longer. He could always make up the excuse that he had forgotten to charge the phone the night before and the battery had died, an excuse that would have been hard to pass off before the accident because he treated his phone and its charge status as if his own heartbeat relied on its power. A man with no eyebrows could be excused for a few lapses and misdeeds, so if he remained out of contact for a few hours the blackout would just be considered a brief and unfortunate outcome of the accident.

He found the house among a small cluster or ranches with oxidized aluminum siding and yards of half grass and half dirt. Monstrous pickup trucks rested in the driveways and the smell of wood smoke hung in the air. He parked in the driveway. A plastic shutter leaned against the house under the window it had previously dressed. The screen door hung slightly open and some of the mesh had been torn. A sickly hedge grew spindly arms and the grass looked like it hadn't been mowed in a month. Two rotted and smashed newspapers lay in the driveway in front of the deputy's truck. The driveway terminated at a garage in the backyard that leaned to the left and looked to have a broken door. A scattering of seedlings broke through the asphalt and caught trash and dead leaves.

The deputy eased himself out of the car. He had become aware that his face no longer throbbed, but where his hands and feet were located had become an open question. The air smelled of past floods and rot. The air temperature had to be peaking at that very moment, the moment that the deputy accidentally kicked loose a chunk of asphalt as he walked down the driveway. He thought something, a bush, a tree, the air, would spontaneously burst into flames. He should have driven home and rested the unharmed side of his face against his wife's cool breasts. He would ask her to rub his feet and if, during the process of relaxing him, the idea struck her to perform a long and slow session of fellatio all the better. First an apology, no? A soul-baring, burden-lifting apology? Not about the infidelity, though. She despised donuts and raged against the stupidity of people cramming their faces with such obvious poison. To find out that he had slept with, ruined their marriage over, stepped away from fidelity and truthfulness, and abandoned his role as a present, full-time and engaged father over a donut cook and peddler would be the ultimate rejection of her values and beliefs. A revelation like that would be such an explosion that not a single brick of their foundation would be left on which to rebuild. No, he would apologize for the gunpowder and burning his face and throwing everything into chaos. He would apologize for Paul and for his decision to bring a corpulent whore to their home, parading his perversion in front of their friends and the sheriff, disrobing and fucking in their hot tub and that weird blowjob tale he spun to her over their very own table where they ate as a family. That alone encompassed a mammoth apology, although how could he really know that his old friend had lost his mind and spun into the shadows of reason and society? He couldn't really be sure the story Paul told had any basis in fact. The act had been buried in so many layers of revulsion, rationalizations, repression and outright denial that it could have been a momentary homosexual impulse, a shared thought, a what-if discussion, a "what if I unzipped my pants and showed you my erection" dare that was never acted upon, an impulse that had been crushed by the weight of their true heterosexual selves. In the intervening decades he never had another occurrence, so how strong could the impulse be? A half a dozen times he had imagined being forced to his knees and taking the sheriff's cock in his mouth while Clarisse watched, but the image had almost nothing to do with homosexuality and almost everything to do with coercion, humiliation and capitulation. The fact that the act happened to be homosexual in nature was nothing but coincidence.

 Paul Newcombe's face rose above the stew of his thoughts and the deputy suddenly had an idea. He would call the Ramada Inn and check if Paul had stayed in town. Maybe the jail time had scared him enough that he had abandoned his plan of ruining the deputy's life. Although, the fact that he had been released and the charges had been dropped after purposefully exposing himself to a church full of octogenarians looking for one last gentle buggy ride down memory lane must have given him encouragement to create more havoc. The deputy had his phone in his hand, even though he had turned it off. It always remained in his hand or within close reach. He carried it like a talisman or a worry stone or a rosary. His fingertips always had to play across its surface and feel its smooth edges. He powered the phone on and called the hotel and asked if Paul had remained. The clerk told him that Paul had taken the room for the balance of the week and had not indicated he would be checking out.

As he spoke with the clerk a call came through from the sheriff's department and buzzed under the clerk's voice. The deputy turned the phone back off and found himself standing in the middle of the front lawn. The front door had been opened and a shadow stood behind the broken screen door. For an awkward moment the deputy and the shadow stared at each other. The deputy had momentarily forgotten his official command and lost his advantage. He could only hope the shock of seeing a uniformed sheriff's deputy standing before him threw the shadow off enough for the deputy to collect himself.

"Do you have a reason for standing on my lawn?" the shadow said in flat and slow tone. The rhythm of the question sounded like the revolution of something warped and swollen.

"I was making a call."

"'Do you have to make a call in the middle of my front yard?"

"I've come to ask you some questions about a missing person, a girl." Silence came back at the deputy. "Amber Miller. Are you related or know Amber Miller?"

The shadow retreated into the house and the light through the screen became a muddle of gray shades. The deputy stepped around land mines of dog shit on the way to the front door, calculating the real possibility that he had stepped in a coil as he made his phone call. He rattled the screen. He rattled the screen again and called through the door. A man cleared phlegm from his throat and, taking advantage of a momentarily clear passage, said that the deputy could enter the house. The deputy's senses sharpened, even through the swamp of his prescription, and he stepped through the door, fully expecting an ambush.

Instead, he found a man slumped in an easy chair in the corner of a dark room. The air smelled of burned fish. An oxygen tank nestled in a two-wheel silver cart stood by the chair. A clear tube snaked-up the arm of the chair, over the shoulder of the man, to a cannula that draped over his ears and hung under his nose. He had broken in the easy chair to the point where no one else would be comfortable sitting in it unless they happened to be the exact height, weight and proportion as the man. The walls of the room stood free of decoration. Other than the easy chair, a couch covered with the same fabric, a crushed yellow velvet that looked like it had entombed 5,000 days of dust and odors, and a small octagonal coffee table with the cheapest walnut veneer, nothing else was in the room. The deputy noticed the absence of a television or any other diversion like a newspaper or magazine. Maybe he kept it all in his bedroom and stayed in bed most of the day, staring at the screen, breathing through his tank. The carpet rose in a high shag and the bright green color shone through the deep shadow in which it lay.

"Is there something I can help you with?" the man said as he clutched a sputum rag in his right hand, ready for something to break loose.

"I'm looking into the disappearance of Amber Miller."

"I heard you before."

"Do you know the girl?"

"I saw you on television on that station out of Columbus."

"You have a television?"

"It's in the bedroom. I spend most of my time there."

"Ah," the deputy felt a surge of confidence having guessed the man's circumstances correctly. "A lot of people saw that story."

"Do you believe it's Amber?" the man said in a strangely toneless way as if he had practiced it many times and all emotion had been blanched from the question.

"I don't know, sir. I'm just following up on all the possible leads we may have."

"I believe you had eyebrows and hair when you were on the television. Are you getting radiation?"

"No sir, I had an accident."

The sputum moved, seizing the man in a coughing fit, which ended with the offending blockage in the folds of the rag,

"I can't say I'm not ready to go. I'm through with this life. I can't really put my finger on what was the point to all of it. The life of a milkweed. Sprout unwanted. Grow ugly, tough and remain unwanted. Die underfoot, broken, and unmourned."

"Did you know the girl, Amber Miller?"

"My name is Miller...she came out of her momma squalling and angry. Tiny little fists punching the air and little feet kicking, striking out against the world.

Face smashed and eyes blind for a moment, but it was like she knew she wouldn't like what she saw when she could see it. The hag nurses and the white walls. She cried and fought them through the shots, the weighing and the cleaning and when they squirted that gel into her eyes and didn't stop until they put her against her momma's breast. They were always very close. I always said it was like Amber didn't exactly grow in her momma's womb, but sort of broke off of her, like a clone or maybe a seed. I helped make her somehow, but it was apparent pretty early that all of me, I mean all of me, was routed out. I'm not sure my contribution made it much past the womb. Maybe I was left in the afterbirth, rejected after my job was done. Sometimes friends and family said the girl had my ears, but I always thought they were just being kind. Those ears could have been made of plaster molds of her mother's ears. She was always a fighter, though, kind of a loner. She improved on her mother's beauty, but she lost all the softness. It wasn't like she was mean or cold, she just seemed to be made of tougher stuff, unbreakable, indifferent like iron. When she disappeared and the days kept creeping by with no form or reason, her mother rotted from the inside. The doctors called it cancer, said she had several tumors the size of my fist inside her, but anyone close to her knew it was Amber's disappearance that got her. The agony just ate her alive, hollowed her out. I always thought that if it had been turned around and her mother had disappeared Amber would not have worried herself to death. She wasn't soft like that. Look at me. By all rights I should been dead six years ago. But here I am. I guess Amber looked like her mother, but inside her heart and her will were all me."

"I requisitioned the investigation report at the time of her disappearance, but the file was nearly empty. There was a card with this address and your initial filing of a missing person's form, but nothing beyond that. What happened during the investigation that you remember?"

"Why is it when some children go missing the world stops, bloodhounds are released, neighbors join hands and walk through abandoned fields or they dig up basements, tear down walls, clear-cut forests in search of a body and other times the only reaction the disappearance gets is the checking of a box, completing a form, and filing it away as an unfortunate and unintentional consequence of the freedoms we enjoy?"

The deputy thought of how much of his day consisted of sitting in front of a computer screen filling out official forms, spying contradictions that could be exploited by a defense attorney, reliving arrests in official language, breaking down chaos and emotion into logical and linear nuggets as society's arbiter, the dispassionate eye, the chronicler of lament, woe, the end of luck, and the aftermath of sudden violence. He became aware of the silence hanging between them and felt compelled to answer the question, even though both knew the rhetoric barely masked his rage.

"That's not a question I can answer."

"Why are you here?"

"A skull was found in a gravel pit..."

"Probably an Indian burial mound."

"The tests indicate the body was buried around twenty years ago."

"Was there a body?"

"I misspoke. No body has been recovered."

"Not misspoke. More likely you are trying to spare my feelings. It's much worse to just find a head."

"My apologies."

"Apology? Why else would they put it in the news? But why are you here?" A flash of anger flickered across the man's face and his body rallied enough to shake off some of its vulnerability.

"I'm following one of the few leads I have."

"But to what purpose? To solve the mystery of the rolling skull? Have you asked me yet if I want Amber's disappearance solved?"

"What do you mean?"

"I mean I have created every variation to the story that could be created. Must you tell me now that there's an official version of the truth? I'm in the last months of my life. Of course, with my milkweed genes I might be unfortunate enough to live a few more years, but why do I need the official story? The so-called objective truth? I've witnessed her decapitation. I've seen it. I've heard her last screams, but I've also seen her walk away from our house with a plan, get on a bus, and ride all the way to California, probably Los Angeles, where she lives to this very day, too ashamed to call me because of the guilt she feels about leaving without a word. Maybe she didn't want us as parents. Didn't want to be from Waverly, Ohio. She just needed to start life anew. She had to cut the umbilical cord from her mother once and for all and the only way she could have done so was leaving without a goodbye. I've seen every extreme and everything in between, so I don't have much interest in the official story. What can you tell me that I don't already know?"

"I'm trying to find the truth and possibly bring the perpetrator to justice. We can arrest someone only if we know the true story."

The man began a laugh but phlegm choked it off before it could gather strength. The ensuing coughs sounded like the desperate last breaths of a drowning man. The deputy tensed at the edge of the couch cushion, ready to implement a remedy. The need for action came before he decided what remedy he could put in place, but he relaxed once something broke off from the man's throat and ended splayed on the shag. The man's breathing returned to a wheezing normalcy.

"I don't mean to mock you, Deputy. I'm sure what you do is very hard and depressing. Your love of the rules, of laws, must outweigh the misery. You can make up a truth if you're convincing enough, if you get the prosecutor on your side. You can just about convince anybody of anything. It becomes the true story because you want it to be so, the only story. Once you have one story, justice follows. At any one time you get 12 fools to believe your version and you blot out all other possibilities."

"Sir, if I could ask you a few questions?"

"I heard that monster, Kinnell, admitted to killing and burying the body, but you let him go. It seems to me you had a true story staring you in the face and you threw it out. It was a goddamn fish that jumped right into your boat, but I'm guessing you thought that after all these years it shouldn't be so easy. Maybe sometimes it is that easy. Maybe a whole big mystery was really just created by a lack of trying, you ever think of that?"

"You knew Kinnell?"

"That family of lunatics lived about a half mile away from here, which you think would have been far enough away that our paths wouldn't have crossed, but the radius of their influence extended well past our house. If you think about one of those radar photos of hurricanes and that's what I can tell you about the Kinnells."

"How many were in the family?"

"As many as they could squeeze out of the old lady's child-bearing years. Maybe fifteen, all criminals, sociopaths and retards. Their house wasn't much bigger than mine and I heard old man Kinnell made his own beds out of stolen 2 x 4s and plywood. He must have stacked them four high and two to a bed."

"Do you know if they still live there?"

"No, first old man Kinnell died of some kind of poisoning. He worked at Piketon at the uranium plant. A lot of people who came out of that plant didn't have long retirements. Radiation just ate them up from the inside. Anyway, after he died the family collapsed. The old lady drank enough grain alcohol to make four people go insane. A handful of them either left or died, but the majority still live in the area spreading that special brand of Kinnell havoc and evil. You dismissed that one who confessed to killing Amber, thinking he would have been too young to hurt and bury her, but you didn't think that a little monster might have brothers and sisters who could have guided him, taught him the ways of the family. Maybe one of the bigger monsters committed the act and made the little one think he did it, who carried his guilt with him all these years until he's convinced himself that he's the one who did the deed. You see, Deputy, I've watched them in my imagination and I'm all but convinced they had something to do with the disappearance of my poor Amber."

The deputy thought his blood pressure might have dropped by half and wondered how he would stay conscious through the entire interview.

"Have you ever told the police about this?"

"The Kinnells were suspects in every crime in the county. The old man served time in the penitentiary and he was about the meanest sonofabitch you could ever meet. Stories started attaching themselves to him, some true and some flat-out myths, but I think it's reasonable to say that he beat a man to death with a crowbar right in the middle of the street in front of a crowd, that he shot a girlfriend of his in the back, that he had a fierce dependency on hard liquor, and that he passed along his rage and misanthropy to his children with fists, kicks and screaming so fierce they either had to turn mean themselves or collapse under the torrent of his words. Everybody suspected them. The police, the neighbors, but you would have had to call in the National Guard to root them out of their house. I think the police were afraid for their own lives but more so the lives of their families. Kinnell was no ordinary hillbilly. He had two of his sons come visit me and my wife once I started making noise about the lack of progress in the investigation and after I started telling people they should arrest Kinnell. They told me without saying exactly that if I valued my life and the life of my wife I would learn to shut up and not spread lies about their father. I remember telling them that without Amber my life had no meaning, no purpose and they could do me a favor by putting me out of my misery. The oldest one, the one I imagine took the full brunt of the old man's madness, had a dead eye and a permanent knot on his forehead like it was some kind of horn bursting to get out or sawed off, he looked at me and gave me this wide grin and said, 'We all have our crosses.' Don't think I was intimidated, because I wasn't in the least bit. Like I said, I had no reason to go on. I couldn't stop my heart without committing an act of violence and I just couldn't bring myself to do it. It was the milkweed in me. I can't tell if I'm ultimately a coward or not or if I'm addicted to pain and misery. My wife, she didn't last all that long. She died in the house. By that time I had lost my job because most days I couldn't get out of bed. Twenty years of perfect attendance didn't matter. They treated me like a damned criminal. They found me in the lunchroom and escorted me off the property with a security guard on my hip. But's that not the point I was trying to tell you. When I watched my wife waste away, when I wiped her ass and scooped the puke off her chest I envied her, and I wondered every day, minute by minute, what the hell made me go on. I can't go one. I think I'll go on, right?"

The man took huge draughts of oxygen and closed his eyes. The deputy wondered if he had been breathing through the mask during his speech or had taken intermittent breaks to breathe because he couldn't remember the man performing the function.

"Do you remember the name of Amber's dentist?"

The man looked at him momentarily like he had emerged from a deep reverie and lowered the mask.

"Do you want to hear the saddest part of my story? A story that may hold the secret of why I hold on?" The man waited for an answer.

"Yes, sure."

"Sometimes I imagine one of those Kinnell boys eloping with Amber and thinking they slipped out of town and they don't want to be found by either family. He because he wants to escape the insanity and criminality of his family and she because she would have known how such a match would have driven me crazy. She thinks it's better to disappear than admit to illicit love. They all couldn't have turned mean, right? One of them had to stay reasonably good and maybe that goodness was the wellspring of his love for Amber. Maybe she was a lifeline of sorts. I think of them living in some backwater Florida town, on the edge of a wasteland, living under different names and without a phone or a proper address. That is the form my hope takes. That is the sunshine that gives the milkweed life. Try as I might, I can come up with nothing better than that. A kernel of goodness amidst abject poverty. If that's not sad, I don't know what is."

The mask covered his mouth again. The deputy searched for something to ask or a comforting statement to make it known he had been listening. The man did not wait for such a cue. The mask came down.

"Truth is, we lost Amber a couple of years before she disappeared. Around fifteen she started drinking and performing oral sex behind the 7-11 where the kids used to hang out. The cops caught her in the act more than once. The drinking led to the sex, we knew that. She was getting a reputation. We tried everything we could think of to get her to stop, but she came by it honestly. Her mother and I got lit up on a pretty regular basis, but our drinking only led to arguments and sleeping. We didn't want Amber to turn out like us, a couple of drunks working bullshit jobs. But we made a mistake. When she missed her curfew we started locking her out of the house. At first she would sleep in the bushes or on the deck out back, maybe a couple of times in the back seat of the car or the garage, but then she started finding other couches and beds to sleep in, at a cost I'm sure. She dropped out of school. I lost track of her. Sometimes I would see her in a car or walking on the street. She would talk to me, but she made it clear that she wasn't coming back. We thought about going to the police, but how would we have kept her in her room? We would've had to use chains."

"So, it is distinctly possible she left the area and hasn't contacted you. But if you would give me the name of her dentist so I can track down her dental records…"

"You know what the Kinnells are? They are what grows after society has collapsed, after the fire or flood. They are ciphers, blanks, without motive or purpose. They are the impulse, the blackness, left when every structure, man-made or instinctual, has disintegrated. They are chaos. They are the end of the world."

He raised the oxygen mask to his face and breathed for a minute as the deputy leaned back on the couch and waited. The shifting of his position caused his field of vision to narrow and almost go black before rallying and keeping the deputy conscious.

"There is a story that is told about them. One evening the neighbors heard screams and the breaking of a window and they came out of their houses and they saw one of the daughters naked and bleeding, crawling across the lawn. The old man came out, naked too, with half a boner bobbing in front of him. He swung a belt and whipped her bare ass and back until she stopped crawling. He caught her by the ankle and dragged her back inside, not before turning on the congregation of neighbors and screaming that if they knew what's good for them they'd forget about everything they had seen. Not one of them called the police. They said it was a family matter. They liked telling the story, though. I heard it straight from the mouth of one of the witnesses, but the neighbor never said anything about his own culpability, never saw his lack of action as the true crime. The Kinnells will always be in the shadows, waiting for the collapse to move in. When you give up, become afraid, refuse to consider the value of a single human life, then it becomes possible for a girl like Amber to disappear without a trace and without much official consideration."

"Sir, I need the dentist's name," the deputy said in a sharp bark that surprised both of them.

"Professor Guggenson."

"Sir?"

"I called him professor because he had shoulder-length hair and a goatee, all white, and tan skin like a Cherokee. Smelled of pipe smoke and hickory. I heard he may have been a cousin of Roy Rogers or that might have been a gimmick to drum up business."

"Do you know his real name?"

"His first name was Sylvester, but he's been dead for more than a decade. I remember how he died. He had a flat tire on the interstate and pulled off on the inside berm. The professor was pretty old by then and he tried to hoof it across three lanes of speeding traffic and never made it past the second lane. It's hard to judge the speed of a car coming at you at 80 miles per hour, especially when you are an old man with bad hips."

"Someone probably took over the practice, no?"

"Such as it was. I'm not sure there was much or a practice left to buy. His look didn't play all that well in these parts. He could have been Roy Rogers' twin brother and still no one would have trusted opening their mouth for him."

"I can find out easy enough. There aren't that many dentists around here and I have access to all the business transfers. I can find out with one phone call."

"Guignol and Associates. Just up Route 23. They're in the same building where the Professor practiced. I would ask you, Deputy, of doing me the favor of waiting for me to die before you match the records. There's no need to torture an old, worn-out man."

"But don't you want to know for certain? Finally lay her to rest if it turns out that it is her."

"And why ruin the mystery now?"

"But you don't even know it's her. We could have stumbled on almost anyone. Even the archeologists from Cleveland are skeptical of the coroner's finding. They want to test the skull themselves if they can get a release."

"I had a feeling that I never had when I saw you on television. Something about the rolling reminded me of Amber. It was her last wild ride, freaking out the driver, making a show of herself, yowling into the void that she once prowled the earth. She was something. Just like her mother before the worry got her."

"I'll follow up with the dentist and if you can think of anything else I'm going to give you my card," he said as he reached into his front shirt pocket to find his business cards, but he inadvertently fingered the spare oxy and paused, realizing his face had indeed gone numb and that for the first time in days he had forgotten he had been burned. He forgot about the card and withdrew his hand from his pocket without another word.

The man didn't follow with an inquiry as to why the deputy suddenly abandoned his purpose, because he had no intention of calling him with the hundred other thoughts he had developed over the course of the intervening decades that could have assisted the deputy in his investigation. Speaking about it once again had convinced him that Amber belonged in the shadows, in her small, miserable town under a storm of mosquitoes or in the dirt, dreaming of a life never lived.

"Deputy, I have done you a favor in speaking with you. I ask you to return the favor and talk to my fucking neighbors to keep their dog from shitting in my yard. I can't even bend over anymore and those mongrels shit at will on my lawn. You think those cretins would pick up after them? Look at my yard when you leave."

The deputy nodded and touched his jaw to test the depth of the numbness. After several probes of increasing strength and duration he surmised he could only feel the pressure of his fingers and the rawness of his nerves had been effectively blunted. He stood up and wobbled as a rush of blood weakened his equilibrium. He drifted to the front door and broke into the sunlight. He couldn't remember if he had given the man a parting word or acknowledged his help. He would look foolish if he went back inside and asked, especially if he had already said goodbye or thanked the man. But he did remember the request and something about a man hooked to an oxygen tank being unable to clear the waste of a neighbor's pet incited in him a small knot of fury and the desire for immediate justice as he looked at the houses to the left and right and the three across the street that likely housed the offending cur. He picked the house to the right that had a torn-up lawn, all bare patches and holes, and a chain bolted to the cement block foundation in the front.

He strode over to the front door of the house, an identical ranch covered in oxidized aluminum siding, and pounded on the door with a fist. The sound unleashed a tumult from within. Five or six dogs barked a desperate warning, each trying to out-do the other in pitch and volume. The deputy closed his eyes and felt the sway of his body, his eroding balance, and his inability to stay with the spin of the earth. A voice spoke to his right and somewhat behind. He waited until he could be sure that turning his head wouldn't send him sprawling onto the lawn to acknowledge the voice. A man stood at the corner of the house, gray t-shirt, jeans, work boots, hair cropped close to his skull, and skin burned from outside work.

The deputy eyed him up and down, then said, "Are your dogs shitting in your neighbor's lawn?"

"What?" The man might have conjured several reasons for a visit from the law but this had not been one of them.

"You heard what I said. I asked you a simple question."

The man didn't respond but squared off and tensed his body as if ready to jump to a physical conclusion before any reasonable explanation could be developed. The deputy took his gun out of its holster and held it at his side as he took three menacing steps toward the man, who watched the pistol in alarm and froze his body from any movement.

"Do your dogs defecate in the neighbor's yard?"

"Sometimes, yes, they get out."

"And when this happens do you clean it up?"

"Yes, I do."

"Then how do you explain that your neighbor doesn't own a dog, yet he has a yard filled with shit?"

"Other people have dogs around here."

"I bet they fucking do. Pit Bulls and Rottweilers, crazy mongrels and half-wolves, breeds for tough guys and fucking peasants. Suitable for the dog ring fighting and chewing the face off any trespasser, because, God knows, something has to protect the troves of treasure you have squirreled behind those rotted walls. God knows you need six dogs to protect that flat screen hanging on your wall."

The man licked his lips and could not effectively hide his anger. "You have a gun, so you can say anything, right?"

"That's right. I have a lethal combination of a gun and a badge. Right here in my hand is a soapbox and a bully pulpit." He laughed hard at the sound combination of bully pulpit, but the laughter died as soon as it began. "And since I have the gavel, so to speak, and I'm a goddamn front yard judge, and telling you to go get a shovel and a nice big bag. A working man like you has a shovel, right?"

"Now?"

"Yes, now. I can't stand here all fucking day. There are dogs shitting all over the county. I'm one man against a tidal wave. Now go get the shovel."

The man disappeared around the corner of the house and the deputy questioned his own ability to perform police work. He had just let the man out of sight. He could come charging around the corner, swinging the shovel like an invading Jute or send two barrels of shotgun pellets screaming in his direction or he could have run through the backyard to the nearest woods, afraid the deputy would find the meth lab in the garage or the raised bed of pot plants growing near the house or see the expired tags on the license plates of his truck. He squeezed the handle of the gun, waiting for the lapse to develop into a further complication, but within a few minutes the man came back dragging a shovel and shuffling his feet.

"Good man, now you're going to walk over to your neighbor's yard and pick up every pile of dog shit, front and back and I'm going to stand watching you, making sure you do it."

"You can't do this."

"I'm doing it. Would you like to call your lawyer?"

"I don't have a lawyer."

"Shame. Every man bent on befouling the world with the waste of his mongrels should have a lawyer in his hip pocket, because you know there's going to be nothing but trouble coming at you. Now get to fucking work."

"You need to stop cursing at me."

"I have certain rights bestowed upon me by Scioto County, cursing being one of them."

"You know this is Pike County, right? You have no jurisdiction here."

"The rights are inalienable and can be enacted wherever I see injustice. Now, get to...fucking...work."

The deputy checked his impulse to point the gun at the neighbor while he shoveled, thinking it might be worse for him if it became known that he used the weapon in such a manner, but he didn't know what to do with the pistol in his hand because what was the difference between aiming it at the man and having it hanging at his side? Both spoke of coercion and now that he had introduced the gun into the interaction between them, raised the ante to the brink of violence, he couldn't very well slide it back into his holster and give the man the advantage should be want to turn the shovel into a weapon. A picket line of nerves awoke along his jawline, the first pricks that signaled the return of pain. He touched the spare oxy, rolled it with his fingertip, but waited to swallow the pill until he went back to the truck. He focused on the man delivering the shit parcels into the garbage bag, but drifted away after following a few scoops and deposits.

    He glanced at his wrist but his watch was absent. Where had he left his watch? How had he skipped that step in his morning preparation and why was he only noticing it now? Sleeping on the couch had altered his routine. His wallet, keys, watch and phone lay scattered from their usual resting spots. He very much wanted to know the time, even looking at the position of the sun in the sky, which, of course, told him nothing except it looked and felt like afternoon. He had left his phone in the truck as well. He worried that the dentist office would be closing. He could call and ask for the records as he had convinced himself the mystery of the rolling skull had been solved. He had indeed found the owner of it, like he said he would. But what then? What would the sheriff do to him then? Would he make him a school crossing guard or would he guard the Head as long as Scioto County owned it? Something humiliating would happen now that he had solved a twenty-five year case within two months of finding the skull. The sheriff would view it the same as if the deputy had filed the paperwork with the Board of Elections to make a run against him. And now that the sheriff had all but cast him out maybe he would make a run at him. The past three elections had been landslides, but only crazies had run against him, the last being a storefront preacher who had gathered enough signatures to get on the ballot through his ragged and dispossessed congregation. His only qualification seemed to be a strong desire to return to biblical justice (i.e. castration for adulterers, amputated hands for thieves, beheadings for murderers, and cutting off the nose to spite one's face). The last was an example of campaign jocularity that sailed completely over the heads of a very small gathering of supporters who attended the candidate's only campaign speech. His idea of campaigning, besides the aforementioned speech, was to pray for the destruction of his opponent as his own subsequent elevation into a democratically elected office. And even the preacher pulled down 28% of the vote and while 72-28% qualified as a landside of monumental proportions, the lesson in the results was that there existed a 28% anti-incumbency core, voters who would risk the threat of castration and amputation because of their hatred for the sheriff. He would have to hope to sway 22% of tepid support that now existed for the sheriff, voters willing to give him a chance, because he had a fresh face (his eyebrows and hair would have grown in by then and his skin would have returned to its normal shade) and new ideas, voters who would be concerned about despotism in the hands of a man who played with dolls. If he could get a picture of the sheriff's desk he could count on knocking off a few points of the sheriff's support, because a segment of adults do not understand the fascination with characters meant to appeal to the minds of children. But he would have to worry about losing some of the anti-incumbency support, because once they caught a glimpse of the sheriff's internal life they may realize they share the same love of saturated color and absurd muscles. The sheriff could be attacked in so many ways that it might not be worth the risk of losing more support than gaining with the use of such a picture.

The deputy suddenly broke his reverie. He had lost the neighbor with the shovel and bag of shit. The front yard looked clean. The grass had been scalped in several spots, but all the piles were gone. It felt like a victory of sorts for the man with the oxygen tank and the deputy had authored it without the muddle of citations, court appointments, lawyers, arguments presented and defended from both sides, all the while losing the thread that a man without a dog had a yard full of shit and that a man with a pack of dogs admitted being guilty of the crime. Now, thanks to the deputy, the yard was free of shit and the neighbor had been put in his place.

Just then the man reappeared around the corner of the house, still holding his shovel and a half-full garbage bag in the other. He walked past the deputy and deposited the bag at the curb, turned and tried to make it back to his house, using the widest angle he could to both avoid the deputy and come reasonably close to his front door. The deputy barked an unintelligible command at him and he stopped, but in a small show of dignity, pride or rebellion he refused to turn toward the deputy.

"Keep an eye on those bare spots you dug. If they don't fill in after a couple of weeks you'll need to seed them. I'll be back around and if I see more shit on the man's yard I'll arrest you and if I hear about you hassling him in any way I'll also have you arrested. Got it?"

The neighbor had already plotted six different and increasingly more violent paths to revenge as he cleaned the dog shit. He began by spelling out a cryptic message in gasoline on the grass, something like "Judas," but since the man's actions really did not resemble those of the unfaithful apostle in any way, he moved on to more explicit words and settled on "Fuck You" as an appropriate response to this humiliation. From there the plans became more elaborate, premeditated as to the time of day, the brand of duct tape used, and a script of words to be spoken before performing each deed. Each plan became a higher step on the ladder of insanity, until the sixth path of retribution included a kidnapping scheme, torture with a knife, and a confession extracted between terrified sobs, before the man cut the tube to his oxygen tank and watched the man slowly suffocate. By the time the deputy stopped him on his way to his front door, the man felt woozy, his equilibrium following the same route of collapse as his rational self had, and he considered wielding the shovel like a battle-axe and smashing the cop's head into a pulpy mass. He caught himself, though, and a dose of panic finished off the fantasies, his escape from fatal consequences much like a pedestrian musing over the result of stepping into fast and heavy traffic or a motorist contemplating swerving into the oncoming lane, preparing themselves to take the first step or pulling the wheel hard to the left before remembering something that had been giving them a reason to live.

    The deputy watched the progress of the neighbor until he jabbed the shovel into the dirt of his own lawn and disappeared behind the front door of his house. He lurched toward his truck. The response of his toes past the webbing and his heels had grown wooden so every step became a surprise and he resembled an ice skater unsure of his blades. By the time he made it to the truck he was perspiring again and he fingered the spare oxy. He wondered if it would melt under his touch and he tasted his fingertips once he withdrew them. He tasted metal, dirt, and maybe the residue of the pill. Either the taste or the herky-jerky walk set off a jangle of nerves across his temple and the bloom of a headache behind his eye, so he fished out the pill with a quick movement and threw it on the back of his tongue.

    He spied the toys he had bought at the drugstore and the idea of going home gathered momentum. He would ask forgiveness, rest his head on his wife's lap and confess. No, not confess, but ask for help, tell her the trouble he had created, the trouble that threatened to finally hunt him down, knock him to the ground, drag him to the nearest tree with a hanging branch, and tie him up by the ankles until he died. He should retreat back to his home and all its jumbled comfort: the stained furniture, the littered floor, the load of dirty plates rotting in the dishwasher, the varying masses of mold growing from forgotten cans or jars pushed to the back of the refrigerator, the mound of bills with ever-increasing balances, the phone calls from collection agents who ran the gamut of roles between mafia hit man and concerned British mom worried about the state of their financial affairs, the cruel little accountings of their lack of discipline, of a lack of enough salary to raise a family, the lack of coordination between husband and wife as to what to buy in what pay period and a miscalculation concerning to what extent their desires could be satiated. He could barely meet the minimum balances in a good month when nothing else in the house broke or the children didn't need something. An extraordinary expense, like car tires or a tooth cavity, plunged them further into debt and at this arc they would either be completely bankrupt in a couple of years or they would struggle for the next twenty-five, always skating the line of complete ruin. Or he would get a different job, like sheriff, and his wife could start working again, which may have had worse odds than beating an entrenched incumbent, because every time he brought up the possibility of their destitution and the possibility of her helping by bringing in some income her eyes glazed over and her words were reduced to a mumble, a response she produced when the conversation turned toward a subject she had no interest in or that she wanted over in the shortest amount of time possible.

Somehow, earning a wage of any kind did not fit the conception she had of herself, and more than a dozen times, as their conversations spiraled downward as he laid out the desperation in which they were sinking he refrained from saying something about putting her extraordinarily expensive college degree to use in something other than experimental lesbianism and a deep aversion to the working class, because had he given voice to such a criticism he very well could have sunk the marriage irrevocably. Such a volley would strike deep in the heart of the misalignment of their marriage; they ignored mismatched class, history, family dynamics, work ethic, and political views. When the deputy thought about mortgages, pensions, debts versus assets, and continually calculated the year of his retirement, which sadly crept up a few months for every passing year, Jenny thought about a place where she would never know someone like the sheriff, where she might have neighbors with shared values, and where the children could have a chance of growing up without internalizing oppression, grasping at materialism, hypnotized by the television, fattened-up with sugar, where their minds wouldn't be stunted and narrowed, where fear and stereotyping wouldn't take the place of thinking and living in the world.

They couldn't have a conversation about money, because his deputy's salary simply was not enough to support their way of living and Jenny refused to acknowledge its power over them. She had floated through high school and college with the knowledge her family was awash with money, so she continued to indulge the girls with ballet lessons, expensive day camps, music lessons, and massive wardrobes that ran the gamut from princess fantasies to soccer cleats. He could probably start collecting overtime or get a second job altogether, because they would never be comfortable as long as he was a simple deputy. The best they could hope for would be to crawl out of debt over a long stretch of time, although bankruptcy was far more likely.

22

One More Time

The comfort of lying his injured face on his wife's lap suddenly felt impossible and sentimental, a hollow remnant of an intimacy that may have never been. He changed his course of action. He would drive to Sabina's trailer and try to restart the affair before too much time had passed. If he worked and focused on staying as her lover he could prevent the sheriff from pushing him aside. The truck started with a roar as if he sat directly on the engine block and all the pulses and surges exploded around his head. His hands felt disconnected from his arms, but although they were acting independently they managed to steer reasonably well and kept the truck out of an obvious drunken weave.

When he turned the final bend toward Sabina's trailer he saw the sheriff's car parked out front in the grass. Her trailer sat in a cluster of five others, not really enough population for the cluster to be considered its own 'park' but not so isolated for her to be considered a misanthrope living in a field alone. The deputy kept driving and tried to stare through the windows as he passed. He imagined them together on her foam mattress, his girth all but suffocating her, and he felt anger and embarrassment. She had told him she had moved on to the sheriff, but he hadn't guessed it had advanced so far. They had obviously been seeing each other even before the accident for him to have been invited inside the trailer. Sabina carefully reeled out her affections, teased and parsed, analyzed and retreated. She loved the game and consummation, even after an achingly long and frustrating courtship. Any subsequent pursuits by the same suitor felt diminished and not a little boring to her.

He backed his truck behind a stand of trees a half a mile down the road. The sheriff would drive this way if he wanted to go to his house or the department, the only two places on earth the sheriff ever talked about, so the deputy thought it the best place to see when he left. The sheriff could possibly spot his car from the road. He had uncanny observation skills and even a brief flash of a fender might be enough for him to stop and investigate. What would the deputy say? His shift had probably not yet ended. The clock on his dashboard had stopped working months ago and he hadn't bothered to get it fixed. He could have turned on his phone but inquiries from his wife and the department waited for him through voicemail and text. He wanted to remain lost for a few hours longer, but he could think of no good story as a cover should the sheriff find him behind the trees, a half mile from Sabina's trailer.

He stared through the window at the patch of weeds in front of him and the barren asphalt beyond. Shade sliced across the clearing and enveloped the truck. The green around him hung leaden from the trees and sprouted like reeds of iron from the ground. The patch of sky he could see looked smudged with white and a deepening brown. Under the trees the light failed as a path with many branches ended in a tangle of underbrush and thorns. A crow wheeled above the trees screaming to another that rested on a branch below. The sheriff did pass the deputy about an hour after he started the surveillance, but the sheriff did not notice a flash of fender and glass as he passed. The deputy also did not notice because he had fallen asleep and his mouth hung agape. A slight, raspy snore escaped his throat. When he finally did awake night had fallen and clouds of fireflies drifted through the trees. His neck hurt and the balance of his body felt like his blood had stopped moving and lay in stagnant pools in his hands and feet.

He turned on his phone and saw that he had twelve text messages from his wife and three voicemails from the sheriff's office. Clarisse or another deputy would have left the message as the sheriff did not like to hear his voice recorded, no matter the banality of the subject, because he feared his words being spliced together to create a sentence he never uttered and the more rational fear of voters hearing his unscripted language and his true thoughts concerning their misdeeds and neediness. The deputy couldn't muster the will to listen to the screeds the messages no doubt contained, although a powerful sense of guilt prodded him to at least read his wife's texts since she could be trying to inform him of some unimaginable tragedy concerning the children. So the twelve in order read:

> July 24, 2013 9:02 AM
> How are you doing? I don't think you should have gone into work.

> July 24, 2013 9:45 AM
> Hello?

> July 24, 2013 9:49 AM
> Does S have you in a meeting? Can u talk?

> July 24, 2013 11:06 AM
> Hello, are u alive? Do you have your phony?

> July 24, 2013 11:07 AM
> I meant phone. GD autocorrect.

> July 24, 2013 11:08 AM
> If you don't have your phone. How would you answer?

> July 24, 2013 2:22 PM
> S office called. They are looking for you. You're pissing the world off.

> July 24, 2013 2:53 PM
> S office called again. This time the man himself. Things aren't good G. He said you left your post at the head. Didn't call. Acting erratic. Are you with that friend of yours and the prostitute he brought to party?????? Fuck you.

> July 24, 2013 5:32 PM
> Kids starving. Getting pizza. They want u here. We miss you.

> July 24, 2013 7:15 PM
> Fuck you!!!!!!!!!!!!! G, we care about you.

July 24, 2013 8:15 PM

????????????xs8686_%areannnahuuhuhhuhuhhumcmcxRATCAN -- - -

-@@$}}}}}}4343432f39jmn baqwqd;dnnq34jfhnfwrr

    The deputy surmised the last text had been written by one of his daughters as Jenny put her to sleep with one of the stories she loved to hear. His finger hovered over the keyboard as a thousand replies raced through his mind. He could still probably explain it all away, the meeting with the sheriff, the guard duty at the Head, leaving his post, the oxy prescription, and following the lead of the missing girl. He could edit out his visit to the donut shop and making the neighbor clean up the dog shit or he could leave in his bullying as a sign of an unhinged mind that could help explain his daylong disappearance. He could blame a dead battery or his forgetfulness because of his condition or his loss of a sense of time and ability to manage schedules. He did not send a reply.

    He turned off the phone again and drove to Sabine's trailer. He found, or course, the sheriff long gone and only one dim light on in one window. The deputy knew it to be her bedroom and even this brief acknowledgement of their past carnality caused him to become hard, not completely rigid but enough to change the purpose of the visit from comfort to pleasure. She answered the door in silk shorts and a silk chemise with no bra to stay her heavy breasts. If there had been a question whether he would try to restart their affair the same day she had broken it off, her outfit drowned all the more reasonable courses of action or uncertainty.

    "You, I did not expect," Sabina said as she blocked the doorway, neither retreating and granting him access nor slamming the door and refusing him outright. "I told you this morning to come see me when you grew hair back on your head. I do not see any hair, Deputy. Not even the presence of a wig to try to make me happy."

    "Let me in, Sabina, I'm not in the mood to play games right now."

    "As you wish," she said as she pivoted her body, leaving a narrow space through which the deputy had to shuffle. "I must ask what exactly you are in the mood for?"

    The deputy straddled the doorway awkwardly, one foot on the level of the floor, one foot on the first step of the stairs leading up to the door, leaving him several inches shorter than her. He wished, as he often did when he spent time with her, that she would drop the coquetry and display an emotion not twisted and manipulated for use in the game between them. Something open, real, and honest.

She still hadn't moved and he paused, gazing up at her chin and allowing her to look down her nose at him.

"What is it you want?"

"I want it to be like it was before."

"Impossible. You had eyebrows and hair then."

"They'll grow back."

"Can you be sure? I have seen burns through which hair never grew again. I do not know if you have disfigured yourself. Come back when that question is answered and I will tell you then what I feel about your new face."

"Oh, for God's sake, this is getting ridiculous." The deputy lurched forward and bumped her slightly as he made his way through the door.

Once in, he had few places to go: the galley kitchen to the left, the living room in front of him, or the bedroom, which lay at the terminus of a short hallway to the right. He wished to act with purpose, but each direction had its advantages and disadvantages. Walking into the bedroom would be his closing argument in their daylong disagreement concerning the state of his face and their affair. There existed a better than average chance that she would acquiesce because of the familiarity of the pattern and one or two extraordinary sense memories of their lovemaking, but looming behind this possibility stood the more probable outcome of outright mockery or a hardening of her resolve because he had pushed through when she very clearly had told him to take a step back. He could make an interim stop on the way to the bedroom by ducking into the bathroom, thus somewhat explaining away his lurch into the trailer and his brusqueness towards her, and he could wait to see where she landed, whether she walked in the bedroom and prepared herself for him or remained resolved and hung back. He could head to the living room, really just two steps in front of him, and settle in one of the chairs as a nod to formality and propriety, a slow reeling out of lust, the build-up to the point of bursting, but he had no time for a delay. He could explain away only so many hours and since he had fallen asleep in the truck he had less time than he would have had. Besides, introducing formality now seemed ludicrous, when they had not made it past the threshold of the trailer so many times. He thought he could explain his absence on the pills, but he couldn't quite convince himself, given that everyone he knew eyed his erratic behavior and thought he had cracked-up, that blaming further peculiarities on an overuse of a prescription drug would be the wisest and most effective excuse he could use, since he carried a gun for a living. So, he settled on the kitchen, or more properly called a kitchenette, since it consisted of a dwarf refrigerator, a narrow stove and sink pushed against the far wall with a foot or two of counter space on either side, with a round, two-person café table resting in the void between the kitchen space and the living room, its top littered with mail, magazines and a dirty cereal bowl.

He opened the refrigerator and found a case of Miller High Life sitting on the main shelf. The Miller had been a recent addition, it being the only beer the sheriff would drink. Anyone who wanted to curry favor with him had to stock a load of it when he visited, something the deputy himself worried about the day of the party as he ran out to buy a second case a few hours before the official start just to be sure the sheriff would remain happy. Behind the case stood two Heinekens, the brand he had been drinking lately, and he did not miss the differences in quantity and brand marketing wrestling in the refrigerator. If the amount and type of beer in a woman's refrigerator revealed her interests, her trend, then he had all but been forgotten. By drinking one of the remaining Heinekens he thought he might be draining half of the feeling she still felt for him or did this visit mean he came for the first of his last two withdrawals? And the brand. He couldn't say he actually preferred the taste of Heineken to any other beer, but it remained on the market as a vaguely European and readily available alternative to American domestics, and the sheriff would never drink it, hated the fact the deputy did, and felt uneasy when he saw the bottle in the deputy's hand, so if beer brands could help differentiate the two men for the woman they both chased then a side-by-side comparison between Miller and Heineken satisfied the condition, at least in the minds of the two men.

He fished out one of his beers and rummaged through a drawer for a bottle opener. The fact the bottle needed an opener was something else that drove the sheriff to distraction, since he felt partial to cans and twist-off bottles. The deputy popped the cap and it slipped through his fingers, skittering across the floor. He positioned himself behind the table, as if occupying the best defensive position in the room, and took a long drink as he watched Sabina advance toward him.

"The sheriff has been looking for you."

"When did you see the sheriff?"

"He came over not three hours ago. We spent some time together. He told me the whole story, again, but this time he added the things you did today. His question to you is whether you want to continue working for him and the department."

"He told you to ask me that?"

"He said you would be coming tonight."

"Did he? Well, he considers himself to be a master of human behavior. What else did he say?"

"Deputy, why are you standing in the corner behind the table like you are caged and trapped? Come to the couch and we can talk maybe a little bit. Maybe you can tell me your troubles."

"I've got one trouble. I see you stocked up on High Life and I'm wondering how it is that you could start up something with that fiend. I mean, look at you. I've got a hard-on the size of a cane pole looking at you wearing those shorts and that top. I'm having a hard time thinking of him pawing you."

"Some of us work for fiends and some of us love fiends. Which are you, Deputy?"

"You don't love him."

"I am not sure. Please sit down, Greg. I do not like you behind the table."

The deputy acquiesced and shuffled out from behind the table and sunk in the abused cushions of her sleeper sofa. His instincts to stay standing had been right if the purpose of the visit was to remain awake, because as he drained the beer the alcohol began a slow dance with the oxy and the weight of the day, the crush of his thoughts, and the warm, familiar comfort of the couch battered any momentum he had gathered to have sex with Sabina. She skipped the open cushion next to him and settled on a chair, positioned the farthest from the couch of all the seating choices. Fortunately, the room was so small her choice passed unnoticed as a slight as she was still close enough to comfortably talk. The chemise barely clung to her breasts and the deputy hoped a simple thought, a simple act of will and effort, could make the strap fall from her shoulders.

"That is better. You are more comfortable. Deputy, what is it that is happening to you? Do you know?"

"You ask a good question. At the moment I've got some alcohol joining forces with a host of oxys in my blood."

"You know that is not what I am talking about."

"It all started when my old friend Paul came to town."

"What did he do, exactly? He introduced you, a policeman, to the idea of prostitution? He popped the bubble in which you were living?"

"He brought the past with him."

"You can't think about past things too often, especially if you are feeling down. You'll make yourself say the dumbest things or act ignorantly or try to be the biggest clown just to try to forget how you once acted. You don't have to justify every impulse you have ever had. It is better to just live, now. You probably don't even remember clearly what happened so long ago. A depressed man does not think clearly so why should they remember clearly?"

"You think I am depressed?"

"I think you are not a deputy."

"Has the sheriff said something? Has he already filed the paperwork?"

"I think you are misspending your life and you know it. You are married to a lesbian so you visit me. You do not like your job so you try very hard one day to convince yourself you are good at it and you like it and the next day you are terrible, the worst deputy in the county, leaving that poor rock unguarded and threatening a man with your gun to pick up waste from a dog."

The deputy became alert and the look of surprise caught her attention.

"Yes, the sheriff knows the story already, I believe. He talked to the man himself. Fortunate for you the man swore at the sheriff and you know that never ends well."

"I can explain that. I can," the deputy said as he settled back into the cushions and felt another crushing wave of sleep pushing down on him.

"What else to say about you? You love your children, but you've imagined a life of seeing them every other weekend and having them live with you a week a month. You thought you were running away from your past, whatever small darkness lies there, but the act of running makes it grow, throws it in your path around the corner up ahead. You feel so bad you hurt your beautiful face and you make me run into the arms of the sheriff."

"You could have a little patience," he thought he said but he couldn't be sure if he had pronounced all the syllables or if any part of the sentence was audible as his energy had taken another downward shift, throwing into question whether he was awake or asleep.

Sabina watched his face carefully. Sleep looked inevitable. She didn't want to say something that would rally him and she wondered if he would notice a long gap of silence before he lost consciousness. But she had her own anger to process given the deputy talked about patience, and her own need to respond to his self-centeredness won out over her desire to see him sleep. She compromised between the two competing interests, though, and said what she had to say without raising her voice.

"I have no reason to be patient. I am not your wife, so I don't have to wait for you to either kill yourself or solve the demons inside you. Your face will heal this time, but you'll do again something, maybe more serious, and you will ask we to wait again. You have been fucking me for two years. You came whenever you liked and I did whatever you wanted. A good deal for the deputy. I liked being your whore. I like hearing your problems and schemes, your hatred of your wife and your hatred of your boss, knowing that none of it made any difference to me, not even the sex. I didn't want you to leave your wife. If you had I wouldn't have continued with the affair. But you can't talk of patience when I made no demands on you for two years. I let you have everything, do everything, on your time, when you could sneak away from work or your family. But if now you want to kill yourself I cannot go on. I have given you everything, but I will not mourn you. I will not wait to mourn for you. I will not watch. I told you before I am not a voyeur in my heart. Your death has nothing to do with me so you can do that by yourself."

She couldn't be sure when the deputy actually fell asleep, but she could be reasonably sure he understood nothing she said. She watched him sitting upright, holding his empty beer bottle in is hand, and felt a low grade remorse that she would not sleep with him again. She questioned her resolve and wondered if she had hardened her position prematurely, that maybe she should give him a couple of weeks to see if he rose from the funk in which he had fallen, waiting long enough to determine if it was a temporary state. She waited several minutes before taking the bottle from his hands and gently pushing him onto his side to a more comfortable position that would allow for a longer sleep.

Her calculation had proved correct. The deputy slept through the night and awoke to the sheriff's fleshy face hanging over him as he shook his shoulder.

"Wake up, son, my lord, you're very nearly dead to the world."

The deputy stared at the face before him and sat up only after he had determined he had stopped dreaming some time ago.

"Why are you here, Sheriff? Where's Sabina?"

"Where's Sabina?" the sheriff said through a grin. "She's been making donuts for a couple of hours already. Poor woman spent a sleepless night behind her locked and dead-bolted door. Why is that, Deputy?"

"She didn't have to lock her door. She's being dramatic."

The pain had come back to his face and scalp. He could barely move his neck from the strange angle at which his head rested during his sleep. He reflexively touched his shirt pocket for the pill and thought he would not take one in front of the sheriff no matter how great the pain.

"You're in no position to argue with the lady's discomfort. You showed up in the middle of the night without an invitation, drunk by all reports. Sabina tells me she told you just yesterday morning to stay away from her, but here you are. What am I supposed to tell your wife?"

"That's something you need to stay out of," the deputy barked as he forgot for a moment the hierarchical relationship between the sheriff and him and let the anger flash through his eyes and voice.

The sheriff's skin had a green tint, sickly, as the decoration of the trailer did him no favors, and a faint whiff of stale beer rose from his pores. The deputy imagined him to be a great sponge dipped into an even bigger mug of foamy Miller High Life.

"Son, I don't concern myself with private affairs unless they come snuggle up on my lap. Not that your wife would be into that sort of thing, unless maybe I was a lady sheriff, and then she would come over and give me a snuggle. But what I mean is if she hadn't been calling me every hour through the night then maybe it wouldn't be my business. She doesn't know where you are and she's worried herself sick over it. Now, because you can't handle your own family business, I'm involved. Now I owe her an explanation as to where I found you and what state I found you in. So, I'll ask you again. What am I supposed to say?"

"Say whatever you want."

"Haven't you ever come across a rhetorical question before? You have kids and I'm not going to be responsible for breaking up a family, no matter how broken it already seems to be. The point is that you put me in a position where I have to outright lie to her or hide the truth as I found it. She won't believe a word I'll say and I'll look like a fool for spinning the tale. You, better than anyone, know how smart she is and how easily she sees through bullshit. But bullshit I'll have to lay down for you, because even though your indiscretions have sullied my reputation and the reputation of the department I'll have to cover for you. There's only one thing I will ask in return."

"What's that?" the deputy asked even though he knew the answer.

"Stay away from Sabina. You had your fun, now move on. She's moved on and there's not one reason why you should be on that couch in this trailer."

"You always get your way, don't you, Sheriff?"

"I don't exactly wallow in hubris. Even if you're on top the ground is constantly shifting under you. Show me a penthouse apartment and I'll show you the cracks in the foundation deep underground. Show me a horde of treasure and I'll show you where it's rusting or rotting."

"Silver and gold don't rust or rot."

"The point is, Deputy, that I watched my wife die slowly, horribly. I haven't thumped my chest or considered myself king since. I survive. I can't help myself."

"But you're taking Sabina for your own."

"She's come to me on her own. She's a free woman and she does what she pleases. Even though, if she tells me you've come around here again you're going to have me to deal with. I won't look kindly on it."

"What if she invites me?"

"If she invites you then I'm assuming she wouldn't tell me about it. But you'll have a decision to make and you can do what you want, but I'll guarantee you she won't be inviting you here anymore, that you can count on."

"I'm sure you have everything worked out, Sheriff."

"Why don't you go home and take the rest of the week off, make up to Jenny, play with your daughters, and get your head straight. Maybe once your eyebrows start growing back you'll start feeling better and you'll be able to handle your responsibilities again."

"I'll go home, but I have to make a few stops first."

"Where would you have to go that's more pressing than making up to your wife and saving your marriage?"

"I need someone from the office to request dental records for a dentist office up on 23 called Guignol and Associates. They'll ask for records of an Amber Miller, dates back twenty-five years. She was a patient of Sylvester Guggenheim."

"Is she your skull?"

"There's a pretty good chance. And the family knew the Kinnells. There's a whole theory I could weave on who could have done it. I mean, it could have been a family project and the littlest Kinnell could have watched it all. No wonder he's confessing."

"You can't let it go. You get a little taste of attention and look where it's led you."

"It's not for the attention."

"All with a burned-off face."

The deputy rose to his feet too quickly and the subsequent drop in blood pressure (he had been susceptible to orthostatic hypotension since his teens) made him wobble and reach out his hands to steady himself.

"Give me a day or two and I think I can have it all wrapped up."

"At this point your time is your own."

"What does that mean?"

"I didn't know where you were."

"When?"

"You left your post at the Head. Once word leaked out that you went AWOL I had to craft a proper response. If I don't address a breakdown in discipline then the department will rot from the inside."

"Meaning?"

"Suspension. The length of which will depend on a review of the facts. The fact that you visited a pill mill and were high on oxy during your shift doesn't bode well for you."

"You sent me there, Sheriff."

"But you didn't tell me you were going there at that time. You left your post. Do you see a pattern here? You don't tell me where you are. You don't tell your wife where you are. Tell me, what would have happened if a contingent from Kentucky had come during the time you left the Head unguarded? We would have been the laughingstock of the state. You know the governor is getting personally involved in the dispute. He can't decide whether to have coffee with the governor of Kentucky or send a team of assassins. Either way it will be worked out."

"So who's guarding it now? Who watched overnight?"

"Since your shift has begun you are the one who is supposed to be over there. I know you're trying to make the case that the duty itself was not as urgent or critical as I've made it out to be and that I may have made the assignment up as some sort of punishment or retribution for a past indiscretion or as a tool in our struggle over the soft and lovely Sabina, but it's a bad line of inquiry to take, since the last time I looked I was still the sheriff and I had the management rights clause of the collective bargaining agreement in my back pocket that allows me to make assignments and keep the proper order of the department."

The deputy thought it best to make himself keep quiet. The sheriff stood before him as the one man capable of scuttling his career and sending his family reeling toward bankruptcy and foreclosure. Sabina had called the sheriff and embarrassed him, no, humiliated him in front of his rival. He shouldn't need any more hints as to whom she had chosen, incredibly chosen, since he could see no path back to her with this betrayal. He chuckled softly to himself, because he had just caught himself creating an elaborate lie just to assuage his hurt feelings. He knew he wished a naked Sabina had waked him from his troubled sleep and he knew he would come to her if she called and, if she wore an ensemble like she had the night before, all would be forgiven within minutes of contact.

"You're right, boss. I've forgotten myself. This injury has scrambled my brains and I'm just not myself. You know me to be loyal and consistent. I'll be back to the way I was. I don't want problems between us. Becoming a deputy has been one of the great achievements in my life. To screw that up would kill me," the deputy said without sarcasm, although even he wasn't sure if the mea culpa was entirely sincere or if he instinctively created it because he sensed how close to the edge of the sheriff's patience he had come.

"Then go home, Deputy."

The problem with being known for wielding sarcasm as a first choice in any type of situation was passing off sincerity when he most needed it, which was the very problem the deputy confronted when the sheriff considered his statement of loyalty. He rolled the deputy's words around, watched the changes in his face, and his gut told him that about 95 percent of what the deputy said should be classified as bullshit, but the sheriff chose to take the words at face value and ignore the forced tone of his voice and the weight of the deputy's history.

"I can't say I was unlike you. I've come to work with my gallbladder in tatters and my colon in flames, but I'm still following through on the suspension. I can't let you get away with any of it. The other deputies will get ideas in their heads and the next time one of them decides to go AWOL they'll point back to the time I let Deputy Auro off the hook. I wouldn't win an arbitration for the next five years."

"Ok, Sheriff, you tell me when I can come back. I'll be waiting."

The sheriff nodded his head, both acknowledging the submission the deputy had just offered and letting the vagueness as to the length of time the suspension would last hang in the air, as if there existed a possibility that he would not be returning to the department at all. If that happened, he saw two clear paths of action, either run against the sheriff in the next election or move his tattered family to a city with more opportunity that didn't always smell of muddy water.

With the conversation at its end, the sheriff would never be the first to leave Sabina's trailer. He would be sure to be the master of the final humiliation, watching the deputy retreat from territory he once held. So, the deputy played his part by staggering toward the door, unsteady on his feet because of a general numbness in his toes and an equilibrium threatening to descend into a spin with every step. The deputy nodded his head as a final note of parting and made the threshold without collapsing.

The fresh air outside revived him a little. A shirtless man, one of Sabina's neighbors, sat on a flimsy lawn chair outside his trailer alternately sipping a beer and taking drags from a cigarette, watching the deputy's progress toward the truck. He had seen the sheriff's car pull in and came outside to see if any arrests had been made. He had seen the deputy come and go in his Trailblazer and sometimes an official department cruiser and more than once watched them fuck in the doorway. Now with the sheriff himself here, he figured the lesson to be learned was to stay far away from Sabina because she had a taste for the law. When the deputy looked back toward Sabina's trailer and saw the sheriff standing in the doorway, his arms folded across his chest, making sure to take in the deputy's full retreat, the man on the chair thought he might be an eyewitness to a shootout, but he was disappointed. The sheriff had come out on the step to wait for that last backwards glance to stomp on the deputy's yearning for things lost, nothing more.

The deputy pulled himself into the truck and took another oxy. He wanted to look back again, through the rearview mirror because it was angled just right to catch the front door, but he worried that the sheriff would see his eyes in the mirror and would know that he had looked, plunging him further down the humiliation scale toward a level that would be considered abject. He forced his eyes to look onto the hood of the truck and a small patch of ground in front of him as he drove away. He imagined the sheriff grinning, arms still folded, until his truck left his sight. Then he would crawl into Sabina's bed and bury his face in the musk of the sheets.

23

Back to Paul

The deputy drove to the Ramada Inn in search of Paul, thinking he had fled without officially checking out of his room. What would be the point of staying now? He had already blasted apart the Roy Rogers festival, had created a scandal for the ages, his dick now firmly lodged in the memories of the audience alongside their all-time favorite western hero. He imagined the festival coming to a halt and losing its nostalgic wholesomeness forever because the disgraced Blue Cowboy, one of its principal architects, could never set foot in Ohio again, ruined also by a simple flap of Paul's dick. Roy Rogers probably never even showed his dick to Dale Evans, let alone a theater full of fans, so how could the two ever be reconciled?

When he parked his truck and made his way to the front entrance of the hotel he realized the drive had done nothing for his equilibrium and either a small pothole in the pavement made him trip or, given his unsteady state, he misjudged the distance his feet would have to descend in order to strike solid ground. With the tripping, limping and staggering the deputy did not project the most imposing image as he entered the hotel and asked for Paul's room number, during which he became aware of his rumpled uniform and the acidic taste of his mouth as breath passed along his tongue. He focused on the elevators and duck-walked through the open doors. With Paul the loss of authority wouldn't matter as he never accepted the deputy's position in the first place, so arriving at his hotel door sporting his burned face, soiled clothes and unsteady gait would not be shocking. Knowing Paul, he might even he expecting the deputy to show up in just such a state.

The deputy rapped on the door with a knuckle, waited a few seconds, and rapped again. Sounds of stirring and a low moan came from behind the door. The deputy tried the handle but the lock held. He pounded with a fist and Paul responded that he would be at the door in a second. Soon footsteps padded near the door, followed by the sound of pissing and the flush of the toilet. The peephole darkened. The two stared at each other through the fisheye lens. Paul gathered in the entire scene of the maniacal-looking deputy standing in the hallway, but the deputy saw only a patch of the Paul's pupil. Paul thought it a good sign that the deputy didn't have his gun drawn and he hadn't yet tried to kick down the door.

The door opened and Paul greeted him wearing just a pair of boxer shorts. His hair sprouted in several intersecting angles as his face remained scrunched in support of his eyes that apparently struggled to adjust to the increase of light.

"And what do I owe this unexpected visit?" Paul said through a grin.

"There's no way this visit is unexpected. You've been looking over your shoulder waiting for me. If you hadn't expected or wanted another visit from me you would have left town the moment they let you out of jail, just like Blue Cowboy and that whore you were hanging with."

"They both left town rather suddenly. That poor old man has been wandering around the hotel telling everybody that will listen how a whore stole his money, that he paid upfront for a week and if she was going to leave she should have had the decency to give him a refund. I know he's told me the same thing at least three times. I heard he even button-holed the manager and asked him to do something. Can you imagine asking the hotel manager to intercede on your behalf in a handshake deal with a whore? I heard the manager was less than pleased to have gained firsthand knowledge of prostitution in his hotel, he being, of course, a Christian man of high moral character and he's said publicly that if the Roy Rogers name was now attracting vermin he would consider revoking their reservation for the coming years."

"Good work, Paul, you've almost brought down the festival all by yourself."

"I never brought her into town. She came on her own accord."

"Said the gasoline to the match."

"I'm not sure you should be bringing fire imagery into the conversation given your tendencies."

"Funny. Now let me in. We have some things to discuss that shouldn't be said in the hallway," said the deputy as he relied on his will to push past his desire to go inside, lie down, and sleep for another eight hours.

"By all means. I've forgotten my manners. Please come in."

Paul turned on his heel and retreated into the room, casting a sideways glance at the bed and laughing once he passed the corner of the bathroom wall. The deputy could not see why he laughed at so he took five heavy steps into the room. Once he also passed the corner he saw a woman lying face down, naked and her legs spread.

The flesh looked pale and old with cellulite cascading down her thighs and a mass of gray hair lying in a tangle around her head.

"You could have told me you had a visitor," said the deputy.

"Would you have believed me? Wouldn't you have come in to verify the accuracy of my statements?"

"She's not dead is she?"

"There you go again with that occupational frame of mind. Why would she be dead? I think tales of hard fucking killing people are greatly exaggerated. Maybe a man can fuck himself into a heart attack but I've never heard of sex taking out a woman. I'll give you this, though, she is a deep sleeper. I've been up an hour and she hasn't made one sign of waking. I've made enough noise to wake the dead, even though I'm not saying she bears any resemblance to a person in a dead state."

The deputy gave Paul a long, hard look. He knew from experience that everything he said could be part of a larger agenda or a complex joke, sometimes days or weeks in the making. He thought of the possibility of this scene being staged for his benefit, but the timing seemed impossible since he had come unannounced and not even Paul could have the resources and patience to create and stage something in the hopes the deputy might visit.

The deputy approached the bait. The woman looked older than he first thought and when he picked up her wrist and found her pulse he thought he may have touched the actual throbbing vein through her translucent skin. The wrist felt like an injured bird held in the palm of his hand. Fortunately, the pulse beat strong.

"Seriously, you're into grannies now?" The deputy asked as he maintained his hold on the wrist, thinking that letting it go to face the brutality of the world would send him into despair.

"You'd be amazed what showing your cock to an audience of septuagenarians will do for your sex life. I've had more action in the last 24 hours than I've had in the past five years. Seems like I'm a bigger attraction than a casino or buffet."

"How exactly did you turn out to be such a sick bastard?"

"I don't know, you were there for my formative years, you tell me. Let me in on the dark truth."

Just then the lady stirred and turned over and the deputy reluctantly released her wrist. The move revealed a face broken up into a thousand tiny fissures but remarkably full and firm breasts that shocked the deputy until he realized that he had to be staring at implants as they had defied time and gravity much too well. She blinked away the sleep and focused on the deputy.

"Oh, Paul brought a friend, in a uniform no less," she said as she opened her legs in a supremely submissive and inviting way.

The deputy leaned forward. Why shouldn't he seek a little comfort in a woman's arms after the week he had been through? The nurse at the doctor's office, the pharmacist, Sabina, his wife, Amber Miller, the threesome in his hot tub: all flashed though his mind. They were everywhere, these alluring women who beckoned him to bed, who could restore faith and equilibrium with the simple act of disrobing, who could incite eroticism by walking, reaching for a high shelf, or bending over to pick up something thought lost, who carried the burden of the desirable with weariness, and who sparingly shared their own erotic yearnings lest they be considered a whore. Even Clarisse, that old boat whore with her tanned skin and her too red hair, the viper the sheriff kept in his breast pocket, could disarm him with a length of cleavage or a too tight pair of pants or a sandal that revealed her immaculately painted toenails. Why not mount this old woman and mold her flesh back into a youthful form? Even take twenty years of age from her, stretch out half the wrinkles, grab handfuls of ass, and enjoy a moment, even if Paul chose to watch. But the deputy hesitated a moment too long and a flash of fire replaced the submissiveness of the woman. She clamped her legs shut like a door had closed. She swung her legs off the edge of the bed and stood up so close to the deputy that her breasts pushed against his chest.

"You're no deputy. I can see that," she said with venom.

Paul laughed in mockery, delighted to witness another humiliation of his old friend as he chose to interpret the preceding scene not as a man turning away from a women he found unattractive but as a man impotent in the face of bald opportunity. Paul could not understand turning down a woman no matter her age, size, personality, or physical form, since the act itself was so gratifying. Everything else was ego and holding out for fantasies that never came true.

"Well, darling, who is, really? Don't blame the deputy for his inadequacies. We can only be who we are," Paul said to the naked back of the woman.

She backed away from the deputy and slid a black thong that she found crumpled on the carpet. She pulled a sundress over her head, preferring to go braless since her new tits never sagged, and the more she adjusted and unruffled and the imperfections of her body had been covered, the twenty years the deputy had hoped to shave from her fell completely away, so that had he seen her in the inverse, clothed then naked, he no doubt would have fucked her, given the radiance of her personality. She saw how he looked at her as she fluffed her hair and felt a small victory.

"Will you be around later, lover?" she asked as she took a few steps toward Paul.

"I will if you plan on coming back."

She slid a hand down his boxers and gave his penis a tug.

"Get your rest. I'll bring a friend of mine who's been feeling poorly since she had her gallbladder removed. Poor thing is nothing but a collection of ailments so she could use a little cheering up."

"I'm just the man for the job."

"I see that you are," she said as she looked at her hand that now held half of an erection. "Too bad your friend is here or we could start the morning off right."

Paul looked to the deputy to see if he would clear out of the room long enough for him to fuck her, but he had decided to ignore the obvious hint and stood with his arms folded across his chest as he stared at the carpet.

"Well, seems like I have official business with the deputy. Come back in an hour with your friend and we'll make a day of it."

She kissed him on the lips and reluctantly released her grip. She left without giving the deputy another consideration. As Paul watched her leave he wore a genuine smile, and then he turned to the deputy.

"Stick around, friend. I'm sure her friend is just as smoking hot, if they've taken out the stitches and the incision has healed."

"No thanks."

"I keep forgetting you are married. I suppose it's like living as a celibate, being married, passing up opportunities, ignoring all these women. Of course, if your pecker can't rise to the occasion what difference does it make? You might as well live life as a celibate just for the companionship."

"Not really like that at all."

"I could be making the mistake of assuming that you've kept the faith and remained true to those nasty vows."

"Why would you make any other assumption?"

Paul let silence be his answer as he finally became conscious of just how ill and deranged the deputy looked and played with the notion he had come to his hotel room to kill him. Any further taunting of his impotency did not seem like a wise course. He would have to make some concessions to the intervening years since he had last seen his friend. Personalities warp over time like a piece of wood left out in the weather and what might have been thought anomalies in their youth rise to the surface and dominate older men. How easy would it be for the deputy's anomaly to find expression through the gun hanging off his hip?

"Why have you come, Greg, in all seriousness?" Paul asked as he adopted a tone of earnestness, which didn't fully hit the mark, but was effective enough to alter the tone of the conversation. "I can't imagine you are all that much interested with my love life."

The deputy could not express why he had come to Paul's room instead of going home other than it seemed preferable.

"I wanted to see if you had stayed in town. I wanted to ask you why the fuck you came down here and pulled out your cock in a church and why you brought a full-blown prostitute to my house and fucked her in my hot tub for my wife to see. And now I want to know how many grandmas you're going to rape before you get your fill and sneak out of town. That's why I came here."

"It sounds bad when you say it like that, but there are some inaccuracies in your telling. Now technically the play did take place in a church, but it very much was not acting as a house of God at that very moment. We were performing before a theater audience and not a congregation and a veteran theatergoer should expect the unexpected. As I was out onstage I starting channeling Roy Roger's ruddy schlong. I got an image of his size and girth and I wanted to give up an offering to him, to the audience, to Blue Cowboy and Third Eye in the context of the play. You can't tell me it didn't work, that it wasn't great theater. No one has given me a hassle since. Actually it's quite the contrary, as you just saw. People who saw the performance think I'm a damn artist.

"As for your party I needed a date and I know no one in town except Third Eye. I don't think she was all that out of place, really, and we weren't exactly alone in the hot tub. If you hadn't burned your face off you and your wife probably would have been in there with us. And we didn't fuck in the water and it wasn't Third Eye who I fucked. I fucked that crazy nurse as the ladies fingered and licked in the tub. I performed on the grass, really, as a matter of courtesy to you. I didn't want to spunk up your water. The fact that your wife caught sight of us I didn't know and is unfortunate. It was dark and we tried to be discreet, but, man, her ass was there for the taking. I couldn't turn that down no more than if I was dying of thirst and you offered me a glass of water."

"And you define discreet as fucking a woman on my lawn?"

Paul laughed and when he regained enough composure to speak he said, "It's a valid point, I guess, but nothing happened in the water and I never touched Third Eye that night, so her being there had nothing to do with the outcome. You or your wife have some crazy friends beside me."

"The fact is that I still had to drain the tub and scrub the sides or else my wife would never get into again. She even threatened to make me get rid of it. She said hot tubs lead to nothing but trouble."

"In your condition? I'm sure scrubbing the tub could have waited. Your wife is one harsh task master making you do that."

The deputy couldn't remember if he drained the tub or if the task remained to be done, but in either case the inconvenience and waste remained the same. He couldn't argue with the statement about his wife. Maybe her harshness and control had led him to this point, to act this way, even though he didn't want to cede a single point to his old friend.

"My wife doesn't have to tell me. I know disgusting. I wouldn't get in that water or have my kids get in that water after a whore had been fucked in it."

"There must be a dead spot in your brain or has the bone of your skull grown so thick that new information, correct information, cannot penetrate and replace your wrong assumptions. Third Eye was not fucked in the tub unless you count fingering from a I'll-try-lesbianism-for-a-night divorcee as fucking and if I know Third Eye like I think I do she wouldn't have worked up much of a lather given the woman's fear of touching her clit."

The deputy felt rage welling in his chest and a knot of gall hung at the top of his throat. He would have considered launching himself at Paul and pounding his face, something he had coming to him since he had made the decision to bring the whore to his home, but he didn't trust the coordination between mind and body and if he made a move he had more than a seventy percent chance of landing on his face without landing a single blow,

"Consider it a ritual cleansing. Think of hosing off excrement from an altar or scrubbing menstrual blood out of a bridal gown. I don't want my family splashing around in disease and filth. That's not so hard to understand, I hope," he said and the words helped him regain some composure and a portion of his anger subsided, but it still could have consumed him based on Paul's response.

Of course Paul could feel the same possibility and remembered he shouldn't push the deputy too far, even if the deputy clung to the most wildly inaccurate and outrageous assumption, even if he felt a wild diatribe forming in his own mind that he readied to execute.

"Ok, Greg, I see you're not going to let this go until I formally apologize for my behavior. I get it, so let me tell you a little bit of where I'm coming from. I want to live life in this full way. I want to fill my lungs with air until they feel like they are going to burst or my blood is so heavy with oxygen I pass out or my heart stops from too much work. I work at City Hall with the undead. You can't believe some of these people. I don't even know what they do or what they are thinking. I don't think they even think about their lives passing them by, that they're not doing much else than surviving. And what are they surviving for? To watch more television? To eat more frozen dinners? I get crazy thinking about it. I want to live for them. I want to do all the things I want to do and all the things they should be doing with their lives. So I take a couple of chances. I could have come to your party alone and made a bunch of excuses that I don't even believe and hoped to meet a single woman, but those friends of your wife wouldn't have given me the time of day without Third Eye on my arm or I could have declined the offer all together and whacked off to porn in the hotel room. But the choice I made was to bring Third Eye with me and I ended up in your hot tub with three naked women and I fucked one of them on the grass while the other two watched. You can't find fault with that. I know it was your hot tub and all that, but I have a hard time feeling bad about your inconvenience when I think about the night I had, you know what I'm saying? I mean I started this vacation with no plans, no prospects, not a sniff of a woman, and I throw myself into Portsmouth and look what I get."

The deputy felt worn down and dull. His anger had slipped from him, leaving a void that had not yet been filled. He recognized Paul as a teenager in the speech and remembered worrying about his libertine philosophy even then. Life with his father had been a shutting off of experience, the denial of temptation, the fear and hatred of women, the rejection of sensation other than pain inflicted in the name of Christ, and mistrust of the world outside the text of the Bible. Had his father heard the same speech Paul had just given he would have simplistically said that Paul had embraced the devil, like he said a thousand times before to explain away behavior with which he disagreed. This explanation never really worked much magic or created much fear in the deputy and he actually owed a debt of gratitude to Paul for giving him dark thoughts that he often mused on at the dinner table when the drone of thanksgiving prayers lasted well after the food had gone cold. He thought of himself and his family hanging on by their fingertips above an abyss of immense proportions that contained all the evil thoughts and deeds the world of men and women had ever had. His father pounded into his head that once a person lost his grip and fell into the miasma their hope of ever returning to a pure state depended solely on an act of mercy from God. Bolstered by Paul's blasphemy he imagined himself letting go and falling a mile or more, seized by the hand of gravity and thrown downward into pitch black to find a blue pool softly illuminated from beneath the water and on the shore a crowd of nude men and women talked softly to each other, sipping drinks, eating small fruits, gazing languidly at the flesh in repose about them and breathing slowly the salubrious air. He climbed out of the silken water and fills a space on the beach. Two women or perfect proportion took a position on either side and began talking about how lucky he had been to escape the foulness of his father's vision. He leaned back, closed their eyes, and their words glided over him like a summer wind.

Even now the deputy can feel himself wanting to fall into the comfort of dissolution and chaos, to blast away the remaining, meager structure of his life and let himself be taken by whatever current passed him by. But his mistrust of Paul stayed his impulse, because he did not want to follow him if the eventual destination led him to pulling out his cock onstage, of that much he was sure.

"I've identified the skull that brought you to Portsmouth. She was a teenage girl, decapitated by a family of killers and creeps. You met one of them the night you came into town, the one I beat in the cell. Turns out he's probably telling the truth, but we let him go. I'm going to go and pick him up and bring him in again."

"Really? Are you going to arrest him alone or are you going to bring the whole department? He's twice your size."

"You're going to help me."

"Am I?"

"Sure, you're open to adventure. You like to throw yourself into the mercy of the currents. What could be more fun than to be in on the arrest of a monster and the solving of a decades old crime?"

"Maybe the newscasters will come back."

"Maybe. Maybe they'll gush over my efficient police work. Maybe they'll run a show for all those old ladies who watch TV to make them feel comfortable and smug that although sometimes justice is delayed it is always served. Imagine the pussy you'll get."

"That's inspiring," said Paul as he did consider how he could parlay a television appearance into further opportunities to explore his deviance.

"I know. This is the world I live in."

"There's nothing inspiring about being a housing inspector, unless you get off on decay and rot and squalor. Some people live worse than animals. In some of the houses I visit I'd rather be the cockroach or rat than the human, because at least if you're a cockroach the filth wouldn't be so degrading. It's not something they did and have the power to change."

"I see the same houses."

"You're not charged with finding a way to get them clean, to keep them from burying themselves alive, to keep the roofs from collapsing on their heads, to make them remember there's a line of decency that no one should live below."

"You're not suggesting that you may have a harder job than I do?"

"Don't underestimate what I do. I've stumbled across the worst of humanity. It wears you down."

"I'm giving you an opportunity to see what I do. It'll give you a chance to arrest one of the cretins. I can tell you it does feel good to throw one of them in jail, sort of like defending a small village from hordes of wild men. A small act of civilization against a wave of chaos."

"This can't be kosher with the sheriff."

"Since when are you concerned about the rules?"

"It's not for me that I'm concerned, although he did tell me to get out of town when he released me."

"Oh, Paul, how sweet of you to think of me, but forgive me if I have a hard time reconciling your sudden concern about me and your philosophy of going where life takes you. Life is offering you an opportunity to follow me. And just like your experience with the whore you never know where it will lead. Maybe you'll find the woman you will marry or you may end up in a hot tub with six naked women and maybe you'll grow another cock to take care of them all. Who the hell knows?"

Paul stared at the deputy for a few moments before he smiled to mask his mistrust of the offer. He couldn't figure out what the deputy had in mind, but he did know that following him would not end with a sexual indulgence.

"Ok, sure, why not, right? What clothes should I wear?"

"If you didn't pack your housing inspector uniform then I would suggest wearing jeans and a shirt. Shoes are necessary as well."

Paul opened his mouth to refute the suggestion that the city issued him a uniform to wear when performing his duties, but as the deputy's response continued he realized the inherent sarcasm of the words and refused the bait.

"Are you going to watch me dress?" Paul said to recover some ground.

"No, I'll be waiting in front of the hotel. You might want to scrub off some of that septuagenarian vagina juice before you come on official business."

"She wasn't a day over 65, that would be my guess."

"Impressive nevertheless. You're a regular Tennessee stud."

Paul couldn't believe he had lost the upper hand in the conversation to the deputy in his obvious weakened state, so to stop him from landing blows he pulled down his boxers and kicked them off his feet.

"Jesus Christ, I've seen your cock enough for three lifetimes. Give me a chance to get the fuck out of here. You know, it's only a matter of time before you start trolling around high schools to show off your pecker to an unsuspecting fresh young girl or boy. Exhibitionism is still frowned upon, Paul, and illegal through most of the country. You'd still be in jail if the sheriff didn't want to humiliate me."

"Career trouble?"

The deputy had made a misstep, so he retreated from the room and waved a hand to dismiss the question. He walked out the door and into the elevator. The old man who had sat in the front row next to him at the play walked in behind him. He sported a western shirt and a new bolo tie. The waist of his pants was several inches too big and was belted tight above his hips as if he had experienced a sudden weight loss. The deputy thought the old man may still be shrinking even as he walked onto the elevator, that by the time they reached the first floor he would be no bigger than a dwarf. The doors closed and the old man eyed the deputy, then stared at the floor buttons before speaking.

"I used to know Rogers. I was twenty years his junior and I thought I wanted a movie career. I went to Hollywood like every other hick without a plan and actually got a few walk-on parts. I had two lines in *Fort Laramie Roundup*, but I got no farther than that. Casting directors rejected me for my nose and height. They said I was too short to be a leading man or a villain, and my nose just threw off the balance of my face. It could have been an asset in comedies, but my timing was godawful and I'm not embarrassed to tell you that I don't understand most jokes. I don't get what makes them funny. But I met Rogers through a mutual friend and he had me to his ranch. He was a real decent fella. I can tell you he had a big heart on and off the screen."

"I'm not part of the festival. I'm not a fan," the deputy interjected.

"I know who you are. You arrested my friend. I haven't seen her since you released her."

"I didn't release her. The sheriff decided to release her."

"The sheriff is a good man. He reminds me a little bit of Rogers. He has sense."

"Your point is?"

"Turns out that I made a fortune in natural gas through my connections I made through Rogers. I made so much money I couldn't even figure out how to invest all of it. I still have piles of it in bank accounts of banks that I don't even remember the names of. Fortunately, I have a ledger somewhere where it's written all down, but I'll never be able to spend all of it so what's the difference. I would have preferred being a singing cowboy star, but the truth is I probably made ten times as much as old Roy ever did."

The doors opened and the two men stepped out. The deputy tried to walk away but the old man reached out a hand and gently stayed his arm. The deputy turned, annoyed.

"That's very fortunate for you," he said with a snarl.

"Roy introduced me to Ronald Reagan. Too bad I didn't like the sonofabitch. This was when he was still an actor of course, but there was something about him that made me angry, like he knew better than anyone else how to live. I ended up giving him buckets of cash for his campaigns over the years, but that was strictly as a favor to Roy. Roy believed in him. I couldn't argue too much if it kept the Democrats out of power. Nothing worse on God's green earth than a Democrat with a plan."

"And why wouldn't you do as Roy said? You have to stay in his good graces."

"You don't believe me. No one believes the old. You think it's nothing but dementia and nostalgia and that I don't know what is what or the difference between the two."

"Why wouldn't I believe you?"

"I don't know if I'll ever find my love again. You cost me time with her. I don't have all that much time left and I don't like to have my passions denied. It was completely unnecessary to arrest her."

"Among her other crimes, sir, she exposed herself in public and I was a witness. The sheriff might have chosen to not press charges, but that doesn't change the fact of what I saw. I don't think the public wants a police officer to ignore obvious violations of the law," the deputy said as he began to feel impatient with the conversation and he folded his arms in front of his chest.

"If there is a law against a woman revealing her breasts then it should be repealed or ignored."

"I can do neither."

"Darlene said you were mad because your friend embarrassed you. That's why she was arrested. I don't think anyone will argue with you on arresting him. Nobody wanted to see the boy's pecker."

"Except they're lining up outside his hotel room to get another look."

"What?"

"This had nothing to do with the hot tub."

"What do you mean?"

"She didn't tell you about her little escapade in my hot tub?"

"You've met her? You know her?"

"What's to know, sir? Of course I know her. Everybody knows her. She may have fucked or blown every single man in Ohio. Why wouldn't I know her? Why wouldn't I get my share?"

"She's not like that."

Years ago he may have laughed, but he had seen the insidious effect delusion could play in a person's life, as the deluded only find their way back to a clear mind the moment a knife is plunged into their heart or a bullet tears through an artery. Instead, he felt a weight pushing on the top of his skull and pressure building inside his brain. The deluded were such a burden.

"No? Then tell me what she is like," the deputy said without much force or genuine interest.

"I'm convinced she's an angel on earth."

"Who obviously wants to express her love for mankind."

"Listen, you don't know what it's like to have a kidney so swollen you can barely piss or to live past all the friends and family you've ever known. A full and productive life can turn to torture in a matter of weeks. So, to find a little comfort at my age is no small feat. Darlene has done that for me."

"If I see her I'll tell her you're looking for her. My bet is she left town when she was told to. She's a smart woman and knows trouble when she sees it."

"You remember who I know and the money I have. Think about what my money can do it a town like this. You leave her alone. She's a good girl. If I hear you even look in her direction I'll bring all my money down on your head. I'll have you back guarding that rock for the rest of your career."

"What do you know about that?"

"You'd be surprised what I know," the old man said as he broke into a wide grin that had the opposite effect of brightening his wizened face. He became a sinister force around which the lobby and the traffic of hotel guests and clerk spun. "In the land of the poor, cash is king."

The old man's smile faded as he became distracted by the smell of fried eggs and coffee drifting from the dining room. His sinister face became a muddle of competing thoughts and sensations and he shuffled away from the deputy toward the smell of the food without another word. The deputy watched his frail frame disappear into the dining room as rage again rose within him, without an appropriate outlet through which to express its full bloom. An elderly lady dressed as Dale Evans with makeup applied in the style for reposing in a coffin asked the deputy where she might find a restroom and a bellboy to carry her bags from her room. The deputy looked down to see if he still wore his uniform, which had lost any resemblance of starch on Sabine's couch. Tilting his nose opened a direct line between his nostrils and the pungent smell emanating from his armpits. The uniform made him official in any situation, the arm of management, the keeper of rules, the seer of the future, the geographer of landscapes, a locksmith, a tinker, a help desk attendant, a carpenter, an electrician, and a priest.

He summoned the authority he had practiced for so many years, directed the old woman to the restrooms, and strode over to the desk and barked at the clerks that she needed assistance with her luggage. The clerk quailed under the orders. The deputy maintained the set jaw, the piercing eyes, and the erect posture as he navigated through the front lobby and out to the front parking lot where he swore an unintelligible combination of curses to the parked cars and the cracked asphalt.

His phone vibrated in his pocket. He hadn't remembered charging it or turning it on. When he fished it out he saw a photo of her lounging in the hot tub in a bikini, hair wet, head tilted back, mouth slightly open, a candid snapshot that he had used as his phone's wallpaper until recently relegating it to call ID status, a picture that never failed to arouse the eroticism of their relationship. Because of his softened state of mind, he answered the call.

"Are you coming home, ever?" Jenny said in a flat tone.

"Why wouldn't I come home?"

"Oh, I don't know. You don't call us for 24 hours or even text to say you're alive and I'm not supposed to wonder?"

"I'm sorry about that. I wanted to call. I wanted to come home."

"And?"

"I couldn't. I didn't. I had a fucked-up day."

"The sheriff told me. Where did you sleep?"

"What did the sheriff say?"

"Where did you sleep?"

"In my car." He regretted the lie. He had missed an opportunity to unburden himself.

"Do I know her?"

"Who? "

"Who you spent the night with. You've never been able to sleep in the car. Remember your dreams about assassins?"

"What did the sheriff say? He's turned against me, Jenny. I don't know why but I think he wants to fire me."

"Why does the sheriff matter? He told me he put you on the rock duty to keep you out of trouble and allow you to draw down a paycheck while you recovered. He said he didn't think you were ready to come back to work, so he thought he'd put you someplace safe. He knows about our finances. He knows we can't afford to miss a paycheck."

"Are you angry?"

Jenny let out a shriek, followed by an unhinged cackle. "Holy Christ, what kind of question is that? I'm angrier than I've even been in my life. Does that sum it up for you? The only thing saving you is that I'm glad you're alive, for the girls' sake. I was worried. I didn't want them to lose their daddy, this young. As for me..."she truncated the thought with a dismissive growl.

The deputy could summon nothing in response. He should have called her a half a dozen times during the day, but he hadn't. He could have easily kept the ruse going, but he hadn't.

"Do I know her?" she asked again.

The deputy could not let another opportunity pass because the truth would be coming out sooner or later in this conversation, so he said, "You don't eat donuts, so I'm sure you don't know her."

Jenny let out a small gasp, a reflective auditory response to humiliation and the shock of her suspicions being confirmed so simply.

"I slept on her couch. Nothing happened. I needed a place to rest, to sleep."

"You couldn't sleep at home? Nothing happened this time. The only reason nothing happened this time is that you burned off half of your face! You throw your family away for a donut whore? You are insane."

"I didn't mean to throw away my family."

"As long you didn't get caught. But now that you are caught, what do you think will happen? What do you think you just did?"

The deputy became alarmed as he felt panic rushing in from all sides. She spoke with little emotion as if she had mulled over these thoughts and constructed and deconstructed the sentences so many times they had lost most of their emotional power or she had become resigned to their impact.

"You act like you know."

"I've known since the beginning, or what I thought was the beginning. You left a trail of clues so obvious I couldn't ignore it. Voicemails on your phone, emails, notes in your pocket, unexplained gaps of time, the smell of perfume on your clothes, coming home from work showered. I could never quite figure out the powdered sugar, but you've given me the final piece of the puzzle, unless there are others which, by some miracle, you've managed to hide."

"The sheriff told you, didn't he?"

"Yes, Greg, he gave me the first warning, but don't blame anything on him. This is a grave you've dug yourself. You're the one who gave him something to tell me."

"He's trying to destroy me. I don't know why he's turned against me, but he has."

"Come home. We'll sort it all out, but we can't do that unless you're here. I need you here. The girls need you here. They miss their daddy. I need to talk to you face to face."

"I'll try, but I don't think I can come home right now."

"What could be more important to you than us, the us that is left? The girls need you. What else do I have to say?"

The deputy eyed Paul leaving the hotel and scanning the parking lot for him. The deputy gave a wave and Paul started toward him and came within a few feet of him, even though he saw the deputy speaking on the phone.

"We'll talk later."

"I can't believe you're getting off the phone. Come home. We need to talk, Greg. Come home."

"I can't talk about it right now, but you'll understand when I'm done why I couldn't talk."

"I don't believe you. You're practically fired. You're doing nothing official. You're not acting under the authority of the sheriff's department. Come home."

The deputy walked a few steps away from Paul and turned his back to him, but he followed to remain well within earshot.

"You have to believe me."

"Because you've never told a lie."

"That's completely different." The words tasted like ash and stomach acid and he wished he had never uttered them.

"I don't think you are well. I don't think you should be out doing anything. I think you should come home and rest. When you are feeling better we will talk and work things out. You'll feel better if you see the kids. They're so worried about you and they just want to see you."

"I bought them presents, but you won't believe it now. I didn't mean for them to be make-up gifts. I bought them yesterday because I felt a physical ache not seeing them. I feel like I haven't seen them in weeks with the burn. I haven't touched them."

"Then come home and see them."

"I'll see you soon. We'll get through this."

Jenny let out an exasperated sigh and clicked the phone off. She looked across the table to the sheriff and shook her head as if she hadn't been successful.

"Did he say where he was going or where he was?"

"No, I forgot to ask."

"I should have never let him go. I thought he would come right home. I've suspended him so nothing he does now is official department business, but I'm kicking myself. After the report I got from Waverly I'm really worried about him. Call him back and ask where he is and I'll send someone to pick him up."

"And bring him here? He could just leave again. What would stop him?"

"I'll put him under house arrest if I have to. If that doesn't work I'll throw him into a jail cell until he comes to his senses."

Jenny felt uncomfortable with the sheriff in her dining room. The house felt sullied or violated. He had a blatant way of letting his eyes drift down to her breasts and not changing his line of sight through the entire conversation. No matter what defense she employed, crossing her arms, pulling a sweater closed over her cleavage, flashing anger with her own eyes that demonstrated her exasperation over his behavior, he could not be dissuaded from his overt appreciation. Normally, she wouldn't have let him, especially the way she had been dressed in yoga pants and a tank top when she answered the door, but he came up the lawn with a look of deep concern in his eyes and she thought he had come to tell her that Greg had been injured or killed, a possibility that always gnawed at the edges of her thoughts. As the sheriff's car turned into the driveway and crept up the gravel, and he hobbled to the door with his fat man's gait, she searched his face for clues of the coming news and felt the impossibility of a dream she had played over and over again coming true. Once he stepped over the threshold the announcement of Greg's death would tumble through his lips.

"Thank you, Sheriff, I'll call you when he comes back."

"I'm sorry to be the bearer of bad news. Sometimes a little bit of fame can go to a person's head. A man talks to Diane Sawyer and he starts thinking they're special and all the rules don't apply to him, even the basic ones like don't play with fire or be faithful to your wife or don't think about running against your boss in an election."

"Greg isn't going to run for sheriff. He never said a word about it."

"I know what people are going to do before they do it. I know what he's thinking. He may never have spoken about it, but he's thinking about it, I'm sure of that. Although, I'd say that fantasy is pretty much over at this point."

"You wouldn't, by any chance, have come over here to tell me..." Jenny stopped short, distracted by the wide grin hanging on his face and the awfulness of the thought that the sheriff had come to her house to tell her of Greg's affair, not for the sake of her well-being or to provide solid evidence of Greg's suddenly troubled path, but as a piece of his agenda to retain power over the county until his death. She suspected he harbored ideas of exerting control through his surrogates even after his death. She felt deep pity for her husband for working under this devil for ten years. Was there any question why his sanity would have begun to fray? That he too, like the rest of the county, had succumbed to the sheriff's ambition and his lack of social conscience. Surely, their marriage had been blown apart and reduced to rubble, but she searched within this devastating metaphor for a moment where she could see herself and Greg picking through the debris, finding an intact photograph, or a few whole dinner plates, maybe an unsoiled blanket, all the usable pieces they could repurpose. She wanted the sheriff out of her house and wondered if he would ever get tired of leering at her.

24

Investigation

When the deputy hung up his phone he became aware of how uncomfortably close Paul stood to him. He set himself in a defensive position, legs spread, arms bent and hands in front, something akin to a linebacker ready to drill a running back bursting through the line. Paul took a step or two back, also expecting the deputy to tackle him to the ground.

"Whoa, Kemosabe, trouble in paradise?" asked Paul, who stopped after back-pedaling to a safe distance.

"That phone call was none of your business."

"Of course not. I didn't hear a word…that's not exactly true. I heard everything you said and a stray word or two from your wife. But it's all about context. The whole thing could have been about the weather for all I know and not the break-up of your marriage."

"Get in the truck," the deputy ordered.

They climbed into the truck and the deputy started the engine. Had he really just confessed his adultery to his wife over the phone in a hotel parking lot? Was he not going to rush home and beg her to keep the family together? Maybe they could leave Portsmouth altogether, even though they were so underwater on the house they could never sell it for what they owed on it and they had no savings to pay for the difference between the selling price and what the bank wanted to settle the mortgage. They could let the place fall into foreclosure. It was the smart play. So many houses had fallen into foreclosure the past couple of years the shame of not being able to meet your obligations had almost ceased to exist. People realized that worldwide forces caused their calamity and a family could not be judged on their inability to manage their meager bank accounts and real estate investments in the face of voracious greed. What chances did they really have when armies of bankers and lawyers crafted rules they didn't understand in a language they couldn't read?

Of course, the worldwide financial conspiracy hatched by leagues of pirates honestly couldn't be applied to them other than to say the meltdown in the housing market had trapped them in their undervalued house and given them fewer options for escape. They could do it, though. They could abandon their home with all the improvements they made: the new windows, the rebuilt roof over the porch, the remodeled bathrooms, the new carpet, and the hot tub. They would most likely land in an apartment and have no room for a hot tub. What would happen? They would have bad credit for seven years. They already had bad credit, anyway. People were forced to sell when they lost a job or became too ill to work or in cases of divorce, but if they stayed together, if Jenny could see her way towards forgiving him, the decision to abandon their home would be theirs alone. It would be a strategic retreat. It would make the possibility of starting a new life tangible, but moving all their possessions seemed like a daunting task. They would have to sell most of what they owned for pennies on the dollar, no doubt, and he would have to hire movers for the rest. He couldn't do it by himself. Would the girls care where they lived as long as they brought along some of their toys? But they did so love the woods. It would be sad to take them from nature and coop them up in an apartment in the city. They had become use to roaming...he stopped to see himself in the side or rearview mirrors to confirm that security and stability for his family had only been a momentary illusion and that the truth had been laid bare, but he didn't want to crane his neck to catch the reflection and give Paul a hint to his thoughts. Escape would never be achieved anyway, not with all their maze of entanglements. Why had he told her about Sabine? He could have denied the accusation, told her the sheriff had become obsessed with ruining him, which now had to considered stronger than a possibility. He could direct the conversation back to the revelation that he and Paul exchanged blowjobs when they were teenagers. Of the two images the first had the most impact on their marriage and certainly would have thrown off his wife from the line of inquiry into his infidelity. How could he now face her with his own confession echoing in her head and the sheriff's corroboration of actually finding him asleep on the couch blocking any possibility for obfuscation, of presenting half-truths, of dismissing Jenny's suspicions with shocked incredulity and feigned sincerity? Now, they had no choice but to confront whatever had been festering for years, to cleanse the wound and inspect the mutual damage.

"Where are we going?" Paul said, to break the silence more than to gain any further knowledge. The deputy had told him they would be arresting Kinnell and that was enough information to satisfy his curiosity, but he thought he should keep the deputy talking to gauge the depth of his instability.

"We're going to the place we always pick up Kinnell."

"Always?"

"He's been arrested thirty times, at least. Usually just drunk and disorderly. We stick him in the cell until he sobers up. Sometimes he starts hitting people and we bring him in for assault. Most times the charges don't stick, the losers of the fight and the witnesses come down with amnesia or they have a change of heart. They'd be fine sending him to jail, but they must look up sentencing guidelines and realize he would also get out of jail. I don't think that's something they want to face, Kinnell with a grudge. He's mean when he's sober, but a godawful sumabitch when he's drunk, especially when he gets ahold of that homebrew gasoline that's a favorite among the dregs of society."

"What are the chances he'll be drunk?"

"You might want to flip the probability question around and ask what are the chances he'll be sober because I think that drunkenness is now his natural state. Sobriety would be the anomaly. So, there's a zero percent chance that he won't be chemically altered, that'd be my guess."

"What do you want me to do, exactly?"

"I don't know. Try not to get killed, that would be a start."

"I've seen this guy, remember? I think you call for backup when you find him. I mean like practically the entire sheriff's department."

"What fun would that be? Truth is no one on the department would be able to come. The arrest is not going to be unofficial until I bring him in. The sheriff is not going to recognize me until then."

"He said that he was going to suspend you? I thought he was just trying to avoid a lawsuit by saying he was going to do it. I didn't think he would actually do it."

"Why the fuck did he tell you that?" The deputy suddenly had a sense that everyone knew more about the machinations ruining his life than he ever could.

"When he released me and Blue Cowboy and Third Eye. He gathered us together and apologized for the night in jail, said he hoped his department hadn't interfered with our art, and said he hoped we would come back to Portsmouth next year for the festival. I think he even asked for and got Third Eye's number and told her to expect a call."

"You never know who you're going to piss off when you're doing my job. Sometimes you can get mighty forces against you, even when you stop an obvious act of indecent exposure."

"I didn't pull out my cock in a shopping mall, Greg, or outside an elementary school. I was onstage performing theater to an audience full of adults who've seen a cock or two in their lifetime."

"I'm not going to argue the point. There were minors in the audience and you went off script. Your cock had nothing to do with that play, and you know it. I could have forgiven the whore for flashing her tits because it looked more like an actual accident and she covered up right away, but she needed to be arrested for overall bad judgment."

"So now you're the judge of the community standard."

"Basically, why not?"

"The sheriff and the community didn't agree. I got an apology and you got suspended. Besides, haven't we already covered this ground enough?"

The deputy glared out the window, his knuckles white from a hard grip on the wheel. He clenched his jaw so hard and intensely the pain came throbbing back. He hesitated in retrieving the pill from his pocket, because he didn't want Paul to see him take it, but he quickly shed the discretion as he decided he didn't give a good goddamn if Paul saw him choke down the entire bottle of oxy. The pill stuck on a patch of dryness in his throat and melted enough to leave an acrid trail.

Either Paul did not notice or he chose not to see the act, retreating as he did from the deputy's rage and imbalance. The sheriff had not made a personal appearance at the jail and no apology had ever been uttered by anyone. He figured his incessant masturbation in the cell had turned all the deputies against him, but with Third Eye so close and caged he couldn't help but rub himself raw. Third Eye remained naked and the smell of her pussy made him tremble. He wanted to bury himself in her flesh, to feel the fat fold around him, to drape a breast over either shoulder, and to lose himself in her comfort. The bars between them drove him to the edge of frenzy. No, the sheriff would never apologize to him, but the fact that the deputy thought it a possibility gave Paul an idea as to the breadth of the estrangement between the sheriff and his subordinate. Paul could have helped him navigate through the trouble. He had had his share of bad directors and acrimonious relationships with most of them, so he had developed at least two perfect strategies for undermining a supervisor's agenda, especially if any part of the agenda happened to be against him. The deputy would refuse his help, though, because Paul had been classified as a deviant and a nuisance.

They drove in silence, each trapped in a loop of their own thoughts, until they came to a rough edge of the city. The houses and streets looked like they had been battered by a tremendous force. Some of the houses on the grid had been wiped out, burned to the ground with the charred remains poking through the uncut grass. The yards were covered in junk, rusted and broken, and as he passed by Paul could not discern the detail of the collections. Were those washing machines and tricycles? Mopeds and gray and warped construction lumber? Did saplings grow through the circle of a trampoline? Did waist-high weeds provide cover for a battalion of scattered plastic toys? Was there a column of discarded tires used as a lookout or an expression of art by one of the inhabitants? If not art, then was it a simple ordering of some of the chaos vomited from the house and garage? If not tires, then was it a single, standing column, blackened with soot, of a temple consumed by fire.

The deputy stopped in front of a house without landscaping, not even an accidental growth of saplings or weeds, except for two small islands of brown grass about the size of a coffee table flanking either side of a crumbled concrete sidewalk that connected the street to the front door. Sections of the wooden siding had been without paint for a decade or more and had turned to weather gray. Dirty curtains covered every window except one that had been covered with newspaper that had yellowed under the sunlight. The roof looked soft and concave and one could imagine a bird landing on the depression and the whole surface giving way. The screen door had been torn off and lay in a mangle under the window in front where normally an evergreen bush would be planted. Paul recognized a lost cause within seconds. This house had severe structural damage and, given the detailed report he could write, should have been clawed back to the earth by a backhoe.

The deputy walked to the door and Paul trailed behind. Bottles, both shattered and whole, lay in the dirt alongside chicken bones and soggy and crushed-flat pizza boxes. Constellations of bottle caps had been ground underfoot. The deputy rapped hard against the door, but he did not identify himself as being from the sheriff's department. He paused, then pounded some more without giving someone time to respond to the first knock. He put his hands on his hips and Paul imagined for a moment the deputy drawing his pistol and shooting the lock off the door. Paul hung back, standing between the islands of grass and feeling completely exposed because should some violence break out on the doorstep he had nothing to hide behind except the deputy's truck that rested some twelve strides away. Running to the car would expose his back for a considerable length of time and would give the worst shot enough opportunity to fire a bullet into his spine.

The front door jerked open and an elderly woman who if she had ever been above the height of five feet had now shrunk far below that mark. Her sliver hair hung down to the middle of her back in a ponytail. The bones of her face showed clearly through her skin, which had not been ravaged by wrinkles or discoloration but had gained translucence. She wore a sleeveless sun dress, light blue with tiny yellow flowers cascading down her frame, which revealed two full sleeves of tattoos on both arms. The arms had lost muscle and the canvases hung in drapes off her bones, which helped to obfuscate the fact that the design, color and execution of the tattoos were amateurish and hideous. The ink had faded to a blue-green-gray and the images had bled together into amorphous blobs. Paul had concocted a disease that manifested itself with skin discoloration before realizing the stain had been self-inflicted. A cigarette hung from her lips and she squinted against the smoke curling up her face.

"I'm looking for Kinnell," the deputy said as a way of introduction.

"There's a whole lot of Kinnells around here. You have a good chance of finding one if you pull over any old car. There's a good chance a Kinnell or a relation will be behind the wheel."

"You know I mean, Garrison."

"You just gone and release him. Why would you want him again for?"

"I want to ask him a few questions in relation to a capital crime."

"Well, what about it? Maybe I can answer your questions for you."

"About the death of Amber Miller."

From the distance where he stood Paul saw the woman's countenance change, something like a shadow passing across her face or a slow petrification that froze her lower jaw in place.

"I don't know why he started talking about that. He was just a boy when she disappeared and even though he was always the strongest sumofabitch on the block I think doing something like that was beyond his years by a mile. The sheriff and prosecutor agreed. They let him go."

"But you lived near the Millers?"

"We done lived near everyone. This town is small and everybody knows everything."

"I'm thinking Garrison saw something, maybe assisted in some way. Any one of your brood is more than capable of committing murder."

"Listen to Johnny Laws disparaging my family. You might be right calling us thieves and roughnecks but we're not killing folk. No one ever accused us of nothing like that. You all made us outcasts and now you want to heap all of your sins on us."

"Amber would be forty-some years old now. Probably would have had kids of her own."

The old lady cackled and took a long drag of her cigarette.

"What do I care about that? I don't care what that little whore would have been. Maybe she would have been a politician's wife with dreams of the White House or maybe she'd be dancing with her cunt wrapped around a pole for any asshole who still wanted to watch her flabby ass shake. I don't give a good goddamn. I'm supposed to feel sorry for every little bitch who gets herself in a situation she can't get out of? I worry about my boy Garrison taking up the world's crimes. I ain't going to lie to you. You know his crimes. The boy has a temper, a rage he gets from his daddy, especially when he gets drinking. I don't doubt that if he doesn't quit his fighting he's going to kill some other old drunk and I've told him that. With his size and strength it's a damn miracle it hasn't happened yet, I've told him that too. The boy doesn't hit girls. He could break most of them in half. I told him if he ever so much as touched a girl, no matter how much a whore or bitch she is, he'd have to answer to me. The boy has seen me castrate a bull before. I even held up them two big balls close to his face and told him they would be his if he ever laid a hand on a girl. I'd of like scare him to death. He wasn't much more than ten and I don't even think his balls had come down yet, but he remembered what I said when he did finally see them. So, the way I see things is that the boy saw you on TV and got it into his head he had something to do with it. He's a sensitive sumofabitch. You wouldn't know by looking at him but he's been called a devil since he started growing oversized. Ain't nobody thought he could be good, but as his auntie I'm telling you he could have never done nothing like it. But here you are getting ready to charge him with something he could have never done just to get yourself back on TV and make yourself look good, maybe make a run for sheriff yourself. But you ain't going to be successful with that as long as I'm alive. Ain't no way my the sumofabitch is going to pay for the sins of a whore."

"Ma'am, I'm still going to talk to him whether you want to let me or not. He can have a lawyer present, but he is an adult and has to answer for his own actions.

Right now we're just having a conversation, but if you keep obstructing me I'll throw you in jail too and we can talk through the bars."

"Deputy, my cherry was popped a long time ago as far as jail goes. You think y'all can threaten me with a cage? I know it's the only thing you got, that and that gun and all them lawyers and judges wanting to make money off us folks, but you're going to get exactly nowhere trying to scare me into talking. You think I give a good goddamn where I sleep. Put me in a cage and I wouldn't have to keep this house from falling down on my head."

"I'm just giving you the scenario if you obstruct my investigation."

"Well, Deputy, the fact of the matter is that Garrison ain't here, anyway. He run off with a girl a couple days after the sheriff released him. I couldn't even tell you where he is right now if I wanted."

"You don't know where he run off to? Maybe a relative's house in another state? I can't imagine Garrison getting a job and taking care of himself."

"You don't know the girl he run off with then. She's in love with him as hard and fierce as anybody was ever in love. She'll take care of Garrison."

"Did they leave Ohio?"

"Couldn't say. But why would they stay here? Garrison ain't on parole yet and he wouldn't be skipping bail if he leaves, so the last time I checked he can come and go as he pleases without asking permission from Johnny Laws. It's a big, open country for a couple of young people."

"Ma'am expect a warrant to be coming his way."

"For what exactly?"

"For Amber Miller."

"Hell's bells, Deputy, I know the sheriff didn't send you over here. We had a long conversation about Garrison and we both done agreed that maybe it would be best if he left town until the ruckus with that skull died down. Sheriff said himself that he didn't want an innocent boy taking the blame for something he could never have done. Sometimes that goddamn TV can put thoughts in a person's head until they start thinking they're the Queen of England or they killed some young whore or maybe they've a New York City detective with brains trying to solve crimes that nobody cared about when they happened."

"That's clever. Did the sheriff tell you that as well?"

"Sheriff understands Garrison."

"We'll see what the sheriff says once he sees the evidence. Garrison's not going to be protected from what he's got coming to him."

"I can't wait to see the evidence. The boy was under ten years old when she disappeared. He could have never done nothing like that. Why can't you understand the basics?"

"We've been over this. I need to ask Garrison a few questions. He brought this on himself. He confessed to the crime in front of every deputy in the department."

"Ain't you ever been drunk, Deputy? Ain't you ever said something you didn't mean? Ain't you ever wanted to act like more than you are? Just leave the sumofabitch alone. That's all I'm asking."

"If it comes out that he's innocent then he'll be able to drink himself to death and beat-up anyone who stands in his path toward his destination."

Paul walked the distance from where he stood to a spot just left of the deputy and broke into the conversation.

"Ma'am, what's the name of Garrison's girlfriend?"

"Who the hell are you?"

"I'm a deputy in training ma'am. I'm observing Deputy Auro all month with the hopes of breaking into the force. If you would indulge me."

"You look too old to be training."

"Paul, stop, go back into the truck," the deputy said as he wheeled toward Paul.

"Deputy, please, how else will I learn? Ma'am what's her name?"

'Paul, I asked you to stop."

"Why do you want to know?" she said as she eyed Paul suspiciously. She figured he had more on the ball and could do more damage than the enfeebled deputy.

"Well, I figure it this way, ma'am. Garrison, might not have any outstanding warrants and he might not be breaking parole by leaving the state, but chances are that his girlfriend has one or both and things won't go so well for her if she's gone and made herself a mess all for the love of your boy. I suppose it will be easy enough to find out who she is. We can go to any one of the half dozen bars we passed the last mile and a half and ask who Garrison Kinnell is running with these days. I mean, I have to think your son is just short of being some kind of celebrity. He's not likely to go anywhere without being noticed and recognized, since he is a giant among men, something Deputy Auro understands since his brush with fame. Once we find out who she is and what's she's done we're going to put her away if she has broken her probation and I'm thinking that if Garrison likes her as much as she likes him he's going to take it hard being away from her. By the time he's done he might confess to the assassination of William McKinley and his ability to spawn killer tornadoes with the thoughts in his mind. See, once we go to the watering holes and find out the girl's name we're going to go to her parents' house, or her friends, anybody that happens to know her and one of these people are going to tell us where they've gone, because she's told someone. She may have even told the whole crowd at their favorite bar and all the regulars might have wished them well or given them money because they were tired of Garrison cracking skulls and punching their faces into mush. Then, we're going to have to tag them fugitives from the law and that's a label you never want. The law will just keep coming after them. It'll be like trying to stop the tide or the wind. The pursuer always determines the length of the chase."

"You can't take away that boy. He's the only comfort I have left."

The deputy and Paul stared at the woman, trying to determine if her intent had been to pass off vulnerability as an actual emotion that had some influence over her. Neither believed it although her countenance did not betray anything contrary to complete sincerity.

"How can we help him if we don't know where he is? If he gets himself worked up and on the run there's no telling what he could do and that girl with him is not going to be able to stop him."

The woman laughed long and hard until she choked on phlegm that had freed itself from her sinuses, all but destroying the minor ploy she tried to pass off.

"Who wants to stop him?" she asked. "He's my avenging angel. I born him out of my pussy as a scourge to all you. He'll take my vengeance. He'll tear you all to the ground until there's nothing but mud in his hands. He'll drink your goddamn blood and eat your flesh for Thanksgiving dinner. He'll take your throat in his hands and crush your windpipe and the last thing your eyes will see is his rage radiating from his eyes and the reflection or your weak and powerless fear. You can try to beat him, Deputy, like you did when he was locked up in your cage, but you best not let him get ahold of you cause no amount of beating him will stop him. My advice is for you and your friend here to leave him be. The sheriff understands his rage for what it is. It comes from the blackest pit. It's stirred and cooked by the foulest witches. The Kinnells have all done and seen too much. We can channel all that evil and make it dance on the end of a stick or we can let it consume us and make us stronger than everything that's ever been. Garrison's father showed him what evil could do on this earth, so if I were you two I wouldn't expect Garrison to join society and live by the laws of man. That Piketon hellhole gave my man cancer and killed him young. I'll be goddamned if I care what that sumofabitch does to all of you."

The deputy could feel a surge of outrage building as she spoke, the source of which was his own father. How many times had his father evoked the image of a thin battle line repulsing wave after wave of naked demons using their faith as a shield and their righteousness as their sword? Was this the moment for which he had been prepared? Faced with the forces of chaos, sin, corruption, violence, impulse, sex, murder, and degradation of the human soul, wasn't he supposed to stand in the path of this frenzy and either try to stop its advance or be ripped apart trying? Hadn't his father warned him to be prepared, to keep himself honest, true, and strong because he would never know when the challenge would occur, in what form it would come, and what would be expected of him at the time of the confrontation. He shook the anger off and tried to clear his head, but his past indoctrinations could not so easily be cleaned.

"Ok, ma'am, we'll do it the hard way. We'll still find him, but we will be angry when we do." Paul punctuated his disgust by spitting in the dirt and covered the gob with dust with a twist of his toe.

"That means nothing to me. It will mean nothing to Garrison."

Paul cocked his head toward the deputy and said, "Let's go."

The deputy followed and didn't realize he had assumed a subordinate role until he slid behind the wheel of the truck and started the engine. They followed Paul's plan by visiting six bars within a tight radius of the Kinnell homestead. Two were closed, not because they visited outside the posted hours of operation, but one bartender still lay sick in bed with fire in his belly and a head that felt split open with his brain exposed and the second had passed out behind the bar after a night raiding the stock, teetering on the edge of alcohol poisoning, and couldn't hear the deputy pounding on the door. The next three acknowledged they knew of Kinnell and that he did sometimes haunt their establishments, but they said they knew nothing of the girlfriend and wouldn't even guess where he had gone. The only hint of the terror that Kinnell inflicted on this corner of the world was provided by a patron sitting at a square bar. His face hovered over a half-gone whiskey sour and when he heard the deputy say Kinnell's name he raised his head and said that he hoped someone would have the courage to send him back into the jaws of Satan from which he had been spit. The deputy asked him to elaborate and the man waved him off, muttering something about a vow he had made to never talk to the law no matter what the circumstances.

At the last bar, the Blasted Buck, they finally came across someone willing to talk. The bartender and owner who had banished Kinnell a dozen times from his bar for fighting said he never witnessed him start the trouble, but he could sure as hell finish whatever had been started. Usually, some pint-sized Napoleon drank his courage up until invincibility flowed through his veins and he convinced himself he could have had a career in boxing or mixed martial arts. At that moment at the apex of his high and in deference to his lost career, he would challenge Kinnell, as any mountain climber worth being called the name eyes Everest with the confidence of the insane. The bartender noticed that Kinnell always started slow and witnesses always concluded that the challengers had an early advantage, meaning that if someone had enough power in his punch to knock Kinnell completely out early in the fight, he could win without getting a beating in return. Unfortunately for the challengers, the force of such a punch lay outside the limits of human ability, and any advantage they thought they had turned sour as Kinnell loosened up and routed them, beat them, and created a near-death experience for one and all who thought they had been up for the challenge.

The bartender had given Kinnell a lifetime ban after the last beating left his opponent bleeding from the ears and convulsing amongst a turned-over table and a broken chair. He had come back the next night without any recollection of the fight except for the bruises on his knuckles. That same night he had a little woman by his side, June Kasper, and they hadn't been apart since, as far as the bartender could tell.

"She's just like him," the bartender growled, "except about a quarter of his size, but probably three times as smart and six times as fierce. That boy will do anything she says. If she told him to cut off his finger he'd do it without question, that's what I'm talking about. Hell, he'd even probably present the digit to her wrapped in a bow. See, I felt I could handle Kinnell when she wasn't in the picture, even when he was insanely drunk. As long as you don't provoke him, he's fine. He'll just sit there a like a fat idiot and not bother no one. He'd never pick a fight. I imagine it's pretty boring for a boy like that to fight anyway. He knows he can kick everyone's ass six ways to Sunday. But it's a completely different story with June. She knows what she wants to do with his strength. It's like she has a bull at her command. I think she had some kind of agenda. She wants something, but I'll be damned if I can figure it out. Maybe she's just getting back at the world for her being so small and a woman who probably hasn't been treated with a whole bunch of kindness coming up. So, when they come into the bar I figure I got to deal with a pissed-off woman with a 400 pound fist. There's no guessing what mischief they're going to get into. I've had her come into the bar and tell me they were going to drink for free because I was going to hire him as a bouncer for the night and he would make sure no trouble started. I told her that the only trouble there was going to be would be started by her and Kinnell. When I said that she slapped her hand on the bar and told me that I should change the name of the establishment to "Death Wish" to more accurately reflect my life's philosophy. I think she's taken a couple of classes over at Shawnee State so she thinks she can talk like that sometimes. I let them drink. It sounds like I am a coward, but it only cost me a bottle or two, but my choice was to break out the shotgun and chase them off, which would have been just fine if it was just Kinnell, but with June at his side that's not much of an option. She'll meet force with more devious force. I would have expected her to come back after I closed and set fire to the place and come to my house and slit the throat of me and my wife. I could have called you all and you could have took them down to jail and kept them there until they sobered up and when they got out they would have come back and then June would have set fire to the place. The only solution to that problem was to give them what they wanted and hope they don't bust up everything I got."

"You didn't need to take that," said the deputy defensively as he felt blame for the impotency of the law.

"Not much to take, really. June got it into her head to order Wild Turkey and Johnnie Walker, but I have a couple of bottles filled with Old Crow and diesel fuel just for them. They wouldn't know the difference anyhow. Sometimes peace can be bought with ten or twenty bucks, know what I mean?"

"When's the last time you saw them?" Paul chimed in.

"I wish you'd stop doing that. I ask the questions," the deputy responded.

"If I wait for you to ask the questions we'll be here until morning."

"I saw them a couple of days ago. They came in and drank a gallon a piece, I think. They paid, but they were looking desperate and talking crazy as usual."

"Did they happen to mention where they might be going?" Paul continued.

"Ya, they talked about it all goddamn night. June's not exactly the shy and retiring type. She pretty much never stops talking."

"Where?"

The deputy wanted to step in but had had a hard time following the conversation and hoped that Paul would remember some of the details.

"Jupiter Hill. They kept talking about someplace called Jupiter Hill."

"Where's that?"

"I haven't been there so I don't know exactly."

"Is it a town or a city?"

"Sort of, I guess. From what I could understand it's more like a settlement. A temporary town. More like tents, campers and such. June knows somebody that went to live out there. By the sound of it they weren't planning on coming back, but they're both so goddamn crazy it's hard to know what's true and what's just talk. They better have a whole lot of liquor out in Jupiter Hill or they won't survive more than a few days."

"Were they definitely going there?"

The bartender laughed bitterly and humorlessly. "As definite as you can be with a couple of drunk crazies. I've heard a few stories in my time and I've heard more plans to reshape the world than Congress, and not a single one of them ever came true or probably were ever even remembered in the morning. I can tell you this, though. June had a car. I don't know where the hell she got it, but I saw they had packed up the back seat with stuff they thought they might need. They wanted me to come out and look to see that they were serious. They were proud of their plan. Of course, they could have crashed into a telephone pole on the next block. Kinnell doesn't drive I don't think and June was so drunk she could barely stay on her feet."

"Anything else that you can remember that's worth telling us?" the deputy finally asked, which seemed unnecessary to Paul since the bartender had obviously told them everything he could remember.

"No, deputy, that's about it, I guess. I just hope they are serious about moving away. It'd be like a plague or an invading army finally moving on, know what I mean? They've worn out their welcome at least six times over."

They left the bar and sat in the truck in the street. Paul conducted a quick search on the deputy's phone and came up with four hits from official news stories that made passing references to Jupiter Hill in South Dakota.

"South fucking Dakota? I guess that's the end of the chase. If they rot out on the Plains who's going to know the difference?" Paul laughed.

"Maybe the end for you. I'm going."

"You don't even know if they went. You base your decisionon one internet search and that's the research you're basing your chase on. What if there's another Jupiter Hill? What if there's a dozen? Maybe it's a goddamn franchise."

"Kinnell is guilty. They ran. I have a gut feeling that's where they went. You heard the bartender say they were packed up."

"I'm not one for advice, Greg, but you should probably go home and get some rest. Talk to the sheriff and your wife and decide tomorrow if you're going to go."

"I'll drop you off at the hotel."

"Do you even have official jurisdiction to arrest someone in South Dakota? How would you even arrest them, anyway? They don't have an outstanding warrant. You never checked on the woman's record to see if she's violating her parole. I mean, what are you doing? None of this would stand up in court, anyway. We have a hard enough time getting convictions of slumlords. Capital cases I'm sure have some rules, right? We just can't kidnap a couple a crazies off the street and expect to get a conviction."

"I told you before this is unofficial."

"I don't think I understand. What are you going to do?"

"I'm not asking you to understand."

Paul didn't think the deputy would make it much past Illinois, let alone all the way to South Dakota, which had to be 1,000 miles away. He had some time to mull over a decision given it would take a half hour to get back to the hotel, but his thoughts raced on their own, pushed along by the deputy's own self-destructive momentum. He couldn't imagine passing up an opportunity to see the conclusion of the chase, even if it ended in an empty field once named Jupiter Hill. Even that, to witness the deputy's final humiliation as he returned empty-handed to his ruined life, sounded better than going back to work in the caverns of City Hall.

"What the hell? I don't think I've ever been to South Dakota. That's Roy Rogers country, right?"

"I wouldn't know."

"I thought he owned the west."

"I couldn't say."

"Let's make Blue Cowboy proud and go west and get our man, and his crazy fucking girlfriend."

The deputy tried to keep a professional demeanor and not betray that he felt thrilled at the prospect of hunting down a fugitive in the wilds of the west. He started the truck and roared down the street.

Part III

25

June

When June saw Kinnell emerge from the hallway that led to the jail cells a little cry escaped from the back of her throat. She had been so worried about him that she imagined him shot or stabbed, lying bleeding on the street, crying for help that no one would give. The bruises on his face and arms looked freshly made. That bastard sheriff had him beaten for no reason and every time they arrested her poor Baby Bear they thrashed him a little more. Not that they could ever hurt him with sticks or fists, which is why, she thought, that she had been dreaming of him shot and dying. Nothing had been so perfect in her life and she had never done anything to deserve the happiness she felt, so why wouldn't it be torn away from her with a bullet or a blade. If some fucker attacked him from the right angle with him unaware of the threat he could get a blade into him. The knife better hit the heart or an eye because anywhere else would just make him mad. Also, June thought it fortunate that her Baby Bear never learned to drive or he most likely would have wrapped himself around a telephone pole or a tree years ago. Now the worst that could happen was he might fall over and scrape his chin or sprain his wrist when the alcohol took ahold of him and drove him to his knees without mercy.

They made him wear an orange jumpsuit and he carried his torn and bloody clothes under his arm. He looked so trapped, so processed, but when he saw June standing on the other side of the desk a glint came back into his eye and suddenly his body that had looked so caged a moment before now seemed poised to smash the room, the chairs, the desk into splinters. June imagined him forming two fists and bringing them down onto the necks of the deputies, crushing their bones and severing their spinal cords and killing them outright without them knowing what had hit them. Maybe he'd tramp through the jail until he found the sheriff's office and smash his collection of dolls before beating the sonofabitch to death.

June had been in the sheriff's office the day before. She had come to explain to him that she didn't have the bail money to get Kinnell released and that she had no hope of ever raising enough and the thought of Baby Bear locked up in a cage drove her mad with fear and loneliness. The sheriff explained that he didn't set bail, that a judge had that responsibility. June told the sheriff that everyone knew that everything went through the sheriff, that nobody sneezed without him knowing whether or not they used a Kleenex or wiped the snot on their sleeve. The sheriff laughed, of that she was proud, but then of course he told her a blowjob might convince him to make a call on Kinnell's behalf, but even a call from him might not make that much of a difference because Kinnell had been in front of the judge so many times for so many violations that his arrest history read like a recitation of the state criminal code.

June crouched on her knees between the sheriff's legs and worked his cock with her hand and mouth until he became hard and eventually satisfied him under the watchful eyes of his collection of superheroes. Those little plastic faces, mostly so beautiful and impossibly perfect, condemned her love of Kinnell but she told them through the flashing of angry eyes that a simple and quick blowjob didn't even scratch the surface of what she would do for her Baby Bear. Anyway, it wasn't like she didn't expect to perform some act when she asked for a meeting and the sheriff granted her request, because she knew him to be an old pervert who use to come and watch her dance twice a week during her brief time as a stripper. Her parents had kicked her out of their house without much else than the clothes on her back. At seventeen she had no assets except her tight ass and flat stomach, so she started dancing before something worse happened like getting trapped in a marriage and having babies before she could drink in a bar legally. She might have been young and dumb, but she understood she didn't know what she wanted out of a man let alone how to get it from him. Back then the sheriff would sit in the shadows nursing his beer, sometimes in his uniform and sometime not. After an hour or so of grim concentration he would ask her over to his table for a private talk and dance.

He never said much. Sometimes he asked her the same questions about her age and whether or not she did drugs, like he hadn't remembered the answers from the week before. She lied about her age, of course, as did all the other girls. Some were too old and had too many kids to generate much of a fantasy, unless the guy was on some kind of rescue trip, so they shaved off the offensive years and only admitted to kids if they had an obvious caesarian scar. Most were too young, like her, from fucked-up families and on the run for one reason or another. He seemed to like to hear her prattle on about nothing as sometimes he would half close his eyes and a creepy smile would seep across his face as she talked. He'd want to buy her a drink and the owners instructed her to ordered a champagne or top shelf liquor, such as it was in that dump of a club, but she hated all of that and would order a Diet Dr. Pepper instead. Everything she did amused him, like he cast her in the role of a pet puppy, except after a while his demeanor would change and all the delight and amusement would harden on his face and he'd start peppering her with questions about the size and shape of her labia or ask her to describe the biggest donkey dick she had ever had in her mouth and how much of it she had been able to take. Sometimes he would ask earnestly about what position facilitated a stronger and longer climax as if he had been sent by a newspaper or magazine to gather the data. She lied about everything and realized it didn't matter if she changed the answers week to week, like donning a different wig and changing her makeup, as he would accept any persona she created.

Then, after he exhausted his questions they walked to a private booth that held a filthy couch and a string of dusty paper lanterns. Technically, the patron couldn't touch the dancer, but the owners told her and the other girls to let the sheriff do as he pleased. He liked to hold her hips and move her to the music, although she felt he moved her a half beat behind the rhythm of the song. As he moved her he stared at her pussy, barely covered behind a thin triangle of cloth, for the entire length of the song. Then he would slowly peel down the G-string, another serious violation of the law because everybody knew that alcohol could not be served in the same room where views of pussies were offered. He would set her on his knee, facing away from him, and make her grind on his pant leg, squeezing her ass so hard that she thought he might be bruising her. He'd unclip her top and push it from her shoulders and he would then run his hands from her shoulders to her ass, which felt more like a tickle than anything remotely erotic. His hands felt so calloused and rough that June thought a lizard could be groping her and somehow that made it seem more bearable.

By the time he allowed her to turn around he had unleashed his ruddy, fully engorged cock. The first time it happened she jumped backwards as if he had pulled a rat out of his pocket. But he gave her a half grin that dared her to do something with it. The first time she turned away from him and sat on it. As she felt it slide into her pussy she wanted to cry for moment but she found as she continued that she really just wanted to punch him in the face over and over again. And he came inside her, the fucker. He never put on a condom and never made a move to pull out when he was about to come and afterwards she started worrying about carrying the sheriff's child or picking up a disease from him. She felt a little part of herself harden with the knowledge, a brutal wisdom, that no one would look after her and any mistake, whether made in confusion or coercion, would be relentlessly punished. Fortunately, she had her period a few days later and nothing came of the disease fear, and she realized that she could not make a life as a stripper, because her rage would build until she killed one of the men with her hands.

But for a year she could find no work and nobody wanted to marry her, so the sheriff became a twice-a-week regular and made her perform as he wished. He never just let her dance and grind through his pants until he came. She would take him in her mouth or maybe drip massage oil on her palm to work him with her hand, so that he would forget about entering her pussy, but most times he demanded more. She submitted. He was the sheriff, distended, malevolent, perverted, and he could harm her, destroy her, although after he had fucked her in the pussy there didn't seem like she had much left to destroy.

The sheriff would never know he had been her first. Not technically, she guessed, because a neighbor boy had popped her cherry at fifteen with his finger or cock, as there had been so much confusion and panic and they had been drinking whiskey he had stolen from his dad's liquor cabinet that that the lower half of her had gone numb and she could never confirm he had been inside of her. She might have screamed, or punched, or kicked the poor boy while he still had his pants off and his cock had lost its power, because she wanted him to know that she felt nothing and that she would never repeat the act with him as long as she lived. She couldn't remember what made her mad. Maybe the smirk on the dude's face like he had just accomplished some great feat, that he had got her naked and had basically fucked the air for all the good it had done, and made himself come on her belly, like he had done a thousand times before on his own belly.

She wouldn't let the sheriff know the shallowness of her experience, because she feared it might change their relationship in some fundamental way. She didn't want him to feel responsible for her. She didn't want him to think of her at all, although sometimes she looked past his gnarled frame, flabby belly and the length of time it sometimes took to get his turgid member to resemble something close to an erection and conjured up fantasies of marrying the sheriff and getting to experience what it felt like to live in a big house and hire a man to mow the lawn and to go to the supermarket and have the clerks and stockers treat you as a woman of power and means and not some ignorant bitch standing on an even lower rung than the miserable one they occupied. She also thought the sheriff expected experience and weariness and a girl who knew the value of what she sold, and not someone scared and stupid who offered her pussy before even exploring other possibilities of making a living, like maybe one of those store cashier cunts who looked down on her or a dental hygienist or massage therapist if she could get the training. No, she ran straight to stripping because she hated something inside herself and wanted to punish it. If she made the sheriff feel shame he would stop coming to her and his hundred dollar tips for her services would stop. His payments gave her some freedom because hustling dollar bills from the stage and begging dances from the regulars didn't generate all that much income. They were all living off disability checks and pensions and couldn't afford the beer they were drinking, let alone a peek at her pussy. Sometimes a young stud would come rolling in but they were all cock and no money and they thought their beauty gave them access to discounts if not outright free service. Anyway, they all soon understood that she was the sheriff's regular and they tended to shy away from her and only paid for a dance with her when they became so drunk and desperate that they forgot themselves.

After a year she decided one day that she didn't much like being the sheriff's whore and she quit the club and never once went back. The sheriff never tried to find her as far she knew, although during the first few weeks of her flight she had the habit of looking over her shoulder, expecting to see him in a recently pressed uniform. Sometimes she thought he would be holding roses and a ring and other times she half expected to be shot in the back before she even had a chance to turn around. She drifted in Kentucky off the money she had saved and first worked in a factory making lipstick. After she grew exhausted from the monotony of the never-ending manufacturing process, she got a job working behind a jewelry counter where she wheedled young couples into buying too expensive rings for their doomed betrothals and convinced erring husbands that platinum was considered the "forgiveness" metal, whereas gold signified a promise and silver a minor indulgence. The problem with gold was that it would remind her of past vows now broken and giving her silver would make her think you had an impulse at the grocery checkout line and saw the silver rings or necklaces sitting next to the candy bars and breath mints. Platinum would tell her of his seriousness and his willingness to reinvest in her and their lives together. The owner had taken a chance on her and her "hillbilly charm" as he called it, figuring she would put the buyers at ease because she had been raised like them and understood their aspirations, limited as they were. Some days she felt like she had fallen into a dream as she stood in the air conditioning with cases of jewelry surrounding her, glittering in the light, purring at the steady flow of customers who sought permanence for their lives or talismans to fend off disease, boredom, and rage.

For over two years she worked the retail trade and collected a rack of polyester dresses that clung to her body in a flattering way. For the first time she began seeing a future for herself and nothing looked too horrible. She stood behind the counter, older and fatter with a hairstyle a couple of seasons out of date, and lived in a little house on the edge of rolling farmland. A husband and children walked through her vision in a gray half-light, their flesh neither made manifest nor the idea of them completely forgotten. The acts the sheriff made her perform hung heavy in her memory and she could not entirely convince herself that men would play a significant role in her life, but so many couples came before her seeking their trinkets and holding each other's hands, it was hard to forget the possibility entirely.

From the moment she had left the club she deflected all inquiries and kept men at bay because she had her savings and a better plan than they did, but the jewelry store just wore on her like a river against a stone. The men who came into the store were either in love, falling out of love, or trying to hold onto love slipping through their fingers, so they had the act front and center in their minds when they spoke to her. She had known for a long time that she could not pass as a great beauty. Her teeth were a jumble and her hair hung from her scalp like wet paper. Fat accumulated in odd spots on her body and the diet she learned as a child portended a distended future. But none of that mattered really because she stood before them, not their wife or fiancée, free of the accumulation of betrayals and missteps, not representing a gamble, a desperate marriage, a coerced engagement, pressure, doubt, or the fundamental questioning of marriage as an institution imposed on lustful dogs just looking for a steady fuck. She looked like the one to provide it for them.

So, the whispers, the indecent moans, the winks, and the outright propositions of finding a nearby motel, sometimes attempted with their inattentive wives-to-be standing not five feet from them, bedazzled as they were by the racks of shiny objects, sailed past her and she grinned in return to keep the sale going. Sometimes she carefully flirted back if the dude was good looking, always with her eye on the commission. But this brief life of stability unraveled the day Shaun Vesper walked through the door, looking for a pair of earnings for his sister, so he said. He ended up buying the cheapest pair of silver trinkets they had and asking her out on a date. She relented. She lowered her defenses because he had muscles and sinew rippling under his shirt and he looked as angry as she felt deep under the polyester dresses and cheap hairdos. He had found that something rattling around inside her, maybe her first memory or first emotion, and it was dark, endlessly deep, and full of rage.

She found out within a month that alcohol and a truckload of whatever available drug fueled Shaun's anger as much as anything else. The revelation was a disappointment, but he taught her the proper way to drink and she experimented with an encyclopedia of liquors, cataloging their effects, speed, expense, the predictability and length of the hangovers, while paying particularly close attention which of them goaded her into violent outbursts. Only beer made her docile and dulled her senses, while the others, particularly tequila and bourbon, unleashed her demons on whoever happened to be before her. Shaun took the brunt of the abuse and gave some back and many of their nights together ended with screaming, a flurry of punches, and either one of them lying bleeding on the floor or a wild fuck if they could still perform after all that booze.

Her career in the jewelry store suffered. The right kind of dress could cover the bruises and scratches on her legs and arms, and make-up glossed over any damage to her face, but nothing could mask the difference in her personality. She thought that a door had been permanently opened and the demons of her soul had befouled the rest of her. When she tried to speak of it she likened it to either a jailbreak of a supermax prison or an invading army of huns trampling the countryside and destroying the fields of fresh crops and burning every city they encountered to the ground. The owner of the store didn't know what to do. She looked like the same raw, unfinished hillbilly but now she snarled and spit instead of showing her messed-up teeth in a crooked, sexy smile. The playful banter between her and the customers turned into outright propositions or arguments. Something rancid smelling found its way through the mist of her cloying, drugstore perfume. The light behind her eyes dimmed and her pupils constricted to pin holes, so the owner wondered how her brain received any new visual information. He caught her vomiting behind the building on more than one occasion and doing nothing to freshen the foulness of her breath once she returned to the counter

The owner had his limits so he fired her one afternoon. Her response to him came slowly, like he had presented her with a difficult riddle that took several minutes to untangle before she could be certain of her words. When the meaning came to her she slammed her hand on one of the display cases, thinking she could smash it. She managed to make it rattle, nothing more. She sailed two more punches toward it with no effect, then she set her sights on the owner. A claw raked the right side of his face and he staggered back. She kicked and caught the underside of his scrotum and he dropped to his knees, exposing his head at the perfect height to accept her punches. She sent a flurry towards his face and gouged at his eyes with her glued-on nails. She didn't disagree with his assessment and subsequent action. She knew she had to be fired. She would scare away every last customer if he kept her employed. None of that mattered now that she had begun fighting. Her mind felt such peace when her body turned into a violent machine that she didn't want to stop herself. He could die for his righteousness. Luckily for the owner the months of drinking had compromised her stamina so he escaped with his life when she tired. She stopped to catch her breath and to wipe the blood off her hands as he lay at her feet with his hands covering his face. Her arms suddenly felt leaden so she kicked him one last time before leaving the store.

She left that path of her life the same day. She left her house on the edge of farmlands, the city she had adopted, her cat, and Shaun. She didn't love him, but she would always be grateful to him for teaching her how to drink. He didn't belong on the path she was headed. He'd be nothing more than an indictment of her weakness, a hedging of bets, a transition from the old to the new, and she didn't like thinking she needed that sort of crutch. She had made her own life after she ran away from being the sheriff's whore, and she was a lot smarter now than she had been when she got on the bus with a little roll of cash stuffed down her panties. She would never speak to Shaun again and she would make him wonder what had happened to her. Maybe he would hear on the news that the store owner had been beaten up and he would laugh knowing that she had done the deed, but that would be the only parting gift she would give him.

She refused to run, though. She sat in her house three days waiting for the police to come. If jail would be the next path then she would carve out something behind bars. As she waited she catalogued what she had accumulated in her time at the store: the polyester dresses, a mismatched set of bent silverware, canned soup and fruit in the cupboard, two pair of shoes, a bag of cosmetics, a toothbrush, a razor, three drinking glasses and the perishable food in the refrigerator, but she couldn't consider that much of a possession considering it would only be edible for a few weeks. The house had come furnished so none of that she could call her own. Shaun had given her nothing, not even the cheapest silver trinket earrings. It could have been worse, she guessed, because he could have left her pregnant given that that they never used birth control during their drunken fucks, so heaven sometimes blessed the lowest of the low with small miracles, she thought. Without something like a child to moor her to this past life she could easily drift way to something new.

So she drifted, drank, and never bought polyester dresses again. Sometimes she met men who took care of her for a time and sometimes she earned money for them in factories or restaurants, but they always seemed to dissipate in a haze of booze, pills and apathy. She came to regret leaving the jewelry store and when melancholy took hold of her, usually during a wicked hangover, she would try to construct plans on how to get back before she unmoored herself. Not long after she began the construction of redemption it would collapse under its own weight, half-formed, misshapen, and created from fear and exhaustion more than a need to actually put such a plan in place.

She could see her end very clearly. She had already begun gaining weight in her gut and ass and her neck resembled something inflated. Her anger had taken up residency in her conscious thoughts, so the majority of conversations she had with men which lasted more than a few sentences ended in an argument or violence, if both were in the mood for a scrape. So, to see her own death took little imagination, although there existed thousands of variations on the theme. She winnowed the field and settled on a death under the choking grip applied by one of them, her drunk and bloated body fighting with all its energy against an irresistible force but succumbing in the end because of her stature and weakness.

Her lovers became murderers-in-waiting, so she honed her skills to launch preemptive strikes when she felt the least bit threatened. Just because she saw the end didn't mean she had to accept it, and her lovers withered under the torrent of abuse. Even the strongest and meanest among them could not stand up to her for long. She was the household mutt, ungainly but loyal, that suddenly attacked their hands or throats with no obvious provocation. She remembered the parting line of one of the losers, who said something like, "I'll always wonder how such a little woman with such a sweet and tender pussy could be such a vicious bitch." Her reaction to his big statement, a braying laugh and spitting in his face, completed the memory for him.

All that came to an end when she met Kinnell. She first saw him as he sat on the curb of a street, bleeding from the head with vomit spattered down the front of his shirt. Another man lay nearby on the sidewalk. Half of a clay brick lay between them and June could piece together the evidence, she had been in so many fights, that the unconscious man had used the brick to wound Kinnell in the head but had paid a fearsome price for the strategy. June doubted the vomit had come from Kinnell. The small crowd who witnessed the beginning of the fight had dispersed when Kinnell continued the pummeling and flirted with manslaughter. No one could stop him and no one wanted to be implicated in the man's inevitable death.

June stopped and her boyfriend tried to pull her away, but she shook off his hand as she wondered if Kinnell sitting down matched her full height. Kinnell noticed them and stood up. He wiped the blood from his eyes and smeared it on his pant leg, but the wound bled profusely as scalp injuries do and more blood coursed down his face. He lumbered over to the two of them and June could feel her boyfriend quake. He wanted to run but she had taken his hand and held it tightly. If he tried to break her grip she would kick him in the knees to hobble him to take the beating he deserved. June's heart beat wildly. She had once heard the heart described like a wild animal beating against the cage of ribs, frantic to burst through. She now understood what they meant, but she refined the simile to a fox stepping into a leg trap: frantic, for sure, desperate, yes, with pain radiating through its little body as the teeth of the trap sank into the bone. She had no hope of escape except self-mutilation. Living a free life, hobbled, with the taste of her own blood in her mouth, that was what Kinnell had already done to her heart.

Her boyfriend squeezed her hand so hard she thought her fingers would crack. Kinnell looked down upon them. Blood dripped from his ear and chin. The only weakness she could find on him was his eyes as they blinked against the running blood, but who could reach his eyes with their own arms? She noticed his knuckles had been scraped raw from the beating he had administered, but his hands, one hand really, could crush her windpipe or skull. Was he the giant demon who would bring about her end that she had so often dreamed about?

"What have you seen?" Kinnell asked in voice that sounded like the rumbling of thunder miles away.

The boyfriend unleashed a torrent of denials of having seen anything, but with each word Kinnell hardened and the blood from his wound flowed a little faster.

"I see my future," June purred.

Kinnell turned his gaze toward her with great effort, resembling rusty machinery with inadequate power.

"What did you say?" His words came as thickly as his movements had.

"Somebody best bandage that cut before you bleed out. Your shirt is getting soaked with it."

"Some of that ain't mine."

June released her boyfriend's hand. She could feel him giving the side of her face a hard glare, but she didn't turn to find out what he wanted. She only wanted to look at Kinnell now. She had given the now ex-boyfriend enough of her time and it needed to end anyway. He needed to take his first step toward finding somebody else if that was what he wanted to do. Maybe he could drink alone for a time. Maybe the ex-boyfriend shouted something at her from a safe distance, but neither heard what he said since his opinion meant nothing. Nobody was listening.

"I'm a lot meaner than your girlfriend."

"I don't have a girlfriend."

"Sometimes the world is a mystery and sometimes you just need to fall down on your knees and thank the Lord for blind luck."

"I'm not arguing."

Her heart leapt back and forth and up and down, looking for an egress, but it could find no escape, so it dragged the rest of her body with it, tethered as it was, to the brink of frenzy. The same feeling came back when she saw him emerge from the hallway of jail cells wearing his orange jumpsuit. How had they found one large enough to fit him? She didn't know how hard her heart could beat before it tore itself apart, but she figured she had to be close to the limit of its ability.

She had finished off the sheriff after what had to have been 45 minutes of sucking. She even swallowed his come and licked off the last of the dribble so he wouldn't stain his pants. After he buckled back up he pretended to make a call to the judge and laid out a convincing case for releasing Kinnell, which he won since he had only been talking to himself. He told her she could go pick up her boyfriend. She waited a moment for him to recognize her, or, if he had, to acknowledge that she had once been his whore. She hadn't changed all that much, but he gave her a cold stare and told her to get out of his office before he changed his mind.

"You don't remember," she said.

"I never forget a name or a face. How the hell do you think I have a stranglehold on an elected office?"

She wanted to tell him what he had done was wrong but she remembered Kinnell and the sheriff could just as easily make another phony phone call to revoke the release.

"You might want to brush your teeth or gargle before you kiss your boyfriend."

Kinnell changed back into his street clothes, bloody and ripped as they were, and June waited until they walked to the parking lot before she squeezed him in a hug with all her strength. She had waited because she didn't want to give the deputies a show. Everybody always snickered at the difference of their sizes, which made them look like they had come from two different species. The laughing brought on the rage. One time she and Kinnell were kissing in a bar and an old drunk leered over his beer and said that Kinnell must have an awfully small pecker if he had to take up with a midget. June slapped the bar and shouted for everyone to hear that if the old man was worried about the size of Kinnell's dick he must be thinking whether or not he could take all of it up his ass or how far down his throat it would go once he started sucking it. The ragged audience of early afternoon regulars laughed some before everyone went back to the business of drinking.

"What did they do to you this time, Baby Bear?" she stroked the swirl of bruises around his eye and along his jaw by standing on the tip of her toes and stretching out to her absolute full length.

"No different than the other times."

"I want to kill them. I want to smash their stupid fucking faces."

"I told them. I told them everything."

"What did you tell them?"

"About the girl. About everything. About how I done it."

"What are you talking about, Baby Bear?"

"How I killed that girl they found in the dirt. I done it. I don't remember much about it, like why I done it, but I remember having my hands around her throat and I remember seeing her pale face looking up with her eyes open wide before I start throwing dirt on her. It's like I saw it on TV and it all come flooding back like I was there the whole time."

"When did you do this?"

"I don't know. I was young. My papa was still at home and all my brothers and sisters. I don't remember anyone else around me when I done it."

"What did you tell them?" June could feel the panic rising inside her.

"I told them I saw the light pass out of her eyes. That I've been carrying that around since I could remember."

"Oh shit, oh shit, oh shit." June fell into a moan, consisting of an untold number of such phrases smashed together or lengthened to match the surging of her emotions. Suddenly, her eyes flashed fury. "What about us? Why would you go and bust us up like that? You didn't think of me, did you? What am I supposed to do with my Baby Bear rotting in a jail cell? You big, goddamn ape!"

The first punch landed on his chest. She could not reach his face with much force behind the blows. A storm of blows and kicks followed in a fit of savagery. None of them had an effect on Kinnell, who looked on June with an apologetic droop for having sent her over the edge again. She stopped when she tired and the exhaustion set off a string of sobs that came from desolation and an understanding that she had was now bereft of hope and joy. She fell to her knees and clung to his feet. She would have licked the mud and scum off his boots it if meant she could keep Kinnell for another day. The impulse of pulling out his cock and giving him a blowjob right then and there in the parking lot came upon her in a surge. She would blot out the memory of the sheriff and take every bit of him into her mouth and let him come into her throat and she would lick every last drop of semen from the head, even squeezing the shaft until he had no more. She rose up and grabbed the zipper but a stray thought stopped her, a persistent, rational inquiry that somehow made it intact through all of her emotions.

"Then how come you're out? Why did they let you go?" She knew the sheriff had enjoyed her blowjob but not even he would exchange that for someone who committed murder.

"They don't believe me."

"You told them the truth and they don't believe you?"

"Sheriff himself came in last night and told me to stop wasting his time. He knew my papa even before all the trouble. They both were in Vietnam and caught hell. He said there ain't no honor in making up lies to get attention. He said a boy like me as big as I am and with as many arrests as I already got should be satisfied with the attention I got."

"Did he say anything about me? " Her spell of despair had passed, although the aftermath left her feeling weak and compromised.

"No, he never said nothing about you."

"Maybe he don't know we're together." The force of the statement trailed off as the meaning of her humiliation before the sheriff came to her so thoroughly that she could taste anew his cock on her lips and the smell of his ball sac and asshole filled her sinuses. The weight of her stupidity in trusting anything the sheriff said made her spit the taste from her mouth and she wanted to confess to Kinnell the true cost of his bail, but she worried about his reaction and she didn't want to get him shot over something as irrelevant as a blowjob.

"You know the sheriff knows just about everything in this town."

"Maybe I wasn't worth talking about."

"Why are you saying that?"

"Always remember the sheriff is always working his own plan."

26

Someplace Else is Better than Here

The plan to leave town came together over the next day. They had begun drinking at Silo's and half the bar cleared out when they came in. June couldn't shake the feeling of doom that had settled upon her. A man couldn't go around confessing to murder without there being consequences for both her and Kinnell. He'd end up strapped to a gurney with enough chemicals pouring into his veins to kill a bull moose and sooner or later she'd start selling her ass. The sheriff released Kinnell for purposes only he knew, but he had something up his sleeve. He always did. She couldn't trust Kinnell to keep his mouth shut. Once you started him talking he would tell you every damn stray thing he ever thought or did. When they first started hanging out together she'd know the next day when he fucked some tramp who thought she was up to the challenge of his body. June would simply ask him where he had been and the whole story would come tumbling out, right down to the last detail of how much of him the whore could take inside of her.

She listened until she became heartsick. The rage that followed pushed her to visit the whores and smack them around and scream at them to stay away from her man. She'd confront them anywhere, in front of their husbands, at work, on their church steps, in the grocery stores in front of the town hens pushing loaded shopping carts, but she came to realize that for the women Kinnell symbolized a kind of a mountain that had to be climbed at least once to prove their mettle and give them bragging rights that they had taken all the giant could give or to satiate their curiosity about the mechanics of conjoining with a man twice their size. June retreated from the fighting because sometimes she felt like she was battling an ocean, but she did decide to never leave Kinnell's side. Of course, that didn't stop the whores from trying to bed him, sometimes with her standing right there by his arm. When one of them made the mistake of slurring something dismissive from the corner of her mouth about her size and anger, cooing at him to try a real woman with a sweet disposition and a deep and sweet pussy, June forgot her short-lived passivity and spit, clawed and punched the whore's face who, before she had run up against June's rage, had been considered one of the prettiest faces in town. Word spread about June's possessiveness and craziness and the onslaught slowed down, but every once in a while some whore would get drunk enough to give the mountain and his girl demon a try.

June figured they had to stay sober long enough to start the plan rolling. Otherwise when the sun rose they'd still be at the bar talking about leaving without a chance to do so. She refused a fourth whiskey when the bartender carried the bottle to her to refill her glass, causing a flicker of hope to travel along the bartender's eyebrow as he thought if a drunk like June could show the ability to moderate her intake then the world might not be as miserable as he had come to know. June held her hand over Kinnell's glass too and barked at him when he whimpered that his thirst was far from being quenched.

"I feel like I could drink for the next three days," Kinnell whined, but June wagged a finger at him.

"You know better, Baby Bear. We keep saying we'll get out of town, but we'll be still sitting at this bar when the sheriff shows up after he's changed his mind about arresting you."

After hearing mention of the sheriff the bartender shuffled away, knowing better than to gather any information the sheriff may need or even want to hear. If he made the mistake of giving him a useful rumor or passing along a secret dislodged by drink the bartender would be expected to say something every time the sheriff happened to stop in. Better to ask nothing, know nothing, and pass along nothing.

"You really think we need to leave?" Kinnell asked as a bewildered look passed across his face. The truth was that he had rarely left the county and the thought of running caused him to worry about where he would eat or drink or how he would find his way around strange streets.

"I ain't been surer about anything in my life." June pounded on the bar, causing the bartender to look up as the brief hope drained from his face. June's moderation had lasted all of about three minutes. The bartender shuffled back over and poured two more drinks as June kept her hands below the bar and watched the liquor flow.

They drank to oblivion but decided they needed a car that could take them farther than the county line. They pieced together a list of people they knew who had working cars, guessed the year and the amount of miles logged on each model, and tried to think of what they would have to do to get one of them. They settled on Alan Ray Wallace and his Buick LeSabre as the target most likely to yield results. Alan Ray was related to June and he liked to call himself her uncle although his familial connection couldn't have been more than a third cousin. He had been sniffing after June since she had been five years old, first making her sit on his knee and hugging her for too long, then chasing her around the yard and tickling her until she peed her pants, and finally when she was no more than thirteen getting her to stand straight and still while he stuck his hand down her pants and a finger into her hole. June thought it was the worst thing that ever happened to her and she wanted to puke when he withdrew his hand and wiped his finger on his upper lip, saying something life her pussy smelled like flowers and fried chicken, or some such goddamn lie.

After the family broke apart she didn't see Alan Ray but half a dozen times and every time he wanted a piece of her ass. She had seen him, though, driving around in his LeSabre and the last time they talked he said he had a government job. She figured he could afford to loan them the car and he needed to make up for all he had done to her over the years. June thought they could go to Alan Ray's house and straight out ask him for the car and if he didn't agree then maybe offer up her ass to him. She had fucked for much less, so if it meant that Kinnell could get out of town she would give to him what he wanted all these years. She didn't know why she protected her pussy from him anyway other than he never had anything to give her in return, but now he did.

27

Alan Ray

They walked the three miles to Alan Ray's house. Kinnell sweated buckets and had begun wheezing by the time they arrived. He also complained of sore feet and burning knees, so June thought the need for a car became all the more urgent because she couldn't expect them to walk out of town, hoping to catch a ride from some kind soul willing to pick up a giant and his mad girlfriend. He had grown past walking and she looked at him as if she could diagnose a heart attack or stroke by the grimace on his face.

Kinnell stood in the gravel driveway behind the LeSabre, bent over and looking like he was going to puke. June stood beside him with a hand on his back. She didn't care if the puke splattered her shoes and legs as long as Kinnell didn't die. Alan Ray came out of his front door wearing a baseball cap and running shorts with expensive looking running shoes and no shirt. He didn't have much hair on his chest and his torso looked flabby. He hadn't yet grown indecent boobs, but June thought he looked more woman than man. Something about his softness made her think of fucking him with a dildo. Something metal glinted in the sun and she spotted a piercing through his right nipple and that cemented the case against him. June spat in the driveway when she conjured up the image of Alan Ray's soft body and tit ring bouncing through town on a jog, looking for underage ass, boys or girls.

"That boy alright?" Alan Ray asked as he looked on the stricken Kinnell.

"He's alright. We just walked over here. He's got to catch his breath."

"I don't want him dying in my driveway. How the hell would I ever get my car out?"

"Drive on the fucking grass," June snorted.

"And ruin the treatment I just had done? I don't want wheel ruts through a lawn that just cost me that much money. By the time I'm done it's going to look like a putting green on a golf course. I've even thought about putting one out here to practice my putting."

June inspected the grass and thought it like all the other lawns of mostly clover and dandelions, except the weeds in Alan Ray's lawn seemed fuller and greener.

"You like showing your titties off, Alan Ray? Why don't you put a shirt on?"

Alan Ray looked down at his chest and tried to flex his pectoral muscles but the act was futile. He put his hands on either side of his chest and pushed up, creating a line of cleavage. June, for all her experience with male anatomy, thought he had crossed the line between gross and the truly indecent.

"You can borrow one of my bras if you want to. It will be more comfortable jogging."

Alan Ray dropped his hands. "I've lost thirteen pounds already. Stopped drinking Coke and eating french fries. I'm already up to a mile and three-quarters running and I started just two weeks ago. Anyway, June Bug, since when do you need a bra?"

With a sigh that sounded like a blast from a seven foot tall bellows, Kinnell stood up and both June and Alan Ray stopped and waited to see if Kinnell would topple over. He kept his feet, but even with his mass he looked vulnerable and weak.

"This little girl is going to put you in the grave, Samson. I always knew she had piss and vinegar in her veins, but she brings even the biggest right to their knees."

"Cut the shit, Alan Ray, I didn't come here to flirt with you or see your titties. We need to borrow your car."

"Borrow my car? I'm not going to let you do that. What kind of shit is that?"

"It'll make up for all those things you done to me over the years."

"I didn't do nothing more than any uncle would."

"First, you ain't like a real uncle and second, since I got real uncles I should know how they act. Not a one of them asked me to pull down my panties and put a finger inside me. And you would have done more if I would have let you."

"If that's what you've come over here for, June Bug, then I can surely oblige you."

"I came here for the car, nothing else, especially from the likes of you."

"Well, you can't have the car, that's for sure."

"Alan Ray, you don't know why we need it. We're in a bad spot."

"I've been hearing all about your bad spots. Sooner or later the two of you are going to have stop drinking. Did you ever think maybe that was the source of most of your troubles?"

"I'll give you what you want. I'll do anything you say."

"Look at those license plates." He pointed to the red and white license plates on the car. "You see them. That means it's property of the State of Ohio. I don't own it, but the State lets me use it because I'm driving all over the foothills for my job. I'd lose my job if they found out I gave you the car to use. There are rules to working, you know, and I can't just bend them to suit you."

"I'm not thinking about your job. You understand what I'm offering you, right? I'll spread my legs, bend over, put it in my mouth or my asshole. I don't give a good goddamn about my own self. You can do what you want."

Alan Ray surveyed the road and the line of mailboxes standing like supplicants, waiting to be filled. No one else in the neighborhood stirred. They were either at work or still asleep or shut-ins that never moved much farther than ten feet from their televisions. He reminded himself of the luck he had fallen into when he had been hired by the State. There he stood in his shorts and no shirt in the middle of the afternoon, getting paid. He still worked hard and long hours, but what price could he put on being able to make his own schedule and not report to the same place every day. Once he regained his composure and the heat of his groin subsided some, he looked back to June. Kinnell had shuffled behind her and stood at his full height. Alan Ray felt like a child next to him and he wondered how he could resist if Kinnell compelled him to act against his own best interest. He could let them steal the car and then call the law, but that carried with it a whole set of complications or explanations and he would still have to face Kinnell when he got out of jail.

"Honey, now it might have been true that I had a small crush on you when we were younger, but the years haven't been kind to you, June Bug, or maybe I'd better say you haven't been kind to yourself. The days of me risking all I have for a little bit of time with you are long gone. This is hard telling my niece this, but I wouldn't touch you even if you were paying me money. Besides, I'm not stupid enough to fool around with you when you got that Sasquatch standing behind you."

"I ain't your niece," June muttered under her breath.

Whether Kinnell suddenly tired of the conversation or took offense to the slight directed at him by Alan Ray, he interrupted the dialogue by hurtling himself between them, his face twisted with violence. Alan Ray locked eyes with him and wilted, witnessing his doom. Kinnell scooped him up in his arms and lifted him off the ground. June thought about pulling off Alan Ray's running shorts to humiliate him further, but her thoughts darkened turn once she saw the grip Kinnell had on him and how he slowly crushed him in the vice of his arms. She edged to Kinnell's shoulder to watch Alan Ray's face. His mouth stretched open and his tongue lolled. His eyes shifted toward her when he knew that she watched and they seemed to plead for some mercy or understanding of the responsibilities of a State man. June barely blinked as Alan Ray kicked and threw punches at Kinnell's head. His thrashing had no effect and the struggle stopped soon enough. A look of terrified death spread across his face and June thought that State men didn't die much different than regular men, except maybe they had more regret for the loss of their easy life.

Kinnell continued squeezing until Alan Ray's bones started breaking. June touched his arm and the sensation felt like twenty tasers hitting her at the same time. She told him he had done enough and he released the corpse from his arms, which fell heavily on the gravel drive behind the State car. She told him to pick up the body and carry it inside the house. He had killed Alan Ray in daylight, facing a dozen houses and a street. Even in a neighborhood where no one wanted to know their neighbor's business somebody might have seen the killing. They had to move the body to get the car out of the driveway anyway, but June liked the idea of leaving his obscene flabbiness there on the ground for all the gawkers to see.

Kinnell flung the body over his shoulder and carried it through the front door. Alan Ray had already piss and shit himself but Kinnell didn't seem to mind carrying the mess close to his head. He stopped in the living room next to a full-size pool table. The room held no other furniture except a cue rack hung on the wall and a large flat screen on the opposite wall. A show featuring a hectoring judge wearing an eye patch over his right eye hissed and spit from the screen, but June could not follow his tirade. An open beer rested on the edge of the pool table over the corner pocket.

Kinnell threw the body onto the green felt, scattering the balls of an interrupted game and knocking the beer onto the floor. June considered her cousin's flabby and pale body for a moment, looking so weird and sad in those stupid running shorts and showing off the hanging flesh of his titties, and she thought she should be glad that Kinnell had killed him, given Alan Ray's years, but she surprisingly felt an emotion akin to pity because she realized Alan Ray had been one of a handful of people who had ever shown her any attention and cared whether she lived or died. She guessed a person didn't have many of those kind of people in their life and to kill one seemed like a foolish thing to do, even if he acted like a soft, old pervert.

She looked at Kinnell's broad face. His bald head was blood red. Her stomach fluttered and she nearly swooned. She loved Kinnell's huge moon face as hard as anyone had ever loved anything. Whenever she looked into a mirror she hoped his face would be reflected back at her, but her scrawny, beat visage gave her only mockery.

"I want to have sex," June demanded.

Kinnell looked at Alan Ray and then back to June. "I ain't likely to be able to watch you fuck a corpse, Junie."

"You fucking dope." She jumped at him and grabbed a handful of his shirt. She tried to pull him down but she hung from him like a clothes pin on a line as he looked at her to understand what she wanted him to do. "We'll go to Alan Ray's bedroom and you'll fuck me, Baby Bear, like I owe you a debt."

She pulled him to the back of the house where they found Alan Ray's bedroom, which she had expected to look like one of those private booths at a strip club, too dark and smeared with cum, but she was surprised to find a room suitable for a fussy old lady. It had been decorated with lacy curtains, a floral bedspread of pinks and yellows, copies of paintings of flowers in vases, of meandering streams through bucolic villages, and of women picking apples in prairie dresses and sun hats. His dresser and closet were meticulously clean and organized. All of it smelled like lavender and honeysuckle. June punched and pushed Kinnell to the edge of the bed, where she clawed at his belt and zipper until they came undone and his pants fell to his ankles. She pulled up his shirt but couldn't reach high enough to take it off his shoulders. He helped her strip it off and before he could take his second foot out of his pants she had his penis in her mouth.

After a couple of minutes of receiving her earnest and passionate work, he crashed to the bed. She rode him down as if she surfed the snapping beams and folding walls of an imploding building. The bed skidded across the floor, creaking under his weight. The barflies had been right to speculate on the impossibility of sex between them given their size difference. His cock was proportionate to his body and when she mounted him and took him inside she wondered where all of it could have gone. She had to ride him slow and easy because he had unintentionally beat up her cervix on more than one occasion, although she hated admitting a physical limitation to their love. She winced and slapped his chest, feeling like an insect impaled on a spear.

She hoped that Alan Ray would rise from the dead and come walking into the room. She very much wanted to rewind events and undo his ghastly death and avoid the trouble that would follow, but more than that she wanted him to witness her body spread across the only man she would ever love. She wanted him to watch her ass slide up and down Kinnell's cock and she wanted to turn her head towards him and wink or maybe blow him a kiss or even speak directly to him and tell him that she hated him, that she always hated him, and that he should have helped her when he had the chance, when she was seventeen and alone and unprepared to take care of herself or when she came here today to ask for a simple favor, instead of always trying to take advantage of her or trick her into giving him something that she could not bring herself to give. She wanted him to see how good the fucking could be when it was given freely. She wanted him to think about her love without limitations. And she wanted him to wallow in the blackness and hollowness of his soul, not that she believed a word of the religious babble she heard people talk about, but she couldn't think of a better word to describe the depth of pain she wanted him to feel. She wanted someone to testify that something perfect and good could have been born from the foulest garbage dump, as her love had blossomed from her life.

He ejaculated inside her and the force and heat of it made her shriek. She could never afford to keep up with the birth control pill and both of them hated condoms because the regular size always broke and anyway they wanted nothing between them. The magnum size did work perfectly well, but the drugstore always seemed out of stock, because, June suspected, the local boys lived in worlds of fantasy or used the wrappers as marketing ploys that could prove effective until they pulled their pants down. Sometimes Kinnell had the impulse to pull out and spray her belly and thighs, but just as often he lifted her hips with him or bore down to stay inside of her.

She would accept a baby if it came from Kinnell. She hoped to have a boy that replicated Kinnell's monstrous and beautiful head and his mountainous body. If she birthed a girl she could hope for the same, but more than likely she would be scrawny and weak and not as mean as her mother, because June would love her and that would be her ruin. Kinnell's cock jumped one last time and she felt like she rose from the bed and could keep rising until she bumped against the ceiling, somehow still tethered to him. From there she would look down on Alan Ray's fussy bedroom one last time. Maybe she would use the lace curtains to wipe the spit from her chin and then she would bust through the ceiling and the roof. From there she could go anywhere, through the clouds, skimming over the land or lighting on a tall building to survey the purposeful bustle below her. Maybe Kinnell's cock couldn't stretch that far, but she could keep a talisman of him gripped tight in her hand: a crushed coke can that he had flattened with his own hand or a buckeye he carried in his pocket for months and that he worried with his thumb and forefinger when he tried to quell the rage within him.

From her perch she would use Kinnell's power and cast spells over the populace to make them give them hordes of money or make them docile, weak and unable to stand up against the torrents of her anger. She could also make them all naked, taking away their cars, houses, their fancy haircuts from expensive salons, and their department store clothes, revealing pockets of fat, scars, pockmarks, drooping skin, cellulite, the pimples on their asses and the hair on their backs and around their pussies that grew in wild swirls to remind them that they were no better than anyone else. Even the young, beautiful, and perfectly proportioned would come to realize they based their superiority on a fragile carcass, vulnerable to the sun, unable to provide its own comfort in the chill of the night and impossibly impractical in the dead of winter.

June watched Kinnell who had closed his eyes and who looked more relaxed than a man should after squeezing someone to death. Her whims would doom him. They had wasted too much time in the bedroom. If one of the neighbors or passersby had witnessed the murder then the house would already be surrounded by every cop in the county. The sex could have waited until they had traveled to someplace safe, but where would that be and how long would it take to get there? They would have had to pull over on the side of the road, anywhere, because June could only look at Kinnell for so long before wanting to touch him and have him inside her. On the only long car trip they had once taken to attend the funeral of Kinnell's oldest brother's wife in Cincinnati, they sat in the back seat of another brother's car and she sucked on Kinnell's fingers the length of the trip.

They found the car keys and Alan Ray's wallet with a thick wad of cash, and an array of credit, debit, discount and membership cards. June thought the cards would be helpful to buy gas because the credit card readers were often at the pump.

She didn't like the idea of passing off a card face-to-face because she thought no one would believe a company had given credit to the likes of them. Maybe when she worked at the jewelry store she could have imagined entangling herself with the credit card corporations because when she was making money there always seemed like there was something to buy, something to fix, something to rent to keep up appearances.

Even though June had lived away from Portsmouth and knew there existed thousands of little towns, some half-abandoned or at the end of forgotten highways, places where she and Kinnell could live more or less unnoticed until word spread about the giant and dwarf couple with an appetite for liquor and violence, she fixated on the settlement in South Dakota called Jupiter Hill. Now, rumor and misinformation flew through the bars and jail cells not unlike a breath of cigarette smoke released from a cancerous lung. One drunk called it a gathering of tribes. He said that people had made a town where there hadn't been one before. What had been a tract of godforsaken scrap land had turned into a thriving community of like-minded souls who wanted community for mutual protection. Such a place would not normally appeal to June but another drunk said that a new Sodom had risen where nothing existed before, like a festering boil, swelling with pus and sin, taunting Jesus and God, flaunting its rot and begging to be destroyed. June thought that even if the truth lay somewhere in the middle she could tolerate any goodness or neighborly feeling that might be on display.

June drove to the Blasted Buck first because she needed a drink. She could not find one ounce of liquor, other than four piss weak beers in the fridge, in Alan Ray's house and her thirst kept gnawing at her. Her nerves were worn out as well. When she and Kinnell had walked out of Alan Ray's front door she expected to die in a hail of bullets. When she made it alive to the car and had to consciously remember how to start and steer it, she felt just how worn out her nerves had become. She could think of only one effective medicine for it, bourbon or one of his cousins. One drink turned into a binge and they spent all night sitting at the corner of the bar, drinking on Alan Ray's money.

They would be able to use the cards for a day or so or until somebody found the body and thought of cancelling them. Somebody would check on him or notice the smell, but the devil willing, they would be at Jupiter Hill by then. She blathered about Jupiter Hill, but she couldn't help herself. Keeping a lid on the details of the murder, of Alan Ray's terrified face, the sound his dead flesh made when Kinnell dropped him on the pool table, the slow, perfect fuck in the granny bedroom, was hard enough, so talking about their eventual destination felt like a harmless bleed of steam compared to the full confession she could make. Her musings swung wildly between a riot burning among crevasses and sheer cliffs, of sex and blood sacrifice to gently sloping hills of heather hosting throngs of robed people, insanely smiling and peaceful.

The handful of customers at the bar stayed away from June and Kinnell's corner, so they heard nothing of Jupiter Hill and didn't have to decide which of the versions they would have preferred. The bartender heard it all and he knew to keep pouring when he first saw the fistful of Alan Ray's money. He thought maybe he could make some of the money back that they had stolen from him through bullying him for free drinks. He didn't ask them any questions and wouldn't look them in the eye. He knew better. A person could never guess what might set June off, whether she might think he held his gaze too long at her little tits or if something in the tone of his voice hinted at mockery or whether or not he was analyzing her face for the first signs of being too drunk to have another bourbon. Silence never enraged her so he would pour without speaking, with a deferential tilt of his head, as long as the tilt could not be misconstrued that he was ogling her.

The bartender got them to leave by pointing to the clock and slowly casting his head from side to side. Time had already slipped past the legal hour to pour and he had to keep some semblance of order or the State would eventually shut him down. They staggered out and June took a long time figuring out how to unlock the car door. They stood on either side of the car, swaying, distracted by the moon and the crisp morning air, until June finally solved the key. She would drive. Kinnell had never passed the driving test and never owned a car. June's experience had been limited to driving her boyfriend's cars when they would let her and she once owned a Volkswagen Rabbit for a few months before it caught fire in a spectacular blaze as she waited for a light to change.

June knew generally that South Dakota lay northwest of where they sat drunk, but she had not planned the route or looked at any map to familiarize herself with the interstate numbers or even what states they would have to drive through to get to Jupiter Hill. She remembered how she left and came back from Kentucky and started to follow that road when she saw a sign at the edge of a thick stand of forest that pointed the way to Columbus. She followed that direction and into the murk of the black forest. She became aware of the presence of suicidal deer gathering at the edges of the road, mulling over whether they would end their lives on the State car's grill or passenger side door. She imagined them bolting from the underbrush, running headlong into the car and the last thing their poor, dumb eyes seeing is Kinnell's impossibly monstrous face as if their terror and rage about living as a deer had come alive in the form of her monstrous love.

28

On the Highway, Eventually

She lost time. She drove down crumbling asphalt roads that led to gravel and dirt roads that passed by rotting trailers that looked like they could be staging areas for landfills or the habitats for genius tinkers. She backtracked and managed to drive toward all four points of the compass within an hour. Kinnell was no help to her. The motion of the car further disoriented him. The few words she could expect him to speak receded further inside him. A few times he said he recognized something they had already passed once or twice, but his information lagged behind June's awareness so his contribution acted as an annoyance and not as help. Sometimes a detail would catch his eye and he'd say something like, "My uncle owned a car like that, except it ain't that color," or "How long you think them trees have been growing? They's the tallest damn things I ever did see." In response June tried not to grind her teeth or punch him in the arm.

They found Columbus hours after they should have and when they saw the ribbons of highways and interstates they felt Jupiter Hill had come that much closer. June stopped at a gas station and filled the tank by using one of Alan Ray's cards. The card reader asked for the zip code of the cardholder and she punched in the only one she knew. She passed the test and squeezed the trigger of the handle. As the gas flowed a man on the other side of the pumps eyed her. He looked in his 40s, being soft around the gut and half-bald. He gave her crotch and tits a good long look and she felt a flurry of curses erupting on her tongue, but she remembered that almost anyone could be a cop.

"What department do you work for?" he asked through a smile that was neither friendly nor threatening, but practiced and professional.

"Did I say anything to you about a job? Did I even talk to you?" June fired back.

The smile drained from his face. "I saw the license plate."

June noticeably grimaced when she thought of the red and white plate on

Alan Ray's car. They would have to steal plates from another car because the state plates were a different color scheme and design as the regular Ohio plates and she didn't think they could pass themselves off for very long as State of Ohio workers.

"Well, not everybody likes to blab about what they do, you know what I mean?"

"Not really. Seems like most people like to talk about what they do, unless they're embarrassed for one reason or another about their job."

June looked at him more closely. He had his hair cropped too closely. His shirt held a little too much starch. The crease in his pants split his legs in a crisp ridge as is he had steam ironed them right before he left the car to pump gas. His belt line was in perfect proportion to the rest of his body, harboring no extra calories or lapses of inactivity. Maybe the gut she had seen before had been the bunching of his shirt or a flutter of breeze catching the material.

"You a trooper?"

"No, what gives you that idea?"

"Something about your look. You look like you want to bring order into the world."

"Not really. Just the opposite maybe."

He gave himself a once over and wondered what she saw in him. That very morning he had stood in front of the bathroom mirror and gave himself a thorough inspection, trying to convince and motivate himself to make a life change before his burgeoning obesity fully flowered. He had never felt less like a trooper in his life, but the fact that this hillbilly slut thought so gave him a little encouragement. The idea that he would bring order to the world amused him. The battle he saw in the mirror was just that, between chaos and dissolution and maintaining a shred of order and dignity. One miscalculation on a design could bankrupt the company and cast him into the wilderness or one transgression at a bar with one of the junior staff who sprouted firm young tits and who reeled him in with her ambitious and optimistic plans. No, chaos scratched at his door and he cowered in the hall closet, knowing it was only a matter of time before he let it in.

"If you want to have sex with me, my boyfriend will want to watch. That gets him off." June could not keep her murderous impulses at bay. She very clearly visualized taking the man to a motel room and Kinnell crushing him to death while her panties lay bunched around her ankles. "We usually ask for money, but we don't insist if you haven't got it."

The man looked through the tint of the passenger side window at Kinnell's head in profile, which seemed to fill the interior of the car. He couldn't imagine being able to perform with a monster like that crowding him. Besides, he did have a family to consider and why would he throw them away for this girl? His eyes darted to the pump and fortunately it stopped. He fumbled with the handle and tried not to meet June's eyes, preferring to look anywhere but at her, but he could feel her stare boring into him.

"It's nothing but fun. I got a sweet little ass on me."

The man jumped in his car and pulled away, leaving his receipt hanging from the pump, which would anger him at the end of the month when he reconciled his credit card bill, but his fear had trumped accounting. June entertained the idea of following him and knocking his car off the road or into a tree or they could follow him home and bust down the door and choke him in his living room in front of the television and kick his wife to death in the laundry room and smother his children with the pillows on their beds. She imagined an eight or nine year old, maybe one boy or one girl close in age, athletic and tanned and wriggling to get away from Kinnell with as much chance as mice caught in an owl's talons.

June thought of the man's wife as older but beautiful with a too fat body for her age. She liked to wear tight clothing to accentuate the weight, a victory of sorts over her worrying that she never lost the pounds she gained when she carried her babies. She's a screamer and a fighter and when she sees her husband broken on the floor she thinks of her children and orders them out of her house. June would probably laugh at her. The woman is quick-witted and smart and figures out that June is the head and Kinnell is the body, and if she kills the head the body will surely follow. So, there, in front of the shaking dryer and sloshing washer, the woman seizes June's neck with intent to kill as Kinnell watches impassively, waiting for an order to come from June's mouth, which is effectively blocked by the pressure of the woman's thumbs. June gouges her eyes and the woman momentarily releases her grip, long enough for June to suck air and scream to Kinnell for help. From behind Kinnell grabs either side of the woman's head. From her angle June imagines that he has entered her and a look of perfect pleasure has crossed her face, a look she had seen on her own face in the mirror as she hung barbed on the end of his cock. She hates the woman for stealing this from her and she feels intense satisfaction or maybe even an orgasm flood through her when Kinnell snaps the woman's neck with a hard twist, killing her instantly.

Kinnell does not let the body fall on June and for that she is thankful. She thinks the woman is more beautiful in death, but she gathers it may be a trick due to her own lack of oxygen more than the actual appearance of the woman's dead body. Kinnell throws the corpse to the floor next to June and a consuming impulse to have sex with him seizes her, but she knows they have to run after committing a quadruple homicide.

She did not know how long she stood at the pump with the handle in her hand and no gas flowing into the tank. The man and his imaginary family had long escaped and now a boy of no more than seventeen stood where the man had been, pumping gas but keeping his eyes averted from her. By the looks of his car he had the same start as she had and probably deserved a little mercy for having fucked up parents. She paused, though, before getting into the car and stood in clear sight of the boy. She ran a hand over her stomach and across her breasts as the other hand slipped over her crotch outside her jeans. She threw her head back and moaned. The boy witnessed it all and looked terrified. He had seen Kinnell in the car and June had looked crazy to him when he pulled up and she stared into space, insanely smiling to something in her head. Now this. If he hadn't already paid 40 dollars cash to the clerk he would have run, but he couldn't just run away from the gas that had to last him the next two weeks.

June stopped moaning and snapped her head in the boy's direction. She stared at him until he visibly started squirming and she brayed an indistinguishable line of invective from the back of her throat until she ended clearly with, "And you're never gonna eat a pussy like mine!" She stomped to the driver's side door. "You wouldn't even have a chance if you were a grown man!" She popped open the door and threw herself behind the wheel. "Do you motherfuckers just walk around with boners all day?" she lashed out at Kinnell. "Cuz do you know what it's like feeling like prey all the goddamn day? I might as well have a target on my ass."

"What happened?" Kinnell asked as his faced hardened and his brow looked like a lopsided awning hanging over his eyes.

"Oh, just some kid with a cock down to his knees and eyes bigger than his balls. He thought he'd have a go at me, but like anything would happen when I got my Baby Bear sitting here."

"What did he say?"

"Oh, you know, always the same shit. He liked my titties and if I would come to his parents' basement he'd like to bust my ass so hard I wouldn't shit right for a week."

"The little fucker said that right out there by the pumps?"

"He did, Baby Bear, he did. Right out there by the pumps."

"He's a motherfucker."

"I don't know anything about that. That's between his mom and him. I do know he's an assfucker as he told me as much."

Kinnell pushed open the door and uncurled himself from the front seat. Suddenly he loomed over the pumps and blocked the sun from the boy's vision. He looked up into the shadow, wondering if a cloud had passed between him and the sunlight. He marveled at the silhouette that stood before him. Kinnell raised his arm and jumped at the boy. His fist came down on the boy's nose, which flattened under the force. Blood spurted from his nostrils as he stumbled back and tripped on the hose. He pulled the nozzle from the car but still squeezed the handle. Gas sprayed on his legs, the ground, and his car. Kinnell landed another punch on the boy's jaw and he collapsed, smashing his face on the concrete island. His hand held its grip and a small lake of gas formed around him.

Kinnell shook the punches from his hand and surveyed the station for witnesses. There were too many to fight. One of them would get a call off to the cops before he could knock them out. The station clerk came out from behind the desk and stood in the doorway, keys in hand should Kinnell have robbery in his mind. A mother or two, with both kids locked in car seats and squalling against the hunger in their bellies, stood closest and had seen both punches very clearly. She and Kinnell locked eyes. He took a step forward because he liked the curve of her jeans and the terrified look on her face. Something soft and weak drew him close. But the gauntlet of other eyes stayed his advance: from the motorcycle poser who looked half thug, half soft office drone, from the unemployed salesman dressed in a fraying suit that held a collection of stains he couldn't afford to have cleaned, from a convenience store clerk who wore her uniform as she was on her way to a long shift behind the counter, slinging alcohol, tobacco, sugar and salt. Each one saw enough of Kinnell to give a detailed description, starting with him being a giant with a bald head and fists of stone.

Kinnell stopped his pursuit of the mother in the enticing jeans and turned back toward Alan Ray's car. He walked through the widening lake of gas and in a small act of mercy bent down and released the trigger from the boy's hand. The boy lay unconscious, unmoving, his hair fanned out and soaking in the gas. Kinnell wished he smoked and carried a lighter or matches so he could immolate the boy as an offering to ensure their escape. He couldn't quite conceive to whom the sacrifice would be made, but if the law demanded blood and flesh for what he had done to the Miller girl and Alan Ray, then why couldn't the boy stand in for him, so that he and June could be free to love each other?

"Get in the fucking car, Baby Bear! I'm sure somebody has called the law!"

Kinnell squeezed back into the passenger seat, filling the cabin with gas fumes. June hit the accelerator hard and the car lurched across the parking lot, nearly clipping the motorcyclist on their way to the street. Once they picked up speed June asked Kinnell:

"How hard did you hit him?"

"I hit him as hard as a boy who said those bad things needed to be hit. I bet he ain't never gonna ask another woman to let him fuck her in the ass as long as he lives, if he does live."

"Thank you, Baby Bear, I appreciate you looking after me and if we weren't running away from a string of felonies as long as you are tall I'd tell you to take that big ol' cock of yours out of your pants so I could give it a good sucking."

"June Bug, there ain't never been anyone like you."

"You ain't kidding there, Baby Bear."

June suppressed her sexual impulses long enough to think a few steps ahead and give them a chance at escape. She stopped at a big box home repair store and bought two screwdrivers, a Phillips head and a flat head because she couldn't remember which one she would need to change the license plates, although the parking lot was full of examples. She made Kinnell stay in the car because anyone could remember his size and now he smelled like gasoline and had blood splattered on his shirt from the boy's pulverized nose so it wouldn't take much to spot them.

She picked a car far away from the door, one she thought might belong to a worker of the big box and quickly unscrewed the plates. She took off the state plates and threw them into the trunk, thinking the owner of the car would be less likely to notice missing plates than the foreignness of the new white plates, and put on the stolen ones. She found the highway within a few blocks. She could get used to driving, and thought that maybe they could save up money once they started working to buy a car of their own so she wouldn't have to worry about driving one that was stolen and tied to a murder.

As they rose up the onramp, Kinnell said that he was hungry and June punched him on the bicep. Of course, the mountain of a man did not flinch but restated his need.

"You're going to have to let your stomach gnaw on itself awhile, because we have to get some distance between us and that beating you gave that kid."

"He really said he wanted to use your asshole?"

"That he did, Baby Bear, that he did."

"Sonofabitch little turd."

They drove I-70 West until it intersected with I-75 and they followed it north. By then, Kinnell's stomach roared in protest and June wanted a drink, but she wouldn't stop. Instead, she turned on the radio, so she could be distracted from Kinnell's grumbling. She preferred AM to FM, because on AM the voices of the announcers sounded like they were broadcast from bunkers in the mountains or caves in a river valley, lone hysterical voices giving witness to some unspeakable calamity. With FM she risked hearing music and she could never hear music without wanting to fuck or dance, so in situations where she could do neither she preferred to avoid it altogether. Kinnell groaned a little when she settled on a Christian station that played hectoring sermons 23 hours a day, with the one hour reserved for a talk show produced by the station owner who used his time to rant about the state of the nation and the baseness of human ambitions. Sometimes he became so disgusted with the world he refused to speak and let an hour's worth of dead air unspool over the broadcast area. Periodically he would cough or sneeze just to let the listeners know he was there and that they hadn't made a mistake with their tuner that he offered them a moment in time to wallow with him in his disgust.

At the moment June found the station, the engineer had begun a recording of a local preacher giving a sermon to his flock. It had been recorded a week before on a hot and humid Sunday in a tiny metal building the congregation had called home for a decade. Word had spread that the station would be there to do a recording so the audience had swelled to twice its normal size. The parishioners breathed like a bellows and the preacher started to sweat before he had begun to speak. He had worn his best suit of heavy wool for the recording and refused to take off the jacket, especially after the pit stains had begun to grow under his arms. He began:

"Consider, my friends, the tongue. While it's hard to rank our organs in order of importance and I suppose some of you would right off pick the brain because what are we without our thoughts and our plans and our abilities to solve problems? Others in the congregation would no doubt pick the heart because it gives us blood and is the source of compassion. Being good Christians they know that faith does not come from the head, is not rational and scientific, but springs from a bountiful heart. A small minority may advance the case for genitalia, because without them human life ceases to exist, and the blood of our ancestors would end with us. But today I will make the case for the tongue. While actually a muscle and not an organ at all, the tongue could be the most important part of our amazing bodies.

"The average length of an adult human tongue is four inches. Four inches, my friends, four inches, and to think these four inches can bring the world down around our ears or can lift us up to heaven as if we have been given a first-class ticket on a rising cloud or on a wisp of hot steam or on the back of a swift eagle. But before we look at what is possible let us look at what is probable. Instead of us looking first at what is aspirational let us look at how we live today. Instead of looking at what lies dormant in our hearts, let us look at what is active in our minds.

"The tongue is the conductor of gluttony. We often refer to our bellies as the insatiable beast within ourselves that demands offerings, the gallons of beer, the three-tier cake, foods wrapped in paper or plastic burdened by salt and sugar, the wine of the fields, the butter, the bread, the flesh of animals and the blood of the world, a veritable onslaught of calories and protein thrown down our throats. In service of our stomachs? I think not. Our stomachs are mute and dumb. They are closets; they are our body's landfill, our garbage can, and our compost heap. The stomach demands nothing. It is a passive receptacle. Reverend, you'll ask, what of hunger? Do not hunger pangs come from the stomach? Surely, hunger drives us forward and certainly it has been a motivating factor of human progress and achievement. I cannot disagree. But who is the master of our hunger? The tongue. It is not for the momentary sensation of taste that we pack our bellies to their limit and distend our bodies? Does the stomach ever tell us what is reasonable, the amount we should eat? Does not the stomach just stretch to match our desires and our gluttony? Is not the tongue like some poor, demented addict always wanting more, more sugar, more spice, more barbecue, which happens to be a weakness of mine as you can see from my own accounting of my tongue's urges." Here he shook his belly and a smattering of laughter rippled through the congregation.

"But is gluttony the worst of the tongue's temptations? Where else can its demands take us? Carnality? Again, is the tongue just one weapon in our arsenal to satiate the drive of our loins or is it the master of our desires, pushing us on the folds and crevices of flesh? Is it not the tongue that cracks the whip, searching each other, locking us in combat with each other in a battle that promises neither winners nor losers? It is not the tongue that curls around the knob and pole, creating a little hat or a moist, warm blanket, performing acts that are an abomination in the eyes of God. Does the tongue seek such pleasures for survival? Certainly not as there are scant calories to be found in our desires. Do we perform such acts for taste and gluttony? I think not. Even a freshly showered human body has a tang unique to itself, neither bitter or sweet, sour or savory. Imagine a chewing gum flavored with our taste. Would you ever buy it? I think not or our capitalist friends would have already been selling it and making their millions. The tongue is the seeker, the scout of our animal desires. Without control the tongue would pry our lips and teeth apart, the dumb ineffectual guardians of the mouth, the idiot sentinels with an impossible task. Once past these guards the tongue will seek all flesh. I would kiss every mouth in this congregation, man or woman, not because it is an expression of love but my tongue demands the sensation. Without a conscious effort to stop the insane demands the tongue places upon me, I would fall to my knees in front of each and every one of you, young and old, and give you pleasure until you could take no more. My heart and mind always risk being its slave.

"I know my tongue is insatiable. I know that in my position of power and leadership in the name of the Lord I have many opportunities and temptations to fail my office. I can guess from the ill winds of rumor and gossip that some of you have dreamed of such a scene, have hoped I would be weak, that I would listen to the call of my animal tongue and debase myself. Maybe some of you right now are hoping for your dream to be fulfilled, that I would strip off my raiment and come to you with my tongue and lust ablaze. But surprisingly, today we are not going to speaking of the lust of the tongue or the gluttony of the tongue. Today we are going to consider the tongue's most powerful function. Yes, more powerful than the animal needs of gluttony and sex. What is, my friends, the most powerful force in the lives of men of which the tongue is the author? Any guesses? I think I hear someone in the back say singing, but singing is a subset of speech. That's right, speech.

"Consider Psalm 64, lines 1-10, which reads, 'Hear my voice, O God, in my complaint, preserve my life from dread of the enemy. Hide me from the secret plots of the wicked, from the throng of evildoers, who whet their tongues like swords, who aim bitter words like arrows, shooting from ambush at the blameless, shooting at him suddenly without fear. They hold fast to their evil purpose, they talk of laying snares secretly, thinking 'Who can see them?' I experienced a scene very similar, eerily so, as what the writer of this psalm describes. I had just returned from a visit with Britney McKuhn, who you all know has a terribly sick boy. I was mentally and physically exhausted from crying and praying with Sister Britney over her boy, praying if not for a miraculous cure then salvation in the life to come after we shuffle off this mortal coil. Who should be sitting in my office but emissaries sent from my flock, or so they said. They are sitting in the audience today. Sister Barbara Harper, nice to see you. Brother Gil Horace, thank you for climbing out of bed and seeing a morning for once. And Sister Claudia Snopes, thank you, thank you for your presence. The fourth of the quartet is ill today, Sister Dawn Kirchner. I feel for Dawn because either she is in the grips of that nasty cold virus that's been sweeping through town or she's suffering through a painful, but ultimately cleansing cardiologic episode, commonly known as a change of heart.

"So, now there are three and when I think of this trio I think of a whole host of passages from the Good Book, such as James 3:10, that reads, 'From the same mouth came blessing and cursing. My brothers, things ought not to be so.' And in James 3:11, 'Does a spring pour forth from the same opening both fresh and salt water?' Yes, the troika sits here and prays with us, lets the word of God tumble off their tongues but what else have they used their tongues for? What other words did their tongues flick out of the dark, moist cavities of their mouths, where both bacteria and sin grow and fester. Yes, they called what they had to say 'their concerns,' but I heard not concern but instead a hymnal from the devil's songbook. They acted as your proxy, as your senators, and said they felt my contact with Sister Britney to be inappropriate, considering the vulnerability of the young woman whose boy was born with his heart outside his body with the boy's father serving time for a laundry list of some petty and some felonious crimes and that poor Britney herself was not the most gifted intellectually among us and that she might not be fully aware of what she was doing. Their words, my friends, not mine. They inferred that my prayers and comfort served a more nefarious purpose. I asked them what exactly was nefarious about the word of God. I asked them where's the harm in God taking Sister Britney in his arms and filling her heart with relief, of easing her guilt for birthing a child from a known drug-user and criminal mind, of providing peace and solace and God's glory to this young, vulnerable woman. The troika said there have been rumors of this sort of thing happening before. Namely, that I have taken an inordinate amount of interest in the youngest women of the flock. I think you understand the reference, but I can't help think about our old friend, the lizard tongue lying in wait in his pearly cave. He flicks and slander follows. He waggles and rumors fly. Some of you have passed gossip through your passive lips to the waiting, hot ears that feed more flicking tongues. Some of the worst of you have passed along a rumor that the poor little boy that was born with his heart outside his chest is my very own, and that I haven't been man enough to stand before you and fess up to my transgressions, that I haven't lived up to my office in the eyes of the Lord and my flock, and that I have denied the boy a father he can call by that name. What else can I tell you that I haven't already said? What power does one faithful, honest tongue have against so many bent on tearing me apart, destroying my name, and casting me out to walk in the wilderness alone? I can tell you that my intentions with Sister Britney are honorable. I am her shepherd. She is one of the flock to which I serve and tend. My tongue is committed to the word of God. From it nothing but truth comes, but sometimes we can become deaf to the truth. So, I've asked Sister Britney to join us today. Come up, sister.... Don't be shy....Come up now."

A murmur broke out among the audience as she made her way to the altar, as the congregation needed the brief silence to confer with friends or family that the scene played before their conscious eyes and not in the realm of dreams. Once again, they felt a step behind the preacher's audacity.

"That's right. Stand in front of the microphone. Just talk like you're talking to me," the preacher said as he placed a controlling hand on the small of her back.

A nervous laugh peaked the audio level and the preacher told her to stand farther away from the microphone.

"I'm nervous, you know. I don't get up in front of people." The voice did sound nervous and shaky, which convinced the listener that she hadn't begun with an obvious rhetorical device to get them on her side. "The preacher asked me to come up here and talk and tell you all about what we done together. I can tell you that I just about want to do anything else than be up here, but I guess some of you are saying some bad things about him. He said some of you are worried about me because of my boy and the fact I don't got any parents to speak of. The preacher is a beautiful man. He talks to me and gives me hope. He tells me that God works in mysterious ways and that maybe he will reveal his purpose for having my son born the way he was. The preacher didn't ask me to say this, but I think one of the purposes for Dylan having so much trouble is so I could meet the preacher. I ain't never felt nothing as powerful as I do with him. He carries with him the true spirit of the Lord. I never felt nothing like it with earth love, you know, like I done with Jeremy. Some of you probably know he's in jail now and will be for a couple more years. He ain't getting off early because he doesn't even know what good behavior is. You know Dylan smiles when he hears the preacher's voice. It was the first time I ever did see it. The preacher was reading from the Good Book and I was feeling better and when I looked over I seen Dylan smiling and almost laughing like because he loved it so much. Isn't that worth something? Isn't that enough? I know there's some people worried about me, but honestly I don't see where that's your business. I'm doing about as well as I ever expected with a sick boy and my boyfriend in jail. I need a man in my life. I've needed one since I was about fifteen..."

"Thank you, Sister Britney," the preacher broke in. "My friends, you see that the good sister has not been harmed, is not in chains, comes and goes using her own free will, but your tongues lash at her like she was a common slave, brand her as a fallen woman, cast her out of our loving congregation, make her the other to be despised and spit upon, fetter her with the reputation as a slut, a cheater, and a bitch in heat. All you have to do is look at her and see the temptation of her skin and flesh. One does not need much of an imagination to think of your wicked tongue traversing very square inch of her body, maybe twice or three times, until your tongue felt like it was just going to fall right out of your head. Some of the more mature ladies in the audience might say she dresses provocatively or use the word 'harlot' to describe this innocent soul. Because she wears skintight clothing? Because the amount of material she wears might be equivalent to a pillow case? Did not God create that form? Are we to be afraid of and run from God's beauty? If we exult the flower of the field then why not a woman's hips? If we marvel at the flight of an eagle then why not a graceful walk as she glides across the room? And, finally, if we love the face of a newborn then how can we not love the perfect shape of the breast which nourishes the babe? What is it you would have me do? This creature, in all her perfection, must be saved. She can't be cast aside and thrown on a landfill of your own making, filled with junk created by your prejudices and misconceptions. I am the instrument of God, allowing her to find salvation. Would you deny her this? How could I stop providing for her soul because a handful of you are uncomfortable? Do I let your tongues bind my wrists and ankles as I watch her fall to her ruin or do I put them back in your mouth and follow God's love?"

"I love you, Kevin! I love you! I love you!" Britney screamed. A fumble of the microphone and the shouts of the congregation muffled his response, but amongst the tumult he clearly said, "You are my ruin, but I don't think I care."

The recording stopped and ten seconds of dead air followed, then a commercial for Bibleland Statue and Story Park, which had just opened a few miles south of the radio station. June turned off the radio and tried to shake the sermon from her head. Jesus had played a major role in her sexual awakening. There had been a dearth of images of naked men in her household as they never had access to the internet or even basic cable, so she used Jesus as the basis of her fantasies, especially the images with him in the loin cloth barely clinging to his groin but very clearly outlining the size and shape of his penis. She looked at Kinnell, who could not have looked less like an emaciated, dying martyr, but that only stoked her desire. She tried to imagine poor Kinnell crucified but what wood could hold his weight? What spike could be forged strong enough to pierce his palms and feet?

"June Bug, if we don't get something to eat soon I'm going to start chewing on my fist. We left Columbus three hours ago."

"Awright, Baby Bear, God forbid if we ever skip a meal. Didn't you learn nothing about the lies of the tongue?"

"I wasn't listening. I couldn't hear nothing over the roar of my hunger."

"It was about the falseness of the tongue."

"I don't know what that means."

"Like when you tell something that ain't exactly true just to get what you want."

"I lie all the time. You know that."

"Like I did back at that gas station. That boy never said nothing to me. He didn't even look at me wrong."

"The one I gave a beating to?"

"The same."

Kinnell mulled over the new information and decided it made no difference to him.

"I'm sure he deserved a beating for something."

"You know that's true."

"So, I don't see what that has to do with the sermon."

"Well, it's not a good habit to fall into. You can't always follow your tongue into places, I guess."

"You know I'll lick you clean once this car stops and I get food in my belly. No sermon is going to stop me from doing that."

"You have a dirty mind, Baby Bear. What I meant was more like you saying you killed that girl. Did that tongue of yours make us tear the hell out of town when we didn't have to?"

"I don't know, Junie."

"That'd be a damn shame if it did."

"I don't think that matters much anymore, since I killed Alan Ray."

"There's no question about that. If goddamn Alan Ray would have stopped talking maybe he'd be alive."

"Right back to the tongue."

"It's a goddamn wonder what you can learn from the radio."

June pulled off at the next exit. She knew that once Kinnell started focusing on his hunger nothing could stop his momentum. By now she would have noticed if a cop had followed them from Columbus or they would have run into an ambush had there been one waiting for them. They found a truck stop called the Flying Argo and they stumbled through a convenience store and into a restaurant that had been added on to the original design. They were both sore and disoriented as neither were used to taking long car rides and sitting in place for so long and the gasoline vapor and smells of cooking meat and French fries pushed June to the edge of consciousness and made Kinnell want to rip down the walls to find the kitchen.

They followed a waitress who looked drugged but she was actually so mad at her manager that she planned to slow down to one-eighth of her normal speed to lodge a silent protest against his insults and lewd behavior. Word was that they were getting ready to build a McDonald's at the interchange and that Burger King, KFC, Wendy's and Subway would be close on its heels, so whatever business they had left would be killed, then the goddamn manager could try to get a job with one of those corporations and see if they put up with him grabbing the asses of the help and flicking his tongue like a possessed lizard.

They slid into a booth of impossibly slick surfaces. The benches could have been used for sliding boards and the table an ice rink. They put their hands on the tabletop and recoiled as it repelled human touch just as it repelled spilled soda and crumbs from hastily eaten food. Kinnell began to tell the waitress to bring a platter of food filled with whatever was prepared at that moment, fried chicken, potatoes (anything from mashed to boiled), biscuits, bacon, pancakes, eggs, waffles, pork chops, roast beef, turkey, gravy hush puppies, really anything that could fit on the plate, but June shushed him and pointed to the menu like they suddenly had to be formal. June had no appetite, but she knew to order the biggest portions on the menu so that Kinnell could be spared from having to order two meals, when they could afford to eat out. Many a waitress arched their eyebrows and said something stupid, like, "A little thing like you is going to eat all that?" Because being women they had to comment on another woman's diet or waistline or absence of neck fat. Most times she refrained from telling the old cows that their asses could use their own zip code because she didn't want them to spit in her food, but every once in a while she let fly a retort that stopped them in their tracks.

As she scanned the menu, thinking mostly what Kinnell might like to finish other than what she had a taste for, she acknowledged that she liked having money in her pocket and not having to calculate the total bill. She lowered the menu to tell Kinnell to order whatever he liked because she carried a thick wad of Alan Ray's money, thinking he should be rewarded for keeping mostly quiet in the car ride even though hunger must have been gnawing at him and to make up for cutting him short when he asked for the scraps from the kitchen.

She aborted her sentence as she stared into a blue, unblinking eye, cut from a magazine and taped to a cowboy hat. The eye exploded her thoughts and for a moment her raging mind went blank as if it had been unplugged or blown a fuse. Her gaze traveled down the contours of the hat and met two identical eyes lazing under the brim. If the eye above was the all-seeing sentinel, the two below were corpulent, lazy queens, secure in their power to rule all they saw. The four eyes locked in a long stare, so intense one could imagine two taut wires traveling between their pupils. June broke first because the waitress had come to take her order and had asked her three times what she wanted. She rolled the answer back and forth along her tongue. What in God's name did she want? The woman with the three eyes knew better than she did what she wanted and what she would get. As for food she vaguely pointed at a number on the menu that seemed to have the highest price and offered the biggest portion to make the waitress go away.

When she looked back in the direction of the three eyes they had unfortunately moved along to other interests. They seemed to be tracking a young couple who had just come into the restaurant, a pair of city kids, too styled and too pierced to be locals, looking tentative and lost. June studied the fleshy face that carried the three eyes in a candid side view. She looked soft and sweet, but June thought she recognized something steely and unforgiving about her as well, which was the undertone that attracted her. Her fleshy arms hung heavily and framed a line of cleavage that seemed to start at her chin and plunge downward, far below the edge of her table.

She almost asked Kinnell if he had a sister, but she knew the answer to that question as he did and June had met them, so she revised the question and asked him if he had a lost sister, maybe a baby given up for adoption or lost along a freeway or forgotten long ago in a supermarket. She saw them side by side, Kinnell in front and the three eyes behind; the male and female parts of the same equation. Kinnell blinked his eyes as if awakening.

"That's a funny question, June Bug."

"You don't see what I see."

"What do you see?"

"I don't know if it's real and true. I'd feel stupid if it's just in my mind."

"It must be bothering you."

"I'll tell you when I tell you."

"As it should be, I guess."

They fell back into silence. June loved that they could be silent for hours or sometimes days, each tangled up in their own thoughts and neither of them felt compelled to rattle on about nothing and nothing grew out of their imaginations that blocked them from each other once the silence had been broken.

They ate. June nibbled on a heap of mash potatoes and surrendered her plate when he had all but licked his clean. When he began attacking her food in earnest, Kinnell did not notice June slipping out of the booth and walking behind him to the phenomenon he had not yet seen. She slid into the booth opposite the eyes. Third Eye ate a small iceberg lettuce salad drowning in Italian dressing with a squad of cherry tomatoes that looked like marbles pushed to the side of the plate. Next to the salad a large carbonated drink spit bubbles onto the table.

"Who are you?" June spat out.

"Who do you think I am?" Third Eye returned.

"What's your name?"

"Oh, that," Third Eye said as she struck a pose of thoughtful consideration. "Call me Janus Cat."

"What?"

"You asked me for a name and I gave you one. I think I answered your question."

"That's not a proper name. Who are you really? Are you related to the Kinnells?"

"Would you prefer Diprosopus?"

"No."

"Janus was the God of gates and doors, beginnings and endings. The past and the future. The Romans worshipped him at both planting and harvest and at marriages, which has both a beginning and end in the ceremony. Instead of showing myself with two heads I've left the third eye on my hat for sentimental reasons, as a nod to a past self."

"Why put that name with a cat?"

"Janus cats are born with two faces. It's a defect known as Diprosopus. So, basically, I'm the pussy who's looking forward through your past. I can see the path you will travel by looking at the path on which you have come."

Third Eye sounded so different than Kinnell and had such a different perspective than he ever expressed that the illusion of their familial relationship temporarily wavered, but when she said the word 'pussy' she sent June careening down a steep and dangerous descent, as when her desire for Kinnell seized her. It made her think that something in their blood or genetic makeup set off her raging needs.

"Are you from Portsmouth?"

Third Eye narrowed her eyes, hoping to cast a look of wariness, but to June she looked suddenly tired and older by a decade.

"I've just spent an unfortunate week in that hellhole. That's a place that punishes a woman for having breasts."

"You didn't grow up there?"

"No, originally I'm from Akron. I grew up in the shadows of one of the Goodrich rubber mills. It was closed before I was born, though."

"You have to be related to the man sitting behind me."

Third Eye looked over June's shoulder at the back of Kinnell's head. In fact, his upper body provided a frame for June as his body spilled around her.

"I come from a small family and I am aware of all my relations. We are a small tree with four withered branches."

"But not from Portsmouth?"

"No, sorry to disappoint. Although I've had assurances from the powers-that-be that I won't be hassled should I return, I have chosen to wipe Portsmouth off my map. It no longer exists. My talents will no longer bless the citizenry of that town, because a place that refuses to acknowledge its own needs and desires should paint themselves on that goddamn wall of theirs and jump into the river to wipe the slate clean so somebody else, some other civilization could give the land a try, to see if they could live honest and true. To deny me is to deny your humanity, yourselves."

June's hands shot across the tabletop and seized Third Eye's hands, one holding a fork with a piece of wilted lettuce impaled on the tines and the other resting palm down. June's impulsive movement did not make her flinch, but she appeared amused and knowing as they held hands.

"I don't deny myself anything," June confessed.

"Of course, why should you?"

"I mean anything," June said as she tried to screw her face up to impress the unspoken import of her words. To a woman who had experienced everything the face and words failed to titillate.

"Would you like your future read?"

"You see it for real?"

"For real, child, what do you think the explanation of Janus was all about?"

"I didn't even know what you were talking about when you were saying that."

"Don't you ask questions?"

"I don't know. Usually, I don't much like the answers."

Third Eye laughed heartily, as if hearing something unexpected from a child.

"Are you sure you want your future told, then? Wouldn't I be providing you an answer?"

"As long as it's honest." June didn't like the laughter. She felt people took her less seriously than they would a person of regular height and were always laughing and saying the things she said were cute, when she hadn't meant it that way at all. "What I meant is that most people give you answers wrapped in politics and bullshit, so I don't even know the purpose of asking the question. If you're not going to get the truth why ask the question?"

"I never lie about what I see."

June took her hands away and cast her gaze around the restaurant. She felt like she couldn't say what she wanted to say directly into the eyes.

"I fear that what you'll see won't be good."

"Which is stronger, the fear or the curiosity?"

June let her chin fall to her chest. "I have Alan Ray money. I can pay whatever you want for your services."

"What is Alan Ray money, darling? I accept U.S. currency only."

"You want to do it here?"

Third Eye smiled and returned the favor of taking June's hands in her own.

"What are we talking about here? Curiosity or the future? I could try to channel here but some of the truckers keep themselves together by being Christians. It's the one thing that keeps them from falling apart completely and they don't like me much as it is, but if I start flaunting my talents too much they'll run me out of here. Sometimes one of them will come to me on the sly and they'll act so mad or ashamed, but I tell them that I don't think anybody can keep themselves together just with themselves and Jesus. Even though I provide them comfort in private they would never publicly support me. They say a devil speaks though me and my deeds nourish his soul. They have to make everything so dramatic, but I know this is a long-winded answer to your question. The point is that I have a rented room down the road from here. I planned on being here for a week and not actively court any business, but those in need always seem to find me."

The waitress came with an enormous pile of food heaped on a plate and before June could redirect her to Kinnell Third Eye stopped her before she could put the plate down.

"I'm going to have to take that to go, darling. I'll come pay for it at the counter.

The waitress gave a quick look at June and turned away quickly enough to hide her expression of fear and disgust. She didn't much care for this society of truckers where whores sold themselves openly and the men were ground down by the hardness and monotony of the job. A few of them had taken her to bed and she had enjoyed those moments, she guessed, but she never would have considered taking money for her time. She hoped one of her lovers would stop again at the restaurant that day to kill her own boredom. Although, when she started feeling sorry for herself she remembered her previous job in a children's restaurant that revolved around a family of animatronic apes that apparently formed a band or played everything from Dixieland to pop favorites to heavy metal to acid jazz all the while speeding on amphetamines. Considering her options she decided she should appreciate the lurid appetites of the beaten truckers.

Third Eye gave June directions to the motel where she had planned to recuperate from her week in Portsmouth. She had found a place where the old man would not think to look. At their parting he had offered to marry her. He even showed her a ring that had once been on the finger of his dead wife. He said he couldn't stand to bury it with her because he knew that someday he would meet a woman that would be her equal in all things. He lay his head on her cleavage and started weeping, saying she had made him so happy and that she had driven the despair out of his life. The intimacy between them had trumped that which he and his wife had achieved over 50 years of marriage. When she didn't immediately accept the proposal and stroked the back of his neck in quiet meditation, she could only think of how to escape the room in which they were standing. He lifted his head and tried a more practical argument.

"I don't have many years left. I've built up a fortune over the course of my life and there's no one to give it to. My sweet bride is dead. I would have given her everything and I wish I had been the one to die first, but luck was not with me. I have two sons who I don't get along with. They've caught the smell of death on me and they want to get back into my bank accounts more than they've wanted anything. But they can go to hell and they'll not get a penny. I'm not going to deny myself anything. I'm done with sacrifice. I'm done with them being in my wallet. I want you in my bed and I want you to live off my money when I'm dead. Consider it an appreciation for giving an old man comfort in his last years."

Third Eye kissed the bald crown of his head and told him that he had made her very happy, but she needed time to think about his proposal. He burrowed his nose between her breasts, his face still with tears. She knew she would flee without giving him an answer, ever. He thought he offered her freedom from the struggle, financial security, safe harbor, but he offered something she had never sought. She had not been looking for safe harbor. She very purposely sought squall lines and hurricanes. She threw herself into chaos and existed in the gaps between the unraveling threads of the world. Life with the old man remained an impossibility.

The waitress brought Third Eye's lunch in a Styrofoam box. Kinnell and Third Eye lumbered out of the restaurant, while June raced around them and all but jumped and yapped, much like a small dog would around two larger and slower dogs. June and Kinnell followed Third Eye to her motel room as June drove too close to the bumper of Third Eye's new Grand Cherokee, a recent gift from the old man. They stood close behind her as she unlocked the door and shuffled into the room on her heels. Third Eye realized that Kinnell had yet to speak and she could feel her nerves wilting under the silence. She dismissively laughed at herself for feeling nervous as she thought she had crushed that feeling long ago under layers and layers of experience and knowledge of human behavior. But she couldn't get a bead on Kinnell's vacant eyes and the smell of fresh kill on his clothes. His silence amplified his strangeness as he offered nothing to distract her from it.

29

Future Uncertain

She asked them to take a seat on the two folding chairs set up around a small circular table on which the bat orb rested, draped with a silk handkerchief. She excused herself and locked herself in the bathroom. She hoped to find a door on the other side of the toilet or a window she could squeeze her bulk through because her trepidation had careened toward abject fear seconds after her self-mocking laughter died on her lips. She splashed water on her face and looked hard into the mirror to compose herself. She thought of the old man crying on her breasts, of the men at her feet, of the men and women begging to lick her clean. She summoned command. She whispered a mantra that her cunt radiated power and beauty and no one could resist or harm it, unless she showed weakness and doubt, unless she accepted the possibility of violence and defeat. Her fear would have her killed.

She peeled off her jeans and replaced her underwear with a thong that indecently covered her pussy with a tiny, inverted isosceles triangle. She took off her shirt and bra and decided not to cover her breasts. She checked her face and fixed the smudged mascara. For a moment she closed her eyes and imagined her act, then kicked open the door. She sauntered out, strong and sure, but she almost ran for the door when she caught sight of Kinnell and June sitting on the folding chairs. They looked hungry and lurid, capable of eating the flesh off her bones. She could even envision them working in tandem, clawing at blood and gore, winding her entrails around their necks and fucking each other in a pool of her blood. She didn't let her raging fear break through her mask of control.

"Why are your clothes still on?" she asked acidly. "Both of you, now. You come into the world naked, you go out naked, nowhere in the metaphysical realm do clothes exist or are they necessary. They only cause interference and static. If you want the truth you have to be honest in front of the energy and spirits." She stopped before she oversold the point.

Confusion fell upon them. They looked to each other but remained dumbfounded. June acquiesced first because she processed the information faster and had been prepared for an overt sexual suggestion. But both undressed and stood awkwardly before her, unsure what she wanted them to do as they waited for her command. Third Eye took her time and gave each body a critical examination, dangerously staring at Kinnell's penis until it flinched with arousal. She knew to be careful with June and avoid giving Kinnell too much attention, but she guessed that she had to kick start his lust to back him away from thoughts of vivisection and cannibalism. She had to remind the giant that she could humiliate and control him whenever she pleased.

Her initial success calmed her nerves and she widened her stance so June could get a better look at her cunt. June leaned forward and half-closed her eyes, as if on the cusp of a dream. She looked ready to faint. The kinetic energy dissipated, leaving a shell of moist clay that Third Eye could mold whichever way she pleased. She found herself attracted to June's hard little body with its tiny tits and sinew tracing her bones. She was so unlike herself, projecting no comfort, providing no shelter, offering no maternity, showing a minimal amount of femininity, and conjuring no fantasies. She was a cunt stripped bare of poetry and myth and the power she offered existed not in the mind of the supplicant but on the skin of his organ because of the hard and sure promise her body made to rub him until he came.

"Sit down," Third Eye barked.

They compiled. Third Eye sat on the edge of the bed and pulled the table closer to her. She had not anticipated a third person at the table. When she did have assistance they never sat with her at the table and couples wanting her services did not show up with enough frequency to warrant her lugging around a third chair to every stop on her circuit. She sat a little higher than June and Kinnell although Kinnell's height more than made up the discrepancy. She made sure to have her body turned toward June and her legs spread wide to showcase her pussy.

Third Eye unveiled the critter with a flourish. June gasped. She didn't know what she expected, but a screaming bat had certainly been low on the list of possibilities.

"The future frightens us, exists in pitch black, is malformed when brought into the present, and can oftentimes be so confusing that it is indecipherable. I am the only medium I know of that uses one of our bat friends as a conduit, but we fear bats because of the limitations of our own understanding. We fear the future because we cannot see the obvious signs around us. We live with the seeds of the future every day and only a minor bit of guessing can get us to the truth. The spirits want to help us. They wish to give us knowledge, but we close ourselves off from them. We refuse to listen because we are ignorant and afraid."

Kinnell had taken his penis in his hand and absent-mindedly stroked it, as if out of habit. Third Eye would not let her concentration be broken, although lurking in her thoughts lay an image of what she would have been doing had she accepted the old man's proposal. She could not shake the image of her sitting by a poolside, sipping a sweet drink loaded with rum, reading a trashy novel, as the old man struggled to complete a second lap of the pool. She thought the temptation corny and boring. What would follow five minutes after the scene? Two hours after? What would happen after she had been sunburned and the novel had taken a ludicrous turn? She would make the old man watch her blow the pool boy or the pizza delivery boy or anyone else who happened to walk into their lives just to kill the boredom. The poor old man would kill himself with handfuls of Viagra to keep pace and gallons of whiskey to douse the humiliation and pain.

"What is it you would like to know?" Third Eye said as she placed the tip of her index finger on her clitoris in an act of call-and-response with Kinnell.

"Are we going to make it to Jupiter Hill?" June all but shouted.

Third Eye closed her eyes on the breeze of conditioned air brushing against her cheek, closed her eyes to the pressure on her clit, the slick texture of old carpet under her bare feet, until the answer broke through the meditation with an affirmative shout that pierced a wall of static and a chorus of a thousand other voices.

"Yes, you will reach your destiny," Third Eye said as she kept two of her eyes closed. She had connected with a strong, ardent voice who wanted to talk so she wanted to clutch that thread. Her Sapphic energy pulsed through her clit as much as her ears.

"What's to become of us?" June asked in a quivering voice.

"I can't ask that of them. You know what becomes of all of us. The conduit would consider me a gross amateur if I asked such a question."

"What's going to happen to us when we get to Jupiter Hill?"

"That's closer. Is there something specific on your mind?"

"Is the law going to catch us when we get to Jupiter Hill or will we be safe there?"

"Let's break the question into two parts, beginning with the law."

The energy became playful, dipping and turning in a celebratory dance. Other voices chimed in, all seized with a sudden hilarity, and they whistled a ragged chorus. Then, they brayed that the information they would give her she shouldn't use. No escape. No escape. No escape from past deeds. Your history follows you. Your future is determined by what you've already done. The practicality of passing along such information remained in question. Third Eye remained in harm's way and introducing a dose of fatalism to them seemed close to suicidal intent. The voices grew heavy and slow and the playfulness turned serious. They gave her a sober, direct answer.

"No law reaches Jupiter Hill. It is a country inside a county inside a country. It is nesting doll kind of place. A society of its own. No trials. No juries. No judges in black robes." Third Eye stopped talking because the voices disagreed on some parts and the resulting chatter was impossible to follow, so she hummed to fill the silence.

"What about the second part? The part about being safe?" June had leaned forward even more. She wanted to smell Third Eye's pussy, but, unfortunately, she could only catch the scent of soap and perfume.

Third Eye winced from the force of the answer she received, although not a syllable of it was clear. One thousand voices said yes, one thousand voices said no, and one thousand voices told her to ask another question. After the deadlock, the voices turned on one another in a form of ritual warfare, where they competed to produce the loudest and longest screams to intimidate the other side. Third Eye opened her eyes to clear the cacophony from her head. The luridness of the naked couple seated before her shocked her anew. She who two hours before would have pronounced herself incapable of being shocked by any behavior, ever. She may have even forwarded the notion that some folks were genetically incapable of experiencing fear, or through experience and knowledge understood the very bottom, the molten core, of human behavior so well that nothing could disorient her so completely that she had no idea what would happen next. Two hours ago she would have been dead wrong.

"Sometimes the voices can be confused or they disagree. I don't think they are from the future. They haven't seen what has happened. They can't travel back and forth in time at will. I see them as our consciousness without distraction. Without flesh and bone, cock or cunt, without hunger or thirst. They aren't struggling to find food or keep a lid on their desires. They have no politics. They fear no humiliation.

They are not curious. They couldn't care less how the world works. They know no science and follow no laws. The sun angers them because they cannot feel its warmth or see its light and it does not provide the basics of their life, but they remember it because they retain shards of memory from their former lives. Unfortunately, they cannot come up with a consensus answer to your question. Does it mean there is a strong possibility that you will not be safe on Jupiter Hill? I don't know. It may very well mean that they don't agree of the definition of "safe." Safe in life and limb? Or will a hardship be of an emotional nature or psychologically damaging? Do they think you are asking if you will be inoculated from experience? Kind of like living in a bubble, to use the most common reference for what I mean. It would be safe, no? No one comes to harm inside a bubble, but how long would you last before you suffocate from the dullness of it? Is monotony safe? Would a prison be safe for you? So the point is the problem with unclear answers may reside in the structure of the question or the interpretation of your intent more than a disagreement about the eventual outcome."

"No place is safe," June muttered.

"Or everywhere is," said Kinnell, which caused a measure of relief in Third Eye because he had broken his silence. Now to her he looked less like a cannibal and more like a pubescent boy with an enormous hard-on.

"Exactly," Third Eye said through a smile directed at him. She didn't receive a smile in return and had not expected one. She arched her eyebrows as a silent compliment to his size and girth, although she had seen far longer and bigger. She figured that no man would turn away the compliment even if his rational mind and previous encounters with women told him otherwise. She had seen every shape and size of the male member and complimented every one. Some cynical men who sported smaller sizes tried to scoff at her appreciation, telling her that they knew the scale and their place on it. But they hadn't counted on the fact that she liked penises on the smaller side because it was easier to appreciate and show tenderness toward something so fragile and forlorn-looking. Any moment of pathos she could experience had to be sought after or she risked becoming hardened toward the plight of men, slaves of tiny masters. "Your deeds create safety or danger, for the most part. Every decision leads to another. Pure accident is very rare. The vast majority of harm comes from just plain bad decisions."

"That's why I want to know if it's a good decision to get to Jupiter Hill."

Third Eye didn't need to consult the energy. To answer any other way than an unequivocal "yes" would be suicide. She sought June's eyes and they locked in a stare.

"Yes, it's the best decision you could have made given the circumstances. I see many paths slowly closing, growing dark, becoming tangled in vines and underbrush. I see one lighted path, representing the only decision. To try any of the other paths would have meant certain doom," Third Eye said as she kept her countenance firm and without emotion.

June smiled. It made her happy to know that the spirit world agreed with her decision. Maybe they would have some luck after all. Maybe Jupiter Hill existed as a place where the past didn't matter, where sin melted away, where the promise of a new life gained strength with every rising sun.

"I have one more question," June said with a trace of girlishness in her voice.

"It's going to have to be the last one. I can feel the voices fading as my strength fails me."

"Are Kinnell and I going to get married?"

Third Eye allowed herself a light chuckle, thinking it posed no danger given the lightness of the question. She had heard a variation of the same question from nearly every woman who had come to her for a reading. Each of them gave an obvious clue as to how she wanted the question answered. The fact June even wanted to know surprised Third Eye, but she felt reassured because somewhere inside her June was no different than any other girl.

"Well, hon, it might be easier to ask the man sitting next to you, but I'll consult them if you want."

"He'd marry me if I told him to, but I don't want to have to tell him, if you know what I mean."

Third Eye drifted to the old man waiting at his house with the polished ring of his dead wife and concluded that she might be able to marry him. No man had ever treated her as well, not even her own father, so why run away from a relationship so positive. His wrinkled skin and false teeth didn't bother her; his hunched back and high beltline endeared him to her. Something inside her had become malformed over time, so warped and beaten it would never return to its original shape, and she suspected she had lost the ability to even recognize normality let alone live within its boundaries.

She could marry the old man. The possibility existed and she recognized its existence, but the probability of following through with it resided on a list of other possibilities between self-immolation on a highway overpass and having her tongue surgically altered to resemble that of a snake's. Technically possible, sure, but in the end she thought the old man would die with the ring in his pocket.

She didn't know how long she had drifted away from June and Kinnell to the question the old man had posed. It could have been just seconds, but she knew better than to lower her guard. The fact that she didn't have a belt wrapped around her neck or a knife in her belly yet could only be attributed to her force of will, and if she let her will waver or become distracted, their violence would rush in to fill the void, like water seeking an opportunity to flood. Unfortunately, the voices were unanimous that they would never marry.

"They tell me you will marry," Third Eye lied. "Your love is obvious to everyone with eyes and even those without. Of course you will marry and your happiness will be as long as your good deeds."

"You mean it?"

"It couldn't be any clearer."

Third Eye stayed focused on June because she could make the giant do anything she desired. She could stay alive by keeping the little woman satisfied or distracted. June slipped off the chair and onto her knees. She crawled between Third Eye's legs, kissed her belly, thighs, knees, and feet. June masterfully shepherded Third Eye's body with pressure from her tongue, a push of her forehead, and insistent, powerful hands, so that she positioned her flat on her back, legs up and spread. The cunnilingus lasted an hour before June gravitated toward her asshole. Technically, she reserved the asshole for the old man and a couple of her longest standing clients, but she felt no power to say no and she tried to enjoy June's stamina. Kinnell joined in and dropped his penis across Third Eye's face. She sucked his balls and gave him a hard and fast blowjob, hoping to make him come and therefore subtract him from any further equations. Unfortunately, he shared the same staying power as June, and when he disengaged he was still not satiated. He took June from behind as she still worked on Third Eye. After a few thrusts the licking stopped and Third Eye watched June's face as he fucked her. The love and abandonment etched on her face frightened her. She felt an urge to run, but her legs were pinned beneath them. June cried out as Kinnell grabbed her hips and rotated her counterclockwise. She looked like a toy designed for frustrated men, but Third Eye still had no doubt she was still in full control. She had trained Kinnell and told him what she liked, what technique to use, and at what speed. She could see June barking orders, coaching, and cajoling him until he got it right. What Third Eye witnessed resulted from hours of practice and instruction.

Kinnell did not finish inside June, but set her aside and pulled Third Eye to the edge of the bed so he could fuck her while standing. June watched awhile, letting her jealousy stew and feed her desire. Then, she straddled Third Eye's head, facing Kinnell. She did not really allow Third Eye to use her tongue as she ground her pussy hard on her face. June seemed unconcerned about Third Eye's ability to breathe. Third Eye had imagined dying in many ways but suffocation by pussy had never been one of them. She had to grab June's hips and push up to create a tiny pocket of air. Even then June fought hard against the interruption of sensation and forced herself back down against Third Eye's mouth and nose. Had June been much heavier Third Eye would have surely lost the battle and she only stayed alive because she had enough strength to lift June's body every minute or so and gulp air.

June orgasmed freely as she kissed Kinnell's belly and threw wild punches at his face and chest. Kinnell finished with a shudder that resembled an electric shock from a 220 volt line, a low growl that would have scared any animal within hearing distance, a bucketful of ejaculate that flooded inside Third Eye, who was immediately reminded that he had not used a condom, but that seemed like the least of her worries.

Eventually Kinnell pulled out and June dismounted. Third Eye lay prone, feeling spent and abused. She watched them dress and didn't know whether to remain lying down or to stand up and try to reestablish some command of the room. She couldn't decide which path offered her the best chance to stay alive.

"How much do we owe you?" June asked.

"There's no charge for my services. I work on donations. Whatever you think you can afford," she said by habit because June and Kinnell were obviously not tied to any law enforcement agency, so the parsing of language was unimportant.

June peeled off a hundred dollars from Alan Ray's roll and walked it over to Third Eye. She placed her hand that didn't hold the money on Third Eye's belly.

"I wish we could bring you with us. I feel like you are the missing piece."

"Threesomes only last a moment. Once you try to keep it going they have a habit of exploding in the most spectacular way. Anyway, there's nothing missing between the two of you. Anyone can see that."

"You wouldn't go with us if we asked ya? Is that what you're saying?"

Third Eye thought June had a look of tenderness when she had placed her hand on her belly but that now faded as anger and violence rose.

"Of course I would come with you. I'd follow you to the end of earth and time. I'd lick your sweet pussy every night and you could do anything you wanted with me. I'd be your slave." Third Eye felt like she was begging to be spared.

June pushed Third Eye's thighs apart. Five twenty dollar bills made up the hundred dollar payment and June balled up each bill and shoved them up Third Eye's vagina, expect the last, which she crammed up her asshole. Third Eye cried out with each insertion and could feel her temples and underarms sweating. She thought June might lose her whole roll of cash just for the pure pleasure of causing her pain, but she must have thought about the trip ahead and had the discipline to stop at one hundred. June leaned close to Third Eye's face, her lips an inch or two above her eyes.

"That's for being a dirty whore, for not knowing an opportunity when you see it, for not giving yourself a chance at happiness. I used to be like you. I kept myself deep down inside my core and I didn't give a good goddamn what happened to my body or who did the doing. Then I started thinking that maybe I'd be happier if I stopped being a filthy whore and when I did stop it turned out that I had been right. You could have come away with us to Jupiter Hill, but you turned your back on happiness. You were the missing piece, but whores like you don't give a rat's ass about the possible. You're all pussy and money and now you have money in your pussy. I don't want nothing more to do with you."

She straightened up and barked at Kinnell to follow her out of the room. When they left they didn't bother to close the door and for a moment Third Eye thought about leaving it open as she remained on the bed, her legs spread so that her vagina pointed toward the outside as an impromptu going-out-of-business sale, prices slashed to nothing, willing and able to take all comers who happened to stumble through the motel parking lot. She resisted pulling the money out, even though it was quite uncomfortable, and she was amazed that it had taken a lady midget to think of the idea. How could all the other perverts she had serviced not hit upon it?

The screech of a car starting snapped her to full consciousness. The engine sound grew faint as the car traveled away from the room. Third Eye waited another moment to see if her invitation to rape would be answered before springing off the bed and running to the door. She slammed it shut and slid the flimsy deadbolt in place. She began gathering her possessions, the crystal bat, her pants, a handful or make-up tubes and compacts. She would take whatever she could hold in her hands and dash to her car. She would fly to the old man's house. She would never tell him what had happened, but she would finally accept his proposal. This had been the end, a warning. She began putting on her pants, but she remembered the money inside her and began sobbing. She slid down the face of the door until she sat on the floor. She started with her asshole and pulled the bills out one at a time, throwing the bills on the carpet after she extracted them. What brand of deviance would allow the little woman to do this to her, someone who submitted willingly and gave both of them pleasure? The inquiry ended shortly after it began because who has ever found the bottom of human depravity? Instead of the questioning she began thinking of her new path opening before her. She would make a present of the money to the old man. He would appreciate the scent of her on the bills. She would tell him that she wanted to find a way to commemorate her retirement. She wouldn't tell him that one of the twenties had been in her asshole or that the other four had sopped up Kinnell's ejaculation. She also wouldn't tell him that she had lost her powers in the face of violence and now rape and death had crept into her life.

    She would run back to the old man, accept his proposal, and ask forgiveness for the time it had taken her to decide.

30

On the Hunt

Paul drove Deputy Auro's Trailblazer as the deputy dozed in the passenger seat, his head hanging awkwardly to the side. The sun hung at midday height and waves of heat rose from the ground like flaming crops. The good deputy had taken another oxy, the fifth by Paul's count since they had left Portsmouth. The unburned half of his face was chalk-white with a hint of green and the burned half was red and pulsing, looking like a scalded and skinned animal. The deputy had driven the first six hours of the trip and then he started drifting across the lanes of the highway. At one point Paul thought all four wheels were kicking up grass and he shouted in the deputy's ear that they were both going to die in a horrible mangle. The deputy revived enough to make it to the next rest stop and Paul took over the wheel while the deputy crashed into a troubled sleep.

Paul yelled at the deputy to wake up. He felt hungry and had been driving for ten hours with only two stops to get gas. After the bartender had told him the information about Jupiter Hill, the deputy searched the internet on his phone and found a handful of hits for the name, all pointing in the direction of Rawson, South Dakota. All of the entries were cryptic, asides mentioned in larger context, such as in a screed about the western Dakota housing market with an allusion that maybe the future belonged to places like Jupiter Hill. Another reference popped up in a blog entry from a writer with the moniker Kenneth B. Toking, who fashioned an open letter to family and friends that basically said that everyone he had known or thought he loved could go fuck themselves because he had made the decision to sell everything and give away whatever he couldn't sell and go to Jupiter Hill. The most reliable source came from a short editorial from the Gregory Times-Advocate newspaper that raised an alarm over the population of transients drifting into their county, stating that the area hadn't seen this many immigrants since the state was a territory offering unlimited promise. The writer of this editorial could not guess why these new pioneers had come, since they did not seem to have come for the opportunities in the gas fields, which had created boomtowns all over the state. A second internet search revealed that Rawson had a population of 5 at the time of a 2012 survey, comprised of 1 male and 4 females. The deputy and Paul had planned to go to Rawson, ask questions, and find the Hill from there.

Paul had a vague sense that his requested vacation time might be at an end, but he could have one of the women in the HR Department change the request to include any extra days he might take. He had always made a point to be kind to the gray, faceless women with broad hips, acne along their jawlines, and meager educations who ran City Hall without acknowledgement. He didn't often use these friendships to his advantage but the prospect of hunting down fugitives warranted cashing in a chip to avoid discipline.

The deputy roused himself and stared at Paul a moment with a bewildered and terrified look in his eye. After a moment his eyes narrowed and he focused on the bleak landscape rolling by.

"Where are we?" the deputy asked.

"Closing in. I've driven ten hours, nine hours and 45 minutes of which you snored in that oxy haze you've got yourself in. I'm hungry and I want to eat before we hit Rawson, but God knows if there's a place to eat in this moonscape."

"Let's just get to Rawson. Maybe they'll have food there."

"I'll remind you, Sherlock, that there are a couple hundred inhabitants in the fair city of Bonesteel. I'm not thinking the dining choices there are very vast. Besides, it's still over a hundred miles away. I'm starving and I saw a sign for what passes as a city out here, so I'm getting off."

The deputy nodded. He felt no hunger but he wanted to untwist his body and be away from the truck, maybe stand awhile if his head would allow it.

"Man," Paul continued. "Maybe you should have brought a change of clothes. That uniform isn't exactly undercover threads. Besides, how long have you been wearing it? The cabin is starting to smell like your armpit."

"Who said I wanted to be undercover?"

"The giant and the dwarf will see us coming a mile away. They'll be looking for the law."

"So, you're an expert on fugitives now? Tell me more, Paul. What else should I know?"

"We should have went to that cousin's house. What was his name?"

"Alan Ray."

"Where else would they get a car?"

"Oh, I don't know, dumbshit, they could just steal one of the millions in existence."

"Alan Ray knows something."

"Or we could have gone to see the sheriff. He would have known everything, right down to what underwear the both of them were wearing."

"What are you saying? You're not serious?"

"Bet me I'm not. I've begun to think I've been working for a seer."

"Oh, for fuck's sake. Maybe the best advice I can give you, Greg, is to stop swallowing those goddamn pills. Your brain is mush."

Paul had expected many things in his duel with the deputy, but he did not anticipate that he would become addled. This talk of the other world had all started in good fun when Third Eye told him his fortune and the smell of her and Trucker Cap's sweet pussies filled the air of the hotel room, but the deputy smelled like a toxic combination of cat piss and vomit and any further mention of the metaphysical pushed Paul into a dark mood, seeing how he couldn't really duel a crazy person and expect to win with any satisfaction.

Paul exited the highway and drove a short distance to the east toward a small cluster of buildings. A gas station sat in the center and four buildings formed a semi-circle around the pumps. Two of the buildings were boarded up, having previously burned. Traces of smoke and fire ran up the sides of the buildings from where the windows and doors used to be but were now covered in gray, sagging plywood. Of the buildings still in use, the first sold and repaired farm equipment. Broken, unsold, and outdated pieces lay in a graveyard around the building. Some of the pieces had lain there so long they had sunk into the earth and gave the impression of not slowly sinking but rising from the grave, as if this patch of ground grew twisted and rusted metal weeds. The other building, impossibly, housed a diner that advertised flapjacks and porterhouse steaks with hand-drawn signs in the windows. Given the shabby state of the restaurant Paul surmised the cook and owner had burned the other two buildings by not controlling the temperature of his grease or not changing it often enough.

Deputy Auro staggered in the sunlight, eventually putting his hands on his knees and holding himself rigid until the blackness that encroached on his vision had faded. Paul would not wait for him and strode into the restaurant himself. Inside looked as dismal as outside. The restaurant had a temporary look: the booths, tables and chairs carelessly thrown into the room, the walls hastily painted, the traffic pattern of patrons from a previous incarnation of the building clearly visible on the floor, and naked fluorescent tubes handing from odd angles on the ceiling, effectively lighting every corner of the room but causing vertigo in anyone trying to find a parallel plane or right angle in the blaze of light.

The men populating the tables looked of a singular tribe with massive frames and equally large heads and hands. They could have easily assumed the roles of berserkers jumping off their long boats to sack a coastal village. A waitress floated among them, carrying slabs of pancakes the size of manhole covers and steaks so bloody and fresh they could have been cut from the flanks of the cow in the back of the restaurant next to the rusting farm implements. Even though she carried food to the hungry throng by darting from table to table, the waitress looked more like a conductor than a servant. Nothing in the demeanor of the men indicated they demanded service from her, but they patiently followed her mastery like humble acolytes.

Paul sat in a booth along the wall. An original photograph hung from a rusty nail. The photo captured a grain silo with a distinct rust stain in the shape of Jesus, bearded, loving, his hands held out from his sides as if he wanted to embrace the viewer in a bear hug. At the base of the silo a crowd milled about around white tents, cars of late 80s vintage, and stands selling t-shirts and bumper stickers. In the corner of the photo someone had written, "To a fellow pilgrim. May you always find the silo you seek. –R.J."

Coffee, utensils and napkins appeared before him and he told the waitress what he wanted, two eggs over easy with rye toast, without looking at the menu. He actually couldn't remember the physical act of speaking as he may have been more exhausted than he first thought, but he figured the waitress had been performing her job at such a high level for so long that she guessed his order the moment he broke the plane of the doorway.

The deputy wandered in when Paul had begun attacking his second egg, which seemed to have been laid by an oversized chicken the approximate size of an ostrich as he kept shoveling food in despite feeling comfortably full with no end of the egg in sight. The deputy still wore his sunglasses and still did not look steady on his feet. Paul could sense the other patrons tense up when they spotted the deputy's uniform. He couldn't imagine what these well-bred farmers had done to make them nervous, so he attributed it to a deep respect for authority no matter how small or wan.

"Dare I say it again? You don't look well," Paul said after the deputy finally found the table and sat across from him, bent forward with both arms on the table. "You should eat something. You should not pass up a meal from the priestess who runs this dining room. I feel myself ascending. I am on the cusp of an ecstatic, if not downright religious, experience from the preparation and presentation of these eggs."

"I can't keep anything down."

"I expected more from you. I'm disappointed."

"What do you mean?"

Paul paused and pushed his plate away, almost knocking it up against the deputy's elbows, and wiped his lips and chin deliberately with a napkin. "What do I mean?" He let out a soft burp. "I expected more from you. I remembered you when you were a kid. A goddamn prick. Strong and fucking fierce, man. Any victory I had over you I knew was only temporary. I'd win and you'd just keep coming back at me, you'd keep pounding until you beat me. You'd just never let it go. But, sweet Jesus, look at you now. I came down here because I saw you on television, saw you get a little fame, saw you in that uniform and thought you were the same sonofabitch, only grownup and more dangerous because you had the law behind you. I thought to myself that there's a prick that needs a little deflating. I thought I'd come down here and see if I could cause a little havoc for old time's sake. I thought it would be a great opportunity to settle some old scores, check in on my old pal, and begin a couple of new grudges, you know what I mean. I couldn't have been more wrong. You collapsed long before I ever got here. I hope it wasn't the goddamn TV cameras that got you. Maybe the stress of the job? Maybe being married to a lesbian? Maybe thinking about all that religious crap your dad filled your head with? I think I would have shot my old man once I got old enough to understand he was living his life and making me live my life in fear of fairy tales. But whatever happened to you I find it disappointing. A person needs constants in their life, deputy. You're supposed to be the prick that's always just a little better than me in all things. Not this."

The deputy's eyes had half-closed and he looked more ready to pass out than stay awake. "I don't know, Paul, maybe the fact that I sucked your dick finally caught up to me."

"Jesus, Deputy, lower your voice. This is not exactly the place to discuss homosexual acts. These Vikings will split your head in two if you start flaunting a worldview not in line with their own. Not even your uniform will save you," Paul said in a quick, harsh whisper. "And secondly, it never happened. We never did that, not once, not even a tender little kiss on my ball sac. We smoked pot. Sometimes we did that crazy wrestling, but we never gave each other blowjobs. It didn't happen."

"I remember it."

"You remember it because I wanted you to remember it and you probably wished it would have happened and all you needed was a little nudge. And it was the slightest of nudges. I'm some guy who shows up to your party with a whore and tells your wife and suddenly the story is gospel. You didn't even protest and you should have known it was an obvious lie. You were supposed to get indignant and want to beat the crap out of me and reveal your revulsion towards homosexuals, but instead you accept a major alteration from the true narrative of your life with barely a whimper. You know what it feels like, Greg? It's like I walked up to a twenty story brick building, gave it a kick, and it all came tumbling down, like it was bombed out behind the façade but no one could even guess the extent of the damage. You were ready to go, your job, your marriage, even your goddamn eyebrows, it was all ready to go."

"Why would you do that?" asked the deputy, whose head had inched closer to the table as its weight seemed impossible for his neck to hold up. He wanted to flash his reliable old anger, but he could not kindle anything significant. "It seems like a complete waste of time to me."

"That's exactly what it is not. You want to know what IS a waste of time? Driving through a city every day that's sinking into the ground, slowly moldering and crumbling around your ears and you've been given the task of stemming the tide, of rooting out neglect and apathy, of screaming into the gale and trying to make people care about the place they live. That's not exactly true. Maybe the scream is for them to find capital, jobs, and stability, for them to reengineer their educations and rewire their thoughts so they have the possibility of fighting the bastards with the money. No one can stop the inexorable decline.

"A waste of time is coming to the same office and looking at the same guy with the same do-wop hairdo who records the same conversations over and over again. A waste of time is writing report after report detailing decay, cataloging the depths to which people can fall, witnessing a tide of depravity and misfortune. A waste of time is going on a beach vacation with a woman you hardly know, lying on the sand and listening to the waves rolling in and thinking about nothing. I mean thinking of nothing but her pussy quivering under the tight triangle of cloth, really just inches away, and knowing that little piece of real estate is as remote and impossible to obtain as a penthouse in Manhattan, because nothing you can do or say will make this woman like you better or make her understand that when she accepted the invitation to vacation together that certain arrangements were implied, like sleeping in the same bed and fucking without a torturously long ceremonial rite-of-passage of food, drink, and six hours of endless talk, centered solely on gaining squatter's rights to that little piece of real estate, you know what I mean?

"Settling a score between yourself and an old enemy, something that may have nagged at you for decades? Crashing his party, interjecting a little chaos in what you thought was order, having my own reader-advisor on call, spreading my acting wings, learning I like exhibitionism, and spreading a wee rumor about cock-sucking was definitely not a waste of time and if you don't understand why then I don't think I can help you. What I won't take credit for is the obvious lack of support from those who were supposed to care for you the most. I mean, c'mon, Greg, both your wife and your boss believed me without hesitation. All your wife knew about me was that I brought a whore to her tidy country home and fucked one of her friends in plain sight and as for your boss the previous evening I pulled my cock out in a church in front of a crowd older than my parents and even he accepted me as some font of authority concerning the good deputy. Hell, man, you even believed it yourself! That ought to tell you something about the state of your life. God, if I went in for metaphors I would say you remind me of all those decrepit old houses that I inspect. Rotting, neglected, standing as if by some miracle, but given a strong enough wind they would collapse on the heads of their owners."

"I thought demolition was your job."

"First of all, you're not demolished. You have farther to fall before you turn to dust. You know, I've seen people living in basements, just basements, with no house above their heads. Maybe a tarp or debris or cardboard to keep the rain off. So think about that. Everything gone, but you're still living. You won't leave the spot where the destruction occurred. You're forced to live a subterranean life. That's what we call demolition. Do you think you are there yet? Secondly, I never thought it was my job exactly. I just saw an opportunity."

"What are you even talking about? What score did we have to settle? I don't remember anything unresolved between us. We were never great friends. We were thrown together by the accident of having adjacent backyards. There were no other kids in easy walking distance. Of course we played together, what choice did we have? But I have to tell you, Paul, the moment I left my parent's house I don't think I ever thought of you again. Why would I, really? Had you not called me, I would have probably forgot that you existed at all. Take no offense to that. It's just how I've always been. I look forward. I have no nostalgia for my childhood, except, of course, for the endless prayers at mealtime and my dad rolling around naked in the dirt. Those were really good times."

"I don't believe you had forgotten me."

"Almost completely. I don't remember one thing you liked."

"Do you remember one Christmas I got a Miami Dolphins uniform and you got a New York Jets uniform and we would go into my backyard and pound away at each other in pretend football games? I remember the helmets and pads were plastic and provided no protection at all, but we smashed into each other anyway."

"I remember the Jets uniform because my dad threatened to buy another team. He remembered the Jets of Joe Namath and called them nothing but whoremongers. I have no idea why I even liked them. They must have been on TV a lot or something. I can't say I really remember the backyard games. I mean, a lot has happened since then. Why would I remember that? Anyway, I'm sure I smoked you in football like I did everything else."

"Are you saying, then, that you don't remember the cave?"

"How do I know it really happened or are you using your powers of mind control to plant memories again?"

"It happened."

"Yes, Paul, I remember the cave. I remember a couple of weird wrestling matches in there when you kept insisting that we had to be naked and given your recent arrest for indecent exposure it all starts to make sense. But so what? You sucked my cock in there and I sucked yours. The best thing about that is I cured myself of that curiosity. I knew with absolute certainly I wasn't a homo. But you know what I really remember the cave for? I remember going there myself, escaping really, when I had to get away from the wrath of Jesus. I remember looking through waterlogged Playboys and Penthouses and the odd Hustler like they were rare manuscripts. We always found porn stacks hidden away in the woods when we were kids. It didn't make sense to me at the time but now it's obvious that we found the secret stashes of husbands and dads. One of the stacks could have been my old man's for all I know. I like Playboys when they airbrushed their pussies away. Fully lighted labia scared the crap out of me for a long time. I also remember reading science fiction novels in there because I couldn't bring them in the house, like that one John Christopher series that begins with the *White Mountains*."

"It was actually the Tripod trilogy, not a series, and the other books are *The City of Gold and Lead* and *The Pool of Fire*. They published an apocryphal fourth book that was a piece of shit that I don't even remember the name, an ill-conceived prequel, but I was the one who turned you on to those books. They were my copies and I still have them."

"I don't remember you giving them to me. Those books had a big effect on me. It was like an alien takeover of the world and the aliens lived in these giant domes filled with poisonous air and they took the fittest young boys who were slaves and they had to always wear masks except in these little rooms where there was oxygen. I remember the aliens were shaped like giant potatoes and they traveled around in these tall tripods that terrified the countryside."

"Were those the last books you've read?"

"I'm not much of a reader. I fall asleep after a page or two."

"We talked a lot about those books."

"What do you want? Are you hoping for some relevancy? Do you want me to say that you had this huge impact on my life and that I've never forgotten the contribution you made? Is that behind all this shit? Well, it didn't happen. I suffered through and then we never talked again. Why is that so hard to understand?"

"Then, if it doesn't matter, if I don't matter, then why did you kidnap me and take me on this ridiculous goose chase of yours?"

"I didn't kidnap you. I asked you, dipshit."

"And interrupted what would have been a perfectly fine morning fuck. You know, you were asleep for like eight hours. I could have easily turned around and taken you right back to your wife and the sheriff and you would have never known the difference."

"More proof that I didn't kidnap you, unless you're suffering from Stockholm syndrome, which would make me the world's most effective kidnapper, able to brainwash my victims while I'm asleep."

"Still, I must matter to you more than you're admitting or you wouldn't have brought me along. Is the plan to shoot me and leave me in the badlands to rot? Is that how you're finally going to get back at me?"

"Were you always so goddamn dramatic?"

"My parents kept a pretty tight lid on that impulse. Obviously, they have no influence now."

The waitress came with the bill. The deputy noticed the plate of eggs in front of him for the first time as he had not touched them and they had gone cold.

"Something wrong with the eggs?" she snapped.

"No, there's something wrong with him. The eggs actually cast me into a dream, such is the perfection the cook has given me," said Paul.

The waitress arched an eye toward Paul but remained interested in the deputy.

"He doesn't look well. Has he seen a doctor?"

"He did," Paul interjected before the deputy could respond as keeping up the banter with the waitress seemed important. "Who do you think made him this way?"

"I know he can speak for himself. He is a law man."

"I'm fine. The medication for this burn," said the deputy as he vaguely pointed to his face, "sometimes kills my appetite. I'll have to come back here when I feel a little better. I would hate to miss the local talent."

"You do that and I'll be waiting for you. I'm always here. Next time try the pancakes. You won't be hungry for the balance of a week."

The waitress walked away.

"It must be the fucking uniform. She was ready to blow you where you sat? You had to see that? She wanted nothing to do with me and here you are looking like a scalded rat and women are still crawling all over you. Honestly, it makes me want to retch. It can't be that easy for you."

The deputy was about to respond that it probably was that easy for him when his attention moved to a couple who had just walked through the door. The woman looked worn and tired with dark half-circles under her eyes and her hair pulled back into ponytail. The clothes she wore hung loosely and formlessly from her as if she had lost a third of her previous weight. She scanned the room and acted distressed that no obvious open table presented itself. The man who sauntered in after her looked like a gambler on a long losing streak, possibly stretching for years. He sweated at the temples but a full mane of hair had been meticulously swept backwards. His clothes had been expensive at one time, but they lagged behind a full seven years of the current fashion and had started fraying at the edges. On closer inspection one would have noticed the permanent stain around the collar and a couple of buttons ready to cast themselves off their threads.

The waitress spotted them and cast a, "You wait right there, darlings. A table will open up soon," at them to keep them in the door.

"Let's go. Let's give these people the table," Paul said.

"Are you going to leave a tack on their seat or pour salt in the sugar container?" retorted the deputy.

"Har, har, you understand nothing."

Paul slid out of the booth and waved his hand to catch the attention of the couple. The woman's face relaxed some and the man returned an appreciative nod. Paul walked straight toward them, thinking his act of generosity gave him the introduction he needed to strike up a conversation with them. The deputy untangled himself and tested whether his feet would stay under him when he stood.

"My name's Paul. Where are you from?" He said with a hand extended toward the man, which had to pass close to the woman's bare arm as the man stood slightly behind her. She reflexively turned her body and crossed her arms.

"Milwaukee," said the man. "Originally. We're from a lot of places now."

"That doesn't sound like a particularly happy story."

The man squinted at Paul and crossed his arms as well. Suddenly, a fence of arms confronted him.

"What's it to you," the gambler said as if his words were something very large being pushed through too small an aperture.

"I'm a man who can smell trouble. If I didn't have a job already I'd look to replace cancer-sniffing and drug-sniffing dogs, except I probably wouldn't be that adept at finding those things. I'd probably hire myself out to find melancholy and despair. It's like a musk trailing behind the two of you."

Whatever trace of a smile that had been on the woman's face now vanished irrevocably.

"It's not as bad as all that," said the gambler, unwilling to summon his usual charm. "I'm not even prepared to call it a losing streak, yet. Believe me, I've met folks a whole lot worse off than us."

"Whatever makes you feel better."

"I want to leave," the woman blurted out.

"Look, babe, I could eat enough for the both of us."

"Take the table. I'm leaving anyway. I'll be seeing you at Jupiter Hill, so we can take up where we left off."

The deputy finally made it to where they stood. He felt out of breath and dizzy. The woman searched the gambler's face for some clue why an officer of the law would be approaching them. The gambler shook his attention from Paul and reoriented himself towards this new threat, confident that nothing in their collapse and flight had been strictly illegal, unless he counted the maxed-out credit cards they had left unpaid and to his knowledge the credit card companies did not yet control private militias to enforce their lending contracts.

"Are you ready?" the deputy said to Paul, ignoring the stares of the couple.

"That's a question you should be asking yourself. It took you like five minutes to stand up and walk over here."

"Look, I took the handcuffs off so you could eat comfortably and not cause a spectacle, but if you insist on bothering people I'll put the leg irons on you."

The woman's eyes widened until a clear circle of white could be seen around her iris, creating a hint of insanity.

Paul recovered from momentarily being thrown off balance. "Officer, I was talking to these people about Jupiter Hill."

"You don't need to worry about Jupiter Hill any more. Where you are going is an eight by eight cell in a super max prison."

"I've got a good lawyer."

"I've seen your bank accounts. What you have isn't going to buy you justice. I guess you could tell the jury you didn't do it. That would be original."

"My lawyer will tie you up like a pretzel. He'll fork your tongue. He'll leave a permanent mark of shame on your face. Oh, too late for that, I guess."

"How many times are you going to joke about my face? You've got to get some new material. I guess the good news is that in a few short weeks you'll have some new experiences to make jokes about, anal sex, bad prison food, sadistic guards. I'll have to stop by and see if my burn is still a preoccupation of yours."

"What did he do?" the woman broke in.

"I wouldn't want to frighten you, lady," the deputy countered.

"I can tell you, I don't know what he means by alleged crimes that would frighten a lady. The authorities say I'm guilty of exposing the blackness and emptiness of a man's heart, of thinking that life actually has some continuity and who you are as a child is pretty much how you'll turn out as an adult, no matter how much forgetting and running you do. I'm guilty of believing that creaky old maxim, 'Whenever you go, there you are.' You wouldn't think that these thoughts would be a crime, which the judicial system would hound me, chase me across half a dozen states, and send this bloodhound after me, but that's exactly what happened. Sometimes I wonder if we have entered a new phase of policing, like the authorities think they have physical crime pretty much under control and now they have to root out problematic thoughts and beliefs that run against the grain of their imagined society."

"You can see," the deputy said, "That he likes words, which he likes to create these worlds in which he's blameless and not guilty. The reality is he eviscerated his poor old aunty. We found her cut from her chin to her belly button. And once the docs got around to sorting out the mess they found a couple of organs missing. And he talks of imaginary crimes."

"And you took the handcuffs off of him?" the woman wailed.

"Ma'am, no worries. We're much more sophisticated than we've ever been. Handcuffs are used now for humiliation, for the most part. We've inserted an anal probe that controls him quite effectively. A push of one button and he'd be on the ground, completely immobilized. He has no chance of running or stepping over prescribed boundaries. I take the blame for letting him speak to you."

The gambler smelled the bullshit of the story and showed a wry smile, just happy the deputy had no interest in him.

"You mentioned Jupiter Hill earlier. What do you know about it?" the gambler asked.

"Sir, I wouldn't get too caught up in a desperate man's fantasies."

"We're headed there."

'Of course you are," said Paul. "What did I say? I can spot one of the pilgrims out of a crowd of thousands."

"I would hardly call us pilgrims."

"Castaways? Dispossessed? Refugees? Tourists? Whatever suits you."

The gambler and his wife silently considered their current status and the gambler came up with 'unlucky' and his wife chose 'lost' to describe their state. Neither shared their opinion with the others.

"I think that's about enough socializing. One more word and so help me God I'll set a jolt through your sphincter that would light up Las Vegas for a night," the deputy commanded.

The waitress busted up the conversational circle with a look of authority and impatience. She collected the couple and spirited them away to their table. Along the way the woman whispered into the Gambler's ear and he slowly shook his head in response and placed a comforting hand on the small of her back to try to reassure her that Jupiter Hill was not filled with criminals running from the law but ordinary people looking for a breather, for a place to gather strength before they jump back into the stream and fight against the current.

"I didn't think you had anything left in you," Paul said with a tone of sincere appreciation.

"You never know what reserves of strength you're going to find. Give me the keys. I'm driving."

"Do you honestly think that's a good idea?"

The deputy held out his hand, waiting for Paul to acquiesce.

"Before I give you the keys I have to ask you to do something. You have to change your uniform, man. I am sick of smelling your rotten pits."

"I didn't bring a change of clothes, so give me the keys."

Paul fished in his pocket, then stopped, as he was struck by an idea that made him smile.

"I have a change of clothes that I bet will fit you. It might make you less conspicuous once we hit Jupiter Hill. You can change in the bathroom here."

"That would make me feel better."

"Hold on," Paul said as he raced out of the door.

The deputy busied himself by tracking the waitress as she moved through the restaurant. If she was aware that he watched her she didn't betray it, but she moved with grace and confidence. Nothing about her body was appealing. Her face had hardened and her hair had thinned, but the deputy wondered if the oxy worked as an aphrodisiac because he began plotting how to have sex with her in one of the burned out buildings as Paul returned with a grocery bag of clothes.

"This was a gift and now I give it to you," said Paul.

The deputy tucked the bag under his arm and slipped into the bathroom. When he opened the bag he laughed. He first pulled out a pair of powder blue pants and then the matching shirt with western stitching and fringe along the front. Also included in the bag was a pair of powder blue briefs decorated with the head of a longhorn bull where the cock was supposed to rest and a pair of powder blue socks. The deputy thought about jamming it all back into the bag and giving Paul his due for a funny joke, but the material of the clothes felt so supple and clean that he knew he had to try them on. He stripped off his uniform and threw it in a pile on the floor. He washed his underarms with foam hand soap, kicked off his underwear and gave his crotch a superficial cleansing. The underwear fit perfectly and the ridiculous bull's head jutted out menacingly, although he couldn't help thinking that any woman seeing it would groan in exasperation. The shirt felt a little tight in the shoulders and the pants were about an inch too long, but other than that he couldn't have found a better fit. He wanted to feel ridiculous, but he couldn't summon enough embarrassment to not feel good in the clean clothes. He raised his shoulder to his nose and smelled the laundry detergent, which gave him a degree of comfort. He put on the blue socks and his shoes. Although Paul meant to mock him he knew he could pull off the look. He unpinned his badge from his deputy's uniform and found a new spot over his heart, just above the leather fringe.

He burst out of the bathroom feeling better than he had in days. He winked at the waitress as he strode by and she blushed crimson on her neck and cheeks. Paul almost giggled when he saw the deputy, not believing that he actually put on the clothes.

"The return of the Blue Cowboy," Paul cracked.

"You can't imagine how good these clothes feel."

"You look locked and loaded. Blue Cowboy left them with Third Eye. She said he had something like thirty sets of these blue outfits. I didn't think he would miss one."

"I feel like a new man. Give me the keys."

Paul did and trailed in his wake as the deputy left the restaurant, forgetting his Scioto County's deputy's uniform on the floor of the bathroom with the spare oxy in the front pocket.

31

Jupiter Hill

They drove the remaining 100 miles to Rawson. They passed grain silos that looked like forgotten cathedrals standing alone on the prairie. The sky felt enormously vast and the fields of wheat rolled by without a distinguishing characteristic. Finally they came to a crossroads that was called Rawson. Two houses stood on opposite corners, looking as if the unrelenting prairie wind had stripped them of their paint and the people who used to inhabit them. Paul thought the 2007 census on which they had relied for information may have overstated the population of five. He spotted a hand-painted sign made from a scrap of plywood nailed to a two-by-four and driven into the ground. It read 'Jupiter Hill' in a surprising floral script with delicate serifs trailing off the letters. The arrow could have been shot from a bow given its straightness and trueness and it pointed to the west as if nothing could be more obvious.

They followed the arrow and drove several more miles before they began to worry they had lost the trail. Just when Paul verbalized their collective doubt and asked if they should turn around and ask one of the ghosts in the Rawson houses, they saw a second sign, smaller, less elaborately and carefully painted, that pointed to a gravel and dirt road that wound off to the right through scrub land.

The deputy pulled off the asphalt and followed the gravel path. The road looked well-worn but unimproved. They bounced over ruts, potholes, and a section that transformed itself into a creek bed during heavy rains. They slowly gained elevation, not much, but enough to obscure the horizon by the angle of the gain. The path flattened and turned along a ridge as a valley opened before them, ringed on three sides by rippling hills. In front of them lay a settlement of RVs, tents, trucks, vans and cars with a clear main path, a street really, carved down the middle of the jumble. Some attempt had been made to build semi-permanent structures in the form of lean-tos protecting fire wood, wooden outhouses mixed in a cluster of port-o-potties, and a pavilion in roughly the center of the settlement that looked like a major public works project in relation to the scale around it. Near the pavilion a telephone pole had been erected with two loud speakers screwed into the wood near the top. The pole was standard-issue treated red cedar that would have looked at home in any city. Several other roads intersected the main road and radiated outward both east and west. Two other roads had been planned to run parallel to the main road, and some work had been completed on them in the form of clearing brush and minor road grading, but no order had been established in these outer reaches of the settlement as the pilgrims, newly arrived or without enough possessions to assert themselves along the main drag, lived where they saw fit and with total disregard to any larger communal plan. The outer areas stretched for a mile in either direction if one measured the distance between the pavilion as the center of the settlement to the farthest reaches of the last and least social pilgrim. Movement rippled through the channels between all the structures, looking from the far perch where the deputy and Paul sat like it could be coordinated with a higher purpose in mind, like the pilgrims prepared to build a monument to their existence, an expression of their struggle or their joy, a cathedral or a gas chamber, a playground or a cemetery.

The deputy couldn't decide if the chaos in the outer reaches was consuming the fragile order in the center or the kernel of order in the middle had begun an inexorable march outward to tame the impulses of the suddenly unfettered. He estimated the number of cars and structures to be around two thousand, but he had no way of knowing what that meant for the census of pilgrims as he could not know the typical family size of the dispossessed. He guessed the average had to hover between two and three pilgrims per car or tent for the sake of coming with a number to wrap his thoughts around, so he thought he looked upon a population of some 4-6,000 souls.

They drove along the ridge until they found a switchback road going down. The deputy became aware that their approach could be seen by the entire camp so any hostility directed toward a law enforcement officer entering the settlement could be marshalled or an ambush could be set in place before they would reach the bottom of the hill. He took some comfort that he drove an unmarked SUV and that he had changed into the blue cowboy outfit, although, admittedly, the clothes were a wildcard and could elicit any number of reactions from the pilgrims, especially if they spotted the badge amidst the blaze of blue.

In a nod to his caution, the deputy stopped once they achieved level ground again. Now that they were on the same elevation as the encampment they felt it had grown three times in size. A barricade made of orange highway barrels and two wheel barrows filled with bricks blocked the main street. A makeshift parking lot of a couple dozen cars and trucks lined up to the right. The deputy had no choice but to park his truck in the lot, unless he wanted to smash the barricade which, he thought, would be too aggressive at this point in the search, because all other possible entrances into the settlement had been artfully blocked. To the left, the port-o-potties and outhouses acted as sentinels as they stretched from the base of the hill to a communal landfill. Next to the landfill the homesteads began. The deputy asked himself how anyone could be unlucky enough to live next to a landfill and a field of shitters way out here in the wide open spaces. To the right, behind the parking lot, lay a scattering of boulders deposited by a landslide that occurred an epoch ago. Children scaled the summits and dug in the dirt of the foothills of the miniature mountain range. The largest boulder, set a distance from the rest, held a collection of names of most of the children who had passed through the camp in house paint and spray paint in colors that had once decorated their lost houses and abandoned furniture.

The deputy parked next to a Subaru, the tailgate of which held a bulletin board of bumper stickers protesting the Iraq war, nuclear weapons, class sizes in elementary schools, George Bush, deforestation, global warming, the industrial beef complex, genetically modified organisms and supporting the need for a living wage, equal pay for equal work, abortion rights, and gay marriage, along with whimsical aphorisms. Some of the newer issues covered older issues and created a political wallpaper. The deputy started thinking the settlement might be some kind of leftist happening, but that did not explain June and Kinnell fleeing here.

The deputy slipped a pill on his tongue and swallowed it dry as Paul tumbled out of the passenger side door. He really couldn't tell if he had any pain left in his face, but he figured he would be exposing the burn to the sun and he didn't have a hat, so the prudent course of action was to head off new pain before it began. Paul stretched and performed a quick series of jumping jacks to get his blood pumping. The deputy took an unsteady step on the dirt and braced himself against the truck. The blue uniform boosted his energy and he stood upright. He wished he had snagged one of those "What Would Roy Do?" buttons he had seen the festival attendees wearing because at that moment he wanted to rub one for luck.

They walked together to the barricade. The kids on the rocks spotted them on foot and quickly formed a pack, maybe twenty of them in all. The started up a rehearsed war chant and ran across the open space between the rocks and the men, like a child's version of a Civil War line charge. The deputy instinctively put his hand on his gun, but he didn't think it necessary to take it out of its holster yet. The children surrounded them and began touching them with their forty hands, all the while raising the pitch of the war cry. One pulled on his belt, another slapped his cock and balls. He felt a tug on his gun and two little mouths sank their teeth hard into the base of his thumb and pinky. They had already unsnapped the gun and the deputy fought not to release his grip. They had pinned Paul against the barricades. He realized more quickly than the deputy that they were being mugged, so he began to fight back by trying to slap the hands away. The little hands were very quick and there were too many of them to fend off effectively. Paul resorted to grabbing one small boy by the shirt, thinking maybe to hold him as a hostage until the others relented, but someone behind him stabbed him in the small of the back. Paul released his catch, but he was stabbed again, this time on his right ass cheek. As he clutched the wounds the band pushed hard against him and tumbled him over the barricade. He landed on his belly and every one of his tormentors gave him a kick to the part of the body their little legs could reach. Some in the ribs, some in the head, and another stomped on his hand. When he tried to stand up they slapped him in the face with his own belt, which they had managed to unbuckle and slide out of the loops without him noticing.

  The deputy fared better because his resistance remained passive. He had managed to raise his hands over his head, while keeping a grip on the gun, exposing his ribs and stomach to a pummeling. The children did not use the opportunity but patted and probed, turned out every pocket, relieved him of his belt, wallet, keys, pills and deputy's badge without him knowing how thoroughly they had robbed him. Blood trickled down his hand from the bite marks. With his finger he felt the gun and found in the tug-of-war the safety had been switched off. It easily could have fired and he would have been responsible for shooting a child not much older than his own. He spotted Paul prone on the ground and the blood on his back and decided he needed to end the attack. He squeezed the trigger twice and the resulting explosions froze the children. They rued the missed opportunity of smashing the deputy's ribs when they had the chance. It was a mistake, they promised themselves, they would never make again. They took a couple of steps back from the deputy, providing enough space for him to lower his arms and point the gun at their heads. They ran in every direction and were gone as quickly as they had come.

The deputy felt his turned out pockets and discovered he had been robbed. He looked to the ground to see if anything had been dropped, but he found only the tracks of the pack. He walked over to Paul and helped him to his feet and asked him to turn so he could inspect at least one of the wounds. He lifted his shirt and found that he had been stabbed deeper than he expected. The deputy had seen enough wounds, especially of the stabbing variety, to be reasonably sure the blade had caught only flesh and missed any organs.

"Just ball up your shirt and press right here. Maybe one of these people will give us a bandage."

"I'm going to break the neck of the little cocksucker that did this to me."

"Drop it. You don't know which one stabbed you and you start calling other people's children cocksuckers the family tends to close ranks and you won't get much sympathy and less satisfaction."

"The whole camp had to hear those gun shots."

"And I bet I'm not the only one with a gun." The deputy saw movement in his periphery and he turned his head. "And almost on cue, look what we have here."

Two men, one older and the other not much past his first shave, walked toward them holding shotguns pointed at the ground. The deputy thought they looked more scared than intimidating, and he realized he still held his pistol in his hand, so he slowly raised the gun and slipped it back in his holster. As he performed the action, the deputy noticed the men slowed their steps and raised their shotguns enough so that a shot would land in the knees and thighs of their targets. The deputy squared his shoulders to them and let his hands hang loosely at his side.

"I didn't come here to start trouble amongst honest folks. I've been on the trail of a fugitive from justice, someone's who's confessed to murder, but we seemed to have fun afoul of our welcoming committee. My partner here has been stabbed in the back and ass. It's not what I expected. I had guessed the encampment defied zoning laws, but I didn't expect you all to be a band of outlaws, letting your kids just stab anybody for no reason. Paul, turn around and show these men I'm not lying to them."

Paul did what he was told and moved his balled-up shirt away from the wound. As the men eyed his injury he inspected the shirt to see how much blood had soaked in. Not as much as he thought had and the pain from the wound seemed out of proportion to the damage that had been done. The men looked at each other and shook their heads. They lowered their shotguns.

"Those little fuckers are getting out of control," the younger one said. "Cody best not have been involved in this or I'm going to whup his ass."

"I told you. I think some of this is hardest on the kids. What kind of example are we setting for them?" the older one responded. "They's just kids looking for a structure."

"Don't give them the right to go around stabbing people. One of them is going to get themselves killed, that's all I'm saying."

"Follow me. My wife worked as a nurse's aide for a while. She can dress a wound like nobody's business. Course, the boss will be needing to see you first. You ain't going to die from that wound."

They led them past the barricade to the main thoroughfare. The impression gleaned from the aerial view proved to be correct. This area of the encampment was highly organized as permanency looked to be gaining hold and spreading. The first site to the right consisted of a camper trailer with flat tires but chocked with cement blocks anyway. An indoor/outdoor carpet runner ran from the side door to two plastic Grecian urn planters decorated with faux patina that held lusty bouquets of peonies. A cloth awning with a massive logo of the University of Oklahoma emblazoned across it had been attached to the side of the camper. The dirt around the site had been freshly broomed, the scrub grass picked clean, and the side of the camper washed and waxed. A woman stood in the shadow of the awning near the door, broom in hand, and watched the procession pass. She looked impossibly clean with carefully combed hair and makeup in place. However, she did wear enormous sunglasses that gave her the look of an insect, protection for living the majority of one's life outdoors in the blazing sun. The deputy compared the men to her and they came out looking far shabbier and dirtier than he first thought. Their clothes had begun to wear and fray and their sunburnt skin had been abused by wind and dust along with the sun.

The other properties near the first looked equally clean and kept. Some residents had hung strings of lights along their awnings although one wondered how often they were illuminated given the lack of an established power grid. Others had paper lanterns holding candles. Each had a symbol from the owner's state of origin or affection and a nostalgic call and response bounced along the main road. Oklahoma's neighbor had planted a sign made to resemble a metal road sign that read

"Don't Mess with Texas" across an outline of the state and the requisite red star underneath. Another flew the Delaware state flag, which, to remind everyone of its status as the first state of the union, had the date of ratification , December 7, 1787, inscribed along the bottom of the flag. Next to Delaware hung a Nashville city limits sign. As their escort picked up the pace of their walking several stopped what they were doing to watch them pass. Everyone had heard the shots and wanted to know if they could expect trouble. Maybe the deputy's blue suit gave them comfort or peaked their interest because some of the residents joined the procession at a cautious ten yards behind. More states and cities sounded off: an Ohio State Buckeyes flag with a gray "O" in a field of scarlet, a Wyoming bucking bronco, a Minnesota Vikings flag, a Chicago Cubs pennant, a group of grinning ears of corn that spelled Iowa, a Florida Gators mascot and others who had no loyalty to a city or state but flew the colors of NASCAR drivers, skiing, surfing and video games.

They stepped under the shadow of the pavilion. The structure had been built by skilled hands as the supports were deeply embedded and cemented into the ground and the lines were plum and true. The ceiling soared above them like a rustic, Wolmanized cathedral. They walked past a swarm of flies that fed on offal. Under the roof the pilgrims had collected a variety of furniture, picnic tables, lawn chairs, benches, card tables, banquet tables, pews, and even a massive La-Z-Boy recliner left in a fully reclined position, which had gone threadbare along the arms. The escort led them to the center of the pavilion and asked them to sit at a round banquet table that looked like it could comfortably hold ten. A warp rippled across the surface and in the middle of the table a liter bottle of wine had been repurposed as a candleholder. The nub of candle it held looked homemade as twenty streaks of color cascaded down the bottle slope and terminated in a frozen pool around the candle base. The deputy and Paul sat next to each other on metal folding chairs, leaving a wide expanse for a tribunal to be seated.

The escorts nodded to them and left without another word. Paul looked behind him and then scanned in all directions. The crowd that had followed them had stopped at the pavilion's edge and now milled about in a loose circle. The two men with the shotguns joined them and the circle closed ranks to listen to the news.

"Those little fuckers cut me good," said Paul as tightened the ball of his shirt over the wound.

The deputy thought he looked more pathetic and weak than most men without a shirt. A softness had crept into him, something the deputy hadn't expected.

"Let's refrain from calling them names, shall we? They're people's kids and they're going to take offense," the deputy repeated.

"That boy called them the same thing."

"He's family. He can say whatever he pleases. You know what I'm talking about."

"The little darlings, then, had intent to kill. Let's get out of here."

"Did they leave you with a wallet? Did they leave you my keys? We're not going anywhere unless they want us to."

"You have a gun, deputy, and a uniform of sorts. You are the law."

"Right, I'm the reincarnation of Roy Rogers. I'll just blast our way out of here with four bullets. I've counted two shotguns so far and I'm thinking every homestead has one of two, so I'm no thinking the gun is not going to be much use in getting us out of here."

"Let's fucking walk then. You could go to the nearest town and get some backup."

"Rawson? Should we go there? We could probably borrow their helicopter or urban assault vehicle. That's if we can find it again. That's not a bad idea."

"You're not very resourceful for being a cop."

"I know when not to panic, if that's what you mean? This isn't a motorcycle gang, Paul."

"Ya, the Hell's Angels would never let their children stab you."

"They didn't cut your throat for God's sake. Can you stop whining? It's not helping anything."

A man with a shambling gait broke away from the group of onlookers and approached them. He was very tall and thin and moved by throwing a collection of angles and planes before him. He broke into an easy grin as he walked. The deputy had put his hand on his gun but let it slide off once he determined the man did not carry a weapon, unless it was enclosed in a the small plastic bag that he held with his skeletal fingers.

"Gentlemen, welcome, welcome." His voice cracked the silence with resonance and force. He shook their hands and slid into a chair across the table from them. He threw the bag near the center next to the candle. "This should be all the belongings the children took from you. Count the money if you need to but I can assure you nothing was stolen. The children invent games to fight off boredom. They usually turn on each other and we let them work out their pecking order. It was like they saw fresh meat when they saw the two of you get out of your truck."

"One of your little angels sliced me open," Paul broke in.

"That's a dramatic turn of phrase. I have the offending weapon right here." He leaned back and fished a pocket knife from his pocket. Once he had it in his hand he straightened his back and opened the knife, revealing a dull and rounded blade, resembling a butter knife more than anything else. "As you can see it's not exactly lethal. I'm actually surprised it broke the skin."

"You want to see the wound?" Paul seethed.

"There's no reason to get upset. I talked to the boy himself. He didn't mean to cut you. He was trying a new technique of cutting the back pocket to get your wallet out and you backed into the blade when you were throwing wild punches at them. For the record I believe him. He knows there's nothing to be gained by hurting a new arrival or visitor. He's old enough to understand that. He's been taught that."

"What kind of place is this? The deputy said as he thought of the Subaru with the left-leaning bumper stickers. "Are you trying to start a commune or something?"

A look of confusion passed across the man's face as he searched for reasons the deputy would ask such a ridiculous question. "I think you might be off a few decades with that question. This aims to be no utopia and we're not setting in place a theoretical way of living. You ask me what kind of place this is? I'd say it has more in common with a refugee camp than anything else."

"Refugees from what?" the deputy asked. Paul noticed a hint of the old sneering tone in his voice.

The man caught the tone as well and paused before speaking, working his jaw side to side and closing his eyes halfway in an act of open insolence. "Why have you come to our community and why are you wearing a powder blue suit?"

"We have reason to believe a man and a woman we are tracking came to this location."

"We both know that you have no jurisdiction in South Dakota, Deputy. Besides, within these boundaries we don't recognize the government or its laws. It's a free land."

"You've managed to secede from the union, have you? I'm not surprised that the U.S. government let this piece of godforsaken scrub land go and all of its inhabitants. I mean, it's not like we're losing a bunch of Nobel Laureates, am I right/ The nation might experience a sudden shortage of dishwashers and landscape workers, but we'll survive," said the deputy.

Paul marveled at his summoning a reservoir of inner strength and letting the sarcasm fly, something he had not expected.

"The fact is you are a deputy of Scioto County in Ohio and this is neither Scioto County nor Ohio."

"It's pronounced SEE-O-TOE," interjected Paul.

"So you employ the children as spies?"

"It's on your damn badge, Deputy! The one you were wearing on your chest! You don't have to be much of a spy to figure that one out. I imagine you have a hard time getting the populace to take you seriously wearing a get-up like that."

"We're looking for a bald-headed giant and his violent mate, closest thing to a midget you'd ever want to touch," said Paul.

The man refused to look Paul's way.

"We don't control who comes and goes. There's no police force, zoning, or census-taking."

"Men with shotguns look close enough to a police force."

The man laughed through his nose. "Harvey and Rob have one shotgun shell between them and I think they found it in the dirt after someone fled the camp. If you would have pointed your gun at them I think they would have run. We have ex-military here, a lot of them, I think, but those two have never been trained and never shot a gun in anger."

"So you all are just a collection of common folk, huh? Never mind the stabbing and pointing shotguns at an officer of the law."

The man finally looked Paul's way and took measure of him.

"You are obviously not a cop. You're not even wearing one of them cute blue uniforms, so what's your role in this chase of the giant and his diminutive master?"

"I'm an interested party."

"I can tell you no such couple has come to this part of the camp. Of course, I can't vouch for the outer areas. If you would have come from the southern entrance you would have run smack into chaos. Those areas are mostly populated by single men that have somehow drifted here. They might be on their way to North Dakota to the gas fields. Sometimes they move on when they get work or promise of work, but the desperate ones and the losers get stuck here. Sometimes one of them will come in and beg for something when they reach the end of their endurance, but most of the time we don't have much interaction with them."

"What makes you so different from them?" asked the deputy.

"I never said I was any different. It's just a matter of circumstances and what you've managed to hold on to before you left. Folks have maybe abandoned their lives when they still had something to bring with them. Maybe they were still married, maybe they still had some money squirreled away in a coffee can, but they could do the accounting and knew it wouldn't last long trying to keep up a home and a certain lifestyle. Maybe they still had their car or had made enough payments on their RV to make it worth their while to take it. They might have even gotten lucky and sold their house and made some of the money back they put into. They kept something. Maybe just enough love to see them through. I've seen the best marriages since I've been out here. You couldn't pry them apart with a crowbar. I've also made the best friends I've ever had. There's a different level of intimacy that comes when you're all in the same boat. All the bullshit falls away. Nobody's worried about appearances or what college their kid is going to get into. They don't brag about their work and don't tell you about their cool vacations on remote beaches. Their leisure time is spent surviving so they don't talk about TV or the games they watched. They only have themselves to talk about and how they are going to get through the next day. The people in the outlands have not been so lucky. They tried to stick in the old life until they had absolutely nothing left. First went the jobs and then their savings and 401Ks, if they had any, and the college funds and then they ran up their credit cards to the hilt. Then their families took off or they ran away from their families because they were too humiliated to confess they had run out of ideas and cash. Some of them lost their health or their sanity or their ability to stay away from a bottle. Those men sleeping in the outlands aren't much more than carcasses, if you ask me. They're living, that's something, I guess, and there is still hope if you are drawing breath. But, let me tell you, when you get done talking to them you don't feel much hope for the country."

"So why are you talking this much? Why all the detail?" the deputy asked as he could feel himself getting tired again and losing his edge. The words had a dulling effect on his senses. "You've not seen the giant?"

"Deputy, I have to tell you that asking questions like that make you sound a touch crazy."

"It's a shortcut to asking whether you've seen a very large man, well over 6'8" and 450 pounds, with a massive bald head and hands that look like they could crush coconuts in their grip."

"Shouldn't be hard to find someone like that."

"The question still remains."

"I've not seen him. You are, of course, free to move about the camp as a citizen. You are a free man in a free land, because, as we both know, you are outside of your jurisdiction. I have to warn you, though, I worry that your uniform is going to bring you unwanted attention. Everybody is going to worry you've come for them. I mean, who hasn't had the nightmare of a sparkling cowboy come to arrest them for crimes real or imagined? We are all guilty in one form or another. Crimes have been committed."

"Let me worry about that."

"That is what I will do. Remember, your belongings are in the bag. We don't want to be accused of stealing from the law." The man unfolded himself and stood up. "What could these people have done, really? That you would have to chase them to the very end of the earth. They're not going to hurt society while they are here. I mean, this might be as good as any prison except you are reminded of the vastness and the limitlessness of the world every day, instead of the closeness and meanness. This is like a voluntary gulag and the only way out is to learn that all the shit you cared about before you came didn't mean a thing. You leave once you understand that only compassion matters. Tell me, are you offering the same chance for rehabilitation to the giant and his little mistress?"

"First it's a refugee camp and now it's a gulag. Next, you're going to tell us it's going to be the site of Walt Disney World, South Dakota," said Paul.

"You ever meet a person and know immediately that you don't like them and never will? You're that person for me," the man shot back.

"Surprisingly, he gets that a lot," the deputy said through a grin.

"It's just that you are confusing me. A refugee camp and a gulag are two very different kind of camps. Refugees are victims of a cataclysm, a drought, an earthquake, war, ethnic violence while prisoners of a gulag have been put there by a government or a political faction. They are considered criminals by someone, whether it's fair and just or not. In some cases the same could be said of refugees, but I think of it as an uprooting of whole cities or regimes or ethnicities. A gulag is a collection of individuals brought together by real or trumped-up charges. A refugee camp in usually on neutral territory, I think, while I think a gulag rests in the very bowels of a government. One is open tragedy and the other houses dark secrets and evil impulses."

"I'm much obliged for the lesson in wordsmithing. You're going to find it's not much use around here, unless you want to tell stories to the children. We're had more than our share of lawyers come through, drunks mostly, careers in flames and families long gone. You had to feel some pity for the poor bastards who tried to practice their trade here. It seems they didn't think that most everybody who's washed up here has run afoul of contracts and agreements crafted by lawyers. If we could have afforded tar and feathers we would have restarted the tradition, but as it was we just sent them to the outlands. We also had a couple of reporters visit us, one from France and the other from Argentina. They were cut loose in the country and I think they found us by accident. I guess we were a big story in Buenos Aires, a feature in a Sunday magazine. Death of American promise, that sort of thing."

"He talked to Diana Sawyer and Wolf Blitzer," Paul said as he jerked his thumb in the deputy's direction.

"You don't say," the man said without enthusiasm.

"He found a skull. I know when you say it out loud it doesn't sound that impressive, but this man caught the zeitgeist of the country for a full twelve minutes."

"I didn't find it. I just responded to the discovery. A man working a gravel pit actually found it."

"Right, even less impressive or interesting, if you were to ask me."

"I'm not the one who decided it should be on television," the deputy said defensively.

"Well, we haven't the pleasure of being visited by the networks, but if I see someone holding a camera I'll sic the children on them. This is the underground and most of the people here don't take kindly to being photographed." He broke away from them with a nod and walked toward the group of onlookers, which had grown more boisterous.

Paul thought of a lynch mob and projected that if they were killed who would know to look in a pilgrim's settlement outside Rawson, South Dakota for their bodies? Neither he nor the deputy had told anyone they were coming to this wasteland.

"What do you want to do now?" Paul asked the deputy.

"I want to go find Kinnell and his girlfriend and take them back to Portsmouth. What else would I want to do?"

"I don't know, leave. Go back to your life and your job. News of your purpose here is going to spread. That group of gossips over there are going to tell everyone and Kinnell could run and hide for the next year to come and you wouldn't find him."

"It doesn't make sense to turn around now. I'm going to drive all the way to South Dakota just to turn around the first hour we get here without even trying?"

"It's been my experience that logic can lead you to a whole host of bad decisions."

"You can sit here if you want. I have to get this done," he said as he stood up. "And get back to my wife and kids." Even the deputy knew he had struck a false note. He had not thought of his children for several hours, probably the whole of the trip, and felt no urgency to rush back to them or his wife. He knew the sheriff had told her what he knew about Sabine and given Jenny's sudden anger he may know a whole lot more than the deputy ever suspected he could. Sabine could have told him every detail of the affair. Whatever the depth of her knowledge, his wife owed him an unpleasant conversation and he had no reason to want that to happen sooner than absolutely necessary.

He pulled his wallet and keys out of the plastic. He didn't count his money because he didn't know how much he had when the children accosted them. He pinned the deputy's star on his chest as he waited for Paul to exploit his falseness but Paul stayed silent and watched the crowd disperse, no doubt taking the information about them to every corner of the camp. Paul knew not to split up from the deputy, who had the gun and experience. Almost anything could happen to him if they split up, so he thought. Of course, he wouldn't tell the deputy he needed his protection and he made a big show of acquiescing to his lead by moaning and lurching off the bench.

"I've come this far. Why not see it to the end?" he said as he touched his back wound. "What happened to that guy who said his wife could bandage me up?"

"They forgot about you. They're hoping for infection to weaken our ranks."

"Your default personality is that of an asshole."

They walked from underneath the pavilion into the sunlight. The air felt hotter by ten degrees in the sun and the light made them wince. The deputy staggered to a stop and reached out a hand to grab something. The closest something was Paul, who stepped away from the grasping hand. Paul recovered first and he watched the deputy as he bent over with his hand on his knees until his pupils reacted.

"I can drive the entire way back to Portsmouth with just a couple of piss breaks. You don't have to tell anyone you went to South Dakota. Tell them you blacked-out and remember nothing since you left Indian Head Rock."

"I told you about that?"

"Six times."

The deputy opened the gun and replaced the two bullets he had sent scaring the children. He stood up and tested his equilibrium. He continued walking and Paul followed. The main strip continued south for a hundred yards then dissipated in a jumble of tents and campers. They passed two semi-truck trailers lying flat on the ground without wheels. The doors on the end of the first trailer had been welded shut, but a smaller person-sized door had been cut in the side and a sheet of rubber, cut into vertical strips, hung over the opening. Two windows had also been cut in the side and translucent plastic covered both. Underneath the windows hung window boxes crammed with small pepper and tomato plants. Across the side STEVENS TRANSPORT had been painted in six foot white letters, although the door and windows cut-outs now hampered easy cognition of the words. The entire trailer had been painted a deep ochre, which helped mask the streaks of rust.

The second trailer had once carried grain and the stainless steel skin gleamed in the sun. The walls tapered out at the bottom and the deputy could see no visible doorway, but he did spot a ladder skimming up the side and ending at an open hatch on the top. The wheels had also been removed and even though it had been planted in the ground it retained an aura of sleek mobility, whereas the STEVENS trailer only lacked a pitched roof to approximate the feel of a small ranch house. A head emerged from the hatch but stayed briefly in the open before disappearing again, as if thrown back into the depths of the trailer by the sun. The deputy first likened it to a silver coffin suitable for a mass burial, but he thought the owners might be the envy of the camp come winter when the wind roared through the tents and shredded everything in its path.

They came across a man on the blind side of the trailer as he dabbed a paint brush on the silver skin with a steady, artistic hand. He peered closely at his target and delicately blotted out the imperfection marring the surface.

"Excuse me!" The deputy shouted at him from a distance.

The painter looked away from his work. Paul tracked a small knot of children spying on them from the other side of the trailers. His back throbbed anew and his rage commanded him to run after the little devils, but after a brief assessment of his chances of catching them he decided not to humiliate himself by giving chase.

"Have you seen a giant walking through here? Bald head and a little dirty blonde woman with him?" asked the deputy.

The man gave his work one last moment of concentration before breaking away and taking a few strides toward the deputy and Paul.

"A giant? I think I've seen who you are talking about. I don't cover for no one if the law wants them. I figure you all can sort out the guilt or innocence and I'm not going to deny the law the opportunity of finding justice. Looked to me like they had nothing but a car. I don't know if they even had a change of clothes. They were flashing some money around like it still mattered. I didn't want to tell them that even if I stole all the money they had it wouldn't be enough to live back in the world for more than a month, so what would be the point? They're not going to last through the winter unless someone takes pity on them. We've had people try to live though it in cars, but let me tell you it's a miserable experience. That's why this hatch," he said as he pointed to the top of the trailer, "locks from the inside. Even good people fallen on desperate times can act in desperate ways. You live inside a car for two months in a North Dakota winter and you'd want to pull me out of this marvel and slice my throat. I have the place so well insulated all you need is ambient body heat to make it perfectly comfortable. Stays cool in the summer too. I know it looks like a sweat box but the stainless reflects a lot of the energy and the rest can't get through the insulation. I swear to God I don't think I'd go back to a regular house if I had the chance. I don't pay one dime to a corporation. I don't pay taxes on my right to live on the land. You make your walls thick enough you don't have to worry about anarchy either."

"Where did you see the giant?"

"I talked to them a bit, although the giant didn't talk. It was mostly the dwarf who talked but I can't recall a damn thing she said."

"Where?"

"The giant? I saw them in the outlands, along with the dwarf. Cute little thing. They stirred up a long-buried circus fetish I thought I had dealt with."

"Where are the outlands? That seems a little vague."

"Out there. The fringes of chaos," he said as he pointed west of the camp, then south, then east. "Those people don't have improved sites like us. I think sometimes they have unrealistic notions of migration but most of them get stuck, moneyless and unprepared."

"I thought money didn't have much use out here?" piped in Paul.

"Some of the folks out here like to believe that, I guess, but I don't intend to stay here forever. I might like my trailer and I don't like paying money to the

United Corporations of America, but South Dakota doesn't have much to recommend it other than the infernal wailing of prairie dogs and coyotes. Far as I can tell, money is going to get me out of here. Not the kind of money the giant and dwarf had, but real money, steady money, money that grows when you are not looking at it. Most people here ran afoul of it and that's why they are here, so they're thinking wistfully that day is night, that the world has stopped turning, that all their friends and families have forgotten the titanic failures of their lives and that society has stopped using money to grease every relationship, to motivate every desire, to keep the scorecard of success and failure, of genius and idiocy, or organization and disorganization, or desire, temptation and denial.

"I was what you call a materialist. I won't lie to you. My wife and I had a 5,000 square foot house. It had a great room with floor to ceiling windows that were triple-paned. Whatever season it happened to be it felt you were standing in the midst of it: the swirling snow, the falling leaves, the gentle rain, the perfect early morning light of the day. The ceiling were almost three stories high and we kept the temperature at a perfect 72 degrees all year round. I don't want to think of the money I wasted heating a second and third floor of a great room. We had five and a half bathrooms, a Jacuzzi, hot tub, sauna and a lap pool. Our master suite felt like an apartment. We had a game room with an oak pool table, a classic Pac Man video game, three classic pinball machines, seven flat screens – one in the game room, one in the master suite, one each in the two kids' bedrooms, one in the kitchen, one in the guest suite, and one in the master toilet. I never missed a first down, homerun, or free throw even when I had to take a shit. We had a land line telephone plus four cells, plus cable with every blessed premium channel. We had the fastest fiber optic internet. The whole neighborhood could have jumped on and it wouldn't have made a difference. We had two full refrigerators, one in the kitchen, or course, and one in the utility room to store beer and frozen foods we would never eat. Speaking of the kitchen, you would have thought we were going to run a catering business out of the home. Besides the stainless steel fridge, oh, did I tell you it was a Sub-Zero Pro 48? The rest was Thermador and Viking. Not exactly La Cornue, but still more than we actually needed, since neither my wife nor I really enjoy cooking. If you ever want to see a ridiculous site then put a frozen Lean Cuisine dinner into a Sub-Zero 48. I sometimes have nightmares just about that memory. Every other small applianece we bought could have made a hundred meals a day – straight out of the professional chef catalogs, but to tell you the truth we mostly ate out at restaurants. You know, I have a thing for Indian and Vietnamese cuisine and I'd drive anywhere to get it. I started getting so fat that I joined the most exclusive gym in town and I eventually got my weight under control, but it wasn't easy to concentrate with all the women walking around in tights and yoga pants. We should be thankful we live in an age of such clothing. Those pants give me a reason to denounce my own imagination as I could have never conjured up something so perfect. See, see, there's my materialism again, collecting, gathering, and searching for the perfect view of a woman's ass. But I remained a faithful husband. I already had a trophy at home. My wife looked better than any one of them. She modeled underwear some and had a great early career as a pharmaceutical rep, but those drug companies are worse than the NFL, man. She hit 35 and even though she looked better than ever they gave her the boot. They didn't say she was an old broad because they feared lawsuits, but she trained her replacement who had perky boobs two cup sizes bigger, hair that was a shade blonder, an ass that defied gravity, and who had no qualms about wearing clothes a size or two too small.

"We still rolled along even without her drug job. She went to work in a knickknack and fashion store that one of her rich friends opened up out of boredom. Instead of bedding one of those yoga asses I thought about buying a Porsche, but I couldn't bring myself to do it. Don't mistake it for restraint. I thought maybe I was being too cliché. I mean I had a Lexus already, the big ass sedan version, and the wife drove a Range Rover, so we had sold out to luxury. So instead of the sports car I decided to sink my money into a car restoration. A lot of the old hulks have been picked over by now, so I settled on a 1950 Crosley Hotshot. Goddamn, what a money pit that was. I spent tens of thousands of dollars on resurrecting a car that should have never been built in the first place. I could have dropped a lawn mower engine in it and it would have had more power. Of course, I sold it at a loss, a big loss. The market for that car is weak, which is something I should have researched before I jumped into it, but money can make you cocky. Seems you're standing in a place where ego comes to die. All those things I bought and blew my money on have passed on into the landfill or someone else's garage. The wife and kids are living in a winner's house who still has his lucky streak rolling. And here I am." The painter stretched his arms wide to embrace the entire camp in a sarcastic hug.

The deputy paused, letting the resonance of the painter's monologue recede before returning to the task at hand. Finally, he asked, "When was the last time you saw the giant?"

"You sure are stuck on that, aren't you? What's finding him going to do for you? Is finding him going to get you out of here?"

"We came here to find him. When we catch him we will leave."

"That's not likely. It's never that easy. You should know that."

"You're right. I should know. I've arrested my share."

"Well then, Deputy, he's out there. Go get him." The painter felt his paint brush and scowled at his discovery. "These things are like gold. I paid like a pound of coffee for this."

"Then wouldn't it be more accurate to say that paintbrushes are like coffee?" interjected Paul.

The man closed his eyes halfway and made a show of taking an exasperated breath before turning on his heel and returning to his work.

"Should we split up? We could cover more ground?" asked Paul, who was really just trying to salve his self-inflicted wound of dependence on the deputy and his gun.

"And what would you do if you found him first? You have no weapon. You let children stab you. You know how big he is and you know you would have no chance against him. I mean you've seen him, what would you do?"

Paul conceded the point, silently comforted that he would stay with the deputy.

They walked toward the chaos at the end of the strip. Thin cirrus clouds drifted past the sun like old, worn shrouds. They plunged past the first tent and nearly stepped on a woman on her knees, washing her hair in a bucket. She was topless and the deputy immediately averted his eyes as if he had just walked in on her in a bathroom. Paul hesitated and let a full gaze fall upon her breasts. A profound weariness blunted any outrage she could summon and she preceded to wash her pits with a wet sponge. Three dogs trotted past them, their noses in the air, as if trailing a scent, whining and howling with saliva dripping from their jaws. The deputy felt the sun penetrating his burn. He felt for his shirt pocket and he realized again he was Blue Cowboy without his deputy's uniform and the bottle of pills had either been taken out of his pants by the children or not returned or he had left it in the truck, which had probably been ransacked by now. Sweat befouled the blue clothes.

They walked past two 55 gallon drums roaring with fire. Blue and green smoke curled and puffed in the air and smelled like burning plastic and melting

Styrofoam. A man, stripped to the waist and revealing nothing but bone and sinew, tended the flames. Next to him sat two rusty shopping carts burdened with trash that he had collected from the camp. He incinerated the refuse for free with the expectation of donations to come should he need them. A third cart held organic materials, cantaloupe rinds, orange peels, egg shells, apple cores and the like that had been sorted from the heap and that he would push to the landfill next to the row of latrines. He explained to the pilgrims that you wanted to keep the animals away from you tents and cars as they could cause additional havoc in their lives. He smiled wildly, casting a look of idiocy or impairment as the deputy and Paul passed. Not many of his teeth had survived the vicissitudes of life. In a clear baritone he suddenly half-shouted, half-sung:

> Burn, burn goes the violent flame
> So much industry and manufacturing in the air.
> Once a solid, now a gas
> Its drifts and wafts.
> Blue and green tongues lift my spirits
> A cleansing, wicked flame.
> Once a solid, now a liquid
> Invention and cleverness reduced to ash.
> Roast, roast the poison from my spleen.
> My lord, my lord, idle the factories
> Stop the presses, stop thinking.
> Take a breath
> My tiny flames can't keep pace with your production.
> Let my barrels grow cold as you rest.

Paul stopped to ask the man questions, but the deputy pulled forcibly on his arm to keep him moving. He reluctantly kept pace with the deputy but looked back as he passed. Across the burner's back two thick swaths of dried mud started at his shoulders and disappeared under his belt line. Lines of scabs followed the mud along the periphery of its course. Paul snapped his head back in the direction of the deputy.

"He could have told us about the giant," Paul hissed. "He obviously walks all through the camp and he probably knows where everything is."

"You don't know much about police work. Once you start listening to madmen and fools you might as well consult astrological charts."

"You're too damn conservative. That's your problem."

"I wasn't aware I had a problem. I'm a few hundred yards, probably, from catching Kinnell and not once did I consult a Ouija board."

"Sometimes you have to jump into the current. You can't ignore it's there. There are sign posts and signals. The guy burning the trash is a perfect example. He had information for us. He was thrown directly in out path so we could consult with him. He would have set our course."

The deputy worked for a true magician, a wizard of knowledge, in the person of the sheriff. Nothing Paul said approximated the sheriff's power and understanding of the human species. His genius lay in understanding everything and seeing all the connections as something as tangible as yarn or twine stretching from person to person. The deputy could not summon a dismissive gesture, so he let his silence be the exclamation point of his refusal to wade into a metaphysical swamp of voodoo and whispers.

The path they were following was suddenly blocked by a mound of debris, mostly concrete blocks, car tires and sections of steel culvert large enough to fit a human body. The deputy concluded that someone had collected the materials with the idea of building a structure, but the challenges of the materials, the lack of tools, or a deficit of building knowledge had undone the project. Weeds had begun to grow through the mound and on patches of the surface where dirt and seed had landed. Why had the others left it alone? They could have incorporated the materials into their own designs. The deputy thought of a simple design of a culvert buried in the ground horizontally with another welded on one of the ends vertically to act as an egress. The earth would act as insulation and the inhabitants wouldn't need to fear tornadoes, dust storms or blizzards. He felt himself in the tube, listening to his own breath, drifting off to sleep as a storm raged above him.

They edged around the mound. Paul felt himself bending under the heat of the sun and walking a reasonably straight line had become a near impossibility. They had brought no water, which was a ridiculous mistake, but the benefit of poor planning would be that the chase would break off earlier than the deputy wanted once thirst took hold of him. Around the other side of the mound they came across two badly torn canvas tents, with the openings facing each other. Two pairs of legs, a man next to a woman, stuck out of the flap and through the tears they could see a brief glimpse of their sleeping faces. In the other tent a riot ensued, the participants wrestled and flung their bodies on top of each other. The tent shook with each clash and threatened to come down on their heads. Four nicked and dusty bikes of various child sizes lay in twisted heaps a few feet from the shaking tent. Trampled trash and broken plastic lay in a halo around the site. A plastic cooler lay on its side, disgorged of its contents. The feet of the adults did not stir and they made no attempt to hush the children even when their screaming reached a fever pitch.

The deputy thought of his own daughters. His guilt of having left them, of not speaking to them or hugging them for what had to be days now, had become so enormous that he could no longer support it as a conscious thought. Even if he let himself accept the fact that he had become an unreliable person, a terrible father, that his flaws and lies had been exposed, not even this complete acceptance of his own failings could assuage his burden for abandoning them without a word. He created a cancer of worry in them, shattered the serenity of their world, introduced the possibility that one of their parents could one day just vanish without a word or a kiss. What neurosis would that breed? His thoughts tumbled to the children in the camp. They seemed to have adapted as well if not better than the adults. They formed gangs for protection and created structures the adults had abandoned or forgotten. His daughters would be fine. How many times in his job had he run across children running the houses of their drug-addled or sick-with-cancer or hopelessly muddled parents? The children always found a way to survive no matter the set of circumstances they had been dealt, as he had survived his father as his daughters would survive him.

A shimmer of clear thinking suddenly entered his mind. Why the hell was he stalking Kinnell in the wilds of South Dakota? He suddenly felt like he had broken the surface of water and taken a long, deep breath after being submerged for weeks. He felt saved just for a moment, because having his head above water afforded him the view of the surface and no land, no solid surface came into focus across the plain of the water. How long could he tread before he sank again if nothing came to his aid?

He plunged forward with more purposeful strides and the sudden clearness of his thinking faded with each step as walked deeper into the tangle of tents and their obvious impermanence. Had he retained the ability to analyze the tethers to his previous life, he would have clearly seen the powerful hold his children had on him and he would have pulled himself back toward them along the tether, hand over hand if necessary. He loved them and wanted to protect them but what could he say about them other than that? He could very clearly see their faces and remembered the urge to have their small bodies in his arms, but their interests and personalities had become mixed up so if one of them was now in his arms he would not know what to say to them.

They took a sharp right and came across a lean-to closed on three sides with road signs, tar paper, scrap wood and baling wire. Inside in the cool shadow a woman performed a slow-motion fellatio. Both participants were large as folds of flesh cascaded from the structure of their skeletons and her heavy breasts swung between his legs, which looked like two fallen logs. The lean-to opening created a perfect proscenium arch, although the lighting of the stage area was rather dim. Neither the deputy nor Paul felt any stray sexual urges brought on by the show, but both became held in the grip of curiosity, bordering on sociological observation. The act itself, brought low by the location and the participants, still had a powerful allure. The fact that Paul had used it as a blunt hammer to the deputy's credibility, which may also have been the final blow to his wounded marriage, was not lost in either the deputy's or Paul's thinking.

Paul grinned on the sly and reveled in his inventiveness. He had guessed the macho environment of the sheriff's department would react unfavorably to the possibility that one of their own had engaged in a homosexual act as told by a reliable witness, but he could not have wished for more success. He had had to fight back once the deputy had thrown him in jail, basically for no reason. One simple story brought the deputy down. He considered it the knockout punch in their lifelong rivalry, which, in retrospect, was the very thing he had hoped to do when he decided to vacation in the dark and dying town of Portsmouth.

They finally broke away as the scene changed little except for the woman's head bobbing up and down and walked to the other side of the lean-to. As they passed they heard the man being pleasured mumble a conjurer's chant to either stave off a quick orgasm or to keep his erection viable. On the backside of the structure four men sat on an odd collection of chairs, a metal folding chair next to a La-Z-Boy recliner across from a bar stool next to a captain's chair situated around a warped card table. They played with a set of home poker chips rescued from the dumpster. They obviously had agreed if the pot exceeded the number of chips they could use found objects for their bets as the pile in the middle and the four small piles next to their hands included crushed soda cans, wood chips, folded chewing tobacco pouches and dried-up ink pens. One of the men, unshaven and squinting against the sun, looked up at the deputy.

"You'd think these bastards would throw me a hand every tenth deal or so, but they've set their sights on humiliation and abuse. If I had a gun with three bullets I'd end this misery," he said through a grin.

"If you had a gun with three bullets and pointed it at me, one bullet would end up in your ear, the second in your mouth, and the third right up your asshole," the man across from him splayed out in the La-Z-Boy said.

"Hell, if you had a gun with three bullets you might want to shoot all three up your asshole, or would it take four to make you come?" the third man piped in.

"C'mon, a gun with three bullets is just like your fucking technique. You don't have a full load of come and after three pulls you're finished, nothing but a useless, empty pistol hanging between your legs," the last one said.

After these initial salvos they proceeded with rapid fire patter.

"I've got the eye of a sniper. I'd put each bullet in one of your eyes."

"Am I missing something or is our poker friend threatening physical violence over a streak of bad luck in which he's lost nothing more than a chip from his ego?"

"You're not wrong."

"How many times have you blinded one of your date's eyes?"

"Is it really a date if they're on the clock?"

"The next time I pay for it would be my first."

The three others laughed.

"I could always get one of you to suck me off before I would resort to buying pussy."

They laughed louder.

"You wouldn't even have to ask Ed. He'd perform gratis."

"C'mon, man, you know I'm in no position to give anything away."

"What would you buy a whore with anyway?"

"Promise of shelter in your car?"

"Rock soup?"

"Potable water?"

"A gallon of gasoline?"

"A job lead?"

The first with the unshaven face who started this round of insults looked back to the deputy.

"Are those two done in there?" he asked as he pointed with his thumb toward the lean-to.

The deputy slowly shook his head.

"They're goddamn animals doing it out in the open like that," the unshaven man said.

The others looked around them at the wide open spaces and inadequate shelter around them.

"And where would you have them do it?"

"Maybe put a flap over the front, something."

"Ya, what are we thinking, gents? They could walk over to the flap store and get themselves outfitted with the perfect sex shield flap for their lean-to made of road signs."

"Oh, right, next to the shitters and the feral children there's that new flap store. All the flaps you could ever want under one roof."

"They could have an artisan hand-knot a flap of their own design."

"I hear it's all the rage on the coasts."

"People have to fuck, Will. It's the call of nature, my friend."

"When was the last time you fucked a woman, Will?"

"Don't think what you see now is me. What you see now is the product of a three years of raging hell. I'm a remnant of what I once was. I had a wife with a gentle soul. Cancer ate right through her. She called it her 'case of termites,' and she wasn't far off with that description. The woman loved me and I couldn't lose. When she finally died so high on morphine she didn't know her name, I didn't have the stomach to continue in the old way. I couldn't pay a bill to save my life and I did even less to earn the money to pay the bills, so here I am with you fucks playing poker for scraps of wood."

"That honestly brought a tear to my eye."

"I never knew you had such depth, such feeling."

"Of course, our empathy doesn't gloss over the fact that who we see now is exactly who you are. That past self you're talking about has long been buried."

"Right, who cares really about who you once were? I mean, how can we verify the story anyway? Do you have any pictures of her gentle soul?"

"Lost everything in a house fire."

"Ah, tragic that."

"I suspected you for a victim of a mud slide, but no matter."

"A house fire is so common, especially when you set it yourself for the insurance money."

"I could tell you that I too am not this flabby, bald mess that you see before you. I'm actually 175 pounds or the little child who could run the fastest in his class or the bright toddler who could walk and talk earlier than anyone in the family thought possible or the bright-eyed, squalling baby sucking on his momma's breast. Man, and you should have seen me before I took form when the Gods made it their personal business to drop celestial dumps on my spirit from their golden assholes on high."

"Really, Will, three years of hell doesn't seem like much adversity. We all love our women, but it makes me think you are made of plaster of Paris. One damn rainstorm and you're done for. How can you sit there and whine about one wife dying and you gave up everything?"

"The cancer just ate right through her."

"Don't get lost in the weeds of detail."

"A sure sign of a terrible story. You paint a scene so meticulously that you can smell it and feel it but not a damn thing happens or you've dragged down the pace so much no one cares a lick about what is to come."

"But that detail is important to know. Her death was especially horrific. I can't shake the image of her ruined body and I still hear her screams. Eventually we ran out of insurance money and morphine, so I had to resort to giving her over the counter aspirin, which basically did nothing."

"What? You couldn't have used your imagination? You didn't think about dipping your little toe into the black market? Even in this goddamn landfill of human misery I could find every known pharmaceutical. You have to be willing to pay. You didn't want your wife's death to inconvenience you."

"I didn't have any money at that point."

"I'm not talking about money. I'm talking about what you were willing to do. What were you willing to do, Will?" What would you have done to ease the pain of your bride?"

"Anything. I would have done anything."

"But you didn't do anything. So, this is just a rhetorical exercise."

"Of course we don't know the man you used to be. Maybe the man you were before your brief three years of hell wouldn't have done everything possible, but now as a broken, lonely soul you have reconsidered. You think you should have done something different. Such as, why not smother her with a pillow instead of feeding her aspirin, for God's sake? You didn't really want to ease her suffering."

"I couldn't do it with my own hands. I loved her."

"So you were far from being willing or able to do everything for her. You weren't willing to get your own hands dirty," Paul suddenly blurted, waving his hands dismissively and angrily, carried away by the stream of the conversation. "I mean, it sounds to me that you feel remorse for the loss of beauty in your life, like you lost a favorite, expensive watch, like a beautiful, handcrafted Swiss masterpiece. You feel your life has been halved because this thing is no longer in it. You never considered her. You wouldn't release her or ease her suffering. I hate your fucking story."

"Yes! That's exactly it, Will. We hate your fucking story. Yes, this man has it exactly right. WE...HATE...YOUR...STORY. We hate you for telling it to us. We hate you for thinking it. We hate you for living it. We hate you because what you've revealed about yourself flips our stomachs so violently that it's a wonder we can hold onto our lunches."

The other two men urged him on with shouts and mumbles of agreement as if the British House of Commons had suddenly been called to order.

"Who is this man who makes so much sense? I don't believe we've had the pleasure of meeting. New arrival? I mean, we really need to start looking for a fourth for our poker games as you can tell from the conversation we've been having."

"No, we're just here on an errand. We're looking for someone."

"I saw the badge of your friend. I don't even know what to say about his uniform. I didn't want it to be so. You've probably already been told or seen for yourself that we don't have much use for structures and rules imported from the outside. This might be the last stop before complete anarchy. But the truth is we carry too much of the outside world in our heads. We are the smugglers and the pimps of bad ideas. We are our own undoing. We were rejected by the world but we would all go back in a heartbeat. All the routines have worn grooves in our thinking. Our synapses are lined up and begging to fall in line behind some obvious order. Now the youngest children only know this existence. They know no fences or limits. When they grow up they will become lords and presidents, chief executive officers and mass murderers. There's not a peasant among them. Not a single drone or worker. They'll burn an office building down before they work in a cubicle."

"Who is it you seek?" said the man who had all the abuse heaped upon him as he laid his cards on the table face up because the others had abandoned the hand. He showed a full house, kings over tens. Apparently, the whining about the losing streak had been a bluff all along.

"A giant and his dwarf wife," said the deputy. "That's the easiest way to describe them."

The man in the Lay-Z-Boy settled further in the chair and looked ready to sleep, but he said sharply, "We've seen them."

"Where?"

"Fuck, where is here exactly?"

"As a matter of fact they walked right into our camp here and wanted in on the game. The woman started flashing money, called it her Billy Ray roll."

"Alan Ray roll," the other three said in a ragged chorus. "

"Ok, her Alan Ray roll. When we told them we played for pride they stomped off. I told them I would give up my seat for them, but they were looking for higher stakes. I don't know which one of them would have played."

"The dwarf, definitely. The giant wouldn't have been able to hold the cards in those hands of his.

"We could have separated them from their money. I would have welcomed the money, I'm not lying."

"We could have ganged up on them and split the wad."

"I know. That Alan Ray roll sounds so hillbilly. You need to consider a large wad of cash a talisman. You need a name out of deep Africa or Native American lore, something to dignify the mysticism and magic the bearer feels caring around a transformative paper treasure."

"Right, something like Ahtahkakeep."

"Which means?"

"Star blanket."

"Nice."

"Or Tenskawatawa, which means 'open door,' because what opens doors faster than money? If you want to skip the security of a blanket or the access created by the roll and just go for sweet and lovely, then called it 'Sayen.'"

"Any one of those choices seems more appropriate than Alan Ray."

The deputy felt a tightness in his throat and his face flushing with blood. He knew Alan Ray. He had come to the jail alone to bail Kinnell out a few times.

The deputy remembered his manicured nails and he always had crisp, new money that he counted out slowly on the table when he posted the bail. He should have checked Alan Ray's house before they left town. He would be dead, no doubt. It was one thing to bail Kinnell out for a drunk and disorderly or a simple assault, when you knew that more than likely the charges would be dropped. He guessed that Alan Ray would not finance their escape. They would have had to take it from him, and to take it from him they would have had to kill him. The house would have been the first place the sheriff would have looked. He considered calling the sheriff and confessing his insubordination, his pursuit to South Dakota, and even bringing Paul along in an attempt, he guessed, at impressing him. At the end of the call he would tell the sheriff he believed Alan Ray was dead in his house, killed by June and Kinnell so they could finance their escape from the murder of Amber Miller. That would be his first step toward rehabilitation. Certainly, the sheriff would reconsider or reduce the length of his banishment. He knew that it would take more accolades and citations just to get back where he had once been. The sheriff had come to his party, a sure signal that he was being considered for inheritance of his political capital, that even though he couldn't exactly pick an heir as if the office transferred via bloodlines, an endorsement from the sheriff guaranteed victory in at least the first two election cycles. From there the sheriff would have grown infirm or died, so it would be up to him to maintain his power.

He probably had lost his first chance at making amends. The sheriff, if he got wind that Kinnell and June had fled, would have driven directly to Alan Ray's house. He knew that Alan Ray kept June afloat when her drinking and insanity threatened to crush them both once and for all. He would have seen the connection and danger as clearly as a hemp rope tied to June's barstool and stretching to Alan Ray's front door.

"Are you wounded?" said one of the poker players, whose neck and bald head hosted a field of skin cancer.

"Yes, the children stabbed me when we arrived," Paul said with a tone of petulance.

"It's as I said. They have learned nothing but anarchy," said one of the others.

"Has anyone offered you a bandage? It looks like the blood flowed quite freely."

"There was an offer, but they quickly forgot the promise they made."

"Don't think too poorly of us. Bandages are in short supply. Sometimes the county, when they can afford it, will send out a health worker, but she's concerned with the plague or contagions and she assesses a sample of us to see if there's a tragedy unfolding out here. I can't blame them. Not a one of us pays taxes to the county and we weren't invited. This camp had grown like a cyst on the land. Why would they care about us other than trying to avoid a mass die off and the subsequent burial expenses the county would have to pay?"

"I use to have a wife who would have bandaged you. That was before cataclysm and despair. Now we really can't afford to worry about anyone but ourselves."

"I think it's stopped bleeding."

"You're lucky they didn't nick your kidney. I told them they were making their shivs too long."

The deputy looked to the east through a narrow avenue that looked more accidental than a planned travel route. The path terminated at a car with familiar Ohio license plates. He flinched and reflexively reached for his gun. The sheriff would have known what make and model they were looking for because he would have gone to Alan Ray's house and found a copy of the registration that a middle-aged man would keep in a filing cabinet in his office or he would have called the BMV and asked what car they had given him for his job. He had tied his own hands behind his back. Why had he not sought advantage and information that would keep him alive?

He took a step toward the car, then another. He unsnapped the tether holding his gun in the holster. Then, he reconsidered and pulled the gun out and held it low, pointing toward the ground. He quickened his pace. He kept his eyes on the car, trying to simmer down his adrenalin because he could be wrong about the plate. A baby cried off to the right, a shrieking wail of bottomless hunger. A breeze carried the smell of diesel and rotting garbage. A tent flap fluttered and something scuttled backward into the shadow like a frightened crab. The last oxy had completely worn off and his face throbbed under the sun. He felt raw, peeled open, permanently disfigured and beyond a time when he wouldn't be conscious of his damaged face.

The plate became clearer as he approached, but how many other Ohioans had come to Jupiter Hill? His fingertips tingled and he couldn't be sure it was the last of the oxy sparking out or a fresh surge of adrenalin. He wiped sweat off the undamaged areas of his forehead and jaw. He knew the line where the damage began so well he could have drawn a portrait of his disfigured self without looking in a mirror.

Had he taken two hundred steps or leapt in one bound? The baby's cry became a howl. The intervening distance should have tempered the sound but maybe he had been walking toward the stricken child all along. He stood in front of Alan Ray's car. All four doors were open as if to air or dry it out. An assortment of clothes, a mismatched pair of socks, panties, a small blouse, a sports bra, and a t-shirt that looked big enough to be a blanket, lay on the hood to bake in the sun. The front passenger side tire had gone flat. The deputy walked around to the driver's side past the first open door and looked inside. The driver's seat was tilted way back and a crumpled blanket lay on the floor. The backseat looked more like a bed with a blanket tucked into the crease of the seat with a pillow resting next to a neatly folded top sheet. The odor of sweat, farts and mildew wafted from the interior. He had found their empty nest.

He walked to the back of the car. June sat in the dirt with her head resting on the bumper, her chin pointed toward the sun, and her eyes closed. She was topless but wore a pair of beaten jeans that anyone of her acquaintances in Portsmouth would have recognized. Her breasts were not much more than enlarged nipples and the skin of her torso was bruised, dirty and scarred with dozens of minor scrapes like she had been dragged across desert ground. The deputy's body cast a shadow across her face. She felt the difference in the heat and light and squinted up at the deputy.

"I'm sure as fuck hoping you're not staring at my tits."

"My name is Deputy Greg Auro from Portsmouth, Ohio. I'm here to take you and Kinnell back to answer for your crimes."

June raised a hand to create an awning over her brow.

"Are you saying I'm under arrest?"

"You know I'm looking for Kinnell. I suspect he's close. You should help me, June. It will go easier for him. You don't want to see him hurt."

"You're going to take him back to Portsmouth all by yourself?"

"Why don't you start by putting a shirt on?"

The deputy shifted his weight from one foot to the other, giving June the opportunity to kick at his ankles, first landing her shoe against the one bearing his weight, and then the other as it had not yet been firmly planted on the ground. He staggered backwards as she used her foot to trip him. He landed on his back as June sprang to feet and chased after him. She landed a kick to his ear that sent a shock wave through his brain. She stomped repeatedly on the hand that held the pistol, breaking at least two fingers. By luck the gun stayed in his hand as he withdrew it toward his chest, pointing it in June's general direction.

"Stop! You don't know what you are doing!" he yelled.

A foot came down hard against the burn on his face and he screamed. He fired the gun as a result of squeezing his hand against the pain. He would later imagine that he could hear the bullet tearing through her flesh.

"Oh, my God! Oh, my God!" June screamed. She held her belly and dark blood coursed through her fingers. "You shit! My fucking shit. Oh, my God. My God. My belly is on fire." She fell to her knees. The deputy wished she had put a shirt on.

He rolled onto his stomach and pushed himself up with his free hand. The burn felt as fresh and raw as the first hour of the injury. He switched the gun to his uninjured hand, as both the index and middle fingers were obviously broken. June's protestations had fallen to a mumble. Her jeans were soaked with blood from her waist to her knees. His head had tilted forward and off to the side and she didn't have the strength left to hold her hands tightly against the wound.

The deputy staggered to the front of the car, looking for Kinnell. Paul stood in the narrow path, hands outstretched to his sides to mime the possible questions "What happened?" or "Where did you go?" The gunshot had attracted a burgeoning crowd who stood at the edge of their sites and peered around their tents or cars to see what happened but they did not commit their bodies to future harm in the guise of a stray bullet.

Kinnell burst from the cover of a rusting pull camper and lumbered up behind Paul. The deputy shouted a warning, but his voice was weak. By the time Paul shouted back to ask what the deputy had said Kinnell had reached him. He seized him in a crushing bear hug. He lifted him off the ground and squeezed with all his strength. Paul's tongue rolled out of his mouth and his eyes widened in terror.

The deputy did not have a clean shot at Kinnell and he didn't trust his left hand. He watched for a moment as Kinnell killed Paul. He put his feet back on the ground and twisted his head until his neck snapped. The deputy took a wild shot and hit Paul in the eye, fired again and missed everything but the dirt behind the two men. The third shot blasted Kinnell just below the nose, destroying part of his upper jaw. Kinnell dropped Paul's body and put both hands to his face. The deputy sprinted toward him and pumped two bullets into his chest. He fell over, dead.

The deputy ran to Paul. He lay facing the sky. A ghastly smile contorted his face into one last sneer of mockery, his own death being the subject derided. His missing eye looked more like a conspiratorial wink than a bullet wound. The deputy stared at the remaining eye, checking for a last flicker or consciousness but Paul had died in Kinnell's arms. He knelt down and put a hand on Paul's chest. He thought if he tried long and hard enough he might be able to cry for the death of his old friend, for the break in the link to his childhood. He looked at Paul's lurid face. A fly had already landed on his ruined eye socket. He set his gun down in the dust and tried to straighten his broken fingers, which caused him to wince and collapse upon himself. He wondered if now was the time to start walking, past the chaos of the outer settlement and toward the barren horizon. Maybe in time he could find a little town called Coronado that held all the promise and neuroses of America. There he would find a job stringing wire or he could pass himself off as a medical doctor and treat the broken working class. One night, as the desert radiation finally relented, he would write a long letter to the sheriff to explain himself, tell him of the visit to Amber Miller's father, and advance a theory that justice had been done or that maybe it hadn't. He could ship the drugstore toys to his girls and write a note that described the beauty of the desert sun as it broke above the horizon at dawn, offering promise and renewal. They would think of him for a moment and then return to their lives.